BOOKS BY SARAH J. MAAS

The Throne of Glass series

The Assassin's Blade
Throne of Glass
Crown of Midnight
Heir of Fire
Queen of Shadows
Empire of Storms
Tower of Dawn
Kingdom of Ash

•

The Throne of Glass Coloring Book

A Court of Thorns and Roses series

A Court of Thorns and Roses
A Court of Mist and Fury
A Court of Wings and Ruin
A Court of Frost and Starlight

•

A Court of Thorns and Roses Coloring Book

KINGDOM OF ASH

A *Throne of Glass* NOVEL

SARAH J. MAAS

BLOOMSBURY

NEW YORK LONDON OXFORD NEW DELHI SYDNEY

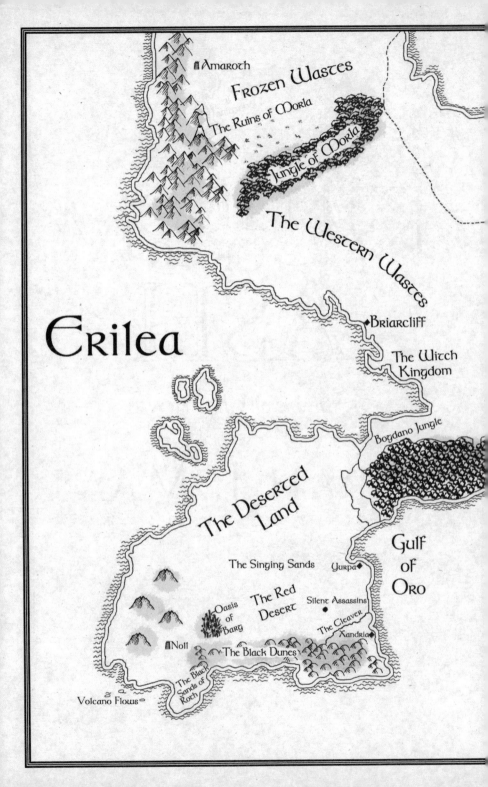

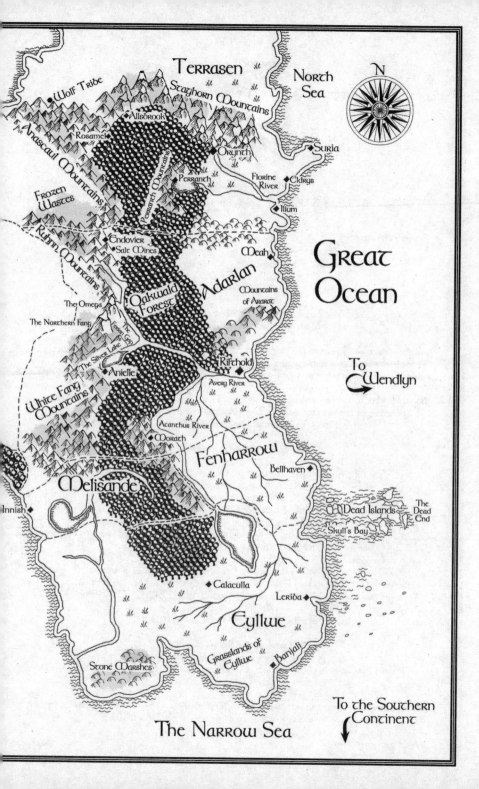

For my parents—
who taught me to believe that girls can save the world

BLOOMSBURY YA
Bloomsbury Publishing Inc., part of Bloomsbury Publishing Plc
1385 Broadway, New York, NY 10018

BLOOMSBURY and the Diana logo are trademarks of Bloomsbury Publishing Plc

First published in the United States of America in October 2018
by Bloomsbury YA
Paperback edition published in October 2019

Bloomsbury books may be purchased for business or promotional use. For information on bulk
purchases please contact Macmillan Corporate and Premium Sales Department at
specialmarkets@macmillan.com

ISBN 978-1-61963-612-5 (paperback)

The Library of Congress has cataloged the hardcover edition as follows:
Names: Maas, Sarah J., author.
Title: Kingdom of ash / by Sarah J. Maas.
Description: New York : Bloomsbury, 2018. | Series: Throne of glass ; [7]
Summary: With Aelin locked in an iron coffin by Queen of the Fae Maeve,
Aedion and Lysandra struggle to defend Terrasen, Chaol, Manon, and Dorian
face their own fates, and Rowan seeks his captured wife and queen.
Identifiers: LCCN 2018034321 (print) • LCCN 2018040101 (e-book)
ISBN 978-1-61963-610-1 (hardcover) • ISBN 978-1-61963-611-8 (e-book)
Subjects: | CYAC: Fantasy. | Kings, queens, rulers, etc.—Fiction. | Fairies—Fiction.
Classification: LCC PZ7.M111575 Kin 2018 (print)| LCC PZ7.M111575 (e-book)|
DDC [Fic]—dc23
LC record available at https://lccn.loc.gov/2018034321

Series design by Regina Flath
Typeset by Westchester Publishing Services
Printed and bound in Great Britain by CPI Group (UK) Ltd, Croydon CRO 4YY

11

To be kept up-to-date about our authors and books, please visit www.bloomsbury.com/newsletters
and sign up for our newsletters, including news about Sarah J. Maas.

The Prince

He had been hunting for her since the moment she was taken from him.

His mate.

He barely remembered his own name. And only recalled it because his three companions spoke it while they searched for her across violent and dark seas, through ancient and slumbering forests, over storm-swept mountains already buried in snow.

He stopped long enough to feed his body and allow his companions a few hours of sleep. Were it not for them, he would have flown off, soared far and wide.

But he would need the strength of their blades and magic, would need their cunning and wisdom before this was through.

Before he faced the dark queen who had torn into his innermost self, stealing his mate long before she had been locked in an iron coffin. And after he was done with her, after that, then he'd take on the cold-blooded gods themselves, hell-bent on destroying what might remain of his mate.

So he stayed with his companions, even as the days passed. Then the weeks.

Then months.

Still he searched. Still he hunted for her on every dusty and forgotten road.

And sometimes, he spoke along the bond between them, sending his soul on the wind to wherever she was held captive, entombed.

I will find you.

The Princess

The iron smothered her. It had snuffed out the fire in her veins, as surely as if the flames had been doused.

She could hear the water, even in the iron box, even with the iron mask and chains adorning her like ribbons of silk. The roaring; the endless rushing of water over stone. It filled the gaps between her screaming.

A sliver of island in the heart of a mist-veiled river, little more than a smooth slab of rock amid the rapids and falls. That's where they'd put her. Stored her. In a stone temple built for some forgotten god.

As she would likely be forgotten. It was better than the alternative: to be remembered for her utter failure. If there would be anyone left to remember her. If there would be anyone left at all.

She would not allow it. That failure.

She would not tell them what they wished to know.

No matter how often her screams drowned out the raging river. No matter how often the snap of her bones cleaved through the bellowing rapids.

She had tried to keep track of the days.

But she did not know how long they had kept her in that iron box. How long they had forced her to sleep, lulled into oblivion by the sweet smoke they'd poured in while they traveled here. To this island, this temple of pain.

She did not know how long the gaps lasted between her screaming and waking. Between the pain ending and starting anew.

Days, months, years—they bled together, as her own blood often slithered over the stone floor and into the river itself.

A princess who was to live for a thousand years. Longer.

That had been her gift. It was now her curse.

Another curse to bear, as heavy as the one placed upon her long before her birth. To sacrifice her very self to right an ancient wrong. To pay another's debt to the gods who had found their world, become trapped in it. And then ruled it.

She did not feel the warm hand of the goddess who had blessed and damned her with such terrible power. She wondered if that goddess of light and flame even cared that she now lay trapped within the iron box—or if the immortal had transferred her attentions to another. To the king who might offer himself in her stead and in yielding his life, spare their world.

The gods did not care who paid the debt. So she knew they would not come for her, save her. So she did not bother praying to them.

But she still told herself the story, still sometimes imagined that the river sang it to her. That the darkness living within the sealed coffin sang it to her as well.

Once upon a time, in a land long since burned to ash, there lived a young princess who loved her kingdom . . .

Down she would drift, deep into that darkness, into the sea of flame. Down so deep that when the whip cracked, when bone sundered, she sometimes did not feel it.

Most times she did.

It was during those infinite hours that she would fix her stare on her companion.

Not the queen's hunter, who could draw out pain like a musician coaxing a melody from an instrument. But the massive white wolf, chained by invisible bonds. Forced to witness this.

There were some days when she could not stand to look at the wolf. When she had come so close, too close, to breaking. And only the story had kept her from doing so.

Once upon a time, in a land long since burned to ash, there lived a young princess who loved her kingdom . . .

Words she had spoken to a prince. Once—long ago.

A prince of ice and wind. A prince who had been hers, and she his. Long before the bond between their souls became known to them.

It was upon him that the task of protecting that once-glorious kingdom now fell.

The prince whose scent was kissed with pine and snow, the scent of that kingdom she had loved with her heart of wildfire.

Even when the dark queen presided over the hunter's ministrations, the princess thought of him. Held on to his memory as if it were a rock in the raging river.

The dark queen with a spider's smile tried to wield it against her. In the obsidian webs she wove, the illusions and dreams she spun at the culmination of each breaking point, the queen tried to twist the memory of him as a key into her mind.

They were blurring. The lies and truths and memories. Sleep and the blackness in the iron coffin. The days bound to the stone altar in the center of the room, or hanging from a hook in the ceiling, or strung up between chains anchored into the stone wall. It was all beginning to blur, like ink in water.

So she told herself the story. The darkness and the flame deep within her whispered it, too, and she sang it back to them. Locked in that coffin hidden on an island within the heart of a river, the princess recited the story, over and over, and let them unleash an eternity of pain upon her body.

Once upon a time, in a land long since burned to ash, there lived a young princess who loved her kingdom . . .

PART ONE

Armies and Allies

CHAPTER 1

The snows had come early.

Even for Terrasen, the first of the autumnal flurries had barreled in far ahead of their usual arrival.

Aedion Ashryver wasn't entirely sure it was a blessing. But if it kept Morath's legions from their doorstep just a little longer, he'd get on his knees to thank the gods. Even if those same gods threatened everything he loved. If beings from another world could be considered gods at all.

Aedion supposed he had more important things to contemplate, anyway.

In the two weeks since he'd been reunited with his Bane, they'd seen no sign of Erawan's forces, either terrestrial or airborne. The thick snow had begun falling barely three days after his return, hindering the already-slow process of transporting the troops from their assembled armada to the Bane's sweeping camp on the Plain of Theralis.

The ships had sailed up the Florine, right to Orynth's doorstep, banners of every color flapping in the brisk wind off the Staghorns: the cobalt and gold of Wendlyn, the black and crimson of Ansel of Briarcliff, the shimmering silver of the Whitethorn royals and their many cousins. The Silent Assassins, scattered throughout the fleet, had no banner, though none was needed to identify them—not with their pale clothes and assortment of beautiful, vicious weapons.

The ships would soon rejoin the rearguard left at the Florine's mouth and patrol the coast from Ilium to Suria, but the footsoldiers—most hailing from Crown Prince Galan Ashryver's forces—would go to the front.

A front that now lay buried under several feet of snow. With more coming.

Hidden above a narrow mountain pass in the Staghorns behind Allsbrook, Aedion scowled at the heavy sky.

His pale furs blended him into the gray and white of the rocky outcropping, a hood concealing his golden hair. And keeping him warm. Many of Galan's troops had never seen snow, thanks to Wendlyn's temperate climate. The Whitethorn royals and their smaller force were hardly better off. So Aedion had left Kyllian, his most trusted commander, in charge of ensuring that they were as warm as could be managed.

They were far from home, fighting for a queen they did not know or perhaps even believe in. That frigid cold would sap spirits and sprout dissent faster than the howling wind charging between these peaks.

A flicker of movement on the other side of the pass caught Aedion's eye, visible only because he knew where to look.

She'd camouflaged herself better than he had. But Lysandra had the advantage of wearing a coat that had been bred for these mountains.

Not that he'd said that to her. Or so much as glanced at her when they'd departed on this scouting mission.

Aelin, apparently, had secret business in Eldrys and had left a note with Galan and her new allies to account for her disappearance. Which allowed Lysandra to accompany them on this task.

No one had noticed, in the nearly two months they'd been maintaining this ruse, that the Queen of Fire had not an ember to show for it. Or that she and the shape-shifter never appeared in the same place. And no one, not the Silent Assassins of the Red Desert, or Galan Ashryver, or the troops that Ansel of Briarcliff had sent with the armada ahead of the bulk of her army, had picked up the slight tells that did not belong to Aelin at all. Nor had they noted the brand on the queen's wrist that no matter what skin she wore, Lysandra could not change.

She did a fine job of hiding the brand with gloves or long sleeves. And if a glimmer of scarred skin ever showed, it could be excused as part of the manacle markings that remained.

The fake scars she'd also added, right where Aelin had them. Along with the laugh and wicked grin. The swagger and stillness.

Aedion could barely stand to look at her. Talk to her. He only did so because he had to uphold this ruse, too. To pretend that he was her faithful cousin, her fearless commander who would lead her and Terrasen to victory, however unlikely.

So he played the part. One of many he'd donned in his life.

Yet the moment Lysandra changed her golden hair for dark tresses, Ashryver eyes for emerald, he stopped acknowledging her existence. Some days, the Terrasen knot tattooed on his chest, the names of his queen and fledgling court woven amongst it, felt like a brand. Her name especially.

He'd only brought her on this mission to make it easier. Safer. There were other lives beyond his at risk, and though he could have unloaded this scouting task to a unit within the Bane, he'd needed the action.

It had taken over a month to sail from Eyllwe with their newfound allies, dodging Morath's fleet around Rifthold, and then these past two weeks to move inland.

They had seen little to no combat. Only a few roving bands of Adarlanian soldiers, no Valg amongst them, that had been dealt with quickly.

Aedion doubted Erawan was waiting until spring. Doubted the quiet had anything to do with the weather. He'd discussed it with his men, and with Darrow and the other lords a few days ago. Erawan was likely waiting until the dead of winter, when mobility would be hardest for Terrasen's army, when Aedion's soldiers would be weak from months in the snow, their bodies stiff with cold. Even the king's fortune that Aelin had schemed and won for them this past spring couldn't prevent that.

Yes, food and blankets and clothes could be purchased, but when the supply lines were buried under snow, what good were they then? All the gold in Erilea couldn't stop the slow, steady leeching of strength caused by months in a winter camp, exposed to Terrasen's merciless elements.

Darrow and the other lords didn't believe his claim that Erawan would strike in deep winter—or believe Ren, when the Lord of Allsbrook voiced his agreement. Erawan was no fool, they claimed. Despite his aerial legion of witches, even Valg foot soldiers could not cross snow when it was ten feet deep. They'd decided that Erawan would wait until spring.

Yet Aedion was taking no chances. Neither was Prince Galan, who had remained silent in that meeting, but sought Aedion afterward to add his support. They had to keep their troops warm and fed, keep them trained and ready to march at a moment's notice.

This scouting mission, if Ren's information proved correct, would help their cause.

Nearby, a bowstring groaned, barely audible over the wind. Its tip and shaft had been painted white, and were now barely visible as it aimed with deadly precision toward the pass opening.

Aedion caught Ren Allsbrook's eye from where the young lord was concealed amongst the rocks, his arrow ready to fly. Cloaked in the same white and gray furs as Aedion, a pale scarf over his mouth, Ren was little more than a pair of dark eyes and the hint of a slashing scar.

Aedion motioned to wait. Barely glancing toward the shape-shifter across the pass, Aedion conveyed the same order.

Let their enemies draw closer.

Crunching snow mingled with labored breathing.

Right on time.

Aedion nocked an arrow to his own bow and ducked lower on the outcropping.

As Ren's scout had claimed when she'd rushed into Aedion's war tent five days ago, there were six of them.

They did not bother to blend into the snow and rock. Their dark fur, shaggy and strange, might as well have been a beacon against the glaring white of the Staghorns. But it was the reek of them, carried on a swift wind, that told Aedion enough.

Valg. No sign of a collar on anyone in the small party, any hint of a ring concealed by their thick gloves. Apparently, even demon-infested vermin could get cold. Or their mortal hosts did.

Their enemies moved deeper into the throat of the pass. Ren's arrow held steady.

Leave one alive, Aedion had ordered before they'd taken their positions.

It had been a lucky guess that they'd choose this pass, a half-forgotten back door into Terrasen's low-lying lands. Only wide enough for two horses to ride abreast, it had long been ignored by conquering armies and the merchants seeking to sell their wares in the hinterlands beyond the Staghorns.

What dwelled out there, who dared make a living beyond any recognized border, Aedion didn't know. Just as he didn't know why these soldiers had ventured so far into the mountains.

But he'd find out soon enough.

The demon company passed beneath them, and Aedion and Ren shifted to reposition their bows.

A straight shot down into the skull. He picked his mark.

Aedion's nod was the only signal before his arrow flew.

Black blood was still steaming in the snow when the fighting stopped.

It had lasted only a few minutes. Just a few, after Ren and Aedion's arrows found their targets and Lysandra had leaped from her perch to shred three others. And rip the muscles from the calves of the sixth and sole surviving member of the company.

The demon moaned as Aedion stalked toward him, the snow at the man's feet now jet-black, his legs in ribbons. Like scraps of a banner in the wind.

Lysandra sat near his head, her maw stained ebony and her green eyes fixed on the man's pale face. Needle-sharp claws gleamed from her massive paws.

Behind them, Ren checked the others for signs of life. His sword rose and fell, decapitating them before the frigid air could render them too stiff to hack through.

"Traitorous filth," the demon seethed at Aedion, narrow face curdling with hate. The reek of him stuffed itself up Aedion's nostrils, coating his senses like oil.

Aedion drew the knife at his side—the long, wicked dagger Rowan Whitethorn had gifted him—and smiled grimly. "This can go quickly, if you're smart."

The Valg soldier spat on Aedion's snow-crusted boots.

Allsbrook Castle had stood with the Staghorns at its back and Oakwald at its feet for over five hundred years.

Pacing before the roaring fire ablaze in one of its many oversized hearths, Aedion could count the marks of every brutal winter upon the gray stones. Could feel the weight of the castle's storied history on those stones, too—the years of valor and service, when these halls had been full of singing and warriors, and the long years of sorrow that followed.

Ren had claimed a worn, tufted armchair set to one side of the fire, his forearms braced on his thighs as he stared into the flame. They'd arrived late last night, and even Aedion had been too drained from the trek through snowbound Oakwald to take the grand tour. And after what they'd done this afternoon, he doubted he'd muster the energy to do so now.

The once-great hall was hushed and dim beyond their fire, and above them, faded tapestries and crests from the Allsbrook family's banner men swayed in the draft creeping through the high windows that lined one side of the chamber. An assortment of birds nested in the rafters, hunkered down against the lethal cold beyond the keep's ancient walls.

And amongst them, a green-eyed falcon listened to every word.

"If Erawan's searching for a way into Terrasen," Ren said at last, "the mountains would be foolish." He frowned toward the discarded trays of food they'd devoured minutes ago. Hearty mutton stew and roasted root vegetables. Most of it bland, but it had been hot. "The land does not forgive easily out here. He'd lose countless troops to the elements alone."

"Erawan does nothing without reason," Aedion countered. "The easiest route to Terrasen would be up through the farmlands, on the northern roads. It's where anyone would expect him to march. Either there, or to launch his forces from the coast."

"Or both—by land and sea."

Aedion nodded. Erawan had spread his net wide in his desire to stomp out what resistance had arisen on this continent. Gone was the guise of Adarlan's empire: from Eyllwe to Adarlan's northern border, from the shores of the Great Ocean to the towering wall of mountains that cleaved their continent in two, the Valg king's shadow grew every day. Aedion doubted that Erawan would stop before he clamped black collars around all their necks.

And if Erawan attained the two other Wyrdkeys, if he could open the Wyrdgate at will and unleash hordes of Valg from his own realm, perhaps even enslave armies from other worlds and wield them for conquest . . . There would be no chance of stopping him. In this world, or any other.

All hope of preventing that horrible fate now lay with Dorian Havilliard and Manon Blackbeak. Where they'd gone these months, what had befallen them, Aedion hadn't heard a whisper. Which he supposed was a good sign. Their survival lay in secrecy.

Aedion said, "So for Erawan to waste a scouting party to find small mountain passes seems unwise." He scratched at his stubble-coated cheek. They'd left before dawn yesterday, and he'd opted for sleep over a shave.

"It doesn't make sense, strategically. The witches can fly, so sending scouts to learn the pitfalls of the terrain is of little use. But if the information is for terrestrial armies . . . Squeezing forces through small passes like that would take months, not to mention risk the weather."

"Their scout just kept laughing," said Ren, shaking his head. His shoulder-length black hair moved with him. "What are we missing here? What aren't we seeing?" In the firelight, the slashing scar down his face was starker. A reminder of the horrors Ren had endured, and the ones his family hadn't survived.

"It could be to keep us guessing. To make us reposition our forces." Aedion braced a hand on the mantel, the warm stone seeping into his still-chilled skin.

Ren had indeed readied the Bane the months Aedion had been away, working closely with Kyllian to position them as far south from Orynth as Darrow's leash would allow. Which, it turned out, was barely beyond the foothills lining the southernmost edge of the Plain of Theralis.

Ren had since yielded control to Aedion, though the Lord of Allsbrook's reunion with *Aelin* had been frosty. As cold as the snow whipping outside this keep, to be exact.

Lysandra had played the role well, mastering Aelin's guilt and impatience. And since then, wisely avoiding any situation where they might talk about the past. Not that Ren had demonstrated a desire to reminisce about the years before Terrasen's fall. Or the events of last winter.

Aedion could only hope that Erawan also remained unaware that they no longer had the Fire-Bringer in their midst. What Terrasen's own troops would say or do when they realized Aelin's flame would not shield them in battle, he didn't want to consider.

"It could also be a true maneuver that we were lucky enough to discover," Ren mused. "So do we risk moving troops to the passes? There are some already in the Staghorns behind Orynth, and on the northern plains beyond it."

A clever move on Ren's part—to convince Darrow to let him station part of the Bane *behind* Orynth, should Erawan sail north and attack from there. He'd put nothing past the bastard.

"I don't want the Bane spread too thin," said Aedion, studying the fire. So different, this flame—so different from Aelin's fire. As if the one before him were a ghost compared to the living thing that was his queen's magic. "And we still don't have enough troops to spare."

Even with Aelin's desperate, bold maneuvering, the allies she'd won didn't come close to the full might of Morath. And all that gold she'd amassed did little to buy them more—not when there were few left to even entice to join their cause.

"Aelin didn't seem too concerned when she flitted off to Eldrys," Ren murmured.

For a moment, Aedion was on a spit of blood-soaked sand.

An iron box. Maeve had whipped her and put her in a veritable coffin. And sailed off to Mala-knew-where, an immortal sadist with them.

"Aelin," said Aedion, dredging up a drawl as best he could, even as the lie choked him, "has her own plans that she'll only tell us about when the time is right."

Ren said nothing. And though the queen Ren believed had returned was an illusion, Aedion added, "Everything she does is for Terrasen."

He'd said such horrible things to her that day she'd taken down the ilken. *Where are our allies?* he'd demanded. He was still trying to forgive himself for it. For any of it. All that he had was this one chance to make it right, to do as she'd asked and save their kingdom.

Ren glanced to the twin swords he'd discarded on the ancient table behind them. "She still left." Not for Eldrys, but ten years ago.

"We've all made mistakes this past decade." The gods knew Aedion had plenty to atone for.

Ren tensed, as if the choices that haunted him had nipped at his back.

"I never told her," Aedion said quietly, so that the falcon sitting in the rafters might not hear. "About the opium den in Rifthold."

About the fact that Ren had known the owner, and had frequented the woman's establishment plenty before the night Aedion and Chaol had hauled in a nearly unconscious Ren to hide from the king's men.

"You can be a real prick, you know that?" Ren's voice turned hoarse.

"I'd never use that against you." Aedion held the young lord's raging dark stare, let Ren feel the dominance simmering within his own. "What I meant to say, before you flew off the handle," he added when Ren's mouth opened again, "was that Aelin offered you a place in this court without knowing that part of your past." A muscle flickered in Ren's jaw. "But even if she had, Ren, she still would have made that offer."

Ren studied the stone floor beneath their boots. "There is no court."

"Darrow can scream it all he wants, but I beg to differ." Aedion slid into the armchair across from Ren's. If Ren truly backed Aelin, with Elide Lochan now returned, and Sol and Ravi of Suria likely to support her, it gave his queen three votes in her favor. Against the four opposing her.

There was little hope that Lysandra's vote, as Lady of Caraverre, would be recognized.

The shifter had not asked to see the land that was to be her home if they survived this war. Had only changed into a falcon on the trek here and flown off for a while. When she'd returned, she'd said nothing, though her green eyes had been bright.

No, Caraverre would not be recognized as a territory, not until Aelin took up her throne.

Until Lysandra instead was crowned queen, if his own did not return.

She *would* return. She had to.

A door opened at the far end of the hall, followed by rushing, light steps. He rose a heartbeat before a joyous *"Aedion!"* sang over the stones.

Evangeline was beaming, clad head to toe in green woolen clothes bordered with white fur, her red-gold hair hanging in two plaits. Like the mountain girls of Terrasen.

Her scars stretched wide as she grinned, and Aedion threw open his arms just before she launched herself on him. "They said you arrived late last night, but you left before first light, and I was worried I'd miss you again—"

Aedion pressed a kiss to the top of her head. "You look like you've grown a full foot since I last saw you."

Evangeline's citrine eyes glowed as she glanced between him and Ren. "Where's—"

A flash of light, and there she was.

Shining. Lysandra seemed to be shining as she swept a cloak around her bare body, the garment left on a nearby chair for precisely this purpose. Evangeline hurled herself into the shifter's arms, half sobbing with joy. Evangeline's shoulders shook, and Lysandra smiled, deeply and warmly, stroking the girl's head. "You're well?"

For all the world, the shifter would have seemed calm, serene. But Aedion knew her—knew her moods, her secret tells. Knew that the slight tremor in her words was proof of the raging torrent beneath the beautiful surface.

"Oh, yes," Evangeline said, pulling away to beam toward Ren. "He and Lord Murtaugh brought me here soon after. Fleetfoot's with him, by the way. Murtaugh, I mean. She likes him better than me, because he sneaks her treats all day. She's fatter than a lazy house cat now."

Lysandra laughed, and Aedion smiled. The girl had been well cared for.

As if realizing it herself, Lysandra murmured to Ren, her voice a soft purr, "Thank you."

Red tinted Ren's cheeks as he rose to his feet. "I thought she'd be safer here than in the war camp. More comfortable, at least."

"Oh, it's the most wonderful place, Lysandra," Evangeline chirped, gripping Lysandra's hand between both of hers. "Murtaugh even took me to Caraverre one afternoon—before it started snowing, I mean. You must see it. The hills and rivers and pretty trees, all right up against the mountains. I thought I spied a ghost leopard hiding atop the rocks, but Murtaugh said it was a trick of my mind. But I swear it was one—even bigger than yours! And the house! It's the loveliest house I ever saw, with a walled garden in the back that Murtaugh says will be full of vegetables and roses in the summer."

For a heartbeat, Aedion couldn't endure the emotion on Lysandra's face as Evangeline prattled off her grand plans for the estate. The pain of longing for a life that would likely be snatched away before she had a chance to claim it.

Aedion turned to Ren, the lord's gaze transfixed on Lysandra. As it had been whenever she'd taken her human form.

Fighting the urge to clench his jaw, Aedion said, "You recognize Cara-verre, then."

Evangeline continued her merry jabbering, but Lysandra's eyes slid toward them.

"Darrow is not Lord of Allsbrook," was all Ren said.

Indeed. And who wouldn't want such a pretty neighbor?

That is, when she wasn't living in Orynth under another's skin and crown, using Aedion to sire a fake royal bloodline. Little more than a stud to breed.

Lysandra again nodded her thanks, and Ren's blush deepened. As if they hadn't spent all day trekking through snow and slaughtering Valg. As if the scent of gore didn't still cling to them.

Indeed, Evangeline sniffed at the cloak Lysandra kept wrapped around herself and scowled. "You smell terrible. All of you."

"Manners," Lysandra admonished, but laughed.

Evangeline put her hands on her hips in a gesture Aedion had seen Aelin make so many times that his heart hurt to behold it. "*You* asked me to tell you if you ever smelled. Especially your breath."

Lysandra smiled, and Aedion resisted the tug on his own mouth. "So I did."

Evangeline yanked on Lysandra's hand, trying to haul the shifter down the hall. "You can share my room. There's a bathing chamber in there." Lysandra conceded a step.

"A fine room for a guest," Aedion muttered to Ren, his brows rising. It had to be one of the finest here, to have its own bathing chamber.

Ren ducked his head. "It belonged to Rose."

His oldest sister. Who had been butchered along with Rallen, the middle Allsbrook sibling, at the magic academy they'd attended. Near the border with Adarlan, the school had been directly in the path of invading troops.

Even before magic fell, they would have had few defenses against ten thousand soldiers. Aedion didn't let himself often remember the slaughter of Devellin—that fabled school. How many children had been there. How none had escaped.

Ren had been close to both his elder sisters, but to high-spirited Rose most of all.

"She would have liked her," Ren clarified, jerking his chin toward Evangeline. Scarred, Aedion realized, as Ren was. The slash down Ren's face had been earned while escaping the butchering blocks, his parents' lives the cost of the diversion that got him and Murtaugh out. Evangeline's scars hailed from a different sort of escape, narrowly avoiding the hellish life her mistress endured.

Aedion didn't let himself often remember that fact, either.

Evangeline continued pulling Lysandra away, oblivious to the conversation. "Why didn't you wake me when you arrived?"

Aedion didn't hear Lysandra's answer as she let herself be led from the hall. Not as the shifter's gaze met his own.

She had tried to speak with him these past two months. Many times. Dozens of times. He'd ignored her. And when they'd at last reached Terrasen's shores, she'd given up.

She had lied to him. Deceived him so thoroughly that any moment between them, any conversation . . . he didn't know what had been real. Didn't want to know. Didn't want to know if she'd meant any of it, when he'd so stupidly left everything laid out before her.

He'd believed this was his last hunt. That he'd be able to take his time with her, show her everything Terrasen had to offer. Show her everything he had to offer, too.

Lying bitch, he'd called her. Screamed the words at her.

He'd mustered enough clarity to be ashamed of it. But the rage remained.

Lysandra's eyes were wary, as if asking him, *Can we not, in this rare moment of happiness, speak as friends?*

Aedion only returned to the fire, blocking out her emerald eyes, her exquisite face.

Ren could have her. Even if the thought made him want to shatter something.

Lysandra and Evangeline vanished from the hall, the girl still chirping away.

The weight of Lysandra's disappointment lingered like a phantom touch.

Ren cleared his throat. "You want to tell me what's going on between you two?"

Aedion cut him a flat stare that would have sent lesser men running. "Get a map. I want to go over the passes again."

Ren, to his credit, went in search of one.

Aedion gazed at the fire, so pale without his queen's spark of magic.

How long would it be until the wind howling outside the castle was replaced by the baying of Erawan's beasts?

⁓

Aedion got his answer at dawn the next day.

Seated at one end of the long table in the Great Hall, Lysandra and Evangeline having a quiet breakfast at the other, Aedion mastered the shake in his fingers as he opened the letter the messenger had delivered moments before. Ren and Murtaugh, seated around him, had refrained from demanding answers while he read. Once. Twice.

Aedion at last set down the letter. Took a long breath as he frowned toward the watery gray light leaking through the bank of windows high on the wall.

Down the table, the weight of Lysandra's stare pressed on him. Yet she remained where she was.

"It's from Kyllian," Aedion said hoarsely. "Morath's troops made landfall at the coast—at Eldrys."

Ren swore. Murtaugh stayed silent. Aedion kept seated, since his knees seemed unlikely to support him. "He destroyed the city. Turned it to rubble without unleashing a single troop."

Why the dark king had waited this long, Aedion could only guess.

"The witch towers?" Ren asked. Aedion had told him all Manon Blackbeak had revealed on their trek through the Stone Marshes.

"It doesn't say." It was doubtful Erawan had wielded the towers, since they were massive enough to require being transported by land, and Aedion's scouts surely would have noticed a one-hundred-foot tower hauled through their territory. "But the blasts leveled the city."

"Aelin?" Murtaugh's voice was a near-whisper.

"Fine," Aedion lied. "On her way back to the Orynth encampment the day before it happened." Of course, there was no mention of her whereabouts in Kyllian's letter, but his top commander had speculated that since there was no body or celebrating enemy, the queen had gotten out.

Murtaugh went boneless in his seat, and Fleetfoot laid her golden head atop his thigh. "Thank Mala for that mercy."

"Don't thank her yet." Aedion shoved the letter into the pocket of the thick cloak he wore against the draft in the hall. *Don't thank her at all*, he almost added. "On their way to Eldrys, Morath took out ten of Wendlyn's warships near Ilium, and sent the rest fleeing back up the Florine, along with our own."

Murtaugh rubbed his jaw. "Why not give chase—follow them up the river?"

"Who knows?" Aedion would think on it later. "Erawan set his sights on Eldrys, and so he has now taken the city. He seems inclined to launch some of his troops from there. If unchecked, they'll reach Orynth in a week."

"We have to return to the camp," Ren said, face dark. "See if we can get our fleet back down the Florine and strike with Rolfe from the sea. While we hammer from the land."

Aedion didn't feel like reminding them that they hadn't heard from Rolfe beyond vague messages about his hunt for the scattered Mycenians and their legendary fleet. The odds of Rolfe emerging to save their asses were as slim as the fabled Wolf Tribe at the far end of the Anascaul Mountains riding out of the hinterland. Or the Fae who'd fled Terrasen a decade ago returning from wherever they'd gone to join Aedion's forces.

The calculating calm that had guided Aedion through battle and butchering settled into him, as solid as the fur cloak he wore. Speed would be their ally now. Speed and clarity.

The lines have to hold, Rowan ordered before they'd parted. *Buy us whatever time you can.*

He'd make good on that promise.

Evangeline fell silent as Aedion's attention slid to the shifter down the table. "How many can your wyvern form carry?"

CHAPTER 2

Elide Lochan had once hoped to travel far and wide, to a place where no one had ever heard of Adarlan or Terrasen, so distant that Vernon didn't stand a chance of finding her.

She hadn't anticipated that it might actually happen.

Standing in the dusty, ancient alley of an equally dusty, ancient city in a kingdom south of Doranelle, Elide marveled at the noontime bells ringing across the clear sky, the sun baking the pale stones of the buildings, the dry wind sweeping through the narrow streets between them. She'd learned the name of this city thrice now, and still couldn't pronounce it.

She supposed it didn't matter. They wouldn't be here long. Just as they had not lingered in any of the cities they'd swept through, or the forests or mountains or lowlands. Kingdom after kingdom, the relentless pace set by a prince who seemed barely able to remember to speak, let alone feed himself.

Elide grimaced at the weathered witch leathers she still wore, her fraying gray cloak and scuffed boots, then glanced at her two companions in the alley. Indeed, they'd all seen better days.

"Any minute now," Gavriel murmured, a tawny eye on the alley's entrance. A towering, dark figure blended into the scant shadows at the half-crumbling archway, monitoring the bustling street beyond.

Elide didn't look too long toward that figure. She'd been unable to stomach it these endless weeks. Unable to stomach him, or the unbearable ache in her chest.

Elide frowned at Gavriel. "We should have stopped for lunch."

He jerked his chin to the worn bag sagging against the wall. "There's an apple in my pack."

Glancing toward the building rising above them, Elide sighed and reached for the pack, riffling through the spare clothes, rope, weapons, and various supplies until she yanked out the fat red-and-green apple. The last of the many they'd plucked from an orchard in a neighboring kingdom. Elide wordlessly extended it to the Fae lord.

Gavriel arched a golden brow.

Elide mirrored the gesture. "I can hear your stomach grumbling."

Gavriel huffed a laugh and took the apple with an incline of his head before cleaning it on the sleeve of his pale jacket. "Indeed it is."

Down the alley, Elide could have sworn the dark figure stiffened. She paid him no heed.

Gavriel bit into the apple, his canines flashing. Aedion Ashryver's father—the resemblance was uncanny, though the similarities stopped at appearance. In the brief few days she'd spent with Aedion, he'd proved himself the opposite of the soft-spoken, thoughtful male.

She'd worried, after Asterin and Vesta had left them aboard the ship they'd sailed here, that she might have made a mistake in choosing to travel with three immortal males. That she'd be trampled underfoot.

But Gavriel had been kind from the start, making sure Elide ate enough and had blankets on frigid nights, teaching her to ride the horses they'd spent precious coin to purchase because Elide wouldn't stand a chance of keeping up with them on foot, ankle or no. And for the times when they had to lead their horses over rough terrain, Gavriel had even braced her leg with his magic, his power a warm summer breeze against her skin.

She certainly wasn't allowing Lorcan to do so for her.

She would never forget the sight of him crawling after Maeve once the queen had severed the blood oath. Crawling after Maeve like a shunned lover, like a broken dog desperate for its master. Aelin had been brutalized, their very location betrayed by Lorcan to Maeve, and still he tried to follow. Right through the sand still wet with Aelin's blood.

Gavriel ate half the apple and offered Elide the rest. "You should eat, too."

She frowned at the bruised purple beneath Gavriel's eyes. Beneath her own, she had no doubt. Her cycle, at least, had come last month, despite the hard travel that burned up any reserves of food in her stomach.

That had been particularly mortifying. To explain to three warriors who could already smell the blood that she needed supplies. More frequent stops.

She hadn't mentioned the cramping that twisted her gut, her back, and lashed down her thighs. She'd kept riding, kept her head down. She knew they would have stopped. Even Rowan would have stopped to let her rest. But every time they paused, Elide saw that iron box. Saw the whip, shining with blood, as it cracked through the air. Heard Aelin's screaming.

She'd gone so Elide wouldn't be taken. Had not hesitated to offer herself in Elide's stead.

The thought alone kept Elide astride her mare. Those few days had been made slightly easier by the clean strips of linen that Gavriel and Rowan provided, undoubtedly from their own shirts. When they'd cut them up, she had no idea.

Elide bit into the apple, savoring the sweet, tart crispness. Rowan had left some coppers from a rapidly dwindling supply on a stump to account for the fruit they'd taken.

Soon they'd have to steal their suppers. Or sell their horses.

A thumping sounded from behind the sealed windows a level above, punctuated with muffled male shouting.

"Do you think we'll have better luck this time?" Elide quietly asked.

Gavriel studied the blue-painted shutters, carved in an intricate lat-ticework. "I have to hope so."

Luck had indeed run thin these days. They'd had little since that blasted beach in Eyllwe, when Rowan had felt a tug in the bond between him and Aelin—the mating bond—and had followed its call across the ocean. Yet when they'd reached these shores after several dreadful weeks on storm-wild waters, there had been nothing left to track.

No sign of Maeve's remaining armada. No whisper of the queen's ship, the *Nightingale*, docking in any port. No news of her returning to her seat in Doranelle.

Rumors were all they'd had to go on, hauling them across mountains piled deep with snow, through dense forests and dried-out plains.

Until the previous kingdom, the previous city, the packed streets full of revelers out to celebrate Samhuinn, to honor the gods when the veil between worlds was thinnest.

They had no idea those gods were nothing but beings from another world. That any help the gods offered, any help Elide had ever received from that small voice at her shoulder, had been with one goal in mind: to return home. Pawns—that's all Elide and Aelin and the others were to them.

It was confirmed by the fact that Elide had not heard a whisper of Anneith's guidance since that horrible day in Eyllwe. Only nudges during the long days, as if they were reminders of her presence. That someone was watching.

That, should they succeed in their quest to find Aelin, the young queen would still be expected to pay the ultimate price to those gods. If Dorian Havilliard and Manon Blackbeak were able to recover the third and final Wyrdkey. If the young king didn't offer himself up as the sacrifice in Aelin's stead.

So Elide endured those occasional nudges, refusing to contemplate what manner of creature had taken such an interest in her. In all of them.

Elide had discarded those thoughts as they'd combed through the streets, listening for any whisper of Maeve's location. The sun had set, Rowan snarling with each passing hour that yielded nothing. As all other cities had yielded nothing.

Elide had made them keep strolling the merry streets, unnoticed and unmarked. She'd reminded Rowan each time he flashed his teeth that there were eyes in every kingdom, every land. And if word got out that a group of Fae warriors was terrorizing cities in their search for Maeve, surely it would get back to the Fae Queen in no time.

Night had fallen, and in the rolling golden hills beyond the city walls, bonfires had kindled.

Rowan had finally stopped growling at the sight. As if they had tugged on some thread of memory, of pain.

But then they'd passed by a group of Fae soldiers out drinking and Rowan had gone still. Had sized the warriors up in that cold, calculating way that told Elide he'd crafted some plan.

When they'd ducked into an alley, the Fae Prince had laid it out in stark, brutal terms.

A week later, and here they were. The shouting grew in the building above.

Elide grimaced as the cracking wood overpowered the ringing city bells. "Should we help?"

Gavriel ran a tattooed hand through his golden hair. The names of warriors who had fallen under his command, he'd explained when she'd finally dared ask last week. "He's almost done."

Indeed, even Lorcan now scowled with impatience at the window above Elide and Gavriel.

As the noon bells finished pealing, the shutters burst open.

Shattered was a better word for it as two Fae males came flying through them.

One of them, brown-haired and bloodied, shrieked while he fell.

Prince Rowan Whitethorn said nothing while he fell with him. While he held his grip on the male, teeth bared.

Elide stepped aside, giving them ample space while they crashed into the pile of crates in the alley, splinters and debris soaring.

She knew a gust of wind kept the fall from being fatal for the broad-shouldered male, whom Rowan hauled from the wreckage by the collar of his blue tunic.

He was of no use to them dead.

Gavriel drew a knife, remaining by Elide's side as Rowan slammed the stranger against the alley wall. There was nothing kind in the prince's face. Nothing warm.

Only cold-blooded predator. Hell-bent on finding the queen who held his heart.

"Please," the male sputtered. In the common tongue.

Rowan had found him, then. They couldn't hope to track Maeve, Rowan had realized on Samhuinn. Yet finding the commanders who served Maeve, spread across various kingdoms on loan to mortal rulers—that, they could do.

And the male Rowan snarled at, his own lip bleeding, *was* a commander. A warrior, from the breadth of his shoulders to his muscled thighs. Rowan still dwarfed him. Gavriel and Lorcan, too. As if, even amongst the Fae, the three of them were a wholly different breed.

"Here's how this goes," Rowan said to the sniveling commander, his voice deadly soft. A brutal smile graced the prince's mouth, setting the blood from his split lip running. "First I break your legs, maybe a portion of your spine so you can't crawl." He pointed a bloodied finger down the alley. To Lorcan. "You know who that is, don't you?"

As if in answer, Lorcan prowled from the archway. The commander began trembling.

"The leg and spine, your body would eventually heal," Rowan went on as Lorcan continued his stalking approach. "But what Lorcan Salvaterre will do to you . . ." A low, joyless laugh. "You won't recover from that, friend."

The commander cast frantic eyes toward Elide, toward Gavriel.

The first time this had happened—two days ago—Elide hadn't been able to watch. That particular commander hadn't possessed any information worth sharing, and given the unspeakable sort of brothel they'd found him in, Elide hadn't really regretted that Rowan had left his body at one end of the alley. His head at the other.

But today, this time . . . *Watch. See*, a small voice hissed in her ear. *Listen.*

Despite the heat and sun, Elide shuddered. Clenched her teeth, bottling up all the words that swelled within her. *Find someone else. Find a way to use your own powers to forge the Lock. Find a way to accept your fates to be trapped in this world, so we needn't pay a debt that wasn't ours to begin with.*

Yet if Anneith now spoke when she had only nudged her these months . . . Elide swallowed those raging words. As all mortals were expected to. For Aelin, she could submit. As Aelin would ultimately submit.

Gavriel's face held no mercy, only a grim sort of practicality as he beheld the shaking commander dangling from Rowan's iron grip. "Tell him what he wants to know. You'll only make it worse for yourself."

Lorcan had nearly reached them, a dark wind swirling about his long fingers.

There was nothing of the male she'd come to know on his harsh face. At least, the male he'd been before that beach. No, this was the mask she'd first seen in Oakwald. Unfeeling. Arrogant. Cruel.

The commander beheld the power gathering in Lorcan's hand, but managed to sneer at Rowan, blood coating his teeth. "She'll kill all of you." A black eye already bloomed, the lid swollen shut. Air pulsed at Elide's ears as Rowan locked a shield of wind around them. Sealing in all sound. "Maeve will kill every last one of you traitors."

"She can try," was Rowan's mild reply.

See, Anneith whispered again.

When the commander began screaming this time, Elide did not look away.

And as Rowan and Lorcan did what they'd been trained to do, she couldn't decide if Anneith's order had been to help—or a reminder of precisely what the gods might do should they disobey.

CHAPTER
3

The Staghorns were burning, and Oakwald with them.

The mighty, ancient trees were little more than charred husks, ash thick as snow raining down.

Embers drifted on the wind, a mockery of how they had once bobbed in her wake like fireflies while she'd run through the Beltane bonfires.

So much flame, the heat smothering, the air itself singeing her lungs.

You did this you did this you did this.

The crack of dying trees groaned the words, cried them.

The world was bathed in fire. Fire, not darkness.

Motion between the trees snared her attention.

The Lord of the North was frantic, mindless with agony, as he galloped toward her. As smoke streamed from his white coat, as fire devoured his mighty antlers—not the immortal flame held between them on her own sigil, the immortal flame of the sacred stags of Terrasen, and of Mala Fire-Bringer before that. But true, vicious flames.

The Lord of the North thundered past, burning, burning, burning.

She reached a hand toward him, invisible and inconsequential, but the proud stag plunged on, screams rising from his mouth.

Such horrible, relentless screams. As if the heart of the world were being shredded.

She could do nothing when the stag threw himself into a wall of flame spread like a net between two burning oaks.

He did not emerge.

The white wolf was watching her again.

Aelin Ashryver Whitethorn Galathynius ran an ironclad finger over the rim of the stone altar on which she lay.

As much movement as she could manage.

Cairn had left her here this time. Had not bothered moving her to the iron box against the adjacent wall.

A rare reprieve. To wake not in darkness, but in flickering firelight.

The braziers were dying, beckoning in the damp cold that pressed to her skin. To whatever wasn't covered by the iron.

She'd already tugged on the chains as quietly as she could. But they held firm.

They'd added more iron. On her. Starting with the metal gauntlets.

She did not remember when that was. Where that had been. There had only been the box then.

The smothering iron coffin.

She had tested it for weaknesses, over and over. Before they'd sent that sweet-smelling smoke to knock her unconscious. She didn't know how long she'd slept after that.

When she'd awoken here, there had been no more smoke.

She'd tested it again, then. As much as the irons would allow. Pushing with her feet, her elbows, her hands against the unforgiving metal. She didn't have enough room to turn over. To ease the pain of the chains digging into her. Chafing her.

The lash wounds etched deep into her back had vanished. The ones that had cleaved her skin to the bone. Or had that been a dream, too?

She had drifted into memory, into years of training in an assassin's keep. Into lessons where she'd been left in chains, in her own waste, until she figured out how to remove them.

But she'd been bound with that training in mind. Nothing she tried in the cramped dark had worked.

The metal of the glove scraped against the dark stone, barely audible over the hissing braziers, the roaring river beyond them. Wherever they were.

Her, and the wolf.

Fenrys.

No chains bound him. None were needed.

Maeve had ordered him to stay, to stand down, and so he would.

For long minutes, they stared at each other.

Aelin did not reflect on the pain that had sent her into unconsciousness. Even as the memory of cracking bones set her foot twitching. The chains jangled.

But nothing flickered where agony should have been rampant. Not a whisper of discomfort in her feet. She shut out the image of how that male—Cairn—had taken them apart. How she'd screamed until her voice had failed.

It might have been a dream. One of the endless horde that hunted her in the blackness. A burning stag, fleeing through the trees. Hours on this altar, her feet shattered beneath ancient tools. A silver-haired prince whose very scent was that of home.

They blurred and bled, until even this moment, staring at the white wolf lying against the wall across from the altar, might be a fragment of an illusion.

Aelin's finger scratched along the curved edge of the altar again.

The wolf blinked at her—thrice. In the early days, months, years of this, they had crafted a silent code between them. Using the few moments she'd been able to dredge up speech, whispering through the near-invisible holes in the iron coffin.

One blink for yes. Two for no. Three for *Are you all right?* Four for *I am here, I am with you.* Five for *This is real, you are awake.*

Fenrys again blinked three times. *Are you all right?*

Aelin swallowed against the thickness in her throat, her tongue peeling off the roof of her mouth. She blinked once. *Yes.*

She counted his blinks.

Six.

He'd made that one up. *Liar,* or something like it. She refused to acknowledge that particular code.

She blinked once again. *Yes.*

Dark eyes scanned her. He'd seen everything. Every moment of it. If he were permitted to shift, he could tell her what was fabricated and what was real. If any of it had been real.

No injuries ever remained when she awoke. No pain. Only the memory of it, of Cairn's smiling face as he carved her up over and over.

He must have left her on the altar because he meant to return soon.

Aelin shifted enough to tug on the chains, the mask's lock digging into the back of her head. The wind had not brushed her cheeks, or most of her skin, in . . . she did not know.

What wasn't covered in iron was clad in a sleeveless white shift that fell to midthigh. Leaving her legs and arms bare for Cairn's ministrations.

There were days, memories, of even that shift being gone, of knives scraping over her abdomen. But whenever she awoke, the shift remained intact. Untouched. Unstained.

Fenrys's ears perked, twitching. All the alert Aelin needed.

She hated the trembling that began to coil around her bones as strolling footsteps scuffed beyond the square room and the iron door into it. The only way in. No windows. The stone hall she sometimes glimpsed beyond was equally sealed. Only the sound of water entered this place.

It surged louder as the iron door unlocked and groaned open.

She willed herself not to shake as the brown-haired male approached. "Awake so soon? I must not have worked you hard enough."

That voice. She hated that voice above all others. Crooning and cold.

He wore a warrior's garb, but no warrior's weapons hung from the belt at his slim waist.

Cairn noted where her eyes fell and patted the heavy hammer dangling from his hip. "So eager for more."

There was no flame to rally to her. Not an ember.

He stalked to the small pile of logs by one brazier and fed a few to the dying fire. It swirled and crackled, leaping upon the wood with hungry fingers.

Her magic didn't so much as flicker in answer. Everything she ate and drank through the small slot in the mask's mouth was laced with iron.

She'd refused it at first. Had tasted the iron and spat it out.

She'd gone to the brink of dying from lack of water when they forced it down her throat. Then they'd let her starve—starve until she broke and devoured whatever they put in front of her, iron or no.

She did not often think about that time. That weakness. How excited Cairn had grown to see her eating, and how much he raged when it still did not yield what he wanted.

Cairn loaded the other brazier before snapping his fingers at Fenrys. "You may see to your needs in the hall and return here immediately."

As if a ghost hoisted him up, the enormous wolf padded out.

Maeve had considered even that, granting Cairn power to order when Fenrys ate and drank, when he pissed. She knew Cairn deliberately forgot sometimes. The canine whines of pain had reached her, even in the box.

Real. That had been real.

The male before her, a trained warrior in everything but honor and spirit, surveyed her body. "How shall we play tonight, Aelin?"

She hated the sound of her name on his tongue.

Her lip curled back from her teeth.

Fast as an asp, Cairn gripped her throat hard enough to bruise. "Such rage, even now."

She would never let go of it—the rage. Even when she sank into that burning sea within her, even when she sang to the darkness and flame, the rage guided her.

Cairn's fingers dug into her throat, and she couldn't stop the choking noise that gasped from her. "This can all be over with a few little words, Princess," he purred, dropping low enough that his breath brushed her mouth. "A few little words, and you and I will part ways forever."

She'd never say them. Never swear the blood oath to Maeve.

Swear it, and hand over everything she knew, everything she was. Become slave eternal. And usher in the doom of the world.

Cairn's grip on her neck loosened, and she inhaled deeply. But his fingers lingered at the right side of her throat.

She knew precisely what spot, what scar, he brushed his fingers over. The twin small markings in the space between her neck and shoulder.

"Interesting," Cairn murmured.

Aelin jerked her head away, baring her teeth again.

Cairn struck her.

Not her face, clad in iron that would rip open his knuckles. But her unprotected stomach.

The breath slammed from her, and iron clanked as she tried and failed to curl onto her side.

On silent paws, Fenrys loped back in and took up his place against the wall. Concern and fury flared in the wolf's dark eyes as she gasped for air, as her chained limbs still attempted to curl around her abdomen. But Fenrys could only lower himself onto the floor once more.

Four blinks. *I am here, I am with you.*

Cairn didn't see it. Didn't remark on her one blink in reply as he smirked at the tiny bites on her neck, sealed with the salt from the warm waters of Skull's Bay.

Rowan's marking. A mate's marking.

She didn't let herself think of him too long. Not as Cairn thumbed free that heavy-headed hammer and weighed it in his broad hands.

"If it wasn't for Maeve's gag order," the male mused, surveying her body like a painter assessing an empty canvas, "I'd put my own teeth in you. See if Whitethorn's marking holds up then."

Dread coiled in her gut. She'd seen the evidence of what their long hours here summoned from him. Her fingers curled, scraping the stone as if it were Cairn's face.

Cairn shifted the hammer to one hand. "This will have to do, I suppose." He ran his other hand down the length of her torso, and she jerked against the chains at the proprietary touch. He smiled. "So responsive." He gripped her bare knee, squeezing gently. "We started at the feet earlier. Let's go higher this time."

Aelin braced herself. Took plunging breaths that would bring her far away from here. From her body.

She'd never let them break her. Never swear that blood oath.

For Terrasen, for her people, whom she had left to endure their own torment for ten long years. She owed them this much.

Deep, deep, deep she went, as if she could outrun what was to come, as if she could hide from it.

The hammer glinted in the firelight as it rose over her knee, Cairn's breath sucking in, anticipation and delight mingling on his face.

Fenrys blinked, over and over and over. *I am here, I am with you.*

It didn't stop the hammer from falling.

Or the scream that shattered from her throat.

CHAPTER
4

"This camp has been abandoned for months."

Manon turned from the snow-crusted cliff where she'd been monitoring the western edge of the White Fang Mountains. Toward the Wastes.

Asterin remained crouched over the half-buried remnants of a fire pit, the shaggy goat pelt slung over her shoulders ruffling in the frigid wind. Her Second went on, "No one's been here since early autumn."

Manon had suspected as much. The Shadows had spotted the site an hour earlier on their patrol of the terrain ahead, somehow noticing the irregularities cleverly hidden in the leeward side of the rocky peak. The Mother knew Manon herself might have flown right over it.

Asterin stood, brushing snow from the knees of her leathers. Even the thick material wasn't enough to ward against the brutal cold. Hence the mountain-goat pelts they'd resorted to wearing.

Good for blending into the snow, Edda had claimed, the Shadow even letting the dark hair dye she favored wash away these weeks to reveal the moon white of her natural shade. Manon's shade. Briar had kept the dye. One of them was needed to scout at night, the other Shadow had claimed.

Manon surveyed the two Shadows carefully stalking through the camp. Perhaps no longer Shadows, but rather the two faces of the moon. One dark, one light.

One of many changes to the Thirteen.

Manon blew out a breath, the wind tearing away the hot puff.

"They're out there," Asterin murmured so the others might not hear from where they gathered by the overhanging boulder that shielded them from the wind.

"Three camps," Manon said with equal quiet. "All long abandoned. We're hunting ghosts."

Asterin's gold hair ripped free of its braid, blowing westward. Toward the homeland they might very well never see. "The camps are proof they're flesh and blood. Ghislaine thinks they might be from the late-summer hunts."

"They could also be from the wild men of these mountains." Though Manon knew they weren't. She'd hunted enough Crochans during the past hundred years to spot their style of making fires, their neat little camps. All the Thirteen had. And they'd all tracked and killed so many of the wild men of the White Fangs earlier this year on Erawan's behalf that they knew their habits, too.

Asterin's gold-flecked black eyes fell on that blurred horizon. "We'll find them."

Soon. They had to find at least *some* of the Crochans soon. Manon knew they had methods of communicating, scattered as they were. Ways to get out a call for help. A call for aid.

Time was not on their side. It had been nearly two months since that day on the beach in Eyllwe. Since she'd learned the terrible cost the Queen of Terrasen must pay to put an end to this madness. The cost that another with Mala's bloodline might also pay, if need be.

Manon resisted the urge to glance over her shoulder to where the King of Adarlan stood amongst the rest of her Thirteen, entertaining Vesta by summoning flame, water, and ice to his cupped palm. A small display of a terrible, wondrous magic. He set three whorls of the elements lazily dancing around each other, and Vesta arched an impressed brow. Manon had seen the way the red-haired sentinel looked at him, had noted that Vesta wisely refrained from acting on that desire.

Manon had given her no such orders, though. Hadn't said anything to the Thirteen about what, exactly, the human king was to her.

Nothing, she wanted to say. Someone as unmoored as she. As quietly angry. And as pressed for time. Finding the third and final Wyrdkey had proved futile. The two the king carried in his pocket offered no guidance, only their unearthly reek. Where Erawan kept it, they had not the faintest inkling. To search Morath or any of his other outposts would be suicide.

So they'd set aside their hunt, after weeks of fruitless searching, in favor of finding the Crochans. The king had protested initially, but yielded. His allies and friends in the North needed as many warriors as they could muster. Finding the Crochans . . . Manon wouldn't break her promise.

She might be the disowned Heir of the Blackbeak Clan, might now command only a dozen witches, but she could still hold true to her word.

So she'd find the Crochans. Convince them to fly into battle with the Thirteen. With her. Their last living Crochan Queen.

Even if it led them all straight into the Darkness's embrace.

The sun arched higher, its light off the snows near-blinding.

Lingering was unwise. They'd survived these months with strength and wits. For while they'd hunted for the Crochans, they'd been hunted themselves. Yellowlegs and Bluebloods, mostly. All scouting patrols.

Manon had given the order not to engage, not to kill. A missing Ironteeth patrol would only pinpoint their location. Though Dorian could have snapped their necks without lifting a finger.

It was a pity he hadn't been born a witch. But she'd gladly accept such a lethal ally. So would the Thirteen.

hat will you say," Asterin mused, "when we find the Crochans?"

non had considered it over and over. If the Crochans would know who Lothian Blackbeak was, that she had loved Manon's father—a rare-born Crochan Prince. That her parents had dreamed, had *believed* they'd created a child to break the curse on the Ironteeth and unite their peoples.

A child not of war, but of peace.

But those were foreign words on her tongue. *Love. Peace.*

Manon ran a gloved finger over the scrap of red fabric binding the end of her braid. A shred from her half sister's cloak. Rhiannon. Named for the last Witch-Queen. Whose face Manon somehow bore. Manon said, "I'll ask the Crochans not to shoot, I suppose."

Asterin's mouth twitched toward a smile. "I meant about who you are."

She'd rarely balked from anything. Rarely feared anything. But saying the words, *those* words . . . "I don't know," Manon admitted. "We'll see if we get that far."

The White Demon. That's what the Crochans called her. She was at the top of their to-kill list. A witch every Crochan was to slay on sight. That fact alone said they didn't know what she was to them.

Yet her half sister had figured it out. And then Manon had slit her throat.

Manon Kin Slayer, her grandmother had taunted. The Matron had likely relished every Crochan heart that Manon had brought to her at Blackbeak Keep over the past hundred years.

Manon closed her eyes, listening to the hollow song of the wind.

Behind them, Abraxos let out an impatient, hungry whine. Yes, they were all hungry these days.

"We will follow you, Manon," Asterin said softly.

Manon turned to her cousin. "Do I deserve that honor?"

Asterin's mouth pressed into a tight line. The slight bump on her nose— Manon had given her that. She'd broken it in the Omega's mess hall for brawling with mouthy Yellowlegs. Asterin had never once complained about it. Had seemed to wear the reminder of the beating Manon bestowed like a badge of pride.

"Only you can decide if you deserve it, Manon."

Manon let the words settle as she shifted her gaze to the western horizon. Perhaps she'd deserve that honor if she succeeded in bringing them back to a home they'd never set eyes on.

If they survived this war and all the terrible things they must do before it was over.

It was no easy thing, to slip away from thirteen sleeping witches and their wyverns.

But Dorian Havilliard had been studying them—their watches, who slept deepest, who might report seeing him walk away from their small fire and who would keep their mouths shut. Weeks and weeks, since he'd settled on this idea. This plan.

They'd camped on the small outcropping where they'd found long-cold traces of the Crochans, taking shelter under the overhanging rock, the wyverns a wall of leathery warmth around them.

He had minutes to do this. He'd been practicing for weeks now—making no bones of rising in the middle of the night, no more than a drowsy man displeased to have to brave the frigid elements to see to his needs. Letting the witches grow accustomed to his nightly movements.

Letting Manon become accustomed to it, too.

Though nothing had been declared between them, their bedrolls still wound up beside each other every night. Not that a camp full of witches offered any sort of opportunity to tangle with her. No, for that, they'd resorted to winter-bare forests and snow-blasted passes, their hands roving for any bit of bare skin they dared expose to the chill air.

Their couplings were brief, savage. Teeth and nails and snarling. And not just from Manon.

But after a day of fruitless searching, little more than a glorified guard against the enemies hunting them while his friends bled to save their lands, he needed the release as much as she did. They never discussed it—what hounded them. Which was fine by him.

Dorian had no idea what sort of man that made him.

Most days, if he was being honest, he felt little. Had felt little for months, save for those stolen, wild moments with Manon. And save for the moments when he trained with the Thirteen, and a blunt sort of rage drove him to keep swinging his sword, keep getting back up when they knocked him down.

Swordplay, archery, knife-work, tracking—they taught him everything he asked. Along with the solid weight of Damaris, a witch-knife now hung from his sword belt. It had been gifted to him by Sorrel when he'd first managed to pin the stone-faced Third. Two weeks ago.

But when the lessons were done, when they sat around the small fire they dared to risk each night, he wondered if the witches could sniff out the restlessness that nipped at his heels.

If they could now sniff out that he had no intention of taking a piss in the frigid night as he wended his way between their bedrolls, then through the slight gap between Narene, Asterin's sky-blue mare, and Abraxos. He nodded toward where Vesta stood on watch, and the red-haired witch, despite the brutal cold, threw a wicked smile his way before he rounded the corner of the rocky overhang and disappeared beyond view.

He'd picked her watch for a reason. There were some amongst the Thirteen who never smiled at all. Lin, who still seemed like she was debating carving him up to examine his insides; and Imogen, who kept to herself and didn't smile at *anyone*. Thea and Kaya usually reserved their smiles for each other, and when Faline and Fallon—the green-eyed demon twins, as the others called them—smiled, it meant hell was about to break loose.

All of them might have been suspicious if he vanished for too long. But Vesta, who shamelessly flirted with him—she'd let him linger outside the camp. Likely from fear of what Manon might do to her if she was spotted trailing after him into the dark.

A bastard—he was a bastard for using them like this. For assessing and monitoring them when they currently risked everything to find the Crochans.

But it made no difference if he cared. About them. About himself, he supposed. Caring hadn't done him any favors. Hadn't done Sorscha any favors.

And it wouldn't matter, once he gave up everything to seal the Wyrdgate.

Damaris was a weight at his side—but nothing compared to the two objects tucked into the pocket of his heavy jacket. Mercifully, he'd swiftly learned to drown out their whispering, their otherworldly beckoning. Most of the time.

None of the witches had questioned why he'd been so easily persuaded to give up the hunt for the third Wyrdkey. He'd known better than to waste his time arguing. So he'd planned, and let them, let Manon, believe him to be content in his role to guard them with his magic.

Reaching the boulder-shrouded clearing that he'd scouted earlier under the guise of aimlessly wandering the site, Dorian made quick work of his preparations.

He had not forgotten a single movement of Aelin's hands in Skull's Bay when she'd smeared her blood on the floor of her room at the Ocean Rose.

But it was not Elena whom he planned to summon with his blood.

When the snow was red with it, when he'd made sure the wind was still blowing its scent away from the witch camp, Dorian unsheathed Damaris and plunged it into the circle of Wyrdmarks.

And then waited.

His magic was a steady thrum through him, the small flame he dared to conjure enough to heat his body. To keep him from shivering to death while the minutes passed.

Ice had been the first manifestation of his magic. He supposed that should give him some sort of preference for it. Or at least some immunity.

He had neither. And he'd decided that if they survived long enough to endure the scorching heat of summer, he'd never complain about it again.

He'd been honing his magic as best he could during these weeks of relentless, useless hunting. None of the witches possessed power, not beyond the Yielding, which they'd told him could only be summoned once—to terrible and devastating effect. But the Thirteen watched with some degree of interest while Dorian kept up the lessons Rowan had started. Ice. Fire. Water. Healing. Wind. With the snows, attempting to coax life from the frozen earth had proved impossible, but he still tried.

The only magic that always leapt at his summons remained that invisible force, capable of snapping bone. That, the witches liked best. Especially since it made him their greatest line of defense against their enemies. Death—that was his gift. All he seemed able to offer those around him. He was little better than his father in that regard.

The flame flowed over him, invisible and steadying.

They hadn't heard a whisper of Aelin. Or Rowan and their companions. Not one whisper of whether the queen was still Maeve's captive.

She had been willing to yield everything to save Terrasen, to save all of them. He could do nothing less. Aelin certainly had more to lose. A mate and husband who loved her. A court who'd follow her into hell. A kingdom long awaiting her return.

All he had was an unmarked grave for a healer no one would remember, a broken empire, and a shattered castle.

Dorian closed his eyes for a moment, blocking out the sight of the glass castle exploding, the sight of his father reaching for him, begging for forgiveness. A monster—the man had been a monster in every possible way. Had sired Dorian while possessed by a Valg demon.

What did it make him? His blood ran red, and the Valg prince who'd infested Dorian himself had delighted on feasting on him, on making him *enjoy* all he'd done while collared. But did it still make him fully human?

Blowing out a long breath, Dorian opened his eyes.

A man stood across the snowy clearing.

Dorian bowed low. "Gavin."

The first King of Adarlan had his eyes.

Or rather Dorian had Gavin's eyes, passed down through the thousand years between them.

The rest of the ancient king's face was foreign: the long, dark brown hair, the harsh features, the grave cast of his mouth. "You learned the marks."

Dorian rose from his bow. "I'm a quick study."

Gavin didn't smile. "The summoning is not a gift to be used lightly. You risk much, young king, in calling me here. Considering what you carry."

Dorian patted the jacket pocket where the two Wyrdkeys lay, ignoring the strange, terrible power that pulsed against his hand in answer. "Everything is a risk these days." He straightened. "I need your help."

Gavin didn't reply. His stare slid to Damaris, still plunged in the snow amid the marks. A personal effect of the king, as Aelin had used the Eye of Elena to summon the ancient queen. "At least you have taken good care of my sword." His eyes lifted to Dorian's, sharp as the blade itself. "Though I cannot say the same of my kingdom."

Dorian clenched his jaw. "I inherited a bit of a mess from my father, I'm afraid."

"You were a Prince of Adarlan long before you became its king."

Dorian's magic churned to ice, colder than the night around him. "Then consider me trying to atone for years of bad behavior."

Gavin held his gaze for a moment that stretched into eternity. A true king, that's what the man before him was. A king not only in title, but in spirit. As few had been since Gavin was laid to rest beneath the foundations of the castle he'd built along the Avery.

Dorian withstood the weight of Gavin's stare. Let the king see what remained of him, mark the pale band around his throat.

Then Gavin blinked once, the only sign of his permission to continue.

Dorian swallowed. "Where is the third key?"

Gavin stiffened. "I am forbidden to say."

"Forbidden, or won't?" He supposed he should be kneeling, should keep his tone respectful. How many legends about Gavin had he read as a child? How many times had he run through the castle, pretending to be the king before him?

Dorian pulled the Amulet of Orynth from his jacket, letting it sway in the bitter wind. A silent, ghostly song leaked from the gold-and-blue medallion—speaking in languages that did not exist. "Brannon Galathynius defied the gods by putting the key in here with a warning to Aelin. The least you could do is give me a direction."

Gavin's edges blurred, but held. Not much time. For either of them. "Brannon Galathynius was an arrogant bastard. I have seen what interfering with the gods' plans brings about. It will not end well."

"Your wife, not the gods, brought this about."

Gavin bared his teeth. And though the man was long dead, Dorian's magic flared again, readying to strike.

"My mate," Gavin snarled, "is the cost of this. My mate, should the keys be retrieved, will vanish *forever*. Do you know what that is like, young king? To have eternity—and then have it ripped away?"

Dorian didn't bother to reply. "You don't wish me to find the third key because it will mean the end of Elena."

Gavin said nothing.

Dorian let out a growl. "Countless people will *die* if the keys aren't put back in the gate." He shoved the Amulet of Orynth back into his jacket, and once again ignored the otherworldly hum pulsing against his bones. "You can't be that selfish."

Gavin remained silent, the wind shifting his dark hair. But his eyes flickered—just barely.

"Tell me where," Dorian breathed. He had mere minutes until even Vesta came looking for him. "Tell me where the third key is."

"Your life will be forfeit, too. If you retrieve the keys and forge the

Lock. Your soul will be claimed as well. Not one scrap of you will live on in the Afterworld."

"There's no one who would really care about that anyway." He certainly didn't. And he'd certainly deserved that sort of end, when he'd failed so many times. With all he'd done.

Gavin studied him for a long moment. Dorian held still beneath that fierce stare. A warrior who had survived the second of Erawan's wars.

"Elena helped Aelin," Dorian pressed, his breath curling in the space between them. "She didn't balk from it, even knowing what it meant for her fate. And neither did Aelin, who will have neither a long life with her own mate, nor eternity with him." *As I will not have, either.* His heart began thundering, his magic rising with it. "And yet you would. You would run from it."

Gavin's teeth flashed. "Erawan could be defeated without sealing the gate."

"Tell me how, and I will find a way to do it."

Yet Gavin fell silent again, his hands clenching at his sides.

Dorian snorted softly. "If you knew, it would have been done long ago." Gavin shook his head, but Dorian plunged ahead. "Your friends died battling Erawan's hordes. Help me avoid the same fate for my own. It might already be too late for some of them." His stomach churned.

Had Chaol made it to the southern continent? Perhaps it would be better if his friend never returned, if he stayed safe in Antica. Even if Chaol would never do such a thing.

Dorian glanced toward the rocky corner he'd rounded. Not much time left.

"And what of Adarlan?" Gavin demanded. "You would leave it kingless?" The question said enough of Gavin's opinion regarding Hollin. "This is how you would atone for years spent idling as its Crown Prince?"

Dorian took the verbal blow. It was nothing but truth, dealt by a man who had served its nameless god. "Does it really matter anymore?"

"Adarlan was my pride."

"It is no longer worthy of it," Dorian snapped. "It hasn't been for a long, long time. Perhaps it deserves to fall into ruin."

Gavin angled his head. "The words of a reckless, arrogant boy. Do you think you are the only one who has endured loss?"

"And yet your own fear of loss makes you choose one woman over the fate of the world."

"If you had the choice—your woman or Erilea—would you have chosen any differently?"

Sorscha or the world. The question rang hollow. Some of the fire within him banked. Yet Dorian dared to say, "You'd delude yourself about the path ahead, yet you served the god of truth." Chaol had told him of their discovery in the catacombs beneath Rifthold's sewers this spring. The forgotten bone temple where Gavin's deathbed confession had been written. "What does *he* have to say about Elena's role in this?"

"The All-Seeing One does not claim kinship with those spineless creatures," Gavin growled.

Dorian could have sworn a dusty, bone-dry wind rattled through the pass. "Then what is he?"

"Can there not be many gods, from many places? Some born of this world, some born elsewhere?"

"That's a question to debate at another time," Dorian ground out. "When we're not at war." He took a long breath. Another one. "Please," he breathed. "Please help me save my friends. Help me make it right."

It was all he really had left—this task.

Gavin again watched him, weighed him. Dorian withstood it. Let him read whatever truth was written on his soul.

Pain clouded the king's face. Pain, and regret, as Gavin finally said, "The key is at Morath."

Dorian's mouth went dry. "Where in Morath?"

"I don't know." Dorian believed him. The raw dread in Gavin's eyes confirmed it. The ancient king nodded to Damaris. "That sword is not ornamental. Let it guide you, if you cannot trust yourself."

"It really tells the truth?"

"It was blessed by the All-Seeing One himself, after I swore myself to him." Gavin shrugged, a half-tamed gesture. As if the man had never really left the wilds of Adarlan where he'd risen from war leader to High King. "You'll still have to learn for yourself what is truth and what is lie."

"But Damaris will help me find the key at Morath?" To break into Erawan's stronghold, where all those collars were made . . .

Gavin's mouth tightened. "I cannot say. But I will tell you this: do not venture toward Morath just yet. Until you are ready."

"I'm ready now." A fool's lie. Gavin knew it, too. It was an effort not to touch his neck, the pale band forever marring his skin.

"Morath is no mere keep," Gavin said. "It is a hell, and it is not kind to reckless young men." Dorian stiffened, but Gavin went on, "You will know when you are truly ready. Remain at this camp, if you can convince your companions. The path will find you here."

Gavin's edges warped further, his face turning murky.

Dorian dared a step forward. "Am I human?"

Gavin's sapphire eyes softened—just barely. "I'm not the person who can answer that."

And then the king was gone.

CHAPTER 5

The commander in the alley had claimed his latest orders had been dispatched from Doranelle.

None of them knew whether to believe him.

Sitting around a tiny fire in a dusty field on the outskirts of a ramshackle city, the blood long since washed from his hands, Lorcan Salvaterre again mulled over the logic of it.

Had they somehow overlooked the simplest option? For Maeve to have been in Doranelle this entire time, hidden from her subjects?

But that commander had been lying filth. He'd spat in Lorcan's face before they'd ended it.

The other commander they'd found today, however, after a week of hunting him down at the nearest seaport, had claimed he'd received orders from a distant kingdom they'd searched three weeks ago. In the opposite direction of Doranelle.

Lorcan toed at the dirt.

None of them had felt like speaking since the commander this afternoon had contradicted the first's claim.

"Doranelle is Maeve's stronghold," Elide said at last, her steady voice filling the heavy quiet. "Simple as it is, it would make sense for her to bring Aelin there."

Whitethorn only stared into the fire. He hadn't washed the blood from his dark gray jacket.

"It would be impossible, even for Maeve, to keep her hidden in Doranelle," Lorcan countered. "We would have heard about it by now."

He wasn't sure when he'd last spoken to the woman before him.

She hadn't balked from how he'd broken Maeve's commanders, though. She'd cringed during the worst of it, yes, but she'd listened to every word Rowan and Lorcan had wrung from them. Lorcan supposed she'd seen worse at Morath—hated that she had. Hated that her monster of an uncle still breathed.

But that hunt would come later. After they found Aelin. Or whatever remained of her.

Elide's eyes grew cold, so cold, as she said, "Maeve managed to conceal Gavriel and Fenrys from Rowan in Skull's Bay. And somehow hid and spirited away her entire fleet."

Lorcan didn't reply. Elide went on, her gaze unwavering, "Maeve knows Doranelle would be the obvious choice—the choice we'd likely reject because it's *too* simple. She anticipated that we'd believe she'd haul Aelin to the farthest reaches of Erilea, rather than right back home."

"Maeve *would* have the advantage of an easily summoned army," Gavriel added, his tattooed throat bobbing. "Which would make rescue difficult."

Lorcan refrained from telling Gavriel to shut his mouth. He hadn't failed to notice how often Gavriel went out of his way to help Elide, to talk to her. And yes, some small part of him was grateful for it, since the gods knew she wouldn't accept any sort of help from *him*.

Hellas damn him, he'd had to resort to giving his cut-up shirt to

Whitethorn and Gavriel to hand to her for her cycle. He'd threatened to skin them alive if they'd said it was his, and Elide, with her human sense of smell, hadn't scented him on the fabric.

He didn't know why he bothered. He hadn't forgotten her words that day on the beach.

I hope you spend the rest of your miserable, immortal life suffering. I hope you spend it alone. I hope you live with regret and guilt in your heart and never find a way to endure it.

Her vow, her curse, whatever it had been, had held true. Every word of it.

He'd broken something. Something precious beyond measure. He'd never cared until now.

Even the severed blood oath, still gaping wide within his soul, didn't come close to the hole in his chest when he looked at her.

She'd offered him a home in Perranth knowing he'd be a dishonored male. Offered him a home with her.

But it hadn't been Maeve's sundering of the oath that had rescinded that offer. It had been a betrayal so great he didn't know how to fix it.

Where is Aelin? Where is my wife?

Whitethorn's wife—and his mate. Only this mission of theirs, this endless quest to find her, kept Lorcan from plunging into a pit from which he knew he would not emerge.

Perhaps if they found her, if there was still enough left of Aelin to salvage after Cairn's ministrations, he'd find a way to live with himself. To endure this . . . person he'd become. It might take him another five hundred years to do so.

He didn't let himself consider that Elide would be little more than dust by then. The thought alone was enough to turn the paltry dinner of stale bread and hard cheese in his stomach.

A fool—he was an immortal, stupid fool for starting down this path with her, for forgetting that even if she forgave him, her mortality beckoned.

Lorcan said at last, "It would also make sense for Maeve to go to the

Akkadians, as the commander today claimed. Maeve has long maintained ties with that kingdom." He, Whitethorn, and Gavriel had been to war and back in that sand-blasted territory. He'd never wished to set foot in it again. "Their armies would shield her."

For it would take an army to keep Whitethorn from reaching his mate.

He turned toward the prince, who gave no indication he'd been listening. Lorcan didn't want to consider if Whitethorn would soon need to add a tattoo to the other side of his face.

"The commander today was much more forthcoming," Lorcan went on to the prince he'd fought beside for so many centuries, who had been as cold-hearted a bastard as Lorcan himself until this spring. "You barely threatened him and he sang for us. The one who claimed Maeve was in Doranelle was still sneering by the end."

"I think she's in Doranelle," Elide cut in. "Anneith told me to listen that day. She didn't the other two times."

"It's something to consider, yes," Lorcan said, and Elide's eyes sparked with irritation. "I see no reason to believe the gods would be that clear."

"Says the male who feels the touch of a god, telling him when to run or fight," Elide snapped.

Lorcan ignored her, that truth. He hadn't felt Hellas's touch since the Stone Marshes. As if even the god of death was repulsed by him. "Akkadia's border is a three-day ride from here. Its capital three days beyond that. Doranelle is over two weeks away, if we travel with little rest."

And time was not on their side. With the Wyrdkeys, with Erawan, with the war surely unleashing itself back on Elide's own continent, every delay came at a cost. Not to mention what each day undoubtedly brought upon the Queen of Terrasen.

Elide opened her mouth, but Lorcan cut her off. "And then, to arrive in Maeve's stronghold exhausted and hungry . . . We won't stand a chance. Not to mention that with the veiling she can wield, we might very well walk right past Aelin and never know it."

Elide's nostrils flared, but she turned to Rowan. "The call is yours, Prince."

Not just a prince, not anymore. Consort to the Queen of Terrasen.

At last, Whitethorn lifted his head. As those green eyes settled on him, Lorcan withstood the weight in his gaze, the innate dominance. He'd been waiting for Rowan to claim the vengeance he deserved, waiting for that blow. Hoping for it. It had never come.

"We've come this far south," Rowan said at last, his voice low. "Better to go to Akkadia than risk venturing all the way to Doranelle to find we were wrong."

And that was that.

Elide only threw a seething glare toward Lorcan and rose, murmuring about seeing to her needs before she went to sleep. Her gait held steady as she crunched through the grass—thanks to the brace Gavriel kept around her ankle.

It should have been his magic helping her. Touching her skin.

Her steps turned distant, near-silent. She usually went farther than necessary to avoid having them hear anything. Lorcan gave her a few minutes before he stalked into the dark after her.

He found Elide already heading back, and she paused atop a little hill, barely more than a hump of dirt in the field. "What do you want."

Lorcan kept walking, until he was at the base of the hill, and stopped. "Akkadia is the wiser choice."

"Rowan decided that, too. You must be so pleased."

She made to stomp past him, but Lorcan stepped into her path. She craned back her neck to see his face, yet he'd never felt smaller. Shorter. "I didn't push for Akkadia to spite you," he managed to say.

"I don't care."

She tried to edge around him, Lorcan easily keeping ahead of her. "I didn't . . ." The words strangled him. "I didn't mean for this to happen."

Elide let out a soft, vicious laugh. "Of course you didn't. Why would you have intended for your wondrous queen to sever the blood oath?"

"I don't care about that." He didn't. He'd never spoken truer words. "I only wish to make things right."

Her lip curled. "I would be inclined to believe that if I hadn't seen you *crawling* after Maeve on the beach."

Lorcan blinked at the words, the hatred in them, stunned enough that he let her walk past this time. Elide didn't so much as look back.

Not until Lorcan said, "I didn't crawl after Maeve."

She halted, hair swaying. Slowly, she glanced over her shoulder. Imperious and cold as the stars overhead.

"I crawled . . ." His throat bobbed. "I crawled after Aelin."

He shut out the bloody sand, the queen's screams, her final, pleading requests to Elide. Shut them out and said, "When Maeve severed the oath, I couldn't move, could barely breathe."

Such agony that Lorcan couldn't imagine what it would be like to sever the oath on his own, without bidding. It was not the sort of pain one walked away from.

The oath could be stretched, drawn thin. That Vaughan, the last of their cadre, still undoubtedly roamed the wilds of the North in his "hunt" for Lorcan was proof enough that the blood oath's restraints might be worked around. But to break it outright of his own will, to find some way to snap the tether, would be to embrace death.

He'd wondered during these months if he should have done just that.

Lorcan swallowed. "I tried to get to her. To Aelin. I tried to get to that box." He added so quietly only Elide could hear it, "I promise."

His word was his bond, the only currency he cared to trade in. He'd told her that once, during those weeks on the road. Nothing flickered in her eyes to tell him she remembered.

Elide merely strode back for the camp. Lorcan remained where he was.

He had done this. Brought this upon her, upon them.

Elide reached the campfire, and Lorcan followed at last, nearing its ring of light in time to see her plop down beside Gavriel, her mouth tight.

The Lion murmured to her, "He wasn't lying, you know."

Lorcan clenched his jaw, making no attempt to disguise his footsteps. If Gavriel's ears were sharp enough to have heard every word of their conversation, the Lion certainly knew he was approaching. And certainly knew better than to shove his nose in their business.

Yet Lorcan still found himself scanning Elide's face, waiting for her answer.

And when she ignored both the Lion and Lorcan, he found himself wishing he hadn't spoken at all.

⁓

Prince Rowan Whitethorn Galathynius, consort, husband, and mate of the Queen of Terrasen, knew he was dreaming.

He knew it, because he could see her.

There was only darkness here. And wind. And a great, yawning chasm between them.

No bottom existed in that abyss, that crack in the world. But he could hear whispers snaking through it, down far below.

She stood with her back to him, hair blowing in a sheet of gold. Longer than he'd seen it the last time.

He tried to shift, to fly over the chasm. His body's innate magic ignored him. Locked in his Fae body, the jump too far, he could only stare toward her, breathe in her scent—jasmine, lemon verbena, and crackling embers— as it floated to him on the wind. This wind told him no secrets, had no song to sing.

It was a wind of death, of cold, of nothing.

Aelin.

He had no voice here, but he spoke her name. Threw it across the gulf between them.

Slowly, she turned to him.

It was her face—or it would be in a few years. When she Settled.

But it wasn't the slightly older features that knocked the breath from him.

It was the hand on her rounded belly.

She stared toward him, hair still flowing. Behind her, four small figures emerged.

Rowan fell to his knees.

The tallest: a girl with golden hair and pine-green eyes, solemn-faced and as proud as her mother. The boy beside her, nearly her height, smiled at him, warm and bright, his Ashryver eyes near-glowing beneath his cap of silver hair. The boy next to him, silver-haired and green-eyed, might as well have been Rowan's twin. And the smallest girl, clinging to her mother's legs . . . A fine-boned, silver-haired child, little more than a babe, her blue eyes harking back to a lineage he did not know.

Children. His children. Their children.

With another mere weeks from being born.

His family.

The family he might have, the future he might have. The most beautiful thing he'd ever seen.

Aelin.

Their children pressed closer to her, the eldest girl peering up to Aelin in warning.

Rowan felt it then. A lethal, mighty black wind sweeping for them.

He tried to scream. Tried to get off his knees, to find some way to them. But the black wind roared in, ripping and tearing everything in its path.

They were still staring at him as it swept them away, too.

Until only dust and shadow remained.

⁓

Rowan jerked awake, his heart a frantic beat as his body bellowed to *move*, to *fight*.

But there was nothing and no one to fight here, in this dusty field beneath the stars.

A dream. That same dream.

He rubbed at his face, sitting up on his bedroll. The horses dozed, no sign of distress. Gavriel kept watch in mountain-lion form just beyond the light of the fire, his eyes gleaming in the dark. Elide and Lorcan didn't stir from their heavy slumber.

Rowan scanned the position of the stars. Only a few hours until dawn.

And then to Akkadia—to that land of scrub and sand.

While Elide and Lorcan had debated where to go, he'd weighed it himself. Whether to fly to Doranelle alone and risk losing precious days in what might be a fool's search.

Had Vaughan been with them, had Vaughan been freed, he might have dispatched the warrior in his osprey form to Doranelle while they continued on to Akkadia.

Rowan again considered it. If he pushed his magic, harnessed the winds to him, the two weeks it would take to reach Doranelle could be done in days. But if he somehow did find Aelin . . . He'd waged enough battles to know he'd need Lorcan and Gavriel's strength before things were over. That he might jeopardize Aelin in trying to free her without their help. Which would mean flying *back* to them, then making the agonizingly slow trip northward.

And with Akkadia so close, the wiser choice was to search there first. In case the commander today had spoken true. And if what they learned in Akkadia led them to Doranelle, then to Doranelle they would go. Together.

Even if it went against every instinct as her mate. Her husband. Even if every day, every hour, that Aelin spent in Maeve's clutches was likely bringing her more suffering than he could stand to consider.

So they'd travel to Akkadia. Within a few days, they'd enter the flat plains, and then the distant dried hills beyond. Once the winter rains began, the plain would be green, lush—but after the scorching summer, the lands were still brown and wheat-colored, water scarce.

He'd ensure they stocked up at the next river. Enough for the horses, too. Food might be in short supply, but there was game to be found on the plains. Scrawny rabbits and small, furred things that burrowed in the cracked earth. Precisely the sort of food Aelin would cringe to eat.

Gavriel noticed the movement at their camp and padded over, massive paws silent even on the bone-dry grass. Tawny, inquisitive eyes blinked at him.

Rowan shook his head at the unspoken question. "Get some sleep. I'll take over."

Gavriel angled his head in a gesture Rowan knew meant, *Are you all right?*

Strange—it was still strange to work with the Lion, with Lorcan, without the bonds of Maeve's oath binding them to do so. To know that they were here by choice.

What it now made them, Rowan wasn't entirely certain.

Rowan ignored Gavriel's silent inquiry and stared into the dwindling fire. "Get some rest while you can."

Gavriel didn't object as he prowled to his bedroll, and plopped onto it with a feline sigh.

Rowan suppressed the twinge of guilt. He'd been pushing them hard. They hadn't complained, hadn't asked him to slow the grueling pace he'd set.

He'd felt nothing in the bond since that day on the beach. Nothing.

She wasn't dead, because the bond still existed, yet . . . it was silent.

He'd puzzled over it during the long hours they'd traveled, during his hours on watch. Even the hours when he should have been sleeping.

He hadn't felt pain in the bond that day in Eyllwe. He'd felt it when Dorian Havilliard had stabbed her in the glass castle, had felt the bond—what he'd so stupidly thought was the *carranam* bond between them—stretching to the breaking point as she'd come so, so close to death.

Yet that day on the beach, when Maeve had attacked her, then had Cairn *whip* her—

Rowan clenched his jaw hard enough to hurt, even as his stomach roiled. He glanced to Goldryn, lying beside him on the bedroll.

Gently, he set the blade before him, staring into the ruby in the center of its hilt, the stone smoldering in the firelight.

Aelin had felt the arrow he'd received during the fight with Manon at Temis's temple. Or enough of a jolt that she'd known, in that moment, that they were mates.

Yet he hadn't felt anything at all that day on the beach.

He had a feeling he knew the answer. Knew that Maeve was likely the cause of it, the damper on what was between them. She'd gone into his head to trick him into thinking Lyria was his mate, had fooled the very instincts that made him a Fae male. It wouldn't be beyond her powers to find a way to stifle what was between him and Aelin, to keep him from knowing that she'd been in such danger, and now to keep him from finding her.

But he should have known. About Aelin. Shouldn't have waited to get the wyverns and the others. Should have flown right to the beach, and not wasted those precious minutes.

Mate. His mate.

He should have known about that, too. Even if rage and grief had turned him into a miserable bastard, he should have known who she was, what she was, from the moment he'd bitten her at Mistward, unable to stop the urge to claim her. The moment her blood had landed on his tongue and it had *sung* to him, and then refused to leave him alone, its taste lingering for months.

Instead, they'd brawled. He'd let them brawl, so lost in his anger and ice. She'd been just as raging as he, and had spat such a hateful, unspeakable thing that he'd treated her like any of the males and females who had been under his command and mouthed off, but those early days still haunted him. Though Rowan knew that if he ever mentioned the brawling they'd done with a lick of shame, Aelin would curse him for a fool.

He didn't know what to do about the tattoo down his face, his neck and arm. The lie it told of his loss, and the truth it revealed of his blindness.

He'd come to love Lyria—that had been true. And the guilt of it ate him alive whenever he thought of it, but he could understand now. Why

Lyria had been so frightened of him for those initial months, why it had been so damn hard to court her, even with that mating bond, its truth unknown to Lyria as well. She had been gentle, and quiet, and kind. A different sort of strength, yes, but not what he might have chosen for himself.

He hated himself for thinking it.

Even as the rage consumed him at the thought, at what had been stolen from him. From Lyria, too. Aelin had been his, and he had been hers, from the start. Longer than that. And Maeve had thought to break them, break *her* to get what she wanted.

He wouldn't let that go unpunished. Just as he could not forget that Lyria, regardless of what truly existed between them, had been carrying their child when Maeve had sent those enemy forces to his mountain home. He would never forgive that.

I will kill you, Aelin had said when she'd heard what Maeve had done. How badly Maeve had manipulated him, shattered him—and destroyed Lyria. Elide had told him every word of the encounter, over and over. *I will kill you.*

Rowan stared into the burning heart of Goldryn's ruby.

He prayed that fire, that rage, had not broken. He knew how many days it had been, knew who Maeve had promised would oversee the torture. Knew the odds were stacked against her. He'd spent two weeks strapped on an enemy's table. Still bore the scar on his arm from one of their more creative devices.

Hurry. They had to hurry.

Rowan leaned forward, resting his brow against Goldryn's hilt. The metal was warm, as if it still held a whisper of its bearer's flame.

He had not set foot in Akkadia since that last, horrible war. Though he'd led Fae and mortal soldiers alike to victory, he'd never had any desire to see it again.

But to Akkadia they would go.

And if he found her, if he freed her . . . Rowan did not let himself think beyond that.

To the other truth that they would face, the other burden. *Tell Rowan that I'm sorry I lied. But tell him it was all borrowed time anyway. Even before today, I knew it was all just borrowed time, but I still wish we'd had more of it.*

He refused to accept that. Would never accept that she would be the ultimate cost to end this, to save their world.

Rowan scanned the blanket of stars overhead.

While all other constellations had wheeled past, the Lord of the North remained, the immortal star between his antlers pointing the way home. To Terrasen.

Tell him he has to fight. He must save Terrasen, and remember the vows he made to me.

Time was not on their side, not with Maeve, not with the war unleashing itself back on their own continent. But he had no intention of returning without her, parting request or no, regardless of the oaths he'd sworn upon marrying her to guard and rule Terrasen.

And tell him thank you—for walking that dark path with me back to the light.

It had been his honor. From the very beginning, it had been his honor, the greatest of his immortal life.

An immortal life they would share together—somehow. He'd allow no other alternative.

Rowan silently swore it to the stars.

He could have sworn the Lord of the North flickered in response.

CHAPTER 6

The winter winds off the rough waves had chilled Chaol Westfall from the moment he'd emerged from his quarters belowdecks. Even with his thick blue cloak, the damp cold seeped into his bones, and now, as he scanned the water, it seemed the heavy cloud cover wasn't likely to break anytime soon. Winter was creeping over the continent, as surely as Morath's legions.

The brisk dawn had revealed nothing, only the roiling seas and the stoic sailors and soldiers who had kept this ship traveling swiftly north-ward. Behind them, flanking them, half of the khagan's fleet followed. The other half still lingered in the southern continent as the rest of the mighty empire's armada rallied. They'd only be a few weeks behind if the weather held.

Chaol sent a prayer on the briny, icy wind that it would. For despite the size of the fleet gathered behind him, and despite the thousand ruk riders who were just taking to the skies from their roosts on the ships for morning hunts over the waves, it might still not be enough against Morath.

And they might not arrive fast enough for that army to make a difference anyway.

Three weeks of sailing had brought them little news of the host his friends had assembled and supposedly brought to Terrasen, and they'd kept far enough from the coast to avoid any enemy ships—or wyverns. But that would change today.

A delicate, warm arm looped through his, and a head of brown-gold hair leaned against his shoulder. "It's freezing out here," Yrene murmured, scowling at the wind-whipped waves.

Chaol pressed a kiss to the top of her head. "The cold builds character."

She huffed a laugh, the steam of her breath torn away by the wind. "Spoken like a man from the North."

Chaol slid his arm around her shoulders, tucking her into his side. "Am I not keeping you warm enough these days, wife?"

Yrene blushed, and elbowed him in the ribs. "Cad."

Over a month later, and he was still marveling at the word: *wife*. At the woman by his side, who had healed his fractured and weary soul.

His spine was secondary to that. He'd spent these long days on the ship practicing how he might fight—whether by horseback or with a cane or from his wheeled chair—during the times when Yrene's power became drained enough that the life-bond between them stretched thin and the injury took over once more.

His spine hadn't healed, not truly. It never would. It had been the cost of saving his life after a Valg princess had taken him to death's threshold. Yet it did not feel like a cost too steeply paid.

It had never been a burden—the chair, the injury. It would not be now.

But the other part of that bargain with the goddess who had guided Yrene her entire life, who had brought her to Antica's shores and now back to their own continent . . . that part scared the hell out of him.

If he died, Yrene went as well.

To funnel her healing power into him so he might walk when her magic was not too drained, their very lives had been entwined.

So if he fell in battle against Morath's legions . . . It would not be just his own life lost.

"You're thinking too hard." Yrene frowned up at him. "What is it?"

Chaol jerked his chin toward the ship sailing nearest their own. On its stern, two ruks, one golden and one reddish brown, stood at attention. Both were already saddled, though there was no sign of Kadara's or Salkhi's riders.

"I can't tell if you're motioning to the ruks or the fact that Nesryn and Sartaq are smart enough to remain in bed on a morning like this." *As we should be*, her golden-brown eyes added tartly.

It was Chaol's turn to nudge her with an elbow. "You're the one who woke *me* up this morning, you know." He brushed a kiss to the column of her neck, a precise reminder of how, exactly, Yrene had awoken him. And what they'd spent a good hour around dawn doing.

Just the warmed silk of her skin against his lips was enough to heat his chilled bones. "We can go back to bed, if you want," he murmured.

Yrene let out a soft, breathless sound that had his hands aching to roam along her bundled-up body. Even with time pressing upon them, hurrying them northward, he'd loved learning all her sounds—loved coaxing them from her.

But Chaol drew his head away from the crook of her neck to gesture again to the ruks. "They're heading on a scouting mission soon." He'd bet that Nesryn and the khagan's newly crowned Heir were currently buckling on weapons and layers. "We've sailed far enough north that we need information on where to moor." So they could decide where, exactly, to dock the armada and march inland as quickly as possible.

If Rifthold was still held by Erawan and the Ironteeth legions, then sailing the armada up the Avery and marching northward into Terrasen would be unwise. But the Valg king might very well have forces lying in wait at any point ahead. Not to mention Queen Maeve's fleet, which had vanished after her battle with Aelin and mercifully remained unaccounted for.

By their captain's calculations, they were just nearing the border

Fenharrow shared with Adarlan. So they needed to decide where, exactly, they were sailing *to*. As swiftly as possible.

They'd already lost precious time skirting the Dead Islands, despite the news that they once more belonged to Captain Rolfe. Word had likely already reached Morath about their journey, but there was no need to proclaim their exact location.

But their secrecy had cost them: he'd had no news on Dorian's location. Not a whisper as to whether he had gone north with Aelin and the fleet she'd gathered from several kingdoms. Chaol could only pray that Dorian had, and that his king remained safe.

Yrene studied the two ruks on the nearby ship. "How many scouts are going?"

"Just them."

Yrene's eyes flared with warning.

"Easier for smaller numbers to stay hidden." Chaol pointed to the sky. "The cloud cover today makes it ideal for scouting, too." When the worry in her face didn't abate, he added, "We will have to fight in this war at some point, Yrene." How many lives did Erawan claim for every day that they delayed?

"I know." She clasped the silver locket at her neck. He'd given it to her, had a master engraver carve the mountains and seas onto the surface. Inside, it still bore the note Aelin Galathynius had left her years ago, when his wife worked as a barmaid in a backwater port, and the queen lived as an assassin under another name. "I just . . . I know it's foolish, but I somehow didn't think it would come upon us this quickly."

He'd hardly call these weeks at sea quick, but he understood what she meant. "These last days will be the longest yet."

Yrene nestled into his side, her arm going around his waist. "I need to check on the supplies. I'll get Borte to fly me over to Hasar's ship."

Arcas, the fierce ruk rider's mount, was still dozing where he slept on the stern. "You might have to wait awhile for that."

Indeed, they'd both learned these weeks *not* to disturb either ruk or rider while they were sleeping. Gods help them if Borte and Aelin ever met.

Yrene smiled, and lifted her hands to cup his face. Her clear eyes scanned his. "I love you," she said softly.

Chaol lowered his brow until it rested against hers. "Tell me that when we're knee-deep in freezing mud, will you?"

She snorted, but made no move to pull away. Neither did he.

So brow to brow and soul to soul, they stood there amid the bitter wind and lashing waves, and waited to see what the ruks might discover.

⁓

She'd forgotten how damn cold it was in the North.

Even while living amongst the ruk riders in the Tavan Mountains, Nesryn Faliq had never been this frozen through.

And winter had not fully descended.

Yet Salkhi showed no hint that the cold affected him as they rushed over cloud and sea. But that might also be because Kadara flew beside him, the golden ruk unfaltering in the bitter wind.

A soft spot—her ruk had developed a soft spot and an undimming admiration for Sartaq's mount. Though Nesryn supposed the same could be said about her and the ruk's rider.

Nesryn tore her eyes from the swirling gray clouds and glanced to the rider at her left.

His shorn hair had grown out—barely. Just enough to be braided back against the wind.

Sensing her attention, the Heir to the khaganate signaled, *All is well?*

Nesryn blushed despite the cold, but signaled back, her numbed fingers clumsy over the symbols. *All clear.*

A blushing schoolgirl. That's what she became around the prince, no matter the fact that they'd been sharing a bed these weeks, or what he'd promised for their future.

To rule beside him. As the future empress of the khaganate.

It was absurd, of course. The idea of her dressed like his mother, in those sweeping, beautiful robes and grand headdresses . . . No, she was better suited to the rukhin leathers, to the weight of steel, not jewels. She'd said as much to Sartaq. Many times.

He'd laughed her off. Had said she might walk around the palace naked if she wished. What she wore or didn't wear wouldn't bother him in the least.

But it was still a ridiculous notion. One the prince seemed to think was the only course for their future. He'd staked his crown on it, had told his father that if being prince meant not being with her, then he'd walk away from the throne. The khagan had offered him the title of Heir instead.

Before they'd left, his siblings had not seemed angered by it, though they'd spent their entire lives vying to be crowned their father's Heir. Even Hasar, who sailed with them, had refrained from her usual, sharp-tongued comments. Whether Kashin, Arghun, or Duva—all still in Antica, with Kashin promised to sail with the rest of his father's forces—had changed their minds about Sartaq's appointment, Nesryn didn't know.

A flutter of activity to her right had her steering Salkhi after it.

Falkan Ennar, shape-shifter and merchant-turned-rukhin-spy, had taken a falcon's form this morning, and wielded the creature's remarkable speed to fly ahead. He must have seen something, for he now banked and swept past them, then soared inland again. *Follow*, he seemed to say.

Sailing to Terrasen was still an option, depending on what they found today along the coast. Whether Lysandra might be there, if she might still be alive, was another matter entirely.

Falkan had sworn that his fortune, his properties, would be her inheritance well before he knew that she'd survived childhood, or received his family's gifts. A strange family from the Wastes, who'd spread across the continent, his brother ending up in Adarlan long enough to sire Lysandra and abandon her mother.

But Falkan had not spoken of those desires since they'd left the Tavan

Mountains, and had instead dedicated himself to helping in whatever manner he could: scouting, mostly. But a time would soon come when they'd need his further assistance, as they had against the *kharankui* in the Dagul Fells.

Perhaps as vital as the army they'd brought with them was the information they'd gleaned there. That Maeve was not a Fae Queen at all, but a Valg imposter. An ancient Valg queen, who had infiltrated Doranelle at the dawn of time, ripping into the two sister-queens' minds and convincing them that they had an elder sister.

Perhaps the knowledge would bring about nothing in this war. But it might shift it in some way. To know that another enemy lurked at their backs. And that Maeve had fled to Erilea to escape the Valg king she'd wed, brother to two others—who in turn had sundered the Wyrdkeys from the gate, and ripped through worlds to find her.

That the three Valg kings had broken into this world only to be halted here, unaware that their prey now lurked on a throne in Doranelle, had been a strange twist of fate. Only Erawan remained here of those three kings, brother to Orcus, Maeve's husband. What would he pay to know who she truly was?

It was a question, perhaps, for others to ponder. To consider how to wield.

Falkan dropped into a swooping dive through the cloud cover, and Nesryn followed.

Cold, misty air ripped at her, but Nesryn leaned into the descent, Salkhi trailing Falkan without command. For a minute, only clouds flowed past, and then—

White cliffs rose from the gray waves, and beyond them dried grasses spread in the last of Fenharrow's northernmost plains.

Falkan soared toward the shore, checking his speed so he didn't lose them.

Kadara kept pace with them easily, and they flew in silence as the coast grew clearer.

The grasses on the plains weren't winter-dried. They'd been burned. And the trees, barren of leaves, were little more than husks.

On the horizon, plumes of smoke stained the winter sky. Too many and too great to be farmers scorching the last of the crops to fertilize the soil.

Nesryn signaled to Sartaq, *I'm taking a closer look.*

The prince signaled back, *Skim the clouds, but don't get below them.*

Nesryn nodded, and she and her ruk disappeared into the thin bottom layer of the clouds. Through occasional gaps, glimpses of the charred land flashed below.

Villages and farmsteads: gone. As if a force had swept in from the sea and razed everything in its path.

But there had been no armada camped by the shore. No, this army had been on foot.

Keeping just within the veil of clouds, Nesryn and Sartaq crossed the land.

Her heart pounded, faster and faster, with every league of seared, barren landscape they covered. No signs of an opposing army or ongoing battles.

They'd burned it for their own sick enjoyment.

Nesryn marked the land, the features she could make out. They'd indeed barely crossed over Fenharrow's borders, Adarlan a sprawl to the north.

But inland, growing closer with each league, an army marched. It stretched for miles and miles, black and writhing.

The might of Morath. Or some terrible fraction of it, sent to instill terror and destruction before the final wave.

Sartaq signaled, *A band of soldiers below.*

Nesryn peered over Salkhi's wing, the drop merciless, and beheld a small group of soldiers in dark armor wending through the trees—an offshoot of the teeming mass far ahead. As if they had been sent to hunt down any survivors.

Nesryn's jaw clenched, and she signaled back to the prince, *Let's go.*

Not back to the ships. But to the six soldiers, beginning the long return trek to their host.

Nesryn and Salkhi plummeted through the sky, Sartaq a blur on her left.

The band of soldiers didn't have the chance to shout before Nesryn and Sartaq were upon them.

Lady Yrene Westfall, formerly Yrene Towers, had counted the supplies about six times now. Every boat was full of them, yet Princess Hasar's ship, the personal escort to the Healer on High, held the most vital mix of tonics and salves. Many had been crafted prior to sailing from Antica, but Yrene and the other healers who had accompanied the army had spent long hours concocting them as best they could on board.

In the dim hold, Yrene steadied her feet against the rocking of the waves and closed the lid on the crate of salve tins, jotting down the number on the piece of paper she'd brought with her.

"The same number as two days ago," an old voice clucked from the stairs. Hafiza, the Healer on High, sat on the wooden steps, hands resting atop the heavy wool skirt covering her skinny knees. "What do you worry will happen to them, Yrene?"

Yrene flicked her braid over a shoulder. "I wanted to make sure I'd counted right."

"Again."

Yrene pocketed the piece of parchment and swept up her fur-lined cloak from where she'd tossed it over a crate. "When we're on the battle-fields, keeping stock of our supplies—"

"Will be vital, yes, but also impossible. When we're on the battle-fields, girl, you'll be lucky if you can even *find* one of these tins amid the chaos."

"That's what I'm trying to avoid."

The Healer on High offered her a sympathetic sigh. "People will die,

Yrene. In horrible, painful ways, they will die, and even you and I will not be able to save them."

Yrene swallowed. "I know that." If they did not hurry, did not make landfall soon and discover where the khagan's army would march, how many more would perish?

The ancient woman's knowing look didn't fade. Always, from the first moment Yrene had laid eyes on Hafiza, she had emanated this calm, this reassurance. The thought of the Healer on High on those bloody battle-fields made Yrene's stomach churn. Even if this sort of thing was precisely why they had come, why they trained in the first place.

But that was without the matter of the Valg, squatting in human hosts like parasites. Valg who would kill them immediately if they knew what the healers planned to do.

What Yrene planned to do to any Valg who crossed her path.

"The salves are made, Yrene." Hafiza groaned as she rose from her perch on the steps and adjusted the lapels of her thick woolen jacket—cut and embroidered in the style of the Darghan riders. A gift from the last visit the Healer on High had made to the steppes, when she'd taken Yrene along with her. "They are counted. There are no more supplies with which to make them, not until we reach land and can see what might be used there."

Yrene clutched her cloak to her chest. "I need to be doing *something*."

The Healer on High patted the railing. "You will, Yrene. Soon enough, you will."

Hafiza ascended the stairs with that, leaving Yrene in the hold amid the stacks of crates.

She didn't tell the Healer on High that she wasn't entirely sure how much longer she'd be a help—not yet. Hadn't whispered a word of that doubt to anyone, even Chaol.

Yrene's hand drifted across her abdomen and lingered.

CHAPTER 7

Morath. The final key was at Morath.

The knowledge hung over Dorian through the night, keeping him from sleep. When he did doze, he awoke with a hand at his neck, grasping for a collar that was not there.

He had to find some way to go. Some way to reach it.

Since Manon would undoubtedly be unwilling to take him. Even if she'd been the one who'd suggested he might be able to take Aelin's place to forge the Lock.

The Thirteen had barely escaped Morath—they were in no hurry to return. Not when their task in finding the Crochans had become so vital. Not when Erawan might very well sense their arrival before they neared the keep.

Gavin had claimed the path would find him here, in this camp. But finding a way to convince the Thirteen to remain, when instinct and urgency compelled them to move on . . . that might prove as impossible a task as attaining the third Wyrdkey.

Their camp stirred in the gray light of dawn, and Dorian gave up on sleep. Rising, he found Manon's bedroll packed, and the witch herself standing with Asterin and Sorrel by their mounts. It was that trio he'd have to convince to remain—somehow.

Already waiting near the mouth of the pass, the other wyverns shifted as they readied for the unbearably cold flight.

Another day, another hunt for a clan of witches who had no desire to be found. And would likely have little desire to join this war.

"We move out in five minutes." Sorrel's rocky voice carried across the camp.

Convincing would have to wait, then. Delaying it was.

Within three minutes, the fire was out and weapons were donned, bedrolls bound to saddles and needs seen to before the long day of flying.

Buckling on Damaris, Dorian aimed for Manon, the witch standing with that preternatural stillness. Beautiful, even here in the blasted snow, a shaggy goat pelt slung over her shoulders. As he neared, her eyes met his in a flash of burnt gold.

Asterin gave him a wicked grin. "Morning, Your Majesty."

Dorian inclined his head. "Where are we wandering today?" He knew the casual words didn't quite meet his eyes.

"We were just debating it," Sorrel answered, the Third's face stony but open.

Behind them, Vesta swore as the buckle on her saddle came undone. Dorian didn't dare to look, to confirm that the invisible hands of his magic had worked.

"We already searched north of here," Asterin said. "Let's keep heading south—make it to the end of the Fangs before we backtrack."

"They might not even be in the mountains," Sorrel countered. "We've hunted them in the lowlands in decades past."

Manon listened with a cool, unruffled expression. As she did every morning. Weighing their words, listening to the wind that sang to her.

Imogen's saddlebag snapped free of its tether. The witch hissed as she dismounted to retie it. How long these little delays could keep them here, he didn't know. Not indefinitely.

"If we abandon these mountains," Asterin argued, "then we'll be far more trackable in the open lands. Both our enemies and the Crochans will spot us before we ever find them."

"It'd be warmer," Sorrel grumbled. "Eyllwe would be a hell of a lot warmer."

Apparently, even immortal witches with steel in their veins could grow tired of the leeching cold.

But to go so far south, into Eyllwe, when they were still near enough to Morath . . . Manon seemed to consider that, too. Her eyes dipped to his jacket. To the keys within, as if she could sense their pulsing whisper, their slide against his power. All that lay between Erawan and his dominion over Erilea. To bring them within a hundred miles of Morath . . . No, she'd never allow it.

Dorian kept his face blandly pleasant, a hand resting on the eye-shaped pommel of Damaris. "This camp has no clues about where they went?"

He knew they hadn't the faintest notion. Knew it, but waited for their answer anyway, trying not to grip Damaris's pommel too hard.

"No," Manon said with a hint of a growl.

Yet Damaris gave no answer beyond a faint warmth in the metal. He didn't know what he'd expected: some verifying hum of power, a confirming voice in his mind.

Certainly not the unimpressive whisper of heat.

Heat for truth; likely cold for lies. But—at least Gavin had spoken true about the blade. He shouldn't have doubted it, considering the god Gavin still honored.

Holding his stare with that relentless, predatory focus, Manon gave the order to move out. Northward.

Away from Morath. Dorian opened his mouth, casting for anything to say, do, to delay this departure. Short of snapping a wyvern's wing, there was nothing—

The witches turned toward the wyverns, where Dorian would ride with one of the sentinels for the next leg of this endless hunt. But Abraxos roared, lunging for Manon with a snap of teeth.

As Manon whirled, Dorian's magic surged, already lashing at the unseen foe.

A mighty white bear had risen from the snow behind her.

Teeth flashing, it brought down its massive paw. Manon ducked, rolling to the side, and Dorian hurled out a wall of his magic—wind and ice.

The bear was blasted back, hitting the snow with an icy thump. It was instantly up again, racing for Manon. Only Manon.

Half a thought had Dorian flinging invisible hands to halt the beast. Just as it collided with his magic, snow spraying, light flashed.

He knew that light. A shifter.

But it was not Lysandra who emerged from the bear's perfectly camouflaged hide.

No, the thing that came out of the bear was made of nightmares.

A spider. A great, stygian spider, big as a horse and black as night.

Its many eyes narrowed on Manon, pincers clicking, as it hissed, *"Blackbeak."*

***

The stygian spider had found her, somehow. After all these months, after the thousands of leagues Manon had traveled over sky and earth and sea, the spider from whom she'd stolen the silk to reinforce Abraxos's wings had found her.

But the spider had not anticipated the Thirteen. Or the power of the King of Adarlan.

Manon drew Wind-Cleaver as Dorian held the spider in place with his magic, the king showing little signs of strain. Powerful—he grew more powerful each day.

The Thirteen closed ranks, weapons gleaming in the blinding sun and snow, the wyverns forming a wall of leathery hides and claws behind them.

Manon stalked a few steps closer to those twitching pincers. "You're a long way from the Ruhnns, sister."

The spider hissed. "You were not so very hard to find, despite it."

"You know this beast?" Asterin asked, prowling to Manon's side.

Manon's mouth curled in a cruel smile. "She donated the Spidersilk for Abraxos's wings."

The spider snarled. "You *stole* my silk, and shoved me and my weavers off a cliff—"

"How is it that you can shape-shift?" Dorian asked, still pinning the spider in place as he approached Manon's other side, one hand gripping the hilt of his ancient sword. "The legends make no mention of that." Curiosity indeed brightened on his face. She supposed the white line through his golden skin on his throat was proof that he'd dealt with far worse. And supposed that whatever bond lay between them was also proof he had little fear of pain or death.

A good trait for a witch, yes. But in a mortal? It would likely wind up getting him killed.

Perhaps it was not a lack of fear, but rather a lack of . . . of whatever mortals deemed vital to their souls. Ripped from him by his father. And that Valg demon.

The spider seethed. "I took two decades from a young merchant's life in exchange for my silk. The gift of his shifting flowed through his life force—some of it, at least." All those eyes narrowed on Manon. "*He* willingly paid the price."

"Kill her, and be done with it," Asterin murmured.

The spider recoiled as much as the king's invisible leash would allow. "I had no idea our sisters had become so cowardly, if they now require magic to skewer us like pigs."

Manon lifted Wind-Cleaver, contemplating where between the spider's many eyes to plunge the blade. "Shall we see if you squeal like one when I do?"

"Coward," the spider spat. "Release me, and we'll end this the old way."

Manon debated it. Then shrugged. "I shall keep this painless. Consider that my debt owed to you." Sucking in a breath, Manon readied for the blow—

"Wait." The spider breathed the word. "*Wait*."

"From insults to pleading," Asterin murmured. "Who is spineless now?"

The spider ignored the Second, her depthless eyes devouring Manon, then Dorian. "Do you know what moves in the South? What horrors gather?"

"Old news," Vesta said, snorting.

"How do you think I found you?" the spider asked. Manon stilled. "So many possessions left at Morath. Your scents all over them."

If the spider had found them here that easily, they had to move out. Now.

The spider hissed, "Shall I tell you what I spied a mere fifty miles south of here? Who I saw, Blackbeak?" Manon stiffened. "Crochans," the spider said, then sighed deeply. Hungrily.

Manon blinked. Just once. The Thirteen had gone equally still. Asterin asked, "You've seen the Crochans?"

The spider's massive head bobbed in a nod before she sighed again. "The Crochans always tasted of what I imagine summer wine to be like. What *chocolate*, as you call it, would taste like."

"Where," Manon demanded.

The spider named the location—vague and unfamiliar. "I will show you where," she said. "I will guide you."

"It could be a trap," Sorrel said.

"It's not," Dorian said, his hand still on the hilt of his sword. Manon studied the clarity of his eyes, the squared shoulders. The pitiless face, yet inquisitive angle to his head. "Let's see if her information holds true—and decide her fate afterward."

Manon blurted, "What." The Thirteen shifted at the denied kill.

Dorian jerked his chin to the shuddering spider. "Don't kill her. Not yet. There's more she might know beyond the Crochans' whereabouts."

The spider hissed, "I do not need a boy's mercy—"

"It is a king's mercy you receive," Dorian said coldly, "and I'd suggest being quiet long enough to receive it." Rarely, so rarely did Manon hear that voice from him, the tone that sent a thrill through her blood and bones. A king's voice.

But he was not her king. He was not the coven leader of the Thirteen. "We let her live and she'll sell us to the highest bidder."

Dorian's sapphire eyes churned, the hand on his sword tightening. Manon tensed at that contemplative, cold stare. The hint of the calculating predator beneath the king's handsome face. He only said to the spider, "You mastered shape-shifting in a matter of months, it seems."

A path would find him here, Gavin had said.

A path into Morath. Not a physical road, not a course of travel, but this.

The unholy terror remained quiet for a beat before she said, "Our gifts are strange and hungry things. We feed not just on your life, but your powers, too, if you possess them. Once magic was freed, I learned to wield the abilities the shape-shifter had transferred to me."

Damaris warmed in his hand. Truth. Every word the spider had spoken had been truth. And this . . . A way into Morath—as something else entirely. In another's skin.

Perhaps a human slave, like Elide Lochan. Someone whose presence would go unmarked.

His raw power had lent itself to every other form of magic, able to move between flame and ice and healing. To shape-shift . . . might he learn it, too?

Dorian only asked the spider, "Do you have a name?"

"A king without his crown asks for a lowly spider's name," she murmured, her depthless eyes setting on him. "You cannot pronounce it in your tongue, but you may call me Cyrene."

Manon ground her teeth. "It doesn't matter what we call you, as you'll be dead soon."

But Dorian cut her a sidelong glance. "The Ruhnns are a part of my kingdom. As such, Cyrene is one of my subjects. I think that gives me the right to decide whether she lives or dies."

"You are *both* at the mercy of my coven," Manon snarled. "Step aside."

Dorian gave her a slight smile. "Am I?" A wind colder than the mountain air filled the pass.

He could kill them all. Whether by choking the air from them or snapping their necks. He could kill them all, and the wyverns included. The knowledge carved out another hollow within him. Another empty spot. Had it ever troubled his father, or Aelin, to bear such power? "Bring her with us—question her more thoroughly at the next camp."

Manon snapped, "You plan to bring *that* with us?"

In answer, the spider shifted, donning the form of a pale-skinned, dark-haired woman. Small and unremarkable, save for those unnerving black eyes. Not pretty, but with a deadly, ancient sort of allure that even a new hide couldn't conceal. And utterly naked. She shivered, rubbing her hands down her thin arms. "Shall this form suffice to travel lightly?"

Manon ignored the spider. "And when she shifts in the night to rip us apart?"

Dorian only inclined his head, ice dancing at his fingertips. "She won't."

Cyrene sucked in a breath. "A rare gift of magic." Her stare turned ravenous as she took in Dorian. "For a rare king."

Dorian only frowned with distaste.

Manon glanced to Asterin. Her Second's eyes were wary, her mouth a tight line. Sorrel, a few feet behind, glowered at the spider, but her hand had dropped from her sword.

The Thirteen, on some unspoken signal, peeled away to their wyverns. Only Cyrene watched them, those horrible, soulless eyes blinking every now and then as her teeth began to clack.

Manon angled her head at him. "You're . . . different today."

He shrugged. "If you want someone to warm your bed who cowers at your every word and obeys every command, look elsewhere."

Her stare drifted to the pale band around his throat. "I'm still not convinced, princeling," she hissed, "that I shouldn't just kill her."

"And what would it take, witchling, to convince you?" He didn't bother to hide the sensual promise in his words, nor their edge.

A muscle flickered in Manon's jaw. Things from legends—that's who surrounded him. The witches, the spider . . . He might as well have been a character in one of the books he'd lent Aelin last fall. Though none of them had ever endured such a yawning pit inside them.

Scowling at her bare feet in the snow, Cyrene's hands twitched at her sides, an echo of the pincers she'd borne moments before.

Dorian tried not to shudder. Suicide to sneak into Morath—once he learned what he needed from this thing.

The weight of Manon's gaze fell upon him again, and Dorian didn't balk from it. Didn't balk from Manon's words as she said, "If you find so little value in your existence that it compels you to trust this thing, then by all means, bring her along." A challenge to look not toward Morath or the spider, but inward. She saw exactly what gnawed on his empty chest, if only because a similar beast gnawed on her own. "We'll find out soon enough whether she spoke true about the Crochans."

The spider had. Damaris had warmed in his hand when Cyrene had spoken.

And when they found the Crochans, when the Thirteen were distracted, he'd learn what he needed from the spider, too.

Manon turned to the Thirteen, the witches thrumming with impatience. "We fly now. We can reach the Crochans by nightfall."

"And what then?" Asterin asked. The only one of them who had permission to do so.

Manon stalked for Abraxos, and Dorian followed, tossing Cyrene a spare cloak as his magic tugged her with him. "And then we make our move," Manon hedged. And for once, she did not meet anyone's stare. Didn't do anything but gaze southward.

The witch was keeping secrets, too. But were hers as dire as his?

CHAPTER
8

Blackness greeted Aelin as she rose to consciousness. Tight, contained blackness.

A shift of her elbows had them digging into the sides of the box, chains reverberating through the small space. Her bare feet could graze the end if she wriggled slightly.

She lifted her bound hands to the solid wall of iron mere inches above her face. Traced the whorls and suns embossed onto its surface. Even on the inside, Maeve had ordered them etched. So Aelin might never forget that this box had been made for her, long before she'd been born.

But—those were her own bare fingertips brushing over the cool, rough metal.

He'd taken off the iron gauntlets. Or had forgotten to put them back on after what he'd done. The way he'd held them over the open brazier, until the metal was red-hot around her hands and she was screaming, screaming—

Aelin pressed her palms flat against the metal lid and pushed.

The shattered arm, the splinters of bone jutting from her skin: gone.

Or had never been. But it had felt real.

More so than the other memories that pressed in, demanding she acknowledge them. Accept them.

Aelin shoved her palms against the iron, muscles straining.

It didn't so much as shift.

She tried again. That she had the strength to do so was thanks to the other *services* Maeve's healers provided: keeping her muscles from atrophying while she lay here.

A soft whine echoed into the box. A warning.

Aelin lowered her hands just as the lock grated and the door groaned open.

Cairn's footsteps were faster this time. Urgent.

"Relieve yourself in the hall and wait by this door," he snapped at Fenrys.

Aelin braced herself as those steps halted. A grunt and hiss of metal, and firelight poured in. She blinked against it, but kept still.

They'd anchored her irons into the box itself. She'd learned that the hard way.

Cairn didn't say anything as he unfastened the chains from their anchor.

The most dangerous time for him, right before he moved her to the anchors on the altar. Even with her feet and hands bound, he took no chances.

He didn't today, either, despite not bothering with the gauntlets.

Perhaps they'd melted away over that brazier, along with her skin.

Cairn yanked her upright as half a dozen guards silently appeared in the doorway. Their faces held no horror at what had been done to her.

She'd seen these males before. On a bloodied bit of beach.

"Varik," Cairn said, and one of the guards stepped forward, Fenrys now at his side by the door, the wolf as tall as a pony. Varik's sword rested against Fenrys's throat.

Cairn gripped her chains, tugging her against his chest as they walked toward the guards, the wolf. "You make a move, and he dies."

Aelin didn't tell him she wasn't entirely sure she had the strength to try anything, let alone run.

Heaviness settled into her.

She didn't fight the black sack shoved over her head as they passed through the arched doorway. Didn't fight as they walked down that hall, though she counted the steps and turns.

She didn't care if Cairn was smart enough to add in a few extras to disorient her. She counted them anyway. Listened to the rush of the river, growing louder with each turn, the rising mist that chilled her exposed skin, slicking the stones beneath her feet.

Then open air. She couldn't see it, but it grazed damp fingers over her skin, whispering of the gaping openness of the world.

Run. Now.

The words were a distant murmur.

She had no doubt the guard's blade remained at Fenrys's throat. That it would spill blood. Maeve's order of restraint bound Fenrys too well— along with that strange gift of his to leap between short distances, as if he were moving from one room to another.

She'd long since lost hope he'd find some way to use it, to bear them away from here. She doubted he'd miraculously reclaim the ability, should the guard's sword strike.

Yet if she heeded that voice, if she ran, was the cost of his life worth her own?

"You're debating it, aren't you," Cairn hissed in her ear. She could feel his smile even through the sack blinding her. "If the wolf's life is a fair cost to get away." A lover's laugh. "Try it. See how far you get. We've a few minutes of walking left."

She ignored him. Ignored that voice whispering to *run, run, run.*

Step after step, they walked. Her legs shook with the effort.

It told her enough about how long she had been here. How long she had not been able to properly move, even with the healers' ministrations to keep her muscles from wasting away.

Cairn led her up a winding staircase that had her rasping for breath, the mist fading away to cool night air. Sweet smells. Flowers.

Flowers still existed. In this world, this hell, flowers bloomed somewhere.

The water's bellow faded behind them to a blessedly dull rushing, soon replaced by merry trickling ahead. Fountains. Cold, smooth tiles bit into her feet, and through the hood flickering fire cast golden ripples. Lanterns.

The air tightened, grew still. A courtyard, perhaps.

Lightning pulsed down her thighs, her calves, warning her to slow, to rest.

Then open air yawned again wide around her, the water once more roaring.

Cairn halted, yanking her against his towering body, his various weapons digging into her chains, her skin. The other guards' clothes rustled as they stopped, too. Fenrys's claws clicked on stone, the sound no doubt meant to signal her that he remained nearby.

She realized why he'd feel the need to do so as a female voice that was both young and old, amused and soulless, purred, "Remove the hood, Cairn."

It vanished, and Aelin needed only a few blinks to take everything in.

She had been here before.

Had been on this broad veranda overlooking a mighty river and water-falls, had walked through the ancient stone city she knew loomed at her back.

Had stood in this very spot, facing the dark-haired queen lounging on a stone throne atop the dais, mist wreathing the air around her, a white owl perched on the back of her seat.

Only one wolf lay sprawled at her feet this time. Black as night, black as the queen's eyes, which settled on Aelin, narrowing with pleasure.

Maeve seemed content to let Aelin look. Let her take it in.

Maeve's deep purple gown glistened like the mists behind her, its long train draped over the few steps of the dais. Pooling toward—

Aelin beheld what glittered at the base of those steps and went still.

Maeve's red lips curved into a smile as she waved an ivory hand. "If you will, Cairn."

The male didn't hesitate as he hauled Aelin toward what lay on the ground.

Shattered glass, piled and arranged in a neat circle.

He halted just outside, the first of the thick shards an inch from Aelin's bare toes.

Maeve motioned to the black wolf at her feet and he rose, plucking up something from the throne's broad arm before trotting to Cairn.

"I thought your rank should at least be acknowledged," Maeve said, that spider's smile never faltering as Aelin beheld what the wolf offered to the guard beside Cairn. "Put it on her," the queen ordered.

A crown, ancient and glimmering, shone in the guard's hands. Crafted of silver and pearl, fashioned into upswept wings that met in its peaked center, encircled with spikes of pure diamond, it shimmered like the moon's rays had been captured within as the guard set it upon Aelin's head.

A terrible, surprising weight, the cool metal digging into her scalp. Far heavier than it looked, as if it had a core of solid iron.

A different sort of shackle. It always had been.

Aelin reined in the urge to recoil, to shake the thing from her head.

"Mab's crown," Maeve said. "Your crown, by blood and birthright. Her true Heir."

Aelin ignored the words. Stared toward the circle of glass shards.

"Oh, that," Maeve said, noting her attention. "I think you know how this shall go, Aelin of the Wildfire."

Aelin said nothing.

Maeve gave a nod.

Cairn shoved her forward, right into the glass.

Her bare feet sliced open, new skin shrieking as it ripped.

She inhaled sharply through her teeth, swallowing her cry just as Cairn pushed her onto her knees.

The breath slammed from her at the impact. At each shard that sliced and dug in deep.

Breathe—breathing was key, was vital.

She pulled her mind out, away, inhaling and exhaling. A wave sweeping back from the shore, then returning.

Warmth pooled beneath her knees, her calves and ankles, the coppery scent of her blood rising to blend into the mists.

Her breath turned jagged as she began shaking, as a scream surged within her.

She bit her lip, canines piercing flesh.

She would not scream. Not yet.

Breathe—*breathe*.

The tang of her blood coated her mouth as she bit down harder.

"A pity that there's no audience to witness this," said Maeve, her voice far away and yet too near. "Aelin Fire-Bringer, wearing her proper Faerie Queen's crown at last. Kneeling at my feet."

A tremor shuddered through Aelin, rocking her body enough that the glass found new angles, new entries.

She drifted further back, away. Each breath tugged her out to sea, to a place where words and feelings and pain became a distant shore.

Maeve snapped her fingers. "Fenrys."

The wolf padded past and sat himself beside her throne. But not before he glanced at the black wolf. Just a turn of the head.

The black wolf returned the look, bland and cold. And that was enough for Maeve to say, "Connall, you may finally tell your twin what you wish to say."

A flash of light.

Aelin inhaled through her nose, exhaled through her mouth, over and over. Barely registered the beautiful dark-haired male who now stood in place of the wolf. Bronze-skinned like his twin, but without the wildness, without the mischief shining from his face. He wore a warrior's layered clothes, black to Fenrys's usual gray, twin knives hanging at his sides.

The white wolf stared up at his twin, rooted to the spot by that invisible bond.

"Speak freely, Connall," Maeve said, her faint smile remaining. The barn owl perched on the back of her throne watched with solemn, unblinking eyes. "Let your brother know these words are your own and not of my command."

A booted foot nudged Aelin's spine, a subtle jab forward. Harder into the glass.

No amount of breathing could draw her far enough away to rein in the muffled whimper.

She hated it—hated that sound, as much as she hated the queen before her and the sadist at her back. But it still made its way out, barely audible over the thundering falls.

Fenrys's dark eyes shot toward her. He blinked four times.

She could not bring herself to blink back. Her fingers curled and uncurled in her lap.

"You brought this upon yourself," Connall said to Fenrys, drawing his brother's attention once more. His voice was as icy as Maeve's. "Your arrogance, your unchecked recklessness—was this what you wanted?" Fenrys didn't answer. "You couldn't let me have this—have any part of this for myself. You took the blood oath not to serve our queen, but so you couldn't be bested by me for once in your life."

Fenrys bared his teeth, even as something like grief dimmed his stare.

Another burning wave washed through her knees, across her thighs. Aelin closed her eyes against it.

She would endure this, would bear down on this.

Her people had suffered for ten years. Were likely suffering now. For their sake, she would do this. Embrace it. Outlast it.

Connall's rumbling voice rippled past her.

"You are a disgrace to our family, to this kingdom. You whored yourself to a foreign queen, and for what? I begged you to control yourself when you were sent to hunt Lorcan. I begged you to be *smart*. You might as well have spat in my face."

Fenrys snarled, and the sound must have been some secret language between them, because Connall snorted. "Leave? Why would I *ever* want to leave? And for what? *That?*" Even with her eyes shut, Aelin knew he pointed toward her. "No, Fenrys. I will not leave. And neither will you."

A low whine cut the damp air.

"That will be all, Connall," Maeve said, and light flashed, penetrating even the darkness behind Aelin's lids.

She breathed and breathed and breathed.

"You know how quickly this can end, Aelin," Maeve said. Aelin kept her eyes shut. "Tell me where you hid the Wyrdkeys, swear the blood oath . . . The order doesn't matter, I suppose."

Aelin opened her eyes. Lifted her bound hands before her.

And gave Maeve an obscene gesture, as filthy and foul as she'd ever made.

Maeve's smile tightened—just barely. "Cairn."

Before Aelin could inhale a bracing breath, hands slammed onto her shoulders. Pushed *down*.

She couldn't stop her scream then.

Not as he shoved her into a burning pit of agony that raced up her legs, her spine.

Oh gods—oh *gods*—

From far away, Fenrys's snarl sliced through her screaming, followed by Maeve's lilting, "Very well, Cairn."

The pressure on her shoulders lightened.

Aelin bowed over her knees. A full breath—she needed to get a full breath down.

She couldn't. Her lungs, her chest, only heaved in shallow, rasping pants.

Her vision blurred, swimming, the blood that had spread beyond her knees rippling with it.

Endure; outlast—

"My eyes told me an interesting tidbit of information this morning," Maeve drawled. "An account that *you* were currently in Terrasen, readying the little army you gathered for war. You, and Prince Rowan, and my two disgraced warriors. Along with your usual group."

Aelin hadn't realized she'd been holding on to it.

That sliver of hope, foolish and pathetic. That sliver of hope that he'd come for her.

She had told him not to, after all. Had told him to protect Terrasen. Had arranged everything for him to make a desperate stand against Morath.

"Useful, to have a shape-shifter to play your part as queen," Maeve mused. "Though I wonder how long the ruse can last without your special gifts to incinerate Morath's legions. How long until the allies you collected start asking why the Fire-Bringer does not burn."

It was no lie. The details, her plan with Lysandra . . . There was no way for Maeve to know them unless they were truth. Could Maeve have made a lucky guess in lying about it? Yes—yes, and yet . . .

Rowan had gone with them. They'd all gone to the North. And had reached Terrasen.

A small mercy. A small mercy, and yet . . .

The glass around her sparkled in the mist and moonlight, her blood a thick stain wending through it.

"I do not wish to wipe away this world, as Erawan does," said Maeve, as if they were no more than two friends conversing at one of Rifthold's finest tea courts. If any still existed after the Ironteeth had sacked the city. "I like Erilea precisely the way it is. I always have."

The glass, the blood, the veranda and moonlight eddied in her vision.

"I have seen many wars. Sent my warriors to fight in them, end them. I have seen how destructive they are. The very glass you lay on comes from one of those wars, you know. From the glass mountains in the South. They once were sand dunes, but dragons burned them to glass during an ancient and bloody conflict." A hum of amusement. "Some claim it's the hardest glass in the world. The most unyielding. I thought, given your own fire-breathing heritage, you might appreciate its origins."

A click of the tongue, and then Cairn was there again, hands on her shoulders.

Pushing.

Harder and harder. Gods, gods, *gods*—

There were no gods to save her. Not really.

Aelin's screams echoed off rock and water.

Alone. She was alone in this. It would be of no use to beg the white wolf to help her.

The hands on her shoulders pulled away.

Heaving, bile burning her throat, Aelin once more curled over her knees.

Endure; outlast—

Maeve simply continued, "The dragons didn't survive that war. And they never rose again." Her lips curved, and Aelin knew Maeve had ensured it.

Other fire-wielders—hunted and killed.

She didn't know why she felt it then. That shred of sorrow for creatures that had not existed for untold centuries. Who would never again be seen on this earth. Why it made her so unspeakably sad. Why it mattered at all, when her very blood was shrieking in agony.

Maeve turned to Connall, remaining in Fae form beside the throne, raging eyes still fixed on his brother. "Refreshments."

Aelin knelt in that glass as food and drink were gathered. Knelt as Maeve dined on cheese and grapes, smiling at her the entire time.

Aelin couldn't stop the shaking that overtook her, the brutal numbness.

Deep, deep, she drifted.

It did not matter if Rowan wasn't coming. If the others had obeyed her wishes to fight for Terrasen.

She would save it in her own way, too. For as long as she could. She owed Terrasen that much. Would never fully repay that debt.

From far away, the words echoed, and memory shimmered. She let it pull her back, pull her out of her body.

She sat beside her father on the few steps descending into the open-air fighting ring of the castle.

It was more temple than brawling pit, flanked by weathered, pale columns that for centuries had witnessed the rise of Terrasen's mightiest warriors. This late in the summer afternoon, it was empty, the light golden as it streamed in.

Rhoe Galathynius ran a hand down his round shield, the dark metal scarred and dinged from horrors long since vanquished. "Someday," he said as she traced one of the long scratches over the ancient surface, "this shield will pass to you. As it was given to me, and to your great-uncle before me."

Her breath was still jagged from the training they'd done. Only the two of them—as he'd promised. The hour once a week that he set aside for her.

Her father placed the shield on the stone step below them, its thunk *reverberating through her sandaled feet. It weighed nearly as much as she did, yet he carried it as if it were merely an extension of his arm.*

"And you," her father went on, "like the many great women and men of this House, shall use it to defend our kingdom." Her eyes rose to his face, handsome and unlined. Solemn and kingly. "That is your charge, your sole duty." He braced a hand on the rim of the shield, tapping it for emphasis. "To defend, Aelin. To protect."

She had nodded, not understanding. And her father had kissed her brow, as if he half hoped she'd never need to.

Cairn ground her into the glass again.

No sound remained in her for screaming.

"I am growing bored of this," Maeve said, her silver tray of food forgotten. She leaned forward on her throne, the owl behind her rustling its wings. "Do you believe, Aelin Galathynius, that I will not make the sacrifices necessary to obtain what I seek?"

She had forgotten how to speak. Had not uttered a word here, anyway.

"Allow me to demonstrate," Maeve said, straightening. Fenrys's eyes flared with warning.

Maeve waved an ivory hand at Connall, frozen beside her throne. Where he'd remained since he'd brought the queen's food. "Do it."

Connall drew one of the knives from his belt. Stepped toward Fenrys.

No.

The word was a cold clang through her. Her lips even formed it as she jerked against the chains, lines of liquid fire shooting along her legs.

Connall advanced another step.

Glass crunched and cracked beneath her. No, *no*—

Connall stopped above Fenrys, his hand shaking. Fenrys only snarled up at him.

Connall raised his knife into the air between them.

She could not surge to her feet. Could not rise against the chains and glass. Could do nothing, *nothing*—

Cairn gripped her by the neck, fingers digging in hard enough to bruise, and ground her again into the blood-drenched shards. A rasping, broken scream cracked from her lips.

Fenrys. Her only tether to life, to this reality—

Connall's blade glinted. He'd come to help at Mistward. He had defied Maeve then; perhaps he'd do it now, perhaps his hateful words had been a deception—

The blade plunged down.

Not into Fenrys.

But Connall's own heart.

Fenrys moved—or tried to. Maw gaping in what might have been a scream, he tried and tried to lunge for his brother as Connall crashed to the tiled veranda. As blood began to pool.

The owl on Maeve's throne flapped its wings once, as if in horror. But Cairn let out a low laugh, the sound rumbling past Aelin's head.

Real. This was real. It had to be.

Something cold and oily lurched through her. Her hands slackened at her sides. The light left Connall's dark eyes, his black hair spilled on the floor around him in a dark mirror to the blood leaking away.

Fenrys was shaking. Aelin might have been, too.

"You tainted something that belonged to me, Aelin Galathynius," Maeve said. "And now it must be purged."

Fenrys was whining, still attempting to crawl to the brother dead on the ground. Fae could heal; perhaps Connall's heart could mend—

Connall's chest rose in a rattling, shallow breath.

It didn't move again.

Fenrys's howl cleaved the night.

Cairn let go, and Aelin slumped onto the glass, hands and wrists stinging.

She let herself lie there, half sprawled. Let the crown tumble off her head and skitter across the floor, dragon-glass spraying where it bounced. Bounced, then rolled, curving across the veranda. All the way to the stone railing.

And into the roaring, hateful river below.

"There is no one here to help you." Maeve's voice was as empty as the gaps between stars. "And there is no one coming for you."

Aelin's fingers curled in the ancient glass.

"Think on it. Think on this night, Aelin." Maeve snapped her fingers. "We're done here."

Cairn's hands wrapped around the chains.

Her legs buckled, feet splitting open anew. She barely felt it, barely felt it through the rage and the sea of fire down deep, deep below.

But as Cairn hauled her up, his savage hands roving, she struck.

Two blows.

A shard of glass plunged into the side of his neck. He staggered back, cursing as blood sprayed.

Aelin whirled, glass ripping her soles apart, and hurled the shard in her other hand. Right at Maeve.

It missed by a hairsbreadth. Scraping Maeve's pale cheek before clattering off the throne behind her. The owl perched just above it screeched.

Rough hands gripped her, Cairn shouting, raging shrieks of *You little bitch*, but she didn't hear them. Not as a trickle of blood snaked down Maeve's cheek.

Black blood. As dark as night.

As dark as the eyes that the queen fixed on her, a hand rising to her cheek.

Aelin's legs slackened, and she didn't fight the guards heaving her away.

A blink, and the blood flowed red. Its scent as coppery as her own.

A trick of the light. A hallucination, another dream—

Maeve peered at the crimson stain coating her pale fingers.

An onyx wind snapped for Aelin, wrapping around her neck.

It squeezed, and she knew no more.

CHAPTER
9

Cairn tied her to the altar and left her.

Fenrys didn't enter until long after she'd awoken.

The blood was still leaking from where Cairn had also left the glass in her legs, her feet.

It was not a wolf who slipped into the stone chamber, but a male.

Each of Fenrys's steps told her enough before she beheld the deadness of his eyes, the pallor of his usually golden skin. He stared at nothing, even as he stopped before where she lay chained.

Beyond words, unsure her throat would even work, Aelin blinked three times. *Are you all right?*

Two blinks answered. *No.*

Lingering salt tracks streaked his cheeks.

Her chains rustled as she stretched a shaking finger toward him.

Silently, he slid his hand into hers.

She mouthed the words, even though he likely couldn't make them out with the slit of the mask's mouth. *I'm sorry.*

His grip only tightened.

His gray jacket was unbuttoned at the top. It gaped open wide enough to reveal a hint of the muscled chest beneath. As if he hadn't bothered to seal it back up in his hurry to leave.

Her stomach turned over. What he'd undoubtedly had to do afterward, with his twin's body still lying on the veranda tiles behind him . . .

"I didn't know he hated me so much," Fenrys rasped.

Aelin squeezed his hand.

Fenrys closed his eyes, drawing in a shaking breath. "She gave me leave only to take out the glass. When it's out, I—I go back over there." He pointed with his chin toward the wall where he usually sat. He made to examine her legs, but she squeezed his hand again, and blinked twice. *No.*

Let him stay in this form for a while longer, let him mourn as a male and not a wolf. Let him stay in this form so she could hear a friendly voice, feel a gentle touch—

She began to cry.

She couldn't help it. Couldn't stop it once it started. Hated every tear and shuddering breath, every jerk of her body that sent lightning through her legs and feet.

"I'll get them out," he said, and she couldn't tell him, couldn't start to explain that it wasn't the glass, the shredded skin down to the bone.

He wasn't coming. He wasn't coming to get her.

She should be glad. Should be relieved. She *was* relieved. And yet . . . and yet . . .

Fenrys drew out a pair of pincers from the tool kit that Cairn had left on a table nearby. "I'll be as quick as I can."

Biting her lip hard enough to draw blood, Aelin turned her head away while the first piece of glass slid from her knee. Flesh and sinew sundered anew.

Salt overpowered the tang of her blood, and she knew he was crying. The scent of their tears filled the tiny room as he worked.

Neither of them said a word.

CHAPTER 10

The world had become only freezing mud, and red and black blood, and the screams of the dying rising to the frigid sky.

Lysandra had learned these months that battle was no orderly, neat thing. It was chaos and pain and there were no grand, heroic duels. Only the slashing of her claws and the rip of her fangs; the clash of dented shields and bloodied swords. Armor that had once been distinguishable quickly turned gore-splattered, and were it not for the dark of her enemy's colors, Lysandra wasn't entirely certain how she would have discerned ally from foe.

Their lines held. At least they had that much.

Shield to shield and shoulder to shoulder in the snowy field that had since become a mud pit, they'd met the legion Erawan had marched through Eldrys.

Aedion had picked the field, the hour, the angle of this battle. The others had pushed for instant attack, but he'd let Morath march far enough inland—right to where he wanted them. Location was as important as numbers, was all he'd said.

Not to Lysandra, of course. He barely said a damn word to her these days. Now certainly wasn't the time to think of it. To care.

Their allies and soldiers believed Aelin Galathynius remained en route to them, allowing Lysandra to don the ghost leopard's form. Ren Allsbrook had even commissioned plated armor for the leopard's chest, sides, and flanks. So light as to not be a hindrance, but solid enough that the three blows she'd been too slow to stop—an arrow to the side, then two slashes from enemy swords—had been deflected.

Little wounds burned along her body. Blood matted the fur of her paws from the slaughtering she'd done amongst the front lines and being torn open on fallen swords and snapped arrows.

But she kept going, the Bane holding firm against what had been sent to meet them.

Only five thousand.

Only seemed like a ridiculous word, but it was what Aedion and the others had used.

Barely enough to be an army, considering Morath's full might, but large enough to pose a threat.

To them, Lysandra thought as she lunged between two Bane warriors and launched herself upon the nearest Valg foot soldier.

The man had his sword upraised, poised to strike the Bane soldier before him. With the angle of his head as he brought the blade up, the Valg grunt didn't spy his oncoming death until her jaws were around his exposed neck.

Hours into this battle, it was instinct to clamp down, flesh splitting like a piece of ripe fruit.

She was moving again before he hit the earth, spitting his throat onto the mud, leaving the advancing Bane to decapitate his corpse. How far away that courtesan's life in Rifthold now seemed. Despite the death around her, she couldn't say she missed it.

Down the line, Aedion bellowed orders to the left flank. They'd let rest some of the Bane upon hearing how few Erawan had sent, and had filled the ranks with a mixture of soldiers from the Lords of Terrasen's own small forces and those from Prince Galan Ashryver and Queen Ansel of the Wastes, both of whom had additional warriors on the way.

No need to reveal they had a small battalion of Fae soldiers courtesy of Prince Endymion and Princess Sellene Whitethorn, or that the Silent Assassins of the Red Desert were amongst them, too. There would be a time when the surprise of their presence would be needed, Aedion had argued during the quick war council they'd conducted upon returning to the camp. Lysandra, winded from carrying him, Ren, and Murtaugh without rest from Allsbrook to the edges of Orynth, had barely listened to the debate. Aedion had won, anyway.

As he won everything, through sheer will and arrogance.

She didn't dare look down the lines to see how he was faring, shoulder to shoulder in the mud with his men. Ren led the right flank, where Lysandra had been stationed. Galan and Ansel had taken the left, Ravi and Sol of Suria fighting amongst them.

She didn't dare see whose swords were still swinging.

They would count their dead after the battle.

There weren't many of the enemy left now. A thousand, if that. The soldiers at her back numbered far more.

So Lysandra kept killing, the blood of her enemy like spoiled wine on her tongue.

~

They won, though Aedion was well aware that victory against five thousand troops was likely fleeting, considering Morath's full host had yet to come.

The rush of battle hadn't yet worn off any of them—which was how Aedion wound up in his war tent an hour after the last of the Valg had fallen, standing around a map-covered table with Ren Allsbrook and Ravi and Sol of Suria.

Where Lysandra had gone, he didn't know. She'd survived, which he supposed was enough.

They hadn't washed away the gore or mud coating them so thoroughly that it had caked beneath their helmets, their armor. Their weapons lay in a discarded pile near the tent flaps. All would need to be cleaned. But later.

"Losses on your side?" Aedion asked Ravi and Sol. The two blond brothers both ruled over Suria, though Sol was technically its lord. They'd never fought in the wars before now, despite being around Aedion's age, but they'd held their own well enough today. Their soldiers had, too.

The Lords of Suria had lost their father to Adarlan's butchering blocks a decade ago, their mother surviving the wars and Adarlan's occupation through her cunning and the fact that her prosperous port-city was too valuable to the empire's trade route to decimate.

Sol, it seemed, took after their even-keeled, clever mother.

Ravi, coltish and brash, took after their late father.

Both, however, hated Adarlan with a deep-burning intensity belied by their pale blue eyes.

Sol, his narrow face flecked with mud, loosed a breath through his nose. An aristocrat's nose, Aedion had thought when they were children. The lord had always been more of a scholar than a warrior, but it seemed he'd learned a thing or two in the grim years since. "Not many, thank the gods. Two hundred at most."

The soft voice was deceptive—Aedion had learned that these weeks. Perhaps a weapon in its own right, to make people believe him gentle-hearted and weak. To mask the sharp mind and sharper instincts behind it.

"And your flank?" Aedion asked Ren.

Ren ran a hand through his dark hair, mud crumbling away. "One hundred fifty, if that."

Aedion nodded. Far better than he'd anticipated. The lines had held, thanks to the Bane he'd interspersed amongst them. The Valg had tried to maintain order, yet once human blood began spilling, they had descended into battle lust and lost control, despite the screaming of their commanders.

All Valg grunts, no princes among them. He knew it wasn't a blessing.

Knew the five thousand troops Erawan had sent, ambushing Galan Ashryver's ships by Ilium before setting upon Eldrys, were just to wear them down. No ilken, no Ironteeth, no Wyrdhounds.

They had still been hard to kill. Had fought longer than most men.

Ravi eyed the map. "Do we pull back to Orynth now? Or head to the border?"

"Darrow ordered us to Orynth, if we survived," Sol countered, frowning at his brother. At the light in Ravi's eyes that so clearly voiced where he wished to go.

Darrow, who was too old to fight, had lingered in the secondary camp twenty miles behind theirs. To be the next line of defense, if five thousand troops somehow managed to destroy one of the most skilled fighting units Terrasen had ever seen. With word now undoubtedly arriving that the battle had gone in their favor, Darrow would likely head back to the capital.

Aedion glanced to Ren. "Do you think your grandfather can persuade Darrow and the other lords to press southward?"

War by committee. It was absurd. Every choice he made, every battlefield he picked, he had to *argue* for it. *Convince* them.

As if these troops weren't for their queen, hadn't come for Aelin when she'd called. As if the Bane served anyone else.

Ren blew out a breath toward the tent's high ceiling. A large space, but unadorned. They hadn't time or resources to furnish it into a proper war tent, setting up only a cot, a few braziers, and this table, along with a copper tub behind a curtain in the rear. As soon as this meeting was over, he'd find someone to fill it for him.

Had Aelin been here, she might have heated it within a heartbeat.

He shut out the tightness in his chest.

Had Aelin been here, one breath from her and the five thousand troops they'd exhausted themselves killing today would have been ash on the wind.

None of the lords around him had questioned where their queen was. Why she hadn't been on the field today. Perhaps they hadn't dared.

Ren said, "If we move the armies south without permission from Darrow and the other lords, we'll be committing treason."

"Treason, when we're saving our own damn kingdom?" Ravi demanded.

"Darrow and the others fought in the last war," Sol said to his brother.

"And lost it," Ravi challenged. "Badly." He nodded toward Aedion. "You were at Theralis. You saw the slaughter."

The Lords of Suria had no love for Darrow or the other lords who had led the forces in that final, doomed stand. Not when their mistakes had led to the deaths of most of their court, their friends. It was of little concern that Terrasen had been so outnumbered that there had never been any hope anyway.

Ravi continued, "I say we head south. Mass our forces at the border, rather than let Morath creep so close to Orynth."

"And let any allies we might still have in the South not have so far to travel when joining with us," Ren added.

"Galan Ashryver and Ansel of the Wastes will go where we tell them—the Fae and assassins, too," Ravi pushed. "The rest of Ansel's troops are making their way northward now. We could meet them. Perhaps have them hammer from the west while we strike from the north."

A sound idea, and one Aedion had contemplated. Yet to convince Darrow . . . He'd head to the other camp tomorrow, perhaps catch Darrow before he returned to the capital. Once he saw to it that the injured were being cared for.

But it seemed Darrow didn't want to wait for the morning.

"General Ashryver." A male voice sounded from outside—young and calm.

Aedion grunted in answer, and it was certainly not Darrow who entered, but a tall, dark-haired, and gray-eyed man. No armor, though his mud-splattered dark clothes revealed a toned body beneath. A letter lay in his hands, which he extended to Aedion as he crossed the tent with graceful ease, then bowed.

Aedion took the letter, his name written on it in Darrow's handwriting.

"Lord Darrow bids you to join him tomorrow," the messenger said, jerking his chin toward the sealed letter. "You, and the army."

"What's the point of the letter," Ravi muttered, "if you're just going to tell him what it says?"

The messenger threw the young lord a bemused glance. "I asked that, too, milord."

"Then I'm surprised you're still employed," Aedion said.

"Not employed," the messenger said. "Just . . . collaborating."

Aedion opened the letter, and it indeed conveyed Darrow's order. "For you to have gotten here so fast, you'd have needed to fly," he said to the messenger. "This must have been written before the battle even started this morning."

The messenger smirked. "I was handed two letters. One was for victory, the other defeat."

Bold—this messenger was bold, and arrogant, for someone at Darrow's beck and call. "What's your name?"

"Nox Owen." The messenger bowed at the waist. "From Perranth."

"I've heard of you," Ren said, scanning the man anew. "You're a thief."

"Former thief," Nox amended, winking. "Now rebel, and Lord Darrow's most trusted messenger." Indeed, a skilled thief would make for a smart messenger, able to slip in and out of places unseen.

But Aedion didn't care what the man did or didn't do. "I assume you're not riding back tonight." A shake of the head. Aedion sighed. "Does Darrow realize that these men are exhausted and though we won the field, it was not an easy victory by any means?"

"Oh, I'm sure he does," Nox said, dark brows rising high with that faint amusement.

"Tell Darrow," Ravi cut in, "that he can come meet *us*, then. Rather than make us move an entire army just to see him."

"The meeting is an excuse," Sol said quietly. Aedion nodded. At Ravi's narrowed brows, his elder brother clarified, "He wants to make sure that we don't . . ." Sol trailed off, aware of the thief who listened to every word. But Nox smiled, as if he grasped the meaning anyway.

Darrow wanted to ensure that they didn't take the army from here and march southward. Had cut them off before they could do so, with this order to move tomorrow.

Ravi growled, at last getting the gist of his brother's words.

Aedion and Ren swapped glances. The Lord of Allsbrook frowned, but nodded.

"Rest wherever you can find a fire to welcome you, Nox Owen," Aedion said to the messenger. "We travel at dawn."

Aedion set out to find Kyllian to convey the order. The tents were a maze of exhausted soldiers, the injured groaning amongst them.

Aedion stopped long enough to greet those men, to offer a hand on the shoulder or a word of reassurance. Some would last the night. Many wouldn't.

He halted at other fires as well. To commend the fighting done, whether the soldiers hailed from Terrasen or the Wastes or Wendlyn. At a few of them, he even shared in their ales or meals.

Rhoe had taught him that—the art of making his men want to follow him, die for him. But more than that, seeing them *as* men, as people with families and friends, who had as much to risk as he did in fighting here. It was no burden, despite the exhaustion creeping over him, to thank them for their courage, their swords.

But it did take time. The sun had fully set, the muddy camp cast in deep shadows amid the fires, by the time he neared Kyllian's tent.

Elgan, one of the Bane captains, clapped him on the shoulder as he passed, the man's grizzled face set in a grim smile. "Not a bad first day, whelp," Elgan grumbled. He'd called Aedion that since those initial days in the Bane's ranks, had been one of the first men here to treat him not as a prince who had lost his kingdom, but as a warrior fighting to defend it. Much of his battlefield training, he owed to Elgan. Along with his life, considering the countless times the man's wisdom and quick sword had saved him.

Aedion grinned at the aging captain. "You fought well, for a grandfather." The man's daughter had given birth to a son just this past winter.

Elgan growled. "I'd like to see you wield a sword so well when you're my age, boy."

Then he was gone, aiming for a campfire that held several other older commanders and captains. They noticed Aedion's attention and lifted their mugs in salute.

Aedion only inclined his head, and continued on.

"Aedion."

He'd know that voice if he were blind.

Lysandra stepped from behind a tent, her face clean despite her muddy clothes.

He halted, finally feeling the weight of the dirt and gore on himself. "What."

She ignored his tone. "I could fly to Darrow tonight. Give him whatever message you want."

"He wants us to move the army back to him, and then to Orynth," Aedion said, making to continue to Kyllian's tent. "Immediately."

She stepped in his path. "I can go, tell him this army needs time to rest."

"Is this some attempt to reenter my good graces?" He was too tired, too weary, to bother beating around the truth.

Her emerald eyes went as cold as the winter night around them. "I don't give a damn about your *good graces*. I care about this army being worn down with unnecessary movements."

"How do you even know what was said in the tent?" He knew the answer as soon as he'd voiced the question. She'd been in some small, unnoticed form. Precisely why so many kingdoms and courts had hunted down and killed any shifters. Unparalleled spies and assassins.

She crossed her arms. "If you don't want me sitting in on your war councils, then say so."

He took in her face, her stiff posture. Exhaustion lay heavy on her, her golden skin pale and eyes haunted. He didn't know where she was staying in this camp. If she even had a tent.

Guilt gnawed on him for a heartbeat. "When, exactly, will our queen make her grand return?"

Her mouth tightened. "Tonight, if you think it wise."

"To miss the battle and only appear to bask in the glory of victory? I doubt the troops would find that heartening."

"Then tell me where, and when, and I'll do it."

"Just as you blindly obeyed our queen, you'll now obey me?"

"I obey no man," she snarled. "But I'm not fool enough to believe I know more about armies and soldiers than you do. My pride is not so easily bruised."

Aedion took a step forward. "And mine is?"

"What I did, I did for her, and for this kingdom. Look at these men, your men—look at the allies we've gathered and tell me that if they knew the truth, they would be so eager to fight."

"The Bane fought when we believed her dead. It would be no different."

"It might be for our allies. For the people of Terrasen." She didn't back down for a moment. "Go ahead and punish me for the rest of your life. For a thousand years, if you wind up Settling."

With Gavriel for his father, he might very well. He tried not to dwell on the possibility. He'd barely interacted with the Fae royals or their soldiers beyond what was necessary. And they mostly kept to themselves. Yet they did not sneer at him for his demi-Fae status; didn't really seem to care what blood flowed in his veins so long as he kept them alive.

"We have enough enemies as it is," Lysandra went on. "But if you truly wish to make me one of them as well, that's fine. I don't regret what I did, nor will I ever."

"Fine," was all he could think to say.

She shrewdly looked him over. As if weighing the man within. "It was real, Aedion," she said. "All of it. I don't care if you believe me or not. But it was real for me."

He couldn't bear to hear it. "I have a meeting," he lied, and stepped around her. "Go slither off somewhere else."

Hurt flashed in her eyes, quickly hidden. He was the worst sort of bastard for it.

But he continued into Kyllian's tent. She didn't come after him.

~

She was a stupid fool.

A stupid fool, to have said anything, and to now feel something in her chest crumpling.

She had enough dignity left not to beg. To not watch Aedion go into Kyllian's tent and wonder if it was for a meeting, or because he was seeking to remind himself of life after so much killing today. To not give one inch of space to the burning in her eyes.

Lysandra made her way toward the comfortable tent Sol of Suria had given her near his. A kind, sharply clever man—who had no interest in women. The younger brother, Ravi, had eyed her, as all men did. But he'd kept a respectful distance, and had talked to *her*, not her chest, so she liked him, too. Didn't mind having a tent in their midst.

An honor, actually. She'd gone from having to crawl into the beds of lords, doing whatever they asked of her with a smile, to fighting beside them. And she was now a lady herself. One whom both the Lords of Suria and the Lord of Allsbrook recognized, despite Darrow spitting on it.

It might have filled her with gladness had battle not worn her out so completely that the walk back to the tent seemed endless. Had the general-prince not filleted her spirit so thoroughly.

Every step was an effort, the mud sucking at her boots.

She turned down an alley of tents, the banners shifting from the white stag on emerald green of the Bane to the twin silver fish on vibrant turquoise of those belonging to the House of Suria. Only fifty more feet to her tent, then she could lie down. The soldiers knew who she was, what she was. None, if they glanced twice in her direction, called out to her in the way men had done in Rifthold.

Lysandra trudged into her tent, sighing in exhausted relief as she shouldered her way through the flaps, aiming for her cot.

Sleep, cold and empty, found her before she could remember to remove her boots.

CHAPTER 11

"You're sure of this?" His heart pounding, Chaol braced a hand on the desk in the quarters he shared with Yrene and pointed to the map that Nesryn and Sartaq had spread before them.

"The soldiers we questioned had been given orders on where to rendezvous," Sartaq said from the other side of the desk, still clad in his rukhin flying clothes. "They were far enough behind the others that they would have needed directions."

Chaol rubbed a hand over his jaw. "And you got a count on the army?"

"Ten thousand strong," Nesryn said, still leaning against the nearby wall. "But no sign of the Ironteeth legions. Only foot soldiers, and about a thousand cavalry."

"As far as you could see from the air," Princess Hasar countered, twirling the end of her long, dark braid. "Who is to say what might be lurking amid the ranks?"

How many Valg demons, the princess didn't need to add. Of all the royal siblings, Hasar had taken Princess Duva's infestation and their sister

Tumelun's murder at her hand the most personally. Had sailed here to avenge both her sisters, and to ensure it didn't happen again. If this war had not been so desperate, Chaol might have paid good coin to see Hasar rip into Valg hides.

"The soldiers didn't divulge that information," Sartaq admitted. "Only their intended location."

At his side, Yrene wrapped her fingers around Chaol's and squeezed. He hadn't realized how cold, how trembling, his hand had become until her warmth seeped into him.

Because the intended target of that enemy army now marching to the northwest . . .

Anielle.

"Your father has not kneeled to Morath," Hasar mused, flicking her heavy braid over the shoulder of her embroidered sky-blue jacket. "It must make Erawan nervous enough that he saw the need to send such an army to crush it."

Chaol swallowed the dryness in his mouth. "But Erawan has already sacked Rifthold," he said, pointing to the capital on the coast, then dragging a finger inland along the Avery. "He controls most of the river. Why not send the witches to sack it instead? Why not sail right up the Avery? Why take an army so far to the coast, then all the way back?"

"To clear the way for the rest," Yrene said, her mouth a tight line. "To instill as much terror as possible."

Chaol blew out a breath. "In Terrasen. Erawan wants Terrasen to know what's coming, that he can take his time and expend forces on destroying swaths of land."

"Does Anielle have an army?" Sartaq asked, the prince's dark eyes steady.

Chaol straightened, hand balling into a fist, as if it could keep the dread pooling in his stomach at bay. Hurry—they had to hurry. "Not one able to take on ten thousand soldiers. The keep might survive a siege, but not indefinitely, and it wouldn't be able to fit the city's population." Only his father's chosen few.

Silence fell, and Chaol knew they were waiting for him to speak, to voice the question himself. He hated every word that came out of his mouth. "Is it worth it to launch our troops here and march to save Anielle?"

Because they couldn't risk the Avery, not when Rifthold sat at its entrance. They'd have to find a place to land and march inland. Across the plains, over the Acanthus, into Oakwald, and to the very foothills of the White Fangs. Days of travel on horseback—the gods knew how long an army would take.

"There might not be an Anielle left by the time we get there," Hasar said with more gentleness than the sharp-faced princess usually bothered with. Enough so that Chaol reined in the urge to tell them that was precisely why they had to move *now*. "If the southern half of Adarlan is beyond help, then we might land near Meah." She pointed to the city in the north of the kingdom. "March near the border, and set ourselves up to intercept them."

"Or we could go directly to Terrasen, and sail up the Florine to Orynth's doorstep," Sartaq mused.

"We don't know what we'll find in either," Nesryn countered quietly, her cool voice filling the room. A different woman in some ways than the one who'd gone with Chaol to the southern continent. "Meah could be overrun, and Terrasen might be facing its own siege. The days it would take for our scouts to fly northward would waste vital time—if they return at all."

Chaol drew in a deep breath, willing his heart to calm. He hadn't the faintest idea where Dorian might be, if he'd gone with Aelin to Terrasen. The soldiers Nesryn and Sartaq had interrogated had not known. What would his friend have chosen? He could almost hear Dorian yelling at him for even hesitating, hear him ordering Chaol to stop wondering where he'd gone and hurry to Anielle.

"Anielle lies near the Ferian Gap," Hasar said, "which is also controlled by Morath, and is another outpost for the Ironteeth and their wyverns. By bringing our forces so far inland, we risk not only the army marching for Anielle, but finding a host of witches at our backs." She met

Chaol's gaze, her face as unflinching as her words. "Would saving the city gain us anything?"

"It is his home," Yrene said quietly, but not weakly, her chin refusing to dip even an inch in the royals' presence. "I'd think that would be all the proof we need to defend it."

Chaol tightened his hand around hers in silent thanks. Dorian would have said the same.

Sartaq studied the map once more. "The Avery splits near Anielle," he murmured, running a finger along it. "It veers southward to the Silver Lake and Anielle, and then the other branch runs northward, past the Ferian Gap, skirting along the Ruhnns and up to nearly the border of Terrasen itself."

"I can read a map, brother," Hasar growled.

Sartaq ignored her, his eyes meeting Chaol's once more. A spark lit their steady depths. "We avoid the Avery until Anielle. March inland. And when the city is secure, we begin a campaign northward, along the Avery."

Nesryn pushed off the wall to prowl to the prince's side. "Into the Ferian Gap? We'd be facing the witches, then."

Sartaq gave her a half grin. "Then it's a good thing we have ruks."

Hasar leaned over the map. "If we secure the Ferian Gap, then we could possibly march all the way to Terrasen, taking the inland route." She shook her head. "But what of the armada?"

"They wait to intercept Kashin's fleet," Sartaq said. "We take the soldiers, the Darghan cavalry, the ruks, and they wait for the rest of the army to arrive and tell them to meet us here."

Hope stirred in Chaol's chest.

"But that still leaves us at least a week behind the army marching for Anielle," Nesryn said.

Truth—they'd never catch up to them in time. Any delay could cost untold lives. "They need to be warned," Chaol said. "Anielle must be warned, and given time to prepare."

Sartaq nodded. "I can be there in a few days' flight."

"No," Chaol said, and Yrene lifted a brow. "If you can spare me a ruk and a rider, I'll go myself. Stay here, and ready the ruks to fly. Tomorrow, if possible. A day or two at most." He gestured to Hasar. "Dock the ships and lead the troops inland, as swiftly as they can march."

Yrene's eyes turned wary, well aware of what and whom he would face in Anielle. The homecoming he had never pictured, certainly not under these circumstances.

"I'm coming with you," his wife said.

He squeezed her hand again, as if to say, *I'm not at all surprised to hear that.*

Yrene squeezed right back.

Sartaq and Hasar nodded, and Nesryn opened her mouth as if she'd object, but nodded, too.

They'd leave tonight, under cover of darkness. Finding Dorian again would have to wait. Yrene chewed on her lip, no doubt calculating what they'd need to pack, what to tell the other healers.

He prayed they'd be swift enough, prayed that he could figure out what the hell to say to his father, after the oath he'd broken, after all that lay between them. And more than that, what he'd say to his mother, and the not-so-young brother he'd left behind when he'd chosen Dorian over his birthright.

Chaol had given Yrene the title owed to her in marrying him: Lady Westfall.

He wondered if he could stomach being called Lord. If it mattered at all, given what bore down upon the city on the Silver Lake.

If it would matter at all if they didn't make it in time.

Sartaq braced a hand on the hilt of his sword. "Hold the defenses for as long as you can, Lord Westfall. The ruks will be a day or so behind you, the foot soldiers a week behind that."

Chaol clasped Sartaq's hand, then Hasar's. "Thank you."

Hasar's mouth curved into a half smile. "Thank us if we save your city."

CHAPTER 12

Everything. She had given everything for this, and had been glad to do it.

Aelin lay in darkness, the slab of iron like a starless night overhead.

She'd awoken in here. Had been in here for . . . a long time.

Long enough she'd relieved herself. Hadn't cared.

Perhaps it had all been for nothing. The Queen Who Was Promised.

Promised to die, to surrender herself to fulfill an ancient princess's debt. To save this world.

She wouldn't be able to do it. She would fail in that, even if she outlasted Maeve.

Outlasted what she might have glimpsed lay beneath the queen's skin. If that had been real at all.

Against Erawan, there had been little hope. But against Maeve as well . . .

Silent tears pooled in her mask.

It didn't matter. She wasn't leaving this place. This box.

She would never again feel the buttery warmth of the sun on her hair, or a sea-kissed breeze on her cheeks.

She couldn't stop crying, ceaseless and relentless. As if some dam had cracked open inside her the moment she'd seen the blood dribble down Maeve's face.

She didn't care if Cairn saw the tears, smelled them.

Let him break her until she was bloody smithereens on the floor. Let him do it over and over again.

She wouldn't fight. Couldn't bear to fight.

A door groaned open and closed. Stalking footsteps neared.

Then a thump on the lid of the coffin. "How does a few more days in there sound to you?"

She wished she could fold herself into the blackness around her.

Cairn told Fenrys to relieve himself and return. Silence filled the room.

Then a thin scraping. Along the top of the box. As if Cairn were running a dagger over it.

"I've been thinking how to repay you when I let you out."

Aelin blocked out his words. Did nothing but gaze into the dark.

She was so tired. So, so tired.

For Terrasen, she had gladly done this. All of it. For Terrasen, she deserved to pay this price.

She had tried to make it right. Had tried, and failed.

And she was so, so tired.

Fireheart.

The whispered word floated through the eternal night, a glimmer of sound, of light.

Fireheart.

The woman's voice was soft, loving. Her mother's voice.

Aelin turned her face away. Even that movement was more than she could bear.

Fireheart, why do you cry?

Aelin could not answer.

Fireheart.

The words were a gentle brush down her cheek. *Fireheart, why do you cry?*

And from far away, deep within her, Aelin whispered toward that ray of memory, *Because I am lost. And I do not know the way.*

Cairn was still talking. Still scraping his knife over the coffin's lid.

But Aelin did not hear him as she found a woman lying beside her. A mirror—or a reflection of the face she'd bear in a few years' time. Should she live that long.

Borrowed time. Every moment of it had been borrowed time.

Evalin Ashryver ran gentle fingers down Aelin's cheek. Over the mask.

Aelin could have sworn she felt them against her skin.

You have been very brave, her mother said. *You have been very brave, for so very long.*

Aelin couldn't stop the silent sob that worked its way up her throat.

But you must be brave a little while longer, my Fireheart.

She leaned into her mother's touch.

You must be brave a little while longer, and remember . . .

Her mother placed a phantom hand over Aelin's heart.

It is the strength of this *that matters. No matter where you are, no matter how far, this will lead you home.*

Aelin managed to slide a hand up to her chest, to cover her mother's fingers. Only thin fabric and iron met her skin.

But Evalin Ashryver held Aelin's gaze, the softness turning hard and gleaming as fresh steel. *It is the strength of* this *that matters, Aelin.*

Aelin's fingers dug into her chest as she mouthed, *The strength of this.*

Evalin nodded.

Cairn's hissed threats danced through the coffin, his knife scraping and scraping.

Evalin's face didn't falter. *You are my daughter. You were born of two mighty bloodlines. That strength flows through you. Lives in you.*

Evalin's face blazed with the fierceness of the women who had come before them, all the way back to the Faerie Queen whose eyes they both bore.

You do not yield.

Then she was gone, like dew under the morning sun.

But the words lingered.

Blossomed within Aelin, bright as a kindled ember.

You do not yield.

Cairn scraped his dagger over the metal, right above her head. "When I cut you up this time, bitch, I'm going to—"

Aelin slammed her hand into the lid.

Cairn paused.

Aelin pounded her fist into the iron again. Again.

You do not yield.

Again.

You do not yield.

Again. Again.

Until she was alive with it, until her blood was raining onto her face, washing away the tears, until every pound of her fist into the iron was a battle cry.

You do not yield.

You do not yield.

You do not yield.

It rose in her, burning and roaring, and she gave herself wholly to it. Distantly, close by, wood crashed. Like someone had staggered into something. Then shouting.

Aelin hammered her fist into the metal, the song within her pulsing and cresting, a tidal wave racing for the shore.

"Get me that gloriella!"

The words meant nothing. He was nothing. Would always be nothing.

Over and over, she pounded against the lid. Over and over, that song of fire and darkness flared through her, out of her, into the world.

You do not yield.

Something hissed and crackled nearby, and smoke poured through the lid.

But Aelin kept striking. Kept striking until the smoke choked her, until its sweet scent dragged her under and away.

And when she awoke chained on the altar, she beheld what she had done to the iron coffin.

The top of the lid had been warped. A great hump now protruded, the metal stretched thin.

As if it had come so very close to breaking entirely.

On a dark hilltop overlooking a sleeping kingdom, Rowan froze.

The others were already halfway down the hill, leading the horses along the dried slope that would take them over Akkadia's border and onto the arid plains below.

His hand dropped from the stallion's reins.

He had to have imagined it.

He scanned the starry sky, the slumbering lands beyond, the Lord of the North above.

It hit him a heartbeat later. Erupted around him and *roared.*

Over and over and over, as if it were a hammer against an anvil.

The others whirled to him.

That raging, fiery song charged closer. Through him.

Down the mating bond. Down into his very soul.

A bellow of fury and defiance.

From down the hill, Lorcan rasped, "Rowan."

It was impossible, utterly impossible, and yet—

"North," Gavriel said, turning his bay gelding. "The surge came from the North."

From Doranelle.

A beacon in the night. Power rippling into the world, as it had done in Skull's Bay.

It filled him with sound, with fire and light. As if it screamed, again and again, *I am alive, I am alive, I am alive.*

And then silence. Like it had been cut off.

Extinguished.

He refused to think of why. The mating bond remained. Stretched taut, but it remained.

So he sent the words along it, with as much hope and fury and unrelenting love as he had felt from her. *I will find you.*

There was no answer. Nothing but humming darkness and the Lord of the North glistening above, pointing the way north. To her.

He found his companions waiting for his orders.

He opened his mouth to voice them, but halted. Considered. "We need to draw Maeve out—away from Aelin." His voice rumbled over the drowsy buzzing of insects in the grasses. "Just long enough for us to infiltrate Doranelle." For even with the three of them together, they might not be enough to take on Maeve.

"If she hears we're coming," Lorcan countered, "Maeve will spirit Aelin away again, not come to meet us. She's not that foolish."

But Rowan looked to Elide, the Lady of Perranth's eyes wide. "I know," he said, his plan forming, as cold and ruthless as the power in his veins. "We'll draw out Maeve with a different sort of lure, then."

CHAPTER 13

The spider spoke true.

Keeping hidden amongst the ice-crusted rocks of a jagged mountain peak, Manon and the Thirteen peered down into the small pass.

At the camp of red-cloaked witches, the location confirmed by the Shadows just an hour ago.

Manon glanced over her shoulder, to where Dorian was nearly invisible against the snow, the spider in her plain human form beside him.

The depthless eyes of the creature met hers, shining with triumph.

Fine. Cyrene, or whatever she called herself, might live. Where it would lead them, she'd see. The horrors the spider had mentioned in Morath—

Later.

Manon scanned the darkening blue skies. None of them had questioned when Manon had sailed off on Abraxos hours earlier. And none of her Thirteen now asked where she'd gone as they monitored their ancient enemy's camp.

"Seventy-five that we can see," Asterin murmured, eyes fixed on the bustling camp. "What in hell are they doing out here?"

Manon didn't know. The Shadows hadn't been able to glean anything.

Tents surrounded small campfires—and every few moments, figures departed and arrived on brooms. Her heart thundered in her chest.

The Crochans. The other half of her heritage.

"We move on your command," Sorrel said, a careful nudge.

Manon drew in a breath, willing the snow-laced wind to keep her cold and steady during this next encounter. And what would come after.

"No nails or teeth," Manon ordered the Thirteen. Then she looked over her shoulder once more to the king and spider. "You may stay here, if you wish."

Dorian gave her a lazy smile. "And miss the fun?" Yet she caught the gleam in his eye—the understanding that perhaps he alone could grasp. That she was not just about to face an enemy, but a potential people. He subtly nodded. "We all go in."

Manon merely nodded back and rose. The Thirteen stood with her.

It was the matter of a few minutes before warning cries rang out.

But Manon kept her hands in the air as Abraxos landed at the edge of the Crochan camp, the Thirteen and their wyverns behind her, Vesta bearing both Dorian and the spider.

Spears and arrows and swords pointed at them with lethal accuracy.

A dark-haired witch stalked past the armed front line, a fine blade in her hand as her eyes fixed on Manon.

Crochans. Her people.

Now—now would be the time to make the speech she'd planned. To free those words that she'd tethered within herself.

Asterin turned toward her in silent urging.

Yet Manon's lips didn't move.

The dark-haired one kept her brown eyes fixed on Manon. Over one shoulder, a polished wood staff gleamed. Not a staff—a broom. Beyond the witch's billowing red cloak, gold-bound twigs shimmered.

High ranking, then, to have such fine bindings. Most Crochans used simpler metals, the poorest just twine.

"What interesting replacements for your ironwood brooms," the Crochan said. The others were as stone-faced as the Thirteen. The witch glanced toward where Dorian sat atop Vesta's mount, likely monitoring all with that clear-eyed cunning. "And interesting company you now keep." The witch's mouth curled slightly. "Unless things have become so sorry for your ilk, Blackbeak, that you have to resort to sharing."

A snarl rumbled from Asterin.

But the witch had identified her—or at least what Clan they hailed from. The Crochan sniffed at the spider-shifter. Her eyes shuttered. "Interesting company indeed."

"We mean you no harm," Manon finally said.

The witch snorted. "No threats from the White Demon?"

Oh, she knew, then. Who Manon was, who they all were.

"Or are the rumors true? That you broke with your grandmother?" The witch brazenly surveyed Manon from head to boot. A bolder look than Manon usually allowed her enemies to make. "Rumor also claims you were gutted at her hand, but here you are. Hale and once more hunting us. Perhaps the rumors about your defection aren't true, either."

"She broke from her grandmother," said Dorian, sliding off Vesta's wyvern and prowling toward Abraxos. The Crochans tensed, but made no move to attack. "I pulled her from the sea months ago, when she lay upon Death's doorstep. Saw the iron shards my friends removed from her abdomen."

The Crochan's dark brows rose, again taking in the beautiful, well-spoken male. Perhaps noting the power that radiated from him—and the keys he bore. "And who, exactly, are you?"

Dorian gave the witch one of those charming smiles and sketched a bow. "Dorian Havilliard, at your service."

"The king," one of the Crochans murmured from near the wyverns.

Dorian winked. "That I am, too."

The head of the coven, however, studied him—then Manon. The spider. "There is more to be explained, it seems."

Manon's hand itched for Wind-Cleaver at her back.

But Dorian said, "We've been looking for you for two months now." The Crochans again tensed. "Not for violence or sport," he clarified, the words flowing in a silver-tongued melody. "But so we might discuss matters between our peoples."

The Crochans shifted, boots crunching in the icy snow.

The coven leader asked, "Between Adarlan and us, or between the Blackbeaks and our people?"

Manon slid off Abraxos at last, her mount huffing anxiously as he eyed their glinting weapons. "All of us," Manon said tightly. She jerked her chin to the wyverns. "They will not harm you." Unless she signaled the command. Then the Crochans' heads would be torn from their bodies before they could draw their swords. "You can stand down."

One of the Crochans laughed. "And be remembered as fools for trusting you? I think not."

The coven leader slashed a silencing glare toward the brown-haired sentinel who'd spoken, a pretty, full-figured witch. The witch shrugged, sighing skyward.

The coven leader turned to Manon. "We will stand down when we are ordered to do so."

"By whom?" Dorian scanned their ranks.

Now would be the time for Manon to say who she was, what she was. To announce why she had truly come.

The coven leader pointed deeper into the camp. "Her."

Even from a distance, Dorian had marveled at the brooms the Crochans sat astride to soar through the sky. But now, surrounded by them . . . No mere myths. But warriors. Ones all too happy to end them.

Bloodred capes flowed everywhere, stark against the snow and gray peaks. Though many of the witches were young-faced and beautiful, there were just as many who appeared middle-aged, some even elderly. How old they must have been to become so withered, Dorian couldn't fathom. He had little doubt they could kill him with ease.

The coven leader pointed toward the neat rows of tents, and the gathered warriors parted, the wall of brooms and weapons shining in the dying light.

"So," an ancient voice said as the ranks stepped back to reveal the one to whom the Crochan had pointed. Not yet bent with age, but her hair was white with it. Her blue eyes, however, were clear as a mountain lake. "The hunters have now become the hunted."

The ancient witch paused at the edge of her ranks, surveying Manon. There was kindness on the witch's face, Dorian noted—and wisdom. And something, he realized, like sorrow. It didn't halt him from sliding a hand onto Damaris's pommel, as if he were casually resting it.

"We sought you so we might speak." Manon's cold, calm voice rang out over the rocks. "We mean you no harm."

Damaris warmed at the truth in her words.

"This time," the brown-haired witch who'd spoken earlier muttered. Her coven leader elbowed her in warning.

"Who are you, though?" Manon instead asked the crone. "You lead these covens."

"I am Glennis. My family served the Crochan royals, long before the city fell." The ancient witch's eyes went to the strip of red cloth tying Manon's braid. "Rhiannon found you, then."

Dorian had listened when Manon had explained to the Thirteen the truth about her heritage, and who her grandmother had bade her to slaughter in the Omega.

Manon kept her chin up, even as her golden eyes flickered. "Rhiannon didn't make it out of the Ferian Gap."

"Bitch," a witch snarled, others echoing it.

Manon ignored it and asked the ancient Crochan, "You knew her, then?"

The witches fell silent.

The crone inclined her head, that sorrow filling her eyes once more. Dorian didn't need Damaris's confirming warmth to know her next words were true. "I was her great-grandmother." Even the whipping wind quieted. "As I am yours."

CHAPTER 14

The Crochans stood down—under the orders of Manon's so-called great-grandmother. Glennis.

She had demanded how, what the lineage was, but Glennis had only beckoned Manon to follow her into the camp.

At least two dozen other witches tended to the several fire pits scattered amongst the white tents, all of them halting their various work as Manon passed. She'd never seen Crochans going about their domestic tasks, but here they were: some tending to fires, some hauling buckets of water, some monitoring heavy cauldrons of what smelled like mountain-goat stew seasoned with dried herbs.

No words sounded in her head while she strode through the ranks of bristling Crochans. The Thirteen didn't try to speak, either. But Dorian did.

The king fell into step beside her, his body a wall of solid warmth, and asked quietly, "Did you know you had kin still living amongst the Crochans?"

"No." Her grandmother hadn't mentioned it in her final taunts.

Manon doubted the camp was a permanent place for the Crochans. They'd be foolish to ever reveal that. Yet Cyrene had discovered it, somehow.

Perhaps by tracking Manon's scent—the parts of it that claimed kinship with the Crochans.

The spider now walked between Asterin and Sorrel, Dorian still showing no sign of strain in keeping her partially bound, though he kept a hand on the hilt of his sword.

A sharp glance from Manon and he dropped it.

"How do you want to play this?" Dorian murmured. "Do you want me to keep quiet, or be at your side?"

"Asterin is my Second."

"And what am I, then?" The smooth question ran a hand down her spine, as if he'd caressed her with those invisible hands of his.

"You are the King of Adarlan."

"Shall I be a part of the discussions, then?"

"If you feel like it."

She felt his rising annoyance and hid her smirk.

Dorian's voice dropped into a low purr. "Do you know what I feel like doing?"

She twisted her head to glare at him incredulously. And found the king smirking.

"You look like you're about to bolt," he said, that smile lingering. "It will set the wrong tone."

He was trying to rile her, to distract her into loosening her iron-hard grip on her control.

"They know who you are," Dorian went on. "Proving that part of it is over. Whether they accept you will be the true matter." Her great-grandmother must have come from the nonroyal part of her bloodline, then. "These do not seem like witches who will be won by brutality."

He didn't know the half of it. "Are you presuming to give me advice?"

"Consider it a tip, from one monarch to another."

Despite who walked ahead of them, behind them, Manon smiled slightly.

He surprised her further by saying, "I've been tunneling into my power since they appeared. One wrong move from them, and I'll blast them into nothing."

A shiver rippled down her back at the cold violence in his voice. "We need them as allies." Everything she was to do today, tonight, was to seal such a thing.

"Then let's hope it doesn't come to that, witchling."

Manon opened her mouth to answer.

But a horn, shrill and warning, blasted through the descending night.

Then the beating of mighty leathery wings boomed across the stars.

The camp was instantly in action, shouts ringing out from the scouts who'd sounded the alarm. The Thirteen closed ranks around Manon, weapons drawn.

The Ironteeth had found them.

Far sooner than Manon had planned.

How the Ironteeth patrol had found them, Dorian didn't know. He supposed the fires would be a giveaway.

Dorian rallied his magic as twenty-six massive shapes swept over the camp.

Yellowlegs. Two covens.

The crone who'd introduced herself as Manon's great-grandmother began shouting commands, and Crochans obeyed, leaping into the newly dark skies on their brooms, bows drawn or swords out.

No time to question how they'd been found, whether the spider had indeed laid a trap—certainly not as Manon's voice rang out, ordering the Thirteen into defensive positions.

Swift as shadows, they raced for where they'd left their wyverns, iron teeth glinting.

Dorian waited until the Crochans were clear of him before unleashing his power. Spears of ice, to pierce the enemy's exposed chests or rip through their wings.

Half a thought had him loosening Cyrene's bonds, though not unleashing her from the power that kept her from attacking. Just giving her enough space to shift, to defend herself. A flash on the other side of the camp told him she had.

The interrogation would come later.

Manon and the Thirteen reached the wyverns, and were airborne within heartbeats, flapping into the chaos above.

The Crochans were so small—so terribly small—against the bulk of the wyverns. Even on their brooms.

And as they swarmed around the two Ironteeth covens, firing arrows and swinging swords, Dorian couldn't get a clear shot. Not with the Crochans darting around the beasts, too fast for him to track. Some of the wyverns bellowed and tumbled from the sky, but many stayed aloft.

Glennis barked orders from the ground, a great bow in her wrinkled hands, aimed upward.

A wyvern soared overhead, so low its spiked, poisonous tail snapped through tent after tent.

Glennis let her arrow fly, and Dorian echoed her blow with one of his own.

A lance of solid ice, careening for the exposed, mottled chest.

Both arrow and ice spear drove home, and black blood spewed downward—before the wyvern and rider went crashing into a peak, and flipped over the cliff face.

Glennis grinned, that aged face lighting. "I struck first." She drew another arrow. Such lightness, even in the face of an ambush.

"I wish you were my great-grandmother," Dorian muttered, and readied his next blow. He'd have to be careful, with the Thirteen looking so much like the Yellowlegs from below.

But the Thirteen did not need his caution, or his help.

They plowed into the lines of the Yellowlegs, breaking them apart, scattering them.

The Yellowlegs might have had the advantage of surprise, but the Thirteen were masters of war.

Crochans tumbled from the skies as they were struck by brutal, spiked tails. Some not even tumbling at all as they came face-to-face with enormous maws and did not emerge again.

"Clear out!" Manon's barked order carried over the fray. "Form lines low to the ground!"

Not an order for the Thirteen, but the Crochans.

Glennis shouted, some magic no doubt amplifying her voice, "Follow her command!"

Just like that, the Crochans fell back, forming a solid unit in the air above the tents.

They watched as Abraxos ripped the throat from a bull twice his size, and Manon fired an arrow through the rider's face. Watched as the green-eyed demon twins rounded up three wyverns between them and sent them crashing onto the mountainsides. Watched as Asterin's blue mare ripped a rider from the saddle, then ripped part of the spine from the wyvern beneath her.

Each of the Thirteen marked a target with every swipe through the gathered attackers.

The Yellowlegs had no such organization.

The Yellowlegs sentinels who tried to break from the Thirteen's path to attack the Crochans below found a wall of arrows meeting them.

The wyverns might have survived, but the riders did not.

And with a few careful maneuvers, the riderless beasts found themselves with throats cut, blood streaming as they crashed onto the nearby peaks.

Pity mingled with the fear and rage in his heart.

How many of those beasts might have been like Abraxos, had they good riders who loved them?

It was surprisingly hard to blast his magic at the wyvern who managed to sail overhead, aiming right for Glennis, another wyvern on its tail.

He made it an easy death, snapping the beast's neck with a burst of his power that left him panting.

He whipped his magic toward the second attacking wyvern, offering it the same quick end, but didn't see the third and fourth that now crashed into the camp, wrecking tents and snapping their jaws at anything in their path. Crochans fell, screaming.

But then Manon was there, Abraxos sailing hard and fast, and she lopped off the head of the nearest rider. The Yellowlegs sentinel still wore an expression of shock as her head flew.

Dorian's magic balked.

The severed head hit the ground near him and rolled.

A room flashed, the red marble stained with blood, the thud of a head on stone the only sound beyond his screaming.

I was not supposed to love you.

The Yellowlegs's head halted near his boots, the blue blood gushing onto the snow and dirt.

He didn't hear, didn't care, that the fourth wyvern soared toward him.

Manon bellowed his name, and Crochan arrows fired.

The Yellowlegs sentinel's eyes stared at no one, nothing.

A gaping maw opened before him, jaws stretching wide.

Manon screamed his name again, but he couldn't move.

The wyvern swept down, and darkness yawned wide as those jaws closed around him.

As Dorian let his magic rip free of its tethers.

One heartbeat, the wyvern was swallowing him whole, its rancid breath staining the air.

The next, the beast was on the ground, corpse steaming.

Steaming, from what he'd done to it.

Not to it, but to himself.

The body he'd turned into solid flame, so hot it had melted through the wyvern's jaws, its throat, and he had passed through the beast's mouth as if it were nothing but a cobweb.

The Yellowlegs rider who'd survived the crash drew her sword, but too late. Glennis put an arrow through her throat.

Silence fell. Even the battle above died out.

The Thirteen landed, splattered in blue and black blood. So different from Sorscha's red blood—his own red blood.

Then there were iron-tipped hands gripping his shoulders, and gold eyes glaring into his own. "Are you daft?"

He only glanced to the Yellowlegs witch's head, still feet away. Manon's own gaze turned toward it. Her mouth tightened, then she let go of him and whirled to Glennis. "I'm sending out my Shadows to scout for others."

"Any enemy survivors?" Glennis scanned the empty skies. Whether his magic surprised them, shocked them, neither Glennis nor the Crochans rushing to tend to their wounded let on.

"All dead," Manon said.

But the dark-haired Crochan who'd first intercepted them stormed at Manon, her sword out. "You did this."

Dorian gripped Damaris, but made no move to draw it. Not while Manon didn't back down. "Saved your asses? Yes, I'd say we did."

The witch seethed. "*You* led them here."

"Bronwen," Glennis warned, wiping blue blood from her face.

The young witch—Bronwen—bristled. "You think it mere coincidence that they arrive, and then we're attacked?"

"They fought with us, not against us," Glennis said. She turned to Manon. "Do you swear it?"

Manon's golden eyes glowed in the firelight. "I swear it. I did not lead them here."

Glennis nodded, but Dorian stared at Manon.

Damaris had gone cold as ice. So cold the golden hilt bit into his skin.

Glennis, somehow satisfied, nodded again. "Then we shall talk—later."

Bronwen spat on the bloody ground and prowled off.

A lie. Manon had lied.

She arched a brow at him, but Dorian turned away. Let the knowledge settle into him. What she'd done.

Thus began a series of orders and movements, gathering the injured and dead. Dorian helped as best he could, healing those who needed it most. Open, gaping wounds that leaked blue blood onto his hands.

The warmth of that blood didn't reach him.

CHAPTER 15

She was a liar, and a killer, and would likely have to be both again before this was through.

But Manon had no regrets about what she'd done. Had no room in her for regret. Not with time bearing down on them, not with so much resting on their shoulders.

For long hours while they worked to repair camp and Crochans, Manon monitored the frosty skies.

Eight dead. It could have been worse. Much worse. Though she would take the lives of those eight Crochans with her, learn their names so she might remember them.

Manon spent the long night helping the Thirteen haul the fallen wyverns and Ironteeth riders to another ridge. The ground was too hard to bury them, and pyres would be too easily marked, so they opted for snow. She didn't dare ask Dorian to use his power to assist them.

She'd seen that look in his eyes. Like he knew.

Manon dumped a stiff Yellowlegs body, the sentinel's lips already blue, ice crusted in her blond hair. Asterin hauled a stout-bodied rider toward her by the boots, then deposited the witch with little fanfare.

But Manon stared at their dead faces. She'd sacrificed them, too.

Both sides of this conflict. Both of her bloodlines.

All would bleed; too many would die.

Would Glennis have welcomed them? Perhaps, but the other Crochans hadn't seemed so inclined to do so.

And the fact remained that they did not have the *time* to waste in wooing them. So she'd picked the only method she knew: battle. Had soared off on her own earlier that day, to where she knew Ironteeth would be patrolling nearby, waited until the great northern wind carried her scent southward. And then bided her time.

"Did you know them?" Asterin asked when Manon remained staring at a fallen sentinel's body. Down the line of them, the wyverns used their wings to brush great drifts of snow over the corpses.

"No," Manon said. "I didn't."

Dawn was breaking by the time they returned to the Crochan camp. Eyes that had spat fire hours earlier now watched them warily, fewer hands drifting toward weapons as they aimed for the large, ringed fire pit. The largest of the camp, and located in its heart. Glennis's hearth.

The crone stood before it, warming her gnarled, bloodied hands. Dorian sat nearby, and his sapphire eyes were indeed damning as he met Manon's stare.

Later. That conversation would come later.

Manon halted a few feet away from Glennis, the Thirteen falling into rank at the outskirts of the fire, surveying the five tents around it, the cauldron bubbling at its center. Behind them, Crochans continued their repairs and healing—and kept one eye upon them all.

"Eat something," Glennis said, gesturing to the bubbling cauldron. To what smelled like goat stew.

Manon didn't bother objecting before she obeyed, gathering one of the small earthenware bowls beside the fire. Another way to demonstrate trust: to eat their food. Accept it.

So Manon did, devouring a few bites before Dorian followed her lead and did the same. When they were both eating, Glennis sat on a stone and sighed. "It's been over five hundred years since an Ironteeth witch and a Crochan shared a meal. Since they sought to exchange words in peace. Interrupted, perhaps, only by your mother and father."

"I suppose so," Manon said mildly, pausing her eating.

The crone's mouth twitched toward a smile, despite the battle, the draining night. "I was your father's grandmother," she clarified at last. "I myself bore your grandfather, who mated a Crochan Queen before she died giving birth to your father."

Another thing they'd inherited from the Fae: their difficulty conceiving and the deadly nature of childbirth. A way for the Three-Faced Goddess to keep the balance, to avoid flooding the lands with too many immortal children who would devour her resources.

Manon scanned the half-ruined camp, though.

The crone read her question in her eyes. "Our men dwell at our homes, where they are safe. This camp is an outpost while we conduct our business." The Crochans had always given birth to more males than the Ironteeth, and had adopted the Fae habit of selecting mates—if not a true mating bond, then in spirit. She'd always thought it outlandish and strange. Unnecessary.

"After your mother never returned, your father was asked to couple with another young witch. He was the sole carrier of the Crochan bloodline, you see, and should your mother and you not have survived the birthing, it would end with him. He didn't know what had happened to either of you. If you were alive, or dead. Didn't even know where to look. So he agreed to do his duty, agreed to help his dying people." Her great-grandmother smiled sadly. "All who met Tristan loved him." Tristan. That had been his name. Had her grandmother even known it before she'd killed him? "A young witch was chosen for him especially. But he did not love her—not with your mother as his true mate, the song of his soul. Tristan made it work nonetheless. Rhiannon was the result of that."

Manon tensed. If Rhiannon's mother were here—

Again, the crone read the question on Manon's face.

"She was slaughtered by a Yellowlegs sentinel in the river plains of Melisande. Years ago."

A flicker of shame went through Manon at the relief that flooded her. To avoid that confrontation, to avoid begging for forgiveness, as she should have done.

Dorian set down his spoon. Such a graceful, casual gesture, considering how he'd felled that wyvern. "How is it that the Crochan line survived? Legend says they were wiped out."

Another sad smile. "You can thank my mother for that. Rhiannon Crochan's youngest daughter gave birth during the siege on the Witch-City. With our armies felled and only the city walls to hold back the Ironteeth legions, and with so many of her children and grandchildren slaughtered and her mate spiked to the city walls, Rhiannon had the heralds announce that it had been a stillbirth. So the Ironteeth would never know that one Crochan might yet live. That same night, just before Rhiannon began her three-day battle against the Ironteeth High Witches, my mother smuggled the baby princess out on her broom." The crone's throat bobbed. "Rhiannon was her dearest friend—a sister to her. My mother wanted to stay, to fight until the end, yet she was asked to do this for her people. Our people. Until the day of her death, my mother believed Rhiannon went to hold the gates against the High Witches as a distraction. To get that last Crochan scion out while the Ironteeth looked the other way."

Manon didn't entirely know what to say, how to voice what roiled within her.

"You will find," Glennis went on, "that you have some cousins in this camp."

Asterin stiffened at that, Edda and Briar also tensing where they lingered at the edge of the fire. Manon's own kin, on the Blackbeak side of her heritage. Undoubtedly willing to fight to keep that distinction for themselves.

"Bronwen," the crone said, gesturing toward the dark-haired coven leader with the gold-bound broom, now monitoring Manon and the Thirteen from the shadows beyond the fire, "is also my great-granddaughter. Your closest cousin."

No kindness shone on Bronwen's face, so Manon didn't bother looking pleasant, either.

"She and Rhiannon were close as sisters," Glennis murmured.

It took a considerable amount of effort not to touch the scrap of red cloak at the end of her braid.

Dorian, Darkness embrace his soul, cut in, "We found you for a reason."

Glennis again warmed her hands. "I suppose it is to ask us to join in this war."

Manon didn't soften her stare. "It is. You, and all the Crochans scattered across the lands."

One of the Crochans in the shadows let out a bark of laughter. "That's rich." Others chuckled with her.

Glennis's blue eyes didn't falter. "We have not rallied a host since before the fall of the Witch-City. You might find it a more difficult task than you anticipated."

Dorian asked, "And if their queen summoned them to fight?"

Snow crunched under stomping steps, and then Bronwen was there, her brown eyes blazing. "Don't answer, Glennis."

Such disrespect, such informality to an elder—

Bronwen leveled her burning stare on Manon. "You are not our queen, despite what your blood might suggest. Despite this little skirmish. We do not, and will never, answer to you."

"Morath found you just now," Manon said coolly. She'd anticipated this reaction. "It will do so again. Whether it is in a few months, or a year, they will find you. And then there will be no hope of beating them." She kept her hands at her sides, resisting the urge to unsheathe her iron claws. "A host of many kingdoms rallies in Terrasen. Join them."

"Terrasen didn't come to our aid five hundred years ago," another voice said, coming closer. The pretty, brown-haired witch from earlier. Her broom, too, was bound in fine metal—silver to Bronwen's gold. "I don't see why we should bother helping them now."

"I thought you lot were a bunch of self-righteous do-gooders," Manon crooned. "Surely this would be your sort of thing."

The young witch bristled, but Glennis held up a withered hand.

It wasn't enough to stop Bronwen, though, as the witch looked Manon over and snarled, "You are not our queen. We will never fly with you."

Bronwen and the younger witch stormed away, the gathered Crochan guards parting to let them pass.

Manon found Glennis wincing slightly. "Our family, you will find, has a hotheaded streak."

Ruthless.

What Manon had done tonight, leading the Ironteeth to this camp . . . Dorian didn't have a word for it other than *ruthless*.

He left Manon and her great-grandmother, the Thirteen looking on, and went in search of the spider.

He found Cyrene where he'd left her, crouched in the shadows of one of the farther tents.

She'd returned to her human form, her dark hair tangled, bundled in a Crochan cloak. As if one of them had taken pity on her. Not realizing the hunger in Cyrene's eyes wasn't for the goat stew.

"Where does the shifting come from?" Dorian asked as he paused before her, a hand on Damaris. "Inside you?"

The spider-shifter blinked up at him, then stood. Someone had given her a worn brown tunic, pants, and boots, too. "That was a great feat of magic you performed." She smiled, revealing sharp little teeth. "What a king it might make you. Unchallenged, unrivaled."

Dorian didn't feel like saying he wasn't entirely sure what manner of king he wished to be, should he live long enough to reclaim his throne. Anyone and anything but his father seemed like a good place to start.

Dorian kept his stance relaxed, even as he asked again, "Where does the shifting come from inside you?"

Cyrene angled her head as if listening to something. "It was strange, mortal king, to find that I had a new place within me with the return of magic. To find that something new had taken root." Her small hand drifted to her middle, just above her navel. "A little seed of power. I will the shift, think of what I wish to be, and the change starts within here first. Always, the heat comes from here." The spider settled her stare on him. "If you wish to be something, king-with-no-crown, then be it. That is the secret to the shifting. Be what you wish."

He avoided the urge to roll his eyes, though Damaris warmed in his grip. *Be what you wish*—a thing far easier said than done. Especially with the weight of a crown.

Dorian put a hand on his stomach, despite the layers of clothes and cloak. Only toned muscle greeted him. "Is that what you do to summon the change: first think of what you want to become?"

"With limits. I need a clear image within my mind, or else it will not work at all."

"So you cannot change into something you have not seen."

"I can invent certain traits—eye color, build, hair—but not the creature itself." A hideous smile bloomed on her mouth. "Use that lovely magic of yours. Change your pretty eyes," the spider dared. "Change their color."

Gods damn him, but he tried. He thought of brown eyes. Pictured Chaol's bronze eyes, fierce after one of their sparring sessions. Not how they had been before his friend had sailed to the southern continent.

Had Chaol managed to be healed? Had he and Nesryn convinced the khagan to send aid? How would Chaol even learn where he was, what had happened to all of them, when they'd been scattered to the winds?

"You think too much, young king."

"Better than too little," he muttered.

Damaris warmed again. He could have sworn it had been in amusement.

Cyrene chuckled. "Do not *think* of the eye color so much as *demand* it."

"How did you learn this without instruction?"

"The power is in me now," the spider said simply. "I listened to it."

Dorian let a tendril of his magic snake toward the spider. She tensed. But his magic brushed up against her, gentle and inquisitive as a cat. Raw magic, to be shaped as he desired.

He willed it toward her—willed it to find that seed of power within her. To learn it.

"What are you doing," the spider breathed, shifting on her feet.

His magic wrapped around her, and he could feel it—each hateful, horrible year of existence.

Each—

His mouth dried out. Bile surged in his throat at the scent his magic detected. He'd never forget that scent, that vileness. He'd bear the mark on his throat forever as proof.

Valg. The spider, somehow, was Valg. And not possessed, but *born*.

He kept his face neutral. Uninterested. Even as his magic located that glowing, beautiful bit of magic.

Stolen magic. As the Valg stole all things.

Took everything they wanted.

His blood became a dull, pounding roar in his ears.

Dorian studied her tiny frame, her ordinary face. "You've been rather quiet regarding the quest for revenge that sent you hunting across the continent."

Cyrene's dark eyes turned to depthless pits. "Oh, I have not forgotten that. Not at all."

Damaris remained warm. Waiting.

He let his magic wrap soothing hands around the seed of power trapped within the black hell inside the spider.

He didn't care to know why and how the stygian spiders were Valg. How they'd come here. Why they'd lingered.

They fed off dreams and life and joy. Delighted in it.

The seed of shape-shifting power flickered in his hands, as if grateful for a kind touch. A human touch.

This. His father had allowed these sorts of creatures to grow, to rule. Sorscha had been slaughtered by these things, their cruelty.

"I can make a bargain with you, you know," Cyrene whispered. "When the time comes, I will make sure you are spared."

Damaris went colder than ice.

Dorian met her stare. Withdrew his magic, and could have sworn that seed of shape-shifting power trapped within her reached for him. Tried to beg him not to go.

He smiled at the spider. She smiled back.

And then he struck.

Invisible hands wrapped around her neck and twisted. Right as his magic plunged into her navel, into where the stolen seed of human magic resided, and wrapped around it.

He held on, a baby bird in his hands, as the spider died. Studied the magic, every facet of it, before it seemed to sigh in relief and fade into the wind, free at last.

Cyrene slumped to the ground, eyes unseeing.

Half a thought and Dorian had her incinerated. No one came to inquire after the stench that rose from her ashes. The black stain that lingered beneath them.

Valg. Perhaps a ticket for him into Morath, and yet he found himself staring at that dark stain on the half-thawed earth.

He let go of Damaris, the blade reluctantly quieting.

He'd find his way into Morath. Once he mastered the shifting.

The spider and all her kind could burn in hell.

~

Dorian's heart was still racing when he found himself an hour later lying in a tent not even tall enough to stand in, on one of two bedrolls.

Manon entered the tent just as he toed off his boots and hauled the heavy wool blankets over him. They smelled of horses and hay, and might very well have been snatched from a stable, but he didn't care. It was warm and better than nothing.

Manon surveyed the tight space, the second bedroll and blanket. "Thirteen is an uneven number," she said by way of explanation. "I've always had a tent to myself."

"Sorry to ruin that for you."

She cut him a drily amused glance before seating herself on the bedroll and unlacing her boots. But her fingers halted as her nostrils flared.

Slowly, she looked over her shoulder at him. "What did you do."

Dorian held her stare. "You did what you had to today," he said simply. "I did as well." He didn't bother trying to touch Damaris where it lay nearby.

She sniffed him again. "You killed the spider." No judgment in her face, just raw curiosity.

"She was a threat," he admitted. And a Valg piece of shit.

Wariness now flooded her eyes. "She could have killed you."

He gave her a half smile. "No, she couldn't have."

Manon assessed him again, and he withstood it. "You have nothing to say about my own . . . choices?"

"My friends are fighting and likely being killed in the North," Dorian said. "We don't have the time to spend weeks winning the Crochans over."

There it was, the brutal truth. To gain some degree of welcome here, they'd had to cross that line. Perhaps such callous decisions were part of wearing a crown.

He'd keep her secret—so long as she wished it hidden.

"No self-righteous speeches?"

"This is war," he said simply. "We're past that sort of thing."

And it wouldn't matter, would it, when his eternal soul would be the asking price to staunch so much of the slaughter? He'd already had it wrecked enough. If crossing line after line would spare any others from harm, he'd do it. He didn't know what manner of king that made him.

Manon hummed, deeming that an acceptable answer. "You know about court intrigue and scheming," she said, deft fingers again flying over the laces and hooks of the boots. "How would you . . . play this, as you called it earlier? My situation with the Crochans."

Dorian rested a hand under his head. "The problem is that they hold all the cards. You need them far more than they need you. The only card you have to play is your heritage—and that they seem to have rejected, even with the skirmish. So how do we make it vital for them? How do you prove that they *need* their last living queen, the last of the Crochan blood-line?" He contemplated it. "There is also the prospect of peace between your peoples, but you . . ." He winced. "You're no longer recognized as Heir. Any bargaining you might have as a Blackbeak would be on behalf of only you and the Thirteen, not the rest of the Ironteeth. It wouldn't be a true peace treaty."

Manon finished with her boots and lay back on her bedroll, sliding the blanket over her as she stared up at the tent's low ceiling. "Did they teach you these things in your glass castle?"

"Yes." Before he'd shattered that castle into shards and dust.

Manon turned on her side, propping her head with a hand, her white hair spilling from its braid to frame her face. "You can't use that magic of yours to simply . . . compel them, can you?"

Dorian huffed a laugh. "Not that I know of."

"Maeve wormed her way into Prince Rowan's mind to convince him to take a false mate."

"I don't even know what Maeve's power *is*," Dorian said, cringing. What the Fae Queen had done to Rowan, what she was now doing to the

Queen of Terrasen . . . "And I'm not entirely certain I want to start exper-
imenting on potential allies."

Manon sighed through her nose. "My training did not include these
things."

He wasn't surprised. "You want my honest opinion?" Her golden eyes
pinned him to the spot as she gave a curt nod. "Find the thing they need,
and use it to your advantage. What would prompt them to rally behind you,
to see you as their Crochan Queen? Fighting in battle tonight won some
degree of trust, but not immediate acceptance. Perhaps Glennis might
know."

"I'd have to risk asking her."

"You don't trust her."

"Why should I?"

"She's your great-grandmother. And didn't order you executed on sight."

"My grandmother didn't until the end, either." No emotion passed
over her face, but her fingers dug into her scalp at her words.

So Dorian said, "Aelin needed Captain Rolfe and his people shaken
out of centuries of hiding in order to rally the Mycenian fleet. She learned
they would only return to Terrasen when a sea dragon reappeared at last,
one of their long-lost allies on the waves. So she engineered it to happen:
provoked a small Valg fleet to attack Skull's Bay while it lay mostly
defenseless, and then used the battle to showcase the sea dragon that
arrived to aid them, summoned from air and magic."

"The shifter," Manon said. Dorian nodded. "And the Mycenians
bought it?"

"Absolutely," Dorian drawled. "Aelin learned what the Mycenians
needed in order to be convinced to join her cause. What sort of thing
might the Crochans require to do the same?"

Manon lay back onto her bedroll, as graceful as a dancer. She toyed with
the end of her braid, the red strip there. "I'll ask Ghislaine in the morning."

"I don't think Ghislaine is going to know."

Those gold eyes slid to his. "You truly believe I should ask Glennis?"

"I do. And I think she will help you."

"Why bother?"

He wondered if the Thirteen could ever see it—that hint of self-loathing that sometimes flickered across her face. "Her mother willingly abandoned her city, her people, her queen in their last hours so she might preserve the royal bloodline. Your bloodline. I think she told you that story tonight so you might realize she will do the same as well."

"Why not say it outright, then?"

"Because, in case you didn't notice, you're not exactly a popular person in this camp, despite your ploy with the Ironteeth. Glennis knows how to play the game. You just need to catch up with her. Find out why they're even here, then plan your next move."

Her mouth tightened, then relaxed. "Your tutors taught you well, princeling."

"Being raised by a demon-infested tyrant did have its benefits, it seems." His words rang flat, even as an edge sharpened inside him.

Her gaze drifted to his throat, to the pale line across it. He could almost feel her stare like a phantom touch.

"You still hate him."

He arched an eyebrow. "Am I not supposed to?"

Her moon-white hair gleamed in the dim light. "You told me he was human. Deep down, he'd remained human, and tried to protect you as best he could. Yet you hate him."

"You'll forgive me if I find his methods of *protecting* me to be unpalatable."

"But it was the demon, not the man, who killed your healer."

Dorian clenched his jaw. "It makes no difference."

"Doesn't it?" Manon frowned. "Most can barely withstand a few months of Valg infestation. You barely withstood it." He tried not to flinch at the blunt words. "Yet he held on for decades."

He held her stare. "If you're trying to cast my father as some sort of noble hero, you're wasting your breath." He debated ending it there, but he asked, "If someone told you that your grandmother was secretly good, that she hadn't wanted to murder your parents and so many others, that she'd been forced to make you kill your own sister, would you find it so easy to believe? To forgive her?"

Manon glanced down at her abdomen—at the scar hidden beneath her leathers. He braced himself for the answer. But she only said, "I'm tired of talking."

Good. So was he.

"Is there something you'd rather do instead, witchling?" His voice turned rough, and he knew she could hear his heartbeat as it began hammering.

Her only answer was to slide over him, strands of her hair falling around them in a curtain. "I said I don't want to talk," she breathed, and lowered her mouth to his neck. Dragged her teeth over it, right through that white line where the collar had been.

Dorian groaned softly, and shifted his hips, grinding himself into her. Her breath became jagged in answer, and he ran a hand down her side.

"Shut me up, then," he said, a hand drifting southward to cup her backside as she nipped at his neck, his jaw. No hint of those iron teeth, but the promise of them lingered, an exquisite sword over his head.

Only with her did he not need to explain. Only with her did he not need to be a king, or anything but what he was. Only with her would there be no judgment for what he'd done, who he'd failed, what he might still have to do.

Just this—pleasure and utter oblivion.

Manon's hand found his belt buckle, and Dorian reached for hers, and neither spoke for some time after that.

The release she found that night—twice—couldn't entirely dull the edge when morning broke, gray and bleak, and Manon approached Glennis's larger tent.

She'd left the king sleeping, bundled in the blankets they'd shared, though she hadn't allowed him to hold her. She'd simply turned onto her side, putting her back to him, and closed her eyes. He hadn't seemed to care, sated and drowsy after she'd ridden him until they'd both found their pleasure, and had been quickly asleep. Had stayed asleep, while Manon had contemplated how, exactly, she was to have this meeting.

Perhaps she should have brought Dorian. He certainly knew how to play these games. To think like a king.

He'd killed that spider like a blue-blooded witch, though. Not an ounce of mercy.

It shouldn't have thrilled her the way it did.

But Manon knew her pride would never recover, and she'd never again be able to call herself a witch, if she let him do this task for her.

So Manon shouldered through Glennis's tent flaps without announcing herself. "I need to speak to you."

She found Glennis buckling on her glamoured cloak before a tiny bronze mirror. "Prior to breakfast? I suppose you got that urgency from your father. Tristan was always rushing into my tent with his various pressing matters. I could barely convince him to sit still long enough to eat."

Manon discarded the kernel of information. Ironteeth didn't *have* fathers. Only their mothers and mothers' mothers. It had always been that way. Even if it was an effort to keep her questions about him at bay. How he'd met Lothian Blackbeak, what had prompted them to set aside their ancient hatred.

"What would it take—to win the Crochans over? To join us in war?"

Glennis adjusted her cape in the mirror. "Only a Crochan Queen may ignite the Flame of War, to summon every witch from her hearth."

Manon blinked at the frank answer. "The Flame of War?"

Glennis jerked her chin toward the tent flaps, to the fire pit beyond. "Every Crochan family has a hearth that moves with them to each camp or home we make; the fires never extinguish. The flame in my hearth dates back to the Crochan city itself, when Brannon Galathynius gave Rhiannon a spark of eternally burning fire. My mother carried it with her in a glass globe, hidden in her cloak, when she smuggled out your ancestor, and it has continued to burn at every royal Crochan hearth since then."

"What about when magic disappeared for ten years?"

"Our seers had a vision that it would vanish, and the flame would die. So we ignited several ordinary fires from that magic flame, and kept them burning. When magic disappeared, the flame indeed winked out. And when magic returned this spring, the flame again kindled, right in the hearth where we had last seen it." Her great-grandmother turned toward her. "When a Crochan Queen summons her people to war, a flame is taken from the royal hearth, and passed to each hearth, one camp and village to the other. The arrival of the flame is a summons that only a true Crochan Queen may make."

"So I only need to use the flame in that pit out there and the army will come to me?"

A caw of laughter. "No. You must first be accepted *as* queen to do that."

Manon ground her teeth. "And how might I achieve *that*?"

"That's not for me to figure out, is it?"

It took all her self-restraint to keep from unsheathing her iron nails and prowling through the tent. "Why are you here—why this camp?"

Glennis's brows rose. "Didn't I tell you yesterday?"

Manon tapped a foot on the ground.

The witch noted the impatience and chuckled. "We were on our way to Eyllwe."

Manon started. "Eyllwe? If you think to run from this war, I can tell you that it's found that kingdom as well." Long had Eyllwe borne the brunt of Adarlan's wrath. In her endless meetings with Erawan, he'd been particularly focused on ensuring the kingdom stayed fractured.

Glennis nodded. "We know. But we received word from our southern hearths that a threat had arisen. We journey to meet with some of the Eyllwe war bands who have managed to survive this long—to take on whatever horror Morath might have sent."

To go south, not north to Terrasen.

"Erawan might be unleashing his horrors in Eyllwe just to divide you," Manon said. "To keep you from aiding Terrasen. He'll have guessed I'm trying to gather the Crochans. Eyllwe is already lost—come with us to the North."

The crone merely shook her head. "That may be. But we have given our word. So to Eyllwe we will go."

CHAPTER 16

Darrow was waiting on horseback atop a hill when the army finally arrived at nightfall. A full day's march, the snow and wind whipping them for every damned mile.

Aedion, atop his own horse, broke from the column of soldiers aiming for the small camp and galloped across the ice-crusted snow to the ancient lord. He gestured with a gloved hand to the warriors behind him. "As requested: we've arrived."

Darrow barely glanced at Aedion as he surveyed the soldiers making camp. Exhausting, brutal work after a long day, and a battle before that, but they'd sleep well tonight. And Aedion would refuse to move them tomorrow. Perhaps the day after that, too. "How many lost?"

"Less than five hundred."

"Good."

Aedion bristled at the approval. It wasn't Darrow's own army, wasn't even Aedion's.

"What did you want that warranted us to haul ass up here so quickly?"

"I wanted to discuss the battle with you. Hear what you learned."

Aedion gritted his teeth. "I'll write a report for you, then." He gathered the reins, readying to steer his horse back to the camp. "My men need shelter."

Darrow nodded firmly, as if unaware of the exhausting march he'd demanded. "At dawn, we meet. Send word to the other lords."

"Send your own messenger."

Darrow cut him a steely look. "Tell the other lords." He surveyed Aedion from his mud-splattered boots to his unwashed hair. "And get some rest."

Aedion didn't bother responding as he urged his horse into a gallop, the stallion charging through the snow without hesitation. A fine, proud beast that had served him well.

Aedion squinted at the wailing snow as it whipped his face. They needed to build shelter—and fast.

At dawn, he'd go to Darrow's meeting. With the other lords.

And Aelin in tow.

A foot of snow fell overnight, blanketing the tents, smothering fires, and setting the soldiers sleeping shoulder to shoulder to conserve warmth.

Lysandra had shivered in her tent, despite being curled into ghost-leopard form by the brazier, and had awoken before dawn simply because sleeping had become futile.

And because of the meeting that was moments away from taking place.

She strode toward Darrow's large war tent, Ansel of Briarcliff at her side, the two of them bundled against the cold. Mercifully, the frigid morning kept any conversation between them to a minimum. No point in talking when the very air chilled your teeth to the point of aching.

The silver-haired Fae royals entered just before them, Prince Endymion giving her—giving *Aelin*—a bow of the head.

His cousin's wife. That's what he believed her to be. In addition to being queen. Endymion had never scented Aelin, wouldn't know that the strange shifter's scent was all wrong.

Thank the gods for that.

The war tent was nearly full, lords and princes and commanders gathered around the center of the space, all studying the map of the continent hanging from one of the wall flaps. Pins jutted from its thick canvas to mark various armies.

So many, too many, clustered in the South. Blocking off aid from any allies beyond Morath's lines.

"She returns at last," a cold voice drawled.

Lysandra summoned a lazy smirk and sauntered to the center of the room, Ansel lingering near the entrance. "I heard I missed some fun yesterday. I figured I'd return before I lost the chance to kill some Valg grunts myself."

A few chuckles at that, but Darrow didn't smile. "I don't recall you being invited to this meeting, Your Highness."

"I invited her," Aedion said, stepping to the edge of the group. "Since she's technically fighting in the Bane, I made her my second-in-command." And thus worthy of being here.

Lysandra wondered if anyone else could see the hint of pain in Aedion's face—pain, and disgust at the imposter queen swaggering amongst them.

"Sorry to disappoint," she crooned to Darrow.

Darrow only turned back to the map as Ravi and Sol filtered in. Sol gave Aelin a respectful nod, and Ravi flashed her a grin. Aelin winked before facing the map.

"After our rout of Morath yesterday under General Ashryver's command," Darrow said, "I believe we should position our troops on Theralis, and ready Orynth's defenses for a siege." The older lords—Sloane, Gunnar, and Ironwood—grunted with agreement.

Aedion shook his head, no doubt already anticipating this. "It announces to Erawan that we're on the run, and spreads us too far from any potential allies from the South."

"In Orynth," said Lord Gunnar, older and grayer than Darrow and twice as mean, "we have walls that can withstand catapults."

"If they bring those witch towers," Ren Allsbrook cut in, "then even Orynth's walls will crumble."

"We have yet to see evidence of those witch towers," Darrow countered. "Beyond the word of an enemy."

"An enemy turned ally," Aelin—Lysandra—said. Darrow cut her a distasteful stare. "Manon Blackbeak did not lie. Nor were her Thirteen aligned with Morath when they fought alongside us."

A nod from the Fae royals, from Ansel.

"Against Maeve," sneered Lord Sloane, a reed-thin man with a hard face and hooked nose. "That battle was against Maeve, not Erawan. Would they have done the same against their own kind? Witches are loyal unto death, and craftier than foxes. Manon Blackbeak and her cabal might very well have played you for desperate fools and fed you the wrong information."

"Manon Blackbeak turned on her own grandmother, the High Witch of the Blackbeak Clan," Aedion said, his voice dropping to a dangerous growl. "I do not think the iron splinters we found in her gut wound were a lie."

"Again," Lord Sloane said, "these witches are crafty. They'll do anything."

"The witch towers are real," Lysandra said, letting Aelin's cool, unfazed voice fill the tent. "I'm not going to waste my breath proving their existence. Nor will I risk Orynth to their power."

"But you'd risk the border towns?" Darrow challenged.

"I plan to find a way to take out the towers before they can pass the foothills," she drawled. She prayed Aedion had a plan.

"With the fire that you've so magnificently displayed," Darrow said with equal smoothness.

Ansel of Briarcliff answered before Lysandra could come up with a suitably arrogant lie. "Erawan likes to play his little mind games, to drum up fear. Let him wonder and worry why Aelin hasn't wielded hers yet.

Contemplate if she's storing it up for something grand." A roguish wink at her. "I do hope it will be horrific."

Lysandra gave the queen a slash of a smile. "Oh, it will be."

She felt Aedion's stare, the well-hidden agony and worry. But the general said, "Eldrys was to thin our numbers, make us doubt Morath's wisdom by sending his grunts here. He wants us to underestimate him. If we move to the border, we'll have the foothills to slow his advance. We know that terrain; he doesn't. We can wield it to our advantage."

"And if he cuts through Oakwald?" Lord Gunnar pointed to the road past Endovier. "What then?"

Ren Allsbrook replied this time. "Then we know that terrain as well. Oakwald has no love for Erawan or his forces. Its allegiance is to Brannon. And his heirs." A glance at her, cold and yet—warming. Slightly.

She offered the young lord a hint of a smile. Ren ignored it, facing the map again.

"If we move to the border," Darrow said, "we risk being wiped out, thus leaving Perranth, Orynth, and every town and city in this kingdom at Erawan's mercy."

"There are arguments to be made for both," Prince Endymion said, stepping forward. The oldest among them, though he looked not a day past twenty-eight. "Your army remains too small to risk dividing in half. All must go—either south, or back north."

"I would vote for the South," said Princess Sellene, Endymion's cousin. Rowan's cousin. She'd been curious about Aelin, Lysandra could tell, but had stayed away. As if hesitant to forge a bond when war might destroy them all. Lysandra had wondered more than once what in the princess's long life had made her that way—wary and solemn, yet not wholly aloof. "There are more routes for escape, if the need arises." She pointed a tanned finger to the map, her braided silver hair shining amongst the folds of her heavy emerald cloak. "In Orynth, your backs will be against the mountains."

"There are secret paths through the Staghorns," Lord Sloane said, utterly unruffled. "Many of our people used them ten years ago."

And so it went on. Debating and arguing, voices rising and falling.

Until Darrow called a vote—amongst the six Lords of Terrasen only. The only official leaders of this army, apparently.

Two of them, Sol and Ren, voted for the border.

Four of them, Darrow, Sloane, Gunnar, and Ironwood, voted to move to Orynth.

Darrow simply said, when silence had fallen, "Should our allies not wish to risk our plan, they may depart. We hold you to no oaths."

Lysandra almost started at that.

Aedion growled, even as worry flashed in his eyes.

But Prince Galan, who had kept silent and watchful, a listener despite his frequent smiles and bold fighting on both sea and land, stepped forward. Looked right at Aelin, his eyes—their eyes—glowing bright. "Poor allies we would indeed make," he said, his Wendlynian accent rich and rolling, "if we abandoned our friends when their choices veered from ours. We promised our assistance in this war. Wendlyn will not back from it."

Darrow tensed. Not at the words, but at the fact that they were directed at her. At Aelin.

Lysandra bowed her head, putting a hand on her heart.

Prince Endymion lifted his chin. "I swore an oath to my cousin, your consort," he said, and the other lords bristled. Since Aelin was not queen, Rowan's own title was still not recognized by them. Only the other lords, it seemed. "Since I doubt we will be welcome in Doranelle again, I would like to think that this may perhaps be our new home, should all go well."

Aelin would have agreed. "You are welcome here—all of you. For as long as you like."

"You are not authorized to make such invitations," Lord Gunnar snapped.

None of them bothered to answer. But Ilias of the Silent Assassins gave a solemn nod that voiced his agreement to stay, and Ansel of Briarcliff merely winked again at Aelin and said, "I came this far to help you beat that bastard into dust. I don't see why I'd go home now."

Lysandra didn't fake the gratitude that tightened her throat as she bowed to the allies her queen had gathered.

A tall, dark-haired young man entered the tent, his gray eyes darting around the gathered company. They widened when they beheld her—Aelin. Widened, then glanced to Aedion as if to confirm. He marked the golden hair, the Ashryver eyes, and paled.

"What is it, Nox," Darrow growled. The messenger straightened, and hurried to the lord's side, murmuring something in his ear. "Send him in," was Darrow's only answer.

Nox stalked out, graceful despite his height, and a shorter, pale-skinned man entered.

Darrow extended a hand for the letter. "You had a message from Eldrys?"

Lysandra smelled the stranger the moment Aedion did.

A moment before the stranger smiled and said, "Erawan sends his regards."

And unleashed a blast of black wind right at her.

CHAPTER 17

Lysandra ducked, but not fast enough to avoid the lash of power that sliced down her arm.

She hit the ground, rolling, as she'd learned under Arobynn's careful tutelage. But Aedion was already in front of her, sword out. Defending his queen.

A flash of light and cold—from Enda and Sellene—and the Morath messenger was pinned to his knees, his dark power lashing against an invisible barrier of ice-kissed wind.

Around the tent, all had fallen back, weapons glinting. Flanking the downed man, Ilias and Ansel had their swords already angled toward him, their defensive poses mirror images. Trained into their very bones by the same master, under the same blistering sun. Neither looked at the other, though.

Ren, Sol, and Ravi had slipped into position at Lysandra's—at Aelin's—side, their own blades primed to spill blood. A fledgling court closing ranks around its queen.

Never mind that the older lords had stumbled behind the safety of the refreshment table, their weathered faces ashen. Only Galan Ashryver had taken up a place near the tent exit, no doubt to intercept their assailant should he try to flee. A bold move—and a fool's one, considering what knelt in the center of the tent.

"Did *no one* smell that he was a Valg demon?" Aedion demanded, hauling Lysandra to her feet with her uninjured arm. But there was no collar on the stranger, no ring on his bare, pale hands.

Lysandra's stomach churned as she clasped a hand to the throbbing gash on her upper arm. She knew what beat within the man's chest. A heart of iron and Wyrdstone.

The messenger laughed, hissing. "Run to your castle. We're—"

He sniffed the air. Looked right at Lysandra. At the blood leaking down her left arm, seeping into the ocean blue of Aelin's worn tunic.

His dark eyes widened with surprise and delight, the word taking form on his lips. *Shifter.*

"Kill him," she ordered the silver-haired Fae royals, her heart thundering.

No one dared tell her to burn him herself.

Endymion raised a hand, and the Valg-possessed man began gasping. Yet not before his eyes darkened wholly, until no white shone.

Not from the death sweeping over him. But as he seemed to convey a message down a long, obsidian bond.

The message that might doom them: Aelin Galathynius was not here.

"Enough of this," Aedion snarled, and fear—real fear blanched his face as he, too, realized what the messenger had just relayed to his master.

The Sword of Orynth flashed, black blood spraying, and the man's head tumbled to the rug-covered ground.

In the silence, Lysandra panted, lifting her hand from her arm to survey the wound. The cut was not deep, but it would be tender for a few hours.

Ansel of Briarcliff sheathed her wolf-headed sword and gripped

Lysandra's shoulder, her red hair swaying as she assessed the injury, then the corpse. "Nasty little pricks, aren't they?"

Aelin would have had some swaggering answer to set them all chuckling, but Lysandra couldn't find the words. She just nodded as the black stain inched over the tent floor. The Fae royals sniffed at the reek, grimacing.

"Clean up this mess," Darrow ordered no one in particular. Even as his hands shook slightly.

By the tent flaps, Nox was gaping at the decapitated Valg. His gray eyes met hers, searching, and then lowered. "He didn't have a ring," Nox murmured.

Snatching up a dangling edge of tablecloth from the untouched refreshment table, Aedion wiped the Sword of Orynth clean. "He didn't need one."

Erawan knew Aelin was not with them. That a shifter had taken her place.

Aedion stalked through the camp, Lysandra-as-Aelin at his heels. "I know," he said over his shoulder, for once ignoring the warriors who saluted him.

She kept following him anyway. "What should we do?"

He didn't stop until he reached his own tent, the reek of that Valg messenger clinging in his nose. That whip of blackness spearing for Lysandra still burning behind his eyes. Her cry of pain ringing in his ears.

His temper roiled, howling for an outlet.

She followed him into the tent. "What should we do?" she asked again.

"How about we start with making sure there aren't any other *messengers* lurking in the camp," he snarled, pacing. The Fae royals had already conveyed that order, and were sending out their best scouts.

"He knows," she breathed. He whirled to face her, finding his cousin—finding *Lysandra* shaking. Not Aelin, though she'd been plenty convincing today. Better than usual. "He *knows* what I am."

Aedion rubbed his face. "He also seems to know we're going to Orynth. Wants us to do just that."

She slumped onto his cot, as if her knees couldn't hold her upright. For a heartbeat, the urge to sit beside her, to pull her to him, was so strong he nearly yielded to it.

The tang of her blood filled the space, along with the wild, many-faced scent of her. It dragged a sensual finger down his skin, whetting his rage into something so deadly he might have very well killed the next male who entered this tent.

"Erawan might hear the news and worry," Aedion said when he could think again. "He might wonder *why* she isn't here, and if she's about to do something that will hurt him. It could force him to show his hand."

"Or to strike us now, with his full might, when he knows we're weakest."

"We'll have to see."

"Orynth will be a slaughterhouse," she whispered, her shoulders curving beneath the weight—not just of being a woman thrust into this conflict, but a woman playing another, who might be able to pretend, but only so far. Who did not truly have the power to halt the hordes marching north. She'd been willing to shoulder that burden, though. For Aelin. For this kingdom.

Even if she'd lied to him about it, she'd been willing to accept this weight.

Aedion slumped down beside her and stared blankly at the tent walls. "We're not going to Orynth."

Her head lifted. Not just at the words, but at how close he sat. "Where are we going, then?"

Aedion surveyed his suit of armor, oiled and waiting on a dummy across the tent. "Sol and Ravi will take some of their men back to the coast to make sure that we don't encounter any more attacks from the sea. They'll rendezvous with what's left of the Wendlynian fleet while Galan and his soldiers stay with us. We'll march as one army down to the border."

"The other lords voted against it." Indeed they had, the old fools.

He'd danced with treason for the past decade. Had made it an art form. Aedion smiled slightly. "Leave that to me."

⁓

The Bane were loyal to none but Aelin Galathynius.

So were the allies she'd gathered. And the forces of Ren Allsbrook and Ravi and Sol of Suria.

And so, apparently, was Nox Owen.

Yet it was Lysandra, not Aedion, who made their flight possible.

She'd been walking back to her own tent—to Aelin's tent, not fit for a queen, but an army captain—when Nox fell into step beside her. Silent and graceful. Well-trained. And likely more lethal than he appeared.

"So, Erawan knows you're not Aelin."

She whipped her head to him. "What?" A quick, vague question to buy herself time. Had Aedion risked telling him the truth?

Nox gave her a half smile. "I figured as much when I saw the surprise on that demon's face."

"You must be mistaken."

"Am I? Or do you not remember me at all?"

She did her best to look down her nose at him, even as the messenger-thief towered over her. Aelin had never mentioned a Nox Owen. "Why should I remember one of Darrow's lackeys?"

"A decent attempt, but Celaena Sardothien looked a *little* more amused when she cut men into ribbons."

He knew—who Aelin was, what she'd been. Lysandra said nothing, and kept walking toward her tent. If she told Aedion, how quickly could Nox be buried under the frozen earth?

"Your secret is safe," Nox murmured. "Celaena—Aelin was a friend. Is still one, I'd hope."

"How." She'd admit no more than that regarding her role in this.

"We fought in the competition together at the glass castle." He snorted. "I had no idea until today. Gods, I was there for Minister Joval as a spy for the rebels. It was my first time out of Perranth. My *first* time, and I wound up unwittingly training alongside my queen." He laughed, low and amazed. "I'd been working with the rebels for years, even as a thief. They wanted me to be their inside eyes on the castle, the king's plans. I reported the strange goings-on until it became too dangerous. Until Cel—Aelin warned me to run. I listened, and came back here. Joval is dead. Fell in a skirmish with a band of rebels by the border this spring. Darrow plucked me up to be his own messenger and spy. So here I am." A sidelong glance at her, awe still on his face. "I am at your disposal, even if you're not . . . you." He angled his head. "Who are you, anyway?"

"Aelin."

Nox smiled knowingly. "Fair enough."

Lysandra paused before the queen's too-small tent, nestled between Aedion's and Ren's own. "What's the cost of your silence? Or does Darrow already know?"

"Why would I tell him? I serve Terrasen, and the Galathynius family. I always have."

"Some might say Darrow has a strong claim to the throne, given his relationship with Orlon."

"I realized today that the assassin I came to call a friend is actually the queen I believed dead. I think the gods are pointing me in a certain direction, don't you?"

She lingered between the tent flaps. Delicious warmth beckoned within. "And if I were to tell you we needed your help tonight, and that the risk was being branded a traitor?"

Nox only sketched a bow. "Then I'd say I owe my friend Celaena a favor for her warning at the castle, plus saving my life before that."

She didn't know why she trusted him. But she'd developed an instinct for men that had always proved correct, even if she had been unable to act on it in the past. Had only been able to brace herself for them.

But Nox Owen—the kindness in his face was true. His words were true. Another ally Aelin had wrangled for them, this time unwittingly.

She knew Aedion would agree to the plan, even if he still hated her. So Lysandra leaned in, her voice dropping to a whisper. "Then listen carefully."

⁓

It was done quietly and without a trace.

Every intricate element played out without issue, as if the gods themselves aided them.

At dinner, Nox Owen laced the wine he'd personally served—as a groveling apology for letting in the Valg soldier—to Lords Darrow, Sloane, Gunnar, and Ironwood. Not to kill them, but to send them into a deep, dreamless sleep.

Even a roaring bear couldn't wake this lout, Ansel of Briarcliff had sniffed when she'd stood over Lord Gunnar's cot, lifted his limp arm, and let it drop.

The lord didn't stir, and Lysandra, wearing a field mouse's form and tucked into the shadows behind the queen, deemed it proof enough.

The four lords' loyal banner men also found themselves sleeping deeply that night, courtesy of the wine that Galan Ashryver, Ilias, Ren, and Ravi had made sure was handed out at their fires.

And when they all awoke the next day, there was only whipping snow beyond their tents.

The camp was gone.

The army with it.

CHAPTER 18

No one in Anielle or the gray-stoned keep looming over its southern edge shouted with alarm at the ruk that descended from the skies and alit upon the battlements.

The keep sentries who'd been on watch had only drawn their weapons, one racing into the dim interior, and pointed them at Chaol and Yrene as they slid off the mighty bird.

The cold on the open ocean was nothing compared to the wind off the wall of mountains the city had been built against, or the blistering chill from the sprawling Silver Lake it curved around, so flat that it looked like a mighty mirror spread beneath the gray sky.

Yrene knew Anielle's layout was as familiar to Chaol as his own body—and knew, from the memories she'd seen in his soul and what he'd told her these months, that the gray shingles of the roofs had been hewn from the slate quarries just to the south, the timber of the houses taken from the tangle of Oakwald lurking beyond the flat plain that bordered the southern side of the lake. A small offshoot of peaks jutted like an arm from the snaking body of the Fangs, hemming in the city between it and the Silver Lake—and it was into the barren slopes that the keep had been built.

Level after level, Westfall Keep rose from the plain to the higher reaches of the mountain behind it, the lowermost gate opening onto the flat expanse of snow, while other levels flowed into the city to its left. It had been built as a fortress, the countless levels, battlements, and gates all designed to outlast an enemy assault. The gray stones bore the scars of just how many it had witnessed and survived, none more so than the thick curtain wall that encompassed the keep.

Intimidating, imposing, unforgiving—Chaol had told her the keep had never been built for beauty or pleasure. Indeed, no colorful banners flapped in the wind. No scent or spices drifted on it, either. Just chill, thick dampness.

From the lichen-crusted upper towers, Yrene knew that one could monitor any movements on the lake or the plain, in the city or the forest, even along the slopes of the Fangs. How many hours had her husband spent on the tower walkways, gazing toward Rifthold, wishing he were anywhere but this cold, dark place?

Chaol stayed close to Yrene, his chin high, as he announced to the dozen guards aiming their swords at them that he was Lord Chaol Westfall, and he wished to see his father. Immediately.

She'd never heard him use that voice. A different sort of authority. A lord's voice.

A lord—and she was a lady, she supposed. Even if flying had forced her to abandon her usual dresses in favor of rukhin leathers, even if she was certain her braided hair had been whipped in about a dozen directions and would take hours and a bath to detangle.

They lingered on the battlements in silence, and Chaol's gloved hand slid into her own, the wind ruffling the fur along his heavy cloak collar. His face revealed nothing but grim determination, yet the hand he squeezed around her own . . . She knew what this homecoming meant.

She'd never forget the memory she'd witnessed of the father who had thrown him down the stone steps a few levels below, granting Chaol the hidden scar just past his hairline. A child. He'd hurled a *child* down those stairs and forced him to make his way to Rifthold on foot.

She doubted her second impression of her father-in-law would be any better.

Certainly not as a gaunt-faced man appeared in a gray tunic and said, "Come this way."

No title, no honorific. No welcome.

Yrene tightened her grip around Chaol's hand. They had come to warn the people of this city—not the bastard who had left such brutal scars upon her husband's soul. Those people deserved the warning, the protection.

Yrene reminded herself of that fact as they entered the gloomy keep interior.

The tall, narrow passageway wasn't much better than the exterior. Slender windows set high in the walls permitted little light, and ancient braziers cast flickering shadows on the stones. Threadbare tapestries hung intermittently, and no sounds—not music, not laughter, not conversation—greeted them.

This drafty, ancient house had been his home? Compared to the khagan's palace, it was a hovel, not fit for ruks to roost.

"My father," Chaol murmured so their escort wouldn't hear, no doubt reading the dismay on Yrene's face, "doesn't believe in wasting his coffers on improvements. If it hasn't collapsed, then it's not broken."

Yrene tried to smile at the attempt at humor, tried to do it for his sake, but her temper roiled with every step down the hall. Their silent escort at last paused before two towering oak doors, the wood as old and rotting as the keep itself, and knocked once.

"Enter."

Yrene felt the tremor that went through Chaol at the cold, sly voice.

The doors swung open to reveal a dark, column-lined hall speared with shafts of watery light.

The only greeting they would get, it seemed, since the man seated at the head of the long, wooden table, large enough to host forty men, did not bother to rise.

Each of their steps echoed through the hall, the roaring, mammoth hearth to their left hardly taking the edge off the cold. A goblet of what seemed to be wine and the remains of the evening meal lay before the Lord of Anielle on the table. No sign of his wife, or other son.

But the face . . . it was Chaol's face, in a few decades. Or would be, if Chaol became as soulless and cold as the man before them.

She didn't know how he did it. How Chaol managed to lower his head in a bow.

"Father."

          ~

Chaol had never been ashamed of the keep until he'd walked through it with Yrene. Had never realized how badly it needed repairs, how neglected it had been.

The thought of her, so full of light and warmth, in this bleak place made him want to run back to the ruk waiting on the parapets and fly to the coast again.

And now, at the sight of her before his father, who had not bothered to rise from his chair, whose half-eaten dinner lay discarded before him, Chaol found his temper in need of a short leash.

His father's fur-lined cloak pooled around him. How many times had he seen him on this chair, at the head of this mighty table, which had once seated some of the finest lords and warriors in Adarlan?

Now it lay empty, a husk of what might have been.

"You walk," his father said, scanning him from head to toe. His attention lingered on the hand Chaol still kept clasped around Yrene's. Oh, he'd surely bring that up soon enough. When it would strike deepest. "Last I heard, you could not so much as wiggle your toe."

"It is thanks to this woman," Chaol said. Yet Yrene stared at his father with a coldness Chaol had never glimpsed before. As if she were thinking of rotting his organs from the inside out. It warmed Chaol enough to say, "My wife. Lady Yrene Towers Westfall."

A kernel of surprise lit his father's face, but swiftly vanished. "A healer, then," he mused, surveying Yrene with an intensity that made Chaol want to start shattering things. "Towers is not a noble house I recognize."

The miserable bastard.

Yrene's chin lifted slightly. "It may not be, milord, but its lineage is no less proud or worthy."

"At least she speaks well," his father said, sipping from his wine. Chaol clenched his free hand so hard his glove groaned. "Better than that other one—the swaggering assassin."

Yrene knew. All of it. She knew every scrap of history, knew whose note she carried in her locket. But it didn't ease the blow, not as his father added, "Who, it turned out, is Queen of Terrasen." A mirthless laugh. "What a prize you might have had then, my son, if you'd managed to keep her."

"Yrene is the finest healer of her generation," Chaol said with deadly quiet. "Her worth is greater than any crown." And in this war, it might very well be.

"You don't need to bother proving my value to him," Yrene said, her icy eyes pinned on his father. "I know precisely how talented I am. I don't require his blessing."

She meant every damn word.

His father turned that aloof stare upon her again, curiosity filling it for a moment.

If he'd been asked, even minutes ago, how he thought this encounter might go, Yrene being utterly unfazed by his father, Yrene going toe to toe with his father, would not have been among the possible outcomes.

His father leaned back in his chair. "You didn't come here to at last fulfill your oath to me, did you."

"That promise is broken, and for that I apologize," Chaol managed to say. Yrene bristled. Before she could tell him not to bother again, Chaol went on, "We came to warn you."

His father lifted a brow. "Morath is on the move, this I know. I've taken the precaution of having your beloved mother and brother removed to the mountains."

"Morath is on the move," Chaol said, fighting the disappointment that he would see neither of the two people he needed to speak to the most, "and it is on its way directly here."

His father, for once, went still.

"Ten thousand troops," Chaol said. "They come to sack the city."

He could have sworn his father paled. "You know this without a doubt?"

"I sailed with an army sent from the khagan, a legion of his ruk riders amongst them. Their scouts discovered the information. The rukhin fly here as we speak, but their Darghan soldiers won't arrive for at least a week or longer." He came forward—just one step. "You need to rally your forces, prepare the city. Immediately."

But his father swirled his wine, frowning at the red liquid within. "There are no forces here—none to make a dent in ten thousand men."

"Then begin the evacuation, and move as many into the keep as you can. Prepare for a siege."

"Last I looked, boy, *I* was still Lord of Anielle. You gladly turned your back on it. Twice."

"You have Terrin."

"Terrin's a scholar. Why do you think I sent him away with his mother like a nursing babe?" His father sneered. "Have you come back to bleed for Anielle, then? To bleed for this city at last?"

"Don't you talk to him like that," Yrene said with dangerous calm.

His father ignored her.

But Yrene stepped up to Chaol's side once more. "I am the heir apparent to the Healer on High of the Torre Cesme. I came at your son's behest, back to the lands of my birth, to help in this war, along with two hundred healers from the Torre itself. Your son spent the last several months forging an alliance with the khaganate, and now *all* of the khagan's armies sail to this continent to save *your* people. So while you sit here in your miserable keep, tossing insults at him, know that he has done what no other could do, and if your city survives, it will be because of *him*, not you."

His father blinked at her. Slowly.

It took all of Chaol's restraint to keep from sweeping Yrene into his arms and kissing her.

But Chaol said to his father, "Prepare for a siege, and get the defenses ready. Or the Silver Lake will run red again beneath the claws of Erawan's beasts."

"I know the history of this city as well as you do."

Chaol debated ending it there, but he asked, "Is that why you didn't kneel to Erawan?"

"Or to the puppet king before him," his father said, picking at his food.

"You knew—that the old king was Valg-possessed?"

His father's fingers stilled on a crust of hearty bread, the only sign of his shock. "No. Only that he was building a host throughout the land that did not seem . . . natural. I am no king's lackey, no matter what you may think of me." He lowered his hand once more. "Of course, in my plans to get you out of harm's way, it seems it only led you closer to it."

"Why bother?"

"I meant what I said in Rifthold. Terrin is not a warrior—not at heart. I saw what was building in Morath, in the Ferian Gap, and required my eldest son to be here, to pick up the sword should I fall. And now you have returned, at the hour when the shadow of Morath has crept around us on all sides."

"All sides but one," Chaol said, motioning toward the White Fangs just barely visible through the windows high above. "Rumor has it Erawan has spent these months hunting down the wild men of the Fangs. If you are so short of soldiers, call for aid."

His father's mouth tightened. "They are half-savage nomads who relish killing our people."

"As ours have relished killing them. Let Erawan unite us."

"And offer them what? The mountains have belonged to us since before Gavin Havilliard sat on his throne."

Yrene muttered, "Offer them the damn moon, if it will convince them to help."

His father smirked. "Can you offer such a thing, as the heir apparent to the Healer on High?"

"Careful," Chaol growled.

His father ignored that, too. "I would rather have my head on a pike than give the wild men of the Fangs an inch of Anielle's land, let alone ask them for aid."

"I hope your people agree," said Yrene.

His father let out one of those joyless laughs. "I like you better than the assassin-queen, I think. Perhaps marrying the rabble will breed some backbone into our bloodline once more."

Chaol's blood roared in his ears, but Yrene's lips curved into a smile. "You're exactly as I'd pictured you to be," she said. His father only inclined his head.

"Prepare this city, this keep," Chaol managed to say through his gritted teeth. "Or you'll deserve everything you bring down upon it."

CHAPTER 19

Fifteen minutes later, Chaol could feel Yrene still trembling as they entered a small yet warm bedroom. One of the few cozy places in this horrible keep. A bed and a half-rusted washing basin filled most of the space, a ewer of steaming water beside it.

Not exactly a bedroom fit for a lord's son. He fought the heat that warmed his cheeks.

"I was disowned, remember," Chaol said, leaning against the shut door, their packs discarded at his feet. "This bedroom is meant for a guest."

"I'm sure your father had it selected just for you."

"I'm sure he did."

Yrene snarled. "He's worse than you portrayed."

Chaol gave her a tired, small smile. "And you were brilliant." Utterly brilliant.

His father, at least, had agreed to begin the evacuations for those on the outskirts of the city, and by the time they'd made their way to this room, the keep had already been abuzz with readying for a siege. If his father needed help planning it, the man hadn't let on. Tomorrow, after they rested tonight, he'd see for himself what his father had in mind.

But for now, after almost two days of flying through the frigid air, he needed to rest.

And his wife, however bold and fearless, needed to rest as well, whether she admitted it or not.

So Chaol pushed off the door, prowling to where Yrene paced in front of the bed. "I'm sorry for what he said to you."

She waved him off. "I'm sorry you ever had to deal with him for longer than that conversation."

Her temper, despite all that loomed, despite the bastard ruling over this city, warmed something in him. Enough so that Chaol closed the distance between them, halting her pacing by taking her hand. He brushed his thumb over her wedding band.

"I wish you were meeting her instead—my mother," he said softly.

The fierceness in her eyes banked. "I do, too." Her mouth quirked to the side. "Though I'm surprised your father cared enough to send them away at a whisper of a threat."

"They're assets to him. I wouldn't be surprised if he sent them with a good part of the trove."

Yrene glanced around in doubt.

"Anielle is one of the richer territories in Adarlan, despite what this keep suggests." He kissed her knuckles, her ring. "There are chambers full of treasure in the catacombs. Gold, jewels, armor—rumor has it the wealth of an entire kingdom is down there."

Yrene let out an impressed hum, but said, "I should have told Sartaq and Nesryn to bring more healers than the fifty we selected." Hafiza would remain with the foot soldiers and cavalry, but Eretia, her second-in-command, would fly with the ruks and lead the group, Yrene included.

"We'll make do with what we have. I doubt there was a single magically gifted healer in this city until an hour ago."

Her throat bobbed. "Can this keep survive a siege long enough for the terrestrial army to get here? It doesn't look like it can withstand another winter, let alone an army at its doorstep."

"This keep has stood for well over a thousand years—it survived Erawan's second army, even when they sacked Anielle. It will outlast this third war of his, too."

"Where will the people evacuate to? The mountains are already covered in snow."

"There are passes through them—dangerous, but they could make it to the Wastes if they stay together and bring enough supplies." Heading north of Anielle was a death trap, with the witches holding the Ferian Gap, and going too far south would take them to Morath's doorstep. To go east would take them in the path of the army they sought to outrun. "They might be able to hide in Oakwald, along the edge of the Fangs." He shook his head. "There are no good options, not at this time of year."

"A lot of them won't make it," she said softly.

"They'll stand a better chance in the Fangs than here," he said with equal quiet. They were still his people, had still shown him kindness, even when his own father had not. "I'll see to it that my father sends some of the soldiers who are too old to fight with them—they'll remember the way."

"I know I'm nothing more than the rabble," Yrene said, and Chaol snickered, "but those who do choose to stay, who are let into the keep . . . Perhaps while we wait for our own forces, I could help find room for them. Supplies. See if there are any healers among them who might have access to the herbs and ingredients we need. Get bandages ready."

He nodded, pride filling his chest to the point of pain. A lady. If not by blood, then by nobility of character. His wife was more of a lady than any other he'd met, in any court.

"Then let us prepare for war, husband," Yrene said, sorrow and dread filling her eyes.

And it was the sight of that kernel of fear, not for herself but what they were undoubtedly soon to take part in, to witness, that had him sweeping her into his arms and laying her upon the bed. "War can wait until morning," he said, and lowered his mouth to hers.

Dawn broke, and the ruks arrived.

So many ruks they blotted out the watery sun, the boom of wings and rustle of feathers filling the skies.

People cried out this time, their voices a herald of the screams to come when that army reached their doorstep.

On the plain before the southern side of the keep, flowing to the lake edge itself, the ruks settled. It had long been kept clear of settlement, the flat expanse riddled with hot springs and prone to annual flooding, though a few stubborn farmers still tried to coax crops from the hard soil.

It had once been part of the lake itself, before the Western Falls tucked into the Fangs had been dammed up, their roaring waters quieted to a trickle that fed the lake. For centuries, Chaol's ancestors had debated breaking the dam, letting that raging river run free once more, now that their ancient forges had given way to a few water-powered mills that could easily be moved elsewhere.

Yet the destruction breaking that dam would cause, even if they gathered every water-wielder in the realm to control the flow, would be catastrophic. The entire plain would flood in a matter of minutes, some of the city being swept away as well. The waters would barrel down from the mountains, destroying everything in their path in a mighty wave that would flow to Oakwald itself. The lowest levels of the keep, the gate that opened onto the plain, would be wholly submerged.

So the dam had stayed, and the grassy plain with it.

The ruks settled themselves in neat rows, and Chaol and Yrene watched from the battlements, other sentries breaking from their posts to join them, as the riders began setting up camp with whatever supplies their mounts had carried. The healers would be brought up later, though a few might remain down in their camp until Morath's legion arrived.

Two dark shapes soared overhead, and the sentries fell back to their posts as Nesryn and Sartaq landed on the battlement wall, a small falcon alighting beside the former's ruk. Falkan Ennar, then.

Nesryn leaped off her ruk in an easy movement, her face grave as any pocket of Hellas's realm. "Morath is three days away, possibly four," she said breathlessly.

Sartaq came up behind her, the ruks needing no hitching post. "We kept high overhead, out of sight, but Falkan was able to get closer." The shifter remained in falcon form by Salkhi.

Yrene stepped forward. "What did you see?"

Nesryn shook her head, her normally golden-brown skin bloodless. "Valg and men, mostly. But they all look fast—vicious."

Chaol reined in his grimace. "No sign of the witches?"

"None," Sartaq said, running a hand over his braided hair. "Though they might be waiting to sweep down from the Ferian Gap when the army arrives here."

"Let's pray they don't," Yrene said, surveying the ruks in the valley below.

A thousand ruks. It had seemed like a gift from the gods, seemed like an impossibly large number. And yet seeing them assembled on the plain . . .

Even the mighty birds might be swept away in the tide of battle.

CHAPTER 20

"Do you know the story of the queen who walked through worlds?"

Seated on the mossy carpet of an ancient glen, one hand toying with the small white flowers strewn across it, Aelin shook her head.

In the towering oaks that formed a lattice over the clearing, small stars blinked and shimmered, as if they'd been snared by the branches themselves. Beyond them, bathing the forest with light bright enough to see by, a full moon had risen. All around them, faint, lilting singing floated on the warm summer air.

"It is a sad story," her aunt said, one corner of her red-painted mouth curling upward as she leaned back on her seat carved into a granite boulder. Her usual place, while they had these lessons, these long, peaceful chats deep into the balmy summer nights. "And an old one."

Aelin lifted an eyebrow. "Aren't I a little old for faerie stories?" She'd indeed just celebrated her twentieth birthday three days ago, in another clearing not too far from here. Half of Doranelle had come, it had seemed, and yet her mate had found a way to sneak her from the revelry. All the way to a secluded pool in the forest's heart. Her face still warmed to think of that moonlit swim, what Rowan had made her feel, how he'd worshipped her in the sun-warmed water.

Mate. The word was still a surprise. As it had been to arrive here at spring's end and see him beside her aunt's throne and simply *know.* And in the months since, their courting . . . Aelin indeed blushed at the thought of it. What they'd done in that forest pool had been the culmination of those months. And an unleashing. The mating marks on her neck—and on Rowan's—proved it. She would not be returning to Terrasen alone when autumn arrived.

"No one is too old for faerie stories," her aunt said, faint smile growing. "And as you are part faerie yourself, I would think you'd have some interest in them."

Aelin smiled back, bowing her head. "Fair enough, Aunt."

Aunt wasn't entirely accurate, not with generations and millennia separating them, but it was the only thing the queen had suggested Aelin call her.

Maeve settled further into her seat. "Long ago, when the world was new, when there were no human kingdoms, when no wars had marred the earth, a young queen was born."

Aelin folded her legs beneath her, angling her head.

"She did not know she was a queen. Amongst her people, power was not inherited, but simply *born.* And as she grew, her strength rose with her. She found the land she dwelled in to be too small for that power. Too dark and cold and grim. She had gifts similar to many wielded by her kind, but she had been given *more*, her power a sharper, more intricate weapon—enough that she was different. Her people saw that power and bowed to it, and she ruled them.

"Word spread of her gifts, and three kings came to seek her hand. To form an alliance between their throne and the one she had built for herself, small as it might have been. For a time, she thought it would be the newness, the challenge that she had always craved. The three kings were brothers, each mighty in his own right, their power vast and terrifying. She picked the eldest among them, not for any particular skill or grace, but for his countless libraries. What she might learn in his lands, what she might *do* with her power . . . It was that knowledge she craved, not the king himself."

A strange story. Aelin's brows rose, but her aunt continued on.

"So they were wed, and she left her small territory to join him in his castle. For a time, she was contented, both by her husband and the knowledge his home offered her. He and his two brothers were conquerors, and spent much of their time away, leashing new lands to their shared throne. She did not mind, not when it gave her freedom to learn as she would. But her husband's libraries contained knowledge even he did not realize was held within. Lore and wisdom from worlds long since turned to dust. She learned that there were indeed *other* worlds. Not the dark, blasted realm in which they lived, but worlds beyond that, living atop one another and never realizing it. Worlds where the sun was not a watery trickle through the ash-clouds, but a golden stream of warmth. Worlds where *green* existed. She had never heard of such a color. Green. Nor had she heard of blue—not the shade of sky that was described. She could not so much as picture it."

Aelin frowned. "A pitiful existence."

Maeve nodded grimly. "It was. And the more she read about these other worlds, where long-dead wayfarers had once roamed, the more she wanted to see them. To know the kiss of the sun on her face. To hear the morning songs of sparrows, the crying of gulls over the sea. The sea—that, too, was foreign to her. An endless sprawl of water, with its own moods and hidden depths. All they had in her lands were shallow, murky lakes and half-dried streams. So while her husband and his two brothers were off waging yet another war, she began to ponder how she might find a way into one of those worlds. How she might *leave*."

"Is such a thing even possible?" Something nagged at her, as if it might indeed be true, but perhaps that was one of her own mother's tales, or even Marion's, tugging on her memory.

Maeve nodded. "It was. Using the very language of existence itself, doors might be opened, however briefly, between worlds. It was forbidden, outlawed long before her husband and his brothers were born. Once the last of the ancient wayfarers had died out, the paths between realms were sealed, their methods of world-walking lost with them. Or so all had thought. But deep in her husband's private library, she found the old spells. She began with small experiments. First, she opened a door to the realm of resting, to find one of those wayfarers and ask her how it was properly done." A knowing smile. "The wayfarer refused to tell her. So the queen began to teach herself. Opening and closing doors long since forgotten or sealed. Peering deep into the workings of the cosmos. Her own world became a cage. She grew tired of her husband's warring, his casual cruelty. And when he went away to war once again, the queen gathered her closest handmaidens, opened a door to a new world, and left the one she'd been born into."

"She left?" Aelin blurted. "She—she just *left* her own world? Permanently?"

"It had never been her world, not really. She had been born to rule others."

"Where did she go?"

That smile grew a bit. "To a fair, lovely world. Where there was no war, no darkness. Not like that in which she had been born. She was made a queen there, too. Was able to hide herself within a new body so that none could know what she was beneath, so that even her own husband would not recognize her."

"Did he ever find her again?"

"No, though he looked. Found out all she'd learned, and taught it to himself and his brothers. They tore apart world after world to find her. And when they arrived at the world where she had made her new home, they did not know her. Even as they went to war, she did not reveal herself. She won, and two of the kings, her husband included, were banished back to their own world. The third remained trapped, his power nearly broken. He crawled off into the depths of the earth, and the victorious queen spent her long, long existence preparing for his return, preparing her *people* for it. For the three kings had gone beyond her methods of world-walking. They had found a way to permanently *open* a gate between worlds, and had made three keys to do so. To wield those keys was to control *all* worlds, to have the power of eternity in the palm of your hand. She wished to find them, only so she might possess the strength to banish any enemies, banish her husband's youngest brother back to his realm. To protect her new, lovely world. It was all she ever wanted: to dwell in peace, without the shadow of her past hunting her."

From far away, that ghost of memory pushed. As if she'd forgotten to douse a flame left burning in her room. "And did the queen find the keys?"

Maeve's smile turned sad. "Do you think she did, Aelin?"

Aelin considered. So many of their chats, their lessons in this glen, held deeper puzzles, questions for her to work through, to help her when she one day took her throne, Rowan at her side.

As if she'd summoned him, the pine-and-snow scent of her mate filled the clearing. A rustle of wings, and there he was, perched in hawk form on one of the towering oaks. Her warrior-prince.

She smiled toward him, as she had for weeks now, when he'd come to escort her back to her rooms in the river palace. It was during those walks from forest to mist-shrouded city that she had come to know him, love him. More than she had ever loved anything.

Aelin again faced her aunt. "The queen was clever, and ambitious. I would think she could do anything, even find the keys."

"So you would believe. And yet they eluded her."

"Where did they go?"

Maeve's dark stare unwaveringly held hers. "Where do you think they went?"

Aelin opened her mouth. "I think—"

She blinked. Paused.

Maeve's smile returned, soft and kind. As her aunt had been to her from the start. "Where do you think the keys are, Aelin?"

She opened her mouth once more. And again halted.

Like an invisible chain yanked her back. Silenced her.

Chain—a chain. She glanced down at her hands, her wrists. As if expecting them to be there.

She had never felt a shackle's bite in her life. And yet she stared at the empty place on her wrist where she could have sworn there was a scar. Only smooth, sun-kissed skin remained.

"If this world were at risk, if those three terrible kings threatened to destroy it, where would you go to find the keys?"

Aelin looked up at her aunt.

Another world. There was another world. Like a fragment of a dream, there was another world, and in it, she had a wrist with a scar on it. Had scars all over.

And her mate, perched overhead . . . He had a tattoo down his face and neck and arm in that world. A sad story—his tattoo told a sad, awful story. About loss. Loss caused by a dark queen—

"Where are the keys hidden, Aelin?"

That placid, loving smile remained on Maeve's face. And yet . . .

And yet.

"No," Aelin breathed.

Something slithered in the depths of her aunt's stare. "No what?"

This wasn't her existence, her life. This place, these blissful months learning in Doranelle, finding her mate—

Blood and sand and crashing waves.

"No."

Her voice was a thunderclap through the peaceful glen.

Aelin bared her teeth, fingers curling in the moss.

Maeve let out a soft laugh. Rowan flapped from the branches to land on the queen's upraised arm.

He didn't so much as fight it when she wrapped her thin white hands around his neck. And snapped it.

Aelin screamed. Screamed, clutching at her chest, at the shredding mating bond—

⁓

Aelin arched off the altar, and every broken and torn part of her body screamed with her.

Above her, Maeve was smiling. "You liked that vision, didn't you?"

Not real. That had not been real. Rowan was alive, he was *alive*—

She tried to move her arm. Red-hot lightning lashed her, and she screamed again.

Only a broken rasp came out. Broken, just as her arm now lay—

Now lay—

Bone gleamed, jutting upward along more places than she could count. Blood and twisted skin, and—

No shackle scars, even with the wreckage.

In this world, this place, she did not have scars, either.

Another illusion, another spun dreamscape—

She screamed again. Screamed at her ruined arm, the unscarred skin, screamed at the lingering echo of the severed mating bond.

"Do you know what pains me most, Aelin?" Maeve's words were soft as a lover's. "It's that you believe I'm the villain in this."

Aelin sobbed through her teeth as she tried and failed to move her arm. Both arms. She cast her gaze through the space, this real-yet-not room.

They'd repaired the box. Had welded a new slab of iron over the lid. Then over the sides. The bottom. Less air trickled in, the hours or days now spent inside in near-suffocating heat. It had been a relief when she'd finally been chained to the altar.

Whenever that had been. If it had even happened at all.

"I have no doubt that your mate or Elena or even Brannon himself filled your head with lies about what I'll do with the keys." Maeve ran a hand over the stone lip of the altar, right through her splattered blood and shards of bone. "I meant what I said. I like this world. I do not wish to destroy it. Only improve it. Imagine a realm where there is no hunger, no pain. Isn't that what you and your cohorts are fighting for? A better world?"

The words were a mockery. A mockery of what she'd promised so many. What she had promised Terrasen, and still owed it.

Aelin tried not to shift against the chains, against her broken arms, against the tight pressure pushing on her skin from the inside. A rising intensity along her bones, in her head. A little more, every day.

Maeve heaved a small sigh. "I know what you think of me, Fire-Bringer. What you assume. But there are some truths that cannot be shared. Even for the keys."

Yet the growing strain cracking within her, smothering the pain . . . perhaps worse.

Maeve cupped her cheek over the mask. "The Queen Who Was Promised. I wish to *save* you from that sacrifice, offered up by a head-strong girl." A soft laugh. "I'd even let you have Rowan. The two of you here, together. While you and I work to save this world."

The words were lies. She knew it, though she couldn't quite remember where one truth ended and the lie began. If her mate had belonged to another before her. Been given away. Or had that been the nightmare?

Gods, the pressure in her body. Her blood.

You do not yield.

"You can feel it, even now," Maeve went on. "The urge of your body to say *yes*." Aelin opened her eyes, and confusion must have glittered there, because Maeve smiled. "Do you know what being encased in iron does to a magic-wielder? You wouldn't feel it immediately, but as time goes on . . . your magic needs release, Aelin. That pressure is your magic screaming it wants you to come free of these chains and release the strain. Your very blood tells you to heed me."

Truth. Not the submission part, but the deepening pressure she knew would be worse than any pain from burnout. She'd felt it once, when plunging as far into her power as she'd ever gone.

That would be nothing compared to this.

"I am leaving for a few days," Maeve said.

Aelin stilled.

Maeve shook her head in a mockery of disappointment. "You are not progressing as quickly as I wished, Aelin."

Across the room, Fenrys let out a warning snarl. Maeve didn't so much as glance at him.

"It has come to my attention that our mutual enemy has been spotted again on these shores. One of them, a Valg prince, was contained a few days' journey from here, near the southern border. It brought with it several collars, no doubt to use on my own people. Perhaps even on me."

No. *No*—

Maeve brushed a hand over Aelin's neck, as if tracing a line where the collar would go. "So I will go myself to retrieve that collar, to see what Erawan's minion might say for itself. I ripped apart the Valg princes who encountered me in the first war," she said quietly. "It shall be rather easy, I suppose, to instead bend them to my will. Well, bend *one* to my will and wrest it from Erawan's control, once I put its collar around your neck."

No.

The word was a steady chant, a rising shriek within her.

"I don't know why I didn't think of it before," Maeve mused.

No.

Maeve poked Aelin's shattered wrist, and Aelin swallowed her scream. "Think on it. And when I return, let's discuss my proposition again. Maybe all that growing strain will make you see more clearly, too."

A collar. Maeve was going to retrieve a Wyrdstone collar—

Maeve turned, black gown swirling with her. She crossed the threshold, and her owl swooped from its perch atop the open door to land upon her shoulder. "I'm sure Cairn will find ways to entertain you while I'm away."

She didn't know how long she lay on the altar after the healers swept in with their sweet-smelling smoke. They'd put the metal gauntlets back on her.

With each hour, the pressure beneath her skin grew. Even in that heavy, drugged sleep. As if once she'd acknowledged it, it wouldn't be ignored. Or contained.

It would be the least of her problems, if Maeve put a collar around her neck.

Fenrys sat by the wall, concern bright in his eyes as he blinked. *Are you all right?*

She blinked twice. *No.*

No, she was not anywhere near to all right. Maeve had been waiting for this, waiting for this pressure to begin, worse than anything Cairn might do. And with the collar Maeve now went to personally retrieve . . .

She couldn't let herself contemplate it. A more horrific form of slavery, one she might never escape, never be able to fight. Not a breaking of the Fire-Bringer, but an erasure.

To take all she was, power and knowledge, and rip it from her. To have her trapped inside while she witnessed her own voice yield the location of the Wyrdkeys. Swear the blood oath to Maeve. Wholly submit to her.

Fenrys blinked four times. *I am here, I am with you.*

She answered in kind. *I am here, I am with you.*

Her magic surged, seeking a way out, filling the gaps between her breath and bones. She couldn't find room for it, couldn't do anything to soothe it.

You do not yield.

She focused on the words. On her mother's voice.

Perhaps the magic would devour her from the inside before Maeve returned.

But she did not know how she'd endure it. Endure another few days of this, let alone the next hour. To ease the strain, just a fraction . . .

She shut down the thoughts that snaked into her mind. Her own or Maeve's, she didn't care.

Fenrys blinked again, the same message over and over. *I am here, I am with you.*

Aelin closed her eyes, praying for oblivion.

⁓

"Get up."

A mockery of words she'd once heard.

Cairn stood above her, a smile twisting his hateful face. And the wild light in his eyes . . .

Aelin went still as he began unfastening her chains.

Guards stomped in. Fenrys snarled.

The pressure writhed against her skin, pounding in her head like a brutal hammer. Worse than the tools of breaking dangling at Cairn's side.

"Maeve wants you moved," he said, that feverish light growing as he hoisted her up and carried her to the box. Let her drop into it so hard the chains clanked against her bones, her skull. Her eyes watered, and she lunged up, but the lid slammed shut.

Darkness, hot and tight, pressed in. The twin to what grew under her skin.

"With Morath creeping onto these shores again, she wants you moved somewhere more *secure* until she returns," Cairn crooned through the lid. Guards grunted, and the box lifted, Aelin shifting, biting her lip against the movement. "I don't give a shit what she does to you once she puts that demon collar around your throat. But until then . . . I'll get you all to myself, won't I? A last little bout of fun for you and me, until you find yourself with a new friend inside you."

Dread coiled in her stomach, smothering the pressure.

Moving her to another location—she had once warned a young healer about that. Had told her if an attacker tried to move her, they would most definitely kill her, and she was to make a final stand before they could.

And that was without the threat of a Wyrdstone collar traveling closer with each passing day.

But Cairn wouldn't kill her, not when Maeve needed her alive.

Aelin focused on her breathing. In and out, out and in.

It didn't keep the oily, sharp fear from taking hold. From making her start shaking.

"You are to join us, Fenrys," Cairn said, laughter in his voice as Aelin slid against the metal of the box while they walked up the stairs. "I wouldn't want you to miss a heartbeat of this."

CHAPTER 21

Rowan knew every path, traveled and hidden, into Doranelle. Both the lush kingdom and the sprawling city it had been named after.

So did Gavriel and Lorcan. They'd sold their horses the night before, Elide bartering for them. The Fae warriors were too recognizable, and if their faces weren't noted, the sheer presence of their power would be. Few wouldn't know who they were.

Unlike the northern border with Wendlyn, no wild wolves guarded the southern roads into the kingdom. But they'd still kept hidden, taking half-forgotten pathways on their trek northward.

And when they were a few days away from the outer limits of the city, they had laid their trap for Maeve.

What he knew the queen might not be able to resist coming to retrieve herself: Wyrdstone collars.

Aelin had not broken yet. He knew it, had felt it. It would likely be driving Maeve mad. So the temptation to use one of the Wyrdstone collars, the arrogance he knew Maeve possessed that would allow her to believe she might control the demon within, wrest it away from Erawan himself . . . it would indeed be too great an opportunity for the queen to pass up.

So they had begun with rumors, fed by Elide at taverns and markets, at the places where Rowan knew Maeve's spies would be listening. Whispers of a Fae garrison who had captured a Valg prince—the strange collars they found on him. The location: an outpost leagues away. The collars: anyone's for the taking.

He didn't bother to pray to the gods that Maeve fell for it. That she didn't send one of her spies instead to retrieve the collars or confirm their existence. A fool's gamble, but the only one they could make.

And as they scaled the steep southern hillocks that would offer them a view of the night-veiled city at last, Rowan's heart thundered in his chest. They might not have Maeve's cloaking abilities, but without the blood oath, they could remain undetected.

Though Maeve's eyes were everywhere, her net of power spread far and wide across this land. And so many others.

Their breathing was labored as they half crawled to the highest of the wooded hills. There were other ways into the city, yes, but none that offered a view of the terrain before them. Rowan hadn't risked flying, not when keen-eyed patrols no doubt searched for a white-tailed hawk, even under cover of darkness.

Only thirty feet to the summit now.

Rowan kept climbing, the others close behind.

She was here. She'd been here the entire time. If they'd come directly to Doranelle—

He didn't let himself consider it. Not as he cleared the hilltop.

Under the sliver of a moon, the gray-stoned city was bathed in white, wreathed in mist from the surrounding rivers and waterfalls. Elide, amid her panting, gasped.

"I—I thought it would be like Morath," she admitted.

The serene city lay in the heart of a river basin. Lanterns still glowed despite the late hour, and he knew that in some squares, music would be playing.

Home. Or it had been. Were its citizens still his people, when he'd wed a foreign queen? When he'd fought and killed so many of them on Eyllwe's waters? He didn't look for the black mourning banners that would be hanging from so many windows.

Beside him, he knew Lorcan and Gavriel were avoiding counting them, too. For centuries, they had known these people, lived amongst them. Called them friends.

But were any aware who was held in their midst? Had they heard her screams?

"That's the palace," Gavriel said to Elide, pointing toward the cluster of domes and elegant buildings set on the eastern edge, right along the lip of the massive waterfall.

None of them spoke as they scanned the column-lined building that housed the queen's private quarters. And their own suites. No lights burned within.

"It doesn't confirm anything," Lorcan said. "Whether Maeve left, or if Aelin remains."

Rowan listened to the wind, scented it, but felt nothing. "The only way to confirm either is to go into the city."

"Are those two bridges the only way in?" Elide frowned toward the twin stone bridges on the southern and northern sides of Doranelle. Both open, both visible for miles around.

"Yes," Lorcan said, his voice tight.

The river was too wide, too wild, to swim. And if any other ways in existed, Rowan had never learned them.

"We should make a wide sweep of the basin," Lorcan said, studying the city in the heart of the plain. To the north, the forested foothills flowed to the towering wall of the Cambrian Mountains. To the west, the plain rolled into farmland, endless and open, to the sea. And in the east, past the waterfall, the grassy plain yielded to ancient forests, more mountains beyond them.

His mountains. The place he'd once called home, where that mountain house had stood until it had been burned. Where he'd buried Lyria and had one day expected to be laid to rest himself.

"We need an exit strategy as well," Rowan said, though he'd already been considering it. Where to run afterward. Maeve would send out her best to hunt them down.

That had once included him. He'd been sent to track and dispatch the Fae who turned too monstrous for even Maeve to stomach, rogue Fae who had no business existing anymore. He'd trained the hunters Maeve would now unleash. Had taught them the veiled paths, the places Fae preferred to hide.

He'd never considered that would someday be used against him.

"We take a day," Lorcan said.

Rowan leveled a cold look at him. "A day is more than we can spare."

Aelin was down there. In that city. He knew it, could feel it. He'd been plunging into his power for the past two days, readying for the killing he'd unleash, the flight they'd make. The strain of holding it back yanked on him, on any lingering control.

Lorcan said, "We'll pay for a hasty plan if we don't take the time. Your mate will pay, too."

His former commander's control was also on a knife's edge. Even Gavriel, calm and steady, was pacing. All of them had descended into their power, drawing it up from the very dregs.

But Lorcan was right. Rowan would say the same if their positions were reversed.

Gavriel pointed to a rocky outcropping on the hill face below them. "It's shielded from sight. We camp there tonight, make our assessments tomorrow. Get some rest."

The idea was abhorrent. Sleeping while Aelin was mere miles away.

His ears strained, as if he might pick up her screams on the wind. But Rowan said, "Fine."

He didn't need to declare that they wouldn't risk a fire. The air was chill, but mild enough that they could survive.

Rowan stepped down the hill face, offering a hand to Elide to help her skirt the dangerous, rocky plunge. She took his hand with shaking fingers.

Still she hadn't balked to come with them, to do any of this.

Rowan found another foothold before turning to assist her. "You don't need to go into the city. We'll decide on the escape route and you can meet us there."

When Elide didn't answer, Rowan looked up at her.

Her eyes weren't on him. But on the city ahead.

Wide with terror. Her scent became drenched in it.

Lorcan was there in a heartbeat, hand at her shoulder. "What is—"

Rowan twisted toward the city. The hilltop had been a border.

Not of the city limits, but of an illusion. A pretty, idyllic illusion for any scouting its fringes to report. For what now surrounded the city on every side, even on the eastern plain . . .

An army. A great army lay camped there.

"She's summoned most of her forces," Gavriel breathed, wind whipping his hair across his face.

Rowan counted the campfires covering the dark terrain like a blanket of stars. He'd never seen such a Fae host assembled. The ones he and the cadre had led into war didn't come close.

Aelin could be anywhere in that force. In the camps, or in the city itself.

They'd have to be clever. Cunning. And if Maeve had not fallen for their diversion . . .

"She brought an army to keep us out?" Elide asked.

Lorcan glanced at Rowan, his dark eyes full of warning. "Or to keep Aelin in."

Rowan surveyed the encamped army. What did those dwelling in

Doranelle, who rarely saw any sort of forces beyond the warriors who sometimes stalked through their city, make of the host?

"We have allies in the city," Gavriel offered. "We could try to make contact. Learn where Maeve is, what the host rallied here to do. If there's been any mention of Aelin."

Rowan's uncle, Ellys, the head of their House, had remained when Maeve's armada had sailed. A hard male, a smart male, but a loyal one. He'd trained Enda in his image, to be a sharp-minded courtier. But he'd also trained Rowan when he could, giving him some of his first lessons in swordplay. He'd grown up in his uncle's household, and it had been the only home he'd known until he'd found that mountain. But would Ellys's loyalty skew toward Maeve or to their own bloodline, especially in the wake of the House of Whitethorn's betrayal in Eyllwe?

His uncle might already be dead. Maeve might have punished him on behalf of all the cousins whom Rowan had begged to aid them. Or Ellys, seeking to reenter Maeve's good graces after their betrayal, might sell them out before they could find Aelin.

And as for the others, the few allies they might have . . .

"Maeve is capable of worming her way into a person's mind," Rowan said. "She likely knows who our allies are and might have already compromised them." He braced a hand on Goldryn's hilt, the warm metal a comforting touch. "We don't risk it."

Lorcan grunted his agreement.

Elide said, "Maeve doesn't know me—or barely does. No one here would recognize me, especially if I can . . . adjust my appearance. Like I did with spreading those lies about the Valg prince. I could try to get into the city tomorrow and see if there's anything to learn."

"No."

Lorcan's reply was a knife in the dark.

Elide said to him, cool and unfazed, "You're not my commander. You're not in my court."

She turned to Rowan. But *he* was.

He outranked her. Rowan tried not to recoil. Aelin had laid this upon him.

Lorcan hissed, "She doesn't know the city layout, doesn't know how to handle the guards—"

"Then we teach her," Gavriel cut in. "Tonight. We teach her what we know."

Lorcan bared his teeth. "If Maeve remains in Doranelle, she will sniff her out."

"She won't," Elide said.

"She found you on that beach," Lorcan snapped.

Elide lifted her chin. "I am going into that city tomorrow."

"And what are you going to do? Ask if Aelin Galathynius has been strutting about town? Ask if Maeve's available for high tea?" Lorcan's snarl ripped through the air.

Elide didn't back down for a heartbeat. "I'm going to ask after Cairn."

They all stilled. Rowan wasn't entirely certain he'd heard her correctly.

Elide steadily surveyed them. "Surely a young, mortal woman is allowed to inquire about a Fae male who jilted her."

Lorcan went pale as the moon above them. "Elide." When she didn't reply, Lorcan whirled on Rowan. "We'll scout, there's another way to—"

Elide only said to Rowan, "Find Cairn, and we find Aelin. And learn if Maeve remains."

Fear no longer bloomed in Elide's eyes. Not a trace remained in her scent.

So Rowan nodded, even as Lorcan tensed. "Good hunting, Lady."

CHAPTER 22

The snow-crusted plains of Terrasen flowed southward, right to the rolling foothills that spread to the horizon.

Earlier this summer, Lysandra had crossed those foothills with her companions—with her queen. Had watched Aelin ascend one, and stride to the carved granite stone jutting from its top. The marker of the border between Adarlan and Terrasen. Her friend had taken a step beyond the stone, and had been home.

Perhaps it made Lysandra a fool, but she had not realized that the next time she'd see the foothills again, wearing the feathers of a bird, it would be in war.

Or as a scout for an army thousands of soldiers strong, marching far behind her. She'd left Aedion to figure out how to explain Aelin's sudden disappearance when she'd departed for this scouting mission. To glean where they might at last intercept Morath's legions—and give the general a lay of the terrain ahead. Fae scouts in their own avian forms had flown to the west and east to see what they might learn as well.

Her silvery falcon's wings wrangled the bitter wind, setting her soaring with a speed that shot liquid lightning through her heart. Beyond the ghost leopard, this form had become a favorite. Swift, sleek, vicious—this body had been built to ride the winds, to run down prey.

The snow had stopped, but the sky remained gray, not a hint of the sun to warm them. The cold was a secondary concern, made bearable by her layers of feathers.

For long miles, she flew and flew, scanning the empty terrain. Villages they had passed through during the summer had been emptied, their inhabitants fleeing north. She prayed they'd found safe harbor before the snows, that the magic-wielders within those villages got far from Morath's nets. There had been a girl in one of the towns who had been blessed with a powerful water gift—had she and her family been taken in behind Orynth's thick walls?

Lysandra caught an updraft and soared higher, the horizon revealing more of itself. The first of the foothills passed below, ridges of light and shadow under the cloudy sky. Getting the army over them would not be a simple task, but the Bane had fought near here before. They undoubtedly knew the path through, despite the snowdrifts piled high in the hollows.

The wind screamed, shoving northward. As if warding her from flying south. Begging her not to continue.

Hills crowned with stones appeared—the ancient border markings. She swept past them. A few hours lingered until darkness fell. She'd fly until night and cold rendered her unable, and find some tree to hunker down in until she could resume scouting at dawn.

She sailed farther south, the horizon bleak and empty.

Until it wasn't.

Until she beheld what marched toward them and nearly tumbled from the sky.

Ren had taught her how to count soldiers, yet she lost track each time she attempted to get a number on the neat lines stomping across Adarlan's northern plains. Right toward the foothills that spanned both territories.

Thousands. Five, ten, fifteen thousand. More.

Again and again, she stumbled on counting. Twenty, thirty.

Lysandra rose higher into the sky. Higher, because winged ilken flew with them, soaring low over the black-armored troops, monitoring all that passed below.

Forty. Fifty.

Fifty thousand troops, overseen by ilken.

And amongst them, on horseback, rode beautiful-faced young men. Black collars at their throats, above their armor.

Valg princes. Five in total, each commanding a legion.

Lysandra counted the force again. Thrice.

Fifty thousand troops. Against the twenty-five thousand they had gathered.

One of the ilken spotted her and flapped upward.

Lysandra banked hard and swept back north, wings beating like hell.

⁓

The two armies met in the snow-covered fields of southern Terrasen.

Terrasen's general-prince had ordered them to wait, rather than rush to meet Morath's legions. To let Erawan's hordes exhaust themselves on the foothills, and to send an advance force of the Silent Assassins to pick off soldiers struggling amid the bumps and hollows.

Only some of the assassins returned.

The dark power of the Valg princes swept ahead, devouring all in their path.

And still, the Fire-Bringer did not blast the Valg to ash. Did nothing but ride at her cousin's side.

Ilken descended upon their camp in the night, unleashing chaos and terror, shredding soldiers with their poison-slick claws before escaping to the skies.

They ripped the ancient border-stones from their grassy hilltops as they passed into Terrasen.

Barely winded, unfazed by the snow, and hardly thinned out, Morath's army left the last of the foothills.

They rushed down the hillsides, a black wave breaking over the land. Right onto the spears and shields of the Bane, the magic of the Fae soldiers keeping the power of the Valg princes at bay.

It could not stand against the ilken, however. They swept through it like cobwebs in a doorway, some spewing their venom to *melt* the magic.

Then the ilken landed, or shattered through their defenses entirely. And even a shape-shifter in the form of a wyvern armed with poisoned spikes could not take them all down.

Even a general-prince with an ancient sword and Fae instincts could not slice through their necks fast enough.

In the chaos, no one noticed that the Fire-Bringer did not appear. That not an ember of her flame glowed in the screaming night.

Then the foot soldiers reached them.

And that cobbled-together army began to sunder.

The right flank broke first. A Valg prince unleashed his power, men lying dead in his wake. It took Ilias of the Silent Assassins sneaking behind enemy lines to decapitate him for the slaughter to staunch.

The Bane's center lines held, yet they lost yard after yard to claws and fangs and sword and shield. So many of the enemy that the Fae royals and their kin couldn't choke the air from their throats fast enough, widely enough. Whatever advances the Fae's magic bought them did not slow Morath for long.

Morath's beasts pushed them northward that first day. And into the night.

And at dawn the next day.

By nightfall on the second, even the Bane's line had buckled.

Still Morath did not stop coming.

CHAPTER 23

Elide had never seen such a place as Doranelle.

The City of Rivers, they called it. She'd never imagined that a city could be built in the heart of several as they met and poured into a mighty basin.

She didn't let the awe show on her face as she strode through the winding, neat streets.

Fear was another companion that she kept at bay. With the Fae's heightened sense of smell, they could detect things like emotion. And though a good dose of fear would aid in her cover, too much would spell her doom.

Yet this place *seemed* like a paradise. Pink and blue flowers draped from windowsills; little canals wended between some of the streets, ferrying people in bright, long boats.

She'd never seen so many Fae, had never thought they'd be utterly normal. Well, as normal as possible, with their grace and those ears and canines. Along with the animals rushing around her, flitting past, so many forms she couldn't keep track of them. All perfectly content to go about their daily business, buying everything from crusty loaves of bread to jugs of some sort of oil to vibrant swaths of fabric.

Yet ruling over everything, squatting in the palace on the eastern side of Doranelle, was Maeve. And this city, Rowan had told Elide, had been built from stone to keep Brannon or any of his descendants from razing it to the ground.

Elide fought the limp that grew with each step farther into the city— farther away from Gavriel's magic. She'd left them in the forested foot-hills where they'd camped the night before, and Lorcan had again tried to argue against her going. But she'd rummaged through their various packs until she'd found what she needed: berries Gavriel had gathered yester-day, a spare belt and dark green cape from Rowan, a wrinkled white shirt from Lorcan, and a tiny mirror he used for shaving.

She hadn't said anything when she'd found the white strips of linen at the bottom of Lorcan's bag. Waiting for her next cycle. She hadn't been able to find the words, anyway. Not with what it would crumple in her chest to even think them.

Elide kept her shoulders loose, though her face remained tight as she paused at the edge of a pretty little square around a burbling fountain. Vendors and shoppers milled about, chatting in the midmorning sunshine. Elide paused by the square's arched entrance, putting her back to it, and fished the little mirror out of her cloak pocket, careful not to jostle the knives hidden there as well.

She flicked open the compact, frowning at her reflection—half of the expression not entirely faked. She'd crushed the berries at dawn and carefully lined her eyes with the juices, turning them red-rimmed and miserable-looking. As if she'd been weeping for weeks.

Indeed, the face that pouted back at her was rather wretched.

But it wasn't the reflection she wanted to see. But rather the square behind her. Surveying it outright might raise too many questions, but if she was merely staring into a compact mirror, no more than a self-conscious girl trying to fix her frazzled appearance . . . Elide smoothed some strands of her hair while monitoring the square beyond.

A hub of sorts. Two taverns lined its sides, judging by the wine barrels that served as tables out front and the empty glasses atop them, yet to be collected. Between the two taverns, one seemed to attract more males, some in warrior garb. Of the three squares she'd visited, the taverns she'd spotted, this was the only one with soldiers.

Perfect.

Elide smoothed her hair again, shut the compact, and turned back to the square, lifting her chin. A girl trying to muster some dignity.

Let them see what they wanted to see, let them look at the white shirt she'd donned in lieu of the leather witches' jacket, the green cape draped over herself belted across the middle, and think her an unfashionable, unworldly traveler. A girl far out of her element in this lovely, well-dressed city.

She approached the seven Fae lounging outside the tavern, sizing up who talked most, laughed loudest, who the five males and two females often turned to. One of the females wasn't a warrior, but rather clothed in soft, feminine pants and a cornflower-blue tunic that fit her lush figure like a glove.

Elide marked the one who they seemed to glance to the most in confirmation and hope of approval. A broad-shouldered female, her dark hair cropped close to her head. She bore armor on her shoulders and wrists—finer than what the other males wore. Their commander, then.

Elide lingered a few feet away, a hand rising to clutch her cape where it draped across her heart, the other fiddling with the golden ring on her finger, the invaluable heirloom little more than a lover's keepsake. Gnawing on her lip, she cast uncertain, darting eyes on the soldiers, on the tavern. Sniffled a little.

The other female—the one in the fine blue clothes—noticed her first. She was beautiful, Elide realized. Her dark hair falling in a thick, glossy braid down her back, her golden-brown skin shone with an inner light. Her eyes were soft with kindness. And concern.

Elide took that concern as invitation and stumbled up to them, head bowing. "I—I—I'm sorry to interrupt," she blurted, speaking more to the dark-haired beauty.

The stammer had always made people uncomfortable, had always made them foolishly off guard and eager to get away. To tell her what she needed to know.

"Is something wrong?" The female's voice was husky—lovely. The sort of voice Elide had always imagined great beauties possessing, the sort of voice that made men fall all over themselves. From the way some of the males around her had been smiling, Elide had no doubt the female had that effect on them, too.

Elide wobbled her lip, chewed on it. "I—I was looking for someone. He said he'd be here, but . . ." She glanced to the warriors, and toyed with the ring on her finger again. "I s-s-saw your uniforms and thought y-you might know him."

The merriment of the little company had died out, replaced by wariness. And pity—from the beauty. Either at the stutter or what she so clearly saw: a young woman pining for a lover who likely was not there.

"What's his name?" asked the taller female, perhaps the other's sister, judging by their same dusky skin and dark hair.

Elide swallowed hard enough to make her throat bob rather pathetically. "I—I hate to bother you," she demurred. "But you all looked very k-k-kind."

One of the males muttered something about getting another round of drinks, and two of his companions decided to join him. The two males who lingered seemed inclined to go as well, but a sharp look from their commander had them staying.

"It's not a bother," the beauty said, waving a manicured hand. She was as short as Elide, though she carried herself like a queen. "Would you like us to fetch you some refreshments?"

People were easy to flatter, easy to trick, regardless of whether they had pointy ears or round.

Elide stepped closer. "No, thank you. I wouldn't want to trouble y-you."

The female's nostrils flared as Elide halted close enough to touch them. No doubt smelling the weeks on the road. But she politely said nothing, though her eyes roved over Elide's face.

"Your friend's name," the commander urged, her gruff voice the opposite of her sister's.

"Cairn," Elide whispered. "His name is Cairn."

One of the males swore; the other scanned Elide from head to toe.

But the two females had gone still.

"H-he serves the queen," Elide said, eyes leaping from face to face, the portrait of hope. "Do you know him?"

"We know him," the commander said, her face dark. "You—you are his lover?"

Elide willed her face to redden, thinking of all the mortifying moments on the road: her cycle, having to explain when she needed to relieve herself . . . "I need to speak with him," was all Elide said. Learning Maeve's whereabouts would come later.

The dark-haired beauty said a shade too quietly, "What is your name, child?"

"Finnula," Elide lied, naming her nursemaid.

"Here's a bit of advice," the second male drawled, sipping from his ale. "If you escaped Cairn, don't go looking for him again."

His commander shot him a look. "Cairn is blood-sworn to our queen."

"Still makes him a prick," the male said.

The female growled, viciously enough that the male wisely went to see about their drinks.

Elide made her shoulders curve inward. "You—you know him, then?"

"Cairn was supposed to meet you here?" the beauty asked instead.
Elide nodded.

The two females exchanged glances. The commander said, "We don't know where he is."

Lie. She saw the look between them, between sisters. The decision to not tell her, either to protect the helpless mortal girl they believed her to be, or out of some loyalty to him. Or perhaps to all Fae who decided to find beds in mortal realms and then ignore the consequences months later. Lorcan had been the result of such a union, and then discarded to the mercy of these streets.

The thought was enough to set her grinding her teeth, but Elide kept her jaw relaxed.

Don't be angry, Finnula had taught her. *Be smart.*

She made note of that. Not to appear too pathetic at the next tavern. Or like a jilted lover who might be carrying his child.

For she'd have to go to another one. And if she got an answer the next time, she'd have to go to another after that to confirm it.

"Is—is the queen in residence?" Elide said, that beseeching, whining voice grating on her own ears. "He s-s-said he travels with her now, but if she is not here—"

"Her Majesty is not at home," the commander said, sharply enough that Elide knew her patience was wearing thin. Elide didn't allow her knees to buckle, didn't allow her shoulders to sag with anything but what they took to be disappointment. "But where Cairn is, as I said, we do not know."

Maeve was not here. They had that in their favor, at least. Whether it was luck or due to their own scheming, she didn't care. But Cairn . . . She'd learn nothing more from these females. So Elide bowed her head. "Th-thank you."

She backed away before the females could say more, and made a good show of waiting by the fountain for five minutes. Fifteen. The clock on the square struck the hour, and she knew they were still watching as she did her best attempt at a dejected walk to the other entrance to the square.

She kept it up for a few blocks, wandering with no direction, until she ducked into a narrow pass-through and heaved a breath.

Maeve was not in Doranelle. How long would that remain true?

She had to find Cairn—swiftly. Had to make her next performance count.

She'd need to be less pathetic, less needy, less weepy. Perhaps she'd added too much redness around her eyes.

Elide fished out the mirror. Swiping her pinky under one eye, she rubbed at some of the red stain. It didn't budge. Moistening the tip of her pinky with her tongue, she ran her finger across her lower lid again. It lessened—slightly.

She was about to do it again when movement flashed in the mirror.

Elide whirled, but too late.

The dark-haired beauty from the tavern was standing behind her.

Lorcan had never felt the weight of the hours so heavily upon him.

While he scouted the southern border of that army, watching the soldiers on their rotations, noting the main arteries of the camp, he kept one eye upon the city.

His city—or it had been. He'd never imagined, even during the childhood he'd spent surviving in its shadows, that it would become an enemy stronghold. That Maeve, while she'd whipped and punished him for any defiance or for her own amusement, would become as great a foe as Erawan. And to send Elide into Maeve's clutches—it had taken all of his will to let her walk away.

If Elide was captured, if she was found out, he wouldn't hear of it, know of it. She had no magic to wield, save for the keen eyes of the goddess at her shoulder and an uncanny ability to remain unnoticed, to play into expectations. There would be no flash of power, no signal to alert him that she was in danger.

But he stayed away. Had watched her cross that bridge earlier, his breath tight in his chest, and pass unquestioned and unnoticed by the guards posted at either end. While Maeve did not allow demi-Fae or humans to live within Doranelle's borders without proving their worth, they could still visit—briefly.

Then he'd gone about scouting. He knew Whitethorn had ordered him to study the southern edge, this edge, because it was precisely where she'd emerge. If she emerged.

Whitethorn and Gavriel had divided up the other camps, the prince claiming the west and north, the Lion taking the eastern camp above the waterfall's basin.

The afternoon sun was sinking toward the distant sea when they returned to their little base.

"Anything?" Rowan's question rumbled to them.

Lorcan shook his head. "Not from Elide, not from my scouting. The sentries' rotations are strict, but not impenetrable. They posted scouts in the trees six miles up." He knew some of them. Had commanded them. Were they now his enemy?

Gavriel shifted and slumped onto a boulder, equally out of breath. "They've got aerial patrols on the eastern camp. And sentries out by the forest's border."

Rowan leaned against a towering pine and crossed his arms. "What manner of birds?"

"Raptors, mostly," Gavriel said. Highly trained soldiers, then. They'd always been the sharpest of the scouts. "I didn't recognize any from your House."

They either had all been in that armada, now in Terrasen, or Maeve had put them down.

Rowan ran a hand over his jaw. "The western plain camp is as tightly guarded. The northern one less so, but the wolves in the passes are likely doing half the work for them."

They didn't bother to discuss what that army might have been gathered to do. Where it might be headed. If Maeve's defeat off the Eyllwe coast might be enough to lead her into an alliance with Morath—and to bring this army to crush Terrasen at last.

Lorcan gazed down the wooded hillside, ears straining for any cracking branches or leaves.

A half hour. He'd wait a half hour before going down that hill.

He forced himself to listen to Whitethorn and Gavriel lay out entry points and exit strategies for each camp, forced himself to join in that debate. Forced himself to also discuss the possible entrances and exits from Doranelle itself, where they might go in the city, how they might get over and back across without bringing down the wrath of that army. An army they'd once overseen and commanded. None of them mentioned it, though Gavriel kept glancing to the tattoos inked on his hands. How many more lives would he need to add before they were through? His soldiers not felled by enemy blows, but by his own blade?

The sun inched closer to the horizon. Lorcan began pacing.

Too long. It had taken too long.

The others had fallen silent, too. Gazing down the hill. Waiting.

A slight tremor rocked Lorcan's hands, and he balled them into fists, squeezing hard. Five minutes. He'd go in five minutes, Aelin Galathynius and their plan be damned.

Aelin had been trained to endure torture. Elide . . . He could see those scars on her from the shackles. See her maimed foot and ankle. She had endured too much suffering and terror already. He couldn't allow her to face another heartbeat of it—

Twigs snapped under light feet, and Lorcan shot upright, a hand going to his sword.

Whitethorn thumbed free the hatchet at his side, a knife appearing in his other hand, and Gavriel drew his sword.

But then a two-note whistle echoed, and Lorcan's legs wobbled so violently he sat back onto the rock where he'd been perched.

Gavriel whistled back, and Lorcan was grateful for it. He wasn't sure he had the breath.

Then she was there, panting from the climb, her cheeks rosy in the cool night air.

"What happened?" Whitethorn asked.

Lorcan scanned her face, her posture.

She was fine. She was unhurt. There was no enemy on her tail.

Elide's eyes met his. Wary and uncertain. "I met someone."

⌇

Elide had thought she was about to die.

Or had at least believed that she was going to be sold out to Maeve when she'd faced the dark-haired beauty in the shadowed alley.

She'd told herself, in those heartbeats, that she'd do her best to withstand the torture sure to come, to keep her companions' location secret even if they broke apart her body. But the prospect of what they'd do to her . . .

The female held up a delicate hand. "I only wish to talk. In private." She gestured farther down the alley, to a doorstop covered with a metal awning. To shield them from any eyes—those on the ground and above.

Elide followed her, a hand sliding to the knife in her pocket. The female led the way, no weapons to be seen, her gait unhurried.

But when they halted in the shadows beneath the awning, the female held up a hand once more.

Golden flame danced between her fingers.

Elide recoiled, and the fire vanished as quickly as it had appeared.

"My name is Essar," the female said softly. "I am a friend—of your friends, I believe."

Elide said nothing.

"Cairn is a monster," Essar said, taking a step closer. "Stay far from him."

"I need to find him."

"You played the part of his mistreated lover well enough. You have to know something about him. What he does."

"If you know where he is, please tell me." She wasn't above begging.

Essar ran an eye over Elide. Then she said, "He was in this city until yesterday. Then he went out to the eastern camp." She pointed with a thumb over a shoulder. "He's there now."

"How do you know?"

"Because he's not terrorizing the patrons of every fine establishment in this town, glutting himself on the coin Maeve gave him when he took the blood oath."

Elide blinked. She had hoped some of the Fae might be opposed to Maeve, especially after the battle in Eyllwe, but to find such outright distaste . . .

Essar then added, "And because my sister—the soldier you spoke with—told me. She saw him in the camp this morning, smirking like a cat."

"Why should I believe you?"

"Because you are wearing Lorcan's shirt, and Rowan Whitethorn's cloak. If you do not believe me, inform them who told you and they will."

Elide cocked her head to the side.

Essar said softly, "Lorcan and I were involved for a time."

They were in the midst of war, and had traveled for thousands of miles to find their queen, and yet the tightness that coiled in Elide's gut at those words somehow found space. Lorcan's lover. This delicate beauty with a bedroom voice had been Lorcan's *lover*.

"I'll be missed if I'm gone for too long, but tell them who I am. Tell them that I told you. If it's Cairn they seek, that is where he shall be. His precise location, I don't know." Essar backed away a step. "Don't go asking after Cairn at other taverns. He isn't well regarded, even amongst the soldiers. And those who do follow him . . . You do not wish to attract their interest."

Essar made to turn away, but Elide blurted, "Where did Maeve go?"

Essar looked over her shoulder. Studied her. The female's eyes widened. "She has Aelin of the Wildfire," Essar breathed.

Elide said nothing, but Essar murmured, "That was . . . that was the power we felt the other night." Essar swept back toward Elide. Gripped her hands. "Where Maeve went a few days ago, I don't know. She did not announce it, did not take anyone with her. I often serve her, am asked to . . . It doesn't matter. What matters is Maeve is not here. But I do not know when she will return."

Relief again threatened to send Elide crumpling to the ground. The gods, it seemed, had not abandoned them just yet.

But if Maeve had taken Aelin to the outpost where they'd lied that the Valg prince had been contained . . .

Elide gripped Essar's hands, finding them warm and dry. "Does your sister know where Cairn resides in the camp?"

For long minutes, then an hour, they had talked. Essar left and returned with Dresenda, her sister. And in that alley, they had plotted.

Elide finished telling Rowan, Lorcan, and Gavriel what she'd learned. They sat in stunned silence for a long minute.

"Just before dawn," Elide repeated. "Dresenda said the watch on the eastern camp is weakest at dawn. That she'd find a way for the guards to be occupied. It's our only window."

Rowan was staring into the trees, as if he could see the layout of the camp, as if he were plotting his way in, way out.

"She didn't confirm if Aelin was in Cairn's tent, though," Gavriel cautioned. "Maeve is gone—Aelin might be with her, too."

"It's a risk we take," Rowan said. A risk, perhaps, they should have considered.

Elide glanced to Lorcan, who had been silent throughout. Even though it had been his lover who had helped them, perhaps guided by Anneith herself. Or at least had been tipped off by the scent on Elide's clothes.

"You think we can trust her?" Elide asked Lorcan, though she knew the answer.

Lorcan's dark eyes shifted to her. "Yes, though I don't see why she'd bother."

"She's a good female, that's why," Rowan said. At Elide's lifted brow, he explained, "Essar visited Mistward this spring. She met Aelin." He cut a glare toward Lorcan. "And asked me to tell *you* that she sends her best."

Elide hadn't seen anything that came close to pining in Essar's face, but gods, she was beautiful. And smart. And kind. And Lorcan had let her go, somehow.

Gavriel cut in, "If we move on the eastern camp, we need to figure out our plan now. Get into position. It's miles away."

Rowan gazed again toward that distant camp.

"If you're debating flying there right now," Lorcan growled, "then you'll deserve whatever misery comes of your stupidity." Rowan flashed his teeth, but Lorcan said, "We all go in. We all go out."

Elide nodded, in agreement for once. Lorcan seemed to stiffen in surprise.

Rowan arrived at that conclusion, too, because he crouched and plunged a knife into the mossy earth. "This is Cairn's tent," he said of the dagger, and fished for a nearby pinecone. "This is the southern entrance to the camp."

And so they planned.

~

Rowan had parted from his companions an hour ago, sending them to take up their positions.

They would not all go in, all go out.

Rowan would break into the eastern camp, taking the southernmost entrance. Gavriel and Lorcan would be waiting for his signal near the east entrance, hidden in the forest just beyond the rolling, grassy hills on that side of the camp. Ready to unleash hell when he sent a flare of his magic, diverting soldiers to their side while Rowan made his run for Aelin.

Elide would wait for them farther in that forest. Or flee, if things went badly.

She'd protested, but even Gavriel had told her that she was mortal. Untrained. And what she'd done today . . . Rowan didn't have the words to convey his gratitude for what Elide had done. The unexpected ally she'd found.

He trusted Essar. She'd never liked Maeve, had outright said she did not serve her with any willingness or pride. But these last few hours before dawn, when so many things could go wrong . . .

Maeve was not here. That much, at least, had gone right.

Rowan lingered in the steep hills above the southern entrance to the camp. He'd easily kept hidden from the sentries in the trees, his wind masking any trace of his scent.

Down below, spread across the grassy eastern plain, the army camp glittered.

She had to be there. Aelin had to be there.

If they had come so close but wound up being the very thing that had caused Maeve to take Aelin away again, to bring her along to the outpost . . .

Rowan pushed against the weight in his chest. The bond within him lay dark and slumbering. No indication of her proximity.

Essar had no idea that Aelin was being kept here until Elide informed her. How many others hadn't known? How well had Maeve hidden her?

If Aelin wasn't in that camp tomorrow, they'd find Cairn, at least. And get some answers then. Give him a taste of what he'd done—

Rowan shut out the thought. He didn't let himself think of what had been done to her.

He'd do that tomorrow, when he saw Cairn. When he repaid him for every moment of pain.

Overhead, the stars shone clear and bright, and though Mala had only once appeared to him at dawn, on the foothills across this very city, though she might be little more than a strange, mighty being from another world, he offered up a prayer anyway.

Then, he had begged Mala to protect Aelin from Maeve when they entered Doranelle, to give her strength and guidance, and to let her walk out alive. Then, he had begged Mala to let him remain with Aelin, the woman he loved. The goddess had been little more than a sunbeam in the rising dawn, and yet he had felt her smile at him.

Tonight, with only the cold fire of the stars for company, he begged her once more.

A curl of wind sent his prayer drifting to those stars, to the waxing moon silvering the camp, the river, the mountains.

He had killed his way across the world; he had gone to war and back more times than he cared to remember. And despite it all, despite the rage and despair and ice he'd wrapped around his heart, he'd still found Aelin. Every horizon he'd gazed toward, unable and unwilling to rest during those centuries, every mountain and ocean he'd seen and wondered what lay beyond . . . It had been her. It had been Aelin, the silent call of the mating bond driving him, even when he could not feel it.

They'd walked this dark path together back to the light. He would not let the road end here.

CHAPTER 24

The Crochans ignored her. And ignored the Thirteen. A few hissed insults as they passed, but one glance from Manon and the Thirteen kept their fists balled at their sides.

The Crochans remained in the camp for a week to tend to their wounded, and so Manon and the Thirteen had remained as well, ignored and hated.

"What is this place?" Manon asked Glennis as she found the crone polishing the handle of a gold-bound broom beside the fire. Two others lay on a cloak nearby. Menial work for the witch in charge of this camp.

"This is an ancient camp—one of the oldest we claim." Glennis's knobbed fingers flew over the broom handle. "Each of the seven Great Hearths has a fire here, as do many others." Indeed, there were far more than seven in the camp. "It was a gathering place for us after the war, and since then, it had become a place to usher in some of our younger witches to adulthood. It is a rite we've developed over the years—to send them into the deep wilds for a few weeks to hunt and survive with only their brooms and a knife. We remain here while they do so."

Manon asked quietly, "Do you know what our initiation rite is?"

Glennis's face tightened. "I do. We all do." Which hearth had the witch she'd killed at age sixteen belonged to? What had her grandmother done with the Crochan heart she'd brought back in a box to Blackbeak Keep, wearing her enemy's cloak as a trophy?

But Manon asked, "When do you head to Eyllwe?"

"Tomorrow. Those who were the most gravely wounded in the skirmish have healed enough to travel—or survive here on their own."

Manon's gut tightened, but she shut out the regret.

Glennis extended one of the brooms to Manon, its base bound with ordinary metal threads. "Do you fly south with us?"

Manon took the broom, the wood zinging against her hand. The wind whispered at her ear of the fast, wicked current between the peaks above.

She and the Thirteen had already decided days ago. If south was where the Crochans went, then south was where they would go. Even if each passing day might spell doom for those in the North.

"We fly with you," Manon said.

Glennis nodded. "That broom belongs to a black-haired witch named Karsyn." The crone jerked her chin toward the tents behind Manon. "She's on duty by your wyverns."

***

Dorian decided he didn't need a hidden place to practice. Which was lucky, since there was no such thing as privacy in the Crochans' camp. Not inside the camp, and certainly not around it, not with the sharp eyes of their sentinels patrolling day and night.

Which is how he wound up sitting before Vesta at Glennis's hearth, the red-haired witch half asleep with boredom. "Learning shifting," she groused, yawning for the tenth time that hour, "seems like a colossal waste of time." She flicked a snow-white hand toward the makeshift training ring where the Thirteen kept up their honed bodies and instincts. "You could be sparring with Lin right now."

"I just watched Lin nearly knock Imogen's teeth down her throat. Forgive me if I'm in no mood to get into the ring with her."

Vesta arched an auburn brow. "No male swaggering from you, then."

"I like my teeth where they are." He sighed. "I'm trying to concentrate."

None of the witches, even Manon, had questioned why he practiced. He'd only mentioned, nearly a week ago, that the spider had made him wonder if he might be able to shift, using his raw magic, and they'd shrugged.

Their focus was on the Crochans. On the trip to Eyllwe that would likely happen any day now.

He hadn't heard any mention of a war band gathering, but if it could divide Morath's forces even slightly to venture south to deal with them, if it distracted Erawan when Dorian went to the Valg king's stronghold . . . He'd accept it.

He'd already offered Manon and Glennis what he knew regarding the kingdom and its rulers. Nehemia's parents and two younger brothers. Adarlan's empire had done its work thoroughly in decimating Eyllwe's army, so any hope on that front was impossible, but if they mustered a few thousand soldiers to head northward . . . It'd be a boon for his friends.

If they could survive, it would be enough.

Dorian closed his eyes, and Vesta fell silent. For days, she'd sat with him when her training and scouting permitted it, watching for any of the shifting that he attempted: changing his hair, his skin, his eyes.

None of it occurred.

His magic had touched that stolen shifter's power—had learned it just enough before he'd killed the spider.

It was now a matter of convincing his magic to *become* like that shifter's power. Whether it had ever been done with raw magic before, he did not know.

Be what you wish, Cyrene had told him.

Nothing. He wished to be nothing.

But Dorian kept peering inward. Into every hollow, empty corner. He need only do it long enough. To master the shifting. To sneak into Morath and find the third key. To then offer up all he was and had been to the Lock and the gate.

And then it would be over. For Erawan, yes, and for him.

Even if it would leave Hollin with the right to the throne. Hollin, who had been sired by a Valg-infested man as well. Had the demon passed any traits to his brother?

The boy had been beastly—but had he been human?

Hollin had not killed their father. Shattered the castle. Let Sorscha die.

Dorian hadn't dared ask Damaris. Wasn't certain what he'd do should the sword reveal what he was, deep down.

So Dorian peered inward, to where his magic flowed in him, to where it could move between flame and water and ice and wind.

But no matter how he willed it, how he pictured brown hair or paler skin or freckles, nothing happened.

~

She was no messenger, but Manon took the hint—and the offer. Along with three other brooms, all for witches across the camp.

It would not be enough to fly with them to Eyllwe. No, she'd have to *learn* about them. Each of these witches.

Asterin, who'd been monitoring from across the fire, fell into step beside her, taking up two of the brooms. "I forgot they used the redwood," her Second said, studying the brooms in her arms. "A hell of a lot easier to carve than the ironwood."

Manon could still feel how her own hands had ached during the long days she'd whittled down her first broom from the log of ironwood she'd found deep in Oakwald. The first two ventures had resulted in snapped shafts, and she'd resolved to carve her broom more carefully. Three tries, one for each face of the Goddess.

She'd been thirteen, mere weeks past her first bleeding, which had brought about the zipping current of power that called to the wind, that flowed through the brooms and carried them into the skies. Each stroke of the chisel, each pound of the hammer that transformed the block of near-impenetrable material, had transferred that power into the emerging broom itself.

"Where'd you leave yours?" Manon asked.

Asterin shrugged. "Somewhere at Blackbeak Keep."

Manon nodded. Hers was currently discarded in the back of a closet in her room at her grandmother's seat of power. She'd thrown it in there after magic had vanished, the broom little more than a cleaning tool without it.

"I suppose we won't be retrieving them now," Asterin said.

"No, we won't," Manon said, scanning the skies. "We fly with the Crochans to Eyllwe tomorrow. To rendezvous with whatever human war band they're to meet."

Asterin's mouth tightened. "Perhaps we'll convince all of them—the Crochans, the Eyllwe war band—to head north."

Perhaps. If they were lucky enough. If they did not squander so much time that Erawan crushed the North into dust.

They reached the first of the witches Glennis had indicated, and Asterin said nothing as Manon motioned her Second to pass over the broom.

The Crochan's nose wrinkled with distaste as she let the broom dangle from two fingers. "Now I'll need it cleaned again."

Asterin gave her a crooked smile that meant trouble was swiftly approaching.

So Manon nudged her Second into another walk, wending between the tents in search of the other owners.

"You really think this is worth our time?" Asterin muttered when the second, then the third witch sneered upon receiving their brooms. "Playing servant to these pampered princesses?"

"I hope so," Manon murmured back as they reached the last of the witches. Karsyn. The dark-haired Crochan was staring toward the ring of wyverns, just where Glennis had said she'd be.

Asterin cleared her throat, and the witch turned, her olive-skinned face tightening.

But she didn't sneer. Didn't hiss.

Mission done, Asterin turned away. But Manon said to the Crochan, jerking her chin toward the wyverns, "It's different from using the brooms. Faster, deadlier, but you also have to feed and water them."

Karsyn's green eyes were wary—but curious. She glanced again at the wyverns huddled against the cold, Asterin's blue mare pressed into Abraxos's side, his wing draped over her.

Manon said, "Erawan made them, using methods we're not quite sure of. He took an ancient template and brought it to life." For there had been wyverns in Adarlan before—long ago. "He meant to breed a host of thoughtless killers, but some did not turn out as such."

Asterin kept quiet for once.

Karsyn spoke at last. "Your wyvern seems like more of a dog than anything."

It was not an insult, Manon reminded herself. The Crochans *kept* dogs as pets. Adored them, as humans did. "His name is Abraxos," Manon said. "He is . . . different."

"He and the blue one are mates."

Asterin started. "They're what?"

The Crochan pointed to the blue mare huddled beside Abraxos. "He is smaller, yet he dotes on her. Nuzzles her when no one is looking."

Manon exchanged a glance with Asterin. Their mounts incessantly flirted, yes, but to *mate*—

"Interesting," Manon managed to say.

"You didn't know they did such things?" Karsyn's brows knotted.

"We knew they bred." Asterin stepped in at last. "But we haven't witnessed it being for . . . choice."

"For love," the Crochan said, and Manon nearly rolled her eyes. "These beasts, despite their dark master, are capable of love."

Nonsense, yet some kernel in her realized it to be true. Instead, Manon said, though she already knew, "What's your name?"

But wariness again flooded Karsyn's eyes, as if remembering whom she spoke to, that there were others who might see them conversing. "Thank you for the broom," the witch said, and strode between the tents.

At least one of the Crochans had spoken to her. Perhaps this journey to Eyllwe would offer her the chance to speak to more. Even if she could feel each passing hour and minute weighing upon them.

Hurry northward, the wind sang, day and night. *Hurry, Blackbeak.*

When Karsyn was gone, Asterin remained staring at Abraxos and Narene, scratching her hair. "You really think they're mated?"

Abraxos lifted his head from where it rested atop Narene's back and looked toward them, as if to say, *It took you long enough to figure it out.*

"What am I supposed to be watching for, exactly?"

Sitting knee to knee in their tiny tent, the wind howling outside, Manon's golden eyes narrowed as she peered into Dorian's face. "My eyes," he said. "Just tell me if they change color."

She growled. "This shape-shifting is really a pressing thing to learn?"

"Indulge me," he purred, and reached inward, his magic flaring.

Brown. You will change from blue to brown.

Liar—he supposed he was a liar for keeping his true reasons from her. He didn't need Damaris to confirm it.

She might forbid him from going to Morath, but there was another possibility, even worse than that.

That she would insist on going with him.

Manon gave him a look that might have sent a lesser man running. "They're still blue."

Gods above, she was beautiful. He wondered when it would stop feeling like a betrayal to think so.

Dorian took a long breath, concentrating again. Ignoring the whispering presence of the two keys in his jacket pocket. "Tell me if it changes at all."

"It's that different from your magic?"

Dorian sat back, bracing his arms behind him as he sought the words to explain. "It's not like other sorts of magic, where it flows through my veins, and half a thought has it changing from ice to flame to water."

She studied him, head angled in a way he'd witnessed the wyverns doing. Right before they devoured a goat whole. "Which do you like the best?"

An unusually personal question. Even though this past week, thanks to the tent's relative warmth and privacy, they'd spent hours tangling in the blankets now beneath them.

He'd never had anything like her. He sometimes wondered if she'd never had anything like him, either. He'd seen how often she found her pleasure when he took the reins, when her body writhed beneath his and she lost control entirely.

But the hours in this tent hadn't yielded any sort of intimacy. Only blessed distraction. For both of them. He was glad of it, he told himself. None of this could end well. For either of them.

"I like the ice best," Dorian admitted at last, realizing he'd let the silence drip on. "It was the first element that came out of me—I don't know why."

"You're not a cold person."

He arched a brow. "Is that your professional opinion?"

Manon studied him. "You can descend to those levels when you are angry, when your friends are threatened. But you are not cold, not at heart. I've seen men who are, and you are not."

"Neither are you," he said a bit quietly.

The wrong thing to say.

Manon stiffened, her chin lifting. "I am one hundred seventeen years old," she said flatly. "I have spent the majority of that time killing. Don't convince yourself that the events of the past few months have erased that."

"Keep telling yourself that." He doubted anyone had ever spoken to her that baldly—relished that he now did, and kept his throat intact.

She snarled in his face. "You're a fool if you believe the fact that I am their queen wipes away the truth that I have killed scores of Crochans."

"That fact will always remain. It's how you make it count now that matters."

Make it count. Aelin had said as much back in those initial days after he'd been freed of the collar. He tried not to wonder whether the icy bite of Wyrdstone would soon clamp around his neck once more.

"I am not a softhearted Crochan. I will never be, even if I wear their crown of stars."

He'd heard the whispers about that crown amongst the Crochans this week—about whether it would be found at last. Rhiannon Crochan's crown of stars, stolen from her dying body by Baba Yellowlegs herself. Where it had gone after Aelin had killed the Matron, Dorian had not the faintest idea. If it had stayed with that strange carnival she'd traveled with, it could be anywhere. Could have been sold for quick coin.

Manon went on, "If that is what the Crochans expect me to become before they join in this war, then I will let them venture to Eyllwe tomorrow alone."

"Is it so bad, to care?" The gods knew he'd been struggling to do so himself.

"I don't know *how* to," she growled.

Ridiculous. An outright lie. Perhaps it was because of the high likelihood that he'd be collared again at Morath, perhaps it was because he was a king who'd left his kingdom in an enemy's grip, but Dorian found himself saying, "You do care. You know it, too. It's what makes you so damn scared of all this."

Her golden eyes raged, but she said nothing.

"Caring doesn't make you weak," he offered.

"Then why don't you heed your own advice?"

"I care." His temper rose to meet hers. And he decided to hell with it—decided to let go of that leash he'd put on himself. Let go of that restraint. "I care about more than I should. I even care about you."

Another wrong thing to say.

Manon stood—as high as the tent would allow. "Then you're a fool." She shoved on her boots and stomped into the frigid night.

I even care about you.

Manon scowled as she turned in her sleep, wedged between Asterin and Sorrel. Only hours remained until they were to move out—to head to Eyllwe and whatever force might be waiting to ally with the Crochans. And in need of help.

Caring doesn't make you weak.

The king was a fool. Little more than a boy. What did he know of anything?

Still the words burrowed under her skin, her bones. *Is it so bad, to care?*

She didn't know. Didn't want to know.

Dawn was not too far off when a warm body slid beside his.

Dorian said into the darkness, "Three to a tent isn't too comfortable, is it?"

"I didn't come back because I agree with you." Manon yanked the blankets over herself.

Dorian smiled slightly, and fell asleep once more, letting his magic warm them both.

When they awoke, something sharp in his chest had dulled—just a fraction.

But Manon was frowning down at him. Dorian sat up, groaning as he stretched his arms as far as the tent would allow. "What is it?" he asked when her brow remained furrowed.

Manon pulled on her boots, then her cape. "Your eyes are brown."

He lifted a hand to his face, but she was already gone.

Dorian stared after her, the camp already hurrying to be off.

Where that edge had dulled in his chest, his magic now flowed freer. As if it, too, had been freed from those inner restraints he'd loosened slightly last night. What he'd opened up, revealed to her. A sort of freedom, that letting go.

The sun was barely in the sky when they began the long flight to Eyllwe.

CHAPTER 25

Cairn had let her rot in the box for a while.

It was quieter here, no endless, droning roar of the river.

Nothing but that pressure, building and building and building under her skin, in her head. She could not outrun it, even in oblivion.

But still the irons dug in, chafing against her skin. Wetness pooled beneath her as time wheeled by. As Maeve undoubtedly brought that collar closer with each hour.

She couldn't remember the last time she'd eaten.

She drifted down again, into a pocket of the dark, where she told herself that story—*the* story—over and over.

Who she was, what she was, what she stood to destroy should she yield to the near-airlessness of the box, to the rising strain.

It wouldn't matter, though. Once that collar went around her neck, how long would it take until the Valg prince within pried from her everything Maeve wished to know? Violated and delved into every inner barrier to mine those vital secrets?

Cairn would begin again soon. It would be wretched. And then the healers would return with their sweet-smelling smoke, as they had come these months, these years, however long it had been.

But she'd seen beyond them, for an instant. Had seen canvas fabric draped overhead, rushes covered with woven rugs beneath their sandaled feet. Braziers smoldered all around.

A tent. She was in a tent. Murmuring sounded outside—not nearby, but close enough for her Fae hearing to pick up. People speaking in both her tongue and the Old Language, someone muttering about the cramped camp conditions.

An army camp, full of Fae.

A more secure location, Cairn had said. Maeve had wanted her here, to guard her from Morath. Until Maeve clamped the cold Wyrdstone collar around her neck.

But then oblivion swept in. When she awoke, cleaned and without an ache, she knew Cairn was soon to begin. His canvas had been wiped bare, ready for him to paint red. His terrible, grand finale, not to pry information from her, not with Maeve's triumph at hand, but for his own pleasure.

Aelin was ready, too.

They hadn't chained her to an altar this time. But to a metal table, set within the center of the large tent. He'd had them bring in the comforts of home—or whatever Cairn might consider home.

A tall chest of drawers stood by one canvas wall. She doubted it held clothes.

Fenrys lay beside it, head on his front paws, sleeping. For once, sleeping. Grief laid heavy on him, dulling his coat, dimming his bright eyes.

Another table had been placed near the one on which she lay. A cloth covered three humped objects on it. Beside the one closest, a patch of black velvet also had been left out. For the instruments he'd use on her. The way a merchant might display his finest jewels.

Two chairs sat facing each other on the other side of the second table, before the large brazier full to the brim with crackling logs. The smoke curled upward, up, up—

A small hole had been cut into the tent's ceiling. And through it . . .

Aelin couldn't fight the trembling in her mouth at the night sky, at the pinpricks of light shining in it.

Stars. Just two, but there were stars overhead. The sky itself . . . it was not the heaviness of full night, but rather a murky, graying black.

Dawn. Likely an hour or so away, if the stars remained out. Perhaps she would last long enough to see sunlight.

Fenrys's eyes shot open, and he lifted his head, ears twitching.

Aelin took steadying breaths as Cairn shoved through the tent flaps, offering a glimpse of fires and lightening darkness beyond. Nothing else.

"Enjoy your rest?"

Aelin said nothing.

Cairn ran a hand down the metal table's edge. "I've been debating what to do with you, you know. How to really savor this, make it special for us both before our time is through."

Fenrys's snarl rumbled through the tent. Cairn just swept the cloth from the smaller table.

Low metal dishes on three legs, piled with unlit logs.

Aelin stiffened as he hauled one over, and set it beneath the foot of the metal table. A smaller brazier, its legs cut short for its bowl to hover barely above the ground.

He set the second brazier below the table's center. The third at the head.

"We've played with your hands before," Cairn said, straightening. Aelin began shaking, began tugging on the chains anchoring her arms above her head. His smile grew. "Let's see how your entire body reacts to flame without your special little gift. Perhaps you'll burn like the rest of us."

Aelin yanked uselessly, her feet sliding against the still-cool metal.

Not like this—

Cairn reached into his pocket and withdrew some flint.

This wasn't just a breaking of her body. But a breaking of *her*—of the fire she'd come to love. To destroy the part of her that sang.

He'd melt her skin and bones until she feared the flame, until she hated it, as she hated those healers who had come again and again to repair her body, to hide what was real from what had been a dream.

Fenrys's snarl rolled on, endless.

Cairn said mildly, "You can scream all you like, if it pleases you."

The table would turn red-hot, and the scent of burning flesh would fill her nose, and she wouldn't be able to stop it, stop him; she would sob in agony, as the burns went so deep, through skin and into bone—

The pressure in her body, her head, faded. It became secondary as Cairn fished a rolled pouch from his other pocket. He set it upon the swath of black velvet, and she could make out the indents of the slender tools inside. "For when heating the table grows boring," he said, patting the tool kit. "I want to see how far the burns go inside your skin."

Bile shot up her throat as he weighed the flint in his hands and stepped closer.

She began fraying then, who she was and had been melting away as her own body would soon melt when this table heated.

The hand she'd been dealt. It was the hand she had been dealt, and she would endure it. Even as a word took form on her tongue.

Please.

She tried to swallow it. Tried to keep it locked in as Cairn crouched beside the table, flint raised.

You do not yield.

You do not yield.

You do not yield.

"Wait."

The word was a rasp.

Cairn paused. Rose from his crouch. "Wait?"

Aelin shook, her breathing ragged. "Wait."

Cairn crossed his arms. "Do you have something you'd like to say at last?"

He'd let her promise anything to him, to Maeve. And then would still light those fires. Maeve would not hear of her yielding for days.

Aelin made herself meet his stare, her gauntlet-covered fingers pressing into the iron slab beneath her.

One last chance.

She'd seen the stars overhead. It was as great a gift as any she'd received, greater than the jewels and gowns and art she'd once coveted and amassed in Rifthold. The last gift she would receive, if she played the hand she'd been dealt. If she played him right.

To end this, end her. Before Maeve could put the Wyrdstone collar around her neck.

Dawn neared, the stars dimming one by one.

Rowan lurked by the southernmost entrance to the camp, his power thrumming.

Cairn's tent lay in the center of the camp. A mile and a half lay between Rowan and his prey.

When the guards began their shift change, he'd rip the air from their lungs. Would rip the air from the lungs of every soldier in his path. How many would he know? How many had he trained? A small part of him prayed the number would be few. That if they knew him, they'd be wise and stand down. He had no intention of stopping, though.

Rowan freed the hatchet from his side, a long knife already glinting in the other.

A killing calm had settled over him hours ago. Days ago. Months ago.

Only a few more minutes.

The six guards at the camp entrance stirred from their watches. The sentries in the trees behind him, unaware of his presence this night, would spot the action the moment their fellow sentries went down. And certainly spot him the moment he broke from the trees, crossing the narrow strip of grass between the forest and camp.

He'd debated flying in, but the aerial patrols had circled all night, and if he faced them, expending more power than he needed to while also fighting off the arrows and magic sure to be firing from below . . . He'd waste vital reserves of his energy. So on foot it would be, a hard, brutal run to the center of the camp. Then out, either with Aelin or Cairn.

Still alive. He had to keep Cairn alive for now. Long enough to clear this camp and reach a spot where they could slice every answer from him.

Go, a quiet voice urged. *Go now.*

Essar's sister had advised to wait until dawn. When the shift was weakest. When she'd make sure certain guards didn't arrive on time.

Go now.

That voice, warm and yet insistent, tugged. Pushed him toward the camp.

Rowan bared his teeth, his breathing roughening. Lorcan and Gavriel would be waiting for the signal, a flare of his magic, when he got far enough into the camp.

Now, Prince.

He knew that voice, had felt its warmth. And if the Lady of Light herself whispered at his ear . . .

Rowan didn't give himself time to consider, to rage at the goddess who urged him to act but would gladly sacrifice his mate to the Lock.

So Rowan steeled himself, willing ice into his veins.

Calm. Precise. Deadly.

Every swing of his blades, every blast of his power, had to count.

Rowan speared his magic toward the camp entrance.

The guards grabbed for their throats, feeble shields wobbling around them. Rowan shattered them with half a thought, his magic tearing the air from their lungs, their blood.

They went down a heartbeat later.

Sentries shouted from the trees, orders of "Sound the alarm!" ringing out.

But Rowan was already running. And the sentries in the trees, their shouts lingering on the wind as they gasped for breath, were already dead.

⁓

The sky slowly bled toward dawn.

Standing at the edge of the forest that bordered the eastern side of the camp, a good two miles of rolling, grassy hills between him and the edge of the army, Lorcan monitored the stirring troops.

Gavriel had already shifted, and the mountain lion now paced near the tree line, waiting for the signal.

It was an effort not to peer behind him, though Lorcan could not see her. They'd left Elide a few miles into the forest, hidden in a copse of trees bordering a glen. Should all go poorly, she'd flee deeper into the hilly woods, up into the ancient mountains. Where far more deadly and cunning predators than Fae still prowled.

She hadn't offered him a parting word, though she'd wished them all luck. Lorcan hadn't been able to find the right words anyway, so he'd left without so much as a look back.

But he glanced back now. Prayed that if they didn't return, she wouldn't come hunting for them.

Gavriel halted his pacing, ears twitching toward the camp.

Lorcan stiffened.

A spark of his power awakened and flickered.

Death beckoned nearby.

"It's too soon," Lorcan said, scanning for any sign of Whitethorn's signal. Nothing.

Gavriel's ears lay flat against his head. And still those flutters of the dying trickled past.

CHAPTER 26

Aelin swallowed once. Twice. The portrait of uncertain fear as she lay chained on the metal table, Cairn waiting for her answer.

And then she said, her voice cracking, "When you finish breaking me apart for the day, how does it feel to know that you are still nothing?"

Cairn grinned. "Some fire left in you, it seems. Good."

She smiled back through the mask. "You were only given the oath for this. For me. Without me, you're nothing. You'll go back to being nothing. Less than nothing, from what I've heard."

Cairn's fingers tightened around the flint. "Keep talking, bitch. Let's see where it gets you."

A rasping laugh broke from her. "The guards talk when you're gone, you know. They forget I'm Fae, too. Can hear like you."

Cairn said nothing.

"At least they agree with me on one front. You're spineless. Have to tie up people to hurt them because it makes you feel like a male." Aelin gave a pointed glance between his legs. "Inadequate in the ways that count."

A tremor went through him. "Would you like me to show you how *inadequate* I am?"

Aelin huffed another laugh, haughty and cool, and gazed toward the ceiling, toward the lightening sky. The last she'd see, if she played this right.

There had always been another, a spare, to take her place should she fail. That her death would mean Dorian's, would send those hateful gods to demand his life to forge the Lock . . . It was no strange thing, to hate herself for it. She'd failed enough people, failed Terrasen, that the additional weight barely landed. She wouldn't have much longer to feel it anyway.

So she drawled toward the sky, the stars, "Oh, I know there's not much worth seeing in that regard, Cairn. And you're not enough of a male to be able to use it without someone screaming, are you?" At his silence, she smirked. "I thought so. I dealt with plenty of your ilk at the Assassins' Guild. You're all the same."

A deep snarl.

Aelin only chuckled and adjusted her body, as if getting comfortable. "Go ahead, Cairn. Do your worst."

Fenrys let out a warning whine.

She waited, waited, maintaining the smirk, the looseness in her limbs.

A hand slammed into her gut, hard enough she bowed around it, the air vanishing from her.

Then another blow, to her ribs, a cry rasping from her. Fenrys barked.

Locks clicked, unlocking. Hot breath tickled her ear as she was yanked up, off the table. "Maeve's orders might hold me at bay, bitch, but let's see how much you talk after this."

Her chained legs failed to get under her before Cairn gripped the back of her head and slammed her face into the edge of the metal table.

Stars burst, blinding and agonizing, as metal on metal on bone cracked through her. She stumbled, falling back, her chained feet sending her sprawling.

Fenrys barked again, frantic and raging.

But Cairn was there, gripping her hair so tightly her eyes watered, and she cried out once more as he dragged her across the floor toward that great, burning brazier.

He hauled her up by her hair and shoved her masked face forward. "Let's see how you mock me now."

The heat instantly singed her, the flames licking so close to her skin. Oh gods, oh gods, the heat of it—

The mask warmed on her face, the chains along her body with it.

Despite herself, her plans, she shoved back, but Cairn held her firm. Pushed her toward the fire as her body strained, fighting for any pocket of cool air.

"I'm going to melt your face so badly even the healers won't be able to fix you," he breathed in her ear, bearing down, her limbs starting to wobble, the heat scorching her skin, the chains and mask.

He shoved her an inch closer to the flame.

Aelin's foot slid back, between his braced legs. Now. It had to be *now*—

"Enjoy the fire-breathing," he hissed, and she let him shove her another inch lower. Let him get off balance, just a fraction, as she slammed her body not up, but *back* into him, her foot hooking around his ankle as he staggered.

Aelin whirled, smashing her shoulder into his chest. Cairn crashed to the ground.

She ran—or tried to. With the chains at her feet, on her legs, she could barely walk, but she stumbled past him, knowing he was already twisting, already rising up.

Run—

Cairn's hands wrapped around her calves and yanked. She went down, teeth singing as they slammed against the mask, drawing blood from her lip.

Then he was over her, raining blows on her head, her neck, her chest.

She couldn't dislodge him, her muscles so drained from disuse, despite the healers keeping the atrophying at bay. Couldn't flip him, either, though she tried.

Cairn fumbled behind them—for an iron poker, heating in the brazier.

Aelin thrashed, trying to get her hands up and over his head, to loop those chains around his neck. But they'd been hooked to the irons at her sides, down her back.

Fenrys's snarling barks rang out. Cairn's hand fumbled again for the poker. Missed.

Cairn glanced behind him to grab the poker, daring to take his eyes off her for a heartbeat.

Aelin didn't hesitate. She rammed her head upward and slammed her masked face into Cairn's head.

He knocked back, and she lunged toward the tent flaps.

He had more restraint than she'd estimated.

He wouldn't kill her, and what she'd done just now, provoking him—

She'd barely made it out of her crouch when Cairn's hands gripped her hair again.

When he hurled her with all his strength against the chest of drawers.

Aelin hit it with a crack that echoed through her body.

Something in her side snapped and she cried out, the sound small and broken, as she collided with the floor.

Fenrys had seen his twin drive a knife through his heart. Had watched Connall bleed out onto the tiles and die. And had then been ordered to kneel before Maeve in that very blood as she'd bade him to *attend* her.

He'd sat in a stone room for two months, witness to what they'd done to a young queen's body, her spirit. Had been unable to help her as she'd screamed and screamed. He'd never stop hearing those screams.

But it was the sound that came out of her as Cairn hurled her into the chest of drawers where Fenrys had watched him arranging his *tools*, the sound she made as she hit the floor, that shattered him entirely.

A small sound. Quiet. Hopeless.

He'd never heard it from her, not once.

Cairn got to his feet and wiped his bloodied, broken nose.

Aelin Galathynius stirred, trying to rise onto her forearms.

Cairn pulled the red-hot poker from the brazier. He pointed it at her like a sword.

Fenrys strained against his invisible bindings as Aelin glanced at him, toward where he'd sat for the past two days, in that same damned spot by the tent wall.

Despair shone in her eyes.

True despair, without light or hope. The sort of despair that wished for death. The sort of despair that began to erode strength, to eat away at any resolve to endure.

She blinked at him. Four times. *I am here, I am with you.*

Fenrys knew it for what it was. The final message. Not before death, but before the sort of breaking that no one would walk away from. Before Maeve returned with the Wyrdstone collar.

Cairn rotated the poker in his hands, heat rippling off its point.

And Fenrys couldn't allow it.

He couldn't allow it. In his shredded soul, in what was left of him after all he'd been forced to see and do, he couldn't allow it.

The blood oath kept his limbs planted. A dark chain that ran into his soul.

He would not allow it. That final breaking.

He pushed upward against the bond's dark chain, screaming, though no sound came from his open maw.

He pushed and pushed and *pushed* against those invisible chains, against that blood-sworn order to obey, to stay down, to watch.

He defied it. All that the blood oath was.

Pain lanced through him, into his very core.

He blocked it out as Cairn pointed the smoldering poker at the young queen with a heart of wildfire.

He would not allow it.

Snarling, the male inside him thrashing, Fenrys bellowed at the dark chain binding him.

He shredded into it, biting and tearing with every scrap of defiance he possessed.

Let it kill him, wreck him. He would not serve. Not another heartbeat. He would not obey.

He would not obey.

And slowly, Fenrys got to his feet.

Pain shuddered Aelin as she lay sprawled, panting, arms straining to hold her head and chest off the ground.

It was not Cairn and the poker she stared at.

But Fenrys, rising upward, his body rippling with tremors of pain, snout wrinkled in rage.

Even Cairn halted. Looked toward the white wolf. "*Stand down.*"

Fenrys snarled, deep and vicious. And still he struggled to his feet.

Cairn pointed the poker at the rug. "*Lie down. That is an order from your queen.*"

Fenrys spasmed, his hackles lifting. But he was standing.

Standing.

Despite the order, despite the blood oath's commands.

Get up.

From far away, the words sounded.

Cairn roared, "*Lie down!*"

Fenrys's head thrashed from side to side, his body bucking against invisible chains. Against an invisible oath.

His dark eyes met Cairn's.

Blood began running from the wolf's nostril.

It'd kill him—to sever the oath. It would break his soul. His body would go soon after that.

But Fenrys put one paw forward. His claws dug into the ground.

Cairn's face paled at that step. That impossible step.

Fenrys's eyes slid toward hers. Neither needed the silent code between them for the word she beheld in his gaze. The order and plea.

Run.

Cairn read the word, too.

And he hissed, "Not with a shattered spine, she can't," before he brought the poker slamming down for Aelin's back.

With a roar, Fenrys leaped.

And with it, he snapped the blood oath completely.

CHAPTER 27

Wolf and Fae went tumbling to the carpet, roaring and tearing.

Fenrys lunged for Cairn's throat, his enormous body pinning the male, but Cairn got his feet between them and *kicked*.

Aelin lurched upright, willing strength to her legs as she came into a kneel beside the chest of drawers. Fenrys slammed into the side of the metal table, but was instantly moving, throwing his body against Cairn.

A low hiss sounded nearby, and Aelin dared look away to find the poker lying to her right.

She twisted her feet toward it. Placed the center of the chains binding her ankles atop the red-hot tip.

Slowly, the links in the center heated.

Wolf and Fae clashed in a tangle of claws and fists and teeth, then leaped apart.

Severing the blood oath—it would kill him.

These were his last breaths, his last heartbeats.

"I'll peel the fur from your bones," Cairn panted.

Fenrys breathed heavily, blood leaking from between his teeth as he placed one paw over the other, circling. His stare did not break from Cairn's as they moved, assessing each other for the killing blow.

The links in the center of the chain began glowing.

Overhead, the sky lightened to gray.

Fenrys and Cairn circled again, step after step.

Wearing him out, wearing him down. Cairn knew the cost of severing the blood oath. Knew he had only to wait it out before Fenrys was dead.

Fenrys knew it, too.

He charged, teeth snapping for Cairn's throat as his paws swiped for the male's shins.

Aelin grabbed the poker, planted her heels, and drove the rod upward. It strained against the heated links in the chain, and she shoved and shoved her feet downward, her arms buckling.

Cairn and Fenrys rolled, and Aelin gritted her teeth, bellowing.

The chain between her legs snapped.

It was all she needed.

She scrambled to her feet, but halted. Fenrys, pinned by Cairn, met her gaze. Snarled in warning and command.

Run.

Cairn whipped his head toward her. Toward the chain hanging free between her ankles. "*You—*"

But Fenrys surged up, his jaws clamping around Cairn's shoulder.

Cairn shouted, arching, grabbing for Fenrys's back.

Fenrys met her stare again, ripping into Cairn's shoulder even as the male shoved them into the edge of the table. Hammered Fenrys's spine into the metal, hard enough that bone cracked.

Run.

Aelin did not hesitate. She sprinted for the tent flaps.

And into the morning beyond.

~

Half a mile to the center of the camp. To the tent.

The soldiers had responded as Rowan anticipated, and he'd killed them accordingly.

Birds of prey dove for him, attacking with wind and ice from above. He shattered their magic with a surge of his own, sending them scattering.

A cluster of warriors charged from behind a row of tents.

Some beheld him and ran back the way they'd come. All soldiers whom he'd trained. And some he hadn't. Yet many stayed to fight.

Rowan ripped through their shields, ripped the air from their lungs. Some found his hatchet swinging for their necks.

Close. So close to that tent. He would signal Lorcan and Gavriel in a moment. When he was close enough to need the diversion for the way out.

Another onslaught of soldiers barreled for him, and Rowan angled his long knife. His power blasted away their fired arrows, then blasted away the archers.

Turning them all to bloodied splinters.

CHAPTER 28

Aelin ran.

Her weakened legs stumbled on the grass, her still-bound hands restricting the full range of motion, but she ran. Picked a direction, any direction but the river mists to her left, and ran.

The sun was rising, and the army camp . . . There was motion behind her. Shouting.

She blocked it out and aimed right. Toward the rising sun, as if it were Mala's own welcoming embrace.

She couldn't get down enough air through the mask's thin slit, but she kept moving, racing past tents, past soldiers who whipped their heads toward her, as if puzzled. She clenched the poker in her ironclad hands, refusing to see what the commotion was, if Cairn raged behind her.

But then she heard them. Bellowed orders.

Rushing steps in the grass behind, closing in. People ahead alerted by their cries.

Bare feet flying over the ground, her exhausted legs screamed to stop.

Still Aelin aimed for the eastern horizon. Toward the trees and mountains, toward the sun cresting over them.

And when the first of the soldiers blocked her path, shouting to stop, she angled the iron poker and did not falter.

~

Death sang to Lorcan.

From the birds of prey that speared farther and farther into the camp, he knew Whitethorn was close to Cairn's tent.

Soon now, they'd get the signal.

Lorcan and Gavriel steadied their breathing, readying their power. It thrummed through them, twin waves cresting.

But death began beckoning elsewhere in the camp.

Closer to them. Moving fast. .

Lorcan scanned the brightening sky, the line of the first tents. The entrance with the guards.

"Someone's making a move this way," Lorcan murmured to Gavriel. "But Whitethorn's still over there."

Fenrys. Or Connall, perhaps. Maybe Essar's sister, who he'd never liked. But he wouldn't give a shit about that if she hadn't betrayed them.

He pointed north of the entrance. "You take that side. Be ready to strike from the flank."

Gavriel sped off, a predator ready to pounce unseen when Lorcan attacked head-on.

Death glimmered. Whitethorn was nearly at the camp's center. And that force approaching their eastern entrance . . .

To hell with waiting.

Lorcan broke from the cover of trees, dark power swirling, primed to meet whatever broke through the line of tents.

Freeing the sword at his side, he searched the sky, the camp, the world as death flickered, as the rising sun gilded the rolling grasses and set the dew steaming.

Nothing. No indication of what, of who—

He'd reached the first of the hollows that flowed to the camp edge, the dips narrow and steep, when Aelin Galathynius appeared.

Lorcan didn't expect the sob in his throat as she raced between the tents, as he beheld the iron mask and the chains on her, hands still bound.

As he beheld the blood soaking her skin, the short white shift, her hair, longer than he'd last seen and plastered to her head with gore.

His knees stopped working, and even his magic faltered at the sight of her wild, desperate race for the camp's edge.

Soldiers ran toward her.

Lorcan surged into motion, flaring his magic up and wide. Not to her, but to Whitethorn, still charging for the center of the camp.

She's here, she's here, she's here, he signaled.

But Lorcan was too far, the grassy bumps and hollows between them now endless, as ten soldiers converged on Aelin, blocking her path toward the open field.

One swung his sword, a strike that would cleave her skull in two.

The fool didn't realize who he faced. What he faced.

That it wasn't a fire-breathing queen bound in iron who charged at him, but an assassin.

With a twist, arms lifting, Aelin met that sword head-on.

Just as she'd planned.

The male's sword fell short of his intended target, but hit precisely where she wished.

In the center of the chains that bound her hands.

Iron snapped.

Then the male's sword was in her freed hands. Then his throat was spraying blood.

Aelin whirled, slamming into the other soldiers who stood between her and freedom. Even as he ran for her, Lorcan could only gape at what unfolded.

She struck before they knew where to turn. Slash, duck, lunge.

She got her other hand on one of their daggers.

Then it was over. Then there was nothing between her and the camp entrance but the six guards drawing their weapons—

Lorcan lashed out with his magic, a lethal net of power that had those guards crashing to their knees. Necks snapped.

Aelin didn't falter as they wilted to the ground. She charged past, aiming straight for the field and hills. To where Lorcan ran for her.

He signaled again. *To me, to me.*

Whether Aelin recognized it, or him, she still raced his way.

Whole. Her body looked whole, and yet she was so thin, her blood-splattered legs straining to keep her upright.

A rolling field of steep bumps and hollows lay between them. Lorcan swore.

She wouldn't make it, not over that terrain, not drained like that—

But she did.

Aelin vanished into the first dip, and Lorcan's magic flared over and over. To her, to Whitethorn.

And then she was up, cresting the hill, and he could see the slowness taking over, the sheer exhaustion from a body at its limit.

Arrows twanged from bows, and a wall of them shot into the sky. Aiming for her on those exposed hills.

Lorcan sent a wave of his power snapping them away.

Still more fired. Single shots this time, from so many directions he couldn't trace their sources. Trained archers, some of Maeve's best. Aelin had to—

She already was.

Aelin began zagging, depriving them of an easy target.

Left to right, she darted over the hills, slower with each bump she cleared, each step toward Lorcan as he raced to her, a hundred yards remaining between them.

An arrow speared for her back, but Aelin lunged to the side, skidding in grass and dirt. She was up again in a heartbeat, weapons still in hand, charging for the hills and hollows between them.

Another arrow aimed for her, and Lorcan made to snap it away. A wall of glittering gold got there first.

From the north, leaping over the hollows, charged Gavriel. Aelin disappeared into a dip in the earth, and when she emerged, the Lion ran at her side, a golden shield around her. Not close to her—but in the air around them. Unable to fully touch her with the iron mask, the chains draped around her torso. The iron gauntlets on her hands.

Soldiers were spilling out of the camp, and Lorcan sent a black wind whipping for them. Where it touched them, they died. And those who did not found an impenetrable shield barring the way to the field.

He spread it as wide as he could. Blood oath or no, they were still his people. His soldiers. He'd prevent their deaths, if he could. Save them from themselves.

Aelin was stumbling now, and Lorcan cleared the last of the hills between them.

He opened his mouth, to shout what, he didn't know, but a cry pierced the blue sky.

The sob that came out of Aelin at the hawk's bellow of fury cracked Lorcan's chest.

But she kept running for the trees, for their cover. Lorcan and Gavriel fell into step beside her, and when she again stumbled, those too-thin legs giving out, Lorcan gripped her under the arm and hauled her along.

Fast as a shooting star, Rowan dove for them. He reached them as they passed the first of the trees, shifting as he landed. They threw themselves into a halt, Aelin sprawling onto the pine-covered ground.

Rowan was instantly before her, hands going to the mask on her face, the chains, the blood coating her arms, her torn body—

Aelin let out another sob, and then moaned, *"Fenrys."*

It took Lorcan a moment to understand. Took her pointing behind them, to the camp, as she said again, as if speech was beyond her, *"Fenrys."* Her breath was a wet rasp. A plea. A broken, bloody plea.

Fenrys remained with Cairn. In the camp. Aelin pointed again, sobbing.

Rowan turned from his mate.

The rage in Rowan's eyes could devour the world. And that rage was about to extract the sort of vengeance only a mated male could command.

Rowan's canines flashed, but his voice was deadly soft as he said to Lorcan, "Take her to the glen." A jerk of his chin to Gavriel. "You're with me."

With a final look toward Aelin, his frozen rage a brewing storm on the wind, the prince and the Lion were gone, charging back toward the chaotic, bloody camp.

CHAPTER 29

With the camp in outright chaos, it was far easier to slip in.

Rowan's power blasted to the western edge, shattering tent and bone. Any soldiers lingering between the camp's eastern edge and the center ran toward it.

Clearing the way. Right to the tent he'd been so close to reaching when Lorcan's power had flared. A signal.

That they'd found her. Or she had found them, it seemed.

And when Rowan had seen her, first from the skies and then beside her, when he smelled the blood, both her own and others', when he beheld the chains and the iron mask clamped over her face, when she was *sobbing* at the sight of him, terror and despair coating her scent—

The rage that roiled through him had no space for mercy. No room for compassion.

There was neither in him as he and Gavriel snuck past the last cluster of tents to the large one situated in a cleared circle of grass. As if no one could stomach being near Cairn.

Fenrys was with her. Or had been.

From the quiet inside, he wondered if the wolf was dead.

Gavriel shifted into his Fae form, and freed a knife at his hip. An exchanged glance conveyed the order for silence as Rowan sent a wisp of wind floating into the tent.

It sang back to him of two life-forms. Both injured. Blood thick in the air. It was all he needed.

Silent as the breeze in the grass, they slipped between the tent flaps. Rowan didn't know where to look first.

At the wolf and Fae male sprawled on the floor.

Or at the iron coffin across the tent.

The iron box they'd locked her in.

Had to reinforce, it seemed, from the sloppy welding on the thick slabs atop it.

The box was so small. So narrow.

The smell of her blood, her fear, saturated the tent. Emanated from that box.

A metal table lay nearby.

And beneath it . . .

Rowan took in the three unlit braziers set beneath it, the chain anchors at the head and foot of the table, and at last looked toward the Fae male left bloodied, but still alive, on the floor across from Fenrys.

Fenrys, whom Gavriel was already crouched over, the golden light of his power wrapped around the blood-soaked fur. Healing him. The white wolf did not rise to consciousness, but his breathing steadied. Good enough.

"Heal him," Rowan said with lethal softness. The Lion looked up, and found that Rowan's gaze was no longer on the wolf. But on Cairn.

Chunks of flesh had been torn from Cairn's body. A lump on his temple told Rowan it had been the blow that had rendered him unconscious. As if Fenrys had slammed Cairn's skull into the side of that metal table. And then collapsed himself mere feet away.

Collapsed, perhaps not from the wounds themselves, but . . . Rowan started. What had happened here, what had been so terrible that the wolf had been able to do the impossible to spare Aelin from enduring it?

Gavriel's tawny eyes flashed with wariness. Rowan pointed at Cairn again. "Heal him."

They did not have much time. Not to do what he wanted. What he needed.

Some of the drawers in the tall chest had been knocked free. Polished tools glinted within.

A pouch of them had also been set on a piece of black velvet beside the metal table.

Her blood sang to him of pain and despair, of utter terror.

His Fireheart.

Gavriel's magic shimmered, golden light settling over Cairn.

Rowan surveyed the tools Cairn had laid out, the ones in the drawer. Carefully, thoughtfully, he selected one.

A thin, razor-sharp knife. A healer's tool, meant for sleek incisions and scraping out rot.

Cairn groaned as unconsciousness gave way. By the time Cairn awoke, chained to that metal table, Rowan was ready.

Cairn beheld who stood over him, the tool in Rowan's tattooed hand, the others he had also laid out on that piece of velvet, and began thrashing. The iron chains held firm.

Then Cairn beheld the frozen rage in Rowan's eyes. Understood what he intended to do with that sharp, sharp knife. A dark stain spread across the front of Cairn's pants.

Rowan wrapped an ice-kissed wind around the tent, blocking out all sound, and began.

CHAPTER 30

The clash of conflict echoed across the land, even from miles away. Deep in the rough hills of an ancient forest, Elide had waited for hours. First shivering in the dark, then watching the sky bleed to gray, then at last blue. And with that final transition, the clamor had started.

She'd alternated between pacing through the mossy glen, weaving amongst the gray boulders strewn between the trees, and sitting in the thrumming silence against one of the towering, wide-trunked trees, making herself as small and quiet as possible. Gavriel had sworn none of the strange or fell beasts in these lands would prowl so close to Doranelle, but she didn't want to risk it. So she remained in the glen, where she'd been told to wait.

Wait for them. Or wait for things to go badly enough that she had to find her own way. Perhaps she'd seek out Essar if it should come to that—

It wouldn't come to that. She swore it over and over. It *couldn't* come to that.

The morning sun was beginning to warm the chilled shade when she saw them.

Saw them, before she heard them, because their feet were silent on the forest floor, thanks to their immortal grace and training. The breath shuddered out of her as Lorcan emerged between two moss-crusted trees, eyes already fixed on her. And a step behind him, staggering along . . .

Elide didn't know what to do. With her body, her hands. Didn't know what to say as Aelin stumbled over root and rock, the mask and the chains clanking, blood soaking her. Not just blood from her own wounds, but those of others.

She was thin, her golden hair so much longer. Too long, even with the time apart. It fell nearly to her navel, most of it dark with caked blood. As if she'd run through a rain of it.

No sign of Rowan or Gavriel. But no grief on Lorcan's face, nothing beyond urgency, given how he monitored the sky, the trees. Searching for any pursuit.

Aelin halted at the edge of the clearing. Her feet were bare, and the thin, short shift she wore revealed no major injuries.

But there was little recognition in Aelin's eyes, shadowed with the mask.

Lorcan said to the queen, "We'll wait here for them."

Aelin, as if her body didn't quite belong to her, lifted her shackled, metal-encased hands. The chain linking them had been severed, and hung in pieces off either manacle. The same with those at her ankles.

She tugged at one of the metal gauntlets. It didn't budge.

She tugged again. The gauntlet didn't so much as shift.

"Take it off."

Her voice was low, gravelly.

Elide didn't know which one of them she'd ordered, but before she could cross the clearing, Lorcan gripped the queen's wrist to examine the locks.

One corner of his mouth tightened. There was no easy way to free them, then.

Elide approached, her limp deep once more with Gavriel's magic occupied.

The gauntlets had been locked at her wrist, overlapping slightly with the shackle. Both had small keyholes. Both were made from iron.

Elide shifted slightly, bracing her weight on her uninjured leg, to get a view of where the mask was bound to the back of Aelin's head.

That lock was more complicated than the others, the chains thick and ancient.

Lorcan had fitted the tip of a slender dagger into the lock of the gauntlet, and was now angling it, trying to pick the mechanism.

"Take it off." The queen's guttural words were swallowed by the moss-crusted trees.

"I'm trying," Lorcan said—not gently, though certainly without his usual coldness.

The dagger scraped in the lock, but to no avail.

"Take it off." The queen began trembling.

"I'm—"

Aelin snatched the dagger from him, metal clicking on metal as she fitted the blade's tip into the lock. The dagger shook in her ironclad hand. "Take it off," she breathed, lips curling back from her teeth. "*Take it off.*"

Lorcan made to grab the dagger, but she angled away. He snapped, "These locks are too clever. We need a proper locksmith."

Panting through her clenched teeth, Aelin dug and twisted the dagger into the gauntlet's lock. A snap cracked through the clearing.

But not the lock. Aelin withdrew the dagger to reveal the broken, chipped point. A shard of metal tumbled from the lock and into the moss.

Aelin stared at the broken blade, at the shard in the greenery cushioning her bare, bloodied feet, her breaths coming faster and faster.

Then she dropped the dagger into the moss. Began clawing at the shackles on her arms, the gauntlets on her hands, the mask on her face.

"Take it off," she begged as she scratched and tugged and yanked. *"Take it off!"*

Elide reached a hand for her, to stop her before she ripped the skin clean off her bones, but Aelin dodged away, staggering deeper into the clearing.

The queen dropped to her knees, bowing over them, and clawed at the mask.

It didn't so much as move.

Elide glanced to Lorcan. He was frozen, eyes wide as Aelin knelt in the moss, as her breathing became edged with sobs.

He had done this. Led them to this.

Elide stepped toward Aelin.

The queen's gauntlets drew blood where they scraped into her neck, her jaw, as she heaved against the mask. *"Take it off!"* The plea turned into a scream. *"Take it off!"*

Over and over, the queen screamed it. *"Take it off, take it off, take it off!"*

She was sobbing amid her screaming, the sounds shattering through the ancient forest. She said no other words. Pleaded to no gods, no ancestors.

Only those words, again and again and again.

Take it off, take it off, take it off.

Movement broke through the trees behind them, and the fact that Lorcan did not go for his weapons told Elide who it was. But any relief was short-lived as Rowan and Gavriel emerged, a massive white wolf hauled between them. The wolf whose jaws had clamped around Elide's arm, tearing flesh to the bone. Fenrys.

He was unconscious, tongue lagging from his bloodied maw. Rowan had barely entered the clearing before he set down the wolf and stalked for Aelin.

The prince was covered in blood. From his unhindered steps, Elide knew it wasn't his.

From the blood coating his chin, his neck . . . She didn't want to know.

Aelin ripped at the immovable mask, either unaware or uncaring of the prince before her. Her consort, husband, and mate.

"Aelin."

Take it off, take it off, take it off.

Her screams were unbearable. Worse than those that day on the beach in Eyllwe.

Gavriel came to stand beside Elide, his golden skin pale as he took in the frantic queen.

Slowly, Rowan knelt before her. "Aelin."

She only tipped her head up to the forest canopy and sobbed.

Blood ran down her neck from the scratches she'd dug into her skin, mingling with what already coated her.

Rowan reached out a trembling hand, the only sign of the agony Elide had little doubt was coursing through him. Gently, he laid his hands on her wrists; gently, he closed his fingers around them. Halting the brutal clawing and digging.

Aelin sobbed, her body shuddering with the force of it. *"Take it off."*

Rowan's eyes flickered, panic and heartbreak and longing shining there. "I will. But you have to be still, Fireheart. Just for a few moments."

"Take it off." The sobs ebbed, tricking into something broken and raw. Rowan ran his thumbs over her wrists, over those iron shackles. As if it were nothing but her skin. Slowly, her shaking eased.

No, not eased, Elide realized as Rowan rose to his feet and stalked behind the queen. But contained, turned inward. Tremors rippled through Aelin's tense body, but she kept still as Rowan examined the lock.

Yet something like shock, then horror and sorrow, flashed over his face, as he surveyed her back. It was gone as soon as it appeared.

A glance, and Gavriel and Lorcan drifted to his side, their steps slow. Unthreatening.

Across the small clearing, Fenrys remained out, his white coat soaked with blood.

Elide only walked to Aelin and took up the spot where Rowan had been.

The queen's eyes were closed, as if it took all her concentration to remain still for another heartbeat, to allow them to look, to not claw at the irons.

So Elide said nothing, demanded nothing from her, save for a companion if she needed one.

Behind Aelin, Rowan's blood-splattered face was grim while he studied the lock fastening the mask's chains to the back of her head. His nostrils flared slightly. Rage—frustration.

"I've never seen a lock like this," Gavriel murmured.

Aelin began shaking again.

Elide put a hand on her knee. Aelin had scraped it raw, mud and grass stuck in her blood-crusted skin.

She waited for the queen to shove her hand away, but Aelin didn't move. Kept her eyes shut, her ragged breathing holding steady.

Rowan gripped one of the chains binding the mask and nodded to Lorcan. "The other one."

Silently, Lorcan grasped the opposite end. They'd sever the iron if they had to.

Elide held her breath as both males strained, arms shaking.

Nothing.

They tried again. Aelin's breathing hitched. Elide tightened her hand on the queen's knee.

"She managed to snap the chains on her ankles and hands," Gavriel observed. "They're not indestructible."

But with the chains on the mask so close to her head, a swipe of a sword was impossible. Or perhaps the mask had been made from far stronger iron.

Rowan and Lorcan grunted as they heaved against the chains. It was of little use.

Panting softly, they paused. Red welts shone on their hands.

They'd tried to use their magic to break the iron.

Silence fell through the clearing. They couldn't linger here—not for much longer. But to take Aelin in the chains, when she was so frantic to be free of them . . .

Aelin's eyes opened.

They were empty. Wholly drained. A warrior accepting defeat.

Elide blurted, scrambling for anything to banish that emptiness, "Was there ever a key? Did you see them using a key?"

Two blinks. As if that meant something.

Rowan and Lorcan yanked again, straining.

But Aelin's stare fell to the moss, the stones. Narrowed slightly, as if the question had settled. Through the small hole in her mask, Elide could barely see her mouth the words. *A key.*

"I don't have it—we don't have them," Elide said, sensing the direction of Aelin's thoughts. "Manon and Dorian do."

"Quiet," Lorcan hissed. Not at the level of her voice, but the deadly information Elide revealed.

Aelin again blinked twice with that strange intentionality.

Rowan snarled at the chains, heaving again.

But Aelin stretched out a hand to the moss and traced a shape.

"What is that?" Elide leaned forward as the queen did it again, her hollow face unreadable.

The Fae males paused at her question, and watched Aelin's finger move through the green.

"A Wyrdmark," Rowan said softly. "To open."

Aelin traced it again, mute and still. As if none of them stood there.

"They work on iron?" Gavriel asked, tracking Aelin's finger.

"She unlocked iron doors in Adarlan's royal library with that symbol," Rowan murmured. "But she needed . . ."

He let his words hang unfinished as he picked up the broken knife Aelin had discarded in the moss nearby and sliced it across his palm.

Kneeling before her, he extended his bloodied hand. "Show me, Fireheart. Show me again." He tapped her ankle—the shackle there.

Silently, her movements stiff, Aelin leaned forward. She sniffed at the blood pooling in his hand, her nostrils flaring. Her eyes lifted to his, like the scent of his blood posed some question.

"I am your mate," Rowan whispered, as if it was the answer she sought. And the love in his eyes, in the way his voice broke, his bloodied hand trembling . . . Elide's throat tightened.

Aelin only looked at the blood pooling in his cupped palm. Her fingers curled, the gauntlet clicking. As if it were another answer, too.

"She can't do it with the iron," Elide said. "If it's on her hands. It interferes with the magic in the blood."

A blink from her, in that silent language.

"It's why she put them on you, isn't it," Elide said, her chest straining. "To be sure you couldn't use your own blood with the Wyrdmarks to free yourself." As if all the other iron wasn't already enough.

Another blink, her face still so hollow and cold. Tired.

Rowan's jaw clenched. But he just dipped his finger into the blood in his palm and offered his hand to her. "Show me, Fireheart," he said again.

Elide could have sworn he shuddered, and not from fear, as Aelin's metal-crusted hand closed around his.

In halting, small movements, she guided his finger to trace the symbol onto the shackle around her ankle.

A soft flare of greenish light, then—

The hiss and sigh of the lock filled the clearing. The shackle tumbled to the moss.

Lorcan swore.

Rowan offered his hand, his blood, again. The shackle around her other ankle yielded to the Wyrdmark.

Then the manacles around her wrists. Then the beautiful, horrible gauntlets thudded to the moss.

Aelin lifted her bare hands to her face, reaching for the lock behind the mask, but halted.

"I'll do it," Rowan said, his voice still soft, still full of that love. He moved behind her, and Elide stared at the horrible mask, the suns and flames carved and embossed along its ancient surface.

A flare of light, a click of metal, and then it slid free.

Her face was pale—so pale, all traces of the sun-kissed coloring gone. And empty. Aware, and yet not.

Wary.

Elide kept still, letting the queen survey her. The males moved to face her, and Aelin looked upon them in turn. Gavriel, who bowed his head. Lorcan, who stared right back at her, his dark gaze unreadable.

And Rowan. Rowan, whose breathing became jagged, his swallow audible. "Aelin?"

The name, it seemed, was an unlocking, too.

Not of the queen she'd so briefly known, but the power inside her.

Elide flinched as flame, golden and blazing, erupted around the queen. The shift burned away into ashes.

Lorcan dragged Elide back, and she allowed it, even as the heat vanished. Even as the flare of power contracted into an aura around the queen, a shimmering second skin.

Aelin knelt there, burning, and did not speak.

The flames flickered around her, though the moss, the roots, did not burn. Didn't so much as steam. And through the fire, Aelin's now-long hair half hiding her nakedness, Elide got a good look at what had been done to her.

Aside from a bruise along her ribs, there was nothing.

Not a mark. Not a callus.

Not a single scar. The ones Elide had marked in those days before Aelin had been taken were gone.

As if someone had wiped them away.

CHAPTER
31

They had taken her scars.

Maeve had taken them all away.

It told Rowan enough about what had been done. When he'd seen her back, the smooth skin where the scars of Endovier and the scars from Cairn's whipping should have been, he'd suspected.

But kneeling, burning in nothing but her skin . . . There were no scars where there should have been. The almost-necklace of them from Baba Yellowlegs: gone. The shackle marks from Endovier: gone. The scar where she'd been forced by Arobynn Hamel to break her own arm: gone. And on her palms . . .

It was upon her exposed palms that Aelin now gazed. As if realizing what was missing.

The scars across her palms, one from the moment they had become *carranam*, the other from her oath to Nehemia, had disappeared entirely.

Like they had never been.

Her flames burned brighter.

Healers could remove scars, yes, but the most likely reason for the lack of them on Aelin, on all the places where he'd once traced them with his hands, his mouth . . .

It was new skin. All of it. Save for her face, since he doubted they would be stupid enough to take off the mask.

Nearly every inch of her was covered in new skin, unvarnished as fresh snow. The blood coating her had burned away to reveal it.

New skin, because they'd needed to replace what had been destroyed. To heal her so they could begin again and again.

Gavriel and Elide had moved to where Fenrys lay, the battlefield healing the former had done on the warrior likely not enough to keep death at bay.

Gavriel said to no one in particular, "He doesn't have much longer."

He'd broken the blood oath. Through sheer will, Fenrys had broken it. And would soon pay the price when his life force bled out entirely.

Aelin's gaze shifted then. From her hands, her horrifically pristine skin, to the wolf across the clearing.

She blinked twice. And then slowly rose.

Unaware or uncaring of her nakedness, she took an unsteady step. Rowan was instantly there—or as close as the flames would allow.

He could push through, shielding himself in ice or simply by cutting off the air that fed her flames. But to cross that line, to shove into her flames when so much, too much, had been stolen from her . . . He didn't let himself think about the distant, wary recognition on her face when she'd seen him—seen all of them. As if she wasn't entirely certain to trust them. Trust this.

Aelin managed another step, teetering.

He glimpsed her neck as she passed. Even the twin bite marks, his mark of claiming, had vanished.

Encased in flame, Aelin walked to Fenrys. The white wolf did not stir.

Sorrow softened her face, even with that quiet distance. Sorrow, and gratitude.

Gavriel and Elide remained on Fenrys's other side as she approached. Backed away a step. Not from fear, but to give her space in this moment of farewell.

They had to go. Lingering here, despite the miles between them and the camp, was folly. They could carry Fenrys until it was over, but . . . Rowan couldn't bring himself to say it. To tell Aelin that it might not be wise to draw out this good-bye the way she needed. They had minutes, at best, to spare before they had to be on the move.

But if scouts or sentries found them, he'd make sure they didn't get close enough to disturb her.

Gavriel and Lorcan seemed to be having the same thought, their eyes meeting from across the clearing. Rowan jerked his chin toward the western tree line in silent order. They stalked for it.

Aelin knelt beside Fenrys, and her flame enveloped them both. The fire gave way to a reddish-gold aura, a shield that he knew would melt the flesh of anyone who tried to cross. It flowed and rippled around them, a bubble of coppery air, and through it, Rowan watched as she ran a hand down the wolf's battered side.

Gavriel had healed most of the wounds, but the blood remained.

Aelin made long, gentle strokes over his fur, her head angled as she spoke too softly for Rowan to hear.

Slowly, painfully, Fenrys cracked open an eye. Agony filled it—agony and yet something like relief, and joy, at the sight of her bare face. And exhaustion. Such exhaustion that Rowan knew death would be a welcome embrace, a kiss from Silba herself, goddess of gentle ends.

Aelin spoke again, the sound either contained or swallowed by her shield. No tears. Only that sorrow—and clarity.

A queen's face, he realized as Lorcan and Gavriel took up spots along the glen's border. It was a queen's face that looked upon Fenrys. A queen who took his massive paw in her hands, pushing back folds of fur and skin to unsheathe a curved claw.

She slid it over her bare forearm, splitting skin. Leaving blood in its wake.

Rowan's breath caught. Gavriel and Lorcan whirled toward them.

Aelin spoke again, and Fenrys blinked once in answer.

She deemed that answer enough.

"Holy gods," Lorcan breathed as Aelin extended her bleeding forearm to Fenrys's mouth. "Holy rutting gods."

For Fenrys's loyalty, for his sacrifice, there was no greater reward she could offer. To keep him from death, there was no other way to save him.

Only this. Only the blood oath.

And as Fenrys managed to lap the blood from her wound, as he swore a silent vow to their queen, blinking a few more times, Rowan's chest became unbearably tight.

Severing the blood oath to one queen had snapped his life force, his soul. Swearing the blood oath to another might very well repair that cleaving, the ancient magic binding Fenrys's fading life to Aelin's.

Three mouthfuls. That's all Fenrys took before he laid his head back on the moss and closed his eyes.

Aelin curled on her side next to him, flames encompassing them both.

Rowan couldn't move. None of them moved.

Aelin mouthed a short, curt word.

Fenrys did not respond.

She spoke again, that queen's face unfaltering.

Live.

She'd use the blood oath to force him to remain on this side of life. Still Fenrys didn't stir.

Across the bubble of flame and heat, Elide put a hand over her mouth, eyes shining bright. She'd read the word on Aelin's lips, too.

Aelin spoke a third time, teeth flashing as she gave Fenrys her first order. *Live.*

Rowan didn't breathe as they waited. Long minutes passed.

Then Fenrys's eyes cracked open.

Aelin held the wolf's gaze, nothing in her face save that grave, unyielding command.

Slowly, Fenrys stirred. His paws shifted beneath him, legs straining. And he rose.

"I don't believe it," Lorcan whispered. "I don't . . ."

But there was Fenrys, standing before their now-kneeling queen. And there was Fenrys, inclining his head, shoulders dipping with him, one paw sweeping before the other. Bowing.

A ghost of a smile graced her mouth, gone before it ever took form.

Aelin remained kneeling, though. Even as Fenrys surveyed them, surprise and relief lighting his dark eyes. His gaze met Rowan's, and Rowan smiled, bowing his head.

"Welcome to the court, pup," he said, his voice thick.

Raw emotion rippled across that lupine face, and then Fenrys turned back to Aelin.

She was staring at nothing. Fenrys nudged her shoulder with his furry head.

She ran an idle hand through the wolf's white coat. Rowan's heart clenched.

Maeve had cleaved into Rowan's own mind to trick his very instincts.

What had she done to her? What had she done these months?

"We need to go," Gavriel said, his own voice thick as he took in Fenrys, standing proud and watchful beside Aelin. "We need to put distance between us and the camp, and find somewhere to halt for the night." Where they'd reassess how and where to leave this kingdom. Heading into the forest, toward the mountains, would be their best bet.

These trees offered plenty of coverage, and plenty of caves in which to hide.

"Can you walk?" Lorcan asked Fenrys.

Fenrys slid dark, baleful eyes to Lorcan.

Oh, that fight would come. That vengeance.

The wolf gave him a curt nod.

Elide reached for one of the packs stashed near the base of a tree. "Which way?"

But Rowan didn't get to answer.

Silent as wraiths, they appeared across the glen. As if they'd simply sparked into existence in the shade of the foliage.

Little bodies, some pale, some black as night, some scaled. Mostly concealed, save for spindly fingers and wide, unblinking eyes.

Elide gasped. "The Little Folk."

Elide hadn't seen a whisper of the Little Folk since the days before Terrasen fell. Then, it had been flashes and rustling within Oakwald's ancient shade. Never so many, never so openly.

Or as open as they would ever allow themselves to be.

The half dozen or so who had gathered across the clearing kept mostly hidden behind root and rock and cluster of leaves. None of the males moved, though Fenrys's ears cocked toward them.

A miracle—that's what had happened with the queen and the wolf.

Though Fenrys seemed drained, his eyes were clear as the Little Folk gathered.

Aelin barely looked toward them.

A pale, spindly hand rose over a moss-speckled boulder and curled. *Come.*

Rowan asked, voice like granite, "You wish us to follow you?"

Again, the hand made the motion. *Come.*

Gavriel murmured, "They know this forest better than even we do."

"And you trust them?" Lorcan demanded.

Rowan's eyes settled on Aelin. "They saved her life once." That night Erawan's assassin had returned for Aelin. "They will do so again now."

⸺

Silent and unseen, they passed through the trees and rocks and streams of the ancient forest.

Rowan kept a step behind Aelin and Fenrys, Gavriel and Elide at the head of their party, Lorcan at the rear, as they followed the Little Folk.

Aelin had said nothing, done nothing except rise when they told her it was time to go. Rowan had offered her his cloak, and she'd allowed it to pass through her bubble of golden, clear flame to wrap around her naked body.

She clutched it at her chest as they walked, mile after mile, her feet bare. If the stones and roots of the forest hurt her, she didn't so much as flinch. She only walked on, Fenrys at her side within that sphere of fire, as if they were two ghosts of memory.

A vision of old, striding through the trees, the queen and the wolf.

The others spoke rarely as the hours and miles passed. As the forested hills gave way to steeper inclines, the boulders larger, the rocks and trees broken in spots.

"From the ancient wars between the forest-spirits," Gavriel whispered to Elide when he noticed her frowning at a hillside full of felled trunks and splintered stone. "Some are still waged by them, wholly unaware and unconcerned with the affairs of any realm but this."

Rowan had never seen the race of ethereal beings far more ancient and secretive than even the Little Folk. But at his mountain home, set high in the range that they strode toward, he'd sometimes heard the shattering of rocks and trees on dark, moonless nights. When there was not a whisper of wind on the air, nor any storm to cause them.

So close—only twenty or so miles to the mountain house he'd built.

He'd planned to take Aelin there one day, though it was nothing but long-vanished ashes. Just to show her where the house had been, where he'd buried Lyria. She was still up there, his mate-who-had-never-been.

And his true mate . . . She strode unwavering through the trees. No more than a wraith.

Still they followed the Little Folk, who beckoned from a tree, a rock, and shrub ahead, and then vanished. Behind Lorcan, a few others hid their trail with clever hands and small magics.

He prayed they had a place to stay for the night. A place where Aelin might sleep, and might remain protected from Maeve's eyes once she realized she'd been tricked.

They were headed eastward—far from the coast. Rowan didn't dare risk telling them they needed to find a port. He'd see where they led them tonight, and then craft their plan for returning to their own continent.

But when the Little Folk appeared before a gargantuan boulder, when they then vanished and reappeared in a sliver cut into the rock itself, bony hands beckoning from within, Rowan found himself balking.

The creature dwelling in the lake beneath Bald Mountain was a mild threat compared to the other things that still hunted in dark and forgotten places.

But the Little Folk beckoned again.

Lorcan appeared at his side. "It could be a trap."

But Elide and Gavriel walked toward it, unfazed.

And behind them, Aelin continued as well. So Rowan followed her, as he would follow her until his last breath, and beyond it.

The cave mouth was tight, but soon opened into a larger passage. Aelin illuminated the space, bathing the black stone walls in a golden glow bright enough to see by.

But her flame was dwarfed when they entered a massive chamber. The ceiling stretched into gloom, but it was not the height of the chamber that made him halt.

Nooks and alcoves had been built into the side of the rock, some equipped with bedrolls, some with what seemed to be piles of clothes, and some with food. A small fire burned near one, and past it, tucked against the wall, a natural stone trough gleamed with water, courtesy of a small stream.

But farther into the cave, on the other side of the chamber, flowing right up to the black rock itself, a great lake stretched into the darkness.

There were countless subterranean lakes and rivers beneath these mountains—places so deep in the earth that even the Fae had not bothered or dared to explore.

This one, it seemed, the Little Folk had claimed for themselves, going so far as to outfit the space with sprawling birch branches against the walls. They'd hung small garlands and wreaths from the white limbs, and amongst the leaves, little bluish lights twinkled.

Magic—old, strange magic, those lights. Like they'd been plucked from the night sky.

Elide was surveying the space, awe written over her features. Gavriel and Lorcan, however, assessed it with a sharper, warier eye. Rowan did the same. The only exit seemed to be the one they'd entered through, and the lake stretched too far to discern if a shore lay beyond it.

Aelin did not pause as she strode for one of the glittering walls. There was none of her usual caution, no dart of her eyes as she weighed the exits and pitfalls, potential weapons to wield.

A trance—it was almost as if she had slipped into a trance, plunged into some depthless ocean inside herself and drifted so far down that they might as well have been birds soaring over its distant surface.

But she walked toward that wall, the birch branches artfully displayed across it. More of the Little Folk within, Rowan realized. Perched on the branches, clinging to them.

Aelin's steps were silent on the stone. Fenrys halted nearby, as if to give her privacy.

Rowan had the vague sense of Lorcan, Elide, and Gavriel heading for the alcove across the cave to inspect the goods that had been laid out.

But he lingered in the center of the space as his mate paused before the shining, living wall. There was no expression on her face, no tension in her body.

Yet she inclined her head to the Little Folk half-hidden in the branches and boughs before her. Her jaw moved—speaking. Brief, short words.

He'd never so much as heard of the Little Folk talking. But there was his queen, his wife, his mate, murmuring with them.

At last, she turned away, her face still blank, her wildfire eyes as flat and cold as the lake. Fenrys fell into step beside her, and Rowan remained in place as Aelin aimed for the small fire.

Safe. The Little Folk must have told her this cave was safe, if she now moved for the fire, her own sphere of it still burning bright.

The others halted their assessment of the supplies.

But Aelin paid them no heed, paid the world no heed, as she took up a spot between the fire and the cave wall, lay upon the bare stone, and closed her eyes.

CHAPTER
32

Dorian had brown eyes for three days before he figured out how to change them back to blue. Asterin and Vesta teased him about it mercilessly as they'd traveled down through the spine of the Fangs, dramatically bemoaning the absence of his *pretty bluebell eyes*, and had sighed to the heavens when the sapphire hue had returned.

His magic could leap between one element and another, yet the ability to shift lay within something else entirely. Lay within a part of him that had always yearned for one thing above all others: to let go. To be free. As Temis, Goddess of Wild Things, was free—uncaged. As he had once wished to be, when he had been little more than a reckless, idealistic prince.

It was the magic's sole command: let go. Let go of who and what he'd become since that collar and emerge into something new, something different.

It was easier realized than enacted. Since his eyes had returned to blue, like the unraveling of some thread within him, he'd been unable to do anything else. Even change them to brown again.

The Crochans and the Thirteen had halted for their midday break under the heavy cover of Oakwald, the trees barren, yet not a hint of snow on the earth. Another day, and they'd reach the rendezvous point. A week after they'd promised the Eyllwe war leaders, but they would arrive.

He sat on a fallen, moss-covered log, gnawing on the strip of dried rabbit. His dinner.

"My head pounds on your behalf, just watching you try so hard," Glennis said from across the clearing. Around them, the Thirteen ate in silence, Manon monitoring all. The Crochans sat amongst them, at least. Quietly, but they sat there.

Which meant they all looked at him now. Dorian lowered the strip of tough meat and inclined his head to the crone. "My head is pounding enough for both of us, I think."

"What are you trying to turn into, exactly? Or who?"

The opposite of what he was. The opposite of the man who'd over-looked Sorscha's presence for years. And offered her only death in the end. He'd be glad to let go of it, if only the magic would allow him.

"Nothing," he said. Many of the Thirteen and Crochans went back to their meager meals at his dull response. "I just want to see if it's possible, for someone with my manner of magic. To even change small features." Not a lie, not entirely.

Manon frowned, as if trying to work out some puzzle she couldn't quite grasp.

"But were you to succeed," Glennis pressed, "who would you wish to be?"

He didn't know. Couldn't conjure an image beyond empty darkness. Damaris, at his side, would have no answer, either.

Dorian peered inward, feeling the sea of magic that roiled inside him.

He traced its shape with careful, invisible hands. Followed a thread within himself not to his gut, but to his still-cracked heart.

Who do you wish to be?

There, like the seed of power that Cyrene had stolen, it lay—the little snarl in his magic. Not a snarl, but a knot—a knot in a tapestry. One that he might weave.

One he might fashion into something if he dared.

Who do you wish to be? he asked the barely woven tapestry within himself. Let the threads and knots take form, crafting the picture within his mind. Starting small.

Glennis chuckled. "Your eyes are green now, king."

Dorian started, heart thundering. The others again halted their lunches, gaping, some leaning in to peer at him more closely. But he fed his magic into the loom within himself, adding to the emerging picture.

"Och, golden hair does not suit you at all." Asterin grimaced. "You look sickly."

Who did he wish to be? Anyone but himself. But what he'd become.

His silent answer sent that magical loom tumbling from his invisible grip, and he knew if he looked, his dark hair and sapphire eyes would have returned. Asterin sighed in relief.

But Manon smiled grimly, as if she'd heard his unspoken answer. And understood.

⁓

Night was full overhead, the Crochans' fires crackling away beneath the lattice of leafless trees, when Glennis asked, "Have any of you seen the Wastes?"

The Thirteen blinked toward the crone. She didn't usually address them all at once, or ask such personal questions.

But at least Glennis spoke to them. Three days of travel, and Manon was no closer to winning the Crochans over than she'd been upon their departure from the Fangs. Though they spoke to her, and occasionally joined Glennis's hearth for meals, it was with as few words as necessary.

Asterin answered for the coven. "No. Not one of us, though I spent some time in a forest on the other side of the mountains. But never that far." Sorrow flickered in the witch's gold-flecked black eyes, as if there was more to the tale than that. Indeed, Sorrel and Vesta, even Manon, looked with a bit of that sorrow at the witch.

Manon asked Glennis, the sole Crochan at this fire under the canopy, "Why do you ask?"

"Curiosity," the crone said. "None of us have been, either. We do not dare."

"For fear of us?" Asterin's golden hair shifted as she leaned closer to the fire. She'd found a strip of leather in the camp to tie across her brow— not the black she'd worn for the past century, but a familiar sight, at least. One thing, it seemed, had not entirely altered.

"For fear of what it will do to us, to see what is left of our once-great city, our lands."

"Nothing but rubble, they say," Manon muttered.

"And would you rebuild it, if you could?" Glennis asked. "Rebuild the city for yourselves?"

"We never discussed what we'd do," Asterin said. "If we could ever go home."

"A plan, perhaps," Glennis mused, "would be wise. A powerful thing to have." Her blue eyes settled on Manon. "Not just for the Crochans, but your own people."

Dorian nodded, though he was not a part of this conversation.

Who did the Thirteen, the Ironteeth and Crochans, wish to be, to build, as a people?

Manon opened her mouth, but the Shadows burst into the ring of their hearth, their faces tight. The Thirteen were instantly on their feet.

"We scouted ahead, to the rendezvous site," Edda panted.

Manon braced herself. A whisper of power flickered through the camp, the only indication that Dorian's magic had coiled around them in a near-impenetrable shield.

"It reeks of death," Briar finished.

CHAPTER
33

They had been too late.

Not just by an hour, or a day. No, judging by the state of the bodies in the leaf-strewn clearing twenty miles south, the week they had been delayed had cost the Eyllwe war band everything.

Morath had left the warriors where they lay, a few red-caped Crochans—the ones who had summoned their northern sisters here— amongst the fallen. The smell of decay was enough to make Manon's eyes water as they surveyed what had been left.

She had done this.

Brought this about, in delaying the Crochans through that skirmish. One look at Dorian, the king lingering at the edge of the clearing with an arm over his nose to ward against the reek, and she knew he thought it, too. The sharpness in his eyes spoke enough.

"Some got away," Edda announced, the Shadow's face grim. "But most didn't."

"They wanted survivors," Bronwen said, loud enough for all to hear. "To sow fear."

Manon studied the shattered trees, the ancient oaks as broken as the bodies on the forest floor. Proof of who, exactly, had been responsible for the massacre.

She had done that, too.

Bronwen said, voice cold and low, "What mortal band could ever hope to survive an attack by one of the Ironteeth legions? Especially when that aerial legion was trained by such a skilled Wing Leader."

"Choose your words carefully," Asterin warned.

But Una, the pretty, brown-haired Crochan and another of Manon's cousins, gripped her silver-bound broom and said, "You trained them. All of you—you trained the witches who did *this*." Una pointed to the decaying bodies, the torn throats, the killing that had not stopped at quick deaths. Not at all. "And you expect us to forget that?"

Silence fell. Even from Asterin. Glennis said nothing.

Manon's hands turned frail. Foreign. The iron within them brittle.

She had done this. The soldiers in the wide clearing were nothing and no one to her, most were mere mortals, and yet . . . A woman lay near Manon's boots, her torso split clean open from navel to sternum. Her brown eyes gazed unseeingly at the shattered canopy overhead, her mouth still gaping in pain.

"I can burn them," Dorian offered no one in particular.

Who had she been, the warrior before her? Who had she fought for? Not kingdoms or rulers, but who in her life had been worth defending?

"We should alert the King and Queen of Eyllwe," Bronwen was saying. "Warn their princes, too. Tell them to lie low. Erawan is beyond taking prisoners."

Manon stared and stared at the slaughtered warrior. What she had once delighted in. What she had once flaunted before the world, and done with not a shred of regret. Only with the wish that her grandmother would approve. That the Ironteeth would approve.

This was what they would be remembered for.

What she would be remembered for.

Erawan's crowned rider. His Wing Leader.

"Don't burn them," Manon said.

Silence fell in the clearing.

But Manon knelt on the festering earth, unsheathed her iron nails, and began digging.

Yanking off her gloves, Asterin lowered herself to the ground nearby. Then Sorrel and Vesta. Then the rest of the Thirteen.

The cold, firm earth did not yield easily. It tore at Manon's fingers, root and rock burning as they scraped at her skin.

Across the clearing, Karsyn, the witch whose broom Manon had returned, made to kneel as well. But Manon held up a filthy, already bleeding hand. The witch halted. "Only the Thirteen," Manon said. "We will bury them." The Crochans stared at her, and Manon ripped away the ancient soil. "We'll bury all of them."

For hours, Manon and the Thirteen knelt in the blood-soaked earth and dug the grave.

Dorian assisted Bronwen and Glennis in drafting messages to the King and Queen of Eyllwe and their two sons. Warning them of the danger—and nothing more. No request for aid, for armies.

Just before dawn, the Crochan messengers returned. Their southern kin who had summoned them here had arrived right after the massacre, too late to save the human war band or the few witches they'd sent ahead. They had flown right to Banjali, where their four covens now aided the King and Queen of Eyllwe.

Not that the Eyllwe royals seemed to need it. No, the other Crochan messenger had returned with a message from the king himself: the loss of the war band was grave indeed, but Eyllwe was not broken by it. Their rebels and gathered forces, while small, were still resisting Morath, still unbroken. They would continue to hold the line in the South, and would do so until their final breaths.

Dorian gleaned the unwritten words, though: they did not have a single soldier to spare for Terrasen. After what he'd seen, Dorian was now inclined to agree.

Eyllwe had given too much, for too long. It was time for the rest of them to shoulder the burden.

Dorian wondered if Manon noted the Crochans who watched her. Not with hatred, but some small degree of respect. Together, the Thirteen dug a massive grave, not even asking their wyverns to haul away the dirt.

The sun rose, then began its descent. Slowly, the grave took form. Large enough for every fallen warrior.

He had to go to Morath. Soon.

Before this occurred again. Before one more mass grave was dug. He couldn't endure the thought of it, worse than the thought of another collar going around his neck.

Night was full overhead by the time Dorian managed to slip away. By the time he found an empty clearing, drew the marks, and plunged Damaris into earth shining with his own blood.

His summons was answered quickly this time.

Yet it was not Gavin who emerged, shimmering, from the night air.

Dorian's magic flared, rallying to strike, as the figure took form.

As Kaltain Rompier, clad in an onyx gown and dark hair unbound, smiled sadly at him.

Every word vanished from Dorian's tongue.

But his magic remained swirling about him, invisible hands eager to crack bone.

Not that there was any life to steal from Kaltain Rompier.

Yet she still held up a slender hand, her gauzy dress and silken hair floating on a phantom wind. "I mean you no harm."

"I didn't summon you." It was the only thing he could think to say.

Kaltain's dark eyes slid toward Damaris, jutting from the circle of Wyrdmarks. "Didn't you?"

He didn't want to contemplate why or how the sword had somehow called her, not Gavin. Whether the sword had a will of its own, or whether the god who'd blessed it had orchestrated this meeting. For whatever truth it deemed necessary to show him.

"I thought you were destroyed at Morath," he rasped.

"I was." Her face was softer than he'd ever seen it in life. "In so many ways, I was."

Manon and Elide had told him what she'd endured. What she'd done for them. He bowed his head. "I'm sorry."

"Whatever for?"

Then the words tumbled out, spilling from where he'd kept them since the Stone Marshes of Eyllwe. "For not seeing as I should have. For not knowing where they took you. For not helping you when I had the chance."

"Did you have the chance?" The question was calm, yet he could have sworn an edge sharpened in her voice.

He opened his mouth to deny it. But he made himself look back—at who he'd been long before the collar, before Sorscha. "I knew you were in the castle dungeon. I was content to let you rot there. And then Perrington—Erawan, I mean, took you to Morath, and I didn't bother to wonder about it." Shame sluiced through him. "I'm sorry," he repeated.

A Crown Prince who had not served his kingdom or his people, not really. Gavin had been right.

Kaltain's edges shimmered. "I was not wholly blameless, you know."

"What happened to you in Morath is in no way your fault."

"No, it wasn't," she agreed, a shadow passing over her face. "But I made choices of my own in going to Rifthold last autumn, in pursuing my ambition for you—your crown. I regret some of them."

His gaze slid to her bare forearm, to the scar that lingered even in death. "You saved my friends," he said, and knelt before her. "You gave up everything to save them, and get the Wyrdkey away from Erawan." He would do the same, if he could survive Morath's horrors. "I am in your debt."

Kaltain stared down at where he knelt. "I never had friends of my own. Not as you have. I always envied you for it. You, and Aelin."

He lifted his head. "You know who she is?"

A hint of a smile. "Death has its advantages."

He couldn't stop his next question. "Is—is it better there? Are you at peace?"

"I am not allowed to say," Kaltain replied softly, her eyes shining with understanding. "And I am not allowed to say who dwells here with me."

He nodded, fighting past the tightness in his chest, the disappointment. But he cocked his head to the side. "Who forbids you from doing so?" If the twelve gods of this land were stranded in Erilea, they certainly didn't rule over other realms.

Kaltain's lips curved upward. "I am not allowed to say, either." When he opened his mouth to ask more, she cut him off. "There are other forces at work. Beyond what is tangible and what is known."

He glanced toward Damaris. "Other gods?"

Kaltain's silence was answer enough. But—another time. He'd contemplate it another time.

"I never thought to summon you," he admitted. "You, who knew Morath's true horrors. I didn't realize . . ." He let the words trail off as he rose to his feet.

"That there'd be anything left of me to summon?" she finished. He winced. "The key ate away much—but not everything."

"Is the third one indeed at Morath, then?"

She nodded gravely. Her body shimmered, fading swiftly. "Though I do not know where he kept it. I wasn't . . . ready to receive the second one before I took matters into my own hands." She ran her slender fingers over the black scar snaking down her arm.

He'd never spoken to her—not really. Had barely given her more than a passing glance, or grimaced his way through polite conversation with her.

And yet here she stood, the woman who had taken out a third of Morath, who had devoured a Valg prince from sheer will alone.

"How did you do it?" he whispered. "How did you break free of its control?" He had to know. If he was walking into hell itself, if it was more than likely he'd wind up with a new collar around his throat, he had to know.

Kaltain studied his neck before she met his stare. "Because I raged against it. Because I did not feel that I deserved the collar."

The truth of her words slammed into him as surely as if she'd shoved his chest.

Kaltain only asked, "You drew the summoning marks for a reason. What is it you wish to know?"

Dorian tucked away the truth she'd thrown at him, the mirror she held up to all he'd once been and had become. He had not been a true prince—not in spirit, not in deeds. He'd tried to be, but too late. He had acted too late. He doubted he was doing much better as king. Certainly not when he'd dismissed Adarlan out of his own guilt and anger, questioned whether it should be saved.

As if there were ever a possibility that it didn't deserve to be.

He asked at last, "Am I ready to go to Morath?"

She alone would know. Had witnessed things far worse than any Manon or Elide had beheld.

Kaltain again glanced to Damaris. "You know the answer."

"You won't try to convince me not to go?"

But Kaltain's mouth tightened as her onyx gown began to blend into the gathered night. "You know what you will face there. It is not for me to tell you if you are ready."

His mouth went dry.

Kaltain said, "Everything you have heard about Morath is true. True, and still there is more that is worse than you can imagine. Stay to the keep. It is Erawan's stronghold, and likely the only place he would trust to store the key."

Dorian nodded, his heart beginning to hammer. "I will."

She took a step toward him, but halted as her edges rippled further. "Don't linger too long, and don't attract his attention. He is arrogant, and wholly self-absorbed, and will not bother to look too closely at what might creep through his halls. Be quick, Dorian."

A tremor went through his hands, but he balled them into fists. "If I can kill him, should I take the chance?"

"No." She shook her head. "You would not walk away from it. He has a chamber deep in the keep—it is where he stores the collars. He will bring you there if he catches you."

He straightened. "I— "

"Go to Morath, as you have planned. Retrieve the key, and nothing more. Or you will find yourself with a collar around your neck again."

He swallowed. "I can barely shift."

Kaltain gave him a half smile as she dissolved into the moonlight. "Can't you?"

And then she was gone.

Dorian stared at the place she'd stood, the Wyrdmarks already vanished. Only Damaris remained standing there, witness to the truth it had somehow sensed he needed to hear.

So Dorian felt for that tangle in his magic, the place where raw power eddied and emerged as whatever he wished.

Let go—the shifting magic's command. Let go of everything. Let go of that wall he'd built around himself the moment the Valg prince had invaded him, and look within. At himself. Perhaps what the sword had asked him to do in summoning Kaltain instead.

Who do you wish to be?

"Someone worthy of my friends," he said into the quiet night. "A king worthy of his kingdom." For a heartbeat, snow-white hair and golden eyes flashed into his mind. "Happy," he whispered, and wrapped a hand around Damaris's hilt. Let go of that lingering scrap of terror.

The ancient sword warmed in his hand, a friendly and swift heat.

It flowed up through his fingers, his wrist. To that place within him where all those truths had dwelled, where it became warmth edged with sharpest pain.

And then the world grew and expanded, the trees rising, the ground approaching—

He made to touch his face, but found he had no hands.

Only soot-black wings. Only an ebony beak that allowed no words past it.

A raven. A—

A soft inhale of air had him twisting his neck—far more easily in this form—toward the trees. Toward Manon, standing in the shadows of an oak, her bloody, filthy hand braced against the trunk as she stared at him. At the transformation.

Dorian fumbled for the thread of power that held him in this strange, light form. Instantly, the world swaying, he grew and grew, back into his human body, Damaris cold and still at his feet. His clothes somehow intact. Perhaps through whatever differences existed between his raw magic and a true shifter's gift.

But Manon's lip curled back from her teeth. Her golden eyes glowed like embers. "When, exactly, were you going to inform me that you were about to retrieve the third Wyrdkey?"

CHAPTER
34

"We need to retreat," Galan Ashryver panted to Aedion as they stood by the water tent deep in their army's ranks, the Crown Prince splattered with blood both red and black.

Three days of fighting in the frigid wind and snow, three days of being pushed northward mile by mile. Aedion had the soldiers on rotation to the front lines, and those who managed to catch a few minutes of sleep returned to the fighting with heavier and heavier feet.

He'd left the front line himself minutes ago, only after Kyllian had ordered him to, going so far as to throw Aedion behind him, the Bane roughly passing him along until he was here, the Crown Prince of Wendlyn gulping down water by the farthest reaches of their forces. The prince's olive skin was ashen, his Ashryver eyes dim as they monitored soldiers rushing or trudging past.

"We retreat here, and we stand to be chased all the way to Orynth." Aedion's raw throat ached with each word.

He had never seen an army so large. Even at Theralis, all those years ago.

Galan handed Aedion his waterskin, and Aedion drank deeply. "I will follow you, cousin, to however this may end, but we cannot keep this up. Not for another full night."

Aedion knew that. Had realized it after the fighting had continued under cover of darkness.

When the men had started asking why Aelin of the Wildfire did not burn away their enemies. Did not at least give them light by which to fight.

Why she had vanished again.

Lysandra had donned her wyvern form to battle the ilken, but she had been forced to yield, to fall behind their lines. Good for killing ilken, yes, but also a large target for Morath's archers and spear-throwers.

Ahead, too close for comfort, screams and clashing weapons rose toward the sky. Even the Fae royals' magic was beginning to waver, their soldiers with them. Where it failed, the Silent Assassins lay waiting, shredding apart Valg and ilken alike with swift efficiency. But there were only so many of them. And still no sign of Ansel of Briarcliff's additional army.

Soon, the red-haired queen had promised with uncharacteristic graveness only hours ago, the legion with her already dwindling rapidly. *The rest of my army will be here soon.*

Snarling rose nearby, cutting through the din of battle. The ghost leopard had not faltered, had barely stopped to rest.

He had to go back out. Had to eat something and go back out. Kyllian could maintain order for a good while, but Aedion was their prince. And with Aelin nowhere in sight . . . it was upon him to keep the soldiers in line.

Though those lines were buckling, like leaks in a dam.

"The Lanis River by Perranth," Aedion murmured as Ilias and the Silent Assassins shot ilken out of the sky, their arrows easily finding their marks. Wings first, they'd learned the hard way. To get them out of the air. Then blades to the head, to decapitate fully.

Or else they'd rise again. And remember who had tried to kill them.

"If we retreat northward," Aedion went on, "get to Perranth and cross the river, we could force them to make the crossing, too. Pick them off that way."

"Is there a bridge?" Galan's face tightened as one of the two remaining Valg princes sent a wave of dark power for a cluster of their soldiers. Men wilted like flowers in a frost.

A blast of wind and ice answered—Sellene or Endymion. Maybe one of their many cousins.

"No bridge big enough. But the river's frozen solid—we might cross it, then melt it."

"With Aelin." A doubtful, careful question.

Aedion gestured toward the source of that answering blast of magic, now warring with the Valg princes' power. "If the Fae royals can make ice, then they can unfreeze it. Right beneath Morath's feet."

Galan's turquoise eyes flickered, either at the plan or the fact that Aelin would not be the one enacting it. "Morath might see through us."

"There's little other option." From Perranth, they'd have access to more supplies, perhaps fresh troops rallying to them from the city itself. To retreat, though . . .

Aedion surveyed the lines being picked off one by one, the soldiers on their last legs.

Retreat and live. Fight and die.

For this resistance would founder, if they kept at this. Here, on the southern plains, they'd be ended.

There was no guarantee Rowan and the others would find Aelin. That Dorian and Manon might retrieve the third Wyrdkey and then give them to his queen, should she get free, should she find them in this mess of a world. No guarantee how many Crochans Manon might rally, if any.

With the armada spread too thin along Terasen's coast to be of any use, only Ansel of Briarcliff's remaining forces could offer some relief. If they weren't all clean-picked bones by then. There was little choice but to hold out until they arrived. Their last allies.

Because Rolfe and the Mycenians . . . there was no guarantee that they would come. No word.

"Order the retreat," Aedion said to the prince. "And get word to Endymion and Sellene that we'll need their power as soon as we begin to run."

To throw all their magic into a mighty shield to guard their backs while they tried to put as many miles between them and Morath as possible.

Galan nodded, shoving his bloody helmet over his dark hair, and stalked through the chaotic mass of soldiers.

A retreat. This soon, this fast. For all his training, the brutal years of learning and fighting and leading, this was what it had come to.

Would they even make it to Perranth?

The order with which the army had marched southward utterly collapsed on the flight back north. The Fae troops stayed at their rear, magic shields buckling, yet holding. Keeping Morath's forces at bay by the foothills while they retreated toward Perranth.

The grumbling amongst the limping, exhausted soldiers trickled past Lysandra as she trudged between them, wearing the form of a horse. She'd allowed a young man onto her back when she'd spied his guts nearly hanging out of his rent armor.

For long miles, his leaking blood had warmed her sides as he lay sprawled over her.

The warm trickle had long stopped. Frozen.

So had he.

She hadn't the heart to dislodge him, to leave his dead body on the field to be trampled. His blood had frozen him to her anyway.

Each step was an effort of will, her own wounds healing faster than the soldiers' around her. Many fell during the march toward Perranth. Some were picked up, hauled by their companions or strangers.

Some did not rise again.

The resistance was not supposed to break apart so soon.

The grumbling worsened the closer to Perranth they got, despite a quick few hours of rest that first night. *Where is the queen? Where is her fire?*

She couldn't fight as Aelin—not convincingly, and not well enough to stay alive. And when the Fire-Bringer fought with no flame ... they might know then.

She has run away. Again.

Two Silent Assassins noticed on the second night that the dead soldier still lay on Lysandra's back.

They said nothing as they gathered warm water to melt the blood and gore that had bound him to her. Then to wash her.

In her roan mare form, she had no words to offer them, had no way to ask if they knew what she was. They treated her with kindness nonetheless.

No one made to reach for the lone horse roaming through the ramshackle camp. Some soldiers had erected tents. Many just slept beside the fires, under cloaks and jackets.

Her ears were ringing. Had been ringing since the first clashing of the battle.

She didn't know how she found his tent, but there it was, flaps open to the night to reveal him standing with Galan, Ansel, and Ren.

The Lord of Allsbrook's brows rose as she entered, her head nearly hitting the ceiling.

A horse. She was still a horse.

Ren staggered toward her, despite the exhaustion surely weighing down every inch of him.

Lysandra fumbled for the thread inside her, the thread back to her human body, the shimmering light that would shrink her into it.

The four of them only stared as she found it, fought for it. The magic ripped the last of the strength from her. By the time she was again in her own skin, she was already falling to the hay-covered floor.

She didn't feel the cold slam into her bare skin, didn't care as she collapsed to her knees.

Ansel was already there, slinging her cloak around her. "Where the hell have you been?"

Even the Queen of the Wastes was pale, her wine-red hair plastered to her head beneath the dirt and blood.

Lysandra had no speech left in her. Could only kneel, clutching the cloak.

"We move an hour before dawn," Aedion said, the order a clear dismissal.

Ansel and Galan nodded, peeling out of the tent. Ren only murmured, "I'll find you some food, Lady," before he exited the tent.

Boots crunched in hay, and then he was knee to knee before her. Aedion.

There was nothing kind on his face. No pity or warmth.

For a long minute, they only stared at each other.

Then the prince growled softly, "Your plan was bullshit."

She said nothing, and couldn't stop her shoulders from curving inward.

"Your plan was *bullshit*," he breathed, his eyes sparking. "How could you ever be her, wear her skin, and think to get away with it? How could you *ever* think you'd get around the fact that our armies are *counting on you* to burn the enemy to ashes, and all you can do is run away and emerge as some beast instead?"

"You don't get to pin this retreat on me," she rasped. The first words she'd spoken in days and days.

"You agreed to let Aelin go to her *death*, and leave us here to be slashed to bloody ribbons. You two told no one of this *plan*, told none of us who might have explained the realities of this war, and that we would need a gods-damned Fire-Bringer and not an untrained, *useless* shape-shifter against Morath."

Blow after blow, the words landed upon her weary heart. "We—"

"If you were so willing to let Aelin die, then you should have let her do it *after* she incinerated Erawan's hordes!"

"It would not have stopped Maeve from capturing her."

"If you'd told us, we might have planned differently, acted differently, and we would not be *here*, damn you!"

She stared at the muddy hay. "Throw me out of your army, then."

"You ruined everything." His words were colder than the wind outside. "You, and her."

Lysandra closed her eyes.

Hay rustled, and she knew he'd risen to his feet, knew it as his words speared from above her bowed head. "Get out of my tent."

She wasn't certain she could move enough to obey, though she wished to. Needed to.

Fight back. She should fight back. Rage at him as he lashed at her, needing an outlet for his fear and despair.

Lysandra opened her eyes, peering up at him. At the rage on his face, the hatred.

She managed to stand, her body bleating in pain. Managed to look him in the eye, even as Aedion said again with quiet cold, "Get out."

Barefoot in the snow, naked beneath her cloak. Aedion glanced at her bare legs, as if realizing it. And not caring.

So Lysandra nodded, clutching Ansel's cloak tighter, and strode into the frigid night.

⁓

"Where is she?" Ren asked, a mug of what smelled like watery soup in one hand, a chunk of bread in the other. The lord scanned the tent as if he would find her under the cot, the hay.

Aedion stared at the precious few logs burning in the brazier, and said nothing.

"What have you done?" Ren breathed.

Everything was about to end. Had been doomed since Maeve had stolen Aelin. Since his queen and the shifter had struck their agreement.

So it didn't matter, what he'd said. He hadn't cared if it wasn't fair, wasn't true.

Didn't care if he was so tired he couldn't muster shame at his pinning on her the blame for the sure defeat they'd face in a matter of days before Perranth's walls.

He wished she'd smacked him, had screamed at him.

But she had let him rage. And had walked out into the snow, barefoot.

He'd promised to save Terrasen, to hold the lines. Had done so for years.

And yet this test against Morath, when it had counted . . . he had failed.

He'd muster the strength to fight again. To rally his men. He just . . . he needed to sleep.

Aedion didn't notice when Ren left, undoubtedly in search of the shifter with whom he was so damned enamored.

He should summon his Bane commanders. See how they thought to manage this disaster.

But he couldn't. Could do nothing but stare into that fire as the long night passed.

CHAPTER 35

She had not trusted this world, this dream. The companions who had walked with her, led her here. The warrior-prince with pine-green eyes and who smelled of Terrasen.

Him, she had not dared to believe at all. Not the words he spoke, but the mere fact that he was *there*. She did not trust that he'd removed the mask, the irons. They had vanished in other dreams, too—dreams that had proved false.

But the Little Folk had told her it was true. All of this. They had said it was safe, and she was to rest, and they would look after her.

And that terrible, relentless pressure writhing in her veins—it had eased. Just enough to think, to breathe and act beyond pure instinct.

She'd siphoned off as much as she dared, but not all. Certainly not all.

So she had slept. She'd done that, too, in those other dreams. Had lived through days and weeks of stories that then washed away like footprints in the sand.

Yet when she opened her eyes, the cave remained, dimmer now. The thrumming power had nestled deeper, slumbering. The ache in her ribs had faded, the slice down her forearm had healed—but the scab remained.

The only mark on her.

Aelin prodded it with a finger. Dull pain echoed in response.

Smooth—not the scab, but her finger. Smooth like glass as she rubbed the pads of her thumb and forefinger together.

No calluses. Not on her fingers, on her palms. Utterly blank, wiped of the imprint from the years of training, or the year in Endovier.

But this new scab, this faint throbbing beneath it—that remained, at least.

Curled on the rock floor, she took in the cave.

The white wolf lay at her back, snoring softly. Their sphere of transparent flame still burned around them, easing the strain ember by ember. But not wholly.

Aelin swallowed, tasting ash.

Her magic opened an eye in response.

Aelin sucked in a breath. Not here—not yet.

She whispered it to the flame. *Not yet*.

But the flame around her and the wolf flared and thickened, blotting out the cave. She clenched her jaw.

Not yet, she promised it. Not until it could be done safely. Away from them.

Her magic pushed against her bones, but she ignored it. Leashed it.

The bubble of flame shrunk, protesting, and grew transparent once more. Through it she could make out a water-carved basin, the slumbering forms of her other companions.

The warrior-prince slept only a few feet from the edge of her fire, tucked into an alcove in the cave wall. Exhaustion lay heavy upon him, though he had not disarmed himself.

A sword hung from his belt, its ruby smoldering in the light of her fire.

She knew that sword. An ancient sword, forged in these lands for a deadly war.

It had been her sword, too. Those erased calluses had fit its hilt so perfectly. And the warrior-prince now bearing it had found the sword for her. In a cave like this one, full of the relics of heroes long since sent to the Afterworld.

She studied the tattoo snaking down the side of his face and neck, vanishing into his dark clothes.

I am your mate.

She had wanted to believe him, but this dream, this illusion she'd been spun . . .

Not an illusion.

He had come for her.

Rowan.

Rowan Whitethorn. Now Rowan Whitethorn Galathynius, her husband and king-consort. Her mate.

She mouthed his name.

He had come for her.

Rowan.

Silently, so smoothly that not even the white wolf awoke, she sat up, a hand clutching the cloak that smelled of pine and snow. His cloak, his scent woven through the fibers.

She rose to her feet, legs sturdier than they'd been. A thought had the bubble of flame expanding as she crossed the few feet toward the sleeping prince.

She peered down at his face, handsome and yet unyielding.

His eyes opened, meeting hers as if he'd known where to find her even in sleep.

An unspoken question arose in those green eyes. *Aelin?*

She ignored the silent inquiry, unable to bear opening that silent channel between them again, and surveyed the powerful lines of his body, the sheer size of him. A gentle wind kissed with ice and lightning brushed against her wall of flame, an echo of his silent inquiry.

Her magic flared in answer, a ripple of power dancing through her.

As if it had found a mirror of itself in the world, as if it had found the countermelody to its own song.

Not once in those illusions or dreams had it done that. Had her own flame leaped in joy at his nearness, his power.

He was here. It was him, and he'd come for her.

The flame melted into nothing but cool cave air. Not melted, but rather sucked inside herself, coiling, a great beast straining at the leash.

Rowan. Prince Rowan.

He sat up slowly, a stillness settling over him.

He knew. He'd said it to her earlier, before she'd let oblivion claim her. *I am your mate.*

They must have told him, then. Their companions. Elide and Lorcan and Gavriel. They'd all been on that beach where everything had gone to hell.

Her magic surged, and she rolled her shoulders, willing it to sleep, to wait—just a while longer.

She was here. They were both here.

What could she ever say to him, to explain it, to make it right? That he'd been used so foully, had suffered so greatly, because of her?

There was blood on him. So much blood, soaking into his dark clothes. From the smears on his neck, the arcs under his fingernails, it seemed he'd tried to wash some off. But the scent remained.

She knew that smell—who it belonged to.

Her spine tightened, her limbs tensing. Working past her clenched jaw, she inhaled sharply. Forced a long breath out through her teeth. Forced herself to work past the scent of Cairn's blood. What it did to her. Her magic thrashed, howling.

And she made herself say to him, to her prince who smelled of home, "Is he alive?"

Cold rage flickered across Rowan's eyes. "No."

Dead. Cairn was dead. The tautness in her body eased—just slightly. Her flame, too, banked. "How?"

No remorse dimmed his face. "You once told me at Mistward that if I ever took a whip to you, then you'd skin me alive." His eyes didn't stray from hers as he said with lethal quiet, "I took it upon myself to bestow that fate on Cairn on your behalf. And when I was done, I took the liberty of removing his head from his body, then burning what remained." A pause, a ripple of doubt. "I'm sorry I didn't give you the chance to do it yourself."

She didn't have it in her to feel a spark of surprise, to marvel at the brutality of the vengeance he'd exacted. Not as the words sank in. Not as her lungs opened up once again.

"I couldn't risk bringing him here for you to kill," Rowan went on, scanning her face. "Or risk leaving him alive, either."

She lifted her palms, studying the unmarked, empty skin.

Cairn had done that. Had shredded her apart so badly they needed to put her back together again. Had wiped away all traces of who and what she'd been, what she'd seen and endured.

She lowered her hands to her sides. "I'm glad," she said, and the words were true.

A shudder went through Rowan, and his head dipped slightly. "Are you . . ." He seemed to grapple with the right word. "Can I hold you?"

The stark need in his voice ripped at her, but she stepped back. "I . . ." She scanned the cave, blocking out the way his eyes guttered at her retreat. Across the chamber, the great lake flowed, smooth and flat as a black mirror. "I need to bathe," she said, her voice low and raw. Even if there wasn't a mark on her beyond dirty feet. "I need to wash it away," she tried again.

Understanding softened his eyes. He pointed with a tattooed hand to the trough nearby. "There are a few extra cloths for you to wash with." Dragging a hand through his silver hair, longer than she'd last seen it—in this world, this truth, at least—he added, "I don't know how, but they also found some of your old clothes from Mistward and brought them here."

But words were becoming distant again, dissolving on her tongue.

Her magic rumbled, pressing against her blood, squeezing her bones. *Out*, it howled. *Out*.

Soon, she promised.

Now. It thrashed. Her hands trembled, curling, as if she could keep it in.

So she turned away, aiming not toward the trough but the lake beyond.

The air stirred behind her, and she felt him following. When Rowan gleaned where she intended to bathe, he warned, "That water is barely above freezing, Aelin."

She just dropped the cloak onto the black stones and stepped into the water.

Steam hissed, wafting around her in billowing clouds. She kept going, embracing the water's bite with each step, even if it failed to pierce the heat of her.

The water was clear, though the gloom veiled the bottom that sloped away as she dove under the frigid surface.

The water was silent. Cool, and welcome, and calm.

So Aelin loosened the leash—only a fraction.

Flame leapt out, devoured by the frigid water. Consumed by it.

It pulled away that pressure, that endless fog of heat. Soothed and chilled until thoughts took form.

With each stroke beneath the surface, out into the darkness, she could feel it again. Herself. Or whatever was left of it.

Aelin. She was Aelin Ashryver Whitethorn Galathynius, and she was Queen of Terrasen.

More magic rippled out, but she held her grip. Not all—not yet.

She had been captured by Maeve, tortured by her. Tortured by Cairn, her sentinel. But she had escaped, and her mate had come for her. Had found her, just as they had found each other despite centuries of bloodshed and loss and war.

Aelin. She was Aelin, and this was not some illusion, but the real world.

Aelin.

She swam out into the lake, and Rowan followed the jutting lip of stone along the shore's edge.

She dropped beneath the surface, letting herself sink and sink and sink, toes grasping only open, cool water, straining for a bottom that did not arrive.

Down into the dark, the cold.

The ancient, icy water pulled away the flame and heat and strain. Pulled and sucked and waved it off.

Cooled that burning core of her until she took form, a blade red-hot from the fire plunged into water.

Aelin. That's who she was.

~

That lake water had never seen sunlight, had flowed from the dark, cold heart of the mountains themselves. It would kill even the most hardened of Fae warriors within minutes.

Yet there was Aelin, swimming as if it were a sun-warmed forest pool.

She treaded water, dipping her head back every now and then to scrub at her hair.

He hadn't realized that she was burning so hotly until she'd stepped into the frigid lake and steam had risen.

Silently, she'd dove in, swimming beneath the surface, the water so clear he could see every stroke of her faintly glowing body. As if the water had peeled away the skin of the woman and revealed the blazing soul beneath.

But that glow faded with each passing breath she emerged to take, dimming further each time she plunged beneath the surface.

Had she wished for him not to touch her because of that internal inferno, or simply because she first wanted to wash away the stain of Cairn? Perhaps both. At least she'd begun speaking, her eyes clearing a bit.

They remained clear as she treaded water, the glow still barely cling-ing, and peered up at where he stood on a sliver of black rock jutting into the lake.

"You could join me," she said at last.

No heat in her words, yet he felt the invitation. Not to taste her body the way he yearned to, needed to in order to know she was here with him, but rather to be *with* her. "Unlike you," he said, trying to steady his voice as the recognition on her face threatened to buckle his knees, "I don't think my magic would warm me so well if I got in."

He wanted to, though. Gods, he wanted to leap in. But he made him-self add, "This lake is ancient. You should get out." Before something came creeping along.

She did no such thing, her arms continuing their sweeping circles in the water. Aelin only stared at him again in that grave, cautious way. "I didn't break," she said quietly. His heart cracked at the words. "I didn't tell them anything."

She didn't say it for praise, to boast. But rather to tell him, her consort, of where they stood in this war. What their enemies might know.

"I knew you wouldn't," he managed to say.

"She . . . she tried to convince me that this was the bad dream. When Cairn was done with me, or during it, I don't know, she'd try to worm her way into my mind." She glanced around the cave, as if she could see the world beyond it. "She spun fantasies that felt so real . . ." She bobbed under the surface. Perhaps she'd needed the cooling water of the lake to be able to hear her own voice again; perhaps she needed the distance between them so she could speak these words. She emerged, slicking back her hair with a hand. "They felt like this."

Half of him didn't want to know, but he asked, "What sort of illusions?"

A long pause. "It doesn't matter now."

Too soon to push—if ever.

Then she asked softly, "How long?"

It took the entirety of his three centuries of training to keep the devastation, the agony for her, from his face. "Two months, three days, and seven hours."

Her mouth tightened, either at the length of time, or the fact that he'd counted every single one of those hours apart.

She ran her fingers through her hair, its strands floating around her in the water. Still too long for two months to have passed. "They healed me after each . . . session. So that I stopped knowing what had been done and what was in my mind and where the truth lay." Erase her scars, and Maeve stood a better chance at convincing her none of this was real. "But the healers couldn't remember how long my hair was, or Maeve wanted to confuse me further, so they grew it out." Her eyes darkened at the memory of why, perhaps, they had needed to regrow her hair in the first place.

"Do you want me to cut it back to the length it was when I last saw you?" His words were near-guttural.

"No." Ripples shivered around her. "I want it so I can remember."

What had been done to her, what she'd survived and what she had protected. Even with all he'd done to Cairn, the way he'd made sure the male was kept alive and screaming throughout, Rowan wished the male were still breathing, if only so he could take longer killing him.

And when he found Maeve . . .

That was not his kill. He'd ended Cairn, and didn't regret it. But Aelin . . . Maeve was hers.

Even if the woman treading water before him didn't seem to have vengeance on her mind. Not so much as a hint of the burning rage that fueled her.

He didn't blame her. Knew it would take time, time and distance, to heal the internal wounds. If they could ever really heal at all.

But he'd work with her, help in whatever way he could. And if she never returned to who she had been before this, he would not love her any less.

Aelin dunked her head, and when she emerged, she said, "Maeve was about to put a Valg collar around my neck. She left to retrieve it." The scent of her lingering fear drifted toward him, and Rowan lurched a step closer to the water's edge. "It's why I—why I got away. She had me moved to the army camp for safekeeping, and I . . ." Her voice stalled, yet she met his stare. Let him read the words she could not say, in that silent way they'd always been able to communicate. *Escape wasn't my intention.*

"No, Fireheart," he breathed, shaking his head, horror creeping over him. "There . . . there was no collar."

She blinked, head angling. "That was a dream, too?"

His heart cracked as he struggled for the words. Made himself voice them. "No—it was real. Or Maeve thought it was. But the collars, the Valg presence . . . It was a lie that we crafted. To draw Maeve out, hopefully away from you and Doranelle."

Only the faint lapping of water sounded. "There was no collar?"

Rowan lowered himself to his knees and shook his head. "I—Aelin, if I'd known what she'd do with the knowledge, what you'd decide to do—"

He might have lost her. Not from Maeve or the gods or the Lock, but from his own damned choices. The lie he'd spun.

Aelin drifted beneath the surface again. So deep that when the flare happened, it was little more than a flutter.

The light burst from her, rippling across the lake, illumining the stones, the slick ceiling above. A silent eruption.

His breathing turned ragged. But she swam toward the surface again, light streaming off her body like tendrils of clouds. It had nearly vanished when she emerged.

"I'm sorry," he managed to say.

Again, that angle of the head. "You have nothing to be sorry for."

He did, though. He'd added to her terror, her desperation. He'd—

"If you had not planted that lie for Maeve, if she had not told me, I don't think we'd be here right now," she said.

He tried to rein in the twisting in his gut, the urge to reach for her, to beg for her forgiveness. Tried and tried.

She only asked, "What of the others?"

She didn't know—couldn't know how and why and where they'd all parted ways. So Rowan told her, as succinctly and calmly as he could.

When he finished, Aelin was quiet for long minutes.

She stared out into the blackness, the rippling of her treading water the only sound. Her body had nearly lost that freshly forged glow.

Then she pivoted back toward him. "Maeve said you and the others were in the North. That you'd been spotted by her spies there. Did you plant that deception for her, too?"

He shook his head. "Lysandra has been thorough, it seems."

Aelin's throat bobbed. "I believed her."

It sounded like a confession, somehow.

So Rowan found himself saying, "I told you once that even if death separated us, I would rip apart every world until I found you." He gave her a slash of a smile. "Did you really believe this would stop me?"

She pursed her mouth, and at last, those agonizing emotions began to surface in her eyes. "You were supposed to save Terrasen."

"Considering that the sun shines, I'd say Erawan hasn't won yet. So we'll save it together."

He didn't let himself think of the final cost of destroying Erawan. And Aelin seemed in no hurry to discuss it, either, as she said, "You should have gone to Terrasen. It needs you."

"I need you more." He didn't balk from the stark honesty roughening his voice. "And Terrasen will need you, too. Not Lysandra masquerading as you, but *you*."

A shallow nod. "Maeve raised her army. I doubt it was only to guard me while she was away."

He'd put the thought aside, to consider later. "It might just be to shore up her defenses, should Erawan win across the sea."

"Do you truly think that's what she plans to do with it?"

"No," he admitted. "I don't."

And if Maeve meant to bring that army to Terrasen, to either unite with Erawan or simply be another force battering their kingdom, to strike when they were weakest, they had to hurry. Had to get back. Immediately. His mate's eyes shone with the same understanding and dread.

Aelin's throat bobbed as she whispered, "I'm so tired, Rowan."

His heart strained again. "I know, Fireheart."

He opened his mouth to say more, to coax her onto land so he might at least hold her if words couldn't ease her burden, but that's when he saw it.

A boat, ancient and every inch of it carved, drifted out of the gloom.

"Get back to shore." The boat wasn't drifting—it was being tugged. He could just barely make out two dark forms slithering beneath the surface.

Aelin didn't hesitate, yet her strokes remained steady as she swam for him. She didn't balk at the hand he extended, and he wrapped his cloak around her while the boat ambled past.

Black, eel-like creatures about the size of a mortal man pulled it. Their fins drifted behind them like ebony veils, and with each propelling sweep of their long tails, he glimpsed milky-white eyes. Blind.

They led the flat-bottomed vessel large enough for fifteen Fae males right to the edge of the lake. A flash of short, spindly bodies through the dimness and the Little Folk had it moored to a nearby stalagmite.

The others must have heard his order to Aelin, because they emerged, swords out. A foot behind them, Elide lingered with Fenrys, the male still in wolf form.

"They can't mean for us to take that into the caves," Lorcan murmured.

But Aelin turned toward them, hair dripping onto the stone at her bare feet. Half a thought from her could have had her dry, yet she made no move to do so. "We're being hunted."

"We know that," Lorcan shot back, and were it not for the fact that Aelin was currently allowing him to rest a hand upon her shoulder, Rowan would have thrown the male into the lake.

But Aelin's features didn't shift from that graveness, that unruffled calm. "The only way to the sea is through these caves."

It was an outrageous claim. They were a hundred miles inland, and there was no record of these mountains ever connecting to any cave system that flowed to the ocean itself. To do so, they'd have to go northward through this range, then veer westward at the Cambrian Mountains, and sail beneath them right to the coast.

"And I suppose they told you that?" Lorcan's face was hard as granite.

"Watch it," Rowan snarled. Fenrys indeed bared his teeth at the darkhaired warrior, fur bristling.

But Aelin said simply, "Yes." Her chin didn't dip an inch. "The land above is crawling with soldiers and spies. Going beneath them is the only way."

Elide stepped forward. "I will go." She cut a cold glance toward Lorcan. "You can take your chances above, if you're so disbelieving."

Lorcan's jaw tightened, and a small part of Rowan relished seeing the delicate Lady of Perranth fillet the centuries-hardened warrior with a few words. "Considering the potential pitfalls of the situation is wise."

"We don't have time to consider," Rowan cut in before Elide could voice the retort on her tongue. "We need to keep moving."

Gavriel stalked forward to study the moored boat and what seemed to be bundles of supplies on its sturdy planks. "How will we navigate our way, though?"

"We'll be escorted," Aelin answered.

"And if they abandon us?" Lorcan challenged.

Aelin leveled unfazed eyes upon him. "Then you'll have to find a way out, I suppose."

A hint—just a spark—of temper belied those calm words.

There was nothing else to debate after that. And they had little to pack. The others gave Aelin privacy to dress by the fire while they inspected the boat, and when his mate emerged again, clad in boots, pants, and various layers beneath her gray surcoat, the sight of her in clothes from Mistward was enough to make his gut clench.

No longer a naked, escaped captive. Yet none of that wickedness, that joy and unchecked wildness illuminated her face.

The rest of their party waited on the boat, seated on the benches built into its high-lipped sides. Fenrys and Elide both sat as seemingly far from Lorcan as they could get, Gavriel a golden, long-suffering buffer between them.

Rowan lingered at the shore's edge, a hand extended for Aelin while she approached. Each of her steps seemed considered—as if she still marveled at being able to move freely. As if still adjusting to her legs without the burden of chains.

"Why?" Lorcan mused aloud, more to himself. "Why go to these lengths for us?"

He got his answer—they all did—a heartbeat later.

Aelin halted a few feet away from the boat and Rowan's outstretched hand. She turned back toward the cave itself. The Little Folk peeked from those birch branches, from the rocks, from behind stalagmites.

Slowly, deeply, Aelin bowed to them.

Rowan could have sworn all those tiny heads lowered in answer.

A pair of bony grayish hands rose above a nearby rock, something glittering held between them, and set the object on the stone.

Rowan went still. A crown of silver and pearl and diamond gleamed there, fashioned into upswept swan's wings.

"The Crown of Mab," Gavriel breathed. But Fenrys looked away, toward the looming dark, his tail curling around him.

Aelin staggered a step closer to the crown. "It—it fell into the river."

Rowan didn't want to know how she'd encountered it, why she'd seen it fall into a river. Maeve had kept her sisters' two crowns under constant guard, only bringing them out to be displayed in her throne room on state occasions. In memory of her siblings, she'd intoned. Rowan had sometimes wondered if it was a reminder that she had outlasted them, had kept the throne for herself in the end.

The grayish hand slipped over the rock's edge again and nudged the crown in silent gesture. *Take it.*

"You want to know why?" Gavriel softly asked Lorcan as Aelin strode for the rock. Nothing but solemn reverence on her face. "Because she is not only Brannon's Heir, but Mab's, too."

A throwback to her great-great-grandmother, Maeve had taunted her. Who had inherited her strength, her immortal lifespan.

Aelin's fingers closed around the crown, lifting it gently. It sparkled like living moonlight between her hands.

My sister Mab's line ran true, Elide claimed Maeve had said on the beach. In every way, it seemed.

But Aelin made no move to don the crown while she approached him once more, her gait steadier this time. Trying not to dwell on the unbearable smoothness of her hand as it wrapped around his, Rowan helped her aboard, then climbed in himself before freeing the ropes tethering them to the shore.

Gavriel went on, awe in every word, "And that makes her their queen, too."

Aelin met Gavriel's gaze, the crown near-glowing in her hands. "Yes," was all she said as the boat sailed into the darkness.

CHAPTER 36

"How long will it take to reach the coast?" Elide's whisper echoed off the river-carved cavern walls.

She'd panicked when the boat had ventured beyond the glow of the shore and into a passageway across the lake, so dark she couldn't see her own hands before her face. To be trapped in such impenetrable dark for hours, days, possibly longer . . .

Had it been like that in the iron coffin? Aelin gave no indication that the smothering dark bothered her, and had shown no inclination to illuminate their way. Hadn't even summoned an ember.

But the Little Folk, it seemed, had come prepared. And within heartbeats of entering the pitch-black river passage, blue light had kindled on a lantern dangling over the curved prow.

Not light, not even magic. But small worms that glowed pale blue, as if they'd each swallowed the heart of a star.

They'd been gathered into the lantern, and their soft light rippled over the water-smooth walls. A gentle, soothing light. At least, for her it was so.

The Fae males sat alert, eyes gleaming with animalistic brightness, using the illumination to mark the caverns they were tugged down by those strange, serpentine beasts.

"We're not traveling swiftly," Rowan answered from where he sat beside Aelin near the back of the boat, Fenrys dozing at the queen's feet. It was large enough for each of them to lie down amongst the benches, or gather near the prow to eat the stockpile of fruits and cheeses. "And we don't know how directly these passageways flow. Several days might be a conservative guess."

"It would take three weeks on foot if we were above," Gavriel explained, his golden hair silvered by the lantern's light. "Perhaps longer."

Elide fiddled with the ring on her finger, twisting the band around and around. She'd rather travel for a month on foot than remain trapped in these dark, airless passages.

But they had no choice. Anneith had not whispered in warning—had not said anything at all before they'd climbed into this boat. Before Aelin had been given an ancient Faerie Queen's crown, her birthright and heritage.

The queen had stashed Mab's crown in one of their packs, as if it were no more than an extra sword belt. She hadn't spoken, and they had not asked her any questions, either.

Instead, she'd spent these past few hours sitting in the back of the boat, studying her unmarked hands, occasionally peering into the black waters beneath them. What she expected to see beyond her own rippling reflection, Elide didn't want to know. The fell and ancient creatures of these lands were too numerous to count, and most not friendly toward mortals.

Leaning against their pile of packs, Elide glanced to her left. Lorcan had positioned himself there, along the edge of the boat. Closer to her than he'd sat in weeks.

Sensing her attention, his dark eyes slid to her.

For long heartbeats, she let herself look at him.

He'd crawled after Maeve on the beach to save Aelin. And he had found her during her escape—had ensured Aelin made it out. Did it wipe away what he'd done in summoning Maeve in the first place? Even if Maeve had set the trap, even if he hadn't known what Maeve intended for Aelin, did it erase his decision to call for her?

The last time they'd spoken as friends, it had been aboard that ship in the hours before Maeve's armada had arrived. He'd told her they needed to talk, and she'd assumed it was about their future, about *them*.

But perhaps he'd been about to tell her what he'd done, that he'd been wrong in acting before Aelin's plans played out. Elide stopped twisting the ring.

He'd done it for her. She knew it. He'd summoned Maeve's armada because he'd believed they were about to be destroyed by Melisande's fleet. He'd done it for her, just as he'd dropped the shield around them that day Fenrys had ripped a chunk out of her arm, in exchange for Gavriel's healing her.

But the queen sitting silently behind them, no trace of that sharp-edged fire to be seen, nor that wicked grin she'd flashed at all who crossed her path . . . Two months with a sadist. With two sadists. That had been the cost, and the burden that Aelin and all of them would bear.

That silence, that banked fire was because of him. Not entirely, but in some ways.

Lorcan's mouth tightened, as if he read the thoughts on her face.

Elide looked ahead again, to where the cavern ceiling dipped so low she could have touched it if she stood. The space squeezed tighter and tighter—

"It's likely a pass-through to a larger cavern," Lorcan murmured, as if he could see that fear on her face, too. Or scent it.

Elide didn't bother responding. But she couldn't help the flicker of gratitude.

They continued on into the ancient, silent darkness, and no one spoke for a while after that.

~

The collar had not been real.

But the army Maeve had summoned was.

And Dorian, Manon with him, was in pursuit of the final Wyrdkey. Should he attain it from Erawan himself, wherever the Valg king stored it, should he gain possession of all three . . .

The lapping of the river against their boat was the only sound, had been the only sound for a while.

Gavriel kept his watch at the prow, Lorcan monitoring from the starboard side, his jaw tight. Fenrys and Elide dozed, the lady's head leaning against his flank, inky black hair spilling over a coat of whitest snow.

Aelin glanced to Rowan, seated beside her, but not touching. Her fingers curled in her lap. A blink into the gloom was the only indication that he was aware of her every movement.

Aelin breathed in his scent, let its strength settle into her a bit deeper.

Dorian and Manon might be anywhere. To hunt for the witch and king would be a fool's errand. Their paths would meet again, or they would not. And if he found the final key and then brought it to her, she would pay what the gods demanded. What she owed Terrasen, the world.

Yet if Dorian chose to end it himself, to forge the Lock . . . her stomach churned. He had the power. As much as she did, if not more so.

It was meant to be her sacrifice. Her blood shed to save them all. To let him claim it . . .

She could. She must. With Erawan no doubt unleashing himself on Terrasen, with Maeve's army likely to cause them untold grief, she could let Dorian do this. She trusted him.

Even if she might never forgive herself for it.

Her debt, it was supposed to have been *her* debt to pay. Perhaps the punishment for failing to do so would be having to live with herself. Having to live with all that had been done to her these months, too.

The blackness of the subterranean river pressed in, wrapped its arms around her and squeezed.

Different from the blackness of the iron box. The darkness she'd found inside herself.

A place she might never escape, not really.

Her power stirred, awakening. Aelin swallowed, refusing to acknowledge it. Heed it.

She wouldn't. Couldn't. Not yet. Until she was ready.

She had seen Rowan's face when she spoke of what his deception with the collar had prompted her to do. Had noted the way her companions looked at her, pity and fear in their eyes. At what had been done to her, what she'd become.

A new body. A foreign, strange body, as if she'd been ripped from one and shoved into another. Different from moving between her forms, somehow. She hadn't tried shifting into her human body yet. Didn't see the point.

Sitting in silence as the boat was pulled through the gloom, she felt the weight of those stares. Their dread. Felt them wondering just how broken she was.

You do not yield.

She knew that had been true—that it had been her mother's voice who had spoken and none other.

So she would not yield to this. What had been done. What remained.

For the companions around her, to lift their despair, their fear, she wouldn't yield.

She'd fight for it, claw her way back to it, who she'd been before. Remember to swagger and grin and wink. She'd fight against that lingering stain on her soul, fight to ignore it. Would use this journey into the dark to piece herself back together—just enough to make it convincing.

Even if this fractured darkness now dwelled within her, even if speech was difficult, she would show them what they wished to see.

An unbroken Fire-Bringer. Aelin of the Wildfire.

She would show the world that lie as well. Make them believe it.

Maybe she'd one day believe it, too.

CHAPTER
37

Days of near-silent travel passed.

Three days, if whatever senses Rowan and Gavriel possessed proved true. Perhaps the latter carried a pocket watch. Aelin didn't particularly care.

She used each of those days to consider what had been done, what lay before her. Sometimes, the roar of her magic drowned out her thoughts. Sometimes it slumbered. She never heeded it.

They sailed through the darkness, the river below so black that they might as well have been drifting through Hellas's realm.

It was near the end of the fourth day through the dark and rock, their escorts hauling the boat tirelessly, that Rowan murmured, "We're entering barrow-wight territory."

Gavriel twisted from his spot by the prow. "How can you tell?"

Sprawled beside him, still in wolf form, Fenrys cocked his ears forward.

She hadn't asked him why he remained in his wolf's body. No one asked her why she remained in her Fae form, after all. But she supposed that if he donned his Fae form, he might feel inclined to talk. To answer questions that he was perhaps not yet ready to discuss. Might begin simply screaming and screaming at what had been done to them, to Connall.

Rowan pointed with a tattooed finger toward an alcove in the wall. Shadow veiled its recesses, but as the blue light of the lantern touched it, gold glittered along the rocky floor. Ancient gold.

"What's a barrow-wight?" Elide whispered.

"Creatures of malice and thought," Lorcan answered, scanning the passageway, a hand drifting to the hilt of his sword. "They covet gold and treasure, and infested the ancient tombs of kings and queens so they might dwell amongst it. They hate light of any kind. Hopefully, this will keep them away."

Elide cringed, and Aelin felt inclined to do the same.

Instead, she dredged up enough speech to ask Rowan, "Are these the same ones beneath the burial mounds we visited?"

Rowan straightened, eyes sparking at her question—or at the fact that she'd spoken at all. He'd kept by her these days, a silent, steady presence. Even when they'd slept, he'd remained a few feet away, still not touching, but just *there*. Close enough that the pine-and-snow scent of him eased her into slumber.

Rowan braced a hand along the boat's rim. "There are many barrow-wight mounds across Wendlyn, but no others between the Cambrians and Doranelle beyond those we went to. As far as we know," he amended. "I didn't realize their tombs had been carved so deep."

"The wights needed some way in, with the tomb doors likely sealed above," Gavriel observed, studying a larger alcove that appeared on the right ahead. Not an alcove, but a dry cave mouth that flowed to the edge of the river before rising out of sight.

"Stop the boat," Aelin said.

Silence at the order, even from Rowan.

Aelin pointed to the lip of shore by the cave mouth. "Stop the boat," she repeated.

"I don't think we can," Elide murmured. Indeed, the two of them had resorted to using a bucket to see to their needs these few days, the males engaging in whatever conversation they could to make the silence more bearable.

But the boat headed for the alcove, its speed banking. Fenrys eased to his feet, sniffing the air as they neared the shore ledge. Rowan and Lorcan leaned out to brace their hands against the stone to keep them from colliding too hard.

Aelin didn't wait for the boat to cease rocking before she grabbed a lantern and leaped onto the river-smooth ground.

Rowan swore, jumping after her. "Stay here," he warned whoever remained on the boat.

Aelin didn't bother to see who obeyed as she strode into the cave.

The queen had been reckless before Cairn and Maeve had worked on her for two months, but it seemed she'd had any bit of common sense flayed from her.

Lorcan refrained from saying that, though, as he found himself and Elide alone in the boat. Gavriel and Fenrys had gone after Rowan and Aelin, their path marked only by the fading gleam of blue light on the walls.

Not firelight. She hadn't shown an ember since they'd entered the cave.

Elide remained sitting across from him on the left side of the boat, her back resting along the curved edge. She had been silent these past few minutes, watching the now-dark cave mouth.

"Barrow-wights are nothing to fear if you're armed with magic," Lorcan found himself saying.

Her dark eyes slid to him. "Well, I don't have any, so forgive me if I remain alert."

No, she'd once told him that while magic flowed in the Lochan blood-line, she had none to speak of. He'd never told her that he'd always considered her cleverness to be a mighty magic on its own, regardless of Anneith's whisperings.

Elide went on, "It's not the wights I'm worried about."

Lorcan assessed the quiet river flowing by, the caves around them, before he said, "It will take time for her to readjust."

She stared at him with those damning eyes.

He braced his forearms on his knees. "We got her back. She's with us now. What more do you want?" *From me*, he didn't need to add.

Elide straightened. "I don't want anything." *From you.*

He clenched his teeth. This was where they'd have it out, then. "How much longer am I supposed to atone?"

"Are you growing bored with it?"

He snarled.

She only glared at him. "I hadn't realized you were even atoning."

"I came here, didn't I?"

"For whom, exactly? Rowan? Aelin?"

"For both of them. And for you."

There. Let it be laid before them.

Despite the blue glow of the lantern, he could make out the pink that spread across her cheeks. Yet her mouth tightened. "I told you on that beach: I want nothing to do with you."

"So one mistake and I am your eternal enemy?"

"She is my *queen*, and you summoned Maeve, then told her where the keys were, and you *stood there while they did that to her.*"

"You have *no* idea what the blood oath can do. *None.*"

"Fenrys broke the oath. He found a way."

"And had Aelin not been there to offer him another, he would have *died.*" He let out a low, joyless laugh. "Perhaps that's what you would have preferred."

She ignored his last comment. "You didn't even try."

"I did," he snarled. "I fought it with everything I had. And it was not enough. If she'd ordered me to slit your throat, I would have. And if I had found a way to break the oath, I would have died, and she might very well have killed you or taken you afterward. On that beach, my only thought was to get Maeve to forget about you, to let *you* go—"

"I don't care about me! I didn't care about me on that beach!"

"*Well, I do.*" His growled words echoed across the water and stone, and he lowered his voice. Worse things than wights might come sniffing down here. "*I* cared about you on that beach. And your queen did, too."

Elide shook her head and looked away, looked anywhere, it seemed, but at him.

This was what came of opening that door to a place inside him that no one had ever breached. This mess, this hollowness in his chest that made him keep needing to make things right.

"Resent me all you like," he said, damning the hoarseness of his words. "I'm sure I'll survive."

Hurt flashed in her eyes. "Fine," she said, her voice brittle.

He hated that brittleness more than anything he'd ever encountered. Hated himself for causing it. But he had limits to how low he'd crawl.

He'd said his piece. If she wanted to wash her hands of him forever, then he would find a way to respect that. Live with it.

Somehow.

~

The cave ascended for a few feet, then leveled out and wended into the stone. A rough-hewn passage carved not by water or age, Rowan realized, but by mortal hands. Perhaps the long-dead kings and lords had taken the subterranean river to deposit their dead before sealing the tombs to sunlight and air above, the knowledge of the pathways dying off with their kingdoms.

A faint glow pulsed from the lantern Aelin held, bathing the cave walls in blue. He'd quickly caught up to her, and now strode at her side, Fenrys trotting at her heels and Gavriel taking up the rear.

Rowan hadn't bothered to free his weapons. Steel was of little use against the wights. Only magic might destroy them.

Why Aelin had needed to stop, what she'd needed to see, he could only guess as the passage opened into a small cavern, and gold gleamed.

Gold all around—and a shadow clothed in tattered black robes lurking by the sarcophagus in the center.

Rowan snarled in warning but Aelin didn't strike.

Her hand curled at her side, but she remained still. The wight hissed. Aelin just watched it.

As if she wouldn't, couldn't, touch her power.

Rowan's chest strained. Then he sent a whip of ice and wind through the cave.

The wight shrieked once, and was gone.

Aelin stared at where it had been for a heartbeat, and then glanced at him over a shoulder. Gratitude shone in her eyes.

Rowan only gave her a nod. *Don't worry about it.*

Yet Aelin turned away, shutting off that silent conversation as she surveyed the space.

Time. It would take time for her to heal. Even if he knew his Fireheart would pretend otherwise.

So Rowan looked, too. Across the tomb, beyond the sarcophagus and treasure, an archway opened into another chamber. Perhaps another tomb, or an exit passage.

"We don't have time to find a way out," Rowan murmured as she strode into the tomb. "And the caves remain safer than the surface."

"I'm not looking for a way out," she said in that calm, unmoved voice. She stooped, swiping up a fistful of gold coins stamped with a forgotten king's face. "We're going to need to fund our travels. And the gods know what else."

Rowan arched a brow.

Aelin shrugged and shoved the gold into the pocket of her cloak. "Unless the pitiful clinking I heard from your coin purse *didn't* indicate you were low on funds."

That spark of wry humor, the taunting . . . She was trying. For his sake, or the others', maybe her own, she was trying.

He could offer her nothing less, too. Rowan inclined his head. "We are indeed in dire need of replenishing our coffers."

Gavriel coughed. "This does belong to the dead, you know."

Aelin added another fistful of coins to her pocket, beginning a circuit around the treasure-laden tomb. "The dead don't need to buy passage on a ship. Or horses."

Rowan gave the Lion a slashing grin. "You heard the lady."

A flash ruptured from where Fenrys had been sniffing at a trunk of jewels, and then a male was standing there. His gray clothes worn, but intact—in better shape than the hollowed-out look in his eyes.

Aelin paused her looting.

Fenrys's throat bobbed, as if trying to remember speech. Then he said hoarsely, "We needed more pockets." He patted his own for emphasis.

Aelin's lips curved in a hint of a smile. She blinked at Fenrys—three times.

Fenrys blinked once in answer.

A code. They'd made up some silent code to communicate when he'd been ordered to remain in his wolf form.

Aelin's smile remained, just barely, as she walked to the golden-haired male, his bronze skin ashen. She opened her arms in silent offer.

To let him decide if he wished for contact. If he could endure it.

Just as Rowan would let her decide if she wished to touch him.

A small sigh broke from Fenrys before he folded Aelin into his arms, a shudder rippling through him. Rowan couldn't see her face, perhaps didn't need to, as her hands gripped Fenrys's jacket, so tightly they were white-knuckled.

A good sign—a small miracle, that either of them wished, *could* be touched. Rowan reminded himself of it, even while some intrinsic, male part of him tensed at the contact. A territorial Fae bastard, she'd once called him. He'd do his best not to live up to that title.

"Thank you," Aelin said, her voice small in a way that made Rowan's chest crack further. Fenrys didn't answer, but from the anguish on his face, Rowan knew no thanks were in order.

They pulled away, and Fenrys cupped her cheek. "When you are ready, we can talk."

About what they'd endured. To unravel all that had happened.

Aelin nodded, blowing out a breath. "Likewise."

She resumed shoving gold into her pockets, but glanced back to Fenrys, his face drawn. "I gave you the blood oath to save your life," she said. "But if you do not want it, Fenrys, I . . . we can find some way to free you—"

"I want it," Fenrys said, no trace of his usual swaggering humor. He glanced to Rowan, and bowed his head. "It is my honor to serve this court. And serve you," he added to Aelin.

She waved a hand in dismissal, though Rowan didn't fail to note the sheen in her eyes as she stooped to gather more gold. Giving her a moment, he strode to Fenrys and clasped his shoulder. "It's good to have you back." He added, stumbling a bit on the word, "Brother."

For that's what they would be. Had never been before, but what Fenrys had done for Aelin . . . Yes, *brother* was what Rowan would call him. Even if Fenrys's own—

Fenrys's dark eyes flickered. "She killed Connall. Made him stab himself in the heart."

A pearl-and-ruby necklace scattered from Gavriel's fingers.

The temperature in the tomb spiked, but there was no flash of flame, no swirl of embers.

As if Aelin's magic had surged, only to be leashed again.

Yet Aelin continued shoving gold and jewels into her pockets.

She'd witnessed it, too. That slaughter.

But it was Gavriel, approaching on silent feet even with the jewels and gold on the floor, who clasped Fenrys's other shoulder. "We will make sure that debt is paid before the end."

The Lion had never uttered such words—not toward their former queen. But fury burned in Gavriel's tawny gaze. Sorrow and fury.

Fenrys took a steadying breath and stepped away, the loss on his face mingling with something Rowan couldn't place. But now wasn't the time to ask, to pry.

They filled their pockets with as much gold as they could fit, Fenrys going so far as to remove his gray jacket to form a makeshift pack. When it was nearly drooping to the floor with gold, the threads straining, he silently headed back down the passageway. Gavriel, still wincing at their shameless looting, stalked after him a moment later.

Aelin continued picking her way amongst the treasure, however. She'd been more selective than the rest of them, examining pieces with what Rowan had assumed was a jeweler's eye. The gods knew she'd owned enough finery to tell what would fetch the highest price at market.

"We should go," he said. His own pockets were near to bursting, his every step weighed down.

She rose from a rusted metal chest she'd been riffling through.

Rowan remained still as she approached, something clenched in her palm. It was only when she stopped close enough for him to touch her that she unfurled her fingers.

Two golden rings lay there.

"I don't know the Fae customs," she said. The thicker ring held an elegantly cut ruby within the band itself, while the smaller one bore a sparkling rectangular emerald mounted atop, the stone as large as her fingernail. "But when humans wed, rings are exchanged."

Her fingers trembled—just slightly. Too many unspoken words lay between them.

Yet now was not the time for that conversation, for that healing.

Not when they had to be on their way as swiftly as possible, and this offer she'd made him, this proof that she still wanted what lay between them, the vows they'd sworn . . .

"I assume the sparkly emerald is for me," Rowan said with a half smile.

She huffed a laugh. The soft, whispered sound was as precious as the rings she'd found for them in this hoard.

She took his hand, and he tried not to shudder in relief, tried not to fall to his knees as she slid the ruby ring onto his finger. It fit him perfectly, the ring no doubt forged for the king lying in this barrow.

Silently, Rowan grasped her own hand and eased on the emerald ring. "To whatever end," he whispered.

Silver lined her eyes. "To whatever end."

A reminder—and a vow, more sacred than the wedding oaths they'd sworn on that ship.

To walk this path together, back from the darkness of the iron coffin. To face what waited in Terrasen, ancient promises to the gods be damned.

He ran his thumb over the back of her hand. "I'll make the tattoo again." She swallowed, but nodded. "And," he added, "I'd like to add another. To me—and to you."

Her brows flicked up, but he squeezed her hand. *You'll have to wait and see, Princess.*

Another hint of a smile. She didn't balk from the silent words this time. *Typical.*

He opened his mouth to voice the question he'd been dying to ask for days now. *May I kiss you?* But she pulled her hand from his.

Admiring the wedding band sparkling on her finger, her mouth tightened as she turned over her palm. "I'll need to retrain."

Not a single callus marked her hands.

Aelin frowned at her too-thin body. "And pack on some muscle again." A slight quiver graced her words, but she curled her hands into fists at her sides and smirked at her clothes—the Mistward clothes. "It'll be just like old times."

Trying. She was dredging up that swagger and trying. So he would, too. Until she didn't need to any more.

Rowan gave her a crooked grin. "Just like old times," he said, following her out of the barrow and back toward the ebony river, "but with far less sleep."

He could have sworn the passageway heated. But Aelin kept going.

Later. That conversation, this unfinished business between them, would come later.

CHAPTER
38

The queen and her consort needed a private moment, it seemed. Elide had been more surprised to see Fenrys in his beautiful male form than the gold that he and Gavriel bore, near-spilling out their pockets.

Lorcan laughed softly as they packed the treasure into their bags. More than some people could dream of. "At least she's thinking one step ahead."

Fenrys stilled where he crouched before his bag, the gold in his hands shimmering like his hair. There was nothing remotely warm in his dark eyes. "We're only in this position because of you."

Elide tensed as Lorcan stiffened. Gavriel halted his packing, a hand drifting to the dagger at his side.

But the dark-haired warrior inclined his head. "So I have been reminded," he said, but didn't glance to Elide.

Fenrys bared his teeth. "When we're out of this," he hissed, "you and I will settle things."

Lorcan's smile was a brutal slash of white. "It shall be my pleasure."

Elide knew he meant it. He'd be glad to take on whatever Fenrys threw his way, to engage in that devastating, bloody conflict.

Gavriel let out a sigh, his tawny eyes meeting Elide's. Nothing could be said or done to convince them otherwise.

Yet Elide found herself drawing in breath to suggest that fighting amongst each other, vengeance or no, wouldn't be fulfilling, when Aelin and Rowan emerged from the passage.

Goldryn hung at the queen's side, undoubtedly given back to her by the prince. Its glittering ruby looked like an amethyst in the blue lantern light, bobbing with each of Aelin's steps.

They'd barely stepped onto the boat when a hissing flitted from the passage they'd vacated.

Tensing, Rowan and Gavriel swiftly shoved the boat from the shore. The creatures tugging them along lurched into motion, pulling them farther into the river.

Blades gleamed, all the immortal warriors deathly still.

Aelin didn't draw Goldryn, though. Didn't lift a burning hand. She merely lingered by Elide, her face like stone.

The hissing grew louder. Shadowed, scabbed hands clawed at the passage archway, recoiling wherever they met the light.

"Someone's pissed about the treasure," Fenrys muttered.

"They can get in line," Aelin said, and Elide could have sworn that the gold in the queen's eyes glowed. A flare of deep-hidden light, then nothing.

An ice-kissed wind snapped through the caves. The hissing stopped.

Shuddering, Elide murmured, "I don't think I should care to return to these lands."

Fenrys chuckled, a sensuous laugh that didn't meet his eyes. "I agree with you, Lady."

They drifted into the blackness for another day, then two. Still the sea did not appear.

Aelin was sleeping, a dreamless, heavy slumber, when a strong hand clasped her shoulder. "Look," Rowan whispered, his breath brushing her ear.

She opened her eyes to pale light.

Not the ocean, she realized as she sat up, the others rousing, undoubtedly at Rowan's word.

Overhead, clinging to the cavern ceiling as if they were stars trapped beneath the rock, small blue lights glowed.

Glowworms, like those in the lantern. Thousands of them, made infinite by the reflection in the black water. Stars above and below.

From the corner of her eye, Aelin glimpsed Elide press a hand to her chest.

A sea of stars—that's what the cave had become.

Beauty. There was still beauty in this world. Stars could still glow, still burn bright, even buried under the earth.

Aelin breathed in the cool cave air, the blue light. Let it flow through her.

Rattle the stars. She'd promised to do that. Had done so much toward it, yet more remained. They had to hurry. How many suffered at Morath's claws?

Beauty remained—and she would fight for it. *Needed* to fight.

It was a constant thrum in her blood, her bones. Right alongside the power that she shoved down deep and dismissed with each breath. *Fight*— one last time.

She'd escaped so she might do it. Would think of all those still defying Morath, defying Maeve, while she trained. She wouldn't hesitate. Didn't dare to pause.

She'd make this time count. In every way possible.

The emerald on her marriage band glistened with its own fire.

Selfish of her, to enforce that bond when her very blood destined her for a sacrificial altar, and yet she had gotten out of the boat to find them. The rings. Raiding the trove had been an afterthought. But if she was to have no scars on her, no reminder of where she'd been and who she was and what she'd promised, then she'd needed this one scrap of proof.

Aelin could have sworn the living stars overhead sang, a celestial choir that floated through the caves.

A star-song carried along the river current, running beside them, for the last miles to the sea.

CHAPTER 39

The enemy's army arrived not in three days, or four, but five.

A blessing and a curse, Nesryn decided. A blessing, for the time it granted them to prepare, for the ruks to carry some of the most vulnerable of Anielle's people to a snow-blasted camp beyond the Fangs.

And a curse for the fear it allowed to fester in the keep, now teeming with those who would not or could not make the journey. By sunset on the fourth day, they could see the black lines marching for them through the swaths of Oakwald that they hewed down.

By dawn on the fifth day, they were near the outskirts of the lake, the plain.

Nesryn sat atop Salkhi on one of the keep's spires, Borte on Arcas beside her.

"For a demon army, they march slower than my *ej*'s own mother."

Nesryn snorted. "Armies have supply trains—and this one had a river to cross and a forest to fell."

Borte sniffed. "Seems like an awful lot of trouble for such a small city."

Indeed, the ruk riders had not been impressed by Anielle, certainly not after camping in Antica before their passage to these lands.

"Save this city, take the Ferian Gap to the north of it, and we could clear a path northward. It might be an ugly place, but it's vital."

"Oh, the land is beautiful," Borte said, gazing toward the lake sparkling under the winter light, steam from the nearby hot springs drifting across its surface. "But the buildings . . ." She made a face.

Nesryn chuckled. "You may be right."

For a few moments, they watched the army creep closer. People were fleeing in the streets now, rushing up the keep's endless steps and battlements.

"I'm surprised Sartaq will let his future empress fly against them," Borte said slyly. The girl had relentlessly teased her these weeks.

Nesryn scowled. "Where's Yeran?"

Borte stuck out her tongue, despite the army inching toward them. "Burning in hell, for all I care."

Even away from their respective aeries and ancient rivalries, the betrothed pair had not warmed to each other. Or perhaps it was part of the game the two of them played, had been playing for years now. To feign loathing, when it was so clear they'd slaughter anyone who posed a threat to the other.

Nesryn lifted her brows, and Borte crossed her arms, her twin braids blowing in the wind. "He's bringing the last two healers to the keep." Indeed, a near-black ruk flapped up from the plain.

"No inclination to finally wed before the battle?"

Borte recoiled. "Why would I?"

Nesryn smirked. "So you might have your wedding night?"

Borte barked a laugh. "Who says I haven't already?"

Nesryn gaped.

But Borte only inclined her head, clicked her tongue at Arcas, and rider and ruk dove into the brisk sky.

Nesryn stared after Borte until she'd reached the plain, passing by

Yeran and his ruk in a daring maneuver that some might have interpreted to be a giant, vulgar gesture to the warrior.

Yeran's dark ruk screeched in outrage, and Nesryn smiled, knowing Yeran was likely doing the same, even with the two healers riding with him.

Yet Nesryn's smile proved short-lived as she again beheld the marching army nearer and nearer with each minute. An unbroken, untiring mass of steel and death.

Would they camp until dawn, or attack at nightfall? Would the siege be quick and lethal, or long and brutal? She'd seen their supply trains. They were prepared to stay for as long as it took to bring this city to rubble.

And wipe out every soul dwelling within.

The bone drums began at sundown.

Yrene stood on the highest parapet of the keep, counting the torches sprawling into the night, and fought to keep her dinner down.

It was no different from the other meals she'd eaten today, she told herself. The meals she had struggled to consume without gagging.

The parapet was filled with soldiers and onlookers alike, all gazing toward the army at the border of the plain that separated them from the city's edge, all listening in hushed silence to the relentless drumming.

A steady, horrible beat. Meant to unnerve, to break one's will.

She knew they'd continue all night. Deprive them of rest, make them dread the dawn.

The keep was as full as it could stand, hallways crammed with bedrolls. She and Chaol had yielded their room to a family of five, the children too young to make the trip to the Wastes, even on a ruk's back. In the frigid air, an infant might go blue with cold in minutes.

Yrene ran a hand over the waist-high stone wall. Thick, ancient stone. She beseeched it to hold out.

Catapults. There were catapults in the army below. She'd heard Falkan's latest report at breakfast. The plain itself was still littered with enough boulders from the days it had been a part of the lake that Morath would have no problem finding things to hurl at them.

The warning had kept Yrene busy all day, relocating families who had taken rooms on the lake side of the keep or those who slept too close to windows or outer walls. Last-minute, and foolish not to consider it before now, but she'd been so focused these past five days on getting everyone *in* that she hadn't thought of things like catapults and shattering blocks of heavy stone.

She'd moved their healing supplies, too. To an inner chamber where it would take the entire keep collapsing to destroy what was inside. The Torre healers had brought what they could from the fleet, but they'd made more when they arrived. Not their best work, not by any means, but Eretia had ordered that the salves and tonics need only to function, not dazzle, and to *keep mixing*.

All was set. All was ready. Or as ready as they might ever be.

So Yrene lingered on the battlements, listening to the bone drums for a while longer.

Chaol told himself it was not his last night with his wife. He'd still made the best of it, and they had rested as much as they could stand before they were up, hours before dawn.

The rest of the keep was awake, too, the ruks restless on the tower roofs and battlements, the click and scrape of their talons on the stones echoing in every hall and chamber.

The drums kept pounding. Had pounded all night.

He'd kissed Yrene good-bye, and she'd seemed like she wanted to say more but had opted to hold him for a long, precious minute before they parted ways.

It would not be the last time he saw her, he promised himself as he aimed for the battlements where his father, Sartaq, and Nesryn had agreed to meet at dawn.

The prince and Nesryn had not yet arrived, but his father stood in armor Chaol had not glimpsed since childhood. Since his father had ridden to serve Adarlan's wishes. To conquer this continent.

It still fit him well, the muted metal scratched and dented. Not the finest piece of armor from the family arsenal beneath the keep, but the sturdiest. A sword hung at his hip, and a shield lay against the battlement wall. Around them, sentries tried not to watch, though their fear-wide eyes tracked every movement.

The drums pounded on.

Chaol came up beside his father, his own dark tunic reinforced with armor at his shoulders, forearms, and shins.

A cane of ironwood had been sheathed down Chaol's back, for when Yrene's magic began to fade, and his chair waited just inside the great hall, for when her power depleted entirely.

What his father had made of it when Chaol had explained yesterday, he hadn't let on. Hadn't said a single word.

Chaol cast a sidelong glance at the man staring toward the army whose fires began winking out one by one under the rising light.

"They used the bone drums during the last siege of Anielle," his father said, not a tremor in his voice. "Legend says they beat the drums for three days and three nights before they attacked, and that the city was so rife with terror, so mad with sleeplessness, that they didn't stand a chance. Erawan's armies and beasts shredded them apart."

"They did not have ruks fighting with them then," Chaol said.

"We'll see how long they last."

Chaol gritted his teeth. "If you do not have hope, then your men will not last long, either."

His father stared toward the plain, the army revealed with each minute.

"Your mother left," the man said at last.

Chaol didn't hide his shock.

His father gripped the stone parapet. "She took Terrin and left. I don't know where they fled. As soon as we realized we'd been surrounded by enemies, she took her ladies-in-waiting, their families. Departed in the dead of night. Only your brother bothered to leave a note."

His mother, after all she'd endured, all she'd survived in this hellish house, had finally walked out. To save her other son—their promise of a future. "What did Terrin say?"

His father smoothed his hand over the stone. "It doesn't matter."

It clearly did. But now wasn't the time to push, to care.

There was no fear on his father's face. Just cold resignation.

"If you do not lead these men today," Chaol growled, "then I will."

His father looked at him at last, his face grave. "Your wife is pregnant."

The shock roiled through Chaol like a physical blow.

Yrene—*Yrene*—

"A skilled healer she might be, but a deft liar, she is not. Or have you not noticed her hand frequently resting on her stomach, or how green she turns at mealtime?"

Such mild, casual words. As if his father weren't ripping the ground out from beneath him.

Chaol opened his mouth, body tensing. To yell at his father, to run to Yrene, he didn't know.

But then the bone drums stopped.

And the army began to advance.

CHAPTER 40

Manon and the Thirteen had buried each and every one of the soldiers massacred by the Ironteeth. Their torn and bleeding hands throbbed, their backs ached, but they'd done it.

When the last of the hard earth had been patted down, she'd found Bronwen lingering at the clearing edge, the rest of the Crochans having moved off to set up camp.

The Thirteen had trudged past Manon. Ghislaine, according to Vesta, had been invited to sit at the hearth of a witch with an equal interest in those mortal, scholarly pursuits.

Only Asterin remained in the shadows nearby to guard her back as Manon asked Bronwen, "What is it?"

She should have tried for pleasantries, for diplomacy, but she didn't. Couldn't muster it.

Bronwen's throat bobbed, as if choking on the words. "You and your coven acted honorably."

"You doubted it, from the White Demon?"

"I did not think the Ironteeth bothered to care for human lives."

She didn't know the half of it. Manon only said, "My grandmother informed me that I am no longer an Ironteeth witch, so it seems who they do or do not care for no longer bears any weight with me." She kept walking toward the trees where the Thirteen had vanished, and Bronwen fell into step beside her. "It was the least I could do," Manon admitted.

Bronwen glanced at her sidelong. "Indeed."

Manon eyed the Crochan. "You lead your witches well."

"The Ironteeth have long given us an excuse to be highly trained."

Something like shame washed through her again. She wondered if she'd ever find a way to ease it, to endure it. "I suppose we have."

Bronwen didn't reply before peeling off toward the small fires.

But as Manon went in search of Glennis's own hearth, the Crochans looked her way.

Some tipped their heads toward her. Some offered grim nods.

She saw to it that the Thirteen were tending to their hands, and found herself unable to sit. To let the weight of the day catch up to her.

Around them, around each fire, Crochans argued quietly on whether to return home or head farther south into Eyllwe. Yet if they went into Eyllwe, what would they do? Manon barely heard as the debate raged, Glennis letting each of the seven ruling hearths arrive at its own decision.

Manon didn't linger to hear what they chose. Didn't bother to ask them to fly northward.

Asterin stalked to Manon's side, offering her a strip of dried rabbit while the Thirteen ate, the Crochans continuing their quiet debates. The wind sang through the trees, hollow and keening.

"Where do we go at dawn?" Asterin asked. "Do we follow them, or head northward?"

Did they cling to this increasingly futile quest to win them over, or did they abandon it?

Manon studied her bleeding, aching hands, the iron nails crusted with dirt.

"I am a Crochan," she said. "And I am an Ironteeth witch." She flexed her fingers, willing the stiffness from them. "The Ironteeth are my people, too. Regardless of what my grandmother may decree. They are my people, Blueblood and Yellowlegs and Blackbeak alike."

And she would bear the weight of what she'd created, what she'd trained, forever.

Asterin said nothing, though Manon knew she listened to every word. Knew the Thirteen had stopped eating to listen, too.

"I want to bring them home," Manon said to them, to the wind that flowed all the way to the Wastes. "I want to bring them all home. Before it is too late—before they become something unworthy of a homeland."

"So what are you going to do?" Asterin asked softly, but not weakly.

Manon finished the strip of dried meat, and swigged from her waterskin.

The answer did not lie in picking one over the other, Crochan over Ironteeth. It never had.

"If the Crochans will not rally a host, then I'll find another. One already trained."

"You cannot go to Morath," Asterin breathed. "You won't get within a hundred miles. The Ironteeth host might be already too far gone to even consider siding with you."

"I'm not going to Morath." Manon slid her frozen hand into her pocket. "I'm going to the Ferian Gap. To whatever of the host remains there under Petrah Blueblood's command. To ask them to join us."

Asterin and the Thirteen had been stunned into silence. Letting them dwell on it, Manon had turned into the trees. Had picked up Dorian's scent and followed it.

And seen him conversing with the spirit of Kaltain Rompier, the woman healed and lucid in death. Freed from her terrible torment. Shock had rooted Manon to the spot.

Then she'd heard of Dorian's plans to infiltrate Morath. Morath, where the third and final Wyrdkey was kept. He'd known, and hadn't told her.

Kaltain had vanished into the night air and then Dorian had shifted. Into a beautiful, proud raven.

He hadn't been training to entertain himself. Not at all.

Manon snarled, "When, exactly, were you going to inform me that you were about to retrieve the third Wyrdkey?"

Dorian blinked at her, his face the portrait of calm assurance. "When I left."

"When you flew off as a raven or a wyvern, right into Erawan's net?"

The temperature in the clearing plunged. "What difference does it make if I told you weeks ago or now?"

She knew there was nothing kind, nothing warm on her face. A witch's face. A Blackbeak's face. "Morath is suicide. Erawan will find you in any form you wear, and you will wind up with a collar around your throat."

"I don't have another choice."

"We agreed," Manon said, pacing a step. "We agreed that looking for the keys was no longer a priority—"

"I knew better than to argue with you about it." His eyes glowed like blue fire. "My path doesn't impact your own. Rally the Crochans, fly north to Terrasen. My road leads to Morath. It always has."

"How can you have looked at Kaltain and not seen what awaits you?" She held up her arm and pointed to where Kaltain's scar had been. "Erawan will *catch you*. You cannot go."

"*We will lose this war if I do not go*," he snapped. "How do you not *care* about that?"

"I care," she hissed. "I care if we lose this war. I care if I fail to rally the Crochans. I care if you go into Morath and do not return, not as something worth living." He only blinked. Manon spat on the mossy ground. "Now do you wish to tell me that caring is not such a bad thing? Well, this is what comes of it."

"This is why I didn't say anything," he breathed.

Her heart turned raging, its pulse echoing through her body, though her words were cold as ice. "You wish to go to Morath?" She prowled up to him, and he didn't back down an inch. "Then prove it. Prove you are ready."

"I don't need to prove anything to you, witchling."

She gave him a brutal, wicked smile. "Then perhaps prove it to yourself. A test." He'd deceived her, had lied to her. This man who she'd believed held no secrets between them. She didn't know why it made her want to shred everything within sight. "We fly to the Ferian Gap with the dawn." He started, but she went on, "Join us. We will have need of a spy on the inside. Someone who can sneak past the guards to tell us what and who lies within." She barely heard herself over the roaring in her head. "Let's see how well you can shape-shift then, princeling."

Manon forced herself to hold his stare. To let her words hang between them.

Then he turned on his heel, aiming for the camp. "Fine. But find yourself another tent to sleep in tonight."

CHAPTER
41

They reached the sea under cover of darkness, warned of its arrival by the briny scent that crept into the cave, then the rougher waters that pushed past, and then finally the roar of the surf.

Maeve's eyes might have been everywhere, but they weren't fixed on the cave mouth that opened onto a cove along Wendlyn's western shore. Nor were they on that cove when the boat landed on its sandy beach, then vanished back into the caves before anyone could so much as attempt to thank the creatures who had hauled them without rest.

Aelin watched the boat until it disappeared, trying not to stare too long at the clean, unstained sand beneath her boots, while the others debated where they might be along the coastline.

A few hours of hurrying northward, into Wendlyn's lands, and they got their answer: close enough to the nearest port.

The tide was with them, and with the gold they'd pilfered from the barrow-wights, it was a matter of Rowan and Lorcan simply crossing their arms before a ship was secured. With Wendlyn's armada sailing for

Terrasen's shores, the rules about border crossings had been revoked. Gone were the several boat transfers to reach the continent across the sea, the security measures. No mere tyrant squatted in Adarlan, but a Valg king with an aerial legion.

It made it easier for the messages she dispatched to go out, too. Whether the letter to Aedion and Lysandra would reach them was up to the gods, she supposed, since they seemed hell-bent on being their puppet masters. Perhaps they might not bother with her now, if Dorian was heading for the third key, if he might take her place.

She did not dwell on it for long.

The ship was a step above ramshackle, all the finer vessels commandeered for the war, but it seemed steady enough to make the weeks-long crossing. For the gold they paid, the captain yielded his own quarters to Aelin and Rowan. If the man knew who they were, what they were, he said nothing.

Aelin didn't care. Only that they sailed with the midnight tide, Rowan's magic propelling them swiftly out to the moonlit sea.

Far from Maeve. From her gathered forces.

From the truth that Aelin might have glimpsed that day in Maeve's throne room, the dark blood that had turned to red.

She hadn't told the others. Didn't know if that moment had been real, or a trick of the light. If it had been another dreamscape, or some fragment that had blended into the very real memory of Connall's death.

She'd deal with it later, Aelin decided as she stood by the prow, the others long since having gone to their own quarters belowdecks. Only Rowan remained, perched on the mainmast as he scanned every horizon for signs of pursuit.

They'd evaded Maeve. For now. Tonight, at least, she wouldn't know where to find them. Until word spread of the strangers in that port, of the ship they'd paid a king's fortune to take them into war-torn hell. The messages Aelin had sent.

At least Maeve didn't know where the Wyrdkeys were. They still had that in their favor.

Though Maeve was likely to bring her army across the sea to hunt them down. Or simply aid in Terrasen's demise.

Aelin's power stirred, a thunderhead groaning in her blood. She ground her teeth and paid it no attention.

Everything relied upon them reaching the continent before Maeve and her forces. Or before Erawan could destroy too much of the world.

Aelin leaned into the sea breeze, letting it seep into her skin, her hair, letting it wash away the dark of the caves, if the dark of the prior months could not be eased entirely. Letting it soothe her fire into slumbering embers.

These weeks at sea would be endless, even with Rowan's magic propelling them.

She'd use each day to train, to work with sword and dagger and bow until her hands were blistered, until new calluses formed. Until the thinness returned to muscle.

She'd rebuild it—what she had been.

Perhaps one last time, perhaps only for a little while, but she'd do it. If only for Terrasen.

Rowan swooped from the mast, shifting as he reached her side at the rail. He surveyed the night-black sea beyond them. "You should rest."

She slid him a glance. "I'm not tired." Not a lie, not in some regards. "Want to spar?"

He frowned. "Training can start tomorrow."

"Or tonight." She held his piercing stare, matched his dominance with her own.

"It can wait a few hours, Aelin."

"Every day counts." Against Erawan, even a day of training would count.

Rowan's jaw tightened. "True," he said at last. "But it can still wait. There are . . . there are things we need to discuss."

The silent words rose in his animal-bright eyes. *About you and me.*

Her mouth went dry. But Aelin nodded.

In silence, they strode into their spacious quarters, its only decoration the wall of windows that overlooked the churning sea behind them. A far cry from a queen's chamber, or any she might have purchased as Adarlan's assassin.

At least the bed built into the wall looked clean enough, the sheets crisp and stainless. But Aelin headed for the oak desk anchored to the floor, and leaned against it while Rowan shut the door.

In the dim lantern light, they stared at each other.

She'd endured Maeve and Cairn; she'd endured Endovier and countless other horrors and losses. She could have this conversation with him. The first step toward rebuilding herself.

Aelin knew Rowan could hear her thundering heart as the space between them went taut. She swallowed once. "Elide and Lorcan told you . . . told you everything that was said on that beach."

A curt nod, wariness flooding his eyes.

"Everything that Maeve said."

Another nod.

She braced herself. "That I'm—we're mates."

Understanding and something like relief replaced that wariness. "Yes."

"I'm your mate," she said, needing to voice it. "And you are mine."

Rowan crossed the room, but halted a few feet from the desk on which she leaned. "What of it, Aelin?" His question was low, rough.

"Don't you . . ." She scrubbed at her face. "You know what she did to you, to . . ." She couldn't say her name. Lyria. "Because of it."

"I do know."

"And?"

"And what do you wish me to say?"

She pushed off the desk. "I wish you to tell me how you feel about it. If . . ."

"If what?"

"If you wish it wasn't so."

His brows narrowed. "Why would I ever wish that?"

She shook her head, unable to answer, and stared over her shoulder toward the sea.

It seemed like he would close the distance between them, but he remained where he was. "Aelin." His voice turned hoarse. "Aelin."

She looked at him then, at the pain in his words.

"Do you know what I wish?" He exposed his palms, one tattooed, the other unmarked. "I wish that you had told me. When you realized it. I wish you had told me then."

She swallowed against the ache in her throat. "I didn't want to hurt you."

"Why would it ever hurt me to know the truth that was already in my heart? The truth I hoped for?"

"I didn't understand it. I didn't understand *how* it was possible. I thought maybe . . . maybe you might be able to have two mates within a lifetime, but even then, I just . . ." She blew out a breath. "I didn't want you to be distressed."

His eyes softened. "Do I regret that Lyria was dragged into this, that the cost of Maeve's game was her life, and the life of the child we might have had? Yes. I regret that, and I wish it had never happened." He would bear the tattoo to remember it for the rest of his days. "But none of that was your fault. I will always carry some of the burden of it, always know *I* chose to leave her for war and glory, and that I played right into Maeve's hands."

"Maeve wanted to ensnare you to get to me, though."

"Then it is her choice, not yours."

Aelin ran a hand over the worn wood of the desk. "In those illusions she spun for me, she showed me variations on one more than all the others." The words were strained, but she forced them out. Forced herself to look at him. "She spun me one dreamscape that felt so real I could smell the wind off the Staghorns."

"What did she show you?" A breathless question.

Aelin had to swallow before she could answer. "She showed me what might have been—if there had been no Erawan, if Elena had dealt with him properly and banished him. If there had been no Lyria, none of that pain or despair you endured. She showed me Terrasen as it would have been today, with my father as king, and my childhood happy, and . . ." Her lips wobbled. "When I turned twenty, you came with a delegation of Fae to Terrasen, to make amends for the rift between my mother and Maeve. And you and I took one look at each other in my father's throne room, and we knew."

She didn't fight the stinging in her eyes. "I wanted to believe that was the true world. That this was the nightmare from which I'd awaken. I *wanted* to believe that there was a place where you and I had never known this suffering and loss, where we'd take one look at each other and know we were mates. Maeve told me she could make it so. If I gave her the keys, she'd make it all possible." She wiped at her cheek, at the tear that escaped down it. "She spun me realities where you were dead, where you'd been killed by Erawan and only in handing over the keys to her would I be able to avenge you. But those realities made me . . . I stopped being useful to her when she told me you were gone. She couldn't get me to talk, to think. Yet in the ones where you and I met, where things were as they should have been . . . that was when I came the closest."

His swallow was audible. "What stopped you?"

She wiped at her face again. "The male I fell in love with was you. It was *you*, who knew pain as I did, and who walked with me through it, back to the light. Maeve didn't understand that. That even if she could create that perfect world, it wouldn't be you with me. And I'd never trade that, trade this. Not for anything."

He extended his hand. An offer and invitation.

Aelin laid hers atop his, and his callused fingers squeezed gently. "I wanted it to be you," he breathed, closing his eyes. "For months and months, even in Wendlyn, I wondered why you weren't my mate instead. It tore me up, wondering it, but I still did." He opened his eyes, and they burned like green fire. "All this time, I wanted it to be you."

She lowered her gaze, but he hooked a thumb and forefinger around her chin and lifted her face.

"I know you are tired, Fireheart. I know that the burden on your shoulders is more than anyone should endure." He took their joined hands and laid them on his heart. "But we'll face this together. Erawan, the Lock, all of it. We'll face it together. And when we are done, when you Settle, we will have a thousand years together. Longer."

A small sound came out of her. "Elena said the Lock requires—"

"We'll face it together," he swore again. "And if the cost of it truly is you, then we'll pay it together. As one soul in two bodies."

Her heart strained to the point of cleaving. "Terrasen needs a king."

"I have no intention of ruling Terrasen without you. Aedion can have the job."

She scanned his face. He meant every word.

He brushed the hair from her face, his other hand still clasping hers to his chest, where his heart pounded a steady, unfaltering rhythm. "Even if I had my choice of any dream-realities, any perfect illusions, I would still choose you, too."

She felt the truth of his words echo into the unbreakable thing that bound their very souls, and tilted her face up toward his. But he made no move beyond it.

She frowned. "Why aren't you kissing me?"

"I thought you might want to be asked first."

"That never stopped you before."

"This first time, I wanted to make sure you were . . . ready." After Cairn and Maeve. After months of having no choices whatsoever.

She smiled despite that truth. "I'm ready to be kissed again, Prince."

He let out a dark chuckle and muttered, "Thank the gods," before he lowered his mouth to hers.

The kiss was gentle—light. Letting her decide how to guide it. So she did.

Sliding her arms around Rowan's neck, Aelin pressed herself against him, arching into his touch as his hands roamed along her back. Yet his mouth remained featherlight on hers. Sweet, exploratory kisses. He'd do it all night, if that was what she wished.

Mate. He was her mate, and she was finally allowed to call him such, to let him be such—

The thought snapped something. Aelin nipped at his bottom lip, scraping a canine against it.

The gesture snapped something in him, too.

With a growl, Rowan swept her into his arms, never tearing his mouth from hers as he carried her to the bed and set her down gently. Off came their boots, their jackets and shirts and pants. And then he was with her, the strength and heat of him pouring into her bare skin.

She couldn't touch him fast enough, *feel* enough of him against her. Even when his mouth roved down her neck, licking over that spot where his claiming marks had been. Even when he roamed farther, worshipping her breasts as she arched up into each lick and suckle. Even when he knelt between her legs, his shoulders spreading her thighs wide, and tasted her, over and over, until she was writhing beneath him.

But something primal in her went quiet and still as Rowan rose over her again, and their eyes locked.

"You're my mate," he said, the words near-guttural. He nudged at her entrance, and she shifted her hips to draw him in, but he remained where he was. Withholding what she ached for until he heard what he needed.

Aelin tipped back her head, baring her neck to him. "You're my mate." Her words were a breathless rush. "And I am yours."

Rowan thrust into her in a mighty stroke as he plunged his teeth into the side of her neck.

She cried out at the claiming, release already barreling along her spine, but he began moving. Moving, while his teeth remained in her, and she moaned with each drive of his hips, the sheer size of him a decadence she would never be able to get enough of. She dragged her nails down his muscled back, then lower, feeling every powerful stroke of him into her.

Rowan withdrew his teeth from her neck, and Aelin claimed his mouth in a savage kiss, her blood a coppery tang on his tongue.

He went wild at that, hoisting her hips to angle himself deeper, harder. The world might have been burning around them for all she cared, all he cared, too.

"Together, Aelin," he promised, and she heard the rest of the words in every place their bodies joined. Together they would face this, together they would find a way.

Release crested within her once more, a shimmering brightness.

And just when it broke, Aelin sank her teeth into Rowan's neck, claiming him as he'd claimed her.

His blood, powerful and wind-kissed, filled her mouth, her soul, and Rowan roared as release shattered through him, too.

For long minutes, they lay tangled in each other.

Together we'll find a way, their mingling breaths, the crashing sea, seemed to echo. *Together.*

CHAPTER 42

Lorcan was given the last watch of the night, which allowed him to witness the sunrise over the now-distant horizon.

Would he ever see it again—Wendlyn, Doranelle, any of that eastern land?

Perhaps not, considering what they sailed to in the west, and the immortal army Maeve had no doubt set on their heels. Perhaps they were all doomed to limited sunrises.

The others roused, venturing onto the deck to learn what the morning brought. Nothing, he almost told them from where he stood by the prow. Water and sun and a whole lot of nothing.

Fenrys spotted him and bared his teeth. Lorcan gave him a mocking smile.

Yes, that fight would come later. He'd welcome it, the chance to ease the tightness from his bones, to let Fenrys tear into him a bit.

He wouldn't kill the wolf, though. Fenrys might try to kill him, but

Lorcan wouldn't do it. Not after what Fenrys had endured—what he'd managed to do.

Elide emerged from belowdecks, hair braided and smooth. As if she'd been up before the dawn. She barely looked his way, though he knew she was well aware of his location. Lorcan blocked out the hollow pang in his chest.

But Aelin spied him, and there was more clarity in her face than there'd been these past few days as she stalked for where he stood. More of that swagger in her gait, too.

The sleeves of her white shirt had been rolled to the elbow, her hair braided back. Goldryn and a long knife hung from her belt. Ready for training. Primed for it, judging by the bristling energy that buzzed around her.

Lorcan met her halfway, descending the small stairs.

Whitethorn lingered nearby, also dressed for sparring, the wariness in his eyes telling Lorcan enough: the prince had no idea what this was about.

But the young queen crossed her arms. "Do you plan to sail with us to Terrasen?"

An unnecessary question for dawn, and in the middle of the sea. "Yes."

"And you plan to join us in this war?"

"I'm certainly not going there to enjoy the weather."

Amusement glittered in her eyes, though her face remained grim. "Then this is how it's going to work."

Lorcan waited for the list of orders and demands, but the queen was only watching him, that amusement fading into something steel-hardened.

"You were Maeve's second-in-command," she said, and Elide turned their way. "And now that you aren't, it leaves you as a powerful Fae male whose allegiances I don't know or really trust. Not when Maeve's army is likely on the move toward the continent at this very moment. So I can't have you in my kingdom, or traveling with us, when you might very well sell information to get back into Maeve's good graces, can I?"

He opened his mouth, bristling at the haughty tone, but Aelin went on. "So I'll make you an offer, Lorcan Salvaterre." She tapped her bare forearm. "Swear the blood oath to me, and I'll let you roam wherever you wish."

Fenrys cursed behind them, but Lorcan barely heard it over the roaring in his head.

"And what, exactly," he managed to say, "do I get out of it?"

Aelin's eyes slid over her shoulder. To where Elide watched, mouth agape. When the queen met Lorcan's gaze again, a touch of sympathy had softened the steely arrogance. "You will be allowed into Terrasen. That is what you will get. Where you choose to live within Terrasen's borders will not be my decision."

Not her decision, or his. But that of the dark-haired female gawking at them.

"And if I refuse?" Lorcan dared ask.

"Then you will never be allowed to set foot in my kingdom, or to travel further with us—not with the keys in the balance, and Maeve's army at our backs." That sympathy remained. "I can't trust you enough to let you join us any other way."

"But you'll let me swear the blood oath?"

"I want nothing from you, and you want nothing from me. The only order I shall ever give you is the one I would ask of any citizen of Terrasen: to protect and defend our kingdom and its people. You can live in a hut in the Staghorns for all I care."

She meant it, too. Swear the blood oath, swear never to harm her kingdom, and she'd give him freedom. And if he refused . . . He would never see Elide again.

"I don't have another choice," Aelin said quietly, so the others might not hear. "I can't risk Terrasen." She still held her arm toward him. "But I would not take something as precious away from you."

"What you don't realize is *that* is no longer a possibility."

Again, that hint of a smile and glance over her shoulder toward Elide. "It is." Her turquoise eyes were bright as she looked back at him, and there was wisdom on Aelin's face that he had perhaps never noticed before. A queen's face. "Believe me, Lorcan, it is."

He shut down the hope that filled his chest, foreign and unwanted.

"But Terrasen will not survive this war, *she* will not survive this war, without you."

And even if the queen before him gave her immortal life to forge the Lock, to stop Erawan, Lorcan's blood oath to protect her kingdom would hold.

"It's your choice," she said simply.

Lorcan allowed himself to look to Elide, foolish as it might be.

She had a hand on her throat, her dark eyes so wide.

It didn't matter if she still offered him a home in Perranth, if the queen spoke true.

But what did matter was that Aelin Galathynius had meant her promise: he was too powerful, his allegiances too murky, for her to allow him to roam with her, to enter her kingdom unfettered. She'd let him go, keep him out of Terrasen, even if Erawan's hordes were descending, just to avoid the other threat at their backs: Maeve.

And Elide would not survive it, this war, if all of them were dead.

He couldn't accept it, that possibility. Foolish and useless as it was, he couldn't allow it to pass. To have either Erawan's beasts or her uncle Vernon come to claim her again.

Fool. He was an ancient, stupid fool.

Yet the god at his shoulder did not tell him to run, or to fight.

His choice, then. He wondered what the goddess who whispered to Elide made of this.

Wondered what the woman herself was going to make of this as he said to Aelin, "Fine."

"Gods spare us," Fenrys murmured.

Aelin's lips curved in that hint of a smile, amused and yet edged with a touch of cruelty, as she glanced to the wolf. "You'll have to let him live, you realize," she said to Fenrys, lifting a brow. "No to-the-death dueling. No vengeance-fighting. Can you stomach it?"

Lorcan bristled as Fenrys looked him over. Lorcan let him see every bit of dominance in his stare.

Fenrys sent all of his raging back. Not as much as what Lorcan possessed, but enough to remind him that the White Wolf of Doranelle could bite if he wished. Lethally.

Fenrys just turned to the queen. "If I tell you he's a prick and a miserable bastard to be around, will it change your mind?"

Lorcan snarled, but Aelin snorted. "Isn't that why we love Lorcan, though?" She gave him a smile that told Lorcan she remembered every detail of their initial encounters in Rifthold—when he'd shoved her face-first into a brick wall. Aelin said to Fenrys, "We'll only invite him to Orynth on holidays."

"So he can ruin the festivities?" Fenrys scowled. "I, for one, cherish my holidays. I don't need a misanthrope raining on them."

Gods above. Lorcan cut Rowan a look, but the warrior-prince was watching his queen carefully. As if he knew precisely what manner of storm brewed beneath her skin.

Aelin waved a hand. "Fine, fine. You won't try to kill Lorcan for what happened in Eyllwe, and in exchange, we won't invite him to anything." Her grin was nothing short of wicked.

This was the sort of court he'd be joining—this whirlwind of . . . Lorcan didn't know what the word was for it. He doubted any of his five centuries had prepared him for it, though.

Aelin extended a hand. "You know how this goes, then. Or are you too old to remember?"

Lorcan glared and knelt, offering up the dagger at his side.

A fool. He was a fool.

And yet his hands shook slightly as he gave the queen the knife.

Aelin weighed the blade, a golden ring capped with an obscenely large emerald adorning her finger. A wedding band. Likely from the barrow-wight trove she'd pilfered. He glanced to where Whitethorn stood to the side. Sure enough, a golden ring lay on the warrior's own finger, a ruby built into the band. And peeking above the collar of Rowan's jacket, two fresh scars lay.

A pair of them now marked the queen's own throat.

"Done gawking?" Aelin asked Lorcan coolly.

He scowled. Even with the holy ritual they were about to partake in, the queen found a way to be irreverent. "Say it."

Her lips curved again. "Do you, Lorcan Salvaterre, swear upon your blood and eternal soul, to be loyal to me, to my crown, and to Terrasen for the rest of your life?"

He blinked. Maeve had intoned a lengthy list of questions in the Old Language when he'd sworn her oath. But he said, "I do. I swear it."

Aelin sliced the dagger across her forearm, and her blood shone bright as the ruby in the sword at her side. "Then drink."

His last chance to back out from this.

But he glanced toward Elide again. And saw hope—just a glimmer of it—lighting her face.

So Lorcan took the queen's arm in his hands and drank.

The taste of her—jasmine, lemon verbena, and crackling embers—filled his mouth. Filled his soul, as something burned and settled within him.

An ember of warmth. Like a piece of that raging magic had come to rest inside his very soul.

Swaying a bit, he let go of her arm.

"Welcome to the court," Aelin said. "Here's your first and only order: protect Terrasen and its people."

The command settled in him, too, another little spark that glowed down deep.

Then the queen pivoted on her heel and walked away—no, walked up to Elide.

Lorcan tried and failed to stand. His body, it seemed, still needed a moment.

So he could only watch as Aelin said to Elide, "I am not offering you the blood oath."

Vow or no, he debated throwing the queen into the ocean for the devastation that clouded Elide's face. But the Lady of Perranth kept her chin high. "Why?"

Aelin took Elide's hand with a gentleness that cooled Lorcan's rising temper. "Because when we return to Terrasen, if I am to be given the throne, then you cannot be bound to me." Elide's brows crossed. "Perranth is the second-most powerful House in Terrasen," Aelin explained. "Four of its lords have decided that I am unfit for the throne. I need a majority to win it back."

"And if I am sworn to you, it jeopardizes the integrity of my vote," Elide finished.

Aelin nodded, and let go of her hand to turn to all of them. In the rising sun, the queen was bathed in gold. "Terrasen is over two weeks away, if the winter storms don't interfere. We'll use this time to train and plan."

"Plan for what?" Fenrys asked, coming closer.

A member of this court. Of Lorcan's own court. The three of them once again bound—and yet freer than they'd ever been. Lorcan half wondered why the queen didn't offer the oath to Gavriel, but she spoke again.

"My task cannot be completed without the keys. I assume that their new bearers will eventually seek me out, if the third is found and they decide not to finish things themselves." She glanced to Rowan, who nodded. As if they'd already discussed this. "So rather than waste vital time roaming the continent in pursuit of them, we will indeed go to Terrasen. Especially if Maeve is bringing her army to its shores as well. And if I am not allowed to lead from my throne, then I shall just have to do so from the battlefields."

She meant to fight. The queen—*Lorcan's* queen—meant to fight against

Morath. And Maeve, should the worst happen. And then she'd die for them all.

"To Terrasen, then," Fenrys said.

"To Terrasen," Elide echoed.

Aelin gazed westward, toward the kingdom that was all that stood between Erawan and conquest. Toward Lorcan's new home. As if she could see the dread-lord's legions unleashing upon it. And Maeve's immortal host creeping at their backs, a host Lorcan and his companions had once commanded.

Aelin merely strode to the center of the deck, the sailors giving them a wide berth. She unsheathed Goldryn and her dagger, then lifted her brows at Whitethorn in silent challenge.

The warrior-prince obeyed, unsheathing his blade and hatchet before sinking into a defensive crouch.

Training—retraining her body. No whisper of her power manifested, yet her eyes burned bright.

Aelin angled her weapons. "To Terrasen," she said at last.

And began.

CHAPTER 43

Dorian began small.

First, by changing his eyes to black. Solid black, like the Valg. Then by turning his skin into an icy, pale shade, the sort that never saw sunlight. His hair, he left dark, but he managed to make his nose more crooked, his mouth thinner.

Not a full shift, but one done in pieces. Weaving the image together in himself, forming the tapestry of his new face, new skin, during the long, silent flight up the spine of the Fangs.

He hadn't told Manon it was likely a suicide mission, too. He'd barely talked to her at all since the forest clearing. They'd left with the dawn, when she'd announced to Glennis and the Crochans what she planned to do. They could fly to the Ferian Gap and return to that hidden camp within the Fangs in four days, if they were lucky.

She'd asked the Crochans to meet them there. To trust her enough to return to their mountain camp and wait.

They had said yes. Maybe it was the grave the Thirteen had dug all day, but the Crochans said yes. A tentative trust—just this once.

So Dorian had flown with Asterin. Had used each frigid hour northward to slowly alter his body.

You want to go to Morath so badly, Manon had hissed again before they'd left, *then let's see if you can do it.*

A test. One he was glad to excel at. If only to throw in her face.

Manon knew of a back door that only the wyverns took into the Northern Fang, along with any human grunts unlucky enough to be bound to this place. Asterin and Manon had left the Thirteen farther in the mountains before approaching, and even then they'd stopped far away enough from any scouts that they'd spent hours hiking on foot, taking Asterin's mare with them. Abraxos had snarled and tugged on the reins, but Sorrel had held him firmly.

The two mammoth peaks flanking the Gap grew larger with each passed mile. Yet as he approached the southern side of the Fang, he hadn't realized how massive, exactly, they were.

Large enough to hold an aerial host. To train and breed them.

This was what his father and Erawan had built. What Adarlan had become.

No wyverns circled in the skies, but their roars and shrieks echoed from the pass as he strode for the ancient gates that opened into the mountain itself. Behind him, led by a chain, Asterin's blue mare followed.

Another trainer bringing back his mount after a trip for some air. The few guards—mortal men—at the gates barely blinked as he appeared around a rocky bend.

Dorian's palms turned sweaty within his gloves. He prayed the shifting held.

He would have no way of knowing, though he supposed few here would recognize his natural face. He'd picked coloring close enough to his own that should the tapestry within himself unravel, someone might dismiss the altering of his skin tone, his eyes, as a trick of the light.

Narene huffed, yanking on the reins. Not wanting to go near this place.

He didn't blame her. The reek from the mountain set his knees wobbling.

But he'd spent years schooling his expression against the headache-inducing perfumes his mother's courtiers wore. How far away that world seemed—that palace of perfume and lace and lilting music. Had they not resisted Erawan, would he have allowed it to still exist? Had they bowed to him, would Erawan have maintained his ruse as Perrington and ruled as a mortal king?

Dorian's legs burned, the hours of walking taking their toll. Manon and Asterin lurked nearby, hidden in the snow and stone. They no doubt marked his every move while he inched closer to the gates.

His parting words with Manon had been brief. Terse.

He'd dropped the two Wyrdkeys into her awaiting palm, the Amulet of Orynth clinking faintly against her iron nails. Only a fool would bring them into one of Erawan's strongholds. "They might not be your priority," Dorian said, "but they remain vital to our success."

Manon's eyes had narrowed as she pocketed the keys, utterly unfazed at holding in her jacket a power great enough to level kingdoms. "You think I'd toss them away like rubbish?"

Asterin suddenly found the snow to be in need of her careful attention.

Dorian shrugged, and unbuckled Damaris, the sword too fine for a mere wyvern trainer. He passed it to Manon, too. An ordinary dagger would be his only weapon—and the magic in his veins. "If I don't come back," he said while she tied the ancient blade to her belt, "the keys must go to Terrasen." It was the only place he could think of—even if Aelin wasn't there to take them.

"You'll come back," Manon said. It sounded like more of a threat than anything.

Dorian smirked. "Would you miss me if I didn't?"

Manon didn't reply. He didn't know why he expected her to.

He'd taken all of a step, when Asterin clasped his shoulder. "In and out, quick as you can," she warned him. "Take care of Narene." Worry indeed shone in the Second's gold-flecked black eyes.

Dorian bowed his head. "With my life," he promised as he approached her mount and grasped the dangling reins. He didn't fail to miss the gratitude that softened Asterin's features. Or that Manon had already turned away from him.

A fool to start down this path with her. He should have known better.

The guards' faces became clear. Dorian embraced the portrait of a tired, bored handler.

He waited for the questioning, but it never came.

They simply waved him through, equally tired and bored. And cold.

Asterin had given him a layout of the Northern Fang and the Omega across from it, so he knew to turn left upon entering the towering hallway. Wyvern bellows and grunts sounded all around, and that rotting scent stuffed itself up his nose.

But he found the stables precisely where Asterin said they'd be, the blue mare patient while he loosely tied her chains to the anchor in the wall.

Dorian left Narene with a soothing pat to her neck, and went to see what the Ferian Gap might reveal.

～

The hours that passed were some of the longest of Manon's existence.

From anticipation, she told herself. Of what she had to do.

Abraxos, unsurprisingly, found them within an hour, his reins sliced from the struggle he'd no doubt waged and won with Sorrel. He waited, however, beside Manon in silence, wholly focused upon the gate where Dorian and Narene had vanished.

Time dripped by. The king's sword was a constant weight at her side.

She cursed herself for needing to prove—to him, to herself—that she refused to let him go into Morath for practical, ordinary reasons. Erawan wasn't at the Ferian Gap. It'd be safer.

Somewhat. But if the Matrons were there . . .

That was why he'd gone. To learn if they were. To see if Petrah truly commanded the host there, and how many Ironteeth were present.

He had not been trained as a spy, but he'd grown up in a court where people wielded smiles and clothes like weapons. He knew how to blend in, how to listen. How to make people see what they wished to see.

She'd sent Elide into the dungeons of Morath, Darkness damn her. Sending the King of Adarlan into the Ferian Gap was no different.

It didn't stop her breath from escaping when Abraxos stiffened, scanning the sky. As if he heard something they couldn't.

And it was the joy that sparked in her mount's eyes that told her.

Moments later, Narene sailed toward them, making a lazy path over the mountains, a dark-haired, pale-skinned rider atop her. He'd truly been able to change parts of himself. Had made his face nearly unrecognizable. And kept it that way.

Asterin rushed toward the mare, and even Manon blinked as her Second threw her arms around Narene's neck. Holding her tight. The mare only leaned her head against Asterin's back and huffed.

Dorian slid off the mare, leaving the reins dangling.

"Well?" Manon demanded.

His eyes—dark as a Valg's—flashed. She didn't try to explain that her knees had been shaking. Still buckled while she handed him his sword, then the two keys, her nails grazing his gloved hand.

Dorian's eyes lightened to that crushing sapphire, his skin becoming golden once more. "The Matrons are not there. Only Petrah Blueblood, and about three hundred Ironteeth from all three clans." His mouth curved in a cruel half smile, cold as the peaks around them. Damning. "The way is clear, Majesty."

The patrols at the Ferian Gap spotted them miles away.

The Thirteen were still allowed to land in the Omega.

Manon had left Dorian in the small pass where they'd gathered the Thirteen. If they did not return within a day, he was to do what he wished. Go to Morath and Erawan's awaiting embrace, if he was that reckless.

There had been no good-byes between them.

Manon kept her heartbeat steady as she sat atop Abraxos just inside the cavernous mouth leading into the Omega, aware of every enemy eye on them, both at their front and back. "I wish to speak to Petrah Blueblood," she declared to the hall.

A young voice answered "I assumed so."

The Blueblood Heir appeared through the nearest archway, an iron band on her brow, blue robes flowing.

Manon inclined her head. "Gather your host in this hall."

Manon hadn't dwelled long on what she'd say.

And as the three hundred Ironteeth witches filed into the hall, some coming off their patrols, Manon half wondered if she should have. They watched her, watched the Thirteen, with a wary disdain.

Their disgraced Wing Leader; their fallen Heir.

When all were gathered, Petrah, still standing in the doorway where she'd appeared, merely said, "My life debt for an audience, Blackbeak."

Manon swallowed, her tongue as dry as paper. Seated atop Abraxos, she could see every shifting movement in the crowd, the wide eyes or hands gripping swords.

"I will not tell you the particulars of who I am," Manon said at last. "For I think you have already heard them."

"Crochan bitch," someone spat.

Manon set her eyes on the Blackbeaks, stone-faced where the others bristled with hatred. It was for them she spoke, for them she had come here.

"All my life," Manon said, her voice wavering only slightly, "I have been fed a lie."

"We don't have to listen to this trash," another sentinel spat.

Asterin snarled at Manon's side, and the others fell silent. Even disgraced, the Thirteen were deadly.

Manon went on, "A lie, about who we are, what we are. That we are monsters, and proud to be." She ran a finger over the scrap of red fabric binding her braid. "But we were *made* into them. Made," she repeated. "When we might be so much more."

Silence fell.

Manon took that as encouragement enough. "My grandmother does not plan to only reclaim the Wastes when this war is done. She plans to rule the Wastes as High Queen. Your *only* queen."

A murmur at that. At the words, at the betrayal Manon made in revealing her Matron's private plans.

"There will be no Bluebloods, or Yellowlegs, not as you are now. She plans to take the weapons you have built here, plans to use our Blackbeak riders, and *make* you into our subjects. And if you do not bend to her, you will not exist at all."

Manon took a breath. Another.

"We have known only bloodshed and violence for five hundred years. We will know it for another five hundred yet."

"Liar," someone shouted. "We fly to glory."

But Asterin moved, unbuttoning her leather jacket, then hoisting up her white shirt. Rising in the stirrups to bare her scarred, brutalized abdomen. "She does not lie."

UNCLEAN

There, the word remained stamped. Would always be stamped.

"How many of you," Asterin called out, "have been similarly branded? By your Matron, by your coven leader? How many of you have had your stillborn witchlings burned before you might hold them?"

The silence that fell now was different from before. Shaking—shuddering.

Manon glanced at the Thirteen to find tears in Ghislaine's eyes as she took in the brand on Asterin's womb. Tears in the eyes of all of them, who had not known.

And it was for those tears, which Manon had never seen, that she faced the host again. "You will be killed in this war, or after it. And you will never see our homeland again."

"What is it that you want, Blackbeak?" Petrah asked from the archway.

"Ride with us," Manon breathed. "Fly with us. Against Morath. Against the people who would keep you from your homeland, your future." Murmuring broke out again. Manon pushed ahead, "An Ironteeth-Crochan alliance. Perhaps one to break our curse at last."

Again, that shuddering silence. Like a storm about to break.

Asterin sat back in the saddle, but kept her shirt open.

"The choice of how our people's future shall be shaped is yours," Manon told each of the witches assembled, all the Blackbeaks who might fly to war and never return. "But I will tell you this." Her hands shook, and she fisted them on her thighs. "There is a better world out there. And I have seen it."

Even the Thirteen looked toward her now.

"I have seen witch and human and Fae dwell together in peace. And it is not a weakness to do so, but a strength. I have met kings and queens whose love for their kingdoms, their peoples, is so great that the self is secondary. Whose love for their people is so strong that even in the face of unthinkable odds, they do the impossible."

Manon lifted her chin. "You are my people. Whether my grandmother decrees it so or not, you are my people, and always will be. But I will fly against you, if need be, to ensure that there is a future for those who cannot fight for it themselves. Too long have we preyed on the weak, relished doing so. It is time that we became better than our foremothers." The words she had given the Thirteen months ago. "There is a better world out there," she said again. "And I will fight for it." She turned Abraxos away, toward the plunge behind them. "Will you?"

Manon nodded to Petrah. Eyes bright, the Heir only nodded back. They would be permitted to leave as they had arrived: unharmed.

So Manon nudged Abraxos, and he leaped into the sky, the Thirteen following suit.

Not a child of war.

But of peace.

CHAPTER 44

"How shall I carve you up today, Aelin?"

Cairn's words were a push of hot breath at her ear as his knife scraped down her bare thigh.

No. No, it couldn't have been a dream.

The escape, Rowan, the ship to Terrasen—

Cairn dug the tip of his dagger into the flesh above her knee, and she gritted her teeth as blood swelled and spilled. As he began twisting the blade, a little deeper with each rotation.

He had done it so many times now. All over her body.

He would only stop when he hit bone. When she was screaming and screaming.

A dream. An illusion. Her escape from him, from Maeve, had been another illusion.

Had she said it? Had she said where the keys were hidden?

She couldn't stop the sob that ripped from her.

Then a cool, cultured voice purred, "All that training, and this is what becomes of you?"

Not real. Arobynn, standing on the other side of the altar, was not real. Even if he looked it, his red hair shining, his clothes impeccable.

Her former master gave her a half smile. "Even Sam held out better than this."

Cairn twisted the knife again, slicing through muscle. She arched, her scream ringing in her ears. From far away, Fenrys snarled.

"You could get out of these chains, if you really wanted," Arobynn said, frowning with distaste. "If you really tried."

No, she couldn't, and everything had been a dream, a lie—

"You *let* yourself remain captive. Because the moment you are free . . ." Arobynn chuckled. "Then you must offer yourself up, a lamb to slaughter."

She clawed and thrashed against the shredding in her leg, not hearing Cairn as he sneered. Only hearing the King of the Assassins, unseen and unnoted beside her.

"Deep down, you're hoping you'll be here long enough that the young King of Adarlan will pay the price. Deep down, you know you're hiding here, waiting for him to clear the path." Arobynn leaned against the side of the altar, cleaning his nails with a dagger. "Deep down, you know it's not really fair, that those gods picked you. That Elena picked you instead of him. She bought you time to live, yes, but *you* were still chosen to pay the price. Her price. And the gods'."

Arobynn ran a long-fingered hand down the side of her face. "Do you see what I tried to spare you from all these years? What you might have avoided had you remained Celaena, remained with me?" He smiled. "Do you see, Aelin?"

She could not answer. Had no voice.

Cairn hit bone, and—

Aelin lunged upward, hands grasping for her thigh.

No chains weighed her. No mask smothered her.

No dagger had been twisted into her body.

Breathing hard, the scent of musty sheets clinging to her nose, the sounds of her screaming replaced by the drowsy chirping of birds, Aelin scrubbed at her face.

The prince who'd fallen asleep beside her was already running a hand down her back in silent, soothing strokes.

Beyond the small window of the ramshackle inn somewhere near Fenharrow and Adarlan's border, thick veils of mist drifted.

A dream. Just a dream.

She twisted, setting her feet to the threadbare carpet on the uneven wood floor.

"Dawn isn't for another hour," Rowan said.

Yet Aelin reached for her shirt. "I'll get warmed up, then." Maybe run, as she had not been able to do in weeks and weeks.

Rowan sat up, missing nothing. "Training can wait, Aelin." They'd been doing it for weeks now, as thorough and grueling as it had been at Mistward.

She shoved her legs into her pants, then buckled on her sword belt. "No, it can't."

⁓

Aelin dodged to the side, Rowan's blade sailing past her head, snipping a few strands from the end of her braid.

She blinked, breathing hard, and barely brought Goldryn up in time to parry his next attack. Metal reverberated through the stinging blisters coating her hands.

New blisters—for a new body. Three weeks at sea, and her calluses had barely formed again. Every day, hours spent training at swordplay and archery and combat, and her hands were still *soft*.

Grunting, Aelin crouched low, thighs burning as she prepared to spring.

But Rowan halted in the dusty courtyard of the inn, his hatchet and sword dropping to his sides. In the first light of dawn, the inn could have passed for pleasant, the sea breeze from the nearby coast drifting through the lingering leaves on the hunched apple tree in the center of the space.

A gathering storm to the north had forced their ship to find harbor last night—and after weeks at sea, none of them had hesitated to spend a few hours on land. To learn what in hell had happened while they'd been gone.

The answer: war.

Everywhere, war raged. But *where* the fighting occurred, the aging innkeeper didn't know. Boats didn't stop at the port anymore—and the great warships just sailed past. Whether they were enemy or friendly, he also didn't know. Knew absolutely nothing, it seemed. Including how to cook. And clean his inn.

They'd need to be back on the seas within a day or two, if they were to make it to Terrasen quickly. There were too many storms in the North to have risked crossing directly there, their captain had said. This time of year, it was safer to make it to the continent's coast, then sail up it. Even if that command and those very storms had landed them here: somewhere between Fenharrow and Adarlan's border. With Rifthold a few days ahead.

When Rowan didn't resume their sparring, Aelin scowled. "What."

It wasn't so much of a question as a demand.

His gaze was unfaltering. As it had been when she'd returned from her run through the misty fields beyond the inn and found him leaning against the apple tree. "That's enough for today."

"We've hardly started." She lifted her blade.

Rowan kept his own lowered. "You barely slept last night."

Aelin tensed. "Bad dreams." An understatement. She lifted her chin and threw him a grin. "Perhaps I'm starting to wear *you* down a bit."

Despite the blisters, she'd gained back weight, at least. Had watched her arms go from thin to cut with muscle, her thighs from reeds to sleek and powerful.

Rowan didn't return her smile. "Let's eat breakfast."

"After that dinner last night, I'm in no hurry." She didn't give him a blink of warning before she launched herself at him, swiping high with Goldryn and stabbing low with her dagger.

Rowan met her attack, easily deflecting. They clashed, broke apart, and clashed again.

His canines gleamed. "You need to eat."

"I need to train."

She couldn't stop it—that need to do *something*. To be in motion.

No matter how many times she swung her blade, she could feel them. The shackles. And whenever she paused to rest, she could feel it, too—her magic. Waiting.

Indeed, it seemed to open an eye and yawn.

She clenched her jaw, and attacked again.

Rowan met each blow, and she knew her maneuvers were descending into sloppiness. Knew he let her continue rather than seizing the many openings to end it.

She couldn't stop. War raged around them. People were dying. And she had been locked in that damned box, had been taken apart again and again, unable to *do* anything—

Rowan struck, so fast she couldn't track it. But it was the foot he slid before her own that doomed her, sending her careening into the dirt.

Her knees barked, skinning beneath her pants, and her dagger scattered from her hand.

"I win," he panted. "Let's eat."

Aelin glared up at him. "Another round."

Rowan just sheathed his sword. "After breakfast."

She growled. He growled right back.

"Don't be stupid," he said. "You'll lose all that muscle if you don't feed your body. So eat. And if you still want to train afterward, I'll train with you." He offered her a tattooed hand. "Though you'll likely hurl your guts up."

Either from the exertion or from the innkeeper's suspect cooking.

But Aelin said, "People are dying. In Terrasen. In—everywhere. People are dying, Rowan."

"Your eating breakfast isn't going to change that." Her lips curled in a snarl, but he cut her off. "I know people are dying. We are going to help them. But *you* need to have some strength left, or you won't be able to."

Truth. Her mate spoke truth. And yet she could see them, hear them. Those dying, frightened people.

Whose screams so often sounded like her own.

Rowan wriggled his fingers in silent reminder. *Shall we?*

Aelin scowled and took his hand, letting him haul her to her feet. *So pushy.*

Rowan slid an arm around her shoulders. *That's the most polite thing you've ever said about me.*

⁓

Elide tried not to wince at the grayish gruel steaming in front of her. Especially with the innkeeper watching from the shadows behind his taproom bar. Seated at one of the small, round tables that filled the worn space, Elide caught Gavriel's eye from where he pushed at his own bowl.

Gavriel raised the spoon to his mouth. Slowly.

Elide's eyes widened. Widened further as he opened his mouth, and took a bite.

His swallow was audible. His cringe barely contained.

Elide reined in her smile at the pure misery that entered the Lion's tawny stare. Aelin and Rowan had been finishing up a similar battle when she'd entered the taproom minutes ago, the queen wishing her luck before striding back into the courtyard.

Elide hadn't seen her sit still for longer than it took to eat a meal. Or during the hours when she'd instructed them in Wyrdmarks, after Rowan had requested she teach them.

It had gotten her out of the chains, the prince had explained. And if the ilken were resistant to their magic, then learning the ancient marks would come in handy with all they faced ahead. The battles both physical and magic.

Such strange, difficult markings. Elide couldn't read her own language, hadn't tried to in ages. Didn't suppose she'd be granted the opportunity anytime soon. But learning these marks, if it helped her companions in any way . . . she could try. *Had* tried, enough to know a few of them now.

Gavriel dared another mouthful of the porridge, offering the innkeeper a tight smile. The man looked so relieved that Elide picked up her own spoon and choked down a bite. Bland and a bit sour—had he put salt in it, rather than sugar?—but . . . it was hot.

Gavriel met her stare, and Elide again restrained her laugh.

She felt, rather than saw, Lorcan enter. The innkeeper instantly found somewhere else to be. The man hadn't been surprised to see five Fae enter his inn last night, so his vanishing whenever Lorcan appeared was certainly due to the glower the male had perfected.

Indeed, Lorcan took one look at Elide and Gavriel and left the dining room.

They'd barely spoken these weeks. Elide hadn't known what to even say.

A member of this court. Her court. Forever.

He and Aelin certainly hadn't warmed toward each other. No, only Rowan and Gavriel really spoke to him. Fenrys, despite his promise to Aelin *not* to fight with Lorcan, ignored him most of the time. And Elide . . . She'd made herself scarce often enough that Lorcan hadn't bothered to approach her.

Good. It was good. Even if she sometimes found herself opening her mouth to speak to him. Watching him as he listened to Aelin's lessons on the Wyrdmarks. Or while he trained with the queen, the rare moments when the two of them weren't at each other's throats.

Aelin had been returned to them. Was recovering as best she could.

Elide didn't taste her next bite of porridge. Gavriel, thankfully, said nothing.

And Anneith didn't speak, either. Not a whisper of guidance.

It was better that way. To listen to herself. Better that Lorcan kept his distance, too.

Elide ate the rest of her porridge in silence.

Rowan was right: she nearly vomited after breakfast. Five minutes in the courtyard and she'd had to stop, that miserable gruel rising in her throat.

Rowan had chuckled when she'd clapped a hand over her mouth. And then shifted into his hawk form to sail for the nearby coast and their awaiting ship, to check in with its captain.

Rolling her shoulders, she'd watched him vanish into the clouds. He was right, of course. About letting herself rest.

Whether the others knew what propelled her, they hadn't said a word.

Aelin sheathed Goldryn and loosed a long breath. Deep down, her power grumbled.

She flexed her fingers.

Maeve's cold, pale face flashed before her eyes.

Her magic went silent.

Blowing out another shuddering breath, shaking the tremor from her hands, Aelin aimed for the inn's open gates. A long, dusty road stretched ahead, the fields beyond barren. Unimpressive, forgotten land. She'd barely glimpsed anything on her run at dawn beyond mist and a few sparrows bobbing amongst the winter-dry grasses.

Fenrys sat in wolf form at the edge of the nearest field, staring out across the expanse. Precisely where he'd been before dawn.

She let him hear her steps, his ears twitching. He shifted as she approached, and leaned against the half-rotted fence surrounding the field.

"Who'd you piss off to get the graveyard shift?" Aelin asked, wiping the sweat from her brow.

Fenrys snorted and ran a hand through his hair. "Would you believe I volunteered for it?"

She arched a brow. He shrugged, watching the field again, the mists still clinging to its farthest reaches. "I don't sleep well these days." He cut her a sidelong glance. "I don't suppose I'm the only one."

She picked at the blister on her right hand, hissing. "We could start a secret society—for people who don't sleep well."

"As long as Lorcan isn't invited, I'm in."

Aelin huffed a laugh. "Let it go."

His face turned stony. "I said I would."

"You clearly haven't."

"I'll let it go when you stop running yourself ragged at dawn."

"I'm not running myself ragged. Rowan is overseeing it."

"Rowan is the only reason you're not limping everywhere."

Truth. Aelin curled her aching hands into fists and slid them into her pockets. Fenrys said nothing—didn't ask why she didn't warm her fingers. Or the air around them.

He just turned to her and blinked three times. *Are you all right?*

A gull's cry pierced the gray world, and Aelin blinked back twice. *No.*

It was as much as she'd admit. She blinked again, thrice now. *Are you all right?*

Two blinks from him, too.

No, they were not all right. They might never be. If the others knew, if they saw past the swagger and temper, they didn't let on.

None of them commented that Fenrys hadn't once used his magic to leap between places. Not that there was anywhere to go in the middle of the sea. But even when they sparred, he didn't wield it.

Perhaps it had died with Connall. Perhaps it had been a gift they had both shared, and touching it was unbearable.

She didn't dare peer inward, to the churning sea inside her. Couldn't.

Aelin and Fenrys stood by the field as the sun arced higher, burning off the mists.

After a long minute, she asked, "When you took the oath to Maeve, what did her blood taste like?"

His golden brows narrowed. "Like blood. And power. Why?"

Aelin shook her head. Another dream, or hallucination. "If she's on our heels with this army, I'm just . . . trying to understand it. Her, I mean."

"You plan to kill her."

The gruel in her stomach turned over, but Aelin shrugged. Even as she tasted ash on her tongue. "Would you prefer to do it?"

"I'm not sure I'd survive it," he said through his teeth. "And you have more of a reason to claim it than I do."

"I'd say we have an equal claim."

His dark eyes roved over her face. "Connall was a better male than—than how you saw him that time. Than what he was in the end."

She gripped his hand and squeezed. "I know."

The last of the mists vanished. Fenrys asked quietly, "Do you want me to tell you about it?"

He didn't mean his brother.

She shook her head. "I know enough." She surveyed her cold, blistered hands. "I know enough," she repeated.

He stiffened, a hand going to the sword at his side. Not at her words, but—

Rowan dove from the skies, a full-out plunge.

He shifted a few feet from the ground, landing with a predator's grace as he ran the last steps toward them.

Goldryn sang as she unsheathed it. "What?"

Her mate just pointed to the skies.

To what flew there.

CHAPTER 45

Rock roared against rock, and Yrene braced a hand on the shuddering stones of Westfall Keep as the tower swayed. Down the hallway, people screamed, some wailing, some lunging over family members to cover them with their bodies while debris rained.

Dawn had barely broken, and the battle was already raging.

Yrene pressed herself into the stones, heart hammering, counting the breaths until the shaking stopped. The last assault, it had been six.

She got to three, mercifully.

Five days of this. Five days of this endless nightmare, with only the blackest hours of the night offering reprieve.

She had barely seen Chaol for more than a passing kiss and embrace. The first time, he'd been sporting a wound to the temple that she'd healed away. The next, he'd been leaning heavily on his cane, covered in dirt and blood, much of it not his own.

It was the black blood that had made her stomach turn. Valg. There were Valg out there. Infesting human hosts. Too many for her to cure. No, that part would come after the battle. If they survived.

Soon, too soon, the injured and dying had begun pouring in. Eretia had organized a sick bay in the great hall, and it was there that Yrene had spent most of her time. Where she'd been headed, after managing a few hours of dreamless sleep.

The tower steadied itself, and Yrene announced to no one in particular, "The ruks are still holding off the tide. Morath only fires the catapults because they cannot breach the keep walls."

It was only partially true, but the families crouched in the hall, their bedrolls and precious few belongings with them, seemed to settle.

The ruks had indeed disabled many of the catapults that Morath had hauled here, but a few remained—just enough to hammer the keep, the city. And while the ruks might have been holding off the tide, it would not be for long.

Yrene didn't want to know how many had fallen. She only saw the number of riders in the great hall and knew it would be too many. Eretia had ordered the injured ruks to take up residence in one of the interior courtyards, assigning five healers to oversee them, and the space was so full you could barely move through it.

Yrene hurried onward, mindful of the debris scattered on the tower stair. She'd nearly snapped her neck yesterday slipping on a piece of fallen wood.

The groans of the injured reached her long before she entered the great hall, the doors flung open to reveal row after row of soldiers, from the khaganate and Anielle alike. The healers didn't have cots for all, so many had been laid on bedrolls. When those had run out, cloaks and blankets piled over cold stone had been used.

Not enough—not enough supplies, and not enough healers. They should have brought more from the rest of the host.

Yrene rolled up her sleeves, aiming for the wash station near the doors.

Several of the children whose families sheltered in the keep had taken up the task of emptying dirty tubs and filling them with hot water every few minutes. Along with the basins by the wounded.

Yrene had balked to let children witness such bloodshed and pain, but there was no one else to do it. No one else so eager to help.

Anielle's lord might have been a grand bastard, but its people were a brave, noble-hearted group. One that had left more of a mark on her husband than his hateful father.

Yrene scrubbed her hands, though she'd washed them before coming down here, and shook them dry. They couldn't waste their precious few cloths on drying their hands.

Her magic had barely refilled, despite the sleep she'd gotten. She knew that if she looked to the battlements, she'd spy Chaol using his cane, perhaps even atop the battle-horse they'd outfitted with his brace. His limp had been deep when she'd last seen him, just yesterday afternoon.

He hadn't complained, though—hadn't asked her to stop expending her power. He'd fight whether he was standing or using the cane or the chair or a horse.

Eretia met Yrene halfway across the hall floor, her dark skin shining with sweat. "They're bringing in a rider. Her throat's been slashed by talons, but she's still breathing."

Yrene suppressed her shudder. "Poison on the talons?" So many of the Valg beasts possessed it.

"The scout who flew by to warn us of her arrival wasn't sure."

Yrene pulled her tool kit from the satchel at her hip, scanning the hall for a place to work on the incoming rider. Not much room—but there, by the washbasins where she'd just cleaned her hands. Enough space. "I'll meet them at the doors." Yrene made to hurry for the gaping entryway.

But Eretia gripped Yrene's upper arm, her thin fingers digging gently into her skin. "You've rested enough?"

"Have you?" Yrene shot back. Eretia had still been here when Yrene had trudged to bed hours ago, and it seemed Eretia had either arrived well before Yrene this morning, or hadn't left at all.

Eretia's brown eyes narrowed. "I am not the one who needs to be careful of how much I push myself."

Yrene knew Eretia didn't mean in regard to Chaol and the link between their bodies.

"I know my limits," Yrene said stiffly.

Eretia gave a knowing look to Yrene's still-flat abdomen. "Many would not risk it at all."

Yrene paused. "Is there a threat?"

"No, but any pregnancy, especially in the early months, is draining. That's without the horrors of war, or using your magic to the brink every day."

For a heartbeat, Yrene let the words settle in. "How long have you known?"

"A few weeks. My magic sensed it on you."

Yrene swallowed. "I haven't told Chaol."

"I'd think if there were ever a time to do so," the healer said, gesturing to the shuddering keep around them, "it would be now."

Yrene knew that. She'd been trying to find a way to tell him for a while. But placing that burden on him, that worry for her safety and the safety of the life growing in her . . . She hadn't wanted to distract him. To add to the fear she already knew he fought against, just in having her here, fighting beside him.

And for Chaol to know that if he fell, it would not be her life alone that now ended . . . She couldn't bring herself to tell him. Not yet.

Perhaps it made her selfish, perhaps stupid, but she couldn't. Even if the moment she'd realized it in the ship's bathing chamber, when her cycle still had not come and she had begun counting the days, she had wept with joy. And then realized what, exactly, carrying a child during war would entail. That this war might very well be still raging, or in its final, horrible days, when she gave birth.

Yrene had decided that she'd do everything in her power to make sure it did not end with her child being born into a world of darkness.

"I'll tell him when the time is right," Yrene said a shade sharply.

From the open hall doors, shouts rose to "Clear the way! Clear the way for the injured!"

Eretia frowned, but rushed with Yrene to meet the townsfolk bearing an already-bloodied stretcher and the near-dead ruk rider atop it.

The horse beneath Chaol shifted but stayed firm where they stood along the lower battlements of the keep walls. Not as fine a horse as Farasha, but solid enough. A bravehearted beast who had taken well to his brace-equipped saddle, which was all he'd asked for.

Walking, Chaol knew, would not be an option when he dismounted. The strain in his spine told him enough about how hard Yrene was already working, the sun barely risen. But he could fight just as well from horseback—could lead these soldiers all the same.

Ahead, stretching too far for him to count, Erawan's army launched at the city for another day of all-out assault on the walls.

The ruks soared, dodging arrows and spears, snatching soldiers from the ground and pulling them apart. Atop the birds, the rukhin unleashed their own torrent of fury in careful, clever passes organized by Sartaq and Nesryn.

But after five days, even the mighty ruks were slowing.

And Morath's siege towers, which they had once easily shattered into scraps of metal and wood, were now making their way to the walls.

"Ready the men for impact," Chaol ordered the grim-faced captain standing nearby. The captain shouted the command down the lines Chaol had gathered just before dawn.

A few bands of Morath soldiers had managed to get grappling hooks into the walls these past two days, hoisting up siege ladders and droves of soldiers with them. Chaol had cut them down, and though the warriors of Anielle had been unsure what to do with the demon-infested men who came to slay them, they'd obeyed his barked commands. Quickly staunched the flow of soldiers over the walls, severing the ties that held the ladders to them.

But the siege towers that approached . . . those would not be so easily dislodged. And neither would the soldiers who crossed the metal bridge that would span the tower and the keep walls.

Behind him, levels up, he knew his father watched. Had already signaled through the lantern system Sartaq had demonstrated how to use that they needed ruks to fly back—to knock the towers down.

But the ruks were making a pass at the far rear of Morath's army, where the commanders had kept the Valg lines in order. It had been Nesryn's idea last night: to stop going for the endless front lines and instead take out those who ordered them. Try to sow chaos and disarray.

The first siege tower neared, metal groaning as wyverns—chained to the ground and wings clipped—hauled it closer. Soldiers already lined up behind it in twin columns, ready to storm upward.

Today would hurt.

Chaol's horse shifted beneath him again, and he patted a gauntlet-covered hand on the stallion's armored neck. The thud of metal on metal was swallowed by the din. "Patience, friend."

Far out, past the reach of the archers, the catapult was reloading. They'd launched a boulder only thirty minutes ago, and Chaol had ducked beneath an archway, praying the tower base it struck did not collapse.

Praying Yrene wasn't near it.

He'd barely seen her during these days of bloodshed and exhaustion. Hadn't had a chance to tell her what he knew. To tell her what was in his heart. He'd settled for a deep but brief kiss, and then rushed to whatever part of the battlements he'd been needed at.

Chaol drew his sword, the freshly polished metal whining as it came free of the sheath. The fingers of his other hand tightened around the handles of his shield. A ruk rider's shield, light and meant for swift combat. The brace that held him in the saddle remained steady, its buckles secure.

The soldiers lining the battlements stirred at the nearing siege tower. The horrors inside.

"They were once men," Chaol called, his voice carrying over the clamor of the battle beyond the keep walls, "they can still die like them."

A few swords stopped quivering.

"You are people of Anielle," Chaol went on, hefting his shield and angling his sword. "Let's show them what that means."

The siege tower slammed into the side of the keep, and the metal bridge at its uppermost level snapped down, crushing the battlement parapets beneath.

Chaol's focus went cold and calculating.

His wife was in the keep behind him. Pregnant with their child.

He would not fail her.

A siege tower had reached the keep walls, and now unloaded soldier after soldier right into the ancient castle.

Despite the distance, Nesryn could see the chaos on the battlements. Just barely make out Chaol atop his gray horse, fighting in the thick of it.

Soaring over the army hurling arrows and spears at them, Nesryn banked left, the ruks behind her following suit.

Across the battlefield, Borte and Yeran, leading another faction of rukhin, banked right, the two groups of rukhin a mirror image swooping toward each other, then back to plow through the rear lines.

Just as Sartaq, leading a third group, slammed from the other direction.

They'd taken out two commanders, but three more remained. Not princes, thank the gods here and the thirty-six in the khaganate, but Valg all the same. Black blood coated Salkhi's armored feathers, coated every ruk in the skies.

She'd spent hours cleaning it off Salkhi last night. All the rukhin had, not willing to risk the old blood interfering with how their feathers caught the wind.

Nesryn nocked an arrow and picked her target. Again.

The Valg commander had evaded her shot the last time. But he would not now.

Salkhi swept low, taking arrow after arrow against his breastplate, in his thick feathers and skin. Nesryn had almost vomited the first time an arrow had found its mark days ago. A lifetime ago. She now also spent hours picking them from his body each night—as if they were thorns from a prickly plant.

Sartaq had spent that time going from fire to fire, comforting those whose mounts were not so fortunate. Or soothing the ruks whose riders hadn't lasted the day. Already, a wagon had been piled high with their *sulde*—awaiting the final journey home to be planted on Arundin's barren slopes.

When Salkhi came close enough to rip several Valg off their horses and shred them apart in his talons, Nesryn fired at the commander.

She didn't see if the shot landed.

Not as a horn cut through the din.

A cry rose from the rukhin, all glancing eastward. Toward the sea.

To where the Darghan cavalry and foot soldiers charged for the unprotected eastern flank of Morath's army, Hasar atop her Muniqi horse, leading the khagan's host herself.

~

Two armies clashed on the plain outside an ancient city, one dark and one golden.

They fought, brutal and bloody, for the long hours of the gray day.

Morath's armies didn't break, though. And no matter how Nesryn and the rukhin, led by Sartaq and Hasar's orders, rallied behind their fresh troops, the Valg kept fighting.

And still Morath's host lay between the khagan's army and the besieged city, an ocean of darkness.

When night fell, too black for even the Valg to fight, the khagan's army pulled back to assess. To ready for the attack at dawn.

Nesryn flew Yrene and Chaol, bloodied and exhausted, down from the again-secured keep walls, so they might join in the war council between the khagan's royal children. All around, soldiers groaned and screamed in agony, healers led by Hafiza herself rushing to tend them before the night gave way to more fighting.

But when they reached Princess Hasar's battle tent, when they had all gathered around a map of Anielle, they had only a few minutes of discussion before they were interrupted.

By the person Chaol least expected to walk through the flaps.

CHAPTER 46

Perranth appeared on the horizon, the dark-stoned city nestled between a cobalt lake and a small mountain range that also bore its name.

The castle had been built along a towering mountain bordering the city, its narrow towers tall enough to rival those in Orynth. The great city walls had been torn down by Adarlan's army and never restored, the buildings along its edges now spilling onto the fields beyond the iced-over Lanis River that flowed between the lake and the distant sea.

It was on those fields that Aedion deemed they'd make their stand.

The ice held as they crossed the river and organized their reduced lines once more.

The Whitethorn royals and their warriors were nearly burnt out, their magic a mere breeze. But they'd kept Morath a day behind with their shields.

A day the army used to rest, hewing wood from whatever trees, barns, or abandoned farmsteads they could find to fuel their fires. A day when Aedion had ordered Nox Owen to go as his emissary into Perranth, the thief's home city, and see if men and women from the city might come to fill their depleted ranks.

Not many. Nox returned with a few hundred even-less-trained warriors. No magic-wielders.

But they did have some weapons, most old and rusted. Fresh arrows, at least. Vernon Lochan had seen to it that his people had remained unarmed, fearing their uprising should they learn the true Heir to Perranth had been held captive in the highest tower of the castle.

But the people of Perranth already had enough of their puppet lord, it seemed.

And at least they had blankets and food to spare. Wagons hauled them in hourly, along with healers—none magically gifted—to patch up the wounded. Those who were too injured to fight were sent on the supply wagons to the city, some piled atop one another.

But a warm blanket and hot meal would not add to their numbers. Or keep Morath at bay.

So Aedion planned, keeping his Bane commanders close. They would make this count. Every inch of terrain, every weapon and soldier.

He didn't see Lysandra. *Aelin* made no appearances, either.

The queen had abandoned them, the soldiers muttered.

Aedion made sure to shut down the talk. Had snarled that the queen had her own mission to save their asses, and if she wanted Erawan to know about it, she would have announced it to them all, since they were so inclined to gossip.

It eased the discontent—barely.

Aelin had not defended them with her fire, had left them to be butchered.

Some part of him agreed. Wondered if it would have been better to ignore the keys, to use the two they possessed and obliterate these armies, rather than destroy their greatest weapon to forge the Lock.

Hell, he would have wept to see Dorian Havilliard and his considerable power at that moment. The king had blasted ilken from the sky, had snapped their necks without touching them. He'd bow before the man if it saved them.

It was midday when Morath's army reached them once more, their mass spilling over the horizon. A storm sweeping across the fields.

He'd warned the people of Perranth to flee into Oakwald, if they could. Locking themselves in the castle would be of little use. It had no supplies to outlast a siege. He'd debated using it for this battle, but their advantage lay in the frozen river, not in letting themselves be cornered to endure a slow death.

No one was coming to save them. There had been no word from Rolfe, Galan's forces were depleted, his ships spread thin on the coast, and no whisper of the remainder of Ansel of Briarcliff's soldiers.

Aedion kept that knowledge from his face as he rode his stallion down the front lines, inspecting the soldiers.

The tang of their fear fogged the frosty air, the weight of their dread a bottomless pit yawning open in their eyes as they tracked him.

The Bane began striking their swords against their shields. A steady heartbeat to override the vibrations of the Morath soldiers marching toward them.

Aedion didn't look for a shifter in the ranks. Ilken flew low over Morath's teeming mass. She'd undoubtedly go for them first.

Aedion halted his horse in the center of their host, the iced-over Lanis almost buried beneath the snow that had fallen the night before. Morath knew it existed, though. Those Valg princes had likely studied the terrain thoroughly. Had likely studied *him* thoroughly, too, his technique and skill. He knew he'd face one of them before it was done, perhaps all of them. It wouldn't end well.

Yet as long as they risked the crossing, he didn't care. Endymion and Sellene, the only Fae still left with a whisper of power, were stationed just behind the first of the Bane.

The eyes of his own soldiers were a phantom touch between his shoulder blades, on his helmeted head. He had not prepared a speech to rally them.

A speech would not keep these men from dying today.

So Aedion drew the Sword of Orynth, hefted his shield, and joined the Bane's steady beat.

Conveying all the defiance and rage in his heart, he clashed the ancient sword against the dented, round metal.

Rhoe's shield.

Aedion had never told Aelin. Had wanted to wait until they returned to Orynth to reveal that the shield he'd carried, had never lost, had belonged to her father. And so many others before that.

It had no name. Even Rhoe had not known its age. And when Aedion had spirited it away from Rhoe's room, the only thing he grabbed when the news came that his family had been butchered, he had let the others forget about it, too.

Even Darrow had not recognized it. Worn and simple, the shield had gone unnoticed at Aedion's side, a reminder of what he'd lost. What he'd defend to his final breath.

The soldiers from their allies' armies picked up the beat as Morath reached the edge of the river. A barked command from the two Valg princes on horseback had the first of the foot soldiers crossing the ice, the ilken holding back near the center. To strike when they'd been worn down.

Ren Allsbrook and their remaining archers kept hidden behind the lines, picking targets amongst those winged terrors.

On and on, Aedion and their army banged their swords against their shields.

Closer and closer, Morath's army spilled onto the frozen river.

Aedion held the beat, their enemy not realizing the sound served another purpose.

To mask the cracking of the ice deep below.

Morath advanced until they were nearly across the river.

Enda and Sellene needed no shouted order. A wind swept over the ice, then slammed into it, between the cracks they'd been creating. Then they shoved the ice apart. Tore it to shreds.

One heartbeat, Morath was marching toward them.

The next, they plunged down, water splashing, shouts and screams filling the air. The ilken shot forward to grab soldiers drowning under the weight of their armor.

But Ren Allsbrook was waiting, and at his bellowed order, the archers fired upon the exposed ilken. Blows to the wings sent them tumbling to the ice, into the water. Going under, some ilken dragged by their own thrashing soldiers.

The Valg princes each lifted a hand, as if they were of one mind. The army halted at the shore. Watching as their brethren drowned. Watching as Endymion and Sellene kept ripping the ice apart, forbidding it to freeze over again.

Aedion dared to smile at the sight of the drowning soldiers.

He found the two Valg princes smiling back at him from across the river. One ran a hand over the black collar at his throat. A promise and reminder of precisely what they'd do to him.

Aedion inclined his head in mocking invitation. They could certainly try.

The Fae royals' power broke at last, heralded by the ice that formed over the drowning soldiers, sealing them beneath the dark water.

A gust of black wind from the Valg princes and their soldiers didn't so much as look down as they began marching over the ice, ignoring the banging fists beneath their feet.

Aedion guided his horse behind the front line, to where Kyllian and Elgan were mounted on their own steeds. Two thousand of the enemy had gone into the river at most. None would emerge.

Barely a dent in the force now advancing.

Aedion didn't have words for his commanders, who had known him for most of his life, perhaps better than anyone. They had no words for him, either.

When Morath reached their shore at last, swords bright in the gray day, Aedion let out a roar and charged.

The ilken had learned that a shape-shifter was amongst them, and wore a wyvern's skin. Lysandra realized it after she'd swept for them, leaping from the army's ranks to slam into a cluster of three.

Three others had been waiting, hiding in the horde below. An ambush.

She'd barely taken out two, snapping off their heads with her spiked tail, before their poisoned claws had forced her to flee. So she'd drawn the ilken back toward her own lines, right into the range of Ren's archers.

They'd gotten the ilken down—barely. Shots to the wings that allowed Lysandra to rip their heads from their bodies.

As they'd fallen, she'd dove for the ground, shifting as she went. She landed as a ghost leopard, and unleashed herself upon the foot soldiers already pushing against Terrasen's joined shields.

The skilled unity of the Bane was nothing against the sheer numbers forcing them back. The Fae warriors, the Silent Assassins—Ansel and Galan's few remaining soldiers spread between them—neither of those lethal units could halt them, either.

So she clawed and tore and sundered, black bile burning her throat. Snow turned to mud beneath her paws. Corpses piled, men both human and Valg screamed.

Aedion's voice shattered down the lines, *"Hold that right flank!"*

She dared a glance toward it. The ilken had concentrated their forces there, slamming into the men in a phalanx of death and poison.

Then another order from the prince, *"Hold fast on the left!"*

He'd repositioned the Bane amongst the right and left flanks to account for their wobbling on the southern plains, yet it was not enough.

Ilken tore into the cavalry, horses shrieking as poisoned talons ripped out their innards, riders crushed beneath falling bodies.

Aedion galloped toward the left flank, some of his Bane following.

Lysandra sliced through soldier after soldier, arrows flying from both armies.

SARAH J. MAAS

Still Morath advanced. Onward and harder, driving the Bane back as if they were little more than a branch blocking their path.

Her breath burned in her lungs, her legs ached, yet she kept fighting.

There would be nothing left of them by sundown if they kept at it like this.

The other men seemed to realize it, too. Looked beyond the demons they fought to the tens of thousands still behind in orderly rows, waiting to kill and kill and kill.

Some of their soldiers began to turn. Fleeing the front lines.

Some outright hurled away their shields and *sprinted* out of the path of Morath.

Morath seized on it. A wave crashing to shore, they slammed into their front line. Right into the center, which had never broken, even when the others had wobbled.

They punched a hole right through it.

Chaos reigned.

Aedion roared from somewhere, from the heart of hell, "*Re-form the lines!*"

The order went ignored.

The Bane tried and failed to hold the line. Ansel of Briarcliff bellowed to her fleeing men to get back to the front, Galan Ashryver echoing her commands to his own soldiers. Ren shouted to his archers to remain, but they too abandoned their posts.

Lysandra slashed through the shins of one Morath soldier, then ripped the throat from another. None of Terrasen's warriors remained a step behind her to decapitate the fallen bodies.

No one at all.

Over. It was over.

Useless, Aedion had called her.

Lysandra gazed toward the ilken feasting on the right flank and knew what she had to do.

CHAPTER
47

Aedion had imagined they'd all be killed where they stood, battling together until the end. Not picked off one by one as they fled.

He'd been forced far behind the lines when Morath plunged through, even the Bane having to peel away from the front. Soon, the rout would be complete.

Arrows still flew from deep behind their ranks, Ren having seized some order, if only to cover their retreat.

Not an orderly march to the north. No, soldiers ran, shoving past one another.

A disgraceful end, unworthy of a mention, unworthy of his kingdom.

He'd stand—he'd stay here until they cut him down.

Thousands of men charged past him, eyes wide with terror. Morath gave chase, their Valg princes smiling as they awaited the feasting sure to come.

Done. It was done, here on this unnamed field before Perranth.

Then a call went across the breaking lines.

The fleeing men began to pause. To turn toward the direction of the news.

Aedion skewered a Morath soldier on his sword before he fully understood the words.

The queen has come. The queen is at the front line.

For a foolish heartbeat, he scanned the sky for a blast of flame.

None came.

Dread settled into his heart, fear deeper than any he'd known.

The queen is at the front line—at the right flank.

Lysandra.

Lysandra had taken on Aelin's skin.

He whirled toward the nonexistent right flank.

Just as the golden-haired queen in borrowed armor faced two ilken, a sword and shield in her hands.

No.

The word was a punch through his body, greater than any blow he'd felt.

Aedion began running, shoving through his own men. Toward the too-distant right flank. Toward the shape-shifter facing those ilken, no claws or fangs or anything to defend her beyond that sword and shield.

No.

He pushed men out of the way, the snow and mud hindering each step as the two ilken pressed closer to the shifter-queen.

Savoring the kill.

But the soldiers slowed their fleeing. Some even re-formed the lines when the call went out again. *The queen is here. The queen fights at the front line.*

Exactly why she had done it. Why she had donned the defenseless, human form.

No.

The ilken towered over her, grinning with their horrible, mangled faces.

Too far. He was still too damn far to do anything—

One of the ilken slashed with a long, clawed arm.

Her scream as poisoned talons ripped through her thigh sounded above the din of battle.

She went down, shield rising to cover herself.

He took it back.

He took back everything he had said to her, every moment of anger in his heart.

Aedion shoved through his own men, unable to breathe, to think.

He took it back; he hadn't meant a word of it, not really.

Lysandra tried to rise on her injured leg. The ilken laughed.

"*Please*," Aedion bellowed. The word was devoured by the screams of the dying. "*Please!*"

He'd make any bargain, he'd sell his soul to the dark god, if they spared her.

He hadn't meant it. He took it back, all those words.

Useless. He'd called her *useless*. Had thrown her into the snow naked.

He took it back.

Aedion sobbed, flinging himself toward her as Lysandra tried again to rise, using her shield to balance her weight.

Men rallied behind her, waiting to see what the Fire-Bringer would do. How she'd burn the ilken.

There was nothing to see, nothing to witness. Nothing at all, but her death.

Yet Lysandra rose, Aelin's golden hair falling in her face as she hefted her shield and pointed the sword between her and the ilken.

The queen has come; the queen fights alone.

Men ran back to the front line. Turned on their heels and raced for her.

Lysandra held her sword steady, kept it pointed at the ilken in defiance and rage.

Ready for the death soon to come.

She had been willing to give it up from the start. Had agreed to Aelin's plans, knowing it might come to this.

One shift, one change into a wyvern's form, and she'd destroy the ilken. But she remained in Aelin's body. Held that sword, her only weapon, upraised.

Terrasen was her home. And Aelin her queen.

She'd die to keep this army together. To keep the lines from breaking. To rally their soldiers one last time.

Her leg leaked blood onto the snow, and the two ilken sniffed, laughing again. They knew—what lurked under her skin. That it was not the queen they faced.

She held her ground. Did not yield one inch to the ilken, who advanced another step.

For Terrasen, she would do this. For Aelin.

He took it back. He took it all back.

Aedion was barely a hundred feet away when the ilken struck.

He screamed as the one on the left swept with its claws, the other on the right lunging for her, as if it would tackle her to the snow.

Lysandra deflected the blow to the left with her shield, sending the ilken sprawling, and with a roar, slashed upward with her sword on the right.

Ripping open the lunging ilken from navel to sternum.

Black blood gushed, and the ilken shrieked, loud enough to set Aedion's ears ringing. But it stumbled, falling into the snow, scrambling back as it clutched its opened belly.

Aedion ran harder, now thirty feet away, the space between them clear.

The ilken who'd gone sprawling on the left was not done. Lysandra's eye on the one retreating, it lashed for her legs again.

Aedion threw the Sword of Orynth with everything left in him as Lysandra twisted toward the attacking ilken.

She began falling back, shield lifting in her only defense, still too slow to escape those reaching claws.

The poison-slick tips brushed her legs just as his sword went through the beast's skull.

Lysandra hit the snow, shouting in pain, and Aedion was there, heaving her up, yanking his sword from the ilken's head and bringing it down upon the sinewy neck. Once. Twice.

The ilken's head tumbled into the snow and mud, the other beast instantly swallowed by the Morath soldiers who had paused to watch.

Who now looked upon the queen and her general and charged.

Only to be met by a surge of Terrasen soldiers racing past Aedion and Lysandra, battle cries shattering from their throats.

Aedion half-dragged the shifter deeper behind the re-formed lines, through the soldiers who had rallied to their queen.

He had to get the poison out, had to find a healer who could extract it immediately. Only a few minutes remained until it reached her heart—

Lysandra stumbled, a moan on her lips.

Aedion swung his shield on his back and hauled her over a shoulder. A glimpse at her leg revealed shredded skin, but no greenish slime.

Perhaps the gods had listened. Perhaps it was their idea of mercy: that the ilken's poison had worn off on other victims before it'd gotten to her.

But the blood loss alone . . . Aedion pressed a hand over the shredded, bloody skin to staunch the flow. Lysandra groaned.

Aedion scanned the regrouping army for any hint of the healers' white banners over their helmets. None. He whirled toward the front lines. Perhaps there was a Fae warrior skilled enough at healing, with enough magic left—

Aedion halted. Beheld what broke over the horizon.

Ironteeth witches.

Several dozen mounted on wyverns.

But not airborne. The wyverns walked on land.

Heaving a mammoth, mobile stone tower behind them. No ordinary siege tower.

A witch tower.

It rose a hundred feet high, the entire structure built into a platform whose make he could not determine with the angle of the ground and the lines of chained wyverns dragging it across the plain. A dozen more witches flew in the air around it, guarding it. Dark stone—Wyrdstone—had been used to craft it, and window slits had been interspersed throughout every level.

Not window slits. Portals through which to angle the power of the mirrors lining the inside, as Manon Blackbeak had described. All capable of being adjusted to any direction, any focus.

All they needed was a source of power for the mirrors to amplify and fire out into the world.

Oh gods.

"*Fall back!*" Aedion screamed, even while his men continued to rally. "*FALL BACK.*"

With his Fae sight, he could just make out the uppermost level of the tower, more open to the elements than the others.

Witches in dark robes were gathered around what seemed to be a curved mirror angled into the hollow core of the tower.

Aedion whirled and began running, carrying the shifter with him. "*FALL BACK!*"

The army beheld what approached. Whether they realized it was no siege tower, they understood his order clearly enough. Saw him sprinting, Aelin over his shoulder.

Manon had never known the range of the tower, how far it might fire the dark magic rallied within it.

There was nowhere to hide on the field. No dips in the earth where he might throw himself and Lysandra, praying the blast went over them. Nothing but open snow and frantic soldiers.

"*RETREAT!*" Aedion's throat strained.

He glanced over a shoulder as the witches atop the tower parted to let through a small figure in onyx robes, her pale hair unbound.

A black light began glowing around the figure—the witch. She lifted her hands above her head, the power rallying.

The Yielding.

Manon Blackbeak had described it to them. Ironteeth witches had no magic but that. The ability to unleash their dark goddess's power in an incendiary blast that took out everyone around them. Including the witch herself.

That dark power was still building, growing around the witch in an unholy aura, when she simply walked off the lip of the tower landing.

Right into the hole in the tower's center.

Aedion kept running. Had no choice but to keep moving, as the witch dropped into the mirror-lined core of the tower and unleashed the dark power within her.

The world shuddered.

Aedion threw Lysandra into the mud and snow and hurled himself over her, as if it would somehow spare her from the roaring force that erupted from the tower, right at their army.

One heartbeat, their left flank was fighting as they retreated once more.

The next, a wave of black-tinted light slammed into four thousand soldiers.

When it receded, there was only ash and dented metal.

CHAPTER 48

The khagan's forces had dealt enough of a blow to Morath that the bone drums had ceased.

Not a sign of sure defeat, but enough to make Chaol's heavily limping steps feel lighter as he entered Princess Hasar's sprawling war tent. Her *sulde* had been planted outside, the roan horsehair blowing in the wind off the lake. Sartaq's own spear had been sunk into the cold mud beside his sister's. And beside the Heir's spear . . .

Leaning on his cane, Chaol paused at the ebony spear that had also been planted, its jet-black horsehair still shining despite its age. Not to signify the royals within, a marker of their Darghan heritage, but to represent the man they served. *Ivory horsehair for times of peace; the Ebony for times of war.*

He hadn't realized the khagan had given his Heir the Ebony to bring to these lands.

At Chaol's side, her dress blood-splattered but eyes clear, Yrene also halted. They'd traveled for weeks with the army, yet seeing the sign of their commitment to this war radiating the centuries of conquest it had overseen . . . It seemed almost holy, that *sulde*. It *was* holy.

Chaol put a hand on Yrene's back, guiding her through the tent flaps and into the ornately decorated space. For a woman who had arrived at Anielle not a moment too late, only Hasar would somehow have managed to get her royal tent erected during battle.

Bracing his muddy cane on the raised wooden platform, Chaol gritted his teeth as he took the step upward. Even the thick, plush rugs didn't ease the pain that lashed down his spine, his legs.

He stilled, leaning heavily on the cane while he breathed, letting his balance readjust.

Yrene's blood-flecked face tightened. "Let's get you into a chair," she murmured, and Chaol nodded. To sit down, even for a few minutes, would be a blessed relief.

Nesryn entered behind them, and apparently heard Yrene's suggestion, for she went immediately to the desk around which Sartaq and Hasar stood, and pulled out a carved wooden chair. With a nod of thanks, Chaol eased into it.

"No gold couch?" Princess Hasar teased, and Yrene blushed, despite the blood on her golden-brown skin, and waved off her friend.

The couch Chaol had brought with him from the southern continent—the couch from which Yrene had healed him, from which he had won her heart—was still safely aboard their ship. Waiting, should they survive, to be the first piece of furniture in the home he'd build for his wife.

For the child she carried.

Yrene paused beside his chair, and Chaol took her slim hand in his, entwining their fingers. Filthy, both of them, but he didn't care. Neither did she, judging by the squeeze she gave him.

"We outnumber Morath's legion," Sartaq said, sparing them from Hasar's taunting, "but how we choose to cleave them while we cut a path to the city still must be carefully weighed, so we don't expend too many forces here."

When the real fighting still lay ahead. As if these terrible days of siege and bloodshed, as if the men hewn down today, were just the start.

Hasar said, "Wise enough."

Sartaq winced slightly. "It might not have wound up that way." Chaol lifted a brow, Hasar doing the same, and Sartaq said, "Had you not arrived, sister, I was hours away from unleashing the dam and flooding the plain."

Chaol started. "You were?"

The prince rubbed his neck. "A desperate last measure."

Indeed. A wave of that size would have wiped out part of the city, the plain and hot springs, and leagues behind it. Any army in its path would have drowned—been swept away. It might have even reached the khagan-ate's army, marching to save them.

"Then let's be glad we didn't do it," Yrene said, face paling as she, too, considered the destruction. How close they had come to a disaster. That Sartaq had admitted to it told enough: he might be Heir, but he wished his sister to know he, too, was not above making mistakes. That they had to think through any plan of action, however easy it might seem.

Hasar, it seemed, got the point, and nodded.

A cleared throat cut through the tent, and they all turned toward the open flaps to find one of the Darghan captains, his *sulde* clenched in his mud-splattered hand. Someone was here to see them, the man stammered. Neither royal asked who as they waved the man to let them in.

A moment later, Chaol was glad he was sitting down.

Nesryn breathed, "Holy gods."

Chaol was inclined to agree as Aelin Galathynius, Rowan Whitethorn, and several others entered the tent.

They were mud-splattered, the Queen of Terrasen's braided hair far longer than Chaol had last seen. And her eyes . . . Not the soft, yet fiery gaze. But something older. Wearier.

Chaol shot to his feet. "I thought you were in Terrasen," he blurted. All the reports had confirmed it. Yet here she stood, no army in sight.

Three Fae males—towering warriors as broad and muscled as Rowan—had entered, along with a delicate, dark-haired human woman.

But Aelin was only staring at him. Staring and staring at him.

No one spoke as tears began sliding down her face.

Not at his being here, Chaol realized as he took up his cane and limped toward Aelin.

But at him. Standing. Walking.

The young queen let out a broken laugh of joy and flung her arms around his neck. Pain lanced down his spine at the impact, but Chaol held her right back, every question fading from his tongue.

Aelin was shaking as she pulled away. "I knew you would," she breathed, gazing down his body, to his feet, then up again. "I knew you'd do it."

"Not alone," he said thickly. Chaol swallowed, releasing Aelin to extend an arm behind him. To the woman he knew stood there, a hand over the locket at her neck.

Perhaps Aelin would not remember, perhaps their encounter years ago had meant nothing to her at all, but Chaol drew Yrene forward. "Aelin, allow me to introduce—"

"Yrene Towers," the queen breathed as his wife stepped to his side.

The two women stared at each other.

Yrene's mouth quivered as she opened the silver locket and pulled out a piece of paper. Hands trembling, she extended it to the queen.

Aelin's own hands shook as she accepted the scrap.

"Thank you," Yrene whispered.

Chaol supposed it was all that really needed to be said.

Aelin unfolded the paper, reading the note she'd written, seeing the lines from the hundreds of foldings and rereadings these past few years.

"I went to the Torre," Yrene said, her voice cracking. "I took the money you gave me, and went to the Torre. And I became the heir apparent to the Healer on High. And now I have come back, to do what I can. I taught every healer I could the lessons you showed me that night, about self-defense. I didn't waste it—not a coin you gave me, or a moment of the time, the life you bought me." Tears were rolling and rolling down Yrene's face. "I didn't waste any of it."

Aelin closed her eyes, smiling through her own tears, and when she opened them, she took Yrene's shaking hands. "Now it is my turn to thank you." But Aelin's gaze fell upon the wedding band on Yrene's finger, and when she glanced to Chaol, he grinned.

"No longer Yrene Towers," Chaol said softly, "but Yrene Westfall."

Aelin let out one of those choked, joyous laughs, and Rowan stepped up to her side. Yrene's head tilted back to take in the warrior's full height, her eyes widening—not only at Rowan's size, but at the pointed ears, the slightly elongated canines and tattoo. Aelin said, "Then let me introduce you, Lady Westfall, to my own husband, Prince Rowan Whitethorn Galathynius."

For that was indeed a wedding band on the queen's finger, the emerald mud-splattered but bright. On Rowan's own hand, a gold-and-ruby ring gleamed.

"My mate," Aelin added, fluttering her lashes at the Fae male. Rowan rolled his eyes, yet couldn't entirely contain his smile as he inclined his head to Yrene.

Yrene bowed, but Aelin snorted. "None of that, please. It'll go right to his immortal head." Her grin softened as Yrene blushed, and Aelin held up the scrap of paper. "May I keep this?" She eyed Yrene's locket. "Or does it go in there?"

Yrene folded the queen's fingers around the paper. "It is yours, as it always was. A piece of your bravery that helped me find my own."

Aelin shook her head, as if to dismiss the claim.

But Yrene squeezed Aelin's closed hand. "It gave me courage, the words you wrote. Every mile I traveled, every long hour I studied and worked, it gave me courage. I thank you for that, too."

Aelin swallowed hard, and Chaol took that as excuse enough to sit again, his back giving a grateful tinge. He said to the queen, "There is another person responsible for this army being here." He gestured to

Nesryn, the woman already smiling at the queen. "The rukhin you see, the army gathered, is as much because of Nesryn as it is because of me."

A spark lit Aelin's eyes, and both women met halfway in a tight embrace. "I want to hear the entire story," Aelin said. "Every word of it."

Nesryn's subdued smile widened. "So you shall. But later." Aelin clapped her on the shoulder and turned to the two royals still by the desk. Tall and regal, but as mud-splattered as the queen.

Chaol blurted, "Dorian?"

Rowan answered, "Not with us." He glanced to the royals.

"They know everything," Nesryn said.

"He's with Manon," Aelin said simply. Chaol wasn't entirely sure whether to be relieved. "Hunting for something important."

The keys. Holy gods.

Aelin nodded. Later. He'd think on where Dorian might now be later. Aelin nodded again. The full story would come then too.

Nesryn said, "May I present Princess Hasar and Prince Sartaq."

Aelin bowed—low. "You have my eternal gratitude," Aelin said, and the voice that came out of her was indeed that of a queen.

Any shock Sartaq and Hasar had shown upon the queen bowing so low was hidden as they bowed back, the portrait of courtly grace. "My father," Sartaq said, "remained in the khaganate to oversee our lands, along with our siblings Duva and Arghun. But my brother Kashin sails with the rest of the army. He was not two weeks behind us when we left."

Aelin glanced to Chaol, and he nodded. Something glittered in her eyes at the confirmation, but the queen jerked her chin at Hasar. "Did you get my letter?"

The letter that Aelin had sent months ago, begging for aid and promising only a better world in return.

Hasar picked at her nails. "Perhaps. I get far too many letters from fellow princesses these days to possibly remember or answer all of them."

Aelin smirked, as if the two of them spoke a language no one else could understand, a special code between two equally arrogant and proud women. But she motioned to her companions, who stepped forward. "Allow me to introduce my friends. Lord Gavriel, of Doranelle." A nod toward the tawny-eyed and golden-haired warrior who bowed. Tattoos covered his neck, his hands, but his every motion was graceful. "My uncle, of sorts," Aelin added with a smirk at Gavriel. At Chaol's narrowed brows, she explained, "He's Aedion's father."

"Well, that explains a few things," Nesryn muttered.

The hair, the broad-planed face . . . yes, it was the same. But where Aedion was fire, Gavriel seemed to be stone. Indeed, his eyes were solemn as he said, "Aedion is my pride."

Emotion rippled over Aelin's face, but she gestured to the dark-haired male. Not someone Chaol ever wanted to tangle with, he decided as he surveyed the granite-hewn features, the black eyes and unsmiling mouth.

"Lorcan Salvaterre, formerly of Doranelle, and now a blood-sworn member of my court." As if that weren't a shock enough, Aelin winked at the imposing male. Lorcan scowled. "We're still in the adjustment period," she loudly whispered, and Yrene chuckled.

Lorcan Salvaterre. Chaol hadn't met the male this spring in Rifthold, but he'd heard all about him. That he'd been Maeve's most trusted commander, her most loyal and fierce warrior. That he'd wanted to kill Aelin, *hated* Aelin. How this had come about, why she was not in Terrasen with her army . . . "You, too, have a tale to tell," Chaol said.

"Indeed I do." Aelin's eyes guttered, and Rowan put a hand on her lower back. Bad—something terrible had occurred. Chaol scanned Aelin for any hint of it.

He stopped when he noticed the smoothness of the skin at her neck. The lack of scars. The missing scars on her hands, her palms. "Later," Aelin said softly. She straightened her shoulders, and another golden-haired male came forward. Beautiful. That was the only way to describe him. "Fenrys . . . You know, I don't actually know your family name."

Fenrys threw a roguish wink at the queen. "Moonbeam."

"It is not," Aelin hissed, choking on a laugh.

Fenrys laid a hand on his heart. "I am blood-sworn to you. Would I lie?"

Another blood-sworn Fae male in her court. Across the tent, Sartaq cursed in his own tongue. As if he'd heard of Lorcan, and Gavriel, and Fenrys.

Aelin gave Fenrys a vulgar gesture that set Hasar chuckling, and faced the royals. "They're barely housebroken. Hardly fit for your fine company." Even Sartaq smiled at that. But it was to the small, delicate woman that Aelin now gestured. "And the only civilized member of my court, Lady Elide Lochan of Perranth."

Perranth. Chaol had combed through the family trees of Terrasen just this winter, had seen the lists of so many royal households crossed out, victim to the conquest ten years ago.

Elide's name had been among them. Another Terrasen royal who had managed to evade Adarlan's butchers.

The pretty young woman took a limping step forward, and bobbed a curtsy to the royals. Her boots concealed any sign of the source of the injury, but Yrene's attention shot right to her leg. Her ankle. "It's an honor to meet all of you," Elide said, her voice low and steady. Her dark eyes swept over them, cunning and clear. Like she could see beneath their skin and bones, to the souls beneath.

Aelin wiped her hands. "Well, that's over and done with," she announced, and strode to the desk and map. "Shall we discuss where you all plan to march once we beat the living shit out of this army?"

CHAPTER 49

Rowan had been speaking to the captain of their ship when the ruk had flown past.

According to her mate, the ruk nearly slammed right into the ship thanks to the dense fog on the sea. A scout—from an armada to the south.

A skeleton crew had remained amongst them, though the scout hadn't been privy to the royals' plans. All she knew was that the khagan's army had gone to Anielle.

Where they would go after that—to Rifthold, to Eyllwe—had not been decided.

So Aelin would help them decide. Make sure that when this business with Anielle was over, the khagan's army marched northward. To Terrasen.

And nowhere else. Whatever she needed to do to convince them, offer them in exchange for it, she'd pay it. Even if hauling ass to Anielle had meant delaying her own return to Terrasen.

She supposed it'd be better to return with an army behind her than alone.

Yet now, standing in the royals' war tent, Aelin still couldn't quite believe just how *many* the khagan had sent. With more to come, Prince Sartaq had claimed.

They'd wended through the neatly organized tents and soldiers, both on foot and the downright awe-inspiring cavalry. The Darghan, the legendary riders from the steppes of the khaganate. The royal family's mother-people, who had taken the continent for themselves.

And then they'd seen the ruks, and even miserable Lorcan had sworn in awe at the mighty, beautiful birds adorned with ornate armor, and the armed riders atop them. The scout had been one thing. An army of them had been glorious.

A glance at Rowan told her that shrewd mind was already calculating a plan.

So Aelin asked casually, flashing the royals a grin, "Where *did* you all plan on going after this?"

Princess Hasar, as shrewd as Aelin's mate, returned her smile—a razor-sharp thing of little beauty. "Doubtless, you're about to begin some scheme to convince us to go to Terrasen."

The room tensed, but Aelin snorted. "Begin? Who says I'm not already in the thick of it?"

"Gods help us," Chaol muttered. Rowan echoed the sentiment.

Hasar opened her mouth, but Prince Sartaq cut in, "Where we march will be decided after Anielle is secured." The prince's face remained grave, calculating—but not cold. Aelin had decided within moments that she liked him. And liked him even more when it came out that he had just been crowned the khagan's Heir. With Nesryn as his potential bride.

Potential, to Aelin's amusement, because Nesryn herself wasn't so keen on being empress of the mightiest empire in the world.

But what Sartaq had said—

Elide blurted, "You mean to not go to Terrasen?"

Aelin kept still, her fingers curling at her sides.

Prince Sartaq said carefully, "It had been our initial plan to go north, but there might be other places like Anielle in need of liberation."

"Terrasen needs aid," Rowan said, his face the portrait of steely calm as he surveyed their new allies and old friends.

"And yet Terrasen has not called for it," Hasar countered, utterly unfazed by the wall of Fae warriors glowering at her. Exactly the sort of person Aelin had hoped she'd be when she wrote to her all those months ago.

Chaol cleared his throat. Gods above, Chaol was *walking* again. And married to Yrene Towers, who had healed him.

A thread in a tapestry. That's what it had felt like the night she'd left the gold for Yrene in Innish. Like pulling a thread in a tapestry, and seeing just how far and wide it went.

All the way to the southern continent, it seemed. And it had rippled back with an army and a healed, happy friend. Or as happy as any of them might be at the moment.

Aelin met Chaol's stare. "Focus on winning this battle," he said, nodding once in understanding at the fire she knew smoldered in her eyes, "and then we shall decide."

Princess Hasar smirked at Aelin. "So be sure to impress us."

Again, that tension rippled through the room.

Aelin held the princess's stare. Smiled slightly. And said nothing.

Nesryn shifted on her feet, as if well aware what that silence could mean.

"How solid are the keep walls?" Gavriel asked Chaol, gently steering the conversation away.

Chaol rubbed at his jaw. "They've withstood sieges before, but Morath has been hammering them for days. The battlements are solid enough, but another few blows from the catapults and towers might start coming down."

Rowan crossed his arms. "The walls were breached today?"

"They were," Chaol said grimly. "By a siege tower. The ruks couldn't arrive in time to pull it down." Nesryn cringed, but Sartaq did not offer an apology. Chaol went on, "We secured the walls, but the Valg soldiers cut down a number of our men—from Anielle, that is."

Aelin surveyed the map, blocking out the challenge of the fierce-eyed princess who was a mirror in so many ways. "So how do we play it? Do we slam through the lines, or pick them off one by one?"

Nesryn stabbed a finger onto the map, right atop the Silver Lake. "What if we pushed them to the lake itself?"

Hasar hummed, all traces of taunting gone. "Morath placed itself foolishly in their greed to sack the city. They didn't estimate being trampled by the Darghan, or picked apart by the rukhin."

Aelin glanced sidelong to Rowan. Found him already staring at her.

We'll convince them to go to Terrasen, her mate said silently.

Chaol leaned forward, back quivering a bit, and ran a finger over the lake's western shore. "This section of the lake, unfortunately, is shallow a hundred yards from the shore. The army might be able to wade out there, draw us into the water."

"A few hours in that water," Yrene countered, mouth a tight line, "would kill them. The hypothermia would set in quickly. Maybe within minutes, depending on the wind."

"That's if the Valg fall victim to such things," Hasar said. "They don't die like true men in most ways, and you claim they hail from a land of darkness and cold." So the royals truly knew about their enemies, then. "We might push them into the water to find they don't care at all. And in doing so, risk exposing our troops to the elements." The princess jabbed the keep walls. "We're better off pushing them right into the stone, breaking them apart against it."

Aelin was inclined to agree.

Lorcan opened his mouth to say something no doubt unpleasant, but footsteps squelching in mud outside the tent had them whirling toward the entrance long before a pretty, dark-haired young woman burst in, twin braids swinging. "You wouldn't believe—"

She halted upon seeing Aelin. Seeing the Fae males. Her mouth popped into an O.

Nesryn chuckled. "Borte, meet—"

Another set of steps in the mud, heavier and slower than Borte's quick movements, and then a young man stumbled in, his skin not the gold-kissed brown of Borte or the royals, but pale. "It's back," he panted, gaping at Nesryn. "For days now, I swore I felt something, noted changes, but today it just all came *back*."

Nesryn angled her head, her curtain of dark hair sliding over an armored shoulder. "Who . . ."

Borte squeezed the young man's arm. "*Falkan*. It's *Falkan*, Nesryn."

Prince Sartaq stalked to Nesryn's side, graceful as any Fae warrior. "How."

But the young man had turned toward Aelin, eyes narrowing. As if trying to place her.

Then he said, "The assassin from the market in Xandria."

Aelin arched a brow. "Hopefully, the horse I stole didn't belong to you."

A cough from Fenrys. Aelin threw the warrior a grin over her shoulder.

The young man's eyes darted over her face, then landed on the enormous emerald on her finger. The even bigger ruby in Goldryn's hilt.

Borte blurted to Nesryn, "One minute, we were eating dinner at the campfire, then the next, Falkan clutched his stomach like he was going to puke up his guts all over everyone"—a glare from Falkan at Borte—"and then his face was *young. He's* young."

"I was always young," Falkan muttered. "I just didn't look it." His gray eyes again found Aelin's. "I gave you a piece of Spidersilk."

For a heartbeat, the then and the now blended and wobbled. "The merchant," Aelin murmured. She'd last seen him in the Red Desert—looking twenty years older. "You sold your youth to a stygian spider."

"You two know each other?" Nesryn gaped.

"The threads of fate weave together in strange ways," Falkan said, then smiled at Aelin. "I never got your name."

Hasar chuckled from the other side of the desk. "You already know it, shifter."

Before Falkan could figure it out, Fenrys stepped forward. "Shifter?"

But Nesryn said, "And Lysandra's uncle."

Aelin slumped into the chair beside Chaol's. Rowan laid a hand on her shoulder, and when she looked up, she found him near laughter. "What's so funny, exactly?" she hissed.

Rowan smirked. "That for once, *you* are the one who gets knocked on your ass by a surprise."

Aelin stuck out her tongue. Borte grinned, and Aelin winked at the girl.

But Falkan said to Aelin and her companions, "You know my niece."

His brother must have been a great deal older to have sired Lysandra. There was nothing of Falkan in her friend's face, though Lysandra had also forgotten her original form.

"Lysandra is my friend, and Lady of Caraverre," Aelin said. "She is not with us," she added upon Falkan's hopeful glance toward the tent flaps. "She's in the North."

Borte had gone back to studying the Fae males. Not their considerable beauty, but their size, their pointed ears, their weapons and elongated canines. Aelin whispered conspiratorially to the girl, "Make them roll over before you offer them a treat."

Lorcan glared, but Fenrys shifted in a flash, the enormous white wolf filling the space.

Hasar swore, Sartaq backing away a step, but Borte beamed. "You are all truly Fae, then."

Gavriel, ever the gallant knight, sketched a bow. Lorcan, the bastard, just crossed his arms.

Yet Rowan smiled at Borte. "Indeed we are."

Borte whirled to Aelin. "Then you are Aelin Galathynius. You look just how Nesryn said."

Aelin grinned at Nesryn, the woman leaning against Sartaq's side. "I hope you only said horrible things about me."

"Only the worst," Nesryn said with dead flatness, though her mouth twitched.

But Falkan whispered, "The queen," and fell to his knees.

Hasar laughed. "He never showed that sort of awe when he met us."

Sartaq lifted his brows. "You told him to turn into a rat and scuttle away."

Aelin hoisted up Falkan by the shoulder. "I can't have my friend's uncle kneeling on the ground, can I?"

"You said you were an assassin." Falkan's eyes were so wide the whites around them gleamed. "You stole horses from the Lord of Xandria—"

"Yes, yes," Aelin said, waving a hand. "It's a long story, and we're in the middle of a war council, so . . ."

"Piss off?" Falkan finished.

Aelin laughed, but glanced to Nesryn and Sartaq. The former jerked her chin to Falkan. "He's become our spy of sorts. He joins us in these meetings."

Aelin nodded, then winked at the shifter. "I suppose you didn't need me to slay that stygian spider after all."

But Falkan tensed, his attention going to Nesryn and Sartaq, to Borte, still gawking at the Fae males. "Do they know?"

Aelin had a feeling she'd need to sit down again. Chaol indeed patted the chair beside him, earning a chuckle from Yrene.

Doing herself a favor, Aelin indeed sat, Rowan taking up his place behind her, both of his hands coming to rest on her shoulders. His thumb ran along the nape of her neck, then drifted over the mating marks again scarring one side thanks to the seawater they'd used to seal them.

But as her muscles soothed beneath that loving touch, her soul with it, her breath remained tight.

It didn't get any better when Nesryn said, "The stygian spiders are Valg."

Silence.

"We encountered their kin, the *kharankui*, deep in the Dagul Fells. They came into this world through a temporary crack between realms, and remained afterward to guard the entrance, should it ever reappear."

"This cannot end well," Fenrys muttered. Elide hummed her agreement.

"They feed on dreams and years and life," Falkan said, a hand on his own chest. "As my friends have said the Valg do."

Aelin had seen Valg princes drain a human of every last drop of youth and vigor and leave only a dried corpse behind. She wouldn't put it past the spiders to have a similar gift.

"What does this mean for the war?" Rowan asked, his thumbs still stroking Aelin's neck.

"Will they join Erawan's forces is the better question," Lorcan challenged with a face like stone.

"They do not answer to Erawan," Nesryn said quietly, and Aelin knew. Knew from the look Chaol gave her, the sympathy and fear, knew in her bones before Nesryn even finished. "The stygian spiders, the *kharankui*, answer to their Valg queen. The only Valg queen. To Maeve."

CHAPTER
50

Rowan's hands tightened on Aelin's shoulders as the words settled into her, hollow and cold. "Maeve is a Valg queen?" he breathed.

Aelin said nothing. Couldn't find the words.

Her power roiled. She didn't feel it.

Nesryn nodded solemnly. "Yes. The *kharankui* told us the entire history."

And so Nesryn did as well. Of how Maeve had somehow found a way into this world, fleeing or bored with her husband, Orcus. Erawan's elder brother. Of how Erawan, Orcus, and Mantyx had torn apart worlds to find her, Orcus's missing wife, and only halted here because the Fae had risen to challenge them. Fae led by Maeve, whom the Valg kings did not know or recognize, in the form she had taken.

The life she had crafted for herself. The minds of all the Fae who had existed that she had ripped into, convincing them that there had been *three* queens, not two. Including the minds of Mab and Mora, the two sister-queens who had ruled Doranelle. Including Brannon himself.

"The spiders claimed," Nesryn went on, "that even Brannon didn't know. Even now, in the Afterworld, he doesn't know. That was how deep Maeve's powers went into his mind, into all their minds. She made herself their true queen."

The words, the truth, pelted Aelin, one after another.

Elide's face was white as death. "But she fears the healers." A nod toward Yrene. "She keeps that owl, you said—an enslaved Fae healer—should the Valg ever discover her."

For that was the other piece of it. The other thing Nesryn had revealed, Chaol and Yrene adding in their own accounts.

The Valg were parasites. And Yrene could cure their human hosts of them. Had done so for Princess Duva. And might be able to do with so many others enslaved with rings or collars.

But what had infested Duva . . . A Valg princess.

Aelin leaned back into her chair, her head resting against the solid wall of Rowan's body. His hands shook against her shoulders. Shook as he seemed to realize what, exactly, had ripped into his mind. Where Maeve's power had come from that allowed her to do so. Why she remained death-less and ageless, and had outlasted any other. Why Maeve's power *was* darkness.

"It is also why she fears fire," Sartaq said, jerking his chin to Aelin. "Why she fears you so."

And why she'd wanted to break her. To be just like that enslaved healer bound in owl form at her side.

"I thought—I managed to cut her once," Aelin said at last. That quiet, ancient darkness pushed in, dragging her down, down, down—"I saw her blood flow black. Then it changed to red." She blew out a breath, pulling out of the darkness, the silence that wanted to devour her whole. Made herself straighten. Peer at Fenrys. "You said that her blood tasted ordinary to you when you swore the oath."

The white wolf shifted back into his Fae body. His bronze skin was ashen, his dark eyes swimming with dread. "It did."

Rowan growled, "It didn't taste any different to me, either."

"A glamour—like the form she maintains," Gavriel mused.

Nesryn nodded. "From what the spiders said, it seems entirely possible that she would be able to convince you that her blood looked and tasted like Fae blood."

Fenrys made a sound like he was going to be sick. Aelin was inclined to do the same.

And from far away—a memory-that-was-not-a-memory stirred. Of summer nights spent in a forest glen, Maeve instructing her. Telling her a story about a queen who walked between worlds.

Who had not been content in the realm in which she'd been born, and had found a way to leave it, using the lost knowledge of ancient wayfarers. World-walkers.

Maeve had told her. Perhaps a skewed, biased tale, but she'd told her. Why? Why do it at all? Some way to win her—or to make her hesitate, should it ever come to this?

"But Maeve hates the Valg kings," Elide said, and even from the silent, drifting place to which Aelin had gone, she could see the razor-sharp mind churning behind Elide's eyes. "She's hidden for this long. Surely she wouldn't ally with them."

"She ran at the chance to get hold of a Valg collar," Fenrys said darkly. "Seemed convinced that she could control the prince inside it."

Not only through Maeve's power, but because she was a demon queen.

Aelin forced herself to take another breath. Another. Her fingers curled, gripping an invisible weapon.

Lorcan had not uttered a word. Had done nothing but stand there, pale and silent. As if he'd stopped being in his body, too.

"We don't know her plans," Nesryn said. "The *kharankui* have not seen her for millennia, and only hear whisperings carried by lesser spiders. But they still worship her, and wait for her return."

Chaol met Aelin's stare, his gaze questioning.

Aelin said quietly, "I was Maeve's prisoner for two months."

Utter silence in the tent. Then she explained—all of it. Why she was not in Terrasen, who now fought there, where Dorian and Manon had gone.

Aelin swallowed as she finished, leaning into Rowan's touch. "Maeve wished me to reveal the location of the two Wyrdkeys. Wanted me to hand them over, but I managed to get them away before she took me. To Doranelle. She wanted to break me to her will. To use me to conquer the world, I thought. But it perhaps now seems she wanted to use me as a shield against the Valg, to guard her always." The words tumbled out, heavy and sharp. "I was her captive until nearly a month ago." She nodded toward her court. "When I got free, they found me again."

Silence fell again, her new companions at a loss. She didn't blame them.

Then Hasar hissed, "We'll make the bitch pay for that, too, won't we?"

Aelin met the princess's dark stare. "Yes, we will."

The truth had slammed into Rowan like a physical blow.

Maeve was Valg.

A Valg queen. Whose estranged husband had once invaded this world and, if Chaol was correct, wished to enter it again, should Erawan succeed in opening the Wyrdgate.

He knew his cadre, or whatever they were now called, was in shock. Knew he himself had fallen into some sort of stupor.

The female they'd served, bowed to . . . Valg.

They had been so thoroughly deceived they had not even tasted it in her blood.

Fenrys looked like he was going to empty the contents of his stomach onto the tent floor. For him, the truth would be the most horrendous.

Lorcan's face remained cold and blank. Gavriel kept rubbing his jaw, his eyes swimming with dismay.

Rowan loosed a long breath.

A Valg queen.

That's who had held his Fireheart. What sort of power had tried to break into her mind.

What power *had* broken into Rowan's mind. All their minds, if she could glamour her blood to look and taste ordinary.

He felt the tension rising in Aelin, a raging storm that nearly hummed into his hands as he gripped her shoulders.

Yet her flames made no appearance. They hadn't shown so much as an ember these weeks, despite how hard they'd trained.

Occasionally, he'd spy Goldryn's ruby gleaming while she held it, as if fire glowed in the heart of the stone. But nothing more.

Not even when they'd tangled in their bed on the ship, when his teeth had found that mark on her neck.

Elide surveyed them all, their silence, and said to their new companions, "Perhaps we should determine a plan of action regarding tomorrow's battle." And give them time, later tonight, to sort through this colossal mess.

Chaol nodded. "We brought a trunk of books with us," he said to Aelin. "From the Torre. They're all full of Wyrdmarks." Aelin didn't so much as blink, but Chaol finished, "If we get through this battle, they're yours to peruse. In case there's anything in them that might help." Against Erawan, against Maeve, against his mate's terrible fate.

Aelin just vaguely nodded.

So Rowan forced himself to shove away the shock and disgust and fear, and focus upon the plan ahead. Only Gavriel seemed able to do the same, Fenrys staying where he was, and Lorcan just staring and staring at nothing.

Aelin remained in her chair, simmering. Roiling.

They planned it quickly and efficiently: they would return with Chaol and Yrene to the keep, to help with the fighting tomorrow. The khaganate royals would push from here, Nesryn and Prince Sartaq leading the ruks, and Princess Hasar commanding the foot soldiers and Darghan cavalry.

A brilliantly trained, lethal group. Rowan had already marked the Darghan soldiers, with their fine horses and armor, their spears and crested helmets, while they'd strode for this tent, and breathed a sigh of relief at their skill. Perhaps the last sigh of relief he'd have in this war. Certainly if the khagan's forces hadn't yet decided *where* they would take this army afterward.

He supposed it was fair—so many territories were now in Morath's path—but when this battle was over, he'd make damn sure they marched northward. To Terrasen.

But tomorrow—tomorrow they'd hammer Morath's legion against the keep walls, Chaol and Rowan leading the men from inside, picking off enemy soldiers.

Aelin didn't volunteer to do anything. Didn't indicate that she'd heard them.

And when they'd all deemed the plan sound, along with a contingency plan should it go awry, Nesryn only said, "We'll find you ruks to carry you back to the keep," before Aelin stormed into the frigid night, Rowan barely keeping up with her.

No embers trailed her. Mud did not hiss beneath her boots.

There was no fire at all. Not a spark.

As if Maeve had snuffed out that flame. Made her fear it.

Hate it.

Aelin cut through the neatly organized tents, past horses and their armored riders, past foot soldiers around campfires, past the ruk riders and their mighty birds, who filled him with such awe he had no words for it. All the way to the eastern edge of the camp and the plains that stretched past, the space wide and hollow after the closeness of the army.

She didn't stop until she reached a stream they'd crossed only hours ago. It was nearly frozen over, but a stomp of her boot had the ice cracking. Breaking free to reveal dark water kissed with silvery starlight.

Then she fell to her knees and drank.

Drank and drank, cupping the water to her mouth. It had to be cold enough to burn, but she kept at it until she braced her hands on her knees and said, "I can't do this."

Rowan sank to a knee, the shield he'd kept around her while she stalked here sealing out the cold wind off the open plain.

"I—I *can't*—." She took a shuddering breath, and covered her face with her wet hands.

Gently, Rowan gripped her wrists and lowered them. "You do not face this alone."

Anguish and terror filled those beautiful eyes, and his chest tightened to the point of pain as she said, "It was a fool's shot against Erawan. But against him *and* Maeve? She gathered an army to her. Is likely bringing that army to Terrasen right now. And if Erawan summons his two brothers, if the other kings return—"

"He needs the two other keys to do that. He doesn't have them."

Her fingers curled, digging into her palms hard enough that the tang of her blood filled the air. "I should have gone after the keys. Right away. Not come here. Not done this."

"It is Dorian's task now, not yours. He will not fail at it."

"It is my task, and always has been—"

"We made the choice to come here, and we will stick to that decision," he snarled, not bothering to temper his tone. "If Maeve is indeed bringing her army to Terrasen, then it only confirms that we were right to come here. That we must convince the khagan's forces to go northward after this. It is the only chance we stand of succeeding."

Aelin ran her hands through her hair. Streams of blood stained the gold. "I cannot win against them. Against a Valg king and queen." Her voice turned to a rasp. "They have already won."

"They have not." And though Rowan hated each word, he growled, "And you survived two months against Maeve with no magic to protect you. Two months of a Valg queen trying to break into your head, Aelin. To break *you*."

Aelin shook. "She did, though."

Rowan waited for it.

Aelin whispered, "I *wanted* to die by the end, before she ever threatened me with the collar. And even now, I feel like someone has *ripped* me from myself. Like I'm at the bottom of the sea, and who I am, who I was, is far up at the surface, and I will *never* get back there again."

He didn't know what to say, what to do other than to gently pull her fingers from her palms.

"Did you buy the swagger, the arrogance?" she demanded, voice breaking. "Did the others? Because I've been trying to. I've been trying like hell to convince myself that it's real, reminding myself I only need to pretend to be how I was just long enough."

Long enough to forge the Lock and die.

He said softly, "I know, Aelin." He hadn't bought the winks and smirks for a heartbeat.

Aelin let out a sob that cracked something in him. "I can't *feel* me— *myself* anymore. It's like she snuffed it out. Ripped me from it. She, and Cairn, and everything they *did* to me." She gulped down air, and Rowan wrapped her in his arms and pulled her onto his lap. "I am so tired," she wept. "I am so, so tired, Rowan."

"I know." He stroked her hair. "I know." It was all there really was to say.

Rowan held her until her weeping eased and she lay still, nestled against his chest.

"I don't know what to do," she whispered.

"You fight," he said simply. "We fight. Until we can't anymore. We fight."

She sat up, but remained on his lap, staring into his face with a rawness that destroyed him.

Rowan laid a hand on her chest, right over that burning heart. "Fireheart."

A challenge and a summons.

She placed her hand atop his, warm despite the frigid night. As if that fire had not yet gone out entirely. But she only gazed up at the stars. To the Lord of the North, standing watch. "We fight," she breathed.

Aelin found Fenrys by a quiet fire, gazing into the crackling flames.

She sat on the log beside him, raw and open and trembling, but . . . the salt of her tears had washed away some of it. Steadied her. Rowan had steadied her, and still did, as he kept watch from the shadows beyond the fire.

Fenrys lifted his head, his eyes as hollow as she knew hers had been.

"Whenever you need to talk about it," she said, her voice still hoarse, "I'm here."

Fenrys nodded, his mouth a tight line. "Thank you."

The camp was readying for their departure, but Aelin scooted closer, and sat beside him in silence for long minutes.

Two healers, marked only by the white bands around their biceps, hurried past, arms full of bandages.

Aelin tensed. Focused on her breathing.

Fenrys marked her line of sight. "They were horrified, you know," he said quietly. "Every time she brought them in to . . . fix you."

The two healers vanished around a tent. Aelin flexed her fingers, shaking the lightness from them. "It didn't stop them from doing it."

"They didn't have a choice."

She met his dark stare. Fenrys's mouth tightened. "No one would have left you in those states. No one."

Broken and bloody and burned—

She gripped Goldryn's hilt. Helpless.

"They defied her in their own way," Fenrys went on. "Sometimes, she'd order them to bring you back to consciousness. Often, they claimed they couldn't, that you'd fallen too deeply into oblivion. But I knew—I think Maeve did, too—that they put you there. For as long as possible. To buy you time."

She swallowed. "Did she punish them?"

"I don't know. It was never the same healers."

Maeve likely had. Had likely ripped their minds apart for their defiance.

Aelin's grip tightened on the sword at her side.

Helpless. She had been helpless. As so many in this city, in Terrasen, in this continent, were helpless.

Goldryn's hilt warmed in her hand.

She wouldn't be that way again. For whatever time she had left.

Gavriel padded up beside Rowan, took one look at the queen and Fenrys, and murmured, "Not the news we needed to hear."

Rowan closed his eyes for a heartbeat. "No, it was not."

Gavriel settled a hand on Rowan's shoulder. "It changes nothing, in some ways."

"How."

"We served her. She was . . . not what Aelin is. What a queen should be. We knew that long before we knew the truth. If Maeve wants to use what she is against us, to ally with Morath, then it changes things. But the past is over. Done with, Rowan. Knowing Maeve is Valg or just a wretched person doesn't change what happened."

"Knowing a Valg queen wants to enslave my mate, and nearly did so, changes a great deal."

"But we know what Maeve fears, why she fears it," Gavriel countered, his tawny eyes bright. "Fire, and the healers. If Maeve comes with that army of hers, we are not defenseless."

It was true. Rowan could have cursed himself for not thinking of it already. Another question formed, though. "Her army," Rowan said. "It's made up of Fae."

"So was her armada," Gavriel said warily.

Rowan ran a hand through his hair. "Will you be able to live with it— fighting our own people?" Killing them.

"Will you?" Gavriel countered.

Rowan didn't answer.

Gavriel asked after a moment, "Why didn't Aelin offer me the blood oath?"

The male hadn't asked these weeks. And Rowan wasn't sure why Gavriel inquired now, but he gave him the truth. "Because she won't do it until Aedion has taken the oath first. To offer it to you before him . . . she wants Aedion to take it first."

"In case he doesn't wish me to be near his kingdom."

"So that Aedion knows she placed his needs before her own."

Gavriel bowed his head. "I would say yes, if she offered."

"I know." Rowan clapped his oldest friend on the back. "She knows, too."

The Lion gazed northward. "Do you think . . . we haven't heard any news from Terrasen."

"If it had fallen, if Aedion had fallen, we would know. People here would know."

Gavriel rubbed at his chest. "We've been to war. *He's* been to war. Fought on battlefields as a *child*, gods be damned." Rage flickered over Gavriel's face. Not at what Aedion had done, but what he'd been made to do by fate and misfortune. What Gavriel had not been there to prevent. "But I still dread every day that passes and we hear nothing. Dread every messenger we see."

A terror Rowan had never known, different from his fear for his mate, his queen. The fear of a father for his child.

He didn't allow himself to look toward Aelin. To remember his dreams while hunting for her. The family he'd seen. The family they'd make together.

"We must convince the khaganate royals to march northward when this battle is over," Gavriel swore softly.

Rowan nodded. "If we can smash this army tomorrow, and convince the royals that Terrasen is the only course of action, then we could indeed be heading north soon. You might be fighting at Aedion's side by Yulemas."

Gavriel's hands clenched at his sides, tattoos spreading over his knuckles. "If he will allow me that honor."

Rowan would make Aedion allow it. But he only said, "Gather Elide and Lorcan. The ruks are almost ready to depart."

CHAPTER 51

Lorcan lingered by the edge of the ruk encampment, barely taking in the magnificent birds or their armored riders as they settled down for the night. A few, he knew, would not yet find their rest, instead bearing them and needed supplies back to the keep towering over the city and plain.

He didn't care, didn't marvel that he was soon to be airborne on one of those incredible beasts. Didn't care that tomorrow, they would all take on the dark army gathered beyond.

He'd fought in more battles, more wars, than he cared to remember. Tomorrow would be little different, save for the demons they'd slay, rather than men or Fae.

Demons like his former queen, apparently.

He had offered himself to her, had *wanted* her, or believed he did. And she had laughed at him. He didn't know what it meant. About her, about himself.

He'd thought his darkness, Hellas's gifts, had been drawn to her, that they'd been matched.

Perhaps the dark god had wanted him not to swear fealty to Maeve, but to kill her. To get close enough to do so.

Lorcan didn't adjust his cape against the gust of frigid air off the distant lake. Rather, he leaned into the cold, into the ice on the wind. As if it might rip away the truth.

"We're leaving."

Elide's low voice cut through the roaring silence of his thoughts.

"The ruks are ready," she added.

There was no fear or pity on her face, her black hair gilded by the torches and campfires. Of all of them, she'd mastered the news with little difficulty, stepping up to the desk as if she'd been born on a battlefield.

"I didn't know," he said, voice strained.

Elide knew what he meant. "We have bigger things to worry about anyway."

He took a step toward her. "I didn't know," he said again.

She tipped her head back to study his face and pursed her mouth, a muscle ticking in her jaw. "Do you want me to give you some sort of absolution for it?"

"I served her for nearly five hundred years. Five hundred *years*, and I just thought her to be immortal and cold."

"That sounds like the definition of a Valg to me."

He bared his teeth. "You live for eons and see what it does to you, *Lady*."

"I don't see why you're so shocked. Even with her being immortal and cold, you loved her. You must have accepted those traits. What difference does it make what we call her, then?"

"I didn't love her."

"You certainly acted like you did."

Lorcan snarled, "Why is that the point you keep returning to, Elide? Why is it the one thing you cannot let go of?"

"Because I'm trying to understand. How you could come to love a monster."

"Why?" He pushed into her space. She didn't balk one step.

Indeed, her eyes were blazing as she hissed, "Because it will help me understand how *I* did the same."

Her voice snagged on the last words, and Lorcan stilled as they settled into them. He'd never . . . he'd never had anyone who—

"Is it a sickness?" she demanded. "Is it something broken within you?"

"Elide." Her name was a rasp on his lips. Lorcan dared reach a hand for her.

But she pulled out of reach. "If you think that because you swore the blood oath to Aelin, it means *anything* for you and me, you're sorely mistaken. You're immortal—I'm human. Let us not forget *that* little fact, either."

Lorcan nearly recoiled at the words, their horrible truth. He was five hundred years old. He should walk away—he shouldn't be so damned bothered by any of this. And yet Lorcan snarled, "You're jealous. That's what truly eats away at you."

Elide barked a laugh that he'd never heard before, cruel and sharp. "Jealous? Jealous of *what*? That demon you served?" She squared her shoulders, a wave cresting before it smashed into the shore. "The only thing that I am jealous of, Lorcan, is that *she* is rid of you."

Lorcan hated that the words landed like a blow. That he had no defenses left where she was concerned. "I'm sorry," he said. "For all of it, Elide."

There, he'd said it, and laid it out before her. "I'm sorry," he repeated.

But Elide's face did not warm. "I don't care," she said, turning on her heel. "And I don't care if you walk off that battlefield tomorrow."

Jealous. The idea of it, of being jealous of *Maeve* for commanding Lorcan's affection for centuries. Elide limped toward the readying party of ruks, grinding her teeth so hard her jaw ached.

She was almost to the first of the saddled birds when a voice said behind her, "You should have ignored him."

Elide halted, finding Gavriel following. "Pardon me?"

The Lion's usually warm face was grave—disapproving. "You might as well have kicked a male already down."

Elide hadn't uttered a cross word to Gavriel in all the time she'd known him, but she said, "I don't see how this is any of your business."

"I have never heard Lorcan apologize for anything. Even when Maeve whipped him for a mistake, he did not apologize to her."

"And that means he earns my forgiveness?"

"No. But you have to realize that he swore the blood oath to Aelin for you. For no one else. So he could remain near you. Even knowing well enough that you will have a mortal lifespan."

The birds shifted on their feet, rustling their wings in anticipation of flight.

She knew. Had known it the moment he'd knelt before Aelin. Weeks later, Elide hadn't known what to do with it, the knowledge that Lorcan had done this for her. The longing to talk to him, to work with him as they had. She'd hated herself for it. For not trying to hold on to her anger longer.

It was why she'd gone after him tonight. Not to punish him, but herself. To remind herself of who he'd sold their queen to, how profoundly mistaken she had been.

And her parting line to him . . . it was a lie. A disgusting, hateful lie.

Elide turned to Gavriel again. "I don't—"

The Lion was gone. And for the cold flight over the army, then over the sea of darkness spread between it and the ancient city, even that wise voice who had whispered for the entirety of her life had gone quiet.

Nesryn lingered by Salkhi, a hand on her mount's feathered side, and watched the party soar into the skies. The twenty ruks hadn't just been bearing Aelin Galathynius and her companions, Chaol and Yrene included, but also more healers, supplies, and a few horses, hooded and corralled into wooden pens that the birds could carry. Including Chaol's own horse, Farasha.

"I wish I could go with them," Borte sighed from where she was rubbing down Arcas. "To fight alongside the Fae."

Nesryn gave her an amused, sidelong glance. "You'll get that opportunity soon enough, if we march to Terrasen after this."

Nearby, a distinctly male snort of derision sounded.

"Go eavesdrop on someone else, Yeran," Borte snapped toward her betrothed.

But the Berlad captain only answered back, "A fine commander you are, mooning over the Fae like a doe-eyed girl."

Borte rolled her eyes. "When they teach me their killing techniques and I use them to wipe you off the map at our next Gathering, you can tell me all about my mooning."

The handsome captain stormed over from his own ruk, and Nesryn ducked her head to hide her smile, finding herself immensely interested in brushing Salkhi's brown feathers. "You'll be my wife then, according to your bargain with my hearth-mother," he said, crossing his arms. "It would be unseemly for you to kill your own husband in the Gathering."

Borte smiled with poisoned sweetness at her betrothed. "I'll just have to kill you some other time, then."

Yeran grinned back, the portrait of wicked amusement. "Some other time, then," he promised.

Nesryn didn't fail to note the light that gleamed in the captain's eyes. Or the way Borte bit her lip, just barely, her breath hitching.

Yeran leaned in to whisper something in Borte's ear that made the girl's eyes widen. And apparently stunned her enough that when Yeran prowled to his ruk, the portrait of swaggering arrogance, Borte blushed furiously and returned to cleaning her ruk.

"Don't ask," she muttered.

Nesryn held up her hands. "I wouldn't dream of it."

Borte's blush remained for minutes afterward, her cleaning near-frantic.

Easy, graceful steps sounded in the snow, and Nesryn knew who approached before the rukhin even straightened to attention. Not at the fact that Sartaq was prince and Heir, but that he was their captain. Of all the rukhin in this war, not just the Eridun aerie.

He waved them off, scanning the night sky and ruks still soaring, shielded by Rowan Whitethorn from any enemy arrows that might find their mark. Sartaq had barely come up beside Nesryn when Borte patted Arcas, tossed her brush into her supply pack, and walked into the night.

Not to give them privacy, Nesryn realized. Not when Yeran prowled from his own ruk's side a heartbeat later, trailing Borte at a lazy pace. The girl looked over her shoulder once, and there was anything but annoyance on her face as she noted Yeran at her heels.

Sartaq chuckled. "At least they're a little more clear about it now."

Nesryn snorted, brush gliding over Salkhi's feathers. "I'm as confused as ever."

"The riders whose tents lie on either side of Borte's aren't."

Nesryn's brows rose, but she smiled. "Good. Not about the riders, but—about them."

"War does strange things to people. Makes everything more urgent." He ran a hand down the back of her head, his fingers twining in her hair before he murmured in her ear, "Come to bed."

Heat flared through her body. "We've a battle to launch tomorrow. Again."

"And a day of death has made me want to hold you," the prince said, giving her that disarming grin she had no defenses against. Especially as he added, "And do other things with you."

Nesryn's toes curled in her boots. "Then help me finish cleaning Salkhi."

The prince lunged so fast for the brush Borte had discarded that Nesryn laughed.

CHAPTER 52

The Crochans had returned to their camp in the Fangs and waited.

Manon and the Thirteen dismounted from the wyverns. Something churned in her gut with each step toward Glennis's fire. The strip of red fabric at the end of her braid became a millstone, weighing her head down.

They were almost to Glennis's hearth when Bronwen fell into step beside Manon.

Asterin and Sorrel, trailing behind, tensed, but neither interfered. Especially not as Bronwen asked, "What happened?"

Manon glanced sidelong at her cousin. "I asked them to consider their position in this war."

Bronwen frowned at the sky, as if expecting to see the Ironteeth trailing them. "And?"

"And we'll see, I suppose."

"I thought you went there to rally them."

"I went," Manon said, baring her teeth, "to make them contemplate who they wish to be."

"I didn't think Ironteeth were capable of such things."

Asterin snarled. "Careful, witch."

Bronwen threw her a mocking smile over a shoulder, then said to Manon, "They let you walk out alive?"

"They did indeed."

"Will they fight—will they turn on Morath and the other Ironteeth?"

"I don't know." She didn't. She truly didn't.

Bronwen fell silent for a few steps. Manon had just entered the ring of Glennis's hearth when the witch said, "We shouldn't have bothered to hope, then."

Manon had no answer, so she walked away, the Thirteen not giving Bronwen a passing glance.

Manon found Glennis stirring the coals of her hearth, the sacred fire in its center a bright lick of flame that needed no wood to burn. A gift from Brannon—a piece of Terrasen's queen here.

Glennis said, "We must move out by midmorning tomorrow. It was decided: we are to return to our home-hearths."

Manon only sat on the rock nearest the crone, leaving the Thirteen to scrounge up whatever food they could find. Dorian had remained back with the wyverns. The last she'd seen of him minutes ago, a few Crochans had been approaching him. Either for pleasure or information, Manon didn't know. She doubted he'd share her bed again anytime soon. Especially if he remained hell-bent on going to Morath.

The thought didn't sit entirely well.

Manon said to Glennis, "Do you think the Ironteeth are capable of change?"

"You would know that answer best."

She did, and she wasn't wholly certain she liked the conclusion she reached. "Did Rhiannon think we could be?" *Did she think* I *could be?*

Glennis's eyes softened, a hint of sorrow gracing them as she added another log to the flame. "Your half sister was your opposite, in so many ways. And like your father in many regards. She was open, and honest, and spoke her feelings, regardless of the consequences. Brash, some called her. You might not know it from how they act now," the crone said, smirking a bit, "but there were more than a few around these various hearths who disliked her. Who didn't want to hear her lectures on our failing people, on how a better solution existed. How our peoples might find peace. Every day, she spoke loudly and to anyone who might listen about the possibility of a united Witch Kingdom. The possibility of a future where we did not need to hide, or be spread so thin. Many called her a fool. Thought her a fool especially when she went to look for you. To see if you agreed with her, despite what your bloody history suggested."

She'd died for that dream, that possibility of a future. Manon had killed her for it.

Glennis said, "So did Rhiannon think the Ironteeth capable of change? She might have been the only witch in the Crochans who did, but she believed it with every shred of her being." Her sagging throat bobbed. "She believed you two could rule it together—the Witch Kingdom. You would lead the Ironteeth, and she the Crochans, and together you would rebuild what fractured long ago."

"And now there is just me." Juggling both.

"Now it is just you." Glennis's stare turned direct, unforgiving. "A bridge between us."

Manon accepted the plate of food Asterin handed her before the Second sat beside her.

Asterin said, "The Ironteeth will turn. You'll see."

Sorrel grunted from the nearest rock, disagreement written across her face.

Asterin gave Manon's Third a vulgar gesture. "They'll turn. I swear it."

Glennis offered a small smile, but Manon said nothing as she dug into her food.

Hope, she had told Elide all those months ago.

But perhaps there would be none for them after all.

⁓

Dorian lingered by the wyverns to answer the questions of the Crochans who either did not want to or were perhaps too skittish to ask the Thirteen what had occurred in the Ferian Gap.

No, a host was not rallying behind them. No, no one had tracked them. Yes, Manon had spoken to the Ironteeth and asked them to join. Yes, they had gotten in and out alive. Yes, she had spoken as both Iron-teeth and Crochan.

At least, Asterin had told him so on the long flight back here. Speaking to Manon, discussing their next steps . . . He didn't bother. Not yet.

And when Asterin herself had gone quiet, he'd fallen deep into thought. Mulled over all he'd seen in the Ferian Gap, every twisted hall and chamber and pit that reeked of pain and fear.

What his father and Erawan had built. The sort of kingdom he'd inherited.

The Wyrdkeys stirred, whispering. Dorian ignored them and ran a hand over Damaris's hilt. The gold remained warm despite the bitter cold.

A sword of truth, yes, but also reminder of what Adarlan had once been. What it might become again.

If he did not falter. Did not doubt himself. For whatever time he had left.

He could make it right. All of it. He could make it right.

Damaris heated in silent comfort and confirmation.

Dorian left the small crowd of Crochans and strode to a sliver of land overlooking a deadly plunge to a snow-and-rock-strewn chasm.

Brutal mountains rippled away in every direction, but he cast his gaze to the southeast. To Morath, looming far beyond sight.

He'd been able to shift into a raven that night in the Eyllwe forest. Now he supposed he only needed to learn how to fly.

He reached inward, to that eddy of raw power. Warmth bloomed in him, bones groaning, the world widening.

He opened his beak, and a throaty caw cracked from him.

Stretching out his sooty wings, Dorian began to practice.

CHAPTER 53

Someone had set fire to her thigh.

Not Aelin, because Aelin was gone, sealed in an iron sarcophagus and taken across the sea.

But someone had burned her down to the bone, so thoroughly that the slightest of movements on wherever she lay—a bed? A cot?—sent agony searing through her.

Lysandra cracked open her eyes, a low groan working its way up her parched throat.

"Easy," a deep voice rumbled.

She knew that voice. Knew the scent—like a clear brook and new grass. Aedion.

She dragged her eyes, heavy and burning, toward the sound.

His shining hair hung limp, matted with blood. And those turquoise eyes were smudged with purple beneath—and utterly bleak. Empty.

A rough tent stood around them, the sole light provided by a lantern swinging in the bitter wind that crept in through the flaps. She'd been piled high with blankets, though he sat on an overturned bucket, still in his armor, with nothing to warm him.

Lysandra peeled her tongue off the roof of her mouth and listened to the world beyond the dim tent.

Chaos. Shouting. Some men screaming.

"We yielded Perranth," Aedion said hoarsely. "We've been on the run for two days now. Another three days, and we'll reach Orynth."

Her brows narrowed slightly. She'd been unconscious for that long?

"We had to put you in a wagon with the other wounded. Tonight's the first we've dared to stop." The strong column of his throat bobbed. "A storm struck to the south. It's slowed Morath down—just enough."

She tried to swallow against the dryness in her throat. The last she remembered, she'd been facing those ilken, never so aware of the limitations of a mortal body, of how even Aelin, who seemed so tall as she swaggered through the world, was dwarfed by the creatures. Then those claws had ripped into her leg. And she'd managed to make a perfect swing. To take one of them down.

"You rallied our army," he said. "We lost the battle, but they didn't run in shame."

Lysandra managed to pull a hand from beneath the blankets, and strained for the jug of water set beside the bed. Aedion was instantly in motion, filling a cup.

But as her fingers closed around it, she noted their color, their shape.

Her own hands. Her own arm.

"You . . . shifted," Aedion said, noting her widened eyes. "While the healer was sewing up your leg. I think the pain . . . You shifted back into this body."

Horror, roaring and nauseating, roiled through her. "How many saw?" Her first words, each as rough and dry as sandpaper.

"Don't worry about it."

She gulped down the water. "They all know?"

A solemn nod.

"What did you tell them—about Aelin?"

"That she has been off on a vital quest with Rowan and the others. And that it is so secret we do not dare speak of it."

"Are the soldiers—"

"Don't worry about it," he repeated. But she could see it in his face. The strain.

They had rallied to their queen, only to realize it had been an illusion. That the might of the Fire-Bringer was not with them. Would not shield them against the army at their heels.

"I'm sorry," she breathed.

Aedion took the empty cup of water before he gripped her hand, squeezing gently. "*I* am sorry, Lysandra. For all of it." His throat bobbed again. "When I saw the ilken, when I saw you against them . . ."

Useless. Lying bitch. The words he'd thrown at her, raged at her, dragged her further from the haze of pain. Sharpened her focus.

"You did this," he said, voice lowering, "for Terrasen. For Aelin. You were willing to *die* for it, gods above."

"I was." Her words came out cold as steel.

Aedion blinked as she withdrew her hand from his. Her leg ached and throbbed, but she managed to sit up. To meet his stare. "I have been degraded and humiliated in so many ways, for so many years," she said, voice shaking. Not from fear, but from the tidal wave that swept up everything inside her, burning alongside the wound in her leg. "But I have *never* felt as humiliated as I did when you threw me into the snow. When you called me a lying bitch in front of our friends and allies. *Never.*" She hated the angry tears that stung her eyes. "I was once forced to crawl before men. And gods above, I nearly crawled for you these months. And yet it takes me nearly dying for you to realize that you've been an ass? It takes me nearly dying for you to see me as human again?"

He didn't hide the regret in his eyes. She had spent years reading men and knew that every agonized emotion in his face was genuine. But it didn't erase what had been said, and done.

Lysandra put a hand on her chest, right over her own shredded heart. "I wanted it to be you," she said. "After Wesley, after all of it, I wanted it to be *you*. What Aelin asked me to do had no bearing on that. What she asked me to do never felt like a burden, because I wanted it to be *you* in the end anyway." She didn't wipe away the tears that slipped down her cheeks. "And you threw me into the snow."

Aedion slid to his knees. Reached for her hand. "I will never stop regretting it. Lysandra, I will never forget a second of it, never stop hating myself for it. And I am so—"

"Don't." She snatched back her hand. "Don't kneel. Don't bother." She pointed to the tent flaps. "There's nothing I have left to say to you. Or you to me."

Agony again rippled across his face, but she shut out what it did to her. What it did to her to see Aedion rise to his feet, groaning softly at some unspecified ache in his powerful body. For a few breaths, he just stared down at her.

Then he said, "I meant every promise I made to you on that beach in Skull's Bay."

And then he was gone.

⁓

Aedion had spent a good portion of his life hating himself for the various things he'd done.

But seeing the tears on Lysandra's face because of *him* . . . He'd never felt like more of a bastard.

He barely heard the soldiers around him, tense and skittish in the snow that blew between their quickly erected tents. How many more wounded would die tonight?

He'd already pulled rank to get Lysandra care from the best healers they had left. And still it was not good enough, the healers not gifted magically. And despite Lysandra's quicker healing abilities, they'd still had to stitch up her leg. And now changed the bandages every few hours. The wound had sealed, mercifully, likely fast enough to avoid infection.

Many of the injured amongst them could not say the same. The rotting wounds, the festering blood within their veins . . . Every morning, more and more bodies had been left behind in the snow, the ground too frozen and with no time to burn them.

Food for Erawan's beasts, the soldiers murmured when they'd moved out. They might as well offer the enemy a free meal.

Aedion shut down that talk, along with any sort of hissing about their flight and defeat. By the time they'd camped tonight, a good third of the soldiers, members of the Bane included, had been assigned various tasks to keep them busy. To make them so tired after a day's fleeing that they didn't have the energy to grumble.

Aedion aimed for his own tent, set just outside the healers' ring of tents where Lysandra lay. Giving her a private tent had been another privilege he'd used his rank to acquire.

He'd almost reached the small tent—no use in building his full war tent when they'd be running again in a few hours—when he spotted the figures huddled by the fire outside.

He slowed his steps to a stalking gait.

Ren rose to his feet, his face tight beneath his heavy hood.

Yet it was the man beside Ren who made Aedion's temper hone itself into a dangerous thing.

"Darrow," he said. "I would have thought you'd be in Orynth by now."

The lord bundled in furs did not smile. "I came to deliver the message myself. Since my most trusted courier seems inclined to select another allegiance."

The old bastard knew, then. About Lysandra's masquerading as Aelin. And Nox Owen's role in moving their army out of his grasp.

"Let's get it over with, then," Aedion said.

Ren tensed, but said nothing.

Darrow's thin lips curved in a cruel smile. "For your acts of reckless rebellion, for your failure to heed our command and take your troops where they were ordered, for your utter defeat at the border and the loss of Perranth, you are stripped of your rank."

Aedion barely heard the words.

"Consider yourself now a soldier in the Bane, if they'll have you. And as for the imposter you've paraded around . . ." A sneer toward the healers' tents.

Aedion snarled.

Darrow's eyes narrowed. "If she is again caught pretending to be Princess Aelin"—Aedion almost ripped out his throat at that word, *Princess*— "then we will have little choice but to sign her execution order."

"I'd like to see you try."

"I'd like to see you stop us."

Aedion smirked. "Oh, it's not me who you'd be dealing with. Good luck to any man who tries to harm a shifter that powerful."

Darrow ignored the promise and held out a hand. "The Sword of Orynth, if you will."

Ren started. "You're out of your mind, Darrow."

Aedion just stared. The ancient lord said, "That sword belongs to a true general of Terrasen, to its prince-commander. As you are no longer the bearer of that title, the sword shall return to Orynth. Until a new, appropriate bearer can be determined."

Ren growled, "That sword is in our possession, Darrow, because of Aedion. Had he not won it back, it would still be rusting in Adarlan's trove."

"He will always have our gratitude for it. If only in that regard, at least."

A dull roar filled Aedion's head. Darrow's hand remained extended.

He deserved this, he supposed. For his failure on these battlefields, his failure to defend the land he'd promised Aelin he'd save. For what he'd done to the shifter who had held his heart from the moment she'd shredded into those Valg soldiers in the sewers of Rifthold.

Aedion unbuckled the ancient sword from his belt. Ren let out a sound of protest.

But he ignored the lord and tossed the Sword of Orynth to Darrow.

The lightness where that sword had been threw off his balance.

The old man stared at the sword in his hands. Even went so far as to run a finger over the bone pommel, the hateful bastard unable to contain his awe.

Aedion just said, "The Sword of Orynth is only a piece of metal and bone. It always has been. It's what the sword inspires in the bearer that matters. The true heart of Terrasen."

"Poetic of you, Aedion," was Darrow's reply before he turned on his heel, aiming for wherever his escort waited beyond the camp's edge. "Your commander, Kyllian, is now general of the Bane. Report to him for orders."

The swirling snows devoured the old lord within a few steps.

Ren snarled, "Like hell you aren't general."

"The Lords of Terrasen decree it, and so it shall be."

"Why aren't you fighting this?" Ren's eyes blazed. "You just handed over that sword—"

"I don't give a shit." Aedion didn't bother to keep his exhaustion, his disappointment and anger, from his voice. "Let him have the sword, and the army. I don't give a shit."

Ren didn't stop him as Aedion ducked into his tent and didn't emerge until dawn.

The Lords of Terrasen had stripped General Ashryver of his sword.

The word spread from campfire to campfire, rippling through the ranks.

The soldier was new to the Bane, had been accepted into their ranks only this summer. An honor, even with war upon them. An honor, though the soldier's family had wept to see him depart.

To fight for Prince Aedion, to fight for Terrasen—it had been worth it, the weight of leaving his farmstead home behind. Leaving behind that sweet-faced farmer's daughter whom he'd never gotten the chance to so much as kiss.

It had been worth it then. But not now.

The friends he'd made in the months of training and fighting were dead.

Huddled around the too-small campfire, the soldier was the last of them, the fresh-faced recruits who'd been so eager to test themselves against the Valg at the start of summer.

In the dead heart of winter, he now called himself a fool. If he bothered to speak at all.

Words had become unnecessary, foreign. As foreign as his half-frozen body, which never warmed, though he slept as close to the fire as he dared. If sleep found him, with the screaming of the wounded and dying. The knowledge of what hunted them northward.

There was no one left to help them. Save them. The queen they'd thought amongst them had been a lie. A shape-shifter's deception. Where Aelin Galathynius now fought, what she had deemed more important than them, he didn't know.

The frigid night pressed in, threatening to devour the small fire before him. The soldier inched closer to the flame, shuddering beneath his worn cloak, every ache and scrape from the day throbbing.

He wouldn't abandon this army, though. Not as some of the others were murmuring. Even with Prince Aedion stripped of his title, even with their queen gone, he wouldn't abandon this army.

He had sworn an oath to protect Terrasen. To protect his family. He'd hold to it.

Even if he now knew he'd never see them again.

Snow was still falling when they renewed their flight.

It fell for the next two days, chasing them northward for each long mile.

Darrow's decree had little bearing. Kyllian outright refused to make any calls without Aedion's approval. Refused to don armor fitting of his rank. Refused to take the war tent.

Aedion knew he'd earned that loyalty long ago. Just as the Bane had earned his. But it didn't stop him from hating it, just a bit. From wishing Kyllian would take over in full.

Lysandra's leg was healed enough to ride, but he saw little of her. She kept to Ren's side, the two of them traveling near the healers, should her stitches pull. When Aedion did glimpse her, she often stared him down until he wanted to vomit.

By the third day, the scouts were rushing to them. Reporting that Morath had gained, and was closing in behind—fast.

Aedion knew how this would go. Saw every trudging step and hunger-tight face around him.

Orynth was half a day off. Were it over easy terrain, they might stand a chance of getting behind its ancient walls. But between them and the city lay the Florine River. Too wide to cross without boats. The nearest bridge too far south to risk.

At this time of the year, it still might not yet have frozen. And even so, with the river so wide and deep, the layer of ice that often coated it only went so far. For their army to cross, they'd have to risk the ice collapsing.

There were other ways to Orynth. To go straight north into the Stag-horns, and cut back south to the city nestled at their foot. But each hour delayed allowed Morath's host to gain ground.

Aedion was riding beside Kyllian when Elgan galloped up beside them, horse puffing curls of hot air into the snow-thick day. "The river is ten miles straight ahead," Elgan said. "We have to make our decision now."

To risk the bridge to the south, or the time it'd take to go to the long route northward. Ren, spotting their gathering, urged his horse closer.

Kyllian waited for the order. Aedion arched a brow. "You're the general."

"Horseshit," Kyllian spat.

Aedion only turned to Elgan. "Any word on the status of the ice?"

Elgan shook his head. "No word on it, or the bridge."

Endless, whirling snow lay ahead. Aedion didn't dare glance behind at the trudging, stooping lines of soldiers.

Ren, as silently as he'd come, pulled back to where he rode at Lysandra's side.

Wings fluttered through the wind and snow, and then a falcon was shooting skyward, one leg awkwardly straight beneath it.

"Keep riding," was all Aedion said to his companions.

Lysandra returned within an hour. She addressed Ren and Ren alone, and then the young lord was galloping to Aedion's side, where Kyllian and Elgan still rode.

Ren's face had gone ashen. "There's no ice on the Florine. And Morath scouts snuck ahead and razed the southern bridge."

"They're herding us northward," Elgan murmured.

Ren nodded. "They'll be upon us by tomorrow morning."

They would not have time to consider making a run for the northern entrance to Orynth. And with the Florine mere miles ahead, too wide and deep to cross, too frigid to dare swim, and Morath closing in from behind, they were utterly trapped.

CHAPTER 54

Chaol hand-fed an apple to Farasha, the beautiful black mare skittish after her unprecedented flight.

It seemed even Hellas's horse could be frightened, though Chaol supposed any wise person would find dangling hundreds of feet in the air to be unnerving.

"Someone else could do that for you." Leaning against the stable wall of the keep, Yrene watched him work, monitoring each deeply limping step. "You should rest."

Chaol shook his head. "She doesn't know what the hell is happening. I'd like to try to calm her before she beds down."

Before battle tomorrow—before they might stand a chance of actually saving Anielle.

He was still working through all that had transpired these months he'd been gone. The battles and losses. Where Dorian had gone with Manon and the Thirteen. Chaol could only pray his friend was successful— and that he didn't take it upon himself to forge the Lock.

Needing to unravel all he'd learned, he'd left Aelin and the others near the Great Hall to find whatever food they could, immediately bringing Farasha down here with him. Mostly for the safety of everyone around the Muniqi horse, since Farasha had tried to take a chunk out of the soldier nearest her the moment her hood had come off. Even the hood hadn't concealed from her what, exactly, was happening to the oversized crate they'd buckled her into.

But Farasha hadn't bitten off his hand before she nibbled at the apple, so Chaol prayed she'd forgive him for the rough flight. Part of him half wondered if the mare knew that his back ached, that he needed his cane, but that he chose to be here.

He ran a hand down her ebony mane, then patted her strong neck. "Ready to trample some Valg grunts tomorrow, my friend?"

Farasha huffed, angling a dark eye at him as if to say, *Are* you?

Chaol smiled, and Yrene laughed softly. "I should head back to the hall," his wife said. "See who needs help." But she lingered.

Their eyes met over Farasha's powerful back.

He came around the horse, still mindful of her biting. "I know," he said quietly.

Yrene angled her head. "Know what?"

Chaol interlaced their fingers. And then laid their hands atop her still-flat abdomen.

"Oh," was all Yrene said, her mouth popping open. "I— *How?*"

Chaol's heart thundered. "It's true, then."

Her golden eyes scanned his. "Do you want it to be?"

Chaol slid a hand against her cheek. "More than I ever realized."

Yrene's smile was wide and lovely enough to fracture his heart. "It's true," she breathed.

"How far along?"

"Almost two months."

He studied her stomach, the place that would soon swell with the child growing inside her. Their child. "You didn't tell me, I'm assuming, because you didn't want me to worry."

Yrene bit her lip. "Something like that."

He snorted. "And when you were waddling around, belly near bursting?"

Yrene whacked his arm. "I'm not going to *waddle*."

Chaol laughed, and tugged her into his arms. "You'll waddle beautifully, was what I meant to say." Yrene's laughter reverberated into him, and Chaol kissed the top of her head, her temple. "We're having a child," he murmured onto her hair.

Her arms came around him. "We are," she whispered. "But how did you know?"

"My father," Chaol grumbled, "apparently possesses better observational skills than I do."

He felt, more than saw, her cringe. "You're not angry I didn't tell you?"

"No. I would have appreciated hearing it from your lips first, but I understand why you didn't want to say anything yet. Stupid as it might be," he added, nipping at her ear. Yrene jabbed him in the ribs, and he laughed again. Laughed, even though every day they'd fought in this battle, every opponent he'd faced, he'd dreaded making a fatal mistake. Had been unable to forget that should he fall, he'd be taking them both with him.

Her arms tightened around him, and Yrene nestled her head against his chest. "You'll be a brilliant father," she said softly. "The most brilliant one to ever exist."

"High praise indeed, coming from a woman who wanted to toss me from the highest window of the Torre a few months ago."

"A healer would never be so unprofessional."

Chaol grinned, and breathed in her scent before he pulled back and brushed his mouth against hers. "I am happier than I can ever express, Yrene, to share this with you. Anything you need, I am yours to command."

Her lips twitched upward. "Dangerous words."

But Chaol ran his thumb over her wedding band. "I'll have to win this war quickly, then, so I can have our house built by the summer."

She rolled her eyes. "A noble reason to defeat Erawan."

Chaol stole another kiss from her. "As much as I would like to show you just how much I am at your command," he said against her mouth, "I have another matter to deal with before bed."

Yrene's brows rose.

He grimaced. "I need to introduce Aelin to my father. Before they run into each other." The man hadn't been near the hall when they'd arrived, and Chaol had been too worried for Farasha's well-being to bother hunting him down.

Yrene cringed, though amusement sparked in her eyes. "Is it bad if I want to join you? And bring snacks?"

Chaol slung an arm around her shoulders, giving Farasha a farewell stroke before they left. Despite the cane, each step was limping, and the pain in his back lanced down his legs, but it was secondary. All of it, even the damned war, was secondary to the woman at his side.

To the future they'd build together.

As well as Yrene's conversation with Chaol had gone, that's how badly things went between Aelin Galathynius and his father.

Yrene didn't bring snacks, but that was only because by the time they reached the Great Hall, they had intercepted his father. Storming toward the room where Aelin and her companions had gone for a reprieve.

"Father," Chaol said, falling into step beside him.

Yrene said nothing, monitoring Chaol's movements. The pain in his back had to be great, if he was limping this deeply, even while her magic refilled. She had no idea where he'd left his chair—if it had been crushed under falling debris. She prayed it had not.

His father snapped, "You fail to wake me when the Queen of Terrasen arrives at my castle?"

"It wasn't a priority." Chaol halted before the door that opened into the small chamber that had been vacated for the queen and knocked.

A grunt was the only confirmation before Yrene's husband shouldered open the door enough to poke his head inside. "My father," Chaol said to whoever was inside, presumably the queen, "would like to see you."

Silence, then the rustling of clothes and steps.

Yrene kept back as Aelin Galathynius appeared, her face and hands clean, but clothes still dirty. At her side stood that towering, silver-haired Fae warrior—Rowan Whitethorn. Whom the royals had spoken of with such fear and respect months ago. In the room, Lady Elide sat against the far wall, a tray of food beside her, and the giant white wolf lay sprawled on the ground, monitoring with half-lidded eyes.

A shock to see the shift, to realize these Fae might be powerful and ancient, but they still had one foot in the forest. The queen, it seemed, preferred the form as well, her delicately pointed ears half-hidden by her unbound hair. Behind her, there was no sign of the golden-haired, melancholy warrior, Gavriel, or the utterly terrifying Lorcan. Thank Silba for that, at least.

Aelin left the door open, though their two court members remained seated. Bored, almost.

"Well, now," was all the queen said as she stepped into the hall.

Chaol's father looked over the warrior-prince at her side. Then he turned his head toward Chaol and said, "I assume they met in Wendlyn. After you sent her there."

Yrene tensed at the taunting in the man's voice. Bastard. Horrible bastard.

Aelin clicked her tongue. "Yes, yes, let's get all that out of the way. Though I don't think your son really regrets it, does he?" Aelin's eyes shifted to Yrene, and Yrene tried not to flinch under that turquoise-and-gold stare. Different from the fire she'd beheld that night in Innish, but still full of that razor-sharp awareness. Different—they were both different from the girls they'd been. A smile curved the queen's mouth. "I think he made out rather well for himself." She frowned up at her consort. "Yrene, at least, doesn't seem like the sort to hog the blankets and snore in one's ear all night."

Yrene coughed as Prince Rowan only smiled at the queen. "I don't mind your snoring," he said mildly.

Aelin's mouth twitched when she turned to Chaol's father. Yrene's own laughter died at the lack of light on the man's face. Chaol was tense as a drawn bowstring as the queen said to his father, "Don't waste your breath on taunts. I'm tired, and hungry, and it won't end well for you."

"This is my keep."

Aelin made a good show of gaping at the ceiling, the walls, the floors. "Is it really?"

Yrene had to duck her head to hide her grin. So did Chaol.

But Aelin said to the Lord of Anielle, "I trust you're not going to get in our way."

A line in the sand. Yrene's breath caught in her throat.

Chaol's father said simply, "Last I looked you were not Queen of Adarlan."

"No, but your son is Hand to the King, which means he outranks you." Aelin smiled with horrific sweetness at Chaol. "Haven't you told him that?"

Yrene and Aelin were no longer the girls they'd been in Innish, yes, but that wildfire still remained in the queen's spirit. Wildfire touched with insanity.

Chaol shrugged. "I figured I'd tell him when the time arose."

His father glowered.

Prince Rowan, however, said to the man, "You've defended and prepared your people admirably. We have no plans to take that from you."

"I don't need the approval of Fae brutes," the lord sneered.

Aelin clapped Rowan on the shoulder. "Brute. I like that. Better than 'buzzard,' right?"

Yrene had no idea what the queen was talking about, but she held in her laugh anyway.

Aelin sketched a mocking bow to the Lord of Anielle. "On that lovely parting note, we're going to finish up our dinners. Enjoy your evening, we'll see you on the battlements tomorrow, and please do rot in hell."

Then Aelin was turning away, a hand guiding her husband inside. But not before the queen threw a grin over her shoulder to Yrene and Chaol and said, eyes bright—with joy and warmth this time, "Congratulations."

How she knew, Yrene had no idea. But the Fae possessed a preternatural sense of smell.

Yrene smiled all the same as she bowed her head—just before Aelin slammed the door in the Lord of Anielle's face.

Chaol turned to his father, any hint of amusement expertly hidden. "Well, you saw her."

Chaol's father shook with what Yrene supposed was a combination of rage and humiliation, and stalked away. It was one of the finest sights Yrene had ever seen.

From Chaol's smile, she knew her husband felt the same.

~

"What a horrible man." Elide finished off her chicken leg before handing the other to Fenrys, who had shifted back into his Fae form. He tore into it with a growl of appreciation. "Poor Lord Chaol."

Aelin, her aching legs stretched out before her as she leaned against the wall, finished off her own portion of chicken, then dug into a hunk of dark bread. "Poor Chaol, poor his mother, poor his brother. Poor everyone who has to deal with him."

At the lone, narrow window of the room, monitoring the dark army hundreds of feet below, Rowan snorted. "You were in rare form tonight."

Aelin saluted him with her hunk of hearty oaten bread. "Anyone who interrupts my dinner risks paying the price."

Rowan rolled his eyes, but smiled. Just as Aelin had seen him smile when they'd both scented what was on Yrene. The child in her.

She was happy for Yrene—for them both. Chaol deserved that joy, perhaps more than anyone. As much as her own mate.

Aelin didn't let the thoughts travel further. Not as she finished her bread and came to the window, leaning against Rowan's side. He slid an arm around her shoulders, casual and easy.

None of them mentioned Maeve.

Elide and Fenrys continued eating in silence, giving them what privacy they could in the small, bare room they'd be sharing, sleeping on bedrolls. The Lord of Anielle, it seemed, did not share her appreciation for luxury. Or basic comforts for his guests. Like hot baths. Or beds.

"The men are terrified," Rowan said, gazing out at the levels of the keep below. "You can smell it."

"They've held this keep for days now. They know what's waiting for them at dawn."

"Their fear," Rowan said, his jaw tightening, "is proof they do not trust our allies. Proof they don't trust the khagan's army to actually save them. It will make for sloppy fighters. Could create a weakness where there shouldn't be one."

"Perhaps you should have told Chaol," Aelin said. "He could give them some motivational speech."

"I have a feeling Chaol has given them plenty. This sort of fear rots the soul."

"What's to be done for it, then?"

Rowan shook his head. "I don't know."

But she sensed he did know. Sensed that he wanted to say something else, and either their current company or some sort of hesitation barred him.

So Aelin didn't push, and surveyed the battlements with their patrolling soldiers, the sprawling, dark army beyond. Baying cries and howls rent the night, the sounds unearthly enough that they dragged a shudder down her spine.

"Is a land battle easier or worse than one at sea?" Aelin asked her husband, her mate, peering at his tattooed face.

She'd only faced the ships in Skull's Bay, and even that had been over relatively quickly. And against the ilken who'd swarmed them in the Stone Marshes, it had been more an extermination than anything. Not what awaited them tomorrow. Not what her friends had fought on the Narrow Sea while she and Manon had been in the mirror, then with Maeve on the beach.

Rowan considered. "They're just as messy, but in different ways."

"I'd rather fight on land," Fenrys grumbled.

"Because no one likes the smell of wet dog?" Aelin asked over her shoulder.

Fenrys laughed. "Exactly because of that." At least he was smiling again.

Rowan's mouth twitched, but his eyes were hard as he surveyed the enemy army. "Tomorrow's battle will be just as brutal," he said. "But the plan is sound."

They'd be on the battlements with Chaol, readying for any desperate maneuvers Morath might attempt when they found themselves being herded and crushed by the khagan's army. Elide would be with Yrene and the other healers in the Great Hall, helping the injured.

Where Lorcan and Gavriel would be, Aelin could only assume. Both had peeled off upon arriving, the latter taking watch somewhere, and the former likely brooding. But they'd probably be fighting right alongside them.

As if her thoughts had summoned him, Gavriel slipped into the room. "The army looks quiet enough," he said by way of greeting, then unceremoniously dropped to the floor beside Fenrys and hauled the platter of chicken toward him. "The men are rife with fear, though. Days of defending these walls have worn on them."

Rowan nodded, not bothering to tell the Lion they'd just discussed this as Gavriel ripped into the food. "We'll have to make sure they don't balk tomorrow, then."

Indeed.

"I was wondering," Elide said to none of them in particular after a moment. "Since Maeve is an imposter, who would rule Doranelle if she was banished with all the other Valg?"

"Or burned to a crisp," Fenrys muttered.

Aelin might have smiled grimly, but Elide's question settled into her.

Gavriel slowly set down the chicken.

Rowan's arm dropped from Aelin's shoulders. His pine-green eyes were wide. "You."

Aelin blinked. "There are others from Mab's line. Galan, or Aedion—"

"The throne passes through the maternal line—to a female only. Or it should have," Rowan said. "You're the sole female with a direct, undiluted claim to Mab's bloodline."

"And your household, Rowan," Gavriel said. "Someone in your household would have a claim on Mora's half of the throne."

"Sellene. It would go to her." Even as a prince, Rowan's own heritage connecting him to Mora's bloodline had thinned to the point of being in name only. Aelin was more closely related to Elide, probably to Chaol, too, than she was to Rowan, despite their distant ancestry.

"Well, Sellene can have it," Aelin said, wiping her hands of dust that was not there. "Doranelle's hers."

She wouldn't set foot in that city again, Maeve or no. She wasn't sure if that made her a coward. She didn't dare reach for her magic's comforting rumble.

"The Little Folk truly knew," Fenrys mused, rubbing his jaw. "What you were."

They had always known her, the Little Folk. Had saved her life ten years ago, and saved their lives these past few weeks. They had known her, and left gifts for her. Tribute, she'd thought, to Brannon's Heir. Not to . . .

Gavriel murmured, "The Faerie Queen of the West."

Silence.

Aelin blurted, "Is that an actual title?"

"It is now," Fenrys muttered. Aelin shot him a look.

"With Sellene as the Fae Queen of the East," Rowan mused.

No one spoke for a good minute.

Aelin sighed up at the ceiling. "What's another fancy title, I suppose?"

They didn't answer, and Aelin tried not to let the weight of that title settle too heavily. All it implied. That she might not only look after the Little Folk on this continent, but with the cadre, begin a new homeland for any Fae who might wish to join them. For any of the Fae who had survived the slaughter in Terrasen ten years ago and might wish to return.

A fool's dream. One that she would likely not come to see. To create.

"The Faerie Queen of the West," Aelin said, tasting the words on her tongue.

Wondering how long she'd get to call herself such.

From the heavy quiet, she knew her companions were contemplating the same. And from the pain in Rowan's eyes, the rage and determination, she knew he was already calculating if it might somehow spare her from the sacrificial altar.

But that would come later. After tomorrow. If they survived.

~

There was a gate, and eternity lay beyond its black archway.

But not for her. No, there would be no Afterworld for her.

The gods had built another coffin, this time crafting it of that dark, glimmering stone.

Stone her fire could never melt. Never pierce. The only way to escape was to become it—dissolve into it like sea-foam on a beach.

Every breath was thinner than the previous one. They had not put any holes in this coffin.

Beyond her confines, she knew a second coffin sat beside hers. Knew, because the muffled screams within still reached her here.

Two princesses, one golden and one silver. One young and one ancient. Both the cost of sealing that gate to eternity.

The air would run out soon. She'd already lost too much of it in her frantic clawing at the stone. Her fingertips pulsed where she'd broken nails and skin.

Those female screams became quieter.

She should accept it, embrace it. Only when she did would the lid open.

The air was so hot, so precious. She could not get out, could not get out—

Aelin hauled herself into waking. The room remained dark, her companions' deep breathing holding steady.

Open, fresh air. The stars just visible through the narrow window.

No Wyrdstone coffin. No gate poised to devour her whole.

But she knew they were watching, somehow. Those wretched gods. Even here, they were watching. Waiting.

A sacrifice. That's all she was to them.

Nausea churned in her gut, but Aelin ignored it, ignored the tremors rippling through her. The heat under her skin.

Aelin turned onto her side, nestling closer into Rowan's solid warmth, Elena's muffled screams still ringing in her ears.

No, she would not be helpless again.

CHAPTER 55

Being in a female form wasn't entirely what Dorian had expected.

The way he walked, the way he moved his hips and legs—strange. So disconcertingly strange. If any of the Crochans had noticed a young witch amongst them pacing in circles, crouching and stretching her legs, they didn't halt their work as they readied the camp to depart.

Then there was the matter of his breasts, which he'd never imagined to be so . . . cumbersome. Not unpleasant, but the shock of bumping his arms into them, the need to adjust his posture to accommodate their slight weight, was still fresh after a few hours.

He'd kept the transformation as simple as he could: he'd picked a young Crochan the night before, one of the novices who might not be needed at all hours or noticed very often, and studied her until she likely deemed him a letch.

This morning, the image of her face and form still planted in his mind, he'd come to the edge of the camp, and simply willed it.

Well, perhaps not simply. The shift remained not an entirely enjoyable sensation while bones adjusted, his scalp tingling with the long brown hair that grew out in shining waves, nose tickling as it was reshaped into a delicate curve.

For long minutes, he'd only stared down at himself. At the delicate hands, the smaller wrists. Amazing, how much strength the tiny bones contained. A few subtle pats between his legs had told him enough about the changes there.

And so he'd been here for the past two hours, learning how the female body moved and operated. Wholly different from learning how a raven flew—how it wrangled the wind.

He'd thought he'd known everything about the female body. How to make a woman purr with pleasure. He was half-tempted to find a tent and learn firsthand what certain things felt like.

Not an effective use of his time. Not with the camp readying for travel.

The Thirteen were on edge. They hadn't yet decided where to go. And hadn't been invited to travel with the Crochans to any of their home-hearths. Even Glennis's.

None of them, however, had looked his way when they'd prowled past. None had recognized him.

Dorian had just completed another walking circuit in his little training area when Manon stalked by, silver hair flowing. He paused, no more than a wary Crochan sentinel, and watched her storm through snow and mud as if she were a blade through the world.

Manon had nearly passed his training area when she went rigid.

Slowly, she turned, nostrils flaring.

Those golden eyes swept over him, swift and cutting.

Her brows twitched toward each other. Dorian only gave her a lazy grin in return.

Then she prowled toward him. "I'm surprised you're not groping yourself."

"Who says I haven't already?"

Another assessing stare. "I would have thought you'd pick a prettier form."

He frowned down at himself. "I think she's pretty enough."

Manon's mouth tightened. "I suppose this means you're about to go to Morath."

"Did I say anything of the sort?" He didn't bother sounding pleasant.

Manon took a step toward him, her teeth flashing. In this body, he stood shorter than her. He hated the thrill that shot through his blood as she leaned down to growl at him. "We have enough to deal with today, princeling."

"Do I look as if I'm standing in your way?"

She opened her mouth, then shut it.

Dorian let out a low laugh and made to turn away. An iron-tipped hand gripped his arm.

Strange, for that hand to feel large on his body. Large, and not the slender, deadly thing he'd become accustomed to.

Her golden eyes blazed. "If you want a softhearted woman who will weep over hard choices and ultimately balk from them, then you're in the wrong bed."

"I'm not in anyone's bed right now."

He hadn't gone to her tent any of these nights. Not since that conversation in Eyllwe.

She took the retort without so much as a flinch. "Your opinion doesn't matter to me."

"Then why are you standing here?"

Again, she opened and closed her mouth. Then snarled, "Change out of that form."

Dorian smiled again. "Don't you have better things to do right now, Your Majesty?"

He honestly thought she might unsheathe those iron teeth and rip out his throat. Half of him wanted her to try. He even went so far as to run one of those phantom hands along her jaw. "You think I don't know why you don't want me to go to Morath?"

He could have sworn she trembled. Could have sworn she arched her neck, just a little bit, leaning into that phantom touch.

Dorian ran those invisible fingers down her neck, trailing them along her collarbones.

"Tell me to stay," he said, and the words had no warmth, no kindness. "Tell me to stay with you, if that's what you want." His invisible fingers grew talons and scraped over her skin. Manon's throat bobbed. "But you won't say that, will you, Manon?" Her breathing turned jagged. He continued to stroke her neck, her jaw, her throat, caressing skin he'd tasted over and over. "Do you know why?"

When she didn't answer, Dorian let one of those phantom talons dig in, just slightly.

She swallowed, and it was not from fear.

Dorian leaned in close, tipping his head back to stare into her eyes as he purred, "Because while you might be older, might be deadly in a thousand different ways, deep down, you're afraid. You don't know *how* to ask me to stay, because you're afraid of admitting to yourself that you want it. You're afraid. Of yourself more than anyone else in the world. You're afraid."

For several heartbeats, she just stared at him.

Then she snarled, "You don't know what you're talking about," and stalked away.

His low laugh ripped after her. Her spine stiffened.

But Manon did not turn back.

Afraid. Of admitting that she felt any sort of attachment.

It was preposterous.

And it was, perhaps, true.

But it was not her problem. Not right now.

Manon stormed through the readying camp where tents were being taken down and folded, hearths being packed. The Thirteen were with the wyverns, supplies stowed in saddlebags.

Some of the Crochans had frowned her way. Not with anger, but something like disappointment. Discontent. As if they thought parting ways was a poor idea.

Manon refrained from saying she agreed. Even if the Thirteen followed, the Crochans would find a way to lose them. Use their power to bind the wyverns long enough to disappear.

And she would not lower herself, lower the Thirteen, to become dogs chasing after their masters. They might be desperate for aid, might have promised it to their allies, but she would not debase herself any further.

Manon halted at Glennis's camp, the only hearth with a fire still burning. A fire that would always remain kindled.

A reminder of the promise she'd made to honor the Queen of Terrasen. A single, solitary flame against the cold.

Manon rubbed at her face as she slumped onto one of the rocks lining the hearth.

A hand rested on her shoulder, warm and slight. She didn't bother to slap it away.

Glennis said, "We're departing in a few minutes. I thought I'd say good-bye."

Manon peered up at the ancient witch. "Fly well."

It was really all there was left to say. Manon's failure was not due to Glennis, not due to anyone but herself, she supposed.

You're afraid.

It was true. She had tried, but not really *tried* to win the Crochans. To let them see any part of her that meant something. To let them see what it had done to her, to learn she had a sister and that she had killed her. She didn't know how, and had never bothered to learn.

You're afraid.

Yes, she was. Of everything.

Glennis lowered her hand from Manon's shoulder. "May your path carry you safely through war and back home at last."

She didn't feel like telling the crone there was no home for her, or the Thirteen.

Glennis turned her face toward the sky, sighing once.

Then her white brows narrowed. Her nostrils flared.

Manon leapt to her feet.

"*Run*," Glennis breathed. "*Run now.*"

Manon drew Wind-Cleaver and did no such thing. "What is it."

"They're here." How Glennis had scented them on the wind, Manon didn't care.

Not as three wyverns broke from the clouds, spearing for their camp.

She knew those wyverns, almost as well as she knew the three riders who sent the Crochans into a frenzy of motion.

The Matrons of the Ironteeth Witch-Clans had found them. And come to finish what Manon had started that day in Morath.

CHAPTER 56

The three High Witches had come alone.

It didn't stop the Crochans from rallying, brooms swiftly airborne—a few of them trembling with what could only be recognition.

Manon's grip on Wind-Cleaver tightened at the slight tremor in her hand as the three witches landed at the edge of Glennis's fire, their wyverns crushing tents beneath them.

Asterin and Sorrel were instantly beside her, her Second's murmur swallowed by the crack of breaking tents. "The Shadows are airborne, but they signaled no sign of another unit."

"None of their covens?"

"No. And no sign of Iskra or Petrah."

Manon swallowed. The Matrons truly had come alone. Had flown in from wherever they'd been gathered, and somehow found them.

Or tracked them.

Manon didn't let the thought settle. That she may have led the three

Matrons right to this camp. The soft snarls of the Crochans around her, pointed *at* Manon, said enough of their opinion.

The wyverns settled, their long tails curling around them, those deadly poison-slick spikes ready to inflict death.

Rushing steps crunched through the icy snow, halting at Manon's side just as Dorian's scent wrapped around her. "Is that—"

"Yes," she said quietly, heart thundering as the Matrons dismounted and did not raise their hands in request for parley. No, they only stalked closer to the hearth, to the precious flame still burning. "Don't engage," Manon warned him and the others, and strode to meet them.

It was not the king's battle, no matter what power dwelled in his veins.

Glennis was already armed, an ancient sword in her withered hands. The woman was as old as the Yellowlegs Matron, yet she stood tall, facing the three High Witches.

Cresseida Blueblood spoke first, her eyes as cold as the iron-spiked crown digging into her freckled brow. "It has been an age, Glennis."

But Glennis's stare, Manon realized, was not on the Blueblood Matron. Or even on Manon's own grandmother, her black robes billowing as she sneered at Manon.

It was on the Yellowlegs Matron, hunched and hateful between them. On the crown of stars atop the crone's thinned white hair.

Glennis's sword shook slightly. And just as Manon realized what the Matron had worn here, Bronwen appeared at Glennis's side and breathed, "Rhiannon's crown."

Worn by the Yellowlegs Matron to mock these witches. To spit on them.

A dull roaring began in Manon's ears.

"What company you keep these days, granddaughter," said Manon's grandmother, her silver-streaked dark hair braided back from her face.

A sign enough of their intentions, if her grandmother's hair was in that plait.

Battle. Annihilation.

The weight of the three High Witches' attention pressed upon her. The Crochans gathered behind her shifted as they waited for her response.

Yet it was Glennis who snarled, in a voice Manon had not yet heard, "What is it that you want?"

Manon's grandmother smiled, revealing rust-flecked iron teeth. The true sign of her age. "You made a grave error, Manon Kin-Slayer, when you sought to turn our forces against us. When you sowed such lies amongst our sentinels regarding our plans—my plans."

Manon kept her chin high. "I spoke only truth. And it must have frightened you enough that you gathered these two to hunt me down and prove your innocence in scheming against them."

The other two Matrons didn't so much as blink. Her grandmother's claws had to have sunk deep, then. Or they simply did not care.

"We came," Cresseida seethed, the opposite in so many ways of the daughter who had given Manon the chance to speak, "to at last rid us of a thorn in our sides."

Had Petrah been punished for letting Manon walk out of the Omega alive? Did the Blueblood Heir still breathe? Cresseida had once screamed in a mother's terror and pain when Petrah had nearly plunged to her death. Did that love, so foreign and strange, still hold true? Or had duty and ancient hatred won out?

The thought was enough to steel Manon's spine. "You came because we pose a threat."

Because of the threat you pose to that monster you call grandmother.

"You came," Manon went on, Wind-Cleaver rising a fraction, "because you are afraid."

Manon took a step beyond Glennis, her sword lifting farther.

"You came," Manon said, "because you have no true power beyond what *we* give you. And you are scared to death that we're about to take it away." Manon flipped Wind-Cleaver in her hand, angling the sword downward, and drew a line in the snow between them. "You came alone for that fear. That others might see what we are capable of. The truth that you have always sought to hide."

Her grandmother tutted. "Listen to you. Sounding just like a Crochan with that preachy nonsense."

Manon ignored her. Ignored her and pointed Wind-Cleaver directly at the Yellowlegs Matron as she snarled, "*That is not your crown.*"

Something like hesitation rippled over Cresseida Blueblood's face. But the Yellowlegs Matron beckoned to Manon with iron nails so long they curved downward. "Then come and fetch it from me, traitor."

Manon stepped beyond the line she'd drawn in the snow.

No one spoke behind her. She wondered if any of them were breathing.

She had not won against her grandmother. Had barely survived, and only thanks to luck.

That fight, she had been ready to meet her end. To say farewell.

Manon angled Wind-Cleaver upward, her heart a steady, raging beat.

She would not greet the Darkness's embrace today.

But they would.

"This seems familiar," her grandmother drawled, legs shifting into attacking position. The other two Matrons did the same. "The last Crochan Queen. Holding the line against us."

Manon cracked her jaw, and iron teeth descended. A flex of her fingers had her iron nails unsheathing. "Not just a Crochan Queen this time."

There was doubt in Cresseida's blue eyes. As if she'd realized what the other two Matrons had not.

There—it was there that Manon would strike first. The one who now wondered if they had somehow made a grave mistake in coming here.

A mistake that would cost them what they had come to protect.

A mistake that would cost them this war.

And their lives.

For Cresseida saw the steadiness of Manon's breathing. Saw the clear conviction in her eyes. Saw the lack of fear in her heart as Manon advanced another step.

Manon smiled at the Blueblood Matron as if to say yes.

"You did not kill me then," Manon said to her grandmother. "I do not think you will be able to now."

"We'll see about that," her grandmother hissed, and charged.

Manon was ready.

An upward swing of Wind-Cleaver met her grandmother's first two blows, and Manon ducked the third. Turning right into the onslaught of the Yellowlegs Matron, who swept up with unnatural speed, feet almost flying over the snow, and slashed for Manon's exposed back.

Manon deflected the crone's assault, sending the witch darting back. Just as Cresseida launched herself at Manon.

Cresseida was not a trained fighter. Not as the Blackbeak and Yellow-legs Matrons were. Too many years spent reading entrails and scanning the stars for the answers to the Three-Faced Goddess's riddles.

A duck to the left had Manon easily evading the sweep of Cresseida's nails, and a countermove had Manon driving her elbow into the Blue-blood Matron's nose.

Cresseida stumbled. The Yellowlegs Matron and her grandmother attacked again.

So fast. Their three assaults had happened in the span of a few blinks.

Manon kept her feet under her. Saw where one Matron moved and the other left a dangerous gap exposed.

She was not a broken-spirited Wing Leader unsure of her place in the world.

She was not ashamed of the truth before her.

She was not afraid.

Manon's grandmother led the attack, her maneuvers the deadliest.

It was from her that the first slice of pain appeared. A rip of iron nails through Manon's shoulder.

But Manon swung her sword, again and again, iron on steel ringing out across the icy peaks.

No, she was not afraid at all.

Dorian had never seen fighting like what unfolded before him. Had never seen anything that fast, that lethal.

Had never seen anyone move like Manon, a whirlwind of steel and iron.

Three against one—the odds weren't in her favor. Not when standing against one of them had left Manon on death's threshold months earlier.

Yet where they struck, she was already gone. Already parrying.

She did not land many blows, but rather kept them at bay.

Yet they did not land many, either.

Dorian's magic writhed, seeking a way out, to stop this. But she had ordered him to stand down. And he'd obey.

Around him, the Crochans thrummed with fear and dread. Either for the fight unfolding or the three Matrons who had found them.

But Glennis did not tremble. At her side Bronwen hummed with the energy of one eager to leap into the fight.

Manon and the High Witches sprang apart, breathing heavily. Blue blood leaked down Manon's shoulder, and small slices peppered the three Matrons.

Manon still remained on the far side of the line she'd drawn. Still held it.

The dark-haired witch in voluminous black robes spat blue blood onto the snow. Manon's grandmother. "Pathetic. As pathetic as your mother." A sneer toward Glennis. "And your father."

The snarl that ripped from Manon's throat rang across the mountains themselves.

Her grandmother let out a crow's caw of a laugh. "Is that all you can do, then? Snarl like a dog and swing your sword like some human filth?

We will wear you down eventually. Better to kneel now and die with some honor intact."

Manon only flung out an iron-tipped hand behind her, fingers splaying in demand as her eyes remained fixed on the Matrons.

Dorian reached for Damaris, but Bronwen moved first.

The Crochan tossed her sword, steel flashing over snow and sun.

Manon's fingers closed on the hilt, the blade singing as she whipped it around to face the High Witches again. "Rhiannon Crochan held the gates for three days and three nights, and she did not kneel before you, even at the end." A slash of a smile. "I think I shall do the same."

Dorian could have sworn the sacred flame burning to their left flared brighter. Could have sworn Glennis sucked in a breath. That every Crochan watching did the same.

Manon's knees bent, swords rising. "Let us finish what was started then, too."

She attacked, blades flashing. Her grandmother conceded step after step, the other two Matrons failing to break past her defenses.

Gone was the witch who had slept and wished for death. Gone was the witch who had raged at the truth that had torn her to shreds.

And in her place, fighting as if she were the very wind, unfaltering against the Matrons, stood someone Dorian had not yet met.

Stood a queen of two peoples.

The Yellowlegs Matron launched an offensive that had Manon yielding a step, then another, swords rising against each slashing blow.

Yielding only those few steps, and nothing more.

Because Manon with conviction in her heart, with utter fearlessness in her eyes, was wholly unstoppable.

The Yellowlegs Matron pushed Manon close enough to the line that her heels nearly touched it. The other two witches had fallen back, as if waiting to see what might happen.

For a hunched crone, the Yellowlegs witch was the portrait of nightmares. Worse than Baba Yellowlegs had ever been. Her feet barely seemed to touch the ground, and her curved iron nails drew blood wherever they slashed.

Manon's swords blocked blow after blow, but she made no move to advance. To push back, though Dorian saw several chances to do so.

Manon took the slashings that left her arm and side bleeding. But she yielded no further ground. A wall against which the Yellowlegs Matron could not advance. The crone let out a snarl, attacking again and again, senseless and raging.

Dorian saw the trap the moment it happened.

Saw the side that Manon left open, the bait laid on a silver platter.

Worked into a fury, the Yellowlegs Matron didn't think twice before she lunged, claws out.

Manon was waiting.

Lost in her bloodlust, the Yellowlegs Matron's horrible face lit with triumph as she went for the easy killing blow that would rip out Manon's heart.

The Blackbeak Matron barked in warning, but Manon was already moving.

Just as those curved claws tore through leather and skin, Manon twisted to the side and brought down Wind-Cleaver upon the Yellowlegs Matron's outstretched neck.

Blue blood sprayed upon the snow.

Dorian did not look away this time at the head that tumbled to the ground. At the brown-robed body that fell with it.

The two remaining Matrons halted. None of the Crochans behind Dorian so much as spoke as Manon stared down pitilessly at the bleeding torso of the Yellowlegs Matron.

No one seemed to breathe at all as Manon plunged Bronwen's sword into the icy earth beneath and bent to take the crown of stars from the Yellowlegs witch's fallen head.

He had never seen a crown like it.

A living, glowing thing that glittered in her hand. As if nine stars had been plucked from the heavens and set to shine along the simple silver band.

The crown's light danced over Manon's face as she lifted it above her head and set it upon her unbound white hair.

Even the mountain wind stopped.

Yet a phantom breeze shifted the strands of Manon's hair as the crown glowed bright, the white stars shining with cores of cobalt and ruby and amethyst.

As if it had been asleep for a long, long time. And now awoke.

That phantom wind pulled Manon's hair to the side, silver strands brushing across her face.

And beside him, around him, the Thirteen touched two fingers to their brow in deference.

In allegiance to the queen who stared down the two remaining High Witches.

The Crochan Queen, crowned anew.

The sacred fire leaped and danced, as if in joyous welcome.

Manon scooped up Bronwen's sword, lifting it and Wind-Cleaver, and said to the Blueblood Matron, the witch appearing barely a few years older than Manon herself, "Go."

The Blueblood witch blinked, eyes wide with what could only be fear and dread.

Manon jerked her chin toward the wyvern waiting behind the witch. "Tell your daughter all debts between us are paid. And she may decide what to do with you. Take that other wyvern out of here."

Manon's grandmother bristled, iron teeth flashing as if she'd bark a counter-command to the Blueblood Matron, but the witch was already running for her wyvern.

Spared by the Crochan Queen on behalf of the daughter who had given Manon the gift of speaking to the Ironteeth.

Within seconds, the Blueblood Matron was in the skies, the Yellow-legs witch's wyvern soaring beside her.

Leaving Manon's grandmother alone. Leaving Manon with swords raised and a crown of stars glowing upon her brow.

Manon was glowing, as if the stars atop her head pulsed through her body. A wondrous and mighty beauty, like no other in the world. Like no one had ever been, or would be again.

And slowly, as if savoring each step, Manon stalked toward her grandmother.

Manon's lips curved into a small smile while she advanced on her grandmother.

Warm, dancing light flowed through her, as unfaltering as what had poured into her heart these past few bloody minutes.

She did not balk. Did not fear.

The crown's weight was slight, like it had been crafted of moonlight. Yet its joyous strength was a song, undimming before the sole High Witch left standing.

So Manon kept walking.

She left Bronwen's sword a few feet away. Left Wind-Cleaver several feet past that.

Iron nails out, teeth ready, Manon paused barely five steps from her grandmother.

A hateful, wasted scrap of existence. That's what her grandmother was.

She had never realized how much shorter the Matron stood. How narrow her shoulders were, or how the years of rage and hate had withered her.

Manon's smile grew. And she could have sworn she felt two people standing at her shoulder.

She knew no one would be there if she looked. Knew no one else could see them, sense them, standing with her. Standing with their daughter against the witch who had destroyed them.

Her grandmother spat on the ground, baring her rusted teeth.

This death, though . . .

It was not her death to claim.

It did not belong to the parents whose spirits lingered at her side, who might have been there all along, leading her toward this. Who had not left her, even with death separating them.

No, it did not belong to them, either.

She looked behind her. Toward the Second waiting beside Dorian.

Tears slid down Asterin's face. Of pride—pride and relief.

Manon beckoned to Asterin with an iron-tipped hand.

Snow crunched, and Manon whirled, angling to take the brunt of the attack.

But her grandmother had not charged. Not at her.

No, the Blackbeak Matron sprinted for her wyvern. Fleeing.

The Crochans tensed, fear giving way to wrath as her grandmother hauled herself into the saddle.

Manon raised a hand. "Let her go."

A snap of the reins, and her grandmother was airborne, the great wyvern's wings blasting them with foul wind.

Manon watched as the wyvern rose higher and higher.

Her grandmother did not look back before she vanished into the skies.

When there was no trace of the Matrons left but blue blood and a headless corpse staining the snow, Manon turned toward the Crochans.

Their eyes were wide, but they made no move.

The Thirteen remained where they were, Dorian with them.

Manon scooped up both swords, sheathing Wind-Cleaver across her back, and stalked toward where Glennis and Bronwen stood, monitoring her every breath.

Wordlessly, Manon handed Bronwen her sword, nodding in thanks.

Then she removed the crown of stars and extended it toward Glennis. "This belongs to you," she said, her voice low.

The Crochans murmured, shifting.

Glennis took the crown, and the stars dimmed. A small smile graced the crone's face. "No," she said, "it does not."

Manon didn't move as Glennis lifted the crown and set it again on Manon's head.

Then the ancient witch knelt in the snow. "What was stolen has been restored; what was lost has come home again. I hail thee, Manon Crochan, Queen of Witches."

Manon stood fast against the tremor that threatened to buckle her legs.

Stood fast as the other Crochans, Bronwen with them, dropped to a knee. Dorian, standing amongst them, smiled, brighter and freer than she'd ever seen.

And then the Thirteen knelt, two fingers going to their brows as they bowed their heads, fierce pride lighting their faces.

"Queen of Witches," Crochan and Blackbeak declared as one voice.

As one people.

CHAPTER 57

An hour before dawn, the keep and two armies beyond it were stirring.

Rowan had barely slept, and instead lain awake beside Aelin, listening to her breathing. That the rest of them slumbered soundly was testament to their exhaustion, though Lorcan had not found them again. Rowan was willing to bet it was by choice.

It was not fear or anticipation of battle that had kept Rowan up— no, he'd slept well enough during other wars. But rather the fact that his mind would not stop looping him from thought to thought to thought.

He'd seen the numbers camped outside. Valg, human men loyal to Erawan, some fell beasts, yet nothing like the ilken or the Wyrdhounds, or even the witches.

Aelin could wipe them away before the sun had fully risen. A few blasts of her power, and that army would be gone.

Yet she had not presented it as an option in their planning last night.

He'd seen the hope shining in the eyes of the people in the keep, the awe of the children as she'd passed. *The Fire-Bringer*, they'd whispered. *Aelin of the Wildfire.*

How soon would that awe and hope crumble today when not a spark of that fire was unleashed? How soon would the men's fear turn rank when the Queen of Terrasen did not wipe away Morath's legions?

He hadn't been able to ask her. Had told himself to, had roared at himself to ask these past few weeks, when even their training hadn't summoned an ember.

But he couldn't bring himself to demand why she wouldn't or couldn't use her power, why they had seen or felt nothing of it after those initial few days of freedom. Couldn't ask what Maeve and Cairn had done to possibly make her fear or hate her magic enough that she didn't touch it.

Worry and dread gnawing at him, Rowan slipped from the room, the din of preparations greeting him the moment he entered the hall. A heartbeat later, the door opened behind him, and steps fell into sync with his own, along with a familiar, wicked scent.

"They burned her."

Rowan glanced sidelong at Fenrys. "What?"

But Fenrys nodded to a passing healer. "Cairn—and Maeve, through her orders."

"Why are you telling me this?" Fenrys, blood oath or no, what he'd done for Aelin or no, was not privy to these matters. No, it was between him and his mate, and no one else.

Fenrys threw him a grin that didn't meet his eyes. "You were staring at her half the night. I could see it on your face. You're all thinking it— why doesn't she just burn the enemy to hell?"

Rowan aimed for the washing station down the hall. A few soldiers and healers stood along the metal trough, scrubbing their faces to shake the sleep or nerves.

Fenrys said, "He put her in those metal gauntlets. And one time, he heated them over an open brazier. There . . ." He stumbled for words, and Rowan could barely breathe. "It took the healers two weeks to fix what he did to her hands and wrists. And when she woke up, there was nothing but healed skin. She couldn't tell what had been done and what was a nightmare."

Rowan reached for one of the ewers that some of the children refilled every few moments and dumped it over his head. Icy water bit into his skin, drowning out the roaring in his ears.

"Cairn did many things like that." Fenrys took up a ewer himself, and splashed some into his hands before rubbing them over his face. Rowan's hands shook as he watched the water funnel toward the basin set beneath the trough. "Your claiming marks, though." Fenrys wiped his face again. "No matter what they did to her, they remained. Longer than any other scar, they stayed."

Yet her neck had been smooth when he'd found her.

Reading that thought, Fenrys said, "The last time they healed her, right before she escaped. That's when they vanished. When Maeve told her that you had gone to Terrasen."

The words hit like a blow. When she had lost hope that he was coming for her. Even the greatest healers in the world hadn't been able to take that from her until then.

Rowan wiped his face on the arm of his jacket. "Why are you telling me this?" he repeated.

Fenrys rose from the trough, drying his face with the same lack of ceremony. "So you can stop wondering what happened. Focus on something else today." The warrior kept pace beside him as they headed for where they'd been told a meager breakfast would be laid out. "And let her come to you when she's ready."

"She's my mate," Rowan growled. "You think I don't know that?" Fenrys could shove his snout into someone else's business.

Fenrys held up his hands. "You can be brutal, when you want something."

"I'd never force her to tell me anything she wasn't ready to say." It had been their bargain from the start. Part of why he'd fallen in love with her.

He should have known then, during those days in Mistward, when he found himself sharing parts of himself, his history, that he'd never told anyone. When he found himself *needing* to tell her, in fragments and pieces, yes, but he'd wanted her to know. And Aelin had wanted to hear it. All of it.

They discovered Aelin and Elide already at the buffet table, grim-faced as they plucked up pieces of bread and cheese and dried fruit. No sign of Gavriel or Lorcan.

Rowan came up behind his mate and pressed a kiss to her neck. Right to where his new claiming marks lay.

She hummed, and offered him a bite of the bread she'd already dug into while gathering the rest of her food. He obliged, the bread thick and hearty, then said, "You were asleep when I left a few minutes ago, yet you somehow beat me to the breakfast table." Another kiss to her neck. "Why am I not surprised?"

Elide laughed beside Aelin, piling food onto her own plate. Aelin only elbowed him as he fell into line beside her.

The four of them ate quickly, refilled their waterskins at the fountain in an interior courtyard, and set about finding armor. There was little on the upper levels that was fit for wearing, so they descended into the keep, deeper and deeper, until they came across a locked room.

"Should we, or is it rude?" Aelin mused, peering at the wooden door.

Rowan sent a spear of his wind aiming for the lock and splintered it apart. "Looks like it was already open when we got here," he said mildly.

Aelin gave him a wicked grin, and Fenrys pulled a torch off its bracket in the narrow stone hallway to illuminate the room beyond.

"Well, now we know why the rest of the keep is a piece of shit," Aelin said, surveying the trove. "He's kept all the gold and fun things down here."

Indeed, his mate's idea of fun things was the same as Rowan's: armor and swords, spears and ancient maces.

"He couldn't have distributed this?" Elide frowned at the racks of swords and daggers.

"It's all heirlooms," said Fenrys, approaching one such rack and studying the hilt of a sword. "Ancient, but still good. Really good," he added, pulling a blade from its sheath. He glanced at Rowan. "This was forged by an Asterion blacksmith."

"From a different age," Rowan mused, marveling at the flawless blade, its impeccable condition. "When Fae were not so feared."

"Are we just going to take it? Without even Chaol's permission?" Elide chewed on her lip.

Aelin snickered. "Let's consider ourselves swords-for-hire. And as such, we have fees that need to be paid." She hefted a round, golden shield, its edges beautifully engraved with a motif of waves. Also Asterion-made, judging by the craftsmanship. Likely for the Lord of Anielle—the Lord of the Silver Lake. "So, we'll take what we're owed for today's battle, and spare His Lordship the task of having to come down here himself."

Gods, he loved her.

Fenrys winked at Elide. "I won't tell if you don't, Lady."

Elide blushed, then waved them onward. "Collect your earnings, then."

Rowan did. He and Fenrys found armor that could fit them—in certain areas. They had to forgo the entire suit, but took pieces to enforce their shoulders, forearms, and shins. Rowan had just finished strapping greaves on his legs when Fenrys said, "We should bring some of this up for Lorcan and Gavriel."

Indeed they should. Rowan eyed other pieces, and began collecting extra daggers and blades, then sections from another suit that might fit Lorcan, Fenrys doing the same for Gavriel.

"You must charge a great deal for your services," Elide muttered. Even while the Lady of Perranth tied a few daggers to her own belt.

"I need some way to pay for my expensive tastes, don't I?" Aelin drawled, weighing a dagger in her hands.

But she hadn't donned any armor yet, and when Rowan gave her an inquiring glance, Aelin jerked her chin toward him. "Head upstairs— track down Lorcan and Gavriel. I'll find you soon."

Her face was unreadable for once. Perhaps she wanted a moment alone before battle. And when Rowan tried to find any words in her eyes, Aelin turned toward the shield she'd claimed. As if contemplating it.

So Rowan and Fenrys headed upstairs, Elide helping to haul their stolen gear. No one stopped them. Not with the sky turning to gray, and soldiers rushing to their positions on the battlements.

Rowan and Fenrys didn't have far to go. They'd be stationed by the gates at the lower level, where the battering rams might come flying through if Morath got desperate enough.

On the level above them, Chaol sat astride his magnificent black horse, the mare's breath curling from her nostrils. Rowan lifted a hand in greeting, and Chaol saluted back before gazing toward the enemy army.

The khaganate would make the first maneuver, the initial push to get Morath moving.

"I always forget how much I hate this part," Fenrys muttered. "The waiting before it begins."

Rowan grunted his agreement.

Gavriel prowled up to them, Lorcan a dark storm behind him. Rowan wordlessly handed the latter the armor he'd gathered. "Courtesy of the Lord of Anielle."

Lorcan gave him a look that said he knew Rowan was full of shit, but began efficiently donning the armor, Gavriel doing the same. Whether the soldiers around them marked that armor, whether Chaol recognized it, no one said a word.

Far out, the gray sky lightening further, Morath stirred to discover the khaganate's golden army already in place.

And as a lone ruk screeched its challenge, the khaganate advanced.

Foot soldiers in perfect lines marched, spears out, shields locked rim to rim. The Darghan cavalry flanked either side, a force of nature ready to herd Morath to where they wanted them. And above, flapping into the skies, the rukhin readied their bows and marked their targets.

"Ready now," Chaol called out to the men of his keep.

Armor clanked as men shifted, their fear stuffing itself up Rowan's nose.

This would be it—today. Whether that hope remained or fractured.

Already, the awakening sky revealed two siege towers being hauled toward them. Right to the wall. Far closer than Rowan had last noted when flying overhead last night. Morath, it seemed, had not been sleeping, either.

The ruks would remain back with their own army, driving Morath to the keep. To be picked off here, one by one.

"We have minutes until that first tower makes contact with the wall," Gavriel observed.

A scan of the battlements, the soldiers atop them, revealed no sign of Aelin.

Lorcan indeed muttered, "Someone better tell her to stop primping and get here."

Rowan snarled in warning.

The clash of armored feet and shields was as familiar as any song. Morath's foot soldiers aimed for the keep walls, spears at the ready. At the other end of the host, soldiers faced away, spears and pikes angled to intercept the khaganate's army.

A horn blasted from deep in the khaganate ranks, and arrows flew.

The mass of Morath soldiers didn't so much as flinch or look behind to see what became of their rear lines.

"Ladders," Fenrys murmured, pointing with his chin toward the ripple through the lines. Massive siege ladders of iron parted the crowd.

"They're making this their all-out assault, then," Lorcan said with equal quiet. All of them careful not to let the nearby men hear. "They'll try to break into the keep before the khaganate can break them."

"Archers!" Chaol's bellow rang out. Behind them, down the battlements, bows groaned.

Fenrys unslung the bow across his back and nocked an arrow into place.

Rowan kept his own bow strapped across his back, the quiver untouched, Gavriel and Lorcan doing the same. No need to waste them on a few soldiers when their aim might be needed with far worse targets later in the day.

But one of them had to be noted felling soldiers. For whatever it would do to rally their spirits. And Fenrys, as fine an archer as Rowan, he'd admit, would do just fine.

Rowan followed the line of Fenrys's arrowhead to where he'd marked one of the bearers of a siege ladder. "Make it impressive," he muttered.

"Mind your own business," Fenrys muttered back, tracking his target with the tip of his arrow as he awaited Chaol's order.

If Aelin didn't arrive within another moment, he'd have to leave the battlements to find her. What in hell had held her up?

Lorcan drew his ancient blade, which Rowan had witnessed felling soldiers in kingdoms far from here, in wars far longer than this one. "They'll head for the gates when that siege tower docks," Lorcan said, glancing from the battlements to the gate a level below, the small bastion of men in front of it. Trees had been felled to prop up the metal doors, but should a solid enough group of enemy soldiers swarm it, they might get those supports and the heavy locks down within minutes. And open the gates to the hordes beyond.

"We don't let them get that far," Rowan said, eyeing up the massive tower lumbering closer. Soldiers teemed behind it, waiting to scale its interior. "Chaol brought the tower down the other day without our help. It can happen again."

"*Volley!*" Chaol's roar echoed off the stones, and arrows sang.

Like a swarm of locusts, they swept upon the soldiers marching below. Fenrys's arrow found its mark with lethal precision.

Within a heartbeat, another was on its tail. A second soldier at the siege ladder fell.

Where the *hell* was Aelin—

Morath didn't halt. Marched right over the soldiers who fell on their front lines.

The pulse of human fear down the battlements rippled against his skin. The cadre would have to strike fast, and strike well, to shake it away.

The siege tower lumbered closer. One glance from Rowan had him and his friends moving toward the spot it would now undeniably strike upon the battlements. Close enough to the stairs down to the gate. Morath had chosen the location well.

Some of the soldiers they passed were praying, a shuddering push of words into the frigid morning air.

Lorcan said to one of them, "Save your breath for the battle, not the gods."

Rowan shot him a look, but the man, gaping at Lorcan, quieted.

Chaol ordered another volley, and arrows flew, Fenrys firing as he walked. As if he were barely bothered.

Still, the whispered prayers continued down the line, swords shaking along with them.

Up by Chaol, the soldiers held firm, faces solid.

But here, on this level of the battlements . . . those faces were pale. Wide-eyed.

"Someone better say something inspiring," Fenrys said through gritted teeth, firing another arrow. "Or these men are going to piss themselves in a minute."

For a minute was all they had left, as the first siege tower inched closer.

"You've got the pretty face," Lorcan retorted. "You'd do a better job of it."

"It's too late for speeches," Rowan cut in before Fenrys could reply. "Better to show them what we can do."

They positioned themselves on the wall. Right in the path of the bridge that would snap down over the battlement.

He drew his sword, then thumbed free the hatchet at his side. Gavriel unsheathed twin blades from across his back, falling into flanking position at Rowan's right. Lorcan planted himself on his left. Fenrys took the rear, to catch any who got through their net.

The mortal men clustered behind them. The gates shuddered under the impact of Morath at last.

Rowan steadied his breathing, readying his magic to rip through Valg lungs. He'd fell a few with his blades first. To show how easily it could be done, that Morath was desperate and victory *would* be near. The magic would come later.

The siege tower groaned as it slowed to a stop.

Just as the wall under them shuddered at its impact, Fenrys whispered, "Holy gods."

Not at the bridge that snapped down, soldiers teeming in the dark depths inside.

But at who emerged from the keep archway behind them. What emerged.

Rowan didn't know where to look. At the soldiers pouring out of the siege tower, leaping onto the battlements, or at Aelin.

At the Queen of Terrasen.

She'd found armor below the keep. Beautiful, pale gold armor that gleamed like a summer dawn. Holding back her braided hair, a diadem lay flush against her head. Not a diadem, but a piece of armor. Part of some ancient set for a lady long since buried.

A crown for war, a crown to wear into battle. A crown to lead armies.

There was no fear on her face, no doubt, as Aelin hefted her shield, flipping Goldryn in her hand once before the first of Morath's soldiers was upon her.

A swift, upward strike cleaved the Morath grunt from navel to chin. His black blood sprayed, but she was already moving, flowing like a stream around a rock.

Rowan launched into movement, his blades finding their marks, but still he watched her.

Aelin slammed her shield against an oncoming warrior, Goldryn slicing through another before she plunged the blade into the soldier she'd deflected.

She did it again, and again.

All while heading toward that siege tower. Unhindered. *Unleashed*.

A call went down the line. *The queen has come*.

Soldiers waiting their turn whirled toward them.

Aelin took on three Valg soldiers and left them dying on the stones.

She planted her line before the gaping maw of that siege tower, right in the path of those teeming hordes. Every moment of the training she'd done on the ship here, on the road, every new blister and callus—all to rebuild herself for this.

The queen has come.

Goldryn unfaltering, her shield an extension of her arm, Aelin glowed like the sun that now broke over the khagan's army as she engaged each soldier that hurtled her way.

Five, ten—she moved and moved and moved, ducking and swiping, shoving and flipping, black blood spraying, her face the portrait of grim, unbreaking will.

"*The queen!*" the men shouted. "*To the queen!*"

And as Rowan fought his way closer, as that cry went down the battlements and Anielle men ran to aid her, he realized that Aelin did not need an ounce of flame to inspire men to follow. That she had been waiting, yanking at the bit, to show them what she, without magic, without any godly power, might do.

He'd never seen such a glorious sight. In every land, every battle, he had never seen anything as glorious as Aelin before the throat of the siege tower, holding the line.

Dawn breaking around them, Rowan loosed a battle cry and tore into Morath.

⌢

This first battle would set the tone.

It would set the tone, and send a message. Not to Morath.

Impress us, Hasar had said.

So she would. So she'd picked the golden armor and her battle-crown. And waited until dawn, until that siege tower slammed into the battlements, before unleashing herself.

To keep the men here from breaking, to wipe away the fear festering in their eyes.

To convince the khaganate royals of what she might do, what she *could* do. Not a threat, but a reminder.

She was no helpless princess. She had never been.

Goldryn sang with each swipe, her mind as cool and sharp as the blade while she assessed each enemy soldier, their weapons, and took them down accordingly. She dimly knew that Rowan fought at her side, Gavriel and Fenrys battling near her left flank.

But she was keenly aware of the mortal men who leaped into the fray with cries of defiance. They'd made it this far. They would survive today, too. And the khaganate royals would know it.

Galloping hooves drowned out the battle, and then Chaol was there, sword flashing, driving into the unending tide that rushed from the tower's entrance.

"To Lord Chaol! To the queen!"

How far they both were from Rifthold. From the assassin and the captain.

Arrows rose from the army beyond the wall, but a wave of icy wind snapped them into splinters before they could find any marks.

A dark blur plunged past, and then Lorcan was at the siege tower's mouth, his sword swinging so fast Aelin could barely follow it. He battled his way across the metal bridge of the tower, into the stairwell beyond. Like he'd fight his way down the ramps and onto the battlefield itself.

Below, a *boom* began. Morath had brought in their battering ram.

Aelin smiled grimly. She'd bring them all down. Then Erawan. And then she'd unleash herself upon Maeve.

At the opposite end of the field, the khagan's army pushed, gaining the field step by step.

Not helpless. Not contained. Never again.

Death became a melody in her blood, every movement a dance as the tide of soldiers pouring from the tower slowed. As if Lorcan was indeed forcing his way down the interior. Those who got past him met her blade, or Rowan's. A flash of gold, and Gavriel had slaughtered his way into the siege tower as well, twin blades a whirlwind.

What Lorcan and the Lion would do upon reaching the bottom, how they'd dislodge the tower, she didn't know. Didn't think about it.

Not from this place of killing and movement, of breath and blood. Of freedom.

Death had been her curse and her gift and her friend for these long, long years. She was happy to greet it again under the golden morning sun.

CHAPTER 58

Elide wasn't even on the battlements, and she already wished to never endure another war again.

The soldiers who were hauled in, their injuries . . . She didn't know how the healers were so calm. How Yrene Westfall worked so steadily while a man was screaming, screaming, screaming as his internal organs poked through the gash in his belly.

The keep shook every now and then, and Elide hated herself for being glad she didn't know what it meant. Even as it ate away at her not knowing how her companions fared. If the khagan's army was close enough so that this nightmare could end soon.

It would be hours yet, the dark-skinned, sharp-eyed healer named Eretia had claimed when Elide had vomited upon seeing a man whose shinbone stuck clean through his leg. Hours yet until it was over, the terse healer had chided, so she'd better finish heaving and get back to work.

Not that there was much Elide could do. Despite the generous gift of power that ran through the Lochan bloodline, she possessed no magic, no gifts beyond reading people and lying. But she helped the healers pin down thrashing men. Rushed to get bandages, hot water, and whatever salves or herbs the healers calmly requested.

None of them shouted. They only raised their voices, magic glowing bright around them, if a soldier was shrieking too loudly for their words to be heard.

The sun was barely over the horizon, judging by the light at the windows set high in the Great Hall, and so many already lay injured. So many.

Still they kept coming, and Elide kept moving, her limp becoming a dull, then a sharp ache. A minor pain, compared to what the soldiers endured. Compared to what they faced on the battlements.

She didn't let herself think of her friends. Didn't let herself think of Lorcan, who had not come to the chamber last night and had not sought them out this morning. As if he didn't want to be near her. As if he'd taken every hateful word she'd spoken to heart.

So Elide aided the clear-eyed healers, held down screaming, pleading men, and did not stop.

Farasha did not balk from the Morath soldiers who made it onto the battlements. From the ones who emerged from the second siege tower that docked down the wall, or those who made it up the ladders.

No, that magnificent horse trampled them, fearless and wicked, just as Chaol had predicted. A horse whose name meant *butterfly*—stomping all over Valg foot soldiers.

Had his breath not been a rasp in his chest, Chaol might have smiled. Had men not been cut down around him, he might have laughed a bit, too.

But Morath was launching itself at the walls and gates with a furor they had not yet witnessed. Perhaps they knew who had come to Anielle and now hewed them down. Aelin and Rowan fought back-to-back, and Fenrys had plowed his way down the battlements to join Chaol by the second siege tower.

Chaol's sword arm didn't falter, despite the exhaustion that began to creep up as an hour, then two passed. Far across the sea of enemy soldiers, the rukhin and Darghan armies herded and smashed Morath between their forces, driving them toward the keep walls.

Morath, it seemed, did not think to surrender. Only to inflict destruction, to break into the keep and slaughter as many as they could before meeting their end.

His shield bloodied and dented, his horse a raging demon herself beneath him, Chaol kept swinging his sword. His wife lay within the keep behind him. He would not fail her.

Nesryn ran out of arrows too soon.

Morath did not flee, even with the might of the Darghan riders and the foot soldiers upon them. So they slowly advanced, leaving bodies clad in black as well as gold armor in their wake. More Morath soldiers than their own, but it was hard—near-unbearable—to see so many go down. To see the beautiful horses of the Darghan riderless. Or felled themselves.

The rukhin took losses, but not as many. Not now that an army fought beneath them.

Sartaq led the center, and from where Nesryn commanded the left flank, she kept an eye on him and Kadara. An eye on Borte and Yeran, leading the right flank to the far western side of the battle, Falkan Ennar in ruk form with them. Perhaps she imagined it, but Nesryn could have sworn the shifter fought with renewed vigor. As if the years returned to him aided his strength.

Nesryn nudged Salkhi, and they dove again, the riders behind her following suit. Arrows and spears rose to meet them, some Morath soldiers fleeing. Nesryn and Salkhi rose back into the air coated in more black blood.

High overhead, twin rukhin scout patrols monitored the battle. As

Nesryn wiped the black blood from her face, one rider dove—right for Sartaq.

Sartaq was soaring away a heartbeat later.

Nesryn knew he'd kick her ass for it, but she shouted to the rukhin captain behind her to hold formation, and steered Salkhi after the prince.

"*Get back in line,*" Sartaq ordered over the wind, his skin unusually ashen.

"What's wrong?" she called. Salkhi flapped harder, falling into line with the prince's ruk.

Sartaq pointed ahead. To the wall of mountains just beyond the lake and city.

To the dam that he'd so casually mentioned breaking to wipe away Morath's army.

With each flap of Salkhi's wings, it became clearer. What had sent him into a mad dash.

A group of Morath soldiers had taken the night not to rest, but to sneak through the abandoned city. To scale the foothills, then the mountain wall. To the dam itself.

Where they now, with battering rams and wicked cunning, sought to unleash it.

Salkhi swept closer. Nesryn reached for an arrow. Her fingers curled around air.

Sartaq, however, had two arrows left, and fired both upon the thirty or so Morath soldiers heaving a mammoth battering ram into the center of the dam. Wood, and stone, and iron, ancient and foreboding. A few cracks, and it would come down.

And then the upper lake and river penned up behind it would rage across the plain.

Morath did not care if its own forces were washed away. They would lose today anyway.

They would not allow the khagan's army to walk off the plain, either.

Both of Sartaq's arrows found their marks, but the two soldiers who went down did not cause the others to drop the battering ram. Again, they heaved the ram back—and swung it forward.

The *boom* of wood on wood echoed up to them.

They soared near enough that the iron enforcements at the tip of the battering ram became clear. Thick iron casing, capped with spikes meant to shred and pierce. If Salkhi and Kadara could reach it, they could rip the ram from their hands—

Metal groaned and clanked, and Sartaq's warning cry shattered across the air.

Salkhi banked on instinct, spying the massive iron bolt before Nesryn did. A bolt fired from a heavy-looking device they must have rolled up here. To keep ruks away.

The bolt went wide, slamming through the mountain rock.

It would have pierced Salkhi's chest, straight into his heart.

Stomach churning, Nesryn soared up again, assessing the soldiers below.

Sartaq signaled from nearby, *Weave in through two different directions. Meet in the center.*

The winds screamed in her ears, but Nesryn tugged on the reins, and Salkhi banked in a wide arc. Sartaq turned Kadara, the mirror image to Nesryn's maneuver.

"Fast as you can, Salkhi!" Nesryn shouted to her ruk.

Gaining on the dam, on the soldiers, Salkhi and Kadara soared toward each other, crossed paths, and arced outward again. Weaving fast as the wind itself. Denying the archers an easy target.

An iron bolt fired for Sartaq and ripped through air above him, nearly grazing his head.

The battering ram slammed into the wood again.

A splintering crack sounded this time. A deep groan, like some terrible beast awakening from a long slumber.

Another iron bolt shot for them and missed. Nesryn and Sartaq wove past each other, flying so fast her eyes streamed. The wind sang, full of the voices of the dying and injured.

And then they were there, Salkhi's talons outstretched as he slammed into the iron machine that had launched those bolts, ripping it apart. Soldiers screamed as the ruk fell upon them, too.

Those at the battering ram got in another thundering *boom* against the dam before Sartaq and Kadara slashed into them. Men went flying, some hitting the dam. Some landing in pieces.

Kadara hurled the battering ram onto the nearby mountain face, wood splintering with the impact. It rolled away into the rocks and vanished.

Heart thundering, the battle on the plain below still raging, Nesryn wheeled Salkhi around and took stock of the dam wall, Sartaq doing the same beside her.

. What they saw made them soar back to the keep as swiftly as the winds could carry them.

Lorcan had battled his way down the first siege tower's dim, cramped interior, slaughtering the soldiers in his path. Gavriel followed behind him, soon catching up as Lorcan found himself holding the entrance to the tower against the countless soldiers trying to get in.

The two of them stemmed the tide, even as a few of the Morath grunts got past their swords. Whitethorn and the queen would be waiting to pick them off.

Lorcan lost track of how long he and Gavriel held the entrance to the siege tower—how long it took until their forces were able to dislodge it.

Their magic would be useless. The entire damn thing was built of iron. The ladders, too. As if Morath had anticipated their presence.

Only the groaning of collapsing metal warned them the tower was coming down, and sent them racing onto the battlefield.

Where they'd found themselves outside the gates. Fenrys and Lord Chaol had appeared at the battlement walls with archers, and fired at the soldiers who'd rushed for Lorcan and Gavriel.

But he and the Lion had already marked their next target: the battering ram still slamming into those ever-weakening gates. And with the archers covering from above, they'd begun slaughtering their way to it. And then slaughtering their way along the ram itself, until it thudded to the ground, then was forgotten in the wave of Morath soldiers who came for them.

Lorcan's breath had been a steady beat, a grounding force as the bodies piled around them.

They need only hold the gate long enough for the khagan's army to overrun the Morath host.

From above, a swift, brutal wind added to the dance of death, ripping the air from the lungs of soldiers charging at them, even as he knew Whitethorn kept fighting on the battlements.

Lorcan again lost track of time. Only vaguely knew the sun was arcing across the sky.

But the khagan's army was gaining the field, inch by inch.

Enough so that the ruks wrenched the siege ladders from the keep walls. Enough so that Lord Chaol shouted down to him and Gavriel to scale a siege ladder and *get the hell back up here.*

Gavriel obeyed, spotting the iron ladder cleared of Morath soldiers, being held in place only long enough for them to climb back up to the battlements.

But the khagan's forces were near. And a nudge at Lorcan's shoulder told him not to run, but to fight.

So Lorcan listened. He didn't bother to shout to Gavriel, now half up the ladder, before he plunged into the fray.

He'd been bred for battle. Regardless of what queen he served, whether she was Fae or Valg or human, *this* was what he had been trained to do. What some part of him sang to do.

Lorcan plowed his own path toward the advancing khagan lines, some Morath soldiers fleeing in his wake. Some falling before he reached them, his magic snapping their lives away.

Soon now. They'd win the field soon, and the song in his blood would quiet.

Part of him didn't want it to end, even as his body began to scream to rest.

Yet when the battle was done, what would remain?

Nothing. Elide had made that clear enough. She loved him, but she hated herself for it.

He hadn't deserved her anyway.

She deserved a life of peace, of happiness. He didn't know such things. Had thought he'd glimpsed them during the months they'd traveled together, before everything went to hell, but now he knew he was not meant for anything like it.

But this battlefield, this death-song around him . . . This, he could do. This, he could savor.

The golden helmets of the khagan's army became clear, their fiery horses unfaltering. Finer than any host he'd fought beside in a mortal kingdom. In many immortal kingdoms, too.

Obeying the death-song in his blood, Lorcan let his shields drop. He did not wish it to be easy. He wanted to *feel* each blow, see his enemy's life drain out beneath his sword.

He didn't care what came of it. No one would care if he made it back to the keep anyway. He didn't balk as he engaged the ten soldiers who charged for him.

Perhaps he deserved what happened next. Deserved it for his pathetic thoughts, or his arrogance in lowering his shields.

One moment, he was handily sending the Morath grunts back to their dark maker. One moment, he was grinning, even as he tasted their vile blood spraying the air.

A flash of metal at his back. Lorcan whirled, sword rising, but too late.

The Valg soldier's blade swept upward. Lorcan arched, bellowing as flesh tore along his spine. No armor—there had been no armor to fit them across their torsos.

The Morath soldier moved again, more adept than the others. Perhaps the man he'd infested had some skill on the battlefield, something the demon wielded to its advantage.

Lorcan could barely lift his sword before the soldier plunged his own into Lorcan's gut.

Lorcan fell, sword clattering. Icy mud sucked at his face, as if it would swallow him whole. Pull him down into the dark depths of Hellas's realm, where he deserved to be.

The earth shook beneath thundering hooves, and arrows screamed overhead.

Then there was roaring. And then blackness.

CHAPTER 59

The khagan's army took no prisoners.

A few of Morath's soldiers tried to escape into the city. Standing beside Aelin on the keep battlements, Rowan watched the ruks pick them off with lethal efficiency.

His ears still rang with the din of battle, his breath a rasping beat echoed by Aelin. Already, the small wounds on him had begun to heal, a tingling itch beneath his stained clothes. The gash he'd taken to his leg, however, would need longer.

Across the plain, stretching toward the horizon, the khagan's army made sure their kills stayed down. Swords and spears flashed in the afternoon light as they rose and fell, severing heads. Rowan had always remembered the chaos and rush of battle, but this—the dazed, weary aftermath—this, he'd forgotten.

Healers already made their way over the battlefield, their white banners stark against the sea of black and gold. Those who needed more intensive help were carried off by ruks and brought right to the chaos of the Great Hall.

Atop the blood-slick battlements, their allies and companions around them, Rowan wordlessly passed Aelin the waterskin. She drank deeply, then handed it to Fenrys.

An unleashing and release. That's what the battle had been for his mate.

"Minimal losses," Princess Hasar was saying, a hand braced on a small section of the battlement wall that was not coated in black or red gore. "The foot soldiers got hit hardest; the Darghan remain mostly intact."

Rowan nodded. Impressive—more than impressive. The khagan's army had been a beautifully coordinated force, moving across the plain as if they were farmers reaping wheat. Had he not been swept into the dance of battle, he might have stopped to marvel at them.

The princess turned to Chaol, seated in a wheeled chair, his face grim. "On your end?"

Chaol glanced to his father, who observed the battlefield with crossed arms. His father said without looking at them, "Many. We'll leave it at that."

Pain seemed to flicker in the bastard's eyes, but he said nothing more.

Chaol gave Hasar an apologetic frown, his hands tightening on the chair's arms. The soldiers of Anielle, however bravely they'd fought, were not a trained unit. Many of those who had survived were seasoned warriors who'd fought the wild men up in the Fangs, Chaol had told Rowan earlier. Most of the dead had not.

Hasar at last looked Aelin over. "I heard you put on a show today."

Rowan braced himself.

Aelin turned from the battlefield and inclined her head. "You look as if you did, too."

Indeed, Hasar's ornate armor was splattered with black blood. She'd been in the thick of it, atop her Muniqi horse, and had ridden right up to the gates. But the princess made no further comment.

Irritation, deep and nearly hidden, flashed in Aelin's eyes. Yet she didn't speak again—didn't push the princess about their next steps. She just watched the battlefield once more, chewing on her lip.

She'd barely stopped during the battle, halting only when there had been no more Valg left to kill. And in the minutes since the walls had been cleared, she'd remained quiet—distant. As if she was still climbing out of that calm, calculating place she'd descended into while fighting. She hadn't bothered to remove any of her armor. The bronze battle-crown was caked with blood, her hair matted with it.

Chaol's father had taken one look at her armor, at Rowan's, and gone white with rage. Yet Chaol had merely wheeled his chair to his father's side, snarling something too soft for Rowan to hear, and the man backed off.

For now. They had bigger things to consider. Things that drove his mate to gnaw on her lip. When Prince Kashin's army might arrive, if they would indeed head northward to Terrasen. If today had been enough to win them over.

Two shapes took form in the sky. Kadara and Salkhi, soaring for the keep at an almost unchecked speed.

People scrambled out of the ruks' way as Sartaq and Nesryn landed on the battlements, sliding off their saddles and stalking right up to them.

"We have a problem," Nesryn said, her face ashen.

Indeed, Sartaq's lips were bloodless. Both of their scents were drenched in fear.

The wheels of Chaol's chair splashed through puddled blood. "What is it?"

Aelin straightened, Gavriel and Fenrys going still.

Nesryn pointed across the city, to the wall of mountains. "We intercepted a group of Morath soldiers toward the end of the battle—trying to bring that dam down."

Rowan swore, and Chaol echoed it.

"I'm assuming they didn't succeed thanks to you," Aelin said, gazing toward that too-near dam, the raging waters of the upper lake and river it held at bay.

"Partially," Sartaq said, a muscle feathering in his jaw. "But we arrived after much damage had already been done."

"Out with it," Hasar hissed.

Sartaq's dark eyes flashed. "We need to evacuate our army off the plain. Right now."

"It's going to break?" Chaol's father demanded.

Nesryn winced. "It likely will."

"It could burst at any moment." Sartaq gestured to the khagan's army on the plain. "We need to get them out."

"There's nowhere for them to go," Chaol's father said. "The water will roar for miles, and this keep cannot hold all your forces."

Indeed, Rowan realized, the keep, despite its high position, couldn't fit the size of the army on the plain. Not even close. And the keep, towering high above, would be the only thing that could withstand the tidal wave of freezing water that would sweep from the mountains and across the plain. Obliterating everything in its path.

Hasar fixed her burning stare on Chaol. "Where do we tell them to run?"

"Summon the ruks," Chaol said. "Have them gather up as many as they can, fly them out to this peak behind us." He motioned to the small mountain into which the keep had been built. "Put them on the rocks, put them anywhere."

"And those that don't make it to the ruks?" the princess pressed, something like panic cracking through her fierce face.

Rowan's own heart thundered. They had won the battle, only for the enemy to get the final say in their victory.

Morath would not allow the khagan's army to walk off the plain.

It would destroy this army, this shred of hope, in a simple, brutal blow.

"Was it a trap all along?" Chaol rubbed at his jaw. "Erawan knew I was bringing an army. Did he pick Anielle *for* this? Knowing I'd come, and he'd use the dam to wipe our host away?"

"Think on it later," Aelin warned, her face as grave as Rowan's. She scanned the plain. "Tell them to run. If they cannot get a ruk, then *run*. If they make it to Oakwald's edge, they might stand a chance if they can climb into a tree."

His mate didn't mention that with a wave that size, those trees would be submerged. Or ripped from their roots.

Gavriel asked, "There's no way to fix the damage done?"

"We checked," Sartaq said, throat bobbing. "Morath knew where to strike."

"What of your magic?" Fenrys asked Rowan. "Could you freeze it—the river?"

He'd already thought of it. Rowan shook his head. "It's too deep and its current too strong." Perhaps if he had all his cousins, but Enda and Sellene were up north, their siblings and kin with them.

"Open the keep gates," Chaol said quietly. "Any nearby are to run here. Those farthest out will have to flee for the forest."

Rowan met Aelin's stare.

Her hands began shaking.

This cannot end here, she seemed to say. Panic—panic indeed flared in her eyes. Rowan gripped her trembling hand and squeezed.

But there was no truth or lie that might soothe her.

No truth or lie to save the army on the plain.

∽

Elide found her companions and their allies not in a council room, but gathered on the battlements. As if bodies and gore didn't lie around them.

She cringed at each step through blood both black and red, trying not to meet the sightless eyes of fallen soldiers. She'd been sent by Yrene to see how Chaol fared—a panting, fearful question from a wife who had not heard anything of his fate since the battle began.

After hours helping the healers, Elide had been desperate to escape the room that reeked of blood and refuse. Yet any relief at the fresh air, at the ended battle, had been short-lived when she saw the bloody battlements. When she noted her companions' pale faces, their tense words. All of them were gazing between the mountains and the battlefield.

Something had gone wrong. Something *was* wrong.

The battlefield stretched into the distance, healers darting amongst the felled bodies with white banners high to indicate their locations. So many. So many dead and wounded. A sea of them.

Elide reached Chaol's side just as Nesryn Faliq leaped atop her beautiful ruk, launching into a dive for the army below. No—the other ruks.

Elide laid a hand on Lord Chaol's shoulder, drawing his attention from where he watched Nesryn fly off. Blood-splattered, but his bronze eyes were clear.

And full of terror.

Any message that Yrene had given Elide faded from her memory. "What's wrong?"

It was Aelin who answered, her bloodied armor strange and ancient. A vision of old. "The dam is going to break," the queen said hoarsely. "And wipe away anyone on the plain."

Oh gods. Oh gods.

Elide glanced between them, and knew the answer to her next question: *What can be done?*

Nothing.

Ruks took to the skies, flapping toward them, soldiers in their talons and clinging to their backs.

"Has anyone warned the healers?" Elide pointed to the white banners waving so far out into the plain. "The Healer on High?" Hafiza was down there, Yrene had said.

Silence. Then Prince Sartaq swore in his own tongue, and sprinted for his golden ruk. He was spearing for the battlefield within seconds, his shouts ringing out. Kadara dipped every few moments, and when she rose again, another small figure was in her talons. Healers. Grabbing as many of them as he could.

Elide whirled to her companions as soldiers began running for the keep, trampling corpse and injured alike. Orders went out in the language of the southern continent, and more soldiers on the battlefield leaped into action.

"What else—what else can we do?" Elide demanded. Aelin and Rowan only stared toward the battlefield, watching with Fenrys and Gavriel as the ruks raced to save as many as they could. Behind them, Princess Hasar paced, and Chaol and his father murmured about where they might fit everyone in the keep. Those who survived.

Elide looked at them again. Looked at all of them.

And then asked quietly, "Where is Lorcan?"

None of them turned.

Elide asked, louder, "Where is Lorcan?"

Gavriel's tawny eyes scanned hers, confusion dancing there. "He . . . he went out onto the battlefield during the fighting. I saw him just before the khagan's troops reached him."

"Where *is* he?" Elide's voice broke. Fenrys faced her now. Then Rowan and Aelin. Elide begged, voice breaking, "*Where is Lorcan?*"

From their stunned silence, she knew they hadn't so much as wondered.

Elide whirled to the battlefield. To that endless stretch of fallen bodies. Soldiers fleeing. Many of the wounded being abandoned where they lay.

So many bodies. So, so many soldiers down there.

"Where." No one answered. Elide pointed toward the battlefield and snarled at Gavriel, "*Where* did you see him join with the khagan's forces?"

"Nearly on the other side of the field," Gavriel answered, voice strained, and pointed across the plain. "I—I didn't see him after that."

"Shit," Fenrys breathed.

Rowan said to him, "Use your magic. Jump to the field, find him, and bring him back."

Relief crumpled Elide's chest.

Until Fenrys said, "I can't."

"You didn't use it once during the battle," Rowan challenged. "You should be fully primed to do it."

Fenrys blanched beneath the blood on his face, and cast pleading eyes to Elide. "I can't."

Silence fell on the battlements.

Then Rowan growled, "You won't." He pointed with a bloody finger to the battlefield. "You'd let him die, and for what? Aelin forgave him." His tattoo scrunched as he snarled again. "*Save him.*"

Fenrys swallowed. But Aelin said, "Leave it, Rowan."

Rowan snarled at her too.

She snarled right back. "*Leave it.*"

Some unspoken conversation passed between them, and the hope flaring in Elide's chest went out as Rowan backed down. Gave Fenrys an apologetic nod. Fenrys, looking like he was going to be sick, just faced the battlefield again.

Elide backed away a step. Then another.

Lorcan couldn't be dead.

She would know if he were dead. She would *know* it, in her heart, her soul, if he were gone.

He was down there. He was down there, in that army, perhaps injured and bleeding out—

No one stopped her as Elide raced inside the keep. Each step limped, pain cracking through her leg, but she didn't falter as she hit the interior stairwell and plunged into the chaos.

She had made him a promise.

She had sworn him an oath, all those months ago.

I will always find you.

Soldiers and healers fled up the stairs, shoving past Elide. The shouting was near-deafening, bouncing off the ancient stones. She battled her way down, sobbing through her teeth.

I will always find you.

Pushing, elbowing, bellowing at the frantic people who ran past her, Elide fought for each step downward. Toward the gates.

People screamed, a never-ending flood surging up the stairs. Still Elide pushed her way down, losing a step here, another there. They did not even look at her, even try to clear a way as they flowed upward. It was only when

Elide lost another step that she roared into the stairwell, "*Clear a path for the queen!*"

No one listened, so she did it again. She filled her voice with command, with every ounce of power that she'd seen the Fae males use to intimidate their opponents. "*Clear a path for the queen!*"

This time, people pressed against the walls. Elide took the small opening, and screamed her order again and again, ankle barking with every step down.

But she made it. Made it to the chaotic lower level, to the open gates teeming with soldiers. Beyond them, bodies stretched into the horizon. Warriors and healers and those bearing the wounded rushed toward any stairwell they could find.

Elide managed all of five limping steps toward the open gate before she knew it would be impossible. To cross the field, to *find* him on the endless plain, before that dam burst and he was swept away. Before he was gone forever.

He was not dead.

He was *not* dead.

I will always find you.

Elide scanned the gates, the skies for any sign of a ruk that might carry her. But they soared to the upper levels, crawling with soldiers and healers, some even depositing their charges onto the mountain face itself. And at ground level, none would hear her cries for help.

No soldiers would stop, either.

Elide scanned the other end of the gates' entryway.

Beheld the horses being led out from their stables by frantic handlers, the beasts bucking at the panic around them as they were hauled toward the teeming ramps.

A black mare reared, her cry a sharp warning before she slashed her hooves at the handler. Lord Chaol's horse. The handler shrieked and fell back, barely grasping the reins as the horse stomped, her ears flat to her head.

Elide did not think. Did not reconsider. She limped for the horses and the stables.

She said to the frantic handler, still backing away from the half-wild horse, "I'll get her."

The man, white-faced, threw her the reins. "Good luck." Then he, too, ran.

The mare—Farasha—yanked so hard on the reins that Elide was nearly hurled across the stones. But she planted her feet, leg screaming, and said to the horse, "I have need of you, fierce-heart." She met Farasha's dark, raging eyes. "I have need of you." Her voice broke. "Please."

And gods above, that horse stilled. Blinked.

Horses and handlers streamed past them, but Elide held firm. Waited until Farasha lowered her head, as if in permission.

The stirrups were low enough thanks to Lord Chaol's long legs that Elide could reach them. She still bit down on her shout as her weight settled on her bad ankle, as she *pushed*, and heaved herself into Farasha's fine saddle. A small mercy, that they had not even had time to unsaddle the horses after battle. A set of what seemed to be braces hung from its sides, surely to keep Lord Chaol stabilized, and Elide unhooked them. Any weight, anything to slow her, had to be discarded.

Elide gathered the reins. "*To the battlefield, Farasha.*"

With a whinnying cry, Farasha plunged into the fray.

Soldiers leaped from their path, and Elide did not stop to apologize, did not stop for anyone, as she and the black mare charged toward the gates. Then through them.

And onto the plain.

CHAPTER 60

Rowan knew his magic would merely delay the inevitable. He'd debated flying to the dam, to see if he might hold the structure in place for just long enough, if he could not halt the river entirely, but the force of the thing on the other side . . . it could not be stopped.

Soldiers and healers raced for the keep, the ruks darting across the battlefield to bear those first in the water's path to safety. But not fast enough. Even without knowing when the dam would break, it would not be fast enough.

Was Lorcan currently amongst those running, or had he managed to get onto a ruk?

"The power," Fenrys said quietly to him, gripping the gore-slick wall. "It was the one thing Connall and I shared."

"I know," Rowan said. He shouldn't have pushed. "I'm sorry."

Fenrys just nodded. "I haven't been able to stomach it since then. I—I'm not even certain I *can* use it again," he said, and repeated, "I'm sorry."

Rowan clapped him on the shoulder. Another thing he'd make Maeve pay for. "You might not have even found him, anyway."

Fenrys's jaw tightened. "He could be anywhere."

"He could be dead," murmured Princess Hasar.

"Or injured," Chaol cut in, wheeling to the wall's edge to survey the battlefield below and distant dam beyond it.

Aelin, a few feet away, gazed toward it as well, her blood-soaked hair ripping free of its braid in the harsh wind. Flowing toward those mountains, the destruction that would soon be unleashed.

She said nothing. Had done nothing since Nesryn and Sartaq brought the news. Her exact sort of nightmare, he realized, to be unable to help, to be forced to watch while others suffered. No words could comfort her, no words could fix this. Stop this.

"I could try to track him," Gavriel offered.

Rowan shook off his creeping dread. "I'll fly out, try to pinpoint him, and signal back to you—"

"Don't bother," said Princess Hasar, and Rowan was about to snarl his retort when she pointed to the battlefield. "She's already ahead of you."

Rowan whirled, the others following suit.

"No," Fenrys breathed.

There, galloping across the plain on a familiar black horse, was Elide.

"Farasha," Chaol murmured.

"She'll be killed," said Gavriel, tensing as if he might jump off the battlements and chase after her. "She'll be—"

Farasha leaped over fallen bodies, weaving between the injured and dead, Elide twisting this way and that in the saddle. And from the distance, Rowan could make out her mouth moving, shouting one word, one name, over and over. *Lorcan*.

"If any of you go down there," Hasar warned, "you'll be killed, too."

It went against every instinct, against the centuries of training and fighting he'd done with Lorcan, but the princess was right. To lose one life was better than several. Especially when he would need his cadre so badly during the rest of this war.

Lorcan would agree—had taught Rowan to make those sorts of hard calls.

Still Aelin remained silent, as if she'd descended deep within herself, and gazed at the battlefield.

At the small rider and the mighty horse racing across it.

Farasha was a tempest beneath her, but the mare did not seek to unseat Elide as they thundered across the body-strewn plain.

"Lorcan!"

Her shout was swallowed by the wind, by the screams of fleeing soldiers and people, by the shriek of the ruks above. *"Lorcan!"*

She searched every corpse she passed for a hint of that shining black hair, that harsh face. So many. The field of the dead stretched on forever, bodies piled several deep.

Farasha leaped over them, cutting sharp turns as Elide pivoted to look and look and look.

Darghan horses and riders ran past. Some to the keep, some to the distant forest along the horizon. Farasha wove between them, biting at those in her path.

"Lorcan!" How small her cry sounded, how feeble.

Still the dam held.

I will always find you.

And her words, her stupid, hateful words to him . . . Had she done this? Brought this upon him? Asked some god to do this?

Her words had all melted away the moment she'd realized he was not on the battlements. The past few months had melted away entirely.

"Lorcan!"

Unfaltering, Farasha kept moving, her black mane streaming in the wind.

The dam had to hold. It *would* hold. Until she brought him back to the keep.

So Elide did not stop, did not look toward the doom that lurked, waiting to be unleashed.

She rode, and rode, and rode.

⁓

Atop the battlement, Chaol didn't know what to watch: the dam, the people fleeing its oncoming destruction, or the young Lady of Perranth, racing across the battlefield atop his horse.

A warm hand settled on his shoulder, and he knew it was Yrene without turning. "I just heard about the dam. I'd sent Elide to see if you were . . ." His wife's words trailed off as she beheld the lone rider charging *away* from the masses thundering for the keep.

"Silba save her," Yrene whispered.

"Lorcan's down there," was all Chaol said by way of explanation.

The Fae males were taut as bowstrings while the young woman crossed the battlefield bit by bit. The odds of her finding Lorcan, let alone before the dam burst . . .

Still Elide kept riding. Racing against death itself.

Princess Hasar said quietly, "The girl is a fool. The bravest I've ever seen, but a fool nonetheless."

Aelin said nothing, her eyes distant. Like she'd retreated into herself at the realization that this sliver of hope was about to be washed away. Her friends with it.

"Hellas guards Lorcan," Fenrys murmured. "And Anneith, his consort, watches over Elide. Perhaps they will find each other."

"Hellas's horse," Chaol said.

They turned toward him, dragging their eyes from the field.

Chaol shook his head and gestured to the field, to the black mare and her rider. "I call Farasha Hellas's horse. I've done so from the moment I met her."

As if meeting that horse, bringing her here, was not as much for him as it was for this. For this desperate race across an endless battlefield.

Yrene clasped his hand, like she understood, too.

Silence fell along their section of the battlement. There were no words left to say.

⌇

"Lorcan!"

Elide's voice broke on the cry. She'd lost count of how many times she'd shouted it now.

No sign of him.

She aimed for the lake. Closer to the dam. He would have chosen the lake for its defensive advantages.

Bodies were a blur beneath, around them. So many Valg lying on the field. Some reached pale hands for Farasha. As if they'd grab her, rip her apart, beg her for help.

The mare trampled them into the mud, bone snapping and skulls cracking.

He had to be out here. Had to be somewhere. Alive—hurt, but alive.

She knew it.

The lake was a gray sprawl to her left, a mockery of the hell to be unleashed at any moment.

"Lorcan!"

They'd reached the heart of the battlefield, and Elide slowed Farasha enough to stand in the stirrups, biting down on the agony in her ankle. She had never felt so small, so inconsequential. A speck of nothing in this doomed sea.

Elide dropped back into the saddle, nudged the horse with her heels, and tugged Farasha farther toward the glittering silver expanse. He had to have gone to the lake.

The horse plunged into motion, her chest heaving like a mighty bellows.

On and on, black and golden armor, blood and snow and mud. The dam still held.

But there—

Elide yanked on the reins, slowing the charging horse.

There, not too far from the water's edge, lay a patch of felled Morath soldiers. A swath of them. Not a single set of golden armor. Even where the khagan's army had swept through, they had lost soldiers. The distribution across the battlefield had by no means been even, but there *had* been corpses in golden armor amongst the mass of black.

Yet here, there were none. No arrows or spears, either, to account for the felling of so many.

A veritable road of Valg demons flowed ahead.

Elide followed it. Scanned every corpse, every helmeted face, her mouth going dry. On and on, the wake of his destruction went.

So many. He had killed so many.

Her breath rasped in her throat as they neared the end of that trail of death, where golden bodies again began to appear.

Nothing. Elide halted Farasha. Gavriel had said he'd last seen him right here. Had he plunged behind their ally's lines and moved on from there?

He might have walked off this field, she realized. Might currently be back at the keep, or in Oakwald, and she would have ridden here for nothing—

"*Lorcan!*" She screamed it, so loud it was a wonder her throat didn't bleed. "*Lorcan!*"

The dam remained intact. Which of her breaths would be her last?

"*LORCAN!*"

A pained groan answered from behind.

Elide twisted in the saddle and scanned the path of Valg dead behind her.

A broad, tanned hand rose from beneath a thick pile of them, and fought for purchase on a soldier's breastplate. Not twenty feet away.

A sob cracked from her, and Farasha cantered toward that straining, bloodied hand. The horse skidded to a halt, gore flying from her hooves. Elide threw herself from the saddle before scrambling toward him.

Armor and blades sliced into her, dead flesh slapping against her skin as she shoved away demon corpses, grunting at their weight. Lorcan met her halfway, that hand becoming an arm, then two—pushing off the bodies piled atop him.

Elide reached him just as he'd managed to dislodge a soldier sprawled over him.

Elide took one look at the injury to Lorcan's middle and tried not to fall to her knees.

His blood leaked everywhere, the wound not closed—not in the way that Fae should be able to heal themselves. The injury that had felled him would have been catastrophic, if it had taken all his power to heal him this little.

But she did not say that. Did not say anything other than, "The dam is about to break."

Black blood splattered Lorcan's ashen face, his dark eyes fogged with pain. Elide braced her feet, swallowing her scream of pain, and gripped him under the shoulders. "We need to get you out of here."

His breathing was a wet rasp as she tried to lift him. He might as well have been a boulder, might as well have been as immovable as the keep itself.

"Lorcan," she begged, voice breaking. "We have to get you out of here."

His legs shifted, drawing an agonized groan. She had never heard him so much as whimper. Had never seen him unable to rise.

"Get up," she said. "*Get up.*"

Lorcan's hands gripped her waist, and Elide couldn't stop her cry of pain at the weight he placed on her, the bones in her foot and ankle grinding together. His legs not even kneeling beneath him, he paused.

"*Do it,*" she begged him. "*Get up.*"

But his dark eyes shifted to the horse.

Farasha approached, steps unsteady over the corpses. She did not so much as flinch as Lorcan grasped the bottom straps of the saddle, his other hand on Elide's shoulder, and moved his legs under him again.

His breathing turned jagged. Fresh blood dribbled from his stomach, flowing over the crusted remains on his jacket and pants.

As he began to rise, Elide beheld the wound slicing up the left side of his back.

Flesh lay open—bone peeking through.

Oh gods. Oh gods.

Elide ducked further under him, until his arm was slung across her shoulders. Thighs burning, ankle shrieking, Elide pushed *up*.

Lorcan pulled at the same time, Farasha holding steady. He groaned again, his body teetering—

"Don't stop," Elide hissed. *"Don't you dare stop."*

His breath came in shallow gasps, but Lorcan got his feet under him, inch by inch. Slipping his arm from Elide's shoulder, he lurched to grip the saddle. To cling to it.

He panted and panted, fresh blood sliding from his back, too.

This ride would be agony. But they had no choice. None at all.

"Now up." She didn't let him hear her terror and despair. "Get into that saddle."

He leaned his brow against Farasha's dark side. Swaying enough that Elide wrapped a careful arm around his waist.

"You didn't rutting die," she snapped. "And you're not dead yet. *We're* not dead yet. So *get in that saddle.*"

When Lorcan did nothing other than breathe and breathe and breathe, Elide spoke again.

"I promised to always find you. I promised you, and you promised me. I came for you because of it; I am here because of it. I am here for *you*, do you understand? And if we don't get onto that horse *now*, we won't stand a chance against that dam. We will die."

Lorcan panted for another heartbeat. Then another. And then, gritting his teeth, his hands white-knuckled on the saddle, he lifted his leg enough to slide one foot into the stirrup.

Now would be the true test: that mighty push upward, the swinging of his leg over Farasha's body, to the other side of the saddle.

Elide positioned herself at his back, so careful of the terrible slash down his body. Her feet sank ankle-deep into freezing mud. She didn't dare look toward the dam. Not yet.

"Get up." Her command barked over the panicked cries of the fleeing soldiers. "Get in that saddle *now*."

Lorcan didn't move, his body trembling.

Elide screamed, "*Get up now!*" And shoved him upward.

Lorcan let out a bellow that rang in her ears. The saddle groaned at his weight, and blood gushed from his wounds, but then he was rising into the air, toward the horse's back.

Elide threw her weight into him, and something cracked in her ankle, so violently that pain burst through her, blinding and breathless. She stumbled, losing her grip. But Lorcan was up, his leg over the other side of the horse. He slouched over it, an arm cradling his abdomen, dark hair hanging low enough to brush Farasha's back.

Clenching her jaw against the pain in her ankle, Elide straightened, and eyed the distance.

A long, bloodied arm dropped into her line of sight. An offer up.

She ignored it. She'd gotten him into the saddle. She wasn't about to send him flying off it again.

Elide backed a step, limping.

Not allowing herself to register the pain, Elide ran the few steps to Farasha and leaped.

Lorcan's hand gripped the back of her jacket, the breath going from her as her stomach hit the unforgiving lip of the saddle, and Elide clawed for purchase.

The strength in Lorcan's arm didn't waver as he pulled her almost across his lap. As he grunted in pain while she righted herself.

But she made it. Got her legs on either side of the horse, and took up the reins. Lorcan looped his arm around her waist, his brutalized body a solid mass at her back.

Elide at last dared to look at the dam. A ruk soared from it, frantically waving a golden banner.

Soon. It would break soon.

Elide gathered Farasha's reins. "To the keep, friend," she said, digging her heels into the horse's side. "Faster than the wind."

Farasha obeyed. Elide rocked back into Lorcan as the mare launched into a gallop, earning another groan of pain. But he remained in the saddle, despite the pounding steps that drew agonized breaths from him.

"*Faster, Farasha!*" Elide called to the horse as she steered her toward the keep, the mountain it had been built into.

Nothing had ever seemed so distant.

Far enough that she could not see if the keep's lower gate was still open. If anyone held it, waited for them.

Hold the gate.

Hold the gate.

Every thunderous beat of Farasha's hooves, over the corpses of the fallen, echoed Elide's silent prayer as they raced across the endless plain.

Hold the gate.

CHAPTER
61

Agony was a song in Lorcan's blood, his bones, his breath.

Every step of the horse, every leap she made over body and debris, sent it ringing afresh. There was no end, no mercy from it. It was all he could do to keep in the saddle, to cling to consciousness.

To keep his arm around Elide.

She had come for him. Had found him, somehow, on this endless battlefield.

His name on her lips had been a summons he could never deny, even when death had held him so gently, nestled beneath all those he'd felled, and waited for his last breaths.

And now, charging toward that too-distant keep, so far behind the droves of soldiers and riders racing for the gates, he wondered if these minutes would be his last. Her last.

She had come for him.

Lorcan managed to glance toward the dam on their right. Toward the ruk rider signaling that it was only a matter of minutes until it unleashed hell over the plain.

He didn't know how it had become weakened. Didn't care.

Farasha leaped over a pile of Valg bodies, and Lorcan couldn't stop his moan as warm blood dribbled down his front and back.

Still Elide kept urging the horse onward, kept them on as straight a path toward the distant keep as possible.

No ruk would come to sweep them up. No, his luck had been spent in surviving this long, in her finding him. His power would do nothing against that water.

The farthest lines of panicked soldiers appeared, and Farasha charged past them.

Elide let out a sob, and he followed the line of her sight.

To the keep gate, still open.

"*Faster, Farasha!*" She didn't hide the raw terror in her voice, the desperation.

Once the dam broke, it would take less than a minute for the tidal wave to reach them.

She had come for him. She had found him.

The world went quiet. The pain in his body faded into nothing. Into something secondary.

Lorcan slid his other arm around Elide, bringing his mouth close to her ear as he said, "You have to let me go."

Each word was gravelly, his voice strained nearly to the point of uselessness.

Elide didn't shift her focus from the keep ahead. "No."

That gentle quiet flowed around him, clearing the fog of pain and battle. "You have to. You have to, Elide. I'm too heavy—and without my weight, you might make it to the keep in time."

"No." The salt of her tears filled his nose.

Lorcan brushed his mouth over her damp cheek, ignoring the roaring pain in his body. The horse galloped and galloped, as if she might outrace death itself.

"I love you," he whispered in Elide's ear. "I have loved you from the moment you picked up that axe to slay the ilken." Her tears flowed past him in the wind. "And I will be with you . . ." His voice broke, but he made himself say the words, the truth in his heart. "I will be with you *always*."

He was not frightened of what would come for him once he tumbled off the horse. He was not frightened at all, if it meant her reaching the keep.

So Lorcan kissed Elide's cheek again, allowed himself to breathe in her scent one last time. "I love you," he repeated, and began to withdraw his arms from around her waist.

Elide slapped a hand onto his forearm. Dug in her nails, right into his skin, fierce as any ruk.

"No."

There were no tears in her voice. Nothing but solid, unwavering steel.

"No," she said again. The voice of the Lady of Perranth.

Lorcan tried to move his arm, but her grip would not be dislodged.

If he tumbled off the horse, she would go with him.

Together. They would either outrun this or die together.

"Elide—"

But Elide slammed her heels into the horse's sides.

Slammed her heels into the dark flank and screamed, *"FLY, FAR-ASHA."* She cracked the reins. *"FLY, FLY, FLY!"*

And gods help her, that horse did.

As if the god that had crafted her filled the mare's lungs with his own breath, Farasha gave a surge of speed.

Faster than the wind. Faster than death.

Farasha cleared the first of the fleeing Darghan cavalry. Passed desperate horses and riders at an all-out gallop for the gates.

Her mighty heart did not falter, even when Lorcan knew it was raging to the point of bursting.

Less than a mile stood between them and the keep.

But a thunderous, groaning crack cleaved the world, echoing off the lake, the mountains.

There was nothing he could do, nothing that brave, unfaltering horse could do, as the dam ruptured.

Rowan began praying for those on the plain, for the army about to be wiped away, as the dam broke.

Standing a few feet away, Yrene was whispering her prayers, too. To Silba, the goddess of gentle deaths. *May it be quick, may it be painless.*

A wall of water, large as a mountain, broke free. And rushed toward the city, the plain, with the wrath of a thousand years of confinement.

"They're not going to make it," Fenrys hissed, eyes on Lorcan and Elide, galloping toward them. So close—so close, and yet that wave would arrive in a matter of seconds.

Rowan made himself stand there, to watch the last moments of the Lady of Perranth and his former commander. It was all he could offer: witnessing their deaths, so he might tell the story to those he encountered. So they would not be forgotten.

The roaring of the oncoming wave became deafening, even from miles away.

Still Elide and Lorcan raced, Farasha passing horse after horse after horse.

Even up here, would they escape the wave's reach? Rowan dared to survey the battlements, to assess if he needed to get the others, needed to get Aelin, to higher ground.

But Aelin was not at his side.

She was not on the battlement at all.

Rowan's heart halted. Simply stopped beating as a ruddy-brown ruk dropped from the skies, spearing for the center of the plain.

Arcas, Borte's ruk. A golden-haired woman dangling from his talons.

Aelin. Aelin was—

Arcas neared the earth, talons splaying. Aelin hit the ground, rolling, rolling, until she uncoiled to her feet.

Right in the path of that wave.

"Oh gods," Fenrys breathed, seeing her, too.

They all saw her.

The queen on the plain.

The endless wall of water surging for her.

The keep stones began shuddering. Rowan threw out a hand to brace himself, fear like nothing he had known ripping through him as Aelin lifted her arms above her head.

A pillar of fire shot up around her, lifting her hair with it.

The wave roared and roared for her, for the army behind her.

The shaking in the keep was not from the wave.

It was not from that wall of water at all.

Cracks formed in the earth, splintering across it. Spiderwebbing from Aelin.

"The hot springs," Chaol breathed. "The valley floor is full of veins into the earth itself."

Into the burning heart of the world.

The keep shook, more violently this time.

The pillar of fire sucked back into Aelin. She held out a hand before her, her fist closed.

As if it would halt the wave in its tracks.

He knew then. Either as her mate or *carranam*, he knew.

"Three months," Rowan breathed.

The others stilled.

"Three months," he said again, his knees wobbling. "She's been making the descent into her power for three months."

Every day she had been with Maeve, bound in iron, she had gone deeper. And she had not tapped too far into that power since they'd freed her because she had *kept* making the plunge.

To gather up the full might of her magic. Not for the Lock, not for Erawan.

But for Maeve's death blow.

A few weeks of descent had taken her powers to devastating levels. Three *months* of it . . .

Holy gods. Holy rutting gods.

And when her fire hit the wall of water now towering over her, when they collided—

"GET DOWN!" Rowan bellowed, over the screaming waters. *"GET DOWN NOW!"*

His companions dropped to the stones, any within earshot doing the same.

Rowan plummeted into his power. Plummeted into it fast and hard, ripping out any remaining shred of magic.

Elide and Lorcan were still too far from the gates. Thousands of soldiers were still too far from the gates as the wave crested above them.

As Aelin opened her hand toward it.

Fire erupted.

Cobalt fire. The raging soul of a flame.

A tidal wave of it.

Taller than the raging waters, it blasted from her, flaring wide.

The wave slammed into it. And where water met a wall of fire, where a thousand years of confinement met three months of it, the world exploded.

Blistering steam, capable of melting flesh from bone, shot across the plain.

With a roar, Rowan threw all that remained of his magic toward the onslaught of steam, a wall of wind that shoved it toward the lake, the mountains.

Still the waters came, breaking against the flames that did not so much as yield an inch.

Maeve's death blow. Spent here, to save the army that might mean Terrasen's salvation. To spare the lives on the plain.

Rowan gritted his teeth, panting against his fraying power. A burnout lurked, deadly close.

The raging wave threw itself over and over and over into the wall of flame.

Rowan didn't see if Elide and Lorcan made it into the keep. If the other soldiers and riders on the plain stopped to gape.

Princess Hasar said, rising beside him, "That power is no blessing."

"Tell that to your soldiers," Fenrys snarled, standing, too.

"I did not mean it that way," Hasar snipped, and awe was indeed stark on her face.

Rowan leaned against the battlements, panting hard as he fought to keep the lethal steam from flowing toward the army. As he cooled and sent it whisking away.

Solid hands slid under his arms, and then Fenrys and Gavriel were there, propping him up between them.

A minute passed. Then another.

The wave began to lower. Still the fire burned.

Rowan's head pounded, his mouth going dry.

Time slipped from him. A coppery tang filled his mouth.

The wave lowered farther, raging waters quieting.

Then roaring turned to lapping, rapids into eddies.

Until the wall of flame began to lower, too. Tracking the waters down and down and down. Letting them seep into the cracks of the earth.

Rowan's knees buckled, but he held on to his magic long enough for the steam to lessen. For it, too, to be calmed.

It filled the plain, turning the world into drifting mist. Blocking the view of the queen in its center.

Then silence. Utter silence.

Fire flickered through the mist, blue turning to gold and red. A muted, throbbing glow.

Rowan spat blood onto the battlement stones, his breath like shards of glass in his throat.

The glowing flames shrank, steam rippling past. Until there was only a slim pillar of fire, veiled in the mist-shrouded plain.

Not a pillar of fire.

But Aelin.

Glowing white-hot. As if she had given herself so wholly to the flame that she had become fire herself.

The Fire-Bringer someone whispered down the battlements.

The mist rippled and billowed, casting her into nothing but a glowing effigy.

The silence turned reverent.

A gentle wind from the north swept down. The veil of mist pulled back, and there she was.

She glowed from within. Glowed golden, tendrils of her hair floating on a phantom wind.

"Mala's Heir," Yrene breathed.

Down on the plain, Elide and Lorcan had halted.

The wind pushed away more of the drifting mist, clearing the land beyond Aelin.

And where that mighty, lethal wave had loomed, where death had charged toward them, nothing remained at all.

⁓

For three months, she had sung to the darkness and the flame, and they had sung back.

For three months, she had burrowed so deep inside her power that she had plundered undiscovered depths. While Maeve and Cairn had worked on her, she had delved. Never letting them know what she mined, what she gathered to her, day by day by day.

A death blow. One to wipe a dark queen from the earth forever.

She'd kept that power coiled in herself even after she'd been freed from the irons. Had struggled to keep it down these weeks, the strain enormous. Some days, it had been easier to barely speak. Some days, swaggering arrogance had been her key to ignoring it.

Yet when she had seen that wave, when she had seen Elide and Lorcan choosing death together, when she had seen the army that might save Terrasen, she'd known. She'd felt the fire sleeping under this city, and knew they had come here for a reason.

She had come here for *this* reason.

A river still flowed from the dam, harmless and small, wending toward the lake.

Nothing more.

Aelin lifted a glowing hand before her as blessed, cooling emptiness filled her at last.

Slowly, starting from her fingertips, the glow faded.

As if she were forged anew, forged back into her body.

Back into Aelin.

Clarity, sharp and crystal clear, filled its wake. As if she could see again, breathe again.

Inch by inch, the golden glow faded into skin and bone. Into a woman once more.

Already, a white-tailed hawk launched skyward.

But as the last of the glow faded, disappearing out through her toes, Aelin fell to her knees.

Fell to her knees in the utter silence of the world, and curled onto her side.

She had the vague sense of strong, familiar arms scooping her up. Of being carried onto a broad feathery back, still in those arms.

Of soaring through the skies, the last of the mist rippling away into the afternoon sun.

And then sweet darkness.

CHAPTER 62

The Crochans did not scatter to the winds.

As one, the Thirteen and the Crochans flew to the southwest, toward the outer reaches of the Fangs. To another secret camp, since the location of the other was well and truly compromised. Farther from Terrasen, but closer to Morath, at least.

A small comfort, Dorian thought, when they found a secure place to camp for the night. The wyverns might have been able to keep going, but the Crochans on their brooms could not fly for so long. They'd flown until darkness had nearly blinded them all, landing only after the Shadows and Crochans had agreed on a secure place to stay.

Watches were set, both on the ground and in the sky. If the two surviving Matrons were to retaliate for their humiliating defeat, it would be now. The Crochans and Asterin had spent much of their time today laying misleading tracks, but only time would tell if they'd escaped.

The night was frigid enough that they took the time to erect tents, the wyverns huddling together against one of the rocky overhangs. And though no fires would have been wiser, the cold threatened to be so lethal that Glennis had taken the sacred flame from the glass orb where it was held while traveling and ignited her fire. Others had followed suit, and while glamours would be in place to hide the camp, the fires, from enemy eyes, Dorian couldn't entirely forget that the Ironteeth Matrons had found them regardless.

They hadn't spoken of where they were going next. What they would do. If they would part ways at last, or remain as one united group.

Manon had not asked or pushed them for an alliance, to go to war. Hadn't demanded to know where they flew, such was their dire need to get far from their camp this morning.

But tomorrow, Dorian thought as he slid under the blankets of his bedroll, a lick of flame of his own making warming the space, tomorrow would force them to confront a few things.

Bone-tired, chilled despite the magic that warmed him, Dorian slumped his head against the roll of supplies he used for a pillow.

Sleep had almost dragged him under when a burst of cold slithered into the tent, then vanished. He knew who it was before she sat beside his bedroll, and when he opened his eyes, he found Manon with her knees drawn up, arms braced atop them.

She stared into the dimness of his tent, the space illumined with silvery light from the glowing stars on her brow.

"You don't have to wear it all the time," he said. "We're allowed to take them off."

Golden eyes slid toward him. "I've never seen you wear a crown."

"The past few months haven't provided much access to the royal collection." He sat up. "And I hate wearing them anyway. They dig mercilessly into my head."

A hint of a smile. "This is not so heavy."

"Since it seems made of light itself, I'd imagine not." Though that crown would weigh heavily in other ways, he knew.

"So you're talking to me," she said, not bothering to segue gracefully.

"I talked to you before."

"Is it because I am now queen?"

"You were queen prior to today."

Her golden eyes narrowed, scanning him for the answer she sought. Dorian let her do it, and returned the favor. Her breathing was steady, her posture at ease for once.

"I thought it would be more satisfying. To see her run." Her grandmother. "When you killed your father, what did you feel?"

"Rage. Hate." He didn't balk from the truth in his words, the ugliness.

She chewed on her lower lip, no sign of those iron teeth. A rare, silent admission of doubt. "Do you think I should have killed her?"

"Some might say yes. But humiliating her like that," he said, considering, "might weaken her and the Ironteeth forces more than her death. Killing her might have rallied the Ironteeth against you."

"I killed the Yellowlegs Matron."

"You killed her, spared the Blueblood witch, and your grandmother fled. That's a demoralizing defeat. Had you killed them all, even killed just your grandmother and the Yellowlegs Matron, it could have turned their deaths into noble sacrifices on behalf of the Ironteeth Clans."

She nodded, her golden eyes settling on him again with that preternatural clarity and stillness. "I am sorry," she said. "For how I spoke when I learned of your plans to go to Morath."

He was stunned enough that he just blinked. Stunned enough that humor was his only shield as he said, "Seems like that Crochan do-gooder behavior is rubbing off on you, Manon."

A half smile at that. "Mother help me if I ever become so dull."

But Dorian's amusement faded away. "I accept your apology." He held her gaze, letting her see the truth in it.

It seemed answer enough for her. Answer, and somehow the final clue to what she sought.

Her golden eyes guttered. "You're leaving," she breathed. "Tomorrow."

He didn't bother to lie. "Yes."

It was time. She had faced her grandmother, had challenged what she'd created. It was time for him to do the same. He didn't need Damaris's confirming warmth or the spirits of the dead to tell him that.

"How?"

"You witches have brooms and wyverns. I've learned to make my own wings."

For a few breaths, she said nothing. Then she lowered her knees, twisting to face him fully. "Morath is a death trap."

"It is."

"I—we cannot go with you."

"I know."

He could have sworn fear entered her eyes. Yet she didn't rage at him, roar at him—didn't so much as snarl. She only asked, "You're not afraid to go alone?"

"Of course I'm afraid. Anyone in their right mind would be. But my task is more important than fear, I think."

Anger flickered over her face, her shoulders tensing.

Then it faded and was replaced by something he had seen only earlier today—that queen's face. Steady and wise, edged with sorrow and bright with clarity. Her eyes dipped to the bedroll, then lifted to meet his own. "And if I asked you to stay?"

The question also took him by surprise. He carefully thought through his answer. "I'd need a very convincing reason, I suppose."

Her fingers went to the buckles and buttons of her leathers, and began to loosen them. "Because I don't want you to go," was all she said.

His heart thundered as she revealed inch after inch of bare, silken skin. Not a seductive removal of her clothing, but rather an offer laid bare.

Her fingers began to shake, and Dorian moved at last, helping her to remove her boots, then her sword belt. He left her jacket open, the swells of her breasts just visible between the lapels. They rose and fell in an uneven rhythm that only turned more unsteady as she reached between them and began to remove his own jacket.

Dorian let her. Let her peel off his jacket, then the shirt beneath.

Outside, the wind howled.

And when they kneeled before each other, bare from the waist up, that crown of stars still atop her head, Manon said softly, "We could make an alliance. Between Adarlan, and the Crochans. And any Ironteeth who might follow me."

It was her answer, he realized. To his request for a convincing reason to remain.

She took his hand, and interlaced their fingers.

It was more intimate than anything they'd shared, more vulnerable than she'd ever allowed herself to be. "An alliance," she said, throat bobbing, "between you and me."

Her golden eyes lifted to his, the offer gleaming there.

To marry. To unite their peoples in the strongest, most unbreakable of terms.

"You don't want that," he said with equal quiet. "You would never want to be shackled to any man like that."

He could see the truth there, in her beautiful face. That she agreed with him. But she shook her head, the starlight dancing on her hair. "The Crochans have not offered to fly to war. I have not yet dared ask them. But if I had the strength of Adarlan beside me, perhaps they might be convinced at last."

If they had not been convinced by today's triumph, then nothing would change their minds. Even their queen offering up the freedom she craved so badly.

That Manon would even consider it, though . . .

Dorian twined a wave of her silver hair around his finger. For a heartbeat, he allowed himself to drink her in.

She would be his wife, his queen. She was already his equal, his match, his mirror in so many ways. And with their union, the world would know it.

But he could see the bars of the cage that would creep closer, tighter, every day. And either break her wholly, or turn her into something neither of them wished her to ever be.

"You would marry me, all so we could aid Terrasen in this war?"

"Aelin is willing to die to end this conflict. Why should she bear the brunt of sacrifice?"

And there it was, her answer, though he knew she didn't realize it.

Sacrifice.

Dorian's other hand went to the buttons of her pants, and freed them with a few, deft maneuvers. Revealing the long, thick scar across her abdomen.

Would he have shown the restraint that Manon did today, had he faced her grandmother?

Absolutely not.

He ran his fingers over the scar. Over it, and then up her stomach. Up and up, her skin pebbling beneath his touch, until he halted just over her heart. Until he laid his palm flat against it, the curve of her breast rising to meet his hand with each unsteady breath she took.

"You were right," she said quietly. "I am afraid." Manon laid her hand over his. "I am afraid that you will go into Morath and return as something I do not know. Something I shall have to kill."

"I know." Those same fears haunted his steps.

Her fingers tightened on his, pressing harder. As if she were trying to imprint his hand upon the heart racing beneath. "Would you stay here, if we had this alliance between us?"

He heard every word left unspoken.

So Dorian brushed his mouth against hers. Manon let out a small sound.

Dorian kissed her again, and her tongue met his, hungry and searching. Then her hands were plunging into his hair, both of them rising onto their knees to meet halfway.

She moaned, her hands sliding from his hair down his chest, down to his pants. She stroked him through the material, and Dorian groaned into her mouth.

Time spun out, and there was only Manon, a living blade in his arms. Their pants joined their shirts and jackets on the ground, and then he was laying her upon his bedroll.

Manon drew her hands from him to remove the glittering crown atop her head, but he halted her with a phantom touch. "Don't," he said, voice near-guttural. "Leave it on."

Her eyes turned to molten gold, going heavy-lidded as she writhed, tipping her head back.

His mouth went dry at the beauty that threatened to undo him, the temptation that his every instinct roared to claim. Not the body, but what she had offered.

He almost said yes, then.

Was almost selfish enough, greedy enough for her, that he nearly said yes. Yes, he would take her as his queen. So he might never have to say farewell to this, so that this magnificent, fierce witch might remain by his side for all his days.

Manon reached for him, fingers digging into his shoulders, and Dorian rose over her, finding her mouth in a plundering kiss.

A shift of her hips, and he was buried, the heated silk of her enough to make him forget that they had a camp around them, or kingdoms to protect.

He did not bother with phantom touches. He wanted her all for himself, skin to skin.

Every thrust into her, Manon answered with a rolling, demanding movement of her own. *Stay.* The word echoed in each breath.

Dorian took one of her legs and hefted it higher, angling him closer. He groaned at the perfection of it, and Manon swallowed the sound with a kiss of her own, a hand clamping on his backside to propel him harder, faster.

Dorian gave Manon what she wanted. Gave himself what he wanted. Over and over and over.

As if this might last forever.

⁓

Manon's breathing was as ragged as Dorian's when they pulled apart at last.

She could barely move her limbs, barely get down enough air as she gazed at the tent ceiling. Dorian, as spent as she, didn't bother to try to speak.

What was left to be said anyway?

She'd laid out what she wanted. Had spoken as much of the truth as she dared voice.

In its wake, a sated sort of clarity shone. Such as she had not felt in a long, long time.

His sapphire eyes lingered on her face, and Manon turned toward him. Slowly removed her crown of stars and set it aside.

Then she drew up the blankets around them both.

He didn't so much as flinch as she scooted closer, into the solid muscle of his body.

No, Dorian only draped an arm over her, and pulled her tightly against him.

Manon was still listening to his breathing when she fell asleep, warm in his arms.

⁓

She awoke at dawn to a cold bed.

Manon took one look at the empty place where the king had been, at the lack of supplies and that ancient sword, and knew.

Dorian had gone to Morath. And had taken the two Wyrdkeys with him.

CHAPTER
63

Aedion and Kyllian kept their panicking troops in line as they marched, all the way to the banks of the Florine.

There was no use running northward. Not when the bone drums began pounding. And grew louder with every passing minute that Aedion ordered their legion into formation.

Stalking for the front lines, his armor so heavy it could have been made of stone, the lack of the ancient sword at his side like some phantom limb, Aedion said to Ren, "I need you to do me a favor."

Ren, buckling on his quiver, didn't bother to look up. "Don't tell me to run."

"Never." Close—they were so close to Theralis. How fitting it would have been to at last die on the field where Terrasen had fallen a decade ago. To have his blood soak into the earth where so many of the court he'd loved had died, for his bones to join theirs, unmarked on the plain.

"I need you to call for aid."

Ren looked up then. His scarred face was leaner than it had been weeks ago. When was the last time any of them had a proper meal? Or a full night's rest? Where Lysandra was, what form she wore, Aedion didn't know. He had not sought her out last night, and she had stayed away from him entirely.

"I'm no one now," Aedion said, the lines of soldiers parting for them. Bane and Fae, Silent Assassin and Wendlynian and Wastes-hailing soldier alike. "But you are Lord of Allsbrook. Send out messengers. Send out Nox Owen. Call for aid. Dispatch them to every direction, to anyone they might find. Tell Nox and the others to beg if they have to, but tell them to say that Terrasen calls for aid."

Only Aelin had the authority to do so, or Darrow and his council, but Aedion didn't care.

Ren halted, and Aedion paused with him, well aware of the soldiers within earshot. Of the Fae hearing many possessed. Endymion and Sellene already stood by the front line of the left flank, their faces grave and weary. A home—that was what they'd lost, what they now fought to gain. If any should survive this. What would his father make of his son, fighting alongside his people at last?

"Will anyone come?" Ren asked, aware of those listening ears, too. Aware of the grim faces that remained with them, despite the death that marched at their backs.

Aedion fitted his helmet onto his head, the metal bitingly cold. "None came ten years ago. But maybe someone will bother this time."

Ren gripped his arm, tugging him close. "There might be nothing left to defend, Aedion."

"Send out the call anyway." He jerked his chin to the lines they'd passed through. Ilias was polishing his blades amongst a cluster of his father's assassins, his attention pinned on the enemy ahead. Preparing to make a final stand on this snowy plain so far from his warm desert. "You insist I'm still your general? Then here's my final order. Call for aid."

A muscle feathered in Ren's jaw. But he said, "Consider it done." Then he was gone.

They didn't bother with good-byes. Their luck was bad enough.

So Aedion continued, alone, to the front lines. Two Bane soldiers stepped aside to make room, and Aedion hefted up his shield, seamlessly fitting it between their unified front. The metal wall against which Morath would strike first, and hardest.

The snows swirled, veiling all beyond a hundred or so feet.

Yet the bone drums pounded louder. Soon the earth shook beneath marching feet.

Their final stand, here on an unnamed field before the Florine. How had it come to this?

Aedion drew his sword, the other soldiers following suit, the cry of ringing metal cutting through the howling wind.

Morath appeared, a line of solid black emerging from the snow.

Each foot they gained, more appeared behind. How far back was that witch tower? How soon would its power be unleashed?

He prayed, for the sake of his soldiers, that it would be quick, and relatively painless. That they would not know much fear before they were blasted into ashes.

The Bane didn't clash their swords on their shields this time.

There was only the marching of Morath, and the drums.

Had they gone to Orynth when Darrow demanded, they would have made it. Had time to cross the bridge, or take the northern route.

This defeat, these deaths, rested upon his shoulders alone.

Down the line, motion caught his eye—just as a fuzzy, massive head poked between Prince Galan and one of his remaining soldiers. A ghost leopard.

Green eyes slid toward him, drained and bleak.

Aedion looked away first. This would be bad enough without knowing she was here. That Lysandra would undoubtedly stay until she, too, fell.

He prayed he went first. So he wouldn't witness it.

Morath drew close enough that Ren's order to the archers rang out.

Arrows flew, fading into the snows.

Morath sent an answering volley that blotted out the watery light.

Aedion angled his shield, crouching low. Every impact reverberated through his bones.

Grunts and screams filled their side of the battlefield. When the volley stopped, when they straightened again, many men did not rise with them.

It was not arrows alone that had been fired, and now peppered the snow.

But heads. Human heads, many still in their helmets. Bearing Ansel of Briarcliff's roaring wolf insignia.

The rest of the army that she'd promised. That they'd been waiting for.

They must have intercepted Morath—and been obliterated.

Shouts rose from the army behind him as the realization rippled through the ranks. One female voice in particular carried over the din, her mournful cry echoing through Aedion's helmet.

The milky, wide eyes of the decapitated head that had landed near his boots stared skyward, the mouth still open in a scream of terror.

How many had Ansel known? How many friends had been amongst them?

It wasn't the time to seek out the young queen, to offer his condolences. Not when neither of them would likely survive the day. Not when it might be the heads of his own soldiers that were launched at Orynth's walls.

Ren ordered another volley, their arrows so few compared to what had been unleashed seconds before. A spattering of rain compared to a downpour. Many found their marks, soldiers in dark armor going down. But they were replaced by those behind them, mere cogs in some terrible machine.

"We fight as one," Aedion called down the line, forcing himself to ignore the scattered heads. "We die as one."

A horn blared from deep within the enemy ranks. Morath began its all-out run on their front line.

Aedion's boots dug into the mud as he braced his shield arm. Like it could possibly hold back the tide stretching into the horizon.

He counted his breaths, knowing they were limited. A ghost leopard's snarl ripped down the line, a challenge to the charging army.

Fifty feet. Ren's archers still fired fewer and fewer arrows. Forty. Thirty.

The sword in his hand was no equal to the ancient blade he'd worn with such pride. But he'd make it work. Twenty. Ten.

Aedion sucked in a breath. The black, depthless eyes of the Morath soldiers became clear beneath their helmets.

Morath's front line angled their swords, their spears—

Roaring fire blasted from the left flank.

His left flank.

Aedion didn't dare take his focus off the enemy upon him, but several of the Morath soldiers did.

He slaughtered them for it. Slaughtered their stunned companions, too, as they whirled toward another blast of flame.

Aelin. *Aelin*—

Soldiers behind him shouted. In triumph and relief.

"Close the gap," Aedion growled to the warriors on either side of him, and pulled back enough to see the source of their salvation, free and safe at last—

It was not Aelin who unleashed fire upon the left flank.

It was not Aelin at all who had crept up through the snow-veiled river.

Ships filled the Florine, near-ghosts in the swirling snows. Some bore the banners of their united fleet.

But many, so many he couldn't count, bore a cobalt flag adorned with a green sea dragon.

Rolfe's fleet. The Mycenians.

Yet there was no sign of the ancient sea dragons who had once gone into battle with them. Only human soldiers marched across the snow, each bearing a familiar-looking contraption, scarves over their mouths.

Firelances.

A horn blasted from the river. And then the firelances unleashed white-hot flame into Morath's ranks, as if they were plumes from hell. Dragons, all of them, spewing fire upon their enemy.

Flame melted armor and flesh. And burned the demons that dreaded heat and light.

As if they were farmers burning their reaped fields for the winter, Rolfe's Mycenians marched onward, firelances spewing, until they formed a line between Aedion and their enemy.

Morath turned and ran.

Outright sprinted, their warning cries rising above the bellowing flames. *The Fire-Bringer has armed them! Her power burns anew!*

The fools did not realize that there was no magic—none beyond pure luck and good timing.

Then a familiar voice rang out. *"Quickly! On board, all of you!"* Rolfe.

For the ships in the river had pulled up, gangways lowered and row-boats already at the shore.

Aedion wasted no time. *"To the river! To the fleet!"*

Their soldiers didn't hesitate. They sprinted for the awaiting armada, onto any ship they could reach, leaping into the longboats. Chaotic and messy, but with Morath on retreat for only the gods knew how long, he didn't care.

Aedion kept his position at the front line, ensuring no soldier lagged behind.

Down the line, Prince Galan and a spotted, furry form did the same. Beside them, red hair waving in the wind, Ansel of Briarcliff held her sword pointed at their enemy. Tears slid down her freckled cheeks. The heads of her men lay scattered in the snow around her.

And ahead of them, still unleashing flame, Rolfe's Mycenians bought them the time to retreat.

Each second dripped by, but slowly, those boats filled. Slowly, their army left the shore, every boat that departed was replaced by another. Many Fae shifted, birds of prey filling the gray sky as they soared over the river.

And when there were none left but a few boats, among them a beautiful ship with a mast carved after an attacking sea dragon, Rolfe roared from the helm, "*Fall back, all of you!*"

The Mycenians and their firelances made a quick retreat, hurrying for the longboats returning to shore.

Lysandra and Ansel ran with them, and Aedion followed suit. It was the longest sprint of his life.

But then he was at the gangplank of Rolfe's ship, the river deep enough that they'd been able to pull up close to the shore. Lysandra, Galan, and Ansel were already past him, and Aedion had barely cleared the deck when the gangway was lifted. Below, around, the Mycenians leaped into their longboats and rowed like hell. Not a single soldier left behind. Only the dead.

Light flashed, and Aedion whirled toward the ship's helm in time to see Lysandra shift from ghost leopard to woman, naked as the day she was born.

Rolfe, to his credit, only looked mildly surprised as she flung her arms around his neck. And to his credit once more, the Pirate Lord wrapped his cloak around her before he gripped her back.

Aedion reached them, panting and so relieved he might vomit upon the shining planks.

Rolfe let go of Lysandra, offering her his cloak completely. As the shifter wrapped it around herself, he said, "You looked like you were in need of a rescue."

Aedion only embraced the man, then nodded toward Rolfe's gloved hands. "I assume we have that map of yours to thank."

"Turns out it's good for something other than plundering." Rolfe smirked. "Ravi and Sol of Suria intercepted us near the northern border," he admitted. "They thought you might be in trouble—and sent us this way." He ran a hand through his hair. "They remain with what's left of your fleet, guarding the coast. If Morath attacks from the sea, they won't have enough ships to stand a chance. I told them that, and they still ordered me here." The Pirate Lord's tan face tightened. "So here I am."

Aedion hardly noticed the sailors and soldiers making the quick sailing to the other side of the river. "Thank you," he breathed. And thank the gods for Ravi and Sol.

Rolfe shook his head, gazing toward the mass of Morath soldiers still retreating. "We surprised them, but it won't hold them off for long."

Lysandra stepped to Rolfe's side. Aedion tried not to cringe at the sight of her bare feet and legs, her uncovered shoulders, as the bitter wind off the river bit at them. "We only need to get to Orynth and behind its walls. From there, we can regroup."

"I can't carry your entire army to Orynth," Rolfe said, gesturing to the soldiers massed on the far shore. "But I can bear you there now, if you would like to arrive in advance to prepare." The Pirate Lord studied the shore, as if looking for someone. "She's not here, is she."

Lysandra shook her head. "No."

"Then we'll make do," was all Rolfe said, the portrait of cool command. His sea-green eyes slid to where Ansel of Briarcliff stood at the ship's rail, staring toward the field of heads left in the snow.

None of them spoke as the young queen slid to her knees, armor thunking on the deck, and bowed her head.

Aedion murmured, "Let me send word to our troops to march to Orynth, and then we'll sail for the city."

"I'll do it," Lysandra said, not looking at him. She didn't bother to say anything else. Cloak falling to the planks, she shifted into a falcon and aimed for where Kyllian now climbed out of a longboat. They exchanged only a few words before Kyllian turned toward Aedion and lifted a hand in farewell.

Aedion raised one in answer, and then Lysandra shifted again. When she landed on the ship, returning to her human form and snatching up the cloak, it was to Ansel that she walked.

In silence, the shifter laid a hand on the queen's armored shoulder. Ansel didn't so much as glance up.

Aedion asked Rolfe, "How many of those firelances do you have?"

The Pirate Lord drew his gaze from Ansel to the black mass fading behind them. His mouth tightened. "Not enough to outlast a siege."

And even the firelances would do nothing, absolutely nothing, once the witch towers reached Orynth's walls.

CHAPTER
64

Hours later, Yrene was still shaking.

At the disaster they'd narrowly avoided, at the deaths she'd witnessed before that wave had struck, at the power of the queen on the plain. The power of the prince who had prevented the ensuing steam from boiling alive any caught in its path.

Yrene had thrown herself back into healing during the chaos since. Had left the royals and their commanders to oversee the aftermath, and had returned to the Great Hall. Healers drifted onto the battlefield, searching for those in need of help.

All of them, every single person in the keep or the skies or on the battlefield, kept glancing toward the now-empty gap between two mountain peaks. Toward the flooded, decimated city, and the demarcation line between life and death. Water and debris had destroyed most of Anielle, the former now trickling toward the Silver Lake.

A vision of what would have been left of them, were it not for Aelin Galathynius.

Yrene knelt over a ruk rider, the woman's chest slashed open from a sword blow, and held out her bloodied, glowing hands.

Magic, clean and bright, flowed from her into the woman, mending torn skin and muscle. The blood loss would take time to recover from—but the woman had not lost so much of it that Yrene needed to expend her energy on refilling its levels.

She needed to rest soon. For a few hours.

She'd been asked to inspect the queen when she'd been carried in to a private chamber by Prince Rowan, the two of them borne off the plain by Nesryn. Yrene hadn't been able to stop her hands from shaking as she'd hovered them over Aelin's unconscious body.

There had been no sign of harm beyond a few already-healing cuts and slices from the battle itself. Nothing at all beyond a sleeping, tired woman.

Who held the might of a god within her veins.

Yrene had then inspected Prince Rowan, who looked in far worse shape, a sizable gash snaking down his thigh. But he'd waved her off, claiming he'd come too near a burnout, and just needed to rest as well.

So Yrene had left them, only to tend to another.

To Lorcan, whose injuries . . . Yrene had needed to summon Hafiza to help her with some of it. To lend her power, since Yrene's had been so depleted.

The unconscious warrior, who had apparently tumbled right off Farasha as he and Elide had passed through the gates, didn't so much as stir while they worked on him.

That had been hours ago. Days ago, it felt.

Yes, she needed to rest.

Yrene aimed for the water station in the back of the hall, her mouth dry as paper. Some water, some food, and perhaps a nap. Then she'd be ready to work again.

But a horn, clear and bright, blared from outside.

Everyone halted—then rushed to the windows. Yrene's smile grew as she, too, found a place to peek out over the battlefield.

To where the rest of the khagan's army, Prince Kashin at its front, marched toward them.

Thank the gods. Everyone in the hall muttered similar words.

From the keep, an answering horn sang its welcome.

Not just one army had been spared here today, Yrene realized as she turned back to the water station. If that wave had reached Kashin . . .

Lucky. They had all been so, so very lucky.

Yet Yrene wondered how long that luck would last.

If it would see them through the brutal march northward, and to the walls of Orynth itself.

Lorcan let out a low groan as he surfaced from the warm, heavy embrace of darkness.

"You are one lucky bastard."

Too soon. Too damn soon after hovering near death to hear Fenrys's drawl.

Lorcan cracked open an eye, finding himself lying on a cot in a narrow chamber. A lone candle illuminated the space, dancing in the golden hair of the Fae warrior who sat in a wooden chair at the foot of his bed.

Fenrys's smirk was a slash of white. "You've been out for a day. I drew the short stick and had to look after you."

A lie. For whatever reason, Fenrys had chosen to be here.

Lorcan shifted his body—slightly.

No hint of pain beyond a dull throb down his back and tight pull across his stomach. He managed to lift his head enough to rip away the heavy wool blanket covering his naked body. Where he'd been able to see his insides, only a thick red scar remained.

Lorcan thumped his head back on the pillow. "Elide." Her name was a rasp on his tongue.

The last he remembered, they'd ridden through the gates, Aelin Galathynius's unholy power spent. Then oblivion had swept in.

"Helping with the healing in the Great Hall," Fenrys said, stretching out his legs before him.

Lorcan closed his eyes, something tight in his chest easing.

"Well, since you're not dead," Fenrys began, but Lorcan was already asleep.

Lorcan awoke later. Hours, days, he didn't know.

The candle was still burning on the narrow windowsill, down to its base. Hours, then. Unless he'd slept so long they'd replaced the candle altogether.

He didn't care. Not when the dim light revealed the delicate woman lying facedown on the end of his cot, the lower half of her body still on the wooden chair where Fenrys had been. Her arms cradled her head, one outstretched toward him. Reaching for his hand, mere inches from hers.

Elide.

Her dark hair spilled across the blanket, across his shins, veiling much of her face.

Wincing at the lingering ache in his body, Lorcan stretched his arm just enough to touch her fingers.

They were cold, their tips so much smaller than his. They contracted, pulling away as she sucked in a sharp, awakening breath.

Lorcan savored every feature as she grimaced at a crick in her neck. But her eyes settled on him.

She went still as she found him staring at her, awake and utterly in awe of the woman who had ridden through hell to find him . . .

Tired. She looked spent, yet her chin remained unbowed.

Lorcan had no words. He'd given her everything on the back of that horse anyway.

But Elide asked, "How do you feel?"

Aching. Exhausted. Yet finding her sitting at his bedside . . . "Alive," he said, and meant it.

Her face remained unreadable, even as her eyes dipped to his body. The blanket had slid down enough to reveal most of his torso, though it still hid the scarred-over wound in his abdomen. Yet he'd never felt so keenly naked.

It was an effort to keep his breathing steady beneath her sharp-eyed gaze. "Yrene said you would have died, if they hadn't gotten to you when they did."

"I would have died," he said, voice like gravel, "if you hadn't braved hell to find me."

Her gaze lifted to his. "I made you a promise."

"So you said."

Was that a hint of color stealing across her pale cheeks? But she didn't balk. "You said some interesting things, too."

Lorcan tried to sit up, but his body gave a burst of pain in protest.

Elide explained, "Yrene warned that though the wounds are healed, some soreness will linger."

Lorcan gritted his teeth around the sharp stab in his back, his stomach. He managed to get onto his elbows, and deemed that progress enough. "It's been a while since I was so gravely injured. I'd forgotten what an inconvenience it is."

A faint smile tugged on her mouth.

His heart halted. The first smile she had given him in months and months. Since that day on the ship, when he'd touched her hand as they'd swayed in their hammocks.

Her smile faded, but the color on her cheeks lingered. "Did you mean it? What you said."

He held her stare. Let some inner wall within him come crumbling down. Only for her. For this sharp-eyed, cunning little liar who had slipped through every defense and ironclad rule he'd ever made for himself. He let her see that in his face. Let her see all of it, as no one had ever done before. "Yes."

Her mouth tightened, but not in displeasure.

So Lorcan said softly, "I meant every word." His heart thundered, so wildly it was a wonder she couldn't hear it. "And I will until the day I fade into the Afterworld."

Lorcan didn't breathe as Elide gently reached out her hand. And interlaced their fingers. "I love you," she whispered.

He was glad he was lying down. The words would have knocked him to his knees. Even now, he was half inclined to bow before her, the true owner of his ancient, wicked heart.

"I have loved you," she went on, "from the moment you came to fight for me against Vernon and the ilken." The light in her eyes stole his breath. "And when I heard you were somewhere on that battlefield, the only thing I wanted was to be able to tell you that. It was the only thing that mattered."

Once, he might have scoffed. Declared that far bigger things mattered, in this war especially. And yet the hand grasping his . . . He'd never known anything more precious.

Lorcan ran his thumb over the back of her hand. "I am sorry, Elide. For all of it."

"I know," she said softly, and no regret or hurt dimmed her face. Only clear, unwavering calm shone there. The face of the mighty lady she was growing into, and had already become, and who would rule Perranth with wisdom in one hand and compassion in the other.

They stared at each other for minutes. For a blessed eternity.

Then Elide untangled their hands and rose. "I should return to help Yrene."

Lorcan caught her hand again. "Stay."

She arched a dark brow. "I'm only going to the Great Hall."

Lorcan caressed his thumb over the back of her hand once more. "Stay," he breathed.

For a heartbeat, he thought she'd say no, and was prepared to be fine with it, to accept these last few minutes as more of a gift than he'd deserved.

But then Elide sat on the edge of his cot, right beside his shoulder, and ran a hand through his hair. Lorcan closed his eyes, leaning into the touch, unable to stop the deep purr that rolled through his chest.

She made a low noise of wonder, perhaps something more, and her fingers stroked again.

"Say it," she whispered, fingers stilling in his hair.

Lorcan opened his eyes, finding her gaze. "I love you."

She swallowed hard, and Lorcan gritted his teeth as he sat up fully. This close, he had forgotten how much he towered over her. Atop that horse, she had been a force of nature, a defiant storm. His blanket slipped dangerously low, but he let it lie where it pooled in his lap.

He didn't miss the dip of her stare. Or the long, upward drag of her eyes along his torso. He could almost feel it, lingering on every muscle and scar.

A soft groan came out of him as she continued to look her fill. Asking for things that he sure as hell was in no shape to give her. And that she might not yet be ready to give him, declarations aside.

He was immediately challenged to prove his resolve as Elide ran slightly shaking fingers across the new scar on his abdomen.

"Yrene said you might always have this," she said, her hand mercifully falling away.

"Then it will be the scar I treasure most." Fenrys would laugh until he cried to hear him speak this way, but Lorcan didn't care. To hell with the rest of them.

Another one of those small smiles curved her lips, and Lorcan's hands tightened in the sheets with the effort it took not to taste that smile, to worship it with his own mouth.

But this new, fragile thing humming between them . . . He would not risk it for all the world.

Elide, thank the gods, had no such worries. None at all, it seemed, as she lifted a hand to his cheek and ran her thumb along it. Every breath was an effort of control.

Lorcan held absolutely still as she brought her mouth to his. Brushed her lips across his own.

She pulled back. "Rest, Lorcan. I'll be here again when you wake."

Anything she asked, he'd give her. Anything at all.

Too shaken by that soft, beautiful kiss to bother with words, he lay back down.

She smiled at his utter obedience, and, as if she couldn't help herself, leaned in once more.

This kiss lingered. Her mouth traced his, and at the slight pressure of her lips, the gentle request, he answered with his own.

The taste of her threatened to undo him entirely, and the tentative brush of her tongue against his own drew another rolling purr from deep in his chest. But Lorcan let Elide explore him, slowly and sweetly, giving her whatever she asked.

And when her mouth became more insistent, when her breathing turned ragged, he slipped a hand around her neck to cup her nape. She opened for him, and at her low moan, Lorcan thought he'd fly out of his skin.

His hand slipped from her nape to run down her back, savoring the warm, unbreakable body beneath the layers of clothes. Elide arched into the touch, another of those small noises coming from her. As if she'd been just as starved for him.

But Lorcan made himself pull away. Made himself withdraw his hand from her lower back. Panting slightly, sharing breath, he said onto her mouth, "Later. Go help the others."

Dark eyes glazed with desire met his, and Lorcan adjusted the fall of the blanket over his lap. "Go help the others," he repeated. "I'll be here when you're ready to sleep."

The unspoken request lingered, and Elide pulled back, studying him once more.

"Sleep only," Lorcan said, not bothering to hide the heat rising in his stare. "For now."

Until she was ready. Until she told him, showed him, she wished to share everything with him. That final claiming.

But until then, he wanted her here. Sleeping at his side, where he might watch over her. As she had watched over him.

Elide's face was flushed as she rose, her hands shaking. Not from fear, but from the same effort that it now took Lorcan not to reach for her.

He'd very much enjoy driving her out of her mind. Slowly teaching her all he knew about pleasure, about wanting. He had little doubt he'd be learning a good number of things from her, too.

Elide seemed to read that on his face, and her cheeks reddened further. "Later, then," she breathed, limping to the door.

Lorcan sent a flicker of his power to wrap around her ankle. The limp vanished.

A hand on the knob, she gave him a small, grateful nod. "I missed that."

He heard the unspoken words as she disappeared into the busy hall.

I missed you.

Lorcan allowed himself a rare smile.

CHAPTER
65

Dorian had gone to Morath.

Had flown from the camp on wings of his own making. He would have chosen some sort of small, ordinary bird, Manon knew. Something even the Thirteen would not have noted.

Manon stood at the edge of the outlook, gazing eastward.

Crunching snow told her Asterin approached. "He left, didn't he."

She nodded, unable to find words. She had offered him everything, and had thought he'd meant to accept it. Had thought he *did* accept it, with what they'd done afterward.

Yet it had been a farewell. One last coupling before he ventured into the jaws of death. He would not cage her, would not accept what she'd given.

As if he knew her better than she knew herself.

"Do we go after him?"

In the breaking light of dawn, the camp was stirring. Today—today they would decide where to go. Today, she'd dare ask the Crochans to follow. Would they heed her?

But to head to Morath, where they would be recognized long before they approached, to head back into hell . . .

The sun rose, full and golden, as if it were the solitary note of a song filling the world.

Manon opened her mouth.

"Terrasen calls for aid!" A young Crochan's voice rang through the camp.

Manon and Asterin whirled, others following suit as the witch sprinted for Glennis's tent. The crone emerged as the witch skidded to a halt. A scout, no doubt, breathless and hair wind-tossed.

"Terrasen calls for aid," the scout panted, bracing her hands on her knees as she bent over to gulp down breaths. "Morath routed them at the border, then at Perranth, and advances on Orynth as we speak. They will sack the city within a week."

Worse news than Manon had anticipated. Even if she'd needed it, waited for it.

The Thirteen closed in, Bronwen a step behind, and Manon didn't dare breathe as Glennis stared toward the immortal flame burning in the fire pit mere feet away. The Flame of War.

Then she turned toward Manon. "What say you, Queen of Witches?"

A challenge and a dare.

Manon lifted her chin at the two paths before her.

One to the east, to Morath. The other northward, to Terrasen and battle.

The wind sang, and in it, she heard the answer.

"I shall answer Terrasen's call," Manon said.

Asterin stepped to her side, fearless as she surveyed the assembled camp. "As shall I."

Sorrel flanked Manon's right. "So shall the Thirteen."

Manon waited, hardly daring to acknowledge the thing that began burning in her chest.

Then Bronwen stepped up, her dark hair blowing in the chill wind. "The Vanora hearth shall fly north."

Another witch squared her shoulders. "So shall the Silian."

And so it went.

Until the leaders of all seven of the Great Hearths stood gathered there.

Until Glennis said to Manon, "Long ago, Rhiannon Crochan rode at King Brannon's side into battle. So has her likeness been reborn, so shall the old alliances be forged anew." She gestured to the eternal flame. "Light the Flame of War, Queen of Witches, and rally your host."

Manon's heart raced, so wildly it pulsed in her palms, but she picked up a birch branch set amongst the kindling.

No one spoke as she plunged it into the eternal flame.

Red and gold and blue leaped upon the wood, devouring it. Manon withdrew the branch only when it had caught, deep and true.

Even the wind did not jostle the flame as Manon lifted it, a torch in the new day.

The Crochan crowd parted, revealing a straight path toward Bronwen's hearth. The witch was already waiting, her coven gathered around her.

Each step was a drumbeat of war. An answer to a question posed long ago.

Bronwen's eyes were bright as Manon stopped.

Manon only said, "Your queen summons you to war."

And touched her flame to that in Bronwen's hearth.

Light flared, bright and dancing.

Bronwen picked up a branch of her own, a long log burning in the fire. "The Vanora will fly."

She withdrew the wood and stalked to the next clan's hearth, where she plunged that kernel of the sacred fire into their pit. Again the light flared, just as Bronwen declared, loud and clear as the breaking day around them, "Your queen summons you to war. The Vanora fly with her. Will you?"

The hearth leader only said, "The Redbriar will fly," and ignited her own torch before hurrying to the next clan's fire.

Hearth to hearth. Until all seven in the camp had accepted and ignited the fire.

Then, and only then, did the young scout from the final clan take her burning torch, grab her broom, and leap into the skies. To find the next clan, to tell them the call had gone out.

Manon and the Thirteen, the Crochans around them, watched until the scout was nothing but a smoldering speck against the sky, then nothing at all.

Manon offered a silent prayer on the wind that the sacred flame the young scout bore would burn steadfast over the long, dangerous miles.

All the way to the killing fields of Terrasen.

Hearth to hearth, the Flame of War went.

Over snow-blasted mountains and amongst the trees of tangled forests, hiding from the enemies that prowled the skies. Through long, bitterly cold nights where the wind howled as it tried to wipe out any trace of that flame.

But the wind did not succeed, not against the flame of the queen.

So hearth to hearth, it went.

To remote villages where people screamed and scattered as a young-faced woman descended from the skies on a broom, waving her torch high.

Not to signal them, but the few women who did not run. Who walked toward the flame, the rider, as she called out, *Your queen summons you to war. Will you fly?*

Trunks hidden in attics were thrown open. Folded swaths of red cloth pulled from within. Brooms left in closets, beside doorways, tucked under beds, were brought out, bound in gold or silver or twine.

And swords—ancient and beautiful—were drawn from beneath floorboards, or hauled down from haylofts, their metal shining as bright and fresh as the day they had been forged in a city now lying in ruin.

Witches, the townsfolk whispered, husbands wide-eyed and disbelieving as the women took to the skies, red cloaks billowing. *Witches amongst us all this time.*

Village to village, where hearths that had never once gone fully dark blazed in answer. Always one rider going out, to find the next hearth, the next bastion of their people.

Witches, here amongst us. Witches, now going to war.

A rising tide of witches, who took to the skies in their red cloaks, swords strapped to their backs, brooms shedding years of dust with each mile northward.

Witches who bade their families farewell, offering no explanation before they kissed their sleeping babes and vanished into the starry night.

Mile after mile, across the darkening world, the call went out, ceaseless and unending as the eternal flame that passed from hearth to hearth.

"*Fly, fly, fly!*" they shouted. "*To the queen! To war!*"

Far and wide, through snow and storm and peril, the Crochans flew.

CHAPTER 66

Aelin awoke to the scent of pine and snow, and knew she was home.

Not in Terrasen, not yet, but in the sense she would *always* be home, if Rowan was with her.

His steady breaths filled her right ear, the sound of the well and truly asleep, and the arm he'd draped across her middle was a solid, warm weight. Silvery light glazed the ancient stones of the ceiling.

Morning—or a cloudy day. The halls beyond the room offered shards of sound that she sorted through, piece by piece, as if she were assembling a broken mirror that might reveal the world beyond.

Apparently, it had been three days since the battle. And the rest of the khagan's army, led by Prince Kashin, his third-eldest son, had arrived.

It was that tidbit that had her rising fully to consciousness, a hand sliding to Rowan's arm. A caress of a touch, just to see how deeply the rejuvenating sleep held him. Three days, they'd slept here, unaware of the world. A dangerous, vulnerable time for any magic-wielder, when their bodies demanded a deep sleep to recover from expending so much power.

That was another sliver she'd picked up: Gavriel sat outside their door. In mountain lion form. People drew quiet when they approached, not realizing that as soon as they passed him, their whispers of *That strange, terrifying cat* could be detected by Fae ears.

Aelin ran a finger over the seam of Rowan's sleeve, feeling the corded muscle beneath. Clear—her head, her body felt *clear*. Like the first icy breath inhaled on a winter's morning.

During the days they'd slept, no nightmare had shaken her awake, hunted her. A small, merciful reprieve.

Aelin swallowed, her throat dry. What had been real, what Maeve had tried to plant in her mind—did it matter, whether the pain had been true or imagined?

She had gotten out, gotten away from Maeve and Cairn. Facing the broken bits inside her would come later.

For now, it was enough to have this clarity back. Even though releasing her power, expending that mighty blow here, had not been her plan.

Aelin slid her gaze toward Rowan, his harsh face softened into handsomeness by sleep. And clean—the gore that had splattered them both was gone. Someone must have washed it away while they slept.

As if he sensed her attention, or just felt the lingering hand on his arm, Rowan's eyes cracked open. He scanned her from head to toe, deemed everything all right, and met her stare.

"Show-off," he muttered.

Aelin patted his arm. "You put on a pretty fancy display yourself, Prince."

He smiled, his tattoo crinkling. "Will that display be the last of your surprises, or are there more coming?"

She debated it—telling him, revealing it. *Maybe.*

Rowan sat up, the blanket sliding from him. *Is this the sort of surprise that will end with my heart stopping dead in my chest?*

She snorted, propping her head with a fist as she traced idle marks over the scratchy blanket. "I sent a letter—when we were at that port in Wendlyn."

Rowan nodded. "To Aedion."

"To Aedion," she said, quietly enough that Gavriel couldn't hear from his spot outside the door. "And to your uncle. And to Essar."

Rowan's brows rose. "Saying what?"

She hummed to herself. "Saying that I was indeed imprisoned by Maeve, and that while I was her captive, she laid out some rather nefarious plans."

Her mate went still. "With what goal in mind?"

Aelin sat up, and picked at her nails. "Convincing them to disband her army. Start a revolt in Doranelle. Kick Maeve off the throne. You know, small things."

Rowan just looked at her. Then scrubbed at his face. "You think a letter could do that?"

"It was strongly worded."

He gaped a bit. "What sort of nefarious plans did you mention?"

"Desire to conquer the world, her complete lack of interest in sparing Fae lives in a war, her interest in Valg things." She swallowed. "I might have mentioned that she's possibly Valg."

Rowan started.

Aelin shrugged. "It was a lucky guess. The best lies are always mixed with truth."

"Suggesting Maeve is Valg is a fairly outlandish lie, even for you. Even if it turned out to be true."

She waved a hand. "We'll see if anything comes of it."

"If it works, if they somehow revolt and the army turns against her . . ." He shook his head, laughing softly. "It'd be a boon in this war."

"I scheme and lie so grandly, and that's all the credit I get?"

Rowan flicked her nose. "You'll get credit if her army doesn't show up. Until then, we prepare as if they are. Which is highly likely." At her frown, he said, "Essar doesn't wield much power, and my uncle doesn't take many risks. Not like Enda and Sellene. For them to overthrow Maeve . . . it would be monumental. If they even survived it."

Her stomach churned. "It's their choice, what they do. I only laid out the facts." Carefully worded facts and half guesses. An absolute gamble, if she was being honest.

Rowan smirked. "And other than attempting to overthrow Maeve's throne? Any other surprises I should know about?"

Her smile faded as she lay back down, Rowan doing the same beside her. "There are no more." At his raised brows, she added, "I swear it on my throne. There are no more left."

The amusement in his eyes guttered. "I don't know whether to be relieved."

"Everything I know, you know. All the cards are on the table now."

With the various armies that had gathered, with the Lock, with all of it.

"Do you think you could do it again?" he asked. "Draw up that much power?"

"I don't know. I don't think so. It required being . . . contained. With the irons."

A shadow darkened his face, and he rolled onto his side, propping up his head. "I've never seen anything like it."

"You never will again." It was the truth.

"If the cost of that much power is what you endured, then I'll be glad not to."

Aelin ran a hand down the powerful muscles of his thigh, fingers snagging in the rip of fabric just above his knee. "I didn't feel you get this wound through the mating bond," she said, grazing the thick ridge of the new scar. A trophy from the battle. She made herself meet his piercing stare. *Did Maeve somehow break that part of it? That part of us?*

"No," he breathed, and stroked the hair from her brow. "I've realized that the bond only conveys the pain of the gravest wounds."

She touched the spot on his shoulder where Asterin Blackbeak's arrow had pierced him all those months ago. The moment she'd known what he was to her.

"It was why I didn't know what was happening to you on the beach," Rowan said roughly. Because the whipping, brutal and unbearable as it had been, hadn't brought her to the brink of death. Only into an iron coffin.

She scowled. "If you're about to tell me that you feel guilty for it—"

"We both have things to grapple with—about what happened these months."

A glance at him, and she knew he was well aware of what still clouded her soul.

And because he was the only person who saw everything she was and did not walk away from it, Aelin said, "I wanted that fire to be for Maeve."

"I know." Such simple words, and yet it meant everything—that understanding.

"I wanted it to make things . . . better." She loosed a long breath. "To wipe it all away." Every memory and nightmare and lie.

"It will take a while, Aelin. To face it, work through it."

"I don't have a while."

His jaw tensed. "That remains to be seen."

She didn't bother arguing. Not as she admitted, "I want it to be over."

He went wholly still, but granted her the space to think, to speak.

"I want it to be over and done with," she said hoarsely. "This war, the gods and the Wyrdgate and the Lock. All of it." She rubbed her temples, pushing past the weight, the lingering stain that no fire might cleanse. "I want to go to Terrasen, to fight, and then I want it to be over."

She'd wanted it to be over since she'd learned the true cost of forging the Lock anew. Had wanted it to be over with each of Cairn's lashes on the beach in Eyllwe. And all he'd done to her afterward. Whatever it might bring about, however it might end, she wanted it to be over.

She didn't know who and what it made her.

Rowan remained silent for a long moment before he said, "Then we will make sure the khagan's host goes north. Then we will return to Terrasen and crush Erawan's armies." He brought her hands to his mouth for a swift kiss. "And then, after all that, we'll see about this damned Lock." Uncompromising will filled his every breath, the air around them.

She let it be enough for both of them. Tucked away his words, his vow, all those promises between them and extended her palm in the air between them.

She summoned the magic—the drop of water her mother's bloodline had given her. Mab's bloodline.

A tiny ball of water took form in her hand. Over the calluses she'd so carefully rebuilt.

She let the gentle, cooling power trickle over her. Let it smooth the jagged bits inside herself and sing them to sleep. Her mother's gift.

You do not yield.

When the Lock took everything, would it claim this part as well? This most precious part of her power?

She tucked away those thoughts, too.

Concentrating, gritting her teeth, Aelin commanded the ball of water to rotate in her palm.

A wobble was all she got in answer.

She snorted. "Faerie Queen of the West indeed."

Rowan huffed a quiet laugh. "Keep practicing. In a thousand years, you might actually be able to do something with it."

She whacked his arm, the droplet of water soaking into the sleeve of his shirt. "It's a wonder I learned anything from you with that sort of encouragement." She shook the wetness from her hand. Right into his face.

Rowan nipped at her nose. "I do keep a tally, Princess. Of all the horrible things that come out of your mouth."

Her toes curled, and she dragged her fingers through his hair, luxuriating in the silken strands. "How shall I pay for this one?"

On the other side of the door, she could have sworn that cat-soft feet quickly padded away.

Rowan smirked, as if sensing Gavriel's swift exit, too. Then his hand flattened on her abdomen, his mouth grazing the underside of her jaw. "I've been thinking of some ways."

But the hand he'd set on her belly pushed down just enough that Aelin let out an *oomph*. And realized that she'd been asleep for three days—and had the bladder to go with it. She winced, shooting to her feet. She swayed, and he was instantly there, steadying her. "Before you ravish me wholly," she declared, "I need to find a bathing room."

Rowan laughed, stooping to gather his sword belt, left neatly by the wall alongside hers. Only Gavriel would have arranged them with such care. "That need indeed trumps what I had planned."

People gawked in the halls, some whispering as they passed.

The queen and her consort. Where do you think they've been these past few days?

I heard they went into the mountains and brought the wild men back with them.

I heard they've been weaving spells around the city, to protect it against Morath.

Rowan was still smirking when Aelin emerged from the communal ladies' bathing room.

"See?" She fell into step beside him as they aimed not for their room and ravishment, but for the hallway where food had been laid out. "You're starting to like the notoriety."

Rowan arched a brow. "You think that everywhere I've gone for the past three hundred years, whispers haven't followed me?" She rolled her eyes, but he chuckled. "This is far better than *Cold-hearted bastard* or *I heard he killed someone with a table leg.*"

"You *did* kill someone with a table leg."

Rowan's smirk grew.

"And you *are* a cold-hearted bastard," she threw in.

Rowan snorted. "I never said those whispers were lies."

Aelin looped her arm through his. "I'm going to start a rumor about you, then. Something truly grotesque."

He groaned. "I dread the thought of what *you* might come up with."

She adopted a harsh whisper as they passed a group of human soldiers. "*You flew back onto the battlefield to peck out the eyes of our enemies?*" Her gasp echoed off the rock. "*And ate those eyes?*"

One of the soldiers tripped, the others whipping their heads to them.

Rowan pinched her shoulder. "Thank you for that."

She inclined her head. "You're very welcome."

Aelin kept smiling as they found food and ate a quick lunch—it was midday, they'd learned—sitting side by side in a dusty, half-forgotten stairwell. Much like the days they'd spent in Mistward, knee to knee and shoulder to shoulder in the kitchen while listening to Emrys's stories.

Though unlike those months this spring, when Aelin set down her plate between her feet, she slid her arms around Rowan's neck and his mouth instantly met hers.

No, it was certainly not at all like their time at Mistward as she crawled into Rowan's lap, not entirely caring that anyone might stride up or down the stairs, and kissed him silly.

They halted, breathless and wild-eyed, before she could decide that it really wouldn't be a bad idea to unfasten his pants right there, or that his hand, discreetly and lazily rubbing that damned spot between her thighs, should be inside her.

If Aelin was being honest with herself, she was still debating hauling him into the nearest closet when they set off to find their companions at last. One glance at Rowan's glazed eyes and she knew he was debating the same.

Yet even the desire heating her blood cooled when they entered the ancient study near the top of the keep and beheld the gathered group. Fenrys and Gavriel were already there, Chaol with them, no sign of Elide or Lorcan.

But Chaol's father, unfortunately, was present. And glowered as they entered the meeting that seemed well under way. Aelin gave him a mocking smile and sauntered up to the large desk.

A tall, broad-shouldered man stood with Nesryn, Sartaq, and Hasar, handsome and brimming with a sort of impatient energy. His brown eyes were welcoming, his smile easy. She liked him immediately.

"My brother," Hasar said, waving a hand without looking up from the map. "Kashin."

The prince sketched a graceful bow.

Aelin offered one back, Rowan doing the same. "An honor," Aelin said. "Thank you for coming."

"You can actually thank my father for that. And Yrene," said Kashin, his use of their language as flawless as his siblings'.

Indeed, Aelin had much to thank the healer for.

Nesryn's sharp eyes scanned Aelin from head to toe. "You're feeling all right?"

"Just needed to rest." Aelin jerked her chin at Rowan. "He requires frequent naps in his old age."

Sartaq coughed, keeping his head down as he continued studying the map.

Fenrys, however, laughed. "Back to your good spirits, I see."

Aelin smirked at Chaol's straight-backed father. "We'll see how long it lasts."

The man said nothing.

Rowan motioned to the desk and asked the royals, "Have you decided—where you shall march now?"

Such a casual, calm question. As if the fate of Terrasen did not rest upon it.

Hasar opened her mouth, but Sartaq cut her off. "North. We shall indeed go north with you. If only to repay you for saving our army—our people."

Aelin tried not to look too relieved.

"Gratitude aside," Hasar said, not sounding very grateful at all, "Kashin's scouts have confirmed that Terrasen is where Morath is concentrating its efforts. So it is there that we shall go."

Aelin wished she had not eaten such a large lunch. "How bad is it?"

Nesryn shook her head, answering for Prince Kashin, "The details were murky. All we know is that hordes were spotted marching northward, leaving a trail of destruction in their wake."

Aelin kept her fists at her sides, avoiding the urge to rub at her face.

Chaol's father said, "I hope that power of yours can be summoned again."

Aelin let an ember of that power smolder in her eyes. "Thank you for the armor," she crooned.

"Consider it an early coronation gift," the Lord of Anielle countered with a mocking smile.

Sartaq cleared his throat. "If you and your companions are recovered, then we'll press northward as soon as we are able." No objections from Hasar at that.

"And march along the mountains?" Rowan asked, scanning the map. Aelin traced the route they'd follow. "We'd have to pass directly before the Ferian Gap. We'll barely clear the other end of this lake before we're in another battle."

"So we draw them out," Hasar said. "Trick them into emptying whatever forces wait in the Gap, then sneak up on them from behind."

"Adarlan controls the entire Avery," Chaol said, drawing an invisible line inland from Rifthold. "To pass north, we have to cross that river anyway. In picking the Gap as our battleground, we'll avoid the mess that would come with fighting in the midst of Oakwald. The ruks, at least, would be able to provide aerial coverage. Not so with the trees."

Rowan nodded. "We'd need to march the majority of the host up into the mountains, then—to come at the Gap from where they'd least expect it. It's rough terrain, though. We'll need to pick our route carefully."

Chaol's father grumbled. Aelin lifted her brows, but his son answered, "I sent out emissaries the day after the battle—into the Fangs. To contact the wild men who live there, if they might know of secret ways through the mountains to the Gap."

Ancient enemies of this city. "And?"

"They do. But at a cost."

"One that shall not be paid," the Lord of Anielle snapped.

"Let me guess: territory," Aelin said.

Chaol nodded. Hence the tension in this room.

She tapped a foot as she surveyed the Lord of Anielle. "And you won't give one sliver of land to them?"

He just glared.

"Apparently not," Fenrys muttered.

Aelin shrugged, and turned to Chaol. "Well, it's settled, then."

"What is settled?" his father ground out.

Aelin ignored him, and winked at her friend. "You're the Hand to the King of Adarlan. You outrank him. You're authorized to act on Dorian's behalf." She gestured to the map. "The land might be a part of Anielle, but it belongs to Adarlan. Go ahead and barter it."

His father started. "*You—*"

"We are going north," Aelin said. "You will not stand in our way." She again let some of her fire kindle in her eyes, set the gold in them burning. "I halted that wave. Consider this alliance with the wild men a way to repay the favor."

"That wave destroyed half my city," the man snarled.

Fenrys let out a low, disbelieving laugh. Rowan snarled softly.

Chaol growled at his father, "You're a bastard."

"Watch your tongue, boy."

Aelin nodded sympathetically to Chaol. "I see why you left."

Chaol, to his credit, winced and returned to the map. "If we can get past the Ferian Gap, then we continue northward."

Past Endovier. That path would take them right past Endovier. Aelin's stomach tightened. Rowan's hand grazed her own.

"We have to decide soon," Sartaq declared. "Right now, we sit between the Ferian Gap and Morath. It would be very easy for Erawan to send hosts to crush us between them."

Hasar turned to Chaol. "Is Yrene anywhere near done?"

He leaned an elbow against the arm of his wheeled chair. "Even with the few survivors, there are too many of them. We'd be here weeks."

"How many injured?" Rowan asked.

Chaol shook his head. "Not injured." His jaw tightened. "Valg."

Aelin frowned. "Yrene's healing the Valg?"

Hasar grinned. "In a manner of speaking."

Aelin waved her off. "Can I see?"

They found Yrene not in the keep, but in a tent on the remnants of the battlefield, leaning over a human man thrashing upon a cot. The man had been restrained to anchors in the floor at his wrists and ankles.

Aelin took one look at those chains and had to swallow.

Rowan laid a hand on her lower back, and Fenrys stepped closer to her side.

Yrene paused, her hands wreathed in white light. Borte, sword out, lingered nearby.

"Is something wrong?" Yrene asked, the glow in her hands fading. The man sagged, going boneless as the healer's assault on the demon inside him halted.

Chaol steered his chair closer to her, the wheels equipped for rougher terrain. "Aelin and her companions want a demonstration. If you're up for it."

Yrene smoothed back the hair that had escaped her braid. "It's not really anything that you can see. What happens is beneath the skin—mind to mind."

"You go up against Valg demons directly," Fenrys said with no small amount of awe.

"They're hateful, cowardly wretches." Yrene crossed her arms and scowled at the man tied to the cot. "Utterly pathetic," she spat toward him—the demon inside him.

The man hissed. Yrene only smiled. The man—the demon—whimpered.

Aelin blinked, unsure whether to laugh or fall to her knees. "Show me. Do whatever it is you do, but show me."

So the healer did. Hands shining, she laid them atop the man's chest. He screamed and screamed and screamed.

Yrene panted, brows scrunching. For long minutes, the shrieking continued.

Borte said, "It's not very exciting with them tied down, is it?"

Sartaq threw her an exasperated glare. As if this were a conversation they'd already had many times. "You can be on mucking duty, if you'd prefer."

Borte rolled her eyes, but turned to Aelin, looking her over with a frankness that Aelin could only appreciate. "Any other missions for me?"

Aelin grinned. "Not yet. Soon, perhaps."

Borte grinned right back. "Please. *Please* spare me from the tedium of this."

Aelin glanced toward the healer radiant with light. "How many does this make today?"

"Ten," Borte grumbled.

Aelin asked Chaol, "And how many can she do every day?"

"Fifteen, at most. Some require more energy than others to expel, so those days it's less."

Aelin tried to do the math on how many infested soldiers were left on the field. "And once they're cured? What do you do with them then?"

"We interrogate them," Chaol said, frowning. "See what their stories are, how they wound up captured. Where their allegiances lie."

"And you believe them?" Fenrys asked.

Hasar patted the hilt of her fine sword. "Our interrogators are skilled at retrieving the truth."

Aelin ignored the roiling in her stomach.

"So you free them," Gavriel said, silent for minutes now, "and then torture them?"

"This is war," Hasar said simply. "We leave them able to function. But we will not risk sparing their lives only to find a new army at our backs."

"Some willingly joined Erawan," Chaol said quietly. "Some willingly took the ring. Yrene can tell, when she's in there, who wanted it or not. She doesn't bother to save those who gladly knelt. So most of those she does save were either fools or taken forcibly."

"Some want to fight for us," Sartaq said. "Those who pass our vetting process are allowed to begin training with the foot soldiers. Not many of them, but a few."

Fine. Fine, and fine.

Yrene gasped, her light flaring bright enough that Aelin squinted.

The man bound to the cot coughed, arching.

Black, noxious vomit sprayed.

Borte grimaced, waving away the smell. Then the black smoke that rippled from his mouth.

Yrene slumped back, Chaol shooting out an arm to brace her. The healer only took a perch on the arm of his chair, a hand on her heaving chest.

Aelin gave her a moment to catch her breath. To manage such a feat was remarkable. To do it while pregnant . . . Aelin shook her head in wonder.

Yrene said to no one in particular, "That demon didn't want to go."

"But it's gone now?" Aelin asked.

Yrene pointed to the man on the cot, now opening his eyes. Brown, not black, gazed upward.

"Thank you," was all the man said, his voice raw.

And human. Utterly human.

CHAPTER 67

Rowan followed Aelin as she meandered across the battlefield, to the edge of the Silver Lake. She stopped only now and then to pick up any worthwhile enemy weapons. There were few.

The others had dispersed, Gavriel lingering to learn how Yrene healed the Valg, Fenrys heading off with Chaol to meet with emissaries from the wild men, and the khaganate royals seeing to their troops.

They would leave in two days, if the weather held. Two days, and then they'd begin the push north.

Thank the gods. Even though they were the last beings Rowan wished to thank.

Aelin halted at the rocky shore, peering across the mirror-flat expanse now choked with debris. She rested a hand atop Goldryn's hilt, flame dancing at her fingers, seemingly into the red stone itself.

"It would take years," she observed, "to heal everyone infected by the Valg."

"Each of those soldiers has a family, friends who would want us to try."

"I know." The chill wind whipped her hair across her face, blowing northward.

"Then why the walk out here?" She'd gone contemplative during their meeting in the tent, her brow furrowing.

"Could Yrene heal *them*? Erawan and Maeve? I don't know why I didn't think of it."

"Is Erawan's body made by him, or stolen? Is Maeve's?" Rowan shook his head. "They might be wholly different."

"I don't see how I can ask Yrene to do it. Ask it of Chaol." Aelin swallowed. "To even put Yrene *near* Erawan or Maeve . . . I can't do it."

Rowan wouldn't be able to, either. Not for a thousand different reasons.

"But is it a mistake to put Yrene's safety above that of this entire world?" Aelin mused, examining one of the enemy daggers she'd pilfered. An unusually fine blade, likely stolen in the first place. "She's the greatest weapon we have, if the keys are not in play. Are we fools not to push to use it?"

It wasn't his choice, his call. But he could offer her a sounding board. "Will you be able to live with yourself if something happens to Yrene, to her unborn child?"

"No. But the rest of the world will live, at least. My guilt would be secondary to that."

"And if you don't push Yrene to try to destroy them, and Erawan or Maeve wins—what then?"

"There is still the Lock. There's still me."

Rowan swallowed. Saw the reason she'd needed to be away from the others, needed to walk. "Yrene is a ray of hope for you. For us. That you might not need to forge the Lock at all. You, or Dorian."

"The gods demand it."

"The gods can go to hell."

Aelin chucked away the dagger. "I hate this. I really do."

He slid an arm around her shoulders. It was all he could offer her.

Over—she'd said she wanted it to be over. He'd do all he could to make it so.

Aelin leaned her head against his chest, and they stared across the cold lake in silence. "Would you let me do it, if I were Yrene? If I were carrying our child?"

He failed to block out the image of that dream—of Aelin, heavily pregnant, their children around her. "I don't *let* you do anything."

She waved a hand. "You know what I mean."

He took a moment to answer. "No. Even if the world ended because of it, I couldn't bear it."

And with that Lock, he might very well have to make that decision, too.

Rowan ran his fingers over the claiming marks on her neck. "I told you that love was a weakness. It would be far easier if we all hated each other."

She snorted. "Give it a few weeks on the road with this army, in those mountains, and we might not be such pleasant allies anymore."

Rowan kissed the top of her head. "Gods help us."

But Aelin pulled away at the words, the phrase that dropped off his tongue. She frowned toward the camped army.

"What?" he asked.

"I want to see those Wyrdmark books Chaol and Yrene brought with them."

~

"What does this say?" Aelin asked Borte, tapping a finger on a scribbled line of text in Halha, the tongue of the southern continent.

Seated beside her at the desk in Prince Sartaq's war tent, the ruk rider craned her neck to study the handwritten note beside a long column of Wyrdmarks. *"A good spell for encouraging your herb beds to grow."*

Across the desk, Rowan snorted. A book lay open before him, his progress through it far slower than Aelin's.

Most of the tomes were wholly written in Wyrdmarks, but annotations scribbled in the margins had driven her to seek out the young rukhin. Borte, thoroughly bored with helping Yrene, had leaped at the chance to assist them, passing Valg duty onto her scowling betrothed.

But for the two hours that Aelin and Rowan had perused the collection Chaol and Yrene had brought from Hafiza's forbidden library atop the Torre, nothing had proved useful.

Aelin sighed at the canvas ceiling of the prince's large tent. Fortunate that Sartaq had brought these trunks with him, rather than leaving them with their armada, but . . . exhaustion nipped at her, fogging the intricate lattice of symbols on the yellowed pages.

Rowan straightened. "This one opens something," he said, flipping the book to face her. "I don't know the other symbols, but that one says 'open.'" Even with the hours of instruction on the journey back to this continent, Rowan and the others had not wholly mastered the language of the half-forgotten marks. But her mate remembered most—as if they'd been planted in his mind.

Aelin carefully studied the line of symbols across the page. Read through them a second time. "It's not what we're looking for." She pulled on her bottom lip. "It's a spell for opening a portal between locations— just in this world."

"Like what Maeve can do?" Borte asked.

Aelin shrugged. "Yes, but this is for close traveling. More like what Fenrys can do." Or had once been able to do, before Maeve had broken it from him.

Borte's mouth quirked to the side. "What's the point of it, then?"

"Entertaining people at parties?" Aelin handed the book back to Rowan.

Borte chuckled, and leaned back in her seat, toying with the end of a long braid. "Do you think the spell exists—to find an alternate way to seal the Wyrdgate?" The question was barely more than a whisper, and yet Rowan shot the girl a warning look. Borte just waved him off.

No. Elena would have told her, or Brannon, if such a thing had existed.

Aelin ran a hand over the dry, ancient page, the symbols blurring. "It's worth a look, isn't it?"

Rowan indeed resumed his careful browsing and decoding. He'd sit here for hours, she knew. And if they found nothing, she knew he'd sit here and reread them all just to be sure.

A way out—an alternate path. For her, for Dorian. For whichever of them would pay the price to forge the Lock and seal the gate. A desperate, foolish hope.

The hours passed, the stacks of books dwindling. Fenrys joined them after a time, unusually solemn as they searched and searched. And found nothing.

When there were no books left in the trunk, when Borte was nodding off and Rowan was pacing through the tent, Aelin did them all a favor and ordered them to return to the keep.

It had been worth a look, she told herself. Even if the leaden weight in her gut said otherwise.

Chaol found his father where he'd left him, seething in his study.

"You cannot give a single acre of this territory to the wild men," his father hissed as Chaol wheeled into the room and shut the door.

Chaol crossed his arms, not bothering to look placating. "I can, and I will."

His father shot to his feet and braced his hands on his desk. "You would spit on the lives of all the men of Anielle who fought and died to keep this territory from their filthy hands?"

"If offering them a small piece of land will mean that future generations of Anielle men and women won't have to fight or die, then I'd think our ancestors would be pleased."

"They are beasts, barely fit to be their own masters."

Chaol sighed, slumping back in his chair. A lifetime of this—that's what Dorian had laid upon him. As Hand, he'd have to deal with lords and rulers just like his father. If they survived. If Dorian survived, too. The thought was enough for Chaol to say, "Everyone in this war is making sacrifices. Most far, far greater than a few miles of land. Be grateful that's all we're asking of you."

The man sneered. "And what if I was to bargain with you?"

Chaol rolled his eyes, reaching to turn his chair back toward the door.

His father lifted a piece of paper. "Don't you wish to know what your brother wrote to me?"

"Not enough to stop this alliance," Chaol said, pivoting his chair away.

His father unfolded the letter anyway, and read, "*I hope Anielle burns to the ground. And you with it.*" A small, hateful smile. "That's all your brother said. My heir—that's how he feels about this place. If he will not protect Anielle, then what shall become of it without you?"

Another approach, to guilt him into relenting. Chaol said, "I'd wager that Terrin's regard for Anielle is tied to his feelings for you."

The aging lord lowered himself into his seat once more. "I wish you to know what Anielle will face, should you fail to protect it. I am willing to bargain, boy." He chuckled. "Though I know how well you hold up your end of things."

Chaol took the blow. "I am a rich man, and need nothing you could offer me."

"Nothing?" His father pointed to a trunk by the window. "What about something more priceless than gold?"

When Chaol didn't speak, his father strode for the trunk, unlocked it with a key from his pocket, and flipped back the heavy lid. Wheeling closer, Chaol peered at its contents.

Letters. The entire trunk was filled with letters bearing his name in an elegant script.

"She discovered the trunk. Right before we got word of Morath marching on us," his father said, his smile mocking and cold. "I should have burned them, of course, but something prompted me to save them instead. For this exact moment, I think."

The trunk was piled thick with letters. All written by his mother. To him. "How long," he said too quietly.

"From the day you left." His father's sneer lingered.

Years. Years of letters, from a mother he had not heard from, had believed hadn't wanted to speak to him, had yielded to his father's wishes.

"You let her believe I didn't write back," Chaol said, surprised to find his voice still calm. "You never sent them, and let her believe I didn't write back."

His father shut the trunk and locked it again. "It would appear so."

"Why." It was the only question that mattered.

His father frowned. "I couldn't allow you to walk away from your birthright, from Anielle, without consequences, could I?"

Chaol clamped onto the arms of his chair to keep from wrapping his hands around the man's throat. "You think showing me this trunk of her letters will make me want to bargain with you?"

His father snorted. "You're a sentimental man. Watching you with that wife of yours only proves it. I'd think you'd bargain quite a bit to be able to read these letters."

Chaol only stared at him. Blinked once, as if it would quell the roaring in his head, his heart.

His mother had never forgotten him. Never stopped writing to him.

Chaol smiled slightly.

"Keep the letters," he said, steering his chair back to the doors. "Now that she's left you, it might be your only way to remember her." He opened the study door and looked over his shoulder.

His father remained beside the trunk, stiff as a sword.

"I don't make bargains with bastards," Chaol said, smiling again as he entered the hall beyond. "I'm certainly not going to start with you."

Chaol gave the wild men of the Fangs a small chunk of territory in South Anielle. His father had raged, refusing to acknowledge the trade, but no one had heeded him, to Aelin's eternal amusement.

Two days later, a small unit of those men arrived at the city's westernmost edge, near the gaping hole where the dam had been, and beckoned the way.

Each of the bearded men rode a shaggy mountain pony, and though their heavy furs hid much of their bulky bodies, their weapons were on sharp display: axes, swords, knives all gleamed in the gray light.

Cain's people—or they had been. Aelin decided not to mention him during their brief introduction. And Chaol, wisely, refrained from admitting that he'd killed the man.

Another lifetime. Another world.

Seated atop a fine Muniqi horse Hasar had lent her, Aelin rode at the front of the company, as it marched from Anielle, Chaol on Farasha to her left, Rowan on his own Muniqi horse to her right. Their companions were scattered behind, Lorcan healed enough to be riding, Elide beside him.

And behind them, snaking into the distance, the army of the khagan moved.

Part of it, at least. Half the ruks and Darghan riders would march under Kashin's banner on the eastern side of the mountains, to draw out the forces from the Ferian Gap into open battle in the valley. While they snuck behind, right through their back door.

Snow lay heavy on the Fangs, the gray sky threatening more, but the rukhin scouts and wild men had assessed that no bad weather would hit them for a while yet—not until they reached the Gap, at least.

Five days' trek, with the army and mountains. It would be three for the army that marched along the lake's edge and river.

Aelin tipped her face toward that cold sky as they began the endless series of switchbacks up the mountainsides. The rukhin could carry much of the heavier equipment, thank the gods, but the climb into the mountains would be the first test.

The khagan's armies had crossed every terrain, though. Mountains and deserts and seas. They did not balk now.

So Aelin supposed she would not, either. For whatever time she had left, until it was over.

This final push north, homeward . . . She smiled grimly at the looming mountains, at the army stretching away behind them.

And just because she could, just because they were headed to Terrasen at last, Aelin unleashed a flicker of her power. Some of the standard-bearers behind them murmured in surprise, but Rowan only smiled. Smiled with that fierce hope, that brutal determination that flared in her own heart, as she began to burn.

She let the flame encompass her, a golden glow that she knew could be spied even from the farthest lines of the army, from the city and keep they left behind.

A beacon glowing bright in the shadows of the mountains, in the shadows of the forces that awaited them, Aelin lit the way north.

PART TWO
Gods and Gates

CHAPTER 68

The black towers of Morath rose above the smoking forges and campfires of the valley below like a cluster of dark swords raised to the sky.

They jutted into the low clouds, some broken and chipped, some still standing proud. The wrath and final act of Kaltain Rompier written all over them.

Spreading his soot-colored wings wide, Dorian caught a wind that reeked of iron and carrion and banked around the fortress. He'd learned to harness winds during these long days of travel, and though he'd covered much of the journey as a swift, red-tailed hawk, he'd shifted this morning into an ordinary crow.

Flocks of them circled Morath, their caws as plentiful as the ringing of hammers on anvils throughout the valley. Even with hell unleashed in the north, there was still more camped down here. More troops, more witches.

Dorian followed the example of the other crows and gave the wyverns a wide berth, flying low as coven after coven went about their scouting or reporting or training. So many Ironteeth. All waiting.

He circled Morath's uppermost towers, scanning the keep, the army in the valley, the wyverns in their lofty aeries. With each flap of his wings, the weight of what he'd hidden in a rocky outcropping ten miles north grew heavier.

It would have been madness to bring the two keys here. So he had buried them in the shale rock, not even daring to mark the spot. He could only pray it was far enough away to avoid Erawan's detection.

At the side of a tower, two servants bearing armloads of laundry emerged from a small door and began winding up the exterior stair, heads bowed as if trying to ignore the army that rippled far below. Or the wyverns whose bellows echoed off the black rock.

There. That door.

Dorian flapped toward it, willing his heart to calm, his scent—the one thing that might doom him—to remain unmarked. But none of the Ironteeth flying overhead noticed the crow-that-did-not-smell-like-a-crow. And the two laundresses winding up the tower stairs didn't call out as he landed on the small stone railing and folded his wings neatly.

A hop, and he was on the stones.

A shift, muscles and bones burning, and the world had become smaller, infinitely deadlier.

And infinitely less aware of his presence.

Dorian's whiskers twitched, his oversized ears cocking. The roar of the wyverns rocked through his small, furred body, and he gritted his teeth—large, almost too big for his little mouth. The reek grew near-nauseating.

He could smell . . . everything. The lingering freshness of the laundry that had passed by. The gamey musk of some sort of broth clinging to the laundresses after their lunch. He'd never thought mice to be extraordinary, yet even soaring as a hawk, he had not felt this alertness, this level of being *awake*.

In a world designed to kill them, he supposed mice needed such sharpness to survive.

Dorian allowed himself one long breath before he squeezed beneath the shut door. And into Morath itself.

His senses might have been sharper, but he had never realized how daunting a set of stairs truly was without human legs.

He kept to the shadows, willing himself into dust and gloom with every pair of feet that strode by. Some were armored, some were booted, some in worn shoes. All the wearers pale and miserable.

No witches, thank the gods. And no Valg princes or their grunts.

Certainly no sign of Erawan.

The tower he'd entered was a servants' stair, one Manon had laid out during one of her various explanations to Aelin. It was thanks to her that he followed a mental map, confirmed by his circling overhead for the past few hours.

Erawan's tower—that's where he'd begin. And if the Valg king was there . . . he'd figure it out. Whether he might repay Erawan for all he'd done, regardless of Kaltain's warning.

His breathing ragged, Dorian reached the bottom of the winding steps, curling his long tail around him as he peered to the dim hallway ahead.

From here, he'd need to cross the entire level, take another staircase up, another hall, and then, if he was lucky, Erawan's tower would be there.

Manon had never gained access to it. Never known what waited up there. Only that it was guarded by Valg at all hours. A good enough place to begin his hunt.

His ears twitched. No approaching steps. No cats, mercifully.

Dorian turned the corner, his grayish brown fur blending into the rock, and scuttled along the groove where the wall met the floor. A guard stood on watch at the end of the hall, staring at nothing. He loomed, large as a mountain, as Dorian approached.

Dorian had nearly reached the guard and the crossroads he monitored when he felt it—the stir, and then the silence.

Even the guard straightened, glancing to the slit of a window behind him.

Dorian halted, tucking himself into a shadow.

Nothing. No cries or shouts, yet . . .

The guard returned to his post, but scanned the hall.

Dorian remained still and quiet, waiting. Had they discovered his presence? Sent out a call?

It couldn't have been as easy as it had seemed. Erawan no doubt had traps to alert him of any enemy presence—

Rushing, light steps sounded around the corner, and the guard turned toward them. "What is it?" the man demanded.

The approaching servant didn't check his pace. "Who knows these days with the company we keep? I'm not lingering to find out." Then the man hurried on, rushing past Dorian.

Not rushing toward something, but *away*.

Dorian's whiskers flicked as he scented the air. Nothing.

Waiting in a hallway would do no good. But to plunge ahead, to seek out whatever might be happening . . . Not wise, either.

There was one place he might hear something. Where people were always gossiping, even at Morath.

So Dorian ventured back down the hall. Down another set of stairs, his little legs barely able to move fast enough. Toward the kitchens, hot and bright with the light of the great hearth.

Lady Elide had worked here—had known these people. Not Valg, but people conscripted into service. People who would undoubtedly talk about the comings and goings of this keep. Just as they had at the palace in Rifthold.

The various servants and cooks were indeed waiting. Staring toward the stairs on the opposite side of the cavernous kitchen. As was the lean, green-eyed tabby cat across the room.

Dorian made himself as small as possible. But the beast paid him no mind, its attention fixed on the stairs. As if it knew, too.

And then steps—quick and hushed. Two women entered, empty trays in their hands. Both wan and trembling.

A man who had to be the head cook asked the women, "Did you see anything?"

One of the women shook her head. "They weren't in the council room yet. Thank the gods."

Her partner's hands wobbled as she set down her tray. "They will be soon, though."

"Lucky you got out before they came," someone said. "Or you might have found yourself part of lunch, too."

Lucky, indeed. Dorian lingered, but the kitchen resumed its rhythms, satisfied two of its own had made it back safely.

The council room—perhaps the same Manon had described. Where Erawan preferred to have his meetings. And if Erawan himself was headed there . . .

Dorian scuttled out, heeding that mental map Manon had crafted. A fool—only a fool would willingly go to see Erawan. Risk it.

Perhaps he had a death wish. Perhaps he truly was a fool. But he wanted to see him. Had to see him, this creature who had ruined so many things. Who stood poised to devour their world.

He had to look at him, this *thing* who had ordered him enslaved, who had butchered Sorscha. And if he was fortunate—maybe he'd kill him.

He could remain in this form and strike. But it would be so much more satisfying to return to his own body, to draw Damaris, and end him. To let Erawan see the pale band around his throat and know who killed him, that he hadn't broken him yet.

And then Dorian would find that key.

The silence showed him the way, perhaps more so than the mental map he'd memorized.

Halls emptied out. The air became thick, cold. As if Erawan's corruption leaked from him.

There were no guards, human or Valg, standing watch before the open doors.

No one to mark the hooded figure who strode in, black cape flowing.

Dorian hurried, skittering after that figure just as the doors shut. His magic swelled, and he willed it to calm, to coil, an asp poised to strike.

One blow to get Erawan down, then he'd shift and draw Damaris.

The figure halted, cloak swaying, and Dorian dashed for the nearest shadow—by the crack between the door and floor.

The chamber was ordinary, save for a table of black glass in its center. And the golden-haired, golden-eyed man seated at it.

Manon had not lied: Erawan had indeed shed Perrington's skin for something far fairer.

Though still dressed in finery, Dorian realized as the Valg king rose, his gray jacket and pants immaculately tailored. No weapons lay at his side. No hint of the Wyrdkey.

But he could *feel* Erawan's power, the wrongness leaking from him. Could feel it, and remember it, the way that power had felt inside him, curdling his soul.

Ice cracked in his veins. Quick—he had to be quick. Strike *now*.

"This is an unexpected delight," Erawan said, his voice young and yet not. He gestured to the spread of food—fruits and cured meats. "Shall we?"

Dorian's magic faltered as two moon-pale, slender hands rose from the folds of the black cloak and pushed back the cowl.

The woman beneath was not beautiful, not in the classical way. Yet with her jet-black hair, her dark eyes, her red lips . . . She was striking. Mesmerizing.

Those red lips curved, revealing bone-white teeth.

Cold licked down Dorian's spine at the pointed, delicate ears peeking above the curtain of dark hair. Fae. The woman—female was Fae.

She removed her cloak to reveal a flowing gown of deepest purple before she settled herself across the table from Erawan. Not an ounce of hesitation or fear checked her graceful movements. "You know why I have come, then."

Erawan smiled as he sat, pouring a goblet of wine for the female, then for himself. And all thoughts of killing vanished from Dorian's head as the Valg king asked, "Is there any other reason you would deign to visit Morath, Maeve?"

CHAPTER 69

Orynth had not been this quiet since the day Aedion and the remnants of Terrasen's court had marched to Theralis.

Even then, there had been a hum to the ancient city erected between the mouth of the Florine and the edge of the Staghorns, Oakwald a ripple of wood to the west.

Then, the white walls had still been shining.

Now they lay stained and grayish, as bleak as the sky, while Aedion, Lysandra, and their allies strode through the towering metal doors of the western gate. Here, the walls were six feet thick, the blocks of stone so heavy that legend claimed Brannon had conscripted giants from the Staghorns to heave them into place.

Aedion would give anything for those long-forgotten giants to find their way to the city now. For the ancient Wolf Tribes to come racing down the towering peaks behind the city, the lost Fae of Terrasen with them. For any of the old myths to emerge from the shadows of time, as Rolfe and his Mycenians had done.

But he knew their luck had run out.

Their companions knew it, too. Even Ansel of Briarcliff had gone as silent as Ilias and his assassins, her shoulders bowed. She had been that way since the heads of her warriors had landed amongst their ranks, her wine-red hair dull, her steps heavy. He knew her horror, her guilt. Wished he had a moment to comfort the young queen beyond a swift apology. But Ilias, it seemed, had taken it upon himself to do just that, riding beside Ansel in steady, quiet company.

The city had been laid at the feet of the towering, near-mythic castle built atop a jutting piece of rock. A castle that rose so high its uppermost turrets seemed to pierce the sky. Once, that castle had glowed, roses and creeping plants draped along its sun-warmed stones, the song of a thousand fountains singing in every hall and courtyard. Once, proud banners had flapped from those impossibly high towers, standing watch over the mountains and forest and river and Plain of Theralis below.

It had become a mausoleum.

No one spoke as they trudged up the steep, winding streets. Grim-faced people either stopped to stare or continued rushing to prepare for the siege.

There was no way to outrun it. Not with the Staghorns at their backs, Oakwald to the west, and the army advancing from the south. Yes, they might flee eastward across the plains, but to where? To Suria, where it would only be a matter of time before they were found? To the hinterlands beyond the mountains, where the winters were so brutal they claimed no mortal could survive? The people of Orynth were as trapped as their army.

Aedion knew he should square his shoulders. Should grin at these people—his people—and offer them a shred of courage.

Yet he couldn't. Couldn't stop himself from wondering how many had lost family, friends, in the battle by the river. In the weeks of fighting before that. How many were still praying that the streaming lines of soldiers making their way toward the city would reveal a loved one.

His fault, his burden. His choices had led them here. His choices had left so many bodies in the snow, a veritable path of them from the southern border, all the way to the Florine.

The white castle loomed, larger with every hill they ascended. At least they had that—the advantage of higher ground.

At least they had that.

~

Darrow and the other lords were waiting.

Not in the throne room, but in the spacious council chamber on the other side of the palace.

The last time Aedion had been in the room, a preening Adarlanian prick had presided over the meeting. The Viceroy of Terrasen, he'd called himself.

It seemed the man had taken his finery, chairs and wall hangings included, and run off the moment the king had been killed.

So an ancient worktable now served as their war desk, an assortment of half-rotting chairs from various rooms in the castle around it. Currently occupied by Darrow, Sloane, Gunnar, and Ironwood. Murtaugh, to Aedion's surprise, was amongst them.

They rose as Aedion and his companions entered. Not out of any respect to Aedion, but for the royals with him.

Ansel of Briarcliff surveyed the piss-poor space, as she'd done for the entirety of the walk through the dim and dreary castle, and let out a low whistle. "You weren't kidding when you said Adarlan raided your coffers." Her first words in hours. Days.

Aedion grunted. "To the copper." He halted before the table.

Darrow demanded, "Where is Kyllian?"

Aedion gave him a smile that didn't reach his eyes. Ren tensed, reading the warning in that smile. "He bade me to go ahead while he led the army here." Lie.

Darrow rolled his eyes, then fixed them upon Rolfe, who was still frowning at the shabby castle. "We have you to thank for the lucky retreat, I take it."

Rolfe fixed his sea-green stare upon the man. "That you do."

Darrow sat again, the other lords following suit. "And you are?"

"Privateer Rolfe," the pirate said smoothly. "Commander in Her Majesty's Armada. And Heir to the Mycenian people."

The other lords straightened. "The Mycenians vanished an age ago," Lord Sloane said. But the man noted the sword at Rolfe's side, the sea dragon pommel. Had no doubt spied the fleet creeping up the Florine.

"Vanished, but did not die out," Rolfe countered. "And we have come to fulfill an old debt."

Darrow rubbed at his temple. Old—Darrow truly looked his age as he leaned against the table edge. "Well, we have the gods to thank for that."

Lysandra said, simmering with rage, "You have Aelin to thank for that."

The man narrowed his eyes, and Aedion's temper honed itself into something lethal. But Darrow's voice was exhausted—heavy, as he asked, "Not pretending today, *Lady*?"

Lysandra only pointed to Rolfe, then Ansel, then Galan. Swept her arm to the windows, to where the Fae royals and Ilias of the Silent Assassins tended to their own on the castle grounds. "All of them. All of them came here because of *Aelin*. Not you. So before you sneer that there is no Her Majesty's Armada, allow me to tell you that there *is*. And you are not a part of it."

Darrow let out a long sigh, rubbing his temple again. "You are dismissed from this room."

"Like hell she is," Aedion growled.

But Murtaugh cut in, "There is someone, Lady, who would like to see you." Lysandra raised her brows, and the old man winced. "I did not wish to risk leaving her in Allsbrook alone. Evangeline is in the northern tower—in my former granddaughter's bedroom. She spotted your approach from the window and it was all I could do to convince her to wait."

A polite, clever way to defuse the brewing storm. Aedion debated telling Lysandra that she could stay, but Lysandra was already moving, dark hair flowing behind her.

When she'd left, Aedion said, "She's fought on the front lines at every battle. Nearly died against our enemies. I didn't see any of you bothering to do the same."

The group of old lords frowned with distaste. Yet it was Darrow who shifted in his seat—slightly. As if Aedion had struck upon a festering wound. "To be too old to fight," Darrow said quietly, "while younger men and women die is not as easy as you would think, Aedion." He glanced down, to the nameless sword at Aedion's side. "It is not easy at all."

Aedion debated telling him to ask the people who'd died if *that* wasn't easy, either, but Prince Galan cleared his throat. "What preparations are under way for a siege?"

The Terrasen lords didn't seem to appreciate being questioned, but they opened their hateful mouths and spoke.

An hour later, the others seen to their rooms, then to baths and hot meals, Aedion found himself following her scent.

She had gone not to the north tower and the ward who awaited her, but to the throne room.

The towering oak doors were cracked, the two rearing stags carved on them staring him down. Once, gold filigree had covered the immortal flame shining between their proud antlers.

During the past decade, someone had peeled off the gold. Either for spite or quick coin.

Aedion slipped through the doors, the cavernous chamber like the ghost of an old friend.

How many times had he bemoaned being forced to dress in his finery and stand beside the thrones atop the dais at the far back of the pillar-lined room? How many times had he caught Aelin nodding off during an endless day of pageantry?

Then, the banners of all the Terrasen territories had hung from the ceiling. Then, the pale marble floors had been so polished he could see his reflection in them.

Then, an antler throne had sat upon the dais, towering and primal. Built from the shed horns of the immortal stags of Oakwald.

Stags now butchered and burned, as the antler throne had been after the battle of Theralis. The king had ordered it done right on the battlefield.

It was before that empty dais that Lysandra stood. Staring at the white marble as if she could see the throne that had once been there. See the other, smaller thrones that had sat beside it.

"I hadn't realized that Adarlan wrecked this place so thoroughly," she said, either scenting him or recognizing the cadence of his footsteps.

"The bones of it are still intact," Aedion said. "For how much longer that will remain true, I don't know."

Lysandra's green eyes slid toward him, dim with exhaustion and sorrow. "Deep down," she said quietly, "some part of me thought I'd live to see her sitting here." She pointed to the dais, to where the antler throne had once been. "Deep down, I thought we might actually make it somehow. Even with Morath, and the Lock, and all of it."

There was no hope in her face.

It was perhaps because of it that she bothered to speak to him.

"I thought so, too," Aedion said with equal quiet, though the words echoed in the vast, empty chamber. "I thought so, too."

CHAPTER 70

The Queen of the Fae had come to Morath.

Dorian forced his heartbeat to calm, his breathing to steady as Maeve sipped from her wine.

"You do not know me, then," the Fae Queen said, studying the Valg king.

Erawan paused, goblet half-raised to his lips. "Are you not Maeve, Queen of Doranelle?"

Aelin. Had Maeve brought Aelin *here*? To be sold to Erawan?

Gods, gods—

Maeve tipped back her head and laughed. "Millennia apart, and you have forgotten even your own sister-in-law."

Dorian was glad he was small and quiet and unmarked. He might have very well swayed.

Erawan went still. "You."

Maeve smiled. "Me."

Those golden eyes roved over the Fae Queen. "In a Fae skin. All this time."

"I'm disappointed you did not figure it out."

The pulse of Erawan's power slithered over Dorian. So similar—so terribly similar to the oily power of that Valg prince. "Do you know what you have—" The Valg king silenced himself. Straightened his shoulders.

"I suppose I should thank you, then," Erawan said, mastering himself. "Without you betraying my brother, I would not have discovered this delightful world. And would not stand primed to conquer it." He sipped from his goblet. "But the question remains: Why come here? Why reveal yourself now? My ancient enemy—perhaps enemy no longer."

"I was never your enemy," Maeve said, her voice unruffled. "Your brothers, however, were mine."

"And yet you married Orcus knowing full well what he is like."

"Perhaps I should have married you when you offered." A small smile—coy and horrible. "But I was so young then. Easily misled."

Erawan let out a low laugh that made Dorian's stomach turn. "You were never those things. And now here we are."

If Aelin was here, if Dorian could find her, perhaps they could take on the Valg queen and king . . .

"Here we are," Maeve said. "You, poised to sweep this continent. And me, willing to help you."

Erawan crossed an ankle over a knee. "Again: Why?"

Maeve's fingers smoothed over the facets of her goblet. "My people have betrayed me. After all I have done for them, all I have protected them, they rose up against me. The army I had gathered refused to march. My nobles, my servants, refused to kneel. I am Queen of Doranelle no longer."

"I can guess who might be behind such a thing," Erawan said.

Darkness flickered in the room, terrible and cold. "I had Aelin of the Wildfire contained. I had hoped to bring her here to you when she was . . . ready. But the sentinel I assigned to oversee her care made a grave error.

I myself will admit that I was deceived. And now she is again free. And took it upon herself to dispatch letters to some influential individuals in Doranelle. She is likely already on this continent."

Relief shuddered through him.

Erawan waved a hand. "In Anielle. Expending her power carelessly."

Maeve's eyes glowed. "She cost me my kingdom, my throne. My circle of trusted warriors. Any neutrality I might have had in this war, any mercy I might have offered, vanished the moment she and her mate left."

They'd found her. Somehow, they'd found her. And Anielle—did he dare hope Chaol might also be there?

Dorian might have roared his victory. But Maeve continued, "Aelin Galathynius will come for me, if she survives you. I do not plan to allow her the chance to do so."

Erawan's smile grew. "So you think to ally with me."

"Only together can we ensure Brannon's bloodline is toppled forever. Never to rise again."

"Then why not kill her, when you had her?"

"Would you have done so, brother? Would you not have tried to turn her?"

Erawan's silence was confirmation enough. Then the Valg king asked, "You lay a great deal before me, sister. Do you expect me to believe you so readily?"

"I anticipated that." Her lips curved. "After all, I have nothing left but my own powers."

Erawan said nothing, as if well aware of the dance the queen led him in.

She extended a moon-white hand toward the center of the room. "There is something else I might bring to the table, should it interest you."

A flick of her slender fingers, and a hole simply appeared in the heart of the chamber.

Dorian started, curling himself farther into shadow and dust. Not bothering to hide his trembling as a horror only true darkness could craft appeared on the other side of that hole. The *portal*.

"I had forgotten you'd mastered that gift," Erawan said, his golden eyes flaring at the thing that now bowed to them, its pincers clicking.

The spider.

"And I'd forgotten that they still bothered to answer to you," Erawan went on.

"When the Fae cast me aside," Maeve said, smiling faintly at the enormous spider, "I returned to those who have always been loyal to me."

"The stygian spiders have become their own creatures," Erawan countered. "Your list of allies remains short."

Maeve shook her head, dark hair shining. "These are not the stygian spiders."

Through the portal, Dorian could make out jagged, ashen rock. Mountains.

"These are the *kharankui*, as the people of the southern continent call them. My most loyal handmaidens."

Dorian's heart thundered as the spider bowed again.

Erawan's face turned cool and bored. "What use would I have for them?" He gestured to the windows beyond, the hellscape he'd crafted. "I have created *armies* of beasts loyal to me. I do not need a few hundred spiders."

Maeve didn't so much as falter. "My handmaidens are resourceful, their webs long-reaching. They speak to me of the goings-on in the world. And spoke to me of the next . . . phase of your grand plans."

Dorian braced himself. Erawan stiffened.

Maeve drawled. "The Valg princesses need hosts. You have had difficulty in securing ones powerful enough to hold them. The khaganate princess managed to survive the one you planted in her, and is mistress of her own body once more."

Valg princesses. In the southern continent. Chaol—

"I'm listening," Erawan said.

Maeve pointed to the spider still bowing at the portal—the portal to the southern continent, opened as easily as a window. "Why bother with human hosts for the six remaining princesses when you might create ones far more powerful? And willing."

Erawan's gold eyes slid to the spider. "You and your kin would allow this?" His first words to the creature.

The spider's pincers clicked, her horrible eyes blinking. "It would be our honor to prove our loyalty to our queen."

Maeve smiled at the spider. Dorian shuddered.

"Immortal, powerful hosts," Maeve purred to the Valg king. "With their innate gifts, imagine how the princesses might thrive within them. Both spider and princess becoming *more*."

Becoming a horror beyond all reckoning.

Erawan said nothing, and Maeve flicked her fingers, the portal and spider vanishing. She rose, graceful as a shadow. "I shall let you consider this alliance, if that is what you wish. The *kharankui* will do as I bid them—and will happily march under your banner."

"Yet what shall I say to my brother, when I see him again?"

Maeve angled her head. "Do you plan to see Orcus again?"

"Why do you think I have spent so long building this army, preparing this world, if not to greet my brothers once more? If not to impress them with what I have made here?"

Erawan would bring the Valg kings back to Erilea, if given the chance. And if he did—

Maeve studied the seated king. "Tell Orcus that I grew bored of waiting for him to come home from his conquests." A spider's smile. "I would much rather have joined him."

Erawan blinked, the only sign of his surprise. Then he waved an elegant hand, and the doors opened on a phantom wind. "I shall think on this, sister. For your brazenness in approaching me, I will allow you to stay as my guest until I decide." Two guards appeared in the hall, and Dorian braced himself, paws tensing on the stones. "They will show you to your room."

To remain in this chamber for too long might lead to his exposure, but he had not sensed the key on the Valg king. Later—he could keep looking later. Contemplate the best way to kill the king, too. If he was foolish enough to risk it. For now . . .

Maeve gathered her cloak, sweeping it around her, and Dorian rushed forward, ducking into its shadows once more as the Fae Queen prowled out.

The guards led her down a hall, up a winding stair, and into a tower adjacent to Erawan's. It was well-appointed in polished oak furniture and crisp linen sheets. Likely a remnant of the years this had been a human stronghold and not a home of horrors.

As the door shut behind Maeve, she leaned into the iron-studded wood and sighed.

"Do you plan to hide in that pathetic form all day?"

Dorian lunged for the gap between the door and the floor, but her black-booted foot slammed down upon his tail.

Pain speared through his bones, but her foot remained in place. His magic surged, lashing, but a dark wind wrapped talons around it, choking. Stifling.

The Fae Queen smiled down at him. "You are not a very skilled spy, King of Adarlan."

CHAPTER 71

Dorian's magic struggled, roaring as her dark power held him in its net. If he could turn into a wyvern and rip her head off . . .

But Maeve smiled, weary and amused, and lifted her foot from his poor tail. Then released her grip on his magic.

He shuddered at the dark, festering power as it caressed talons down his magic, brushed the shimmering, raw core, and vanished.

It was an effort not to gag, not to touch the pale band on his neck just to be sure it was gone.

Maeve's smile remained on her red mouth, his magic still shivering as the feel of her power lingered. The power to break into minds, to rip apart the psyche. A different sort of enemy. One that would require another route. A reckless, fool's route. A courtier's route.

So he shifted, fur becoming skin, paws into hands. When he at last stood before the Fae Queen, man once more, her smile grew. "How handsome you are."

Dorian sketched a bow. He didn't dare reach for Damaris at his side. "How did you know?"

"You did not think I beheld you, your scent and the feel of your power, in Aelin's memories?" She angled her head. "Though my spy did not report your interest in shifting."

Cyrene. Horror crept through him.

Maeve strode deeper into the chamber and took up a seat on the bench before the foot of the bed, as regally as if she sat upon her throne. "How do you think the Matrons knew where to find you?"

"Cyrene was only at the camp for a day," he managed to say.

"Do you truly believe that there are no other spiders, up there in the mountains? They all answer to her, and to me. She needed only whisper once, to the right ones, and they found me. And found the Ironteeth." Maeve ran a hand along the lap of her gown. "Whether Erawan knows of your gifts remains to be seen. Before you killed her, Cyrene certainly informed me that you were . . . different."

He did not regret killing her one bit.

"But that is neither here nor there. Cyrene is dead, and you are a long way from the arms of Manon Blackbeak."

Dorian braced a hand on Damaris's hilt.

Maeve smiled at the ancient sword. "It seems the Queen of Terrasen learned to share. She's acquired quite the trove, hasn't she?" Dorian started. If Maeve knew everything Aelin possessed—

"I know that, too," Maeve said, her dark eyes depthless. Damaris warmed in his grip. "And know the spider did not guess at that truth, at least." She scanned him. "Where are they now, Dorian Havilliard?"

Something slithering and sharp slid along his mind. Trying to get *in*—

Dorian's magic roared. A sheet of ice slammed into those mental talons. Blasted them away.

Maeve chuckled, and Dorian blinked, finding the room also coated with frost. "A dramatic, but effective method."

Dorian smirked at her, "You think I would be foolish enough to allow you into my mind?" Still keeping one hand on the sword, he slid the other into a pocket, if only to hide its shaking. "Or to tell you where they are hidden?"

"It was worth the attempt," Maeve said.

"Why not sound the alarm?" was his only reply.

Maeve leaned back, studying him again. "You want what I want. Erawan has it. Does that not make you and I allies of a sort?"

"You must be mad, to think I would ever give you the keys."

"Am I? What would you do with them, Dorian? Destroy them?"

"What would you do? Conquer the world?"

Maeve laughed. "Oh, nothing so common as that. I would make sure that Erawan and his brothers can never return." Damaris remained warm in his hand. The queen spoke the truth. Or some part of it.

"You'll admit so easily that you plan to betray Erawan?"

"Why do you think I came here?" Maeve asked. "My people have cast me out, and I guessed you would seek out Morath soon enough."

Damaris's warmth did not falter, yet Dorian said, "You cannot think I'd believe you came here to win my allegiance. Not when I saw that you plan to offer Erawan your spiders to assist his princesses." He didn't want to know what the Valg princesses could do. Why Erawan had delayed his unleashing of them.

"A small sacrifice on my part to win his trust." Damaris held warm. "We are not so different, you and I. And I have nothing to lose now, thanks to your friend."

Truth, truth, truth.

And there it was—the opening he'd been waiting for.

Keeping his mind encased in that wall of ice, his magic sizing up the enemy before them, Dorian let his hand slide from Damaris's hilt. Let her see his thawing distrust as he said, "Aelin seems to be skilled at wrecking the kingdoms of other people while protecting her own."

"And at letting others pay her debts."

Dorian stilled, though his magic continued its vigil, monitoring her dark power as it paced the barrier to his mind.

"Isn't that why you are here?" Maeve asked. "To be the sacrifice so that Aelin need not destroy herself?" She clicked her tongue. "Such a terrible waste—for either of you to pay the price for Elena's foolishness."

"It is." Truth.

"Can I tell you what Aelin revealed to me, during those moments I was able to peer into her mind?"

Dorian didn't dare reach for Damaris again. "You enslaved her," he growled. "I don't want to hear a damn thing about it."

Maeve brushed her curtain of hair over a shoulder, humming. "Aelin is glad it's you," she merely said. "She's hoping she'll be too late in returning. That you'll accomplish what you've set out to do and spare her from a terrible choice."

"She has a mate and a kingdom. I don't blame her." The sharpness in his words wasn't entirely faked.

"Don't you? Don't you have a kingdom to look after, one no less powerful and noble than Terrasen?" When he didn't answer, Maeve said, "Aelin has been freed for weeks now. And she has not come to find you."

"The continent is a big place."

A knowing smile. "She could find you, if she wished. And yet she went to Anielle."

He knew what manner of game she played. His magic slipped a fraction. An opening.

Maeve's own lashed for it, seeking a way in. She'd barely crossed the threshold when he gritted his teeth and threw her from his mind again, the wall of ice colliding with her.

"If you want me to ally with you, you're picking one hell of a way to show it."

Maeve laughed softly. "Can you blame me for trying?"

Dorian didn't answer, and stared at her for a long minute. Made a show of considering. Every bit of courtly intrigue and training kept his face unreadable. "You think I'd betray my friends that easily?"

"Is it betrayal?" Maeve mused. "To find an alternative to you and Aelin Galathynius paying the ultimate price? It was what I intended for her all along: to keep her from being a sacrifice to unfeeling gods."

"Those gods are powerful beings."

"Then where are they now?" She gestured to the room, the keep. Silence answered. "They are afraid. Of me, of Erawan. Of the keys." She gave him a serpent's smile. "They are afraid of *you*. You, and Aelin Fire-Bringer. Powerful enough to send them home—or to damn them."

He didn't answer. She wasn't entirely wrong.

"Why not defy them? Why bow to their wishes? What have they ever done for you?"

Sorscha's pained face flashed before his eyes.

"There is no other way," he said at last. "To end this."

"The keys could end it."

To wield them, rather than seal them back into the gate.

"They could do anything," Maeve went on. "Destroy Erawan, banish those gods back to their home if that's what they want." She angled her head. "Open another door to realms of peace and resting."

To the woman who would undoubtedly be there.

The dark, predatory power stalking his mind faded away, pulled back to its mistress.

Aelin had done it once. Opened a door to see Nehemia. It was possible. The encounters with Gavin and Kaltain only confirmed it.

"What if you didn't only ally with me," he asked at last, "but with Adarlan itself?"

Maeve didn't answer. As if she were surprised by the offer.

"A bigger alliance than merely working together to find the key," Dorian mused, and shrugged. "You have no kingdom, and clearly want another. Why not lend your gifts to Adarlan, to me? Bring your spiders to our side."

"A breath ago, you were livid that I enslaved your friend."

"Oh, I still am. Yet I am not so proud to refuse to consider the possibility. You want a kingdom? Then join mine. Ally with me, work with me to get what we need from Erawan, and I shall make you queen. Of a far bigger territory, with a people who will not rise up against you. A new start, I suppose."

When she still did not speak, Dorian leaned against the door. The portrait of courtly nonchalance. "You think I'm trying to trick you. Perhaps I am."

"And Manon Blackbeak? What of your promises to her?"

"I have made her no promises regarding my throne, and she wants nothing to do with them, anyway." He didn't hide the bitterness as he shrugged again. "Marriages have been built on far more volatile foundations than this one."

"Aelin of the Wildfire might very well mark you as an enemy, should we make a true union."

"Aelin will not risk killing an ally—not right now. And she will discover that she is not the only one capable of saving this world. Perhaps she'll even come to thank me, if she's as eager to avoid being sacrificed as you claim."

Maeve's red mouth curved upward. "You are young, and brash."

Dorian sketched a bow again. "I am also exceedingly handsome and willing to offer up my throne in a gesture of good faith."

"I could sell you to Erawan right now and he would reward me handsomely."

"Reward you—as if you are a hound bringing back a pheasant to its master." Dorian laughed, and her eyes flashed. "It was you who just posed this alliance between us, not me. But consider this: Shall you kneel, or shall you rule, Maeve?" He tapped his neck, right over the pale band across it. "I have knelt, and found I have no interest in doing so again. Not for Erawan, or for Aelin, or anyone." Another shrug. "The woman I love is dead. My kingdom is in pieces. What do I have to lose?" He let some of the old ice, the hollowness in his chest, rise to his face. "I'm willing to play this game. Are you?"

Maeve fell silent again. And slowly, those phantom hands crept into the corners of his mind.

He let her see. See the truth she sought.

He withstood it, that probing touch.

At last, Maeve loosed a breath through her nose. "You came to Morath for a key and will leave with a bride."

He nearly sagged with relief. "I will leave with both. And quickly."

"And how do you propose we are to find what we seek?"

Dorian smiled at the Fae Queen. The Valg Queen. "Leave that to me."

Atop Morath's highest tower hours later, Dorian peered at the army camp-fires littering the valley floor, his raven's feathers ruffled in the frozen wind off the surrounding peaks.

The screams and snarling had quieted, at least. As if even Morath's dungeon-masters maintained ordinary hours of working. He might have found the idea darkly funny, if he didn't know what manner of thing was being broken and bred here.

His cousin, Roland, had wound up here. He knew it, though no one had ever confirmed it. Had he survived the transition to Valg prince, or had he merely been a meal for one of the terrors who prowled this place?

He lifted his head, scanning the cloudy sky. The moon was a pale blur behind them, a trickle of light that seemed keen to remain hidden from Morath's watchful eyes.

A dangerous game. He was playing one hell of a dangerous game.

Did Gavin watch him now, from wherever he rested? Had he learned what manner of monster Dorian had allied himself with?

He didn't dare to summon the king here. Not with Erawan so close.

Close enough that Dorian might have attacked. Perhaps he'd been a fool not to. Perhaps he'd be a fool to attempt it, as Kaltain had warned, when it might reveal their mission. When Erawan had those collars on hand.

Dorian cast a glance to the adjacent tower, where Maeve slept. A dangerous, dangerous game.

The dark tower beyond hers seemed to throb with power. The council room down the hall from it was still lit, however. And in the hall—motion. People striding past the torches. Hurrying.

Stupid. Utterly stupid, and yet he found himself flapping into the frigid night. Found himself banking, then swooping to a cracked window along the hallway.

He pushed the window open a bit farther with his beak, and listened.

"Months I've been here, and now he refuses my counsel?" A tall, thin man stomped down the hall. Away from Erawan's council room. Toward the tower door at the end of the hall and the blank-faced guards stationed there.

At his side, two shorter men struggled to keep up. One of them said, "Erawan's motives are mysterious indeed, Lord Vernon. He does nothing without reason. Have faith in him."

Dorian froze.

Vernon Lochan. Elide's uncle.

His magic surged, ice cracking over the windowsill.

Dorian tracked the lanky lord while he stormed past, his dark fur cape drooping to the stones. "I have had faith in him beyond what could be expected," Vernon snapped.

The lord and his lackeys gave the tower door a wide berth as they passed it, turned the corner, and vanished, their voices fading with them.

Dorian surveyed the empty hall. The council room at the far end. The door still ajar.

He didn't hesitate. Didn't give himself time to reconsider as he crafted his plan. And waited.

Erawan emerged an hour later.

Dorian's heart thundered through him, but he kept his position in the hall, kept his shoulders straight and hands behind his back. Precisely how he'd appeared to the guards when he'd rounded the corner, having flown off to a quiet hall before shifting and striding here.

The Valg king surveyed him once, and his mouth tightened. "I thought I'd dismissed you for the night, Vernon."

Dorian bowed his head, willing his breathing steady with each step Erawan made toward him. His magic stirred, recoiling in terror at the creature who approached, but he forced it down deep. To a place where Erawan would not detect it.

As he had not detected Dorian earlier. Perhaps the raw magic in him also erased any traceable scent.

Dorian bowed his head. "I had returned to my chambers, but I realized I had a lingering question, milord."

He prayed Erawan didn't notice the different clothes. The sword that he kept half-hidden beneath his cloak. Prayed Erawan decided that Vernon had gone back to his room, changed, and returned. And prayed that he spoke enough like the Lord of Perranth to be convincing.

A sniveling, groveling man—the sort who'd sell his own niece to a demon king.

"What is it." Erawan stalked down the hall to his tower, a nightmare wrapped in a beautiful body.

Strike him now. Kill him.

And yet Dorian knew he hadn't come here for that. Not at all.

He kept his head down, voice low. "Why?"

Erawan slid golden, glowing eyes toward him. Manon's eyes. "Why what?"

"You might have made yourself lord of a dozen other territories, and yet you graced us with this one. I have long wondered why."

Erawan's eyes narrowed to slits, and Dorian kept his face the portrait of groveling curiosity. Had Vernon asked this before?

A stupid gamble. If Erawan noticed the sword at his side—

"My brothers and I planned to conquer this world, to add it to the trove that we'd already taken." Erawan's golden hair danced with the light of the torches as he walked the long hall. Dorian had a feeling that when they reached the tower at the far end, the conversation would be through. "We arrived at this one, encountered a surprising amount of resistance, and they were banished back. I could do nothing less while trapped here than to repay this world for the blow they dealt us. So I will make this world into a mirror of our homeland—to honor my brothers, and to prepare it for their return."

Dorian sifted through countless lessons on the royal houses of their lands and said, "I, too, know what it is to have a brotherly rivalry." He gave the king a simpering smile.

"You killed yours," Erawan said, bored already. "I love my brothers dearly."

The idea was laughable.

Half the hallway remained until the tower door. "Will you truly decimate this world, then? All who dwell in it?"

"Those who do not kneel."

Maeve, at least, wished to preserve it. To rule, but to preserve it.

"Would they receive collars and rings, or a clean death?"

Erawan surveyed him sidelong. "You have never wondered for the sake of your people. Not even the sake of your niece, failure that she was."

Dorian made himself cringe, and bowed his head. "I apologize again for that, milord. She is a clever girl."

"So clever, it seems, that one confrontation with you and you were scared away."

Dorian again bowed his head. "I will go hunt for her, if that is what you wish."

"I am aware that she no longer has what I seek, and it is now lost to me. A loss you brought about." The Wyrdkey Elide had carried, given to her by Kaltain.

Dorian wondered if Vernon had indeed been lying low for months now—avoiding this conversation. He cringed again. "Tell me how to rectify it, milord, and it will be done."

Erawan halted, and Dorian's mouth went dry. His magic coiled within him, bracing.

But he made himself look the king in the face. Meet the eyes of the creature who had brought about so much suffering.

"Your bloodline proved useless to me, Vernon," Erawan said a shade too softly. "Shall I find another use for you here at Morath?"

Dorian knew precisely what sort of uses the man would have. He lifted supplicating hands. "I am your servant, milord."

Erawan stared at him for long heartbeats. Then he said, "Go."

Dorian straightened, letting Erawan stride a few more feet toward the tower. The blank-faced guards posted at its door stepped aside as he approached.

"Do you truly hate them?" Dorian blurted.

Erawan half-turned toward him.

Dorian asked, "The humans. Aelin Galathynius. Dorian Havilliard. All of them. Do you truly hate them?" *Why do you make us suffer so greatly?*

Erawan's golden eyes guttered. "They would keep me from my brothers," he said. "I will let nothing stand in the way of my reunion with them."

"Surely there might be another way to reunite you. Without such a great war."

Erawan's stare swept over him, and Dorian held still, willing his scent to remain unremarkable, the shift to keep its form. "Where would the fun be in that?" the Valg king asked, and turned back toward the hall.

"Did the former King of Adarlan ask such questions?" The words broke from him.

Erawan again paused. "He was not so faithful a servant as you might believe. And look what it cost him."

"He fought you." Not quite a question.

"He never bowed. Not completely." Dorian was stunned enough that he opened his mouth. But Erawan began walking again and said without looking back, "You ask many questions, Vernon. A great many questions. I find them tiresome."

Dorian bowed, even with Erawan's back to him. But the Valg king continued on, opening the tower door to reveal a lightless interior, and shut it behind him.

A clock chimed midnight, off-kilter and odious, and Dorian strode back down the hall, finding another route to Maeve's chambers. A quick shift in a shadowed alcove had him scuttling along the floor again, his mouse's eyes seeing well enough in the dark.

Only embers remained in the fireplace when he slid beneath the door.

In the dark, Maeve said from the bed, "You are a fool."

Dorian shifted again, back into his own body. "For what?"

"I know where you went. Who you sought." Her voice slithered through the darkness. "You are a fool." When he didn't reply, she asked, "Did you plan to kill him?"

"I don't know."

"You couldn't face him and live." Casual, stark words. Dorian didn't need to touch Damaris to know they were true. "He would have put another collar around your throat."

"I know." Perhaps he should have learned where the Valg king kept them and destroyed the cache.

"This alliance shall not work if you are sneaking off and acting like a reckless boy," Maeve hissed.

"I know," he repeated, the words hollow.

Maeve sighed when he didn't say more. "Did you at least find what you were seeking?"

Dorian lay down before the fire, curling an arm beneath his head. "No."

CHAPTER
72

From a distance, the Ferian Gap did not look like the outpost for a good number of Morath's aerial legion.

Nor did it look, Nesryn decided, like it had been breeding wyverns for years.

She supposed that the lack of any obvious signs of a Valg king's presence was part of why it had remained secret for so long.

Sailing closer to the towering twin peaks that flanked either side—the Northern Fang on one, the Omega on the other—and separated the White Fangs from the Ruhnn Mountains, Nesryn could barely make out the structures built into either one. Like the Eridun aerie, and yet not at all. The Eridun's mountain home was full of motion and life. What had been built in the Gap, connected by a stone bridge near its top, was silent. Cold and bleak.

Snow half blinded Nesryn, but Salkhi swept toward the peaks, staying high. Borte and Arcas came in from the north, little more than dark shadows amid the whipping white.

Far behind them, out in the valley plain beyond the Gap, one half of their army waited, the ruks with them. Waited for Nesryn and Borte, along with the other scouts who had gone out, to report back that the time was ripe to attack. They'd made the river crossing under cover of darkness last night, and those the ruks could not carry had been brought over on boats.

A precarious position to be in, on that plain before the Gap. The Avery forked at their backs, effectively hemming them in. Much of it had been frozen, but not nearly thick enough to risk crossing on foot. Should this battle go poorly, there would be nowhere to run.

Nesryn nudged Salkhi, coming around the Northern Fang from the southern side. Far below, the whirling snows cleared enough to reveal what seemed to be a back gate into the mountain. No sign of sentries or any wyverns.

Perhaps the weather had driven them all inside.

She glanced southward, into the Fangs. But there was no sign of the second half of their army, marching north through the peaks themselves to come at the Gap from the western entrance. A far more treacherous journey than the one they'd made.

But if they timed it right, if they drew out the host in the Gap onto the plain just before the others arrived from the west, they might crush Morath's forces between them. And that was without the unleashed power of Aelin Galathynius. And her consort and court.

Salkhi arced around the Northern Fang. Distantly, Nesryn could make out Borte doing the same around the Omega. But there was no sign of their enemy.

And when Nesryn and Borte did another pass through the Ferian Gap, even going so far as to soar between the two peaks, they found no sign, either.

As if the enemy had vanished.

The White Fangs were utterly unforgiving.

The wild men who led them kept the mountains from being fatal, knowing which passes might be wiped out by snow, which might have an unsteady ice shelf, which were too open to any eyes flying overhead. Even with the army trailing behind, Chaol marveled at the speed of their travel, at how, after three days, they cleared the mountains themselves and stepped onto the flat, snow-blasted western plains beyond.

He'd never set foot in the territory, though it was technically his. The official border of Adarlan claimed the plains past the Fangs for a good distance before they yielded to the unnamed territories of the Wastes. But it still *felt* like the Wastes, eerily quiet and sprawling, a strange expanse that stretched, unbreaking, to the horizon.

Even the stoic khaganate warriors did not look too long toward the Wastes at their left as they rode northward. At night, they huddled closer to their fires.

All of them did. Yrene clung a bit tighter at night, whispering about the strangeness of the land, its hollow silence. *As if the land itself does not sing,* she'd said a few times now, shuddering as she did.

A far better place, Chaol thought as they rode northward, skirting the edge of the Fangs on their right, for Erawan to make his empire. Hell, they might have given it to him if he'd set up his fortress deep on the plain and kept to it.

"We're a day out from the Gap," one of the wild men—Kai—said to Chaol as they rode through an unusually sunny morning. "We'll camp south of the Northern Fang tonight, and tomorrow morning's march will take us into the Gap itself."

There was another reason the wild men had allied with them, beyond the territory they stood to gain. Witches had hunted their kind this spring—entire clans and camps left in bloody ribbons. Many had been reduced to cinders, and the few survivors had whispered of a dark-haired woman with unholy power. Chaol was willing to bet it had been Kaltain, but had not told the wild men that particular threat, at least, had been erased. Or had incinerated herself in the end.

It wouldn't matter to them anyway. Of the two hundred or so wild men who had joined their army since they'd left Anielle, all had come to the Ferian Gap to extract vengeance on the witches. On Morath. Chaol refrained from mentioning that he himself had killed one of their kind almost a year ago.

It might as well have been a decade ago, for all that had happened since he'd killed Cain during his duel with Aelin. Yulemas was still weeks away—if they survived long enough to celebrate it.

Chaol said to the slim, bearded man, who made up for his lack of his clansmen's traditional bulk with quick wit and sharp eyes, "Is there a place that might hide an army this large tonight?"

Kai shook his head. "Not this close. Tonight will be the greatest risk."

Chaol glanced to the distant healers' wagons where Yrene rode, working on any soldiers who had fallen ill or injured on the trek. He hadn't seen her since they'd awoken, but he'd known she'd spent their ride today healing—the tightness in his spine grew with each mile.

"We'll just have to pray," said Chaol, turning to the towering mountain taking shape before them.

"The gods don't come to these lands," was all Kai said before he fell back with a group of his own people.

A horse eased up beside his own, and he found Aelin bundled in a fur-lined cloak, a hand on Goldryn's hilt. Gavriel rode behind her, Fenrys at his side. The former kept an eye upon the western plains; the latter monitoring the wall of peaks to their right. Both golden-haired Fae males remained silent, however, as Aelin frowned at Kai's disappearing form. "That man has a flair for the dramatic that should have earned him a place on some of Rifthold's finest stages."

"Fine praise indeed, coming from you."

She winked, patting Goldryn's ruby pommel. The stone seemed to flare in response. "I know a kindred spirit when I see one."

Despite the battle that waited ahead, Chaol chuckled.

But then Aelin said, "Rowan and the cadre have been tunneling into their power for the past few days." She nodded over her shoulder to Fenrys and Gavriel, then to where Rowan rode at the head of the company, the Fae Prince's silver hair bright as the sun-on-snow around them. "So have I. We'll make sure nothing harms this army tonight." A knowing glance toward the healers' wagons. "Certain areas will be especially guarded."

Chaol nodded his thanks. Having Aelin able to use her powers, having her companions wielding them, too, would make the battle far, far easier. Wyverns might not even be able to get close enough to touch their soldiers if Aelin could blast them from the skies, or Rowan could snap their wings with a gust of wind. Or just rip the air from their lungs.

He'd seen enough of Fenrys's and Gavriel's fighting in Anielle to know that even without as much magic, they'd be lethal. And Lorcan . . . Chaol didn't look over his shoulder to where Lorcan and Elide rode. The dark warrior's powers weren't anything Chaol ever wished to face.

With an answering nod, Aelin trotted to Rowan's side, the ruby in Goldryn's hilt like a small sun. Fenrys followed, guarding the queen's back even amongst allies. Yet Gavriel remained, guiding his horse beside Farasha. The black mare eyed the warrior's roan gelding, but made no move to bite him. Thank the gods.

The Lion gave him a slight smile. "I did not have the chance to congratulate you on your happy news."

An odd thing for the warrior to say, given that they'd barely spoken beyond councils, but Chaol bowed his head. "Thank you."

Gavriel stared toward the snow and mountains—toward the distant north. "I was not granted the opportunity you have, to be present from the start. To see my son grow into a man."

Chaol thought of it—of the life growing in Yrene's womb, of the child they'd raise. Thought of what Gavriel had not experienced. "I'm sorry." It was the only thing, really, to say.

Gavriel shook his head, tawny eyes glowing golden, flecks of emerald emerging in the blinding sun. "I did not tell you for sympathy." The Lion looked at him, and Chaol felt the weight of every one of Gavriel's centuries weighing upon him. "But rather to tell you what you perhaps already know: to savor every moment of it."

"Yes." If they survived this war, he would. Every damn second.

Gavriel angled the reins, as if to lead his horse back to his companions, but Chaol said, "I'm guessing that Aedion has not made it easy for you to appear in his life."

Gavriel's grave face tightened. "He has every reason not to."

And though Aedion was Gavriel's son, Chaol said, "I'm sure you already know this, but Aedion is as stubborn and hotheaded as they come." He jerked his chin toward Aelin, riding ahead, saying something to Fenrys that made Rowan snicker—and Fenrys bark a laugh. "Aelin and Aedion might as well be twins." That Gavriel didn't stop him told Chaol he'd read the lingering wound in the Lion's eyes well enough. "Both of them will often say one thing, but mean something else entirely. And then deny it until their last breath." Chaol shook his head. "Give Aedion time. When we reach Orynth, I have a feeling that Aedion will be happier to see you than he lets on."

"I am bringing back his queen, and riding with an army. I think he'd be happy to see his most hated enemy, if they did that for him." Worry paled the Lion's tanned features. Not for the reunion, but for what his son might be facing in the North.

Chaol considered. "My father is a bastard," he said quietly. "He has been in my life from my conception. Yet he never once bothered to ask the questions you pose," Chaol said. "He never once cared enough to do so. He never once worried. That will be the difference."

"If Aedion chooses to forgive me."

"He will," Chaol said. He'd make Aedion do it.

"Why are you so certain?"

Chaol considered his words carefully before he again met Gavriel's striking gaze. "Because you are his father," he said. "And no matter what might lie between you, Aedion will always *want* to forgive you." There it was, his own secret shame, still warring within him after all his father had done. Even after the trunk full of his mother's letters. "And Aedion will realize, in his own way, that you went to save Aelin not for her sake or Rowan's, but for his. And that you stayed with them, and march in this army, for his sake, too."

The Lion gazed northward, eyes flickering. "I hope you are right." No attempt at denial—that all Gavriel had done and would do was for Aedion alone. That he was marching north, into sure hell, for Aedion.

The warrior began to edge his horse past him again, but Chaol found himself saying, "I wish—I wish I had been so lucky to have you as my father."

Surprise and something far deeper passed across Gavriel's face. His tattooed throat bobbed. "Thank you. Perhaps it is our lot—to never have the fathers we wish, but to still hope they might surpass what they are, flaws and all."

Chaol refrained from telling Gavriel he was already more than enough.

Gavriel said quietly, "I shall endeavor to be worthy of my son."

Chaol was about to mutter that Aedion had better deem the Lion worthy when two forms took shape in the skies high above. Large, dark, and moving fast.

Chaol grabbed for the bow strapped across his back as soldiers cried out, Gavriel's own bow already aimed skyward, but Rowan shouted above the fray, *"Hold your fire!"* Galloping hooves thundered toward them, then Aelin and the Fae Prince were there, the latter announcing, "It's Nesryn and Borte."

Within minutes, the two women had descended, their ruks crusted with ice from the air high above the peaks.

"How bad is it?" Aelin asked, now joined by Fenrys, Lorcan, and Elide.

Borte winced. "It makes no sense. None of it."

Nesryn explained before Chaol could tell the girl to get to the point, "We've gone through the Gap thrice now. Even landed in the Omega." She shook her head. "It's empty."

"Empty?" Chaol asked. "Not a soul there?"

The Fae warriors glanced to one another at that.

"A few of the furnaces were still going, so someone must be there," Borte said, "but there wasn't one witch or wyvern. Whoever remains behind is minimal—likely no more than trainers or breeders."

The Ferian Gap was empty. The Ironteeth legion gone.

Rowan scanned the peak ahead. "We need to learn what they know, then."

Nesryn's nod was grim. "Sartaq already has people on it."

CHAPTER 73

Dorian hunted through Morath in a hundred different skins.

On the silent feet of a cat, or scuttling along the floors as a cockroach, or hanging from a rafter as a bat, he spent the better part of a week listening. Looking.

Erawan still remained unaware of his presence. Perhaps the nature of his raw magic indeed provided him with anonymity—and Maeve had only known to recognize it thanks to whatever she'd pried from Aelin's mind.

At night, Dorian returned to Maeve's tower chamber, where they would go over all he had seen. What she did during the day to keep Erawan from noticing the small, ever-changing presence hunting through his halls, she did not reveal.

She'd brought the spiders, though. Dorian had heard the servants' terrified whispers about the fleeting portal that the queen had opened to allow in six of the creatures to the catacombs. Where they, through some terrible magic, allowed in the Valg princesses.

Dorian couldn't decide whether it was a relief that he had not encountered these hybrids yet. Though he'd seen the emaciated human bodies, mere husks, that were occasionally hauled down the corridors. *Dinner*, the guards carrying them had hissed to the petrified servants. To feed a bottomless hunger. To prime them for battle.

What the spider-princess creations could do, what they *would* do to his friends in the North . . . Dorian couldn't stop recalling what Maeve had said to Erawan. That the Valg princesses had been held here for the second phase of whatever he was planning. Perhaps to ensure that they were well and truly destroyed once the bulk of his armies came through.

It honed his focus as he hunted. Pushed and nudged him onward, even when reason and instinct told him to flee this place. But he would not. Could not. Not without the key.

Sometimes, he could have sworn he felt it. The key. The horrible, otherworldly presence.

But when he'd chase after that wretched power down stairwells and along ancient corridors, only dust and shadows would greet him.

Often, it led him back to Erawan's tower. To the locked iron door and Valg guards posted outside. One of the few remaining places he had not dared to search. Though other possibilities did still remain.

The reek from the subterranean chamber reached Dorian long before he soared down the winding stair, the dim passageway cavernous and looming to his fly's senses. It had been the safest form for the day. The kitchen cat had been on the prowl earlier, and the Ironteeth witches hurried about the keep, readying for what he could only assume was an order to march north.

He'd been hunting for the key since dawn, Maeve occupying Erawan's attention in the western catacombs across the keep. Where those spider-princesses tested their new bodies.

He'd never gone so deep under the keep. Beneath the storage rooms. Beneath the dungeons. He'd only found the stair by the smell that had leaked from behind the ordinary door at its top, the scent detected by the fly's remarkable sense of smell. He'd passed the door so many times now on his fruitless hunting, deeming it a mere supply closet—until chance had intervened today.

Dorian rounded the last turn of the spiral stairs, and nearly tumbled from the air as the smell fully hit him. A thousand times worse in this form, with these senses.

A reek of death, of rot, of hate and despair. The scent that only the Valg could summon.

He'd never forget it. Had never quite left it behind.

Turn back. The warning was a whisper through his mind. *Turn back.*

The lower hall was lit with only a few torches in rusted iron brackets. No guards were posted along its length, or by the lone iron door at its far end.

The reek pulsed along the corridor, emanating from that door. Beckoning.

Would Erawan leave the key so unguarded? Dorian sent his magic skittering along the hall, testing for any hidden traps.

It found none. And when it reached the iron door, it recoiled. It fled.

He spooled his power back into himself, tucking it closer.

The iron door was dented and scratched with age. Nine locks lay along its edge, each more complicated than the last. Ancient, strange locks.

He didn't hesitate. He aimed for the slight gap between the stones and the iron door, and shifted. The fly shrank into a gnat, so small it was nearly a dust mote. He flew beneath the door, blocking out the smell, the terrible pulsing against his blood.

It took him a moment to understand what he looked at in the rough-hewn chamber, illuminated by a small lantern dangling from the arched ceiling. A lick of greenish flame danced within. Not a flame of this world.

Its light slid over the heap of black stone in the center of the room. Pieces of a sarcophagus.

And all around it, built into shelves carved from the mountain itself, gleamed Wyrdstone collars.

Only the instincts of his small, inconsequential body kept Dorian in the air. Kept him circling the lightless chamber. The rubble in the center of the space.

Erawan's tomb—directly beneath Morath. The site where Elena and

Gavin trapped him, and then built the keep atop the sarcophagus that could not be moved.

Where all this mess had begun. Where, centuries later, his father had claimed he and Perrington ventured in their youth, using the Wyrdkey to unlock both door and sarcophagus, and unwittingly freed Erawan.

The demon king had seized the duke's body. His father . . .

Dorian's heart raced as he passed collar after collar, around and around the room. Erawan hadn't needed one to contain his father, not when the man possessed no magic in his veins.

Yet Erawan had said that the man hadn't bowed—not wholly. Had fought him for decades.

He hadn't let himself think on it this past week. On whether his father's final words atop the glass castle had indeed been true. How he'd killed him, without the excuse of the collar to justify it.

His head pounded as he continued to circle the tomb. The collars leaked their unholy stench into the world, pulsing in time with his blood.

They seemed to sleep. Seemed to wait.

Did a prince lurk within each one? Or were these shells, ready to be filled?

Kaltain had warned him of this chamber. This place where Erawan would bring him, should he be caught. Why Erawan had chosen this place to store his collars . . . Perhaps it was a sanctuary, if such a thing could exist for a Valg king. Where Erawan might come to gaze upon the method of his own imprisonment, and remind himself that he would not be contained again. That he'd use these collars to enslave those who'd attempt to seal him back into the sarcophagus.

Dorian's magic thrashed, impatient and frantic. Was there a collar in here designated for him? For Aelin?

Around and around, he flew past the sarcophagus and the collars. No sign of the key.

He knew how the collars would feel against his skin. The icy bite of the Wyrdstone.

Kaltain had fought it. Destroyed the demon within.

He could still feel the weight of his father's knee digging into his chest as he'd pinned him to the marble floor in a glass castle that no longer existed. Still feel the slick stone of the collar against his neck as it sealed. Still see Sorscha's limp hand as he tried to reach for her one last time.

The room spun and spun, his blood throbbing with it.

Not a prince, not a king.

The collars reached for him with invisible, clawing fingers.

He was no better than them. Had learned to enjoy what the Valg prince had shown him. Had shredded apart good men, and let the demon feed off his hate, his rage.

The room began to eddy, spiraling, dragging him into its depths.

Not human—not entirely. Perhaps he didn't want to be. Perhaps he would stay in another form forever, perhaps he'd just submit—

A dark wind snapped through the room. Snatched him in its gaping maw and dragged him.

He thrashed, screaming silently.

He wouldn't be taken. Not like this, not again—

But it hauled him away from the collars. Under the door and out of the room.

Into the palm of a pale hand. Dark, depthless eyes peered down at him. An enormous red mouth parted to reveal bone-white teeth.

"Stupid boy," Maeve hissed. The words were a thunderclap.

He panted, the gnat's body shaking from wingtip to wingtip. One press of her finger and he'd be gone.

He braced himself, waiting for it.

But Maeve kept her palm open. And as she began to walk down the hall, away from the sealed chamber, she said, "What you felt in there—that is why I left their world." She gazed ahead, a shadow darkening her face. "Every day, that was what I felt."

⁓

Kneeling on the floor in a corner of Maeve's chamber, Dorian hurled the contents of his stomach into the wooden bucket.

Maeve watched from the chair by the fire, cruel amusement on her red lips.

"You saw the horrors of the dungeons and did not fall ill," she said when he vomited again. The unspoken question shone in her eyes. *Why today?*

Dorian lifted his head, wiping his mouth on the shoulder of his jacket. "Those collars . . ." He ran a hand over his neck. "I didn't think it would affect me like that. To see them again."

"You were reckless in entering that chamber."

"Would I have been able to get out, if you hadn't found me?" He didn't ask how she'd done so, how she'd sensed the peril. That power of hers no doubt kept track of him wherever he went.

"The collars can do nothing without being attached to a host. But that room is a place of hatred and pain, the memory of it etched into the stones." She examined her long nails. "It snared you. You *let* yourself be snared."

Hadn't Kaltain said nearly the same thing regarding the collars? "It took me by surprise."

Maeve let out a hum, well aware of his lie. But she said, "The collars are one of his more brilliant creations. Neither of his brothers was clever enough to come up with it. But Erawan—he always had a gift for ideas." She leaned back in the chair, crossing her legs. "But that gift also made him arrogant." She nodded to him. "That he let you remain in Rifthold with your father, rather than bring you here, only proves it. He thought he could control you both from afar. Had he been more cautious, he would have brought you to Morath immediately. Begun work on you."

The collars flashed before his eyes, leaking their poisoned, oily scent into the world, beckoning, waiting for him—

Dorian heaved again.

Maeve let out a low laugh that raked talons down his spine. His temper.

Dorian mastered himself and twisted toward her. "You gave over those spiders for his princesses, knowing what they'd endure, knowing how it would feel to be trapped like that, albeit in a different manner." *How*, he didn't say. *How could you do that, when you knew that sort of terror?*

Maeve fell silent for a moment, and he could have sworn something like regret passed over her face. "I would not have done it, unless my need to prove my loyalty compelled me." Her attention drifted to where Damaris hung at his side. "You do not wish to verify my claim?"

Dorian didn't touch the golden hilt. "Do you want me to?"

She clicked her tongue. "You are different indeed. I wonder if some of the Valg did cross over when your father bred your mother."

Dorian cringed. He still hadn't dared to ask Damaris about it—whether he was human. Whether it mattered now.

"Why?" he asked, gesturing to the keep around them. "Why does Erawan do any of this?" A week after he'd asked the Valg king himself, Dorian still wanted to—*needed* to know.

"Because he can. Because Erawan delights in such things."

"You made it sound as if he was the mildest of all three brothers."

"He is." She ran a hand over her throat. "Orcus and Mantyx are the ones who taught him all he knows. Should they return here, what Erawan creates in these mountains will seem like lambs."

He'd heeded that warning from Kaltain, at least. He hadn't dared venture into the caverns beyond the valley. To the stone altars and the monstrosities Erawan crafted upon them.

He asked, "You never had children? With Orcus?"

"Does my future husband truly wish to know?"

Dorian settled back on his heels. "I wish to understand my enemy."

She weighed his words. "I did not allow my body to ripen, to ready for children. A small rebellion, and my first, against Orcus."

"Are the Valg princes and princesses the offspring of the other kings?"

"Some are, some are not. No worthy heir has stepped forward. Though who knows what has occurred in their world in these millennia." Their world. Not her own. "The princes Erawan summoned have not been strong—not as they were. I am certain it annoys Erawan to no end."

"Which is why he has brought over the princesses?"

A nod. "The females are the deadliest. But harder to contain within a host."

The white band of skin on his neck seemed to burn, but he kept his stomach down: this time. "Why did you leave your world?"

She blinked at him, as if surprised.

"What?" he asked.

She angled her head. "It has been a long, long time since I conversed with someone who knows me for what I am. And with someone whose mind remained wholly their own."

"Even Aelin?"

A muscle in her slim jaw feathered. "Even Aelin of the Wildfire. I could not infiltrate her mind entirely, but little things . . . those, I could convince her to see."

"Why did you capture and torture her?" Such a simple way of describing what had happened in Eyllwe and after it.

"Because she would never agree to work with me. And she would never have protected me from Erawan or the Valg."

"You're strong—why not protect yourself? Use those spiders to your advantage?"

"Because our kind only fears certain gifts. Mine, alas, are not those things." She toyed with a strand of her black hair. "I usually keep another Fae female with me. One who has powers that work against the Valg. Different from those Aelin Galathynius possesses." That she didn't specify what those powers were told Dorian not to waste his breath in asking her. "She swore the blood oath to me long ago, and has rarely left my side since. But I did not dare bring her to Morath. To have her here would not have convinced Erawan that I came in good faith." She twirled the strand of hair around a finger. "So you see, I am as defenseless against Erawan as you."

Dorian highly doubted that, but he rose to his feet at last, aiming for the table where water and food had been laid out. A fine spread, for a demon king's castle in the dead of winter. He poured himself a glass of water and gulped down the contents. "Is this Erawan's true form?"

"In a manner of speaking. We are not like the human and Fae, where your souls are invisible, unseen. Our souls have a shape to them. We have bodies that we can fashion around them—adorn them, like jewelry. The form you see on Erawan was always his preferred decoration."

"What do your souls look like beneath?"

"You would find them displeasing."

He suppressed a shudder.

"I suppose that makes us shape-shifters, too," Maeve mused as Dorian aimed for the chair beside hers. He'd spent his nights sleeping on the floor before the fire, one eye watching the queen dozing in the canopied bed behind him. But she had made no move to harm him. Not one.

"Do you feel Valg, or Fae?"

"I am what I am." For a heartbeat, he could almost glimpse the weight of her eons of existence in her eyes.

"But who do you wish to be?" A careful question.

"Not like Erawan. Or his brothers. I never have."

"That's not exactly an answer."

"Do you know who and what you wish to be?" A challenge—and genuine question.

"I'm figuring it out," he said. Strange. So strange, to have this conversation. Sparing them both for the time being, Dorian rubbed at his face. "The key is in his tower. I'm sure of it."

Maeve's mouth tightened.

Dorian said, "There is no way in—not with the guards. And I've flown the exterior enough to know there are no windows, no cracks for me to even creep through." He held her otherworldly stare. Did not shrink from it. "We need to get in. If only to confirm that it's there." She'd once held the keys—she knew what they felt like. That she had come so close then . . .

"And I suppose you expect me to do that?"

He crossed his arms. "I can think of no one else that Erawan would admit inside."

Maeve's solitary blink was her only sign of surprise. "To seduce and betray a king—one of the oldest tricks in the book, as you humans say."

"Can Erawan be seduced by anyone?"

He could have sworn disgust flitted over her pale face before she said, "He can."

~

They did not waste time. Did not wait.

And even Dorian found himself unable to look away as Maeve flicked a hand at herself and her purple gown melted away, replaced by a sheer, flowing black dress. Little more than a robe. Golden thread had been woven through it, artfully concealing the parts of her that only the one who removed the garment would see, and when she turned from the mirror, her face was grave.

"You will not like what you are about to witness." Then she slung her cloak around her, hiding that lush body and sinful gown, and swept out the door.

He shifted into a slithering insect, swift and flexible, and trailed her, lingering at her heels as Maeve wound through the halls. To the base of that tower.

He tucked into a crack in the black wall as Maeve said to the Valg posted outside, "You know who I am. What I am. Tell him I have come."

He could have sworn Maeve's hands trembled slightly.

But one of the guards—whom Dorian had never once seen so much as blink—turned to the door, knocked once, and strode inside.

He emerged moments later, resumed his post, and said nothing.

Maeve waited. Then strolling footsteps sounded from the tower interior.

And when the door opened again, the putrid wind and swirling darkness within threatened to send him running. Erawan, still clad in his clothes despite the late hour, lifted his brows. "We have a meeting tomorrow, sister."

Maeve took a step closer. "I did not come to discuss war."

Erawan stilled. And then said to the guards, "Leave us."

CHAPTER 74

As one, the guards outside Erawan's tower walked away.

Alone, the Valg king blocking the doorway to his tower, Maeve said, "Does that mean I am welcome?" She loosened her grip on her cloak, the front folds falling open to reveal the sheer gown.

Erawan's golden eyes surveyed every inch. Then her face. "Though you may not believe so, you are my brother's wife."

Dorian blinked at that. At the honor of the demon within the male body.

"I do not have to be," Maeve murmured, and Dorian knew, then, why she had warned him before they'd left.

A shake of her head, and her thick black hair turned golden. Her moon-white skin darkened slightly, to a sun-kissed tan. The angular face rounded slightly, dark eyes lightening to turquoise and gold. "We could play like this, if you'd prefer."

Even the voice belonged to Aelin.

Erawan's eyes flared, his chest rising in an uneven breath.

"Would that appeal to you?" Maeve gave a half-smile that Dorian had only seen on the Queen of Terrasen's face.

Disgust and horror roiled through him. He knew—knew there was no true lust in Erawan's eyes for Aelin. No true desire beyond the claiming, the pain.

Maeve's glamour changed again. Golden hair paled to white, turquoise eyes burning to gold.

Icy rage, pure and undiluted, tore through Dorian as Manon now stood before the Valg king. "Or maybe this form, beautiful beyond all reckoning." She peered down at herself, smiling. "Was she your intended queen when this war was over, the Wing Leader? Or merely a prize breeding mare?"

Erawan's nostrils flared, and Dorian focused upon his breathing, on the stones beneath him, anything to keep his magic from erupting at the desire—true desire—that tightened Erawan's face.

But if it got Maeve inside that tower—

Erawan blinked, and that desire winked out. "You are my brother's wife," he said. "No matter whose skin you wear. Should you need release, I'll send someone to your chambers."

With that, he shut the door. And did not emerge again.

Maeve brought Dorian to her meeting the next morning.

In her cloak pocket, as a field mouse, Dorian kept still and listened.

"After all that fuss last night," Erawan was saying, "you turned away what I sent you."

Indeed, not fifteen minutes after they'd returned to Maeve's tower, a knock had sounded. A blank-faced young man had stood there, beautiful and cold. Not a prince—not with the ring he wore. Just an enslaved human. Maeve had sent him away, though not from any kindness.

No, Dorian knew the man had been spared his duties because of his presence, and nothing more. Maeve had told him as much before falling asleep.

"I had hoped for wine," Maeve said smoothly, "not watered-down ale."

Erawan chuckled, and paper rustled. "I have been considering further details of this alliance, sister." The title was a barb, a taunt of last night's rejection. "And I have been wondering: what else shall you bring to it? You stand to gain more than I do, after all. And offering up six of your spiders is relatively little, even if they have been receptive hosts to the princesses."

Dorian's ears strained as he waited for Maeve's reply. She said quietly, more tensely than he'd heard her speak before, "What is it that you want, brother?"

"Bring the rest of the *kharankui*. Open a portal and transport them here."

"Not all will be such willing hosts."

"Not hosts. Soldiers. I do not intend to take chances. There will be no second phase."

Dorian's stomach twisted. Maeve hesitated. "There is a chance, you know, that even with all of this, even if I summon the *kharankui*, you might face Aelin Galathynius and fail." A pause. "Anielle has confirmed your darkest fears. I heard what occurred. The power she summoned to halt that river." Maeve hummed. "That was meant for me, you know. The blast. But should she summon it again, let's say against you on a field of battle . . . Would you be able to walk away, brother?"

"That is why this press northward with your spiders shall be vital," was Erawan's only reply.

"Perhaps," Maeve countered. "But do not forget that you and I together could win. Without the spiders. Without the princesses. Even Aelin Galathynius could not stand against us both. We can go to the North, and obliterate her. Keep the spiders in reserve for other kingdoms. Other times."

She did not wish to sacrifice them. As if she held some fondness for the beings who had remained loyal for millennia.

"And beyond that," Maeve went on, "You know much about walking between worlds. But not everything." Her hand slid into the pocket, and

Dorian braced himself as her fingers ran over his back. As if telling him to listen.

"And I suppose I will only find out when you and I have won this war," Erawan said at last.

"Yes, though I am willing to give you a display. Tomorrow, once I have prepared." Again, that horrible silence. Maeve said, "They are too strong, too mighty, for me to open a portal between realms to allow them through. They would destabilize my magic too greatly in the effort to bring all that they are into this world. But I could show them to you—just for a moment. I could show you your brothers. Orcus and Mantyx."

CHAPTER
75

Darrow and the other Terrasen lords had spent their time wisely these past few months, thank the gods, and Orynth was well stocked against the siege marching closer with each passing hour.

Food, weapons, healing supplies, plans for where the citizens might sleep should they flee into the castle, reinforcements at the places along the city and castle walls where the ancient stone had weakened—Aedion had found little at fault.

Yet after a fitful night's sleep in his old room in the castle—awful and strange and cold—he was prowling one of the lower turrets as dawn broke. Up here, the wind was so much wilder, icier.

Stalking, steady footsteps sounded from the archway behind him. "I spotted you up here on the way down to breakfast," Ren said by way of greeting. The Allsbrook court's quarters had always been in the tower adjacent to Aedion's—when they'd been boys, they'd once spent a summer devising a signaling system to each other's rooms using a lantern.

It was the last summer they had spent in friendship, once it had started to become clear to Ren's father that Aedion was favored to take the blood oath. And then the rivalry had begun.

One summer: thick as thieves and as wild. The next: endless pissing contests, everything from footraces through the courtyards to shoving in the stairwells to outright brawling in the Great Hall. Rhoe had tried to defuse it, but Rhoe had never been a comfortable liar. Had refused to deny to Ren's father that Aedion was the one who'd swear that oath. And by the end of that summer, even the Crown Prince had begun to look the other way when the two boys launched into yet another fight in the dirt. Not that it mattered now.

Would his own father, would Gavriel, have encouraged the rivalry? He supposed it didn't matter, either. But for a heartbeat, Aedion tried to picture it—Gavriel here, presiding over his training. His father and Rhoe, teaching him together. And he knew that Gavriel would have found some way to calm the competition, much in the way he held the peace in the cadre. What manner of man would he have become, had the Lion been here? Gavriel likely would have been butchered with the rest of the court, but . . . he would have been here.

A fool's path, to wander down that road. Aedion was who he was, and most of the time, didn't mind that one bit. Rhoe had been his father in the ways that counted. Even if there had been times when Aedion had looked at Rhoe and Evalin and Aelin and still felt like a guest.

Aedion shook the thought from his head. Being here, in this castle, had addled him. Dragged him into a realm of ghosts.

"Don't expect Darrow to put out a breakfast spread like the ones we used to have," Aedion said. Not that he expected or wanted one. He ate only because his body demanded he do so, ate because it was strength, and he would need it, his people would need it, before long.

Ren surveyed the city, then the Plain of Theralis beyond. The still-empty horizon. "I'll get the archers sorted today. And ensure the soldiers at the gates know how to wield that boiling oil."

"Do *you* know how to wield it?" Aedion arched a brow.

Ren snorted. "What's to learn? You dump a giant cauldron over the side of the walls. Damage done."

It certainly required a bit more skill than that, but it was better than nothing. At least Darrow had made sure they *had* such supplies.

Aedion prayed they'd get the chance to use them. With Morath's witch towers, the odds were that they'd be blasted into rubble before the enemy host even reached either of the two gates into the city.

"What we could really use is some hellfire," Ren muttered. "That'd keep them from the gates."

And potentially melt everyone around them, too.

Aedion opened his mouth to agree when his brows narrowed.

He surveyed the plain, the horizon.

"Out with it," Ren said.

Aedion steered Ren back toward the tower entrance. "We need to talk to Rolfe."

Not about hellfire at the southern and western gates. Not at all.

They waited until cover of darkness, when Morath's spies might not spot the small band of them who crept, mile after mile, across the Plain of Theralis.

Clad in battle-black, they moved over the field that would once more become bathed in blood. When they reached the landmarks that Aedion and Ren had used the daylight hours to plan out, Aedion held up a hand.

The Silent Assassins lived up to their name as Ilias signaled back and they spread out. Amongst them moved Rolfe's Mycenians, bearing their heavy loads.

But it was the shape-shifter who began to work first. Turning herself into a giant badger, bigger than a horse, who scooped out the frozen earth with skilled, strong paws.

The scent of her blood filled the air, but Lysandra didn't stop digging.

And when she'd finished the first pit, she moved on to the next, leaving the group of Silent Assassins and Mycenians to lay their trap, then bury it once more.

The brutal wind moaned past them. Yet they worked through the night, used every minute given to them. And when they were done, they vanished back to the city, invisible once more.

~

Morath appeared on the horizon a day later.

From the castle's highest towers and walkways, every marching line could be counted. One after another after another.

Her hands still bruised and bandaged from digging through frozen earth, Lysandra stood with an assortment of their allies on one of those walkways, Evangeline clinging to her.

"That's fifteen thousand," Ansel of Briarcliff announced as yet another line emerged. No one said anything. "Twenty."

"Morath must be empty to now have so many here," Prince Galan murmured.

Evangeline trembled, not entirely from the cold, and Lysandra tightened her arm around the girl. Down the wall of the walkway, Darrow and the other Terrasen lords spoke quietly. As if sensing Lysandra's attention, Darrow threw a narrow glance her way—that then dipped to the pale-faced, shaking Evangeline. Darrow said nothing, and Lysandra didn't bother to look pleasant, before he turned back to his companions.

"That's thirty," Ansel said.

"We can count," Rolfe snipped.

Ansel lifted a wine-red brow. "Can you really?"

Despite the army marching on them, Lysandra's mouth twitched upward.

Rolfe just rolled his eyes and went back to watching the approaching army.

"They won't arrive until dawn at the earliest," Aedion observed, his face grim.

She had not yet decided what form to take. Where to fight. If ilken still flew in their ranks, then it would be a wyvern, but if closer quarters were required, then . . . she hadn't decided. No one had asked her to be anywhere in particular, though Aedion's request the other night to assist in their wild plan had been a rare reprieve from these days of waiting and dreading.

She'd gladly take days of pacing instead of what approached them.

"Fifty thousand," Ansel said, throwing a wry glance to Rolfe.

Lysandra swallowed against the tightness in her throat. Evangeline pressed her face into Lysandra's side.

And then the witch towers took form.

Like massive lances jutting from the horizon, they appeared through the gray morning light. Three of them, spread out equally amid the army that continued to flow behind them.

Even Ansel stopped counting now.

"I did not think it would be so terrible," Evangeline whispered, hands digging into Lysandra's heavy cloak. "I did not think it would be so wretched."

Lysandra pressed a kiss to the top of her red-gold hair. "No harm shall come to you."

"I am not afraid for myself," Evangeline said. "But for my friends."

Those citrine eyes indeed shone with tears of terror, and Lysandra brushed one away before watching the advancing witch towers creep toward them. She had no words to comfort the girl.

"Any minute now," Aedion murmured, and Lysandra glanced down to the snowy plain.

To the figures that emerged from beneath the snow, clad in white. Flaming arrows nocked in their bows. Morath's front lines were nearly upon them, but those soldiers were not their target.

Down the wall, Murtaugh gripped the ancient stones as a figure that had to be Ren gave the order. Flaming arrows arched and flew, Morath soldiers ducking under their shields.

They did not bother to look beneath their feet.

Neither did the witches leading their three towers.

The flaming arrows struck the earth with deadly accuracy, thanks to the Silent Assassins who wielded those bows.

Right atop the fuse lines that flowed directly into the pits they'd dug. Just as the witch towers passed over them.

Blinding flashes broke apart the black sea of the army. Then the mighty boom.

And then a rain of stone, all Morath's forces whirling to see. Providing the right distraction as Ren, Ilias, and the Silent Assassins raced on foot to the white horses hidden behind a snowdrift.

When the flash cleared, when the smoke was gone, a sigh of relief went down the walkway.

Two of those witch towers had been directly over the pits. Pits that they had filled with the chemical reactors and powders that fueled Rolfe's firelances, then concealed beneath the earth—waiting for a spark to ignite them.

Those two towers now lay in scattered ruin, their wyverns broken beneath them, soldiers squashed under falling stone.

Yet one still stood, the pit it had been closest to exploding too soon. One of the wyverns who had pulled it had been hit by debris from another tower—and lay either dead or injured.

And that third remaining tower had stopped.

A wicked, low horn sounded from the enemy host, and the army halted, too.

"Thank the rutting gods," Rolfe said, head bowing.

But Aedion was still staring at the plain—at the figures on horseback galloping to Orynth's walls. Making sure they all returned.

"How long will that stop them?" Evangeline asked.

Everyone, Darrow included, turned to the girl. No one had an answer. No lie to offer.

So they again faced the army gathered on the plain, its farthest reaches now visible.

"One hundred thousand," Ansel of Briarcliff announced softly.

CHAPTER 76

"It's possible—to *show* a different world?" Dorian asked Maeve when they were again in their tower room.

Maeve slid into a chair, her face distant. "Using mirrors, yes."

Dorian lifted a brow.

"You have seen yourself the power of witch mirrors. What it did to Aelin Galathynius and Manon Blackbeak. Who do you think taught the witches such power? Not the Fae." A small laugh. "And how do you think I have been able to see so far, hear the voices of my eyes, all the way from Doranelle? There are mirrors to spy, to travel, to kill. Even now, Erawan wields them to his advantage with the Ironteeth." With the witch towers.

Maeve lounged, a queen with no crown. "I can show him what he wishes to see."

Dorian opened his mouth, then considered the words.

"An illusion. You don't plan to show him Orcus or Mantyx at all."

She cut him a cool stare. "A sleight of hand—while you enter the tower."

"I can't get in."

"I am a world-walker," Maeve said. "I have traveled between universes. Do you think moving between rooms will be so hard?"

"Something kept you from going to Terrasen all these years."

Maeve's jaw tightened. "Brannon Galathynius was aware of my gifts to move between places. The wards around his kingdom prevent me from doing so."

"So you could not transport Erawan's armies there for him."

"No. I can only enter on foot. There are too many of them, anyway, for me to hold the portal that long."

"Erawan is aware of your gift, so he'll likely have taken steps to guard his own room."

"Yes, and I have spent my time here slowly unraveling them. He is not so skilled a spellworker as he thinks." A smug, triumphant smile.

Yet Dorian asked, "Why not do this from the start?"

"Because I had not yet decided it was worth the risk. Because he had not yet pushed me to bring my handmaidens here, to be mere foot soldiers."

"You care about them—the spiders."

"You will find, Your Majesty, that a loyal friend is a rare thing indeed. They are not so easy to sacrifice."

"You offered up six of them to those princesses."

"And I shall remember that for as long as I live," Maeve said, and some kernel of emotion indeed danced over her face. "They went willingly. I tell myself that whenever I look upon them now and see nothing of the creatures I knew. They wished to help me." Her eyes met his. "Not all Valg are evil."

"Erawan is."

"Yes," she said, and her eyes darkened. "He and his brothers . . . they are the worst of our kind. Their rule was through fear and pain. They delight in such things."

"And you do not?"

Maeve twirled an inky strand around a finger. And didn't answer.

Fine. Dorian went on, "So you shall break past Erawan's wards on his room, open the portal for me, and I'll slip in while you distract him with an illusion about his brothers." He frowned. "As soon as I find the key, he'll know you've deceived him. We'll have to leave quickly."

Her mouth curved. "We will. And go to wherever you have hidden the others."

Dorian kept every expression off his face. "You're certain he won't know he's being tricked?"

"Orcus is his brother. But Orcus was also my husband. The illusion will be real enough."

Dorian considered. "What time do we make our move?"

Nightfall.

That was when Maeve had told Erawan to meet. That liminal space between light and dark, when one force yielded to another. When she would open the portal for Dorian from rooms away.

As the sun set—not that Dorian could see it with the clouds and gloom of Morath—he found himself staring at the wall of Maeve's chamber.

She had left minutes ago, with nothing more than a farewell glance. Their escape route had been plotted, an alternative with it. All should go according to plan.

And the body he now wore, the golden hair and golden eyes . . . Should anyone but Erawan himself stumble into the tower, they would find it occupied by their master.

He did not have room in himself for fear, for doubt. Did not think of the Wyrdstone collars beneath the fortress, or every twisted room and dungeon he'd passed through. Darkness fell beyond the room.

Dorian stepped back as the stones turned dark, dark, dark—then vanished.

The stench of death, of rot, of hate flowed out. Far more putrid than the tomb levels below.

It threatened to buckle his knees, but Dorian drew Damaris. Rallied his power and lifted his left hand, a faint golden light shining from his fingers. Fire.

With a prayer to whatever gods might bother to help him, Dorian stepped through the portal.

CHAPTER 77

Dorian didn't know what he had expected from a Valg king's chamber, but the four-poster bed of carved black wood, the washstand and desk, would have been low on his list of guesses.

Nothing extraordinary. No trove of stolen, ancient weapons or heirlooms, no bubbling potions or spellbooks, no snarling beasts in the corner. No additional of Wyrdstone collars.

A bedroom and nothing more.

He scanned the circular room, even going so far as to peer down the stairwell. A straight shot to the iron door and guards posted outside. No closets. No trapdoors.

He opened the armoire to find row after row of clean clothes. None of the drawers contained anything—and there were no hidden compartments.

But he felt it. That otherworldly, terrible presence. Could feel it all around him—

A small noise had him whirling.

Dorian looked at the bed then. At what he had missed, left lying between obsidian sheets, which nearly swallowed her frail, small body.

The young woman. Her face was hollow, vacant. Yet she stared at him. As if she'd awoken.

A pretty, dark-haired girl. No older than twenty. A near-twin to Kaltain.

Bile burned his throat. And as the girl sat up farther, the sheets falling away to reveal a wasted, naked body, to reveal a too-thin arm and the hideous purplish scar near the wrist . . . He knew why he had felt the key's presence throughout the keep. Moving about. Vanishing.

It had been walking. Trailing its master. Her enslaver.

A collar of black stone had been clamped around her throat.

And yet she sat there in that rumpled bed. Staring at him.

Hollow and vacant—and in pain.

He had no words. There was only ringing silence.

Kaltain had destroyed the Valg prince inside her, but the Wyrdkey had driven her mad. Had given her terrible power, but ripped apart her mind.

Dorian slowly, carefully, took one step closer to the bed. "You're awake," he said, willing his voice to the drawl of the Valg king. Knowing it was her captor she saw.

A blink.

Dorian had witnessed Erawan's experiments, the horrors of his dungeons. Yet this young woman, so starved, the bruises on her skin, the unholy thing in her arm, the unholy thing he'd known had shared this bed with her . . .

He dared to unspool a thread of his power. It neared her arm and recoiled.

Yes, the key was there.

He prowled closer, willing her not to look toward the portal in the wall.

The young woman trembled—just slightly.

He willed himself not to vomit. Not to do anything but look at her with cool command as he said, "Give me your arm."

Her brown eyes scanned his face, but she held out her arm.

He nearly staggered back at the festering wound, the black veins running up from it. Leaking its poison into her. What Kaltain's wound had no doubt looked like, and why the scar remained, even in death.

But he sheathed Damaris and took her arm in his hands.

Ice. Her skin was like ice. "Lie down," he told her.

She shook, but obeyed. Bracing herself. For him.

Kaltain. Oh gods, Kaltain. What she'd endured—

Dorian freed the knife at his side—the one Sorrel had gifted him—and angled it over her arm. Kaltain had done the same to free it, Manon had said.

But Dorian sent a flicker of his healing magic to her arm. To numb and soothe. She thrashed, but he held firm. Let his magic flare through her. She gasped, arching, and Dorian took advantage of her sudden stillness to plunge in the knife, fast and deft.

Three movements, his healing magic still working through her, soothing her as best he could, and the bloodied shard was in his fingers. Pulsing its hollow, sickening power through him.

The final Wyrdkey.

He dropped her arm, sliding the Wyrdkey into his pocket, and turned for the portal.

But a hand wrapped around his, feeble and shaking.

He whirled, a hand going to Damaris, and found her staring up at him. Tears slid down her face.

"Kill me," she breathed. Dorian blinked. "You—you pushed it back." Not the key, but the demon inside her, he realized. Somehow, with that healing magic— "Kill me," she said, and began sobbing. "*Kill me*, please."

Damaris warmed in his hand. Truth. He gaped at her in horror. "I—I can't."

She began clawing at the collar around her throat. As if she'd rip it free. "*Please*," she sobbed. "*Please.*"

He did not have time. To find a way to get that collar off. Wasn't even certain it *could* come off, without that golden ring Aelin had used on him. "I can't."

Despair and agony flooded her eyes. "Please," was all she said. "Please."

Damaris remained warm. Truth. The pleading was nothing but truth.

But he had to go—had to go *now*. He could not take her with him. Knew that thing inside her, however his magic had pushed it back, would emerge again. And scream to Erawan where he was. What he'd stolen.

She wept, hands ripping at her brutalized body. *"Please."*

Would it be a mercy—to kill her? Would it be a worse crime to leave her here, with Erawan? Enslaved to him and the Valg demon inside her?

Damaris did not answer his silent questions.

And he let his hand fall away from the blade entirely as he stared down at the weeping girl.

Manon would have ended it. Freed her in the only way left. Chaol would have taken her with him and damned the consequences. Aelin . . . He didn't know what she would have done.

Who do you wish to be?

He was not any of them. He was—he was nothing but himself.

A man who had known loss and pain, yes. But a man who had known friendship and joy.

The loss and pain—they had not broken him wholly. Without them, would the moments of happiness be as bright? Without them, would he fight so hard to ensure it did not happen again?

Who do you wish to be?

A king worthy of his crown. A king who would rebuild what had been shattered, both within himself and in his lands.

The girl sobbed and sobbed, and Dorian's hand drifted toward Damaris's hilt.

Then a crack sounded. Bone snapping.

One moment, the girl was weeping. The next, her head twisted to the side, eyes unseeing.

Dorian whirled, a cry on his lips as Maeve stepped into the room.

"Consider it a wedding gift, Majesty," she said, her lips curling. "To spare you from that decision."

And it was the smile on her face, the predatory gait of her steps that had his magic rallying.

Maeve nodded toward his pocket. "Well done."

Her dark power leapt upon his mind.

He didn't have the chance to grab for Damaris before he was snared in her dark web.

CHAPTER 78

He was in Erawan's room, and yet not.

Maeve purred to him, "The key, if you will."

Dorian's hand slid into his pocket. To the sliver inside.

"And then we shall retrieve the others," she continued, and beckoned to the portal through which they had both come. He followed her, pulling the shard from his pocket. "Such things I have planned for us, Majesty. For our union. With the keys, I could keep you eternally young. And with your power, second to none, not even Aelin Galathynius, you will shield us from any who might try to return to this world again."

They emerged into their room, and a swipe of Maeve's hand had the portal fading. "Quickly now," she ordered him. "We depart. The wyvern awaits."

Dorian halted in the middle of the chamber. "Don't you think it's rude to leave without a note?"

Maeve twisted toward him, but too late.

Too damn late, as the claws she'd hooked into his mind became mired in it. As flame, white-hot and sizzling, closed upon the piece of her she'd unwittingly laid bare in trying to trap him.

A trap within a trap. One he had formed from the moment he'd seen her. It had been a simple trick. To *shift* his mind, as if he were shifting his body. To make her see one thing when she glimpsed inside it.

To make her see what she wished to believe: his jealousy and resentment of Aelin; his desperation; his naive foolishness. He had let his mind become such things, let it lure her in. And every time she had come close, falling for those slips in his power, his magic had studied her own. Just as it had studied Cyrene's stolen kernel of shape-shifting, so had it learned Maeve's ability to creep into the mind, seize it.

It had only been a matter of waiting for her to make her move, to let her lay the trap she'd close to seal him to her forever.

"You—" A smile from him, and Maeve stopped being able to speak.

Dorian said into the dark chasm of her mind, *I was a slave once. You didn't really think I'd allow myself to be so once again, did you?*

She thrashed, but he held her firm. *You will free me*, she hissed, and the voice was not that of a beautiful queen, but something vicious and cold. Starved and hateful.

You're old as the earth, and yet you thought I would truly fall for your offer. He chuckled, letting a wisp of his fire burn her. Maeve shrieked, silent and endless in their minds. *I'm surprised you fell for* my *trap.*

I will kill you for this.

Not if I kill you first. His fire became a living thing, wrapping around her pale throat. In the real world, in the place where their bodies existed.

You hurt my friend, he said with lethal calm. *It will not be so very difficult to end you for it.*

Is this the king you wish to be? Torturing a helpless female?

He laughed again. *You are not helpless. And if I could, I would seal you in an iron box for eternity.* Dorian glanced to the windows. To the night beyond. He had to go—quickly. But he still said, *The king I wish to be is the opposite of what you are.* He gave Maeve a smile. *And there is only one witch who will be my queen.*

A groan rumbled through the mountain beneath them. Morath shuddered.

Maeve's eyes widened further.

A crack louder than thunder echoed through the stones. The tower swayed.

Dorian's mouth curved upward. *You didn't think I spent all those hours merely searching, did you?*

He wouldn't allow it to exist another day—that chamber with the collars. Not one more day.

So he'd bring down the entire damn keep atop it.

It had not been hard. Little bits of magic, of coldest ice, that wormed through the cracks of Morath's foundation. That ate away at the ancient stone. Bit by bit, a web of instability growing with each hall and room he searched. Until the entire eastern half of the keep was balanced upon his will alone.

Until now. Until half a thought had his magic expanding through those cracks, bearing down upon them.

And so Morath began to crumble.

Smiling at Maeve, Dorian pulled out. Pulled away, even as he held her mind.

The tower shuddered again. Maeve's breath hitched. *You can't leave me like this. He'll find me, he'll take me—*

As you would have taken me? Dorian shifted into a crow, flapping in the air of the chamber.

Morath groaned again, and above it rose a screech of rage, so piercing and unearthly that his bones quailed.

Tell Erawan, Dorian said, halting on the windowsill, *that I did it for Adarlan.*

For Sorscha and Kaltain and all those destroyed by it. As Adarlan itself had been destroyed.

But from utter ruin, it might be built again. If not by him, then by others.

Perhaps that would be his first and only gift to Adarlan as its king: a clean slate, should they survive this war.

Screaming filled the halls. He'd marked where the human servants worked, where they dwelled. They would find, as they fled, that their passageways remained stable. Until every last one of them was out.

Please, Maeve begged, staggering to her knees as the tower swayed again. *Please*.

He should let Erawan find her. Doom her to the life she'd intended for him. For Aelin.

Maeve curled over her knees, her mind and power contained. Waiting in despair for the dark king whom she'd tried so hard to escape. Or for the shuddering fortress to collapse around her.

He knew he would regret it. Knew he should kill her. But to condemn her to what he'd endured . . .

He would not wish it upon anyone. Even if it cost them this war.

He did not think it made him weak. Not at all.

Beyond the window, Ironteeth shot to the skies, wyverns shrieking as Morath's stones began to give way. In the valley below, the army halted to peer at the mountain looming high above them. The shaking tower built atop it.

Please, Maeve said again. Levels beneath them, another bellow of rage thundered from Erawan—closer now.

So Dorian soared into the chaotic night.

Maeve's silent cry of despair followed on his heels. All the way to the peaks overlooking Morath and that rocky outcropping—to the two Wyrdkeys buried under the shale.

He could barely remember his own name as he slid them into his other pocket. As all three of the Wyrdkeys now lay upon him.

Then he reached back into the mind still tethered to his.

It was simple as an incision. To sever the link between their minds—and to sever another part of her.

To tie off the gift that allowed her to jump between places. To open those portals.

World-walker no longer, he said as his raw magic shifted her own. Changed its very essence. *I suggest you invest in a good pair of shoes.*

Then he let go of Maeve's mind.

A hateful, unending scream was the only response.

Dorian shifted again, becoming large and vicious, no more than a pack wyvern flying northward to bring supplies to the aerial legion.

A king—he could be a king to Adarlan in these last days that remained for him. Wipe away the stain and rot of what it had become. So it might start anew. Become who it wished to be.

Dorian caught a swift wind, sailing hard and fast.

And when he looked behind him, at the mountain and valley that reeked of death, at the place where so many terrible things had begun, Dorian smiled and brought Morath's towers crashing down.

CHAPTER 79

Yrene hated the Ferian Gap. Hated the tight air between the two gargantuan peaks, hated the bones and wyvern refuse littering the rocky floor, hated the reek that slithered from whatever openings had been carved into the mountains.

At least it was empty. Though they had not yet decided if that was a blessing.

The two armies now filled the Gap, Hasar's soldiers already preparing to make the crossing back over the Avery into the tangle of Oakwald. *That* trek would take an age, even with the rukhin carrying the wagons and heavier supplies. And then the push northward through the forest, taking the ancient road that lay along the Avery's northern branch.

"Pass me that knife there," Yrene said to Lady Elide, pointing with her chin to her supply kit. Spread on a blanket on the bottom of the covered wagon, a Darghan soldier lay unconscious, cold sweat beading his brow. He hadn't seen a healer after getting a slice to the thigh at the battle for Anielle, and when he'd fallen clean off his horse this morning, he'd been hauled in here.

Elide's hands remained steady as she plucked up the thin knife and passed it to Yrene.

"Will it wake him?" she asked while Yrene bent over the unconscious warrior and examined the infected wound that was gruesome enough to turn most stomachs.

"My magic has him in a deep sleep." Yrene angled the knife. "He'll stay out until I wake him."

Elide, to her credit, didn't retch as Yrene began to clean out the wound, scraping away the dead, infected bits.

"No sign of blood poisoning, thank the gods," Yrene announced as the cloth beside the man became covered in the discarded rot. "But we'll need to put him on a special brew to make sure."

"Your magic can't just do a sweep through him?" Elide tossed the soiled cloth into the nearby waste bucket, and laid down another.

"It can, and I will," Yrene said, fighting her gag as the reek from the wound stuffed itself up her nostrils, "but that might not be enough, if the infection truly wishes to make an appearance."

"You talk about illnesses as if they were living creatures."

"They are, to some degree," Yrene said. "With their own secrets and temperaments. You sometimes have to outsmart them, just as you would any foe."

Yrene took the mirrored lantern from beside the bed and adjusted the plates within to shine a beam of light on the infected slice. When the brightness revealed no further signs of rotting skin, she set down both lantern and knife. "That wasn't as bad as I'd feared," she admitted, and held out her hands over the bloody wound.

Warmth and light rose within her, like a memory of the summer in this frigid mountain pass, and as her hands glowed, Yrene's magic guided her within the man's body. It flowed along blood and sinew and bone, knitting and mending, listening to the aches and fever now running rampant. Soothing them, calming them. Wiping them away.

She was panting when she finished, but the man's breathing had eased. The sweat on his brow had dried.

"Remarkable," Elide whispered, gaping at the now-smooth leg of the warrior.

Yrene just turned her head to the side and vomited into the waste bucket.

Elide leapt to her feet.

But Yrene held up a hand, wiping her mouth with the other. "As joyful as it is to know I shall soon be a mother, the realities of the first few months are . . . not so joyous."

Elide limped to the ewer of drinking water and poured a cup. "Here. Is there anything I can get you? Can—can *you* heal your own sickness, or do you need someone else to?"

Yrene sipped at the water, letting it wash away the bitter bile. "The vomiting is a sign that things are progressing with the babe." A hand drifted to her middle. "It's not something that can really be cured, not unless I had a healer at my side day and night, easing the nausea."

"It's become that bad?" Elide frowned.

"Terrible timing, I know." Yrene sighed. "The best options are ginger— anything ginger. Which I would rather save for the upset stomachs of our soldiers. Peppermint can help, too." She gestured toward her satchel. "I have some dried leaves in there. Just put some in a cup with the hot water and I'll be fine." Behind them, a small brazier held a steaming kettle, used for disinfecting supplies rather than making tea.

Elide was instantly moving, and Yrene watched in silence while the lady prepared the tea.

"I could heal your leg, you know."

Elide stilled, a hand reaching for the kettle. "Really?"

Yrene waited until the lady had pressed a cup of the peppermint tea into her hands before she nodded to the lady's boots. "Can I see the injury?"

Elide hesitated, but took her seat on the stool beside Yrene and tugged off her boot, then the sock beneath.

Yrene surveyed the scarring, the twisted bone. Elide had told her days ago why she had the injury.

"You're lucky you didn't get an infection yourself." Yrene sipped from her tea, deemed it still too hot, and set it aside before patting her lap. Elide obeyed, putting her foot on Yrene's thigh. Carefully, Yrene touched the scars and mangled bones, her magic doing the same.

The brutality of the injury was enough to take Yrene's breath away. And to make her grind her teeth, knowing how young Elide had been, how unbearably painful it was—knowing that her very uncle had done this to her.

"What's wrong?" Elide breathed.

"Nothing—I mean, beyond what you already know."

Such cruelty. Such terrible, unforgivable cruelty.

Yrene coiled her magic back into herself, but kept her hands on Elide's ankle. "This injury would require weeks of work to repair, and with our current circumstances, I don't think either of us can undergo it." Elide nodded. "But if we survive this war, I can help you, if you wish."

"What would it entail?"

"There are two roads," Yrene said, letting some of her magic seep into Elide's leg, soothing the aching muscles, the spots where bone ground against bone with no buffer. The lady sighed. "The first is the hardest. It would require me to completely restructure your foot and ankle. Meaning, I would have to break apart the bone, take out the parts that healed or fused incorrectly, and then regrow them. You could not walk while I did it, and even with the help I could give you for the pain, the recovery would be agonizing." There was no way around that truth. "I'd need three weeks to take apart your bones and put them back together, but you'd need at least a month of resting and learning to walk on it again."

Elide's face had gone pale. "And the other option?"

"The other option would be to not do the healing, but to give you salve—like the one you said Lorcan gave you—to help with the aches. But I will warn you: the pain will never entirely leave you. With the way your bones grind together here"—she gently touched the spot on Elide's upper foot, then a spot down by her toes—"arthritis is already setting in. As the bones continue to grind together, the arthritis, that pain you feel when you walk, will only worsen. There may come a point in a few years— maybe five, maybe ten, it's hard to tell—when you find the pain to be so bad that no salve can help you."

"So I would need the healing then, regardless."

"It's up to you whether you want the healing at all. I only want you to have a better idea of the road ahead." She smiled at the lady. "It's up to you to decide how you wish to face it."

Yrene tapped Elide's foot, and the lady lowered it back to the floor before putting her sock back on, then her boot. Efficient, easy motions.

Yrene sipped from her tea, cool enough now to drink. The fresh verve of the peppermint zapped through her, clearing her mind and calming her stomach.

Elide said, "I don't know if I can face that pain again."

Yrene nodded. "With that sort of injury, it would require facing a great many things inside yourself." She smiled toward the wagon entrance. "My husband and I just went through one such journey together."

"Was it hard?"

"Incredibly. But he did it. We did it."

Elide considered, then shrugged. "We'd have to survive this war first, I suppose. If we live . . . then we can talk about it."

"Fair enough."

Elide frowned at the wagon's ceiling. "I wonder what they've learned up there."

Up in the Omega and Northern Fang, where Chaol and the others were now meeting with the breeders and wranglers who had been left behind.

Yrene didn't want to know more than that, and Chaol had not offered any other insight into how they'd be extracting information from the men.

"Hopefully something worth our visit to this awful place," Yrene muttered, then drained the rest of her tea. The sooner they left, the better.

It was as if the gods were laughing at her—at them both. A knock on the wagon doors had Elide limping toward them, just before Borte appeared. Her face uncharacteristically solemn.

Yrene braced herself, but it was Elide whom the ruk rider addressed.

"You're to come with me," Borte said breathlessly. Behind the girl, Arcas waited, a sparrow perched on the saddle. Falkan Ennar. Not a companion, Yrene realized, but an additional guard.

Elide asked, "What's wrong?"

Borte shifted, with impatience or nerves, Yrene couldn't tell. "They found someone in the mountain. They want you up there—to decide what to do with him."

Elide had gone still. Utterly still.

Yrene asked, "Who?"

Borte's mouth tightened. "Her uncle."

Elide wondered if the rukhin would shun her forever if she vomited all over Arcas. Indeed, during the swift, steep flight up to the bridge spanning the Omega and Northern Fang, it was all she could do not to hurl the contents of her stomach all over the bird's feathers.

"They found him hiding in the Northern Fang," Borte had said before she'd hauled Elide into the saddle, Falkan already flying up the sheer face of the pass. "Trying to pretend to be a wyvern trainer. But one of the other trainers sold him out. Queen Aelin called for you as soon as they had him secure. Your uncle, not the trainer, I mean."

Elide hadn't been able to respond. Had only nodded.

Vernon was here. At the Gap. Not in Morath with his master, but *here*.

Gavriel and Fenrys were waiting when Arcas landed in the cavernous opening into the Northern Fang. The rough-hewn rock loomed like a gaping maw, the reek of what lay within making her stomach turn again. Like rotting meat and worse. Valg, undoubtedly, but also a smell of hate and cruelty and tight, airless corridors.

The two Fae males silently fell into step beside her as they entered. No sign of Lorcan, or Aelin. Or her uncle.

Men lay dead in some of the dim hallways that Fenrys and Gavriel led her through, killed by the rukhin when they'd swept in. None of them leaked black blood, but they still had that reek to them. Like this place had infected their very souls.

"They're just up here," Gavriel said quietly—gently.

Elide's hands began shaking, and Fenrys placed one of his own on her shoulder. "He's well restrained."

She knew not with mere ropes or chains. Likely with fire and ice and perhaps even Lorcan's own dark power.

But it did not stop her from shaking, from how small and brittle she became as they turned a corner and beheld Aelin, Rowan, and Lorcan standing before a shut door. Farther down the hall, Nesryn and Sartaq, Lord Chaol with them, waited. Letting them decide what to do.

Letting Elide decide.

Lorcan's grave face was frozen with rage, his depthless eyes like frigid pools of night. He said quietly, "You don't need to go in there."

"We had you brought here," Aelin said, her own face the portrait of restrained wrath, "so you could choose what to do with him. If you wish to speak to him before we do."

One look at the knives at Rowan's and Lorcan's sides, at the way the queen's fingers curled, and Elide knew what their sort of talking would include. "You mean to torture him for information?" She didn't dare meet Aelin's eyes.

"Before he receives what is due to him," Lorcan growled.

Elide glanced between the male she loved and the queen she served. And her limp had never felt so pronounced, so obvious, as she took a step closer. "Why is he here?"

"He has yet to reveal that," Rowan said. "And though we have not confirmed that you are here, he suspects." A glance toward Lorcan. "The call is yours, Lady."

"You will kill him regardless?"

Lorcan asked, "Do you wish us to?" Months ago, she had told him to. And Lorcan had agreed to do it. That had been before Vernon and the ilken had come to abduct her—before the night when she had been willing to embrace death rather than go with him to Morath.

Elide peered inward. They gave her the courtesy of silence. "I would like to speak to him before we decide his fate."

A bow of Lorcan's head was his only answer before he opened the door behind him.

Torches flickered, the chamber empty save for a worktable against one wall.

And her uncle, bound in thick irons, seated on a wooden chair.

His finery was worn, his dark hair unkempt, as if he'd struggled while they'd bound him. Indeed, blood crusted one of his nostrils, his nose swollen.

Shattered.

A glance to her right confirmed the blood on Lorcan's knuckles.

Vernon straightened as Elide stopped several feet away, the door shutting, Lorcan and Aelin mere steps behind. The others remained in the hall.

"What mighty company you keep these days, Elide," Vernon said.

That voice. Even with the broken nose, that silky, horrible voice raked talons along her skin.

But Elide kept her chin up. Kept her eyes upon her uncle. "Why are you here?"

"First you let the brute at me," Vernon drawled, nodding to Lorcan, "then you send in the sweet-faced girl to coax answers?" A smile toward Aelin. "A technique of yours, Majesty?"

Aelin leaned against the stone wall, hands sliding into her pockets. Nothing human in her face. Though Elide marked the way her hands, even within their confines, shifted.

Bound in irons. Battered.

Only weeks ago, it had been the queen herself in Vernon's place. And now it seemed she stood here through sheer will. Stood here, ready to pry the information from Vernon, for Elide's sake.

It strengthened Elide enough that she said to her uncle, "Your breaths are limited. I would suggest you use them wisely."

"Ruthless." Vernon smirked. "The witch-blood in your veins ran true after all."

She couldn't stand it. To be in this room with him. To breathe the same air as the man who had smiled while her father had been executed, smiled while he locked her in that tower for ten years. Smiled while he'd touched Kaltain, done far worse perhaps, then tried to sell Elide to Erawan for breeding. "Why?" she asked.

It was the only question she could really think of, that really mattered. "Why do any of it?"

"Since my breaths are limited," Vernon said, "I suppose it makes no difference what I tell you." A small smile curled his lips. "Because I could," her uncle said. Lorcan growled. "Because my brother, your father, was an insufferable brute, whose only qualification to rule was the order of our birth. A warrior-brute," Vernon spat, sneering toward Lorcan. Then at Elide. "Your mother's preference seems to have passed to you, too." A hateful shake of the head. "Such a pity. She was a rare beauty, you know. Such a pity that she was killed, defending Her Majesty." Heat flared across the room, but Aelin's face remained unmoved. "There might have been a place for her in Perranth had she not—"

"Enough," Elide said softly, but not weakly. She took another step toward him. "So you were jealous. Of my father. Jealous of his strength, his talent. Of his wife." Vernon opened his mouth, but Elide lifted a hand. "I am not done yet."

Vernon blinked.

Elide kept her breathing steady, shoulders back. "I do not care why you are here. I do not care what they plan to do with you. But I want you to know that once I walk from this room, I will never think of you again. Your name will be erased from Perranth, from Terrasen, from Adarlan. There will never be a whisper of you, nor any reminder. You will be forgotten."

Vernon paled—just slightly. Then he smiled. "Erased from Perranth? You say that as if you do not know, *Lady* Elide." He leaned forward as much as his chains would allow. "Perranth now lies in the hands of Morath. *Your* city has been sacked."

The words rippled through her like a blow, and even Lorcan sucked in a breath.

Vernon leaned back, smug as a cat. "Go ahead and erase me, then. With the rubble, it will not be hard to do."

Perranth had been captured by Morath. Elide didn't need to glance over a shoulder to know that Aelin's eyes were near-glowing. Bad—this was far worse than they'd anticipated. They had to move quickly. Get to the North as fast as they could.

So Elide turned toward the door, Lorcan stalking ahead to open it for her.

"That's it?" Vernon demanded.

Elide paused. Slowly turned. "What else could I have to say to you?"

"You did not ask me for details." Another snake's smile. "You still have not learned how to play the game, Elide."

Elide returned his smile with one of her own. "There is nothing more that I care to hear from you." She glanced toward Lorcan and Aelin, toward their companions gathered in the hall. "But they still have questions."

Vernon's face went the color of spoiled milk. "You mean to leave me in their hands, utterly defenseless?"

"I was defenseless when you let my leg remain unhealed," she said, a steady sort of calm settling over her. "I was a child then, and I survived. You're a grown man." She let her lips curl in another smile. "We'll see if you do, too."

She didn't try to hide her limp as she strode out. As she caught Lorcan's eye and beheld the pride gleaming there.

Not a whisper—not one whisper from that voice who had guided her.

Not from fear, but . . . Perhaps she did not need Anneith, Lady of Wise Things. Perhaps the goddess had known she herself was not needed.

Not anymore.

Aelin knew that one word from her, and Lorcan would rip out Vernon's throat. Or perhaps begin with snapping bones.

Or skin him alive, as Rowan had done with Cairn.

As she followed Elide, the Lady of Perranth's head still high, Aelin forced her own breathing to remain steady. To brace herself for what was to come. She could get through it. Push past the shaking in her hands, the cold sweat down her back. To learn what they needed, she could find some way to endure this next task.

Elide halted in the hall, Gavriel, Rowan, and Fenrys taking a step closer. No sign of Nesryn, Chaol, or Sartaq, though one shout would likely summon them in this festering warren.

Gods, the stench of this place. The *feel* of it.

She'd been debating for the past hour whether it was worth it to her sanity and stomach to shift back into her human form—to the blessed lesser sense of smell it offered.

Elide said to none of them in particular, "I don't care what you do with him."

"Do you care if he walks out alive?" Lorcan said with deadly calm.

Elide studied the male whose heart she held. "No." *Good*, Aelin almost said. Elide added, "But make it quick." Lorcan opened his mouth. Elide shook her head. "My father would wish it so."

Punish them all, Kaltain had made Aelin once promise. And Vernon, from what Elide had told Aelin, seemed likely to have been at the top of Kaltain's list.

"We need to question him first," Rowan said. "See what he knows."

"Then do it," Elide said. "But when it's time, make it quick."

"Quick," Fenrys mused, "but not painless?"

Elide's face was cold, unyielding. "You can decide."

Lorcan's brutal smile told Aelin enough. So did the hatchet, twin to Rowan's, gleaming at his side.

Her palms turned sweaty. Had been sweating since they'd bound up Vernon, since she'd seen the iron chains.

Aelin reached for her magic. Not the raging flame, but the cooling droplet of water. She listened to its silent song, letting it wash through her. And in its wake, she knew what she wished to do.

Lorcan took a step toward the chamber door, but Aelin blocked his path. She said, "Torture won't get anything out of him."

Even Elide blinked at that.

Aelin said, "Vernon likes to play games. Then I'll play."

Rowan's eyes guttered. As if he could scent the sweat on her hands, as if he knew that doing it the old-fashioned way . . . it'd send her puking her guts up over the edge of the Northern Fang.

"Never underestimate the power of breaking a few bones," Lorcan countered.

"See what you can get out of him," Rowan said to her instead. Lorcan whirled, mouth opening, but Rowan snarled, "We can decide, here and now, what we wish to be as a court. Do we act like our enemies? Or do we find alternative methods to break them?"

Her mate met her stare, understanding shining there.

Lorcan still seemed ready to argue.

Above the phantom sting of chains on her wrists, the weight of a mask on her face, Aelin said, "We do it my way first. You can still kill him, but we try my way first." When Lorcan didn't object, she said, "We need some ale."

⌒

Aelin slid the tankard of chilled ale across the table to where Vernon now sat, chains loosened enough for him to use his hands.

One false move, and her fire would melt him.

Only the Lion and Fenrys stood in the chamber, stationed by the doors.

Rowan and Lorcan had snarled at her order to stay in the hall, but Aelin had declared that they would only hinder her efforts here.

Aelin sipped from her own tankard and hummed. "An odd day, when one has to compliment their enemy's good taste in ale."

Vernon frowned at the tankard.

"It's not poisoned," Aelin said. "It'd defeat the purpose if it was."

Vernon took a small sip. "I suppose you think plying me with ale and talking like we're steadfast friends will get you what you want to know."

"Would you prefer the alternative?" She smiled slightly. "I certainly don't."

"The methods may differ, but the end result will be the same."

"Tell me something interesting, Vernon, and maybe it will change."

His eyes swept over her. "Had I known you'd grow into such a queen, perhaps I would not have bothered to kneel for Adarlan." A sly smile. "So different from your parents. Did your father ever torture a man?"

Ignoring the taunt, Aelin drank, swishing the ale in her mouth, as if it could wash away the taint of this place. "You tried and failed to win power for yourself. First by stealing it from Elide, then by trying to sell her to Erawan. Morath has sacked Perranth, and no doubt marches on Orynth, and yet we find you here. Hiding." She drank again. "One might think Erawan's favor had shifted elsewhere."

"Perhaps he stationed me here for a reason, Majesty."

Her magic had already felt him out. To make sure no heart of iron or Wyrdstone beat in his chest.

"I think you were cast aside," she said, leaning back and crossing her arms. "I think you outlived your usefulness, especially after you failed to recapture Elide, and Erawan didn't feel like entirely ridding himself of a lackey, but also didn't want you skulking about. So here you are." She waved a hand to the chamber, the mountain above them. "The lovely Ferian Gap."

"It's beautiful in the spring," Vernon said.

Aelin smiled. "Again, tell me something interesting, and perhaps you'll live to see it."

"Do you swear it? On your throne? That you shall not kill me?" A glance toward Fenrys and Gavriel, stone-faced behind her. "Nor any of your companions?"

Aelin snorted. "I was hoping you'd hold out longer before showing your hand." She drained the rest of her ale. "But yes. I swear that neither me nor any of my companions will kill you if you tell us what you know."

Fenrys started. All the confirmation Vernon needed that she meant it—that they had not planned it.

Vernon drank deeply from his ale. Then said, "Maeve has come to Morath."

Aelin was glad she was sitting. She kept her face bored, bland. "To see Erawan?"

"To unite with him."

CHAPTER 80

The room was spinning slightly. Even the droplet of her mother's magic couldn't steady her.

Worse. Worse than anything Aelin had imagined hearing from Vernon's lips.

"Did Maeve bring her army?" Her cool, unruffled voice sounded far, far away.

"She brought no one but herself."

"No army—none at all?"

Vernon drank again. "Not that I saw before Erawan packed me off on a wyvern in the dead of night. Claimed I had asked too many questions and I was *better suited* to be stationed here."

Erawan or Maeve had to have known. Somehow. That they'd wind up here, and planted Vernon in their path. To tell them this.

"Did she say where her army was?" Not Terrasen—if it had gone ahead to Terrasen . . .

"She did not, but I assumed her forces had been left near the coast, to await orders on where to sail."

Aelin shoved aside her rising nausea. "Did you learn what Maeve and Erawan plan to do?"

"Face you, I'd wager."

She made herself lean back in her seat, her face bored, casual. "Do you know where Erawan keeps the third Wyrdkey?"

"What's that?"

Not a misleading question. "A sliver of black stone—like the one planted in Kaltain Rompier's arm."

Vernon's eyes shuttered. "She had the fire gift, too, you know. I tremble to think what might happen if Erawan put the stone within *your* arm."

She ignored him. "Well?"

Vernon finished his ale. "I don't know if he had another beyond what was in Kaltain's arm."

"He did. He does."

"Then I don't know where it is, do I? I only knew of the one my cunning little niece stole."

Aelin refrained from grinding her teeth. Maeve and Erawan—united. And not a whisper of where Dorian and Manon were with the two other keys.

She didn't acknowledge the walls that began pressing in, the cold sweat again sliding down her back. "Why did Maeve ally with Erawan?"

"I was not privy to that discussion. I was dispatched here quickly." A flash of annoyance. "But Maeve somehow has . . . influence over Erawan."

"What happened to the Ironteeth stationed here at the Gap?"

"Called northward. To Terrasen. They were given orders to join with the legion already on its way after routing the army at the border, then at Perranth."

Oh gods. It took all her training to think past the roaring in her head.

"One hundred thousand soldiers march on Orynth," Vernon said, chuckling. "Will that fire of yours be enough to stop them?"

Aelin put a hand on Goldryn's hilt, her heart thundering. "How far are they from the city?"

Vernon shrugged. "They were already within a few days' march when the Ironteeth legion left here."

Aelin calculated the distance, the terrain, the size of their own army. They were two weeks away at best—if the weather didn't hinder them. Two weeks through dense forest and enemy territory.

They'd never make it in time.

"Do Maeve and Erawan go to join them?"

"I'd assume so. Not with the initial group, for reasons I was not told, but they will go to Orynth. And face you there."

Her mouth turned dry. Aelin rose.

Vernon frowned at her. "Don't you wish to ask if I know of Erawan's weaknesses, or any surprises in store for you?"

"I have everything I need to know." She jerked her chin to Fenrys and Gavriel and the former peeled away from the wall to open the door. The latter, however, began tightening Vernon's chains once more. Anchoring him to the chair, binding his hands to the arms.

"Aren't you going to unchain me?" Vernon demanded. "I gave you what you wished."

Aelin took a step into the hall, noting the fury on Lorcan's face. He'd heard every word—including her oath not to let him slaughter Vernon.

Aelin threw Vernon a crooked smile over her shoulder. "I said nothing about unchaining you."

Vernon went still.

Aelin shrugged. "I said none of *us* would kill you. It's not our fault if you can't get out of those chains, is it?"

The blood drained from Vernon's face.

Aelin said quietly, "You chained and locked my friend in a tower for ten years. Let's see how you enjoy the experience." She let her smile turn vicious. "Though, once the trainers here are dealt with, I don't think there will be anyone left to feed you. Or bring you water. Or even hear your screaming. So I doubt you'll make it to ten years before the end claims you, but two days? Three? I can accept that, I think."

"Please," Vernon said as Gavriel reached for the door handle—to seal the man inside.

"Marion saved my life," Aelin said, holding the man's gaze. "And you gleefully bowed to the man who killed her. Perhaps even told the King of Adarlan where to find us. All of us."

"*Please!*" Vernon shrieked.

"You should have conserved that tankard of ale," was all Aelin said before she nodded to Gavriel.

Vernon began screaming as the door shut. And Aelin turned the key.

Silence filled the hall.

Aelin met Elide's wide-eyed stare, Lorcan savagely satisfied at her side.

"It won't be quick this way," Aelin said, extending the key to Elide. The rest of the question hung there.

Vernon kept screaming, pleading for them to come back, to unchain him.

Elide studied the sealed door. The desperate man behind it.

The Lady of Perranth took the outstretched key. Pocketed it. "We should find a better way to seal that room."

"Our worst fears have been confirmed," Aelin said to Rowan, leaning over a railing of one of the Northern Fang's balconies, peering to the army gathered on the Gap floor. To where their companions now headed, the task of permanently sealing the chamber in which Vernon sat chained completed. Where they should be headed, too. But she had paused here. Taken a moment.

Rowan laid a hand on her shoulder. "We will face them together. Maeve and Erawan."

"And the hundred thousand soldiers marching on Orynth?"

"Together, Fireheart," was all he said.

She found only centuries of training and cool calculation within his face. That unbreakable will.

She rested her head against his shoulder, her temple digging into the light armor. "Will we make it? Will there be anything left at all?"

He brushed the hair from her face. "We will try. That is the best we can do." The words of a commander who had walked on and off killing fields for centuries.

He joined their hands, and together they gazed at the army below. The shred of salvation it offered.

Had she been a fool, to expend those three hard-won months of descent into her power on that army, rather than Maeve? Maeve *and* Erawan? Even if she began now, it wouldn't, could never, be the same.

"Don't burden yourself with the what-ifs," Rowan said, reading the words on her face.

I don't know what to do, she said silently.

He kissed the top of her head. *Together.*

And as the wind howled through the peaks, Aelin realized that her mate, perhaps, did not have a solution, either.

CHAPTER 81

"One hundred thousand," Ren breathed, warming his hands before the roaring fire in the Great Hall. They had lost two of the Silent Assassins to Morath archers seeking retaliation for the destruction of the witch towers, but no more than that, mercifully.

Still, the evening meal had been somber. No one had really eaten, not when darkness had fallen and the enemy campfires ignited. More than they could count.

Aedion had lingered here after everyone else had trudged to their own beds. Only Ren had remained, Lysandra escorting a still-trembling Evangeline up to their chamber. What the morning would bring, only the gods knew.

Perhaps the gods had abandoned them again, now that their only way to return home had been locked up in an iron box. Or focused their efforts entirely on Dorian Havilliard.

Ren heaved out a long breath. "This is it, isn't it. There's no one left to come to our aid."

"It won't be a pretty end," Aedion admitted, leaning against the mantel. "Especially once they get that third tower operational again."

They wouldn't have another chance to surprise Morath now.

He jerked his chin at the young lord. "You should get some rest."

"And you?"

Aedion just stared into the flame.

"It would have been an honor," Ren said. "To serve in this court. With you."

Aedion shut his eyes, swallowing hard. "It would have been an honor indeed."

Ren clapped him on the shoulder. Then his departing footsteps scuffed through the hall.

Aedion remained alone in the guttering firelight for another few minutes before he made his way toward bed and whatever sleep he might find.

He'd nearly reached the entrance to the eastern tower when he spied her.

Lysandra halted, a cup of what seemed to be steaming milk in her hands. "For Evangeline," she said. "She can't sleep."

The girl had been shaking all day. Had looked like she'd vomit right at the table.

Aedion only asked, "Can I speak to her?"

Lysandra opened her mouth as if she'd say no, and he was willing to let it drop, but she inclined her head.

They walked in silence the entire way to the north tower, then up and up and up. To Rose's old room. Ren must have seen to it once again. The door was cracked open, golden light spilling onto the landing.

"I brought you some milk," Lysandra announced, barely winded from the climb. "And some company," she added to the girl as Aedion stepped into the cozy room. Despite the years of neglect, Rose's chamber in the royal castle remained unharmed—one of the few rooms to claim such a thing.

Evangeline's eyes widened at the sight of him, and Aedion offered the girl a smile before he perched on the side of her bed. She took the milk that Lysandra offered as the shifter sat on the other edge of the mattress, and sipped once, hands white-knuckled around the cup.

"Before my first battle," Aedion said to the girl, "I spent the entire night in the privy."

Evangeline squeaked, "You?"

Aedion smirked. "Oh yes. Quinn, the old Captain of the Guard, said it was a wonder I had anything left inside me by the time dawn broke." An old ache filled Aedion's chest at the mention of his mentor and friend, the man he'd admired so greatly. Who had made his final stand, as Aedion would, on the plain beyond this city.

Evangeline let out a little laugh. "That's disgusting."

"It certainly was," Aedion said, and could have sworn Lysandra was smiling a bit. "So you're already *much* braver than I ever was."

"I threw up earlier," Evangeline whispered.

Aedion said in a conspiratorial whisper, "Better than shitting your pants, sweetheart."

Evangeline let out a belly laugh that made her clutch the cup to keep from spilling.

Aedion grinned, and ruffled her red-gold hair. "The battle won't be pretty," he said as Evangeline sipped her milk. "And you will likely throw up again. But just remember that this fear of yours? It means you have something worth fighting for—something you care so greatly for that losing it is the worst thing you can imagine." He pointed to the frost-covered windows. "Those bastards out there on the plain? They have none of that." He laid his hand on hers and squeezed gently. "They have *nothing* to fight for. And while we might not have their numbers, *we* do have something worth defending. And because of that, we can overcome our fear. We can fight against them, to the very end. For our friends, for our family . . ." He squeezed her hand again at that. "For those we love . . ." He dared to look up at Lysandra, whose green eyes were lined with silver. "For those we love, we can rise above that fear. Remember that tomorrow. Even if you throw up, even if you spend the whole night in the privy. Remember that we have something to fight for, and it will always triumph."

Evangeline nodded. "I will."

Aedion ruffled her hair once more and walked to the door, pausing on the threshold. He met Lysandra's stare, her eyes emerald-bright. "I lost my family ten years ago. Tomorrow I will fight for the new one I've made."

Not only for Terrasen and its court and people. But also for the two ladies in this room.

I wanted it to be you in the end.

He almost spoke her words then. Almost said them back to Lysandra as something like sorrow and longing entered her face.

But Aedion ducked out of the room, shutting the door behind him.

Lysandra barely slept. Every time she closed her eyes, she saw the expression on Aedion's face, heard his words.

He didn't expect to survive this battle. Didn't expect any of them to.

She should have gone after him. Run down the tower stairs after him. And yet she didn't.

Dawn broke, a bright day with it. So they might see the size of the host waiting for them all the more clearly.

Lysandra braided Evangeline's hair, the girl more straight-backed than she'd been yesterday. She could thank Aedion for that. For the words that had allowed the girl to sleep last night.

They walked in silence, Evangeline's chin high, down to the Great Hall for what might very well be their last breakfast.

They were nearly there when an old voice said, "I would like a word."

Darrow.

Evangeline turned before Lysandra did.

The ancient lord stood in the doorway of what seemed to be a study, and beckoned them inside. "It will not take long," he said upon noting the displeasure still on Lysandra's face.

She was done making herself appear *nice* for men whom she had no interest in being *nice* to.

Evangeline peered at her in silent question, but Lysandra jerked her chin toward the old man. "Very well."

The study was crammed with stacks of books—piles and piles against the walls, along the floors. Well over a thousand. Many half-crumbling with age.

"The last of the sacred texts from the Library of Orynth," Darrow said, aiming toward the desk piled with papers before a narrow glass window. "All that the Master Scholars managed to save ten years ago."

So few. So few compared to what Aelin had said once existed in that near-mythic library.

"I had them brought out of hiding after the king's demise," Darrow said, seating himself behind the desk. "A fool's optimism, I suppose."

Lysandra strode to one of the piles, peering at a title. In a language she did not recognize.

"The remains of a once-great civilization," Darrow said thickly.

And it was the slight catch in his voice that made Lysandra turn. She opened her mouth to demand what he wanted, but glimpsed what sat beside his right hand.

Encased in crystal no larger than a playing card, the red-and-orange flower within seemed to glow—just like the power of its namesake.

"The kingsflame," she breathed, unable to stop herself as she approached.

Aelin and Aedion had told her of the legendary flower, which had bloomed across the mountains and fields the day Brannon had set foot on this continent, proof of the peace he brought with him.

And since those ancient days, only single blossoms had been spotted, so rare that their appearance was deemed a sign that the land had blessed whatever ruler sat on Terrasen's throne. That the kingdom was truly at peace.

The one entombed in crystal on Darrow's desk, Aelin had said, had appeared during Orlon's reign. Orlon, Darrow's lifelong love.

"The Master Scholars grabbed the books when Adarlan invaded," Darrow said, smiling sadly at the kingsflame. "I grabbed this."

The antler throne, the crown—all of it destroyed. Save for this one treasure, as great as any belonging to the Galathynius household.

"It's very beautiful," Evangeline said, coming up to the desk. "But very small."

Lysandra could have sworn the old man's lips twitched toward a smile. "It is indeed," Darrow said. "And so are you."

She didn't expect the softening of his voice, the kindness. And didn't expect his next words, either.

"Battle will be upon us before midday," Darrow said to Evangeline. "I find that I will have need for someone of quick wit and quicker feet to assist me here. To run messages to our commanders in this castle, and fetch me supplies as needed."

Evangeline angled her head. "You wish me to help?"

"You have trained with warriors during your travels with them, I take it."

Evangeline glanced up at Lysandra in question, and she nodded to her ward. They had all overseen Evangeline learning the basics of swordplay and archery while on the road.

The girl nodded to the old lord. "I have some ability, but not like Aedion."

"Few do," Darrow said wryly. "But I shall need someone with a fearless heart and steady hand to help me. Are you that person?"

Evangeline didn't look up to Lysandra again. "I am," she said, chin lifting.

Darrow smiled slightly. "Then head down to the Great Hall. Eat your breakfast, and when you return here, there shall be armor waiting for you."

Evangeline's eyes widened at the mention of armor, no trace of fear dimming them at all.

Lysandra murmured to her, "Go. I'll be down with you in a minute."

Evangeline dashed out, braid flying behind her.

Only when Lysandra was certain she *had* gone downstairs did she say, "Why?"

"I assume that question means you are allowing me to commandeer your ward."

"Why."

Darrow picked up the kingsflame crystal. "Nox Owen is of no use to me now that his allegiance has been made clear, and apparently has vanished to the gods know where, likely at Aedion's request." He turned the crystal over in his thin fingers. "But beyond that, no child should have to watch as her friends are cut down. Keeping her busy, giving her a purpose and some small power will be better than locking her in the north tower, scared out of her wits at every horrible sound and death."

Lysandra did not smile, did not bow her head. "You would do this for the ward of a whore?"

Darrow set down the crystal. "It's the faces of the children that I remember the most from ten years ago. Even more than Orlon's. And Evangeline's face yesterday as she looked out at that army—it was the same despair I saw back then. So you may think me a champion bastard, as Aedion would say, but I am not so heartless as you might believe." He nodded toward the open doorway. "I will keep an eye on her."

She wasn't entirely certain what to say. If she should spit in his face and tell him to hell with his offer.

Yet the brightness in Evangeline's eyes, the way she'd run out of here . . . Purpose. Darrow had offered her purpose and guidance.

So she turned from the room, from the precious trove, the ancient books worth more than gold. Darrow's silent, mournful companions. "Thank you."

Darrow waved her off, and went back to studying whatever papers were on his desk—though his eyes did not move along the pages.

⁓

The battlement walls of the city were lined with soldiers. Each stone-faced at what marched closer.

The witch tower was still down, thank the gods. But even from the distance, Aedion could spy soldiers toiling to repair its damaged wheel. Yet without another wyvern to replace the one felled yesterday, it would not be moving soon.

It wouldn't make today any easier, though. No, today would hurt.

"They'll be within the archers' range in about an hour," Elgan reported. Darrow's orders be damned. Kyllian was still general, yes, but every report his friend received, Aedion got as well.

"Remind them to make their shots count. Pick targets."

The Bane knew that without being told. The others—they had proved their mettle in these battles, but a reminder never hurt.

Elgan aimed for the sections of the city walls that Ren and the Fae nobles had deemed the best advantage for their archers. Against a hundred thousand troops, they might only stand to thin the lines, but to let the enemy charge unchallenged at the walls would be utter folly. And break the spirit of these people before they met their end.

"What is that?" Ren murmured. Pointing to the horizon.

Sharp—Ren's eyes had to be sharper than most humans, since it was still just a smudge on the horizon to Aedion.

A breath passed. The dark smudge began to take form, rising into the blue sky.

Flying toward them.

"Ilken?" Ren squinted as he shielded his eyes against the glare.

"Too big," Aedion breathed.

Closer, the mass flying above the teeming army became clearer. Larger.

"Wyverns," Aedion said, dread curdling in his stomach.

The Ironteeth aerial legion had been unleashed at last.

"Oh gods," Ren whispered.

Against a terrestrial siege, Orynth might have held out—a few days or weeks, but they could have lasted.

But with the thousand or so Ironteeth witches who soared toward them on those wyverns . . . They would not need their infernal towers to destroy this city, the castle. To rip open the city gates and walls and let in Morath's hordes.

The soldiers began to spot the wyverns. People cried out, along the battlements. Up in the castle looming behind them.

This siege would not even get the chance to be a siege.

It would end today. Within a few hours.

Racing feet skidded to a halt, and then Lysandra was there, panting. "Tell me what to do, where to go." Her emerald eyes were wide with terror— helpless terror and despair. "I can change into a wyvern, try to keep them—"

"There are over a thousand Ironteeth," Aedion said, his voice hollow in his ears. Her fear whetted something sharp and dangerous in him, but he refrained from reaching for her. "There is nothing you or we can do."

A few dozen of the Ironteeth had sacked Rifthold in a matter of hours. This host . . .

Aedion focused on his breathing, on keeping his head high as soldiers began to step away from their positions along the walls.

Unacceptable.

"STAY WHERE YOU ARE," he bellowed. *"HOLD THE LINE, AND DO NOT BALK."*

The roared command halted those who'd looked prone to bolt, at least. But it didn't stop the shaking swords, the stench of their rising fear.

Aedion turned to Lysandra and Ren. "Get Rolfe's firelances up on the higher towers and buildings. See if they can burn the Ironteeth from the sky."

When Ren hesitated, Aedion snarled, *"Do it now."*

Then Ren was racing toward where the Pirate Lord stood with his Mycenian soldiers.

"It won't do anything, will it?" Lysandra said softly.

Aedion just said, "Take Evangeline and go. There is a small tunnel in the bottom level of the castle that leads into the mountains. Take her and *go.*"

She shook her head. "To what end? Morath will find us all anyway."

His commanders were sprinting toward him, and for the first time since he'd known them, there was true dread shining in the eyes of the Bane. In Elgan's eyes.

But Aedion kept his attention fixed on Lysandra. "Please. I am begging you. I am *begging you*, Lysandra, to go."

Her chin lifted. "You are not asking our other allies to run."

"Because I am not in love with our other allies."

For a heartbeat, she blinked at him.

Then her face crumpled, and Aedion only stared at her, unafraid of the words he'd spoken. Only afraid of the dark mass that swept toward them, staying within formation above that endless army. Afraid of what that legion would do to her, to Evangeline.

"I should have told you," Aedion said, voice breaking. "Every day after I realized it, all these months. I should have told you every day."

Lysandra began to cry, and he brushed away her tears.

His commanders reached him, ashen and panting. "Orders, General?"

He didn't bother to tell them that he wasn't their general. It wouldn't matter what the hell he was called in a few hours anyway.

Yet Lysandra remained at his side. Made no move to run.

"Please," he said to her.

Lysandra only linked her fingers through his in silent answer. And challenge.

His heart cracked at that refusal. At the hand, shaking and cold, that clung to his.

He squeezed her fingers tightly, and did not let go as he faced his commanders. "We—"

"Wyverns from the north!"

The screamed warning shattered down the battlements, and Aedion and Lysandra ducked as they whirled toward the attack coming at their backs.

Thirteen wyverns raced from the Staghorns, plunging toward the city walls.

And as they shot toward Orynth, people and soldiers screaming and fleeing before them, the sun hit the smaller wyvern leading the attack.

Lighting up wings like living silver.

Aedion knew that wyvern. Knew the white-haired rider atop it.

"HOLD FIRE," he bellowed down the lines. His commanders echoed the order, and all the arrows that had been pointed upward now halted.

"It's . . . ," Lysandra breathed, her hand dropping from his while she walked forward a step, as if in a daze. "It . . ."

Soldiers still fell back from the city walls as Manon Blackbeak and her Thirteen landed along them, right before Aedion and Lysandra.

It was not the witch he had last seen on a beach in Eyllwe.

No, there was nothing of that cold, strange creature in the face that smiled grimly at him. Nothing of her in that remarkable crown of stars atop her brow.

A crown of stars.

For the last Crochan Queen.

Panting, rasping breaths neared, and Aedion glanced away from Manon Blackbeak to see Darrow hurry onto the city walls, gaping at the witch and her wyvern, at Aedion for not firing at her—her, whom Darrow believed to be an enemy come to parley before their slaughter.

"We will not surrender," Darrow spat.

Asterin Blackbeak, her blue wyvern beside Manon's, let out a low laugh.

Indeed, Manon's lips curved in cool amusement as she said to Darrow, "We have come to ensure that you don't, mortal."

Darrow hissed, "Then why has your master sent you to speak with us?"

Asterin laughed again.

"We have no master," Manon Blackbeak said, and it was indeed a queen's voice that she spoke with, her golden eyes bright. "We come to honor a friend."

There was no sign of Dorian amongst the Thirteen, but Aedion was reeling enough that he didn't have the words to ask.

"We came," Manon said, loud enough that all on the city walls could hear, "to honor a promise made to Aelin Galathynius. To fight for what *she* promised us."

Darrow said quietly, "And what was that?"

Manon smiled then. "A better world."

Darrow took a step back. As if disbelieving what stood before him, in defiance of the legion that swept toward their city.

Manon only looked to Aedion, that smile lingering. "Long ago, the Crochans fought beside Terrasen, to honor the great debt we owed the Fae King Brannon for granting us a homeland. For centuries, we were your closest allies and friends." That crown of stars blazed bright upon her head. "We heard your call for aid." Lysandra began weeping. "And we have come to answer it."

"How many," Aedion breathed, scanning the skies, the mountains. "How many?"

Pride and awe filled the Witch-Queen's face, and even her golden eyes were lined with silver as she pointed toward the Staghorns. "See for yourself."

And then, breaking from between the peaks, they appeared.

Red cloaks flowing on the wind, they filled the northern skies. So many he could not count them, nor the swords and bows and weapons they bore upon their backs, their brooms flying straight and unwavering.

Thousands. Thousands of them descended upon Orynth. Thousands of them now swept over the city, his soldiers gaping upward at the stream of fluttering red, undaunted and untroubled by the enemy force darkening the horizon. One by one by one, they alit upon the empty castle battlements.

An aerial legion to challenge the Ironteeth.

The Crochans had returned at last.

CHAPTER 82

Every Crochan who could fly and wield a sword had come.

For days, they had raced northward, keeping deep to the mountains, then cutting low over Oakwald before making a wide circuit to avoid Morath's detection.

Indeed, as Manon and the Thirteen perched on the city walls, the Crochans streaming overhead while they made their way to whatever landing place they might find on the castle battlements, it was still hard to believe they had made it.

And without an hour to spare.

The farther north they had flown, the more Crochans had fallen into the lines. As if the crown of stars Manon wore was a lodestone, summoning them to her.

Every mile, more appeared from the clouds, the mountains, the forest. Young and old, wise-eyed or fresh-faced, they came.

Until five thousand trailed behind Manon and the Thirteen.

"They've completely stopped," breathed the shape-shifter beside Aedion, pointing toward the battlefield.

Far out, Morath's host had halted.

Utterly halted. As if in doubt and shock.

"Your grandmother is with them," Asterin murmured to Manon. "I can feel it."

"I know." Manon turned to the young general-prince. "We shall handle the Ironteeth."

His turquoise eyes were bright as the day above them as he gestured to the plain. "By all means, go right ahead."

Manon's mouth quirked to the side, then she jerked her chin to the Thirteen. "We shall be on your castle's battlements. I leave one of my sentinels here with you, should you need to send word." A nod to Vesta, and the red-haired witch made no move to fly as the others peeled off toward the great, towering palace. Manon had never seen its like—even the former glass castle in Rifthold had been nothing compared to it.

Manon smiled at the old man who had hissed at her, showing all her teeth. "You're welcome," she said, and with a snap of the reins, was airborne.

Morath had halted completely.

As if reassessing their strategy now that the Crochans had appeared from the mists of legend. Not hunted nearly as close to extinction as they'd believed, it seemed.

It left Manon and the army she'd raised the chance to catch their breath, at least.

And a night to sleep, if fitfully. She'd met with the mortal leaders during dinner, when it became apparent that Morath would not be finishing them off today.

Five thousand Crochans would not win this war. They would not stop a hundred thousand soldiers. But they could keep the Ironteeth legions at bay—keep them from sacking the city and letting in the demon hordes.

Long enough for whatever small miracle, Manon didn't know. She hadn't dared ask, and none of the mortals had posed the question, either.

Could the city outlast a hundred thousand soldiers hammering its walls and gates? Perhaps.

But not with the witch tower still operational on the plain. She had little doubt that it was currently being repaired, a new wyvern being hitched up. Perhaps that was why they had halted—to give themselves time to get that tower up again. And blast the Crochans into oblivion.

Only the dawn would reveal what the Ironteeth chose to do. What they'd accomplished.

Manon and the Thirteen, Bronwen and Glennis with them, spent hours organizing the Crochans. Assigning them to certain flanks of the Ironteeth based on Manon's knowledge of their enemy's formations.

She'd created those formations. Had planned to lead them.

And when that was done, when the meeting with the mortal rulers was over, all of them still grim-faced but not quite so near panic, Manon and the Thirteen found a chamber in which to sleep.

A few candles burned in the spacious room, but no furniture filled it. Nothing save the bedrolls they brought in. Manon tried not to look too long at hers, to mark the scent that had faded with every mile northward.

Where Dorian was, what he was doing—she didn't let herself think about.

If only because doing so would send her flying southward again, all the way to Morath.

In the dim room, Manon sat on her bedroll, the Thirteen seated around her, and listened to the chaos of the castle.

The place was little more than a tomb, the ghosts of its riches haunting every corner. She wondered what this room had once been—a meeting room, a place to sleep, a study . . . There were no indicators.

Manon leaned her head back against the cold stones of the wall behind her, her crown discarded by her boots.

Asterin spoke first, cutting through the silence of the coven. "We know their every move, every weapon. And now the Crochans do, too. The Matrons are likely in a panic."

She'd never seen her grandmother in a panic, but Manon huffed a dark laugh. "We shall see tomorrow, I suppose." She surveyed her Thirteen. "You have come with me this far, but tomorrow it will be your own kind that we face. You may be fighting friends or lovers or family members." She swallowed. "I will not blame you if you cannot do it."

"We have come this far," Sorrel said, "because we are all prepared for what tomorrow will bring."

Indeed, the Thirteen nodded. Asterin said, "We are not afraid."

No, they were not. Looking at the clear eyes around her, Manon could see that for herself.

"I'd expected at least *some*," Vesta groused, "from the Ferian Gap to join us."

"They don't understand," Ghislaine said. "What we even offered them."

Freedom—freedom from the Matrons who had forged them into tools of destruction.

"A waste," Asterin grumbled. Even the green-eyed demon twins nodded.

Silence fell again. Despite their clear eyes, her Thirteen were well aware of the limitations of five thousand Crochans against the Ironteeth, and the army beneath it.

So Manon said, looking them each in the eye, "I would rather fly with you than with ten thousand Ironteeth at my side." She smiled slightly. "Tomorrow, we will show them why."

Her coven grinned, wicked and defiant, and touched two fingers to their brows in deference.

Manon returned the gesture, bowing her head as she did. "We are the Thirteen," she said. "From now until the Darkness claims us."

Evangeline had decided that she no longer wished to be page to Lord Darrow, but rather a Crochan witch.

One of the women even went so far as to give the wide-eyed girl an extra red cloak, which Evangeline was still wearing when Lysandra tucked her into bed. She'd help Darrow tomorrow, Evangeline promised as she nodded off. After she made sure the Crochans had all the help they needed.

Lysandra had smiled at that, despite the odds still stacked so high against them. Manon Blackbeak—now Manon Crochan, she supposed— had been blunt in her assessment. The Crochans could keep the Ironteeth at bay, perhaps defeat them if they were truly lucky, but the hosts of Morath were still there to contend with. Once the army marched again, their plans to defend the walls would remain the same.

Unable and unwilling to fall asleep on the cot beside Evangeline's bed, Lysandra found herself wandering the halls of the rambling, ancient castle. What a home it would have made for her and Evangeline. What a court.

Perhaps she'd unconsciously followed his scent, but Lysandra wasn't at all surprised when she entered the Great Hall and found Aedion before the dying fire.

He stood alone, and she had little doubt he'd been that way for a while now.

He turned before she'd barely made it through the doorway. Watched her every step.

Because I am not in love with our other allies. How the words changed everything and yet nothing. "You should be asleep."

Aedion gave her a half smile. "So should you."

Silence fell between them as they stared at each other.

She could have spent all night like that. Had spent many nights like that, in another beast's skin. Just watching him, taking in the powerful lines of his body, the unbreakable will in his eyes.

"I thought we were going to die today," she said.

"We were."

"I'm still angry with you," she blurted. "But . . ."

His brows rose, light she had not seen for some time shining from his face. "But?"

She scowled. "But I shall think about what you said to me. That's all."

A familiar, wicked grin graced his lips. "You'll think about it?"

Lysandra lifted her chin, looking down her nose at him as much as she could while he towered over her. "Yes, I will think about it. What I plan to do."

"About the fact that I am in love with you."

"Och." He knew that the swaggering arrogance would knock her off-kilter. "If that's what you want to call it."

"Is there something else I'm supposed to call it?" He took a single step toward her, letting her decide if she'd allow it. She did.

"Just . . ." Lysandra pressed her lips together. "Don't die tomorrow. That's all I ask."

"So you can have time to think about what you plan to do with my declaration."

"Precisely."

Aedion's grin turned predatory. "May I ask something of you, then?"

"I don't think you're in a position to make requests, but fine."

That wolfish grin remained as he whispered in her ear, "If I don't die tomorrow, may I kiss you when the day is done?"

Lysandra's face heated as she pulled back, yielding a step. She was a trained courtesan, gods above. *Highly* trained. And yet the simple request reduced her knees to wobbling.

She mastered herself, squaring her shoulders. "If you don't die tomorrow, Aedion, then we'll talk. And see what comes of it."

Aedion's wolfish grin didn't so much as falter. "Until tomorrow night, then."

Hell waited for them tomorrow. Perhaps their doom. But she wouldn't kiss him, not now. Wouldn't give that sort of promise or farewell.

So Lysandra walked from the hall, heart racing. "Until tomorrow."

CHAPTER 83

Dorian flew and flew. Along the spine of the Fangs, Oakwald a winter-bare sprawl to his right, he soared northward for nearly two days before he dared to stop.

Picking a clearing amid a tangle of ancient trees, he crashed through the branches, hardly registering the sting through his thick wyvern's hide. He shifted as soon as he hit the snow, his magic instantly thawing the frozen stream wending through the space.

Then he fell to his knees and drank. Deep, panting gulps of water.

Finding food was an easier endeavor than he'd anticipated. He had no need of a snare or arrows to catch the lean rabbit that cowered nearby. No need of knives to skin it. Or a spit.

When his thirst and hunger had been sated, when a glance at the sky told him no enemy approached, Dorian drew the marks. Just one more time.

He had to be on his way soon. But for this, he could delay his flight northward a little while longer. Damaris, it seemed, also agreed. It summoned who he wished this time.

Gavin appeared in the circle of bloody Wyrdmarks, paler and murkier in the morning light.

"You found it, then," the ancient king said by way of greeting. "And left Erawan with one hell of a mess to clean up."

"I did." Dorian put a hand to his jacket pocket. To the terrible power thrumming there. It had taken every ounce of his concentration during his mad flight from Morath to block out its whispering. His shiver was not from the frigid air alone.

"Then why summon me?"

Dorian met the man's gaze. King to king. "I wanted to tell you that I attained it—so you might have a chance to say goodbye. To Elena, I mean. Before the Lock is forged."

Gavin stilled. Dorian didn't shy from the king's assessing stare.

After a moment, Gavin said a shade softly, "Then I suppose I will also be saying farewell to you."

Dorian nodded. He was ready. Had no other choice but to be ready.

Gavin asked, "Have you decided on it, then? That you will be the one sacrificed?"

"Aelin is in the north," Dorian said. "When I find her, I suppose we'll decide what to do." Who would be the one who joined the three keys. And did not walk away from it. "But," he admitted, "I am hoping she might have come up with another solution. One for Elena, too."

Aelin had escaped Maeve. Perhaps she'd be as lucky in finding a way to escape their fate.

A phantom wind blew the strands of Gavin's long hair across his face. "Thank you," he said hoarsely. "For even considering it." But grief shone in the king's eyes. He knew precisely how impossible it would be.

So Dorian said, "I'm sorry. For what success with the Lock will mean for both of you."

Gavin's throat bobbed. "My mate made her choice long ago. She was always prepared to face the consequences, even if I was not."

Just as Sorscha had made her own choices. Followed her own path.

And for once, the memory of her did not ache. Rather, it gleamed, a shining challenge. To make it count. For her, and so many others. For himself, too.

"Do not give up on life so easily," Gavin said. "It is the life I had with Elena that allows me to even consider parting from her now. A good life—as good as any that could be hoped for." He inclined his head. "I wish the same for you."

Before Dorian could voice what surged in his heart at the words, Gavin glanced skyward. His dark brows narrowed. "You need to go." For the booming of wings filled the air. Thousands of wings.

The Ironteeth legion at Morath had still rallied after the keep's collapse, it seemed. And now made its long flight northward to Orynth, likely infinitely more eager to tear into his friends.

He prayed Maeve was not in that host. That she remained licking her wounds in Morath with Erawan. Until the rest of their horrors marched, the spider-princesses with them.

But despite the approaching army, Dorian touched Damaris's hilt and said, "I will take care of it. Of Adarlan. For whatever time I have left. I will not abandon it."

The sword glowed warm.

And Gavin, despite the loss that loomed for him, smiled slightly. As if he felt the warmth of the sword, too. "I know," he said. "I have always known that."

Damaris's warmth held steady.

Dorian swallowed against the tightness in his throat. "When the Wyrdgate is sealed, will I be able to open this sort of portal again?" *Will I be able to see you, seek your counsel?*

Gavin faded. "I don't know." He added quietly, "But I hope so."

Dorian put a hand over his heart and bowed deeply.

And as Gavin disappeared into the snow and sun, Dorian could have sworn the king bowed back.

Minutes later, when wings blotted out the sun, no one noticed the lone wyvern that rose from Oakwald and fell into line with the teeming host.

CHAPTER
84

There was no armor left in the castle's depleted arsenal. And none would have fit wyverns anyway.

What had survived Adarlan's occupation or been acquired since its fall had been distributed, and though Prince Aedion had offered to have a blacksmith weld sheets of metal to form breastplates, Manon had taken one look at the repurposed doors they'd use and known they would be too heavy. Against the Ironteeth legion, speed and agility would be their greatest allies.

So they would head into battle as they always had: with nothing but their blades, their iron teeth and nails, and their cunning.

Standing on a large balcony atop the uppermost tower of the castle of Orynth, Morath's army spread far below, Manon watched the rising sun and knew it could very well be her last.

But the Thirteen, many of them leaning against the balcony rail, did not look eastward.

No, their attention was on the enemy, stirring in the rising light. Or on the two Crochans who stood with Manon, brooms in hand and swords already strapped across their backs.

It had not been a shock to see Bronwen arrive this morning dressed for battle. But Manon had paused when Glennis emerged with a sword, hair braided back.

They had already gone over the details. And had done so thrice last night. And now, in the light of the breaking day, they lingered atop the ancient tower.

Far out, deep in Morath's teeming ranks, a horn rang out.

Slowly, a great beast awakening from a deep sleep, Morath's host began to move.

"It's about time," Asterin muttered beside Manon, her braided hair bound with a strip of leather across her brow.

Ironteeth wyverns became airborne, lumbering against the weight of their armor.

It wouldn't win the day, though. No, the Ironteeth, after a heavy start, soon filled the skies. A thousand at least. Where the Ferian Gap host was, Manon didn't want to know. Not yet.

On the towers of the castle, on the roofs of the city and along the battlement walls, the Crochan army straightened their brooms at their sides, ready for the signal to fly.

A signal from Bronwen, from the carved horn at her side. The horn was cracked and browned with age, the symbols carved into it so worn they were barely visible.

Noting Manon's stare, Bronwen said, "A relic from the old kingdom. It belonged to Telyn Vanora, a young, untried warrior during the last days of the war, who was near the gates when Rhiannon fell. My ancestor." She ran a hand over the horn. "She blew this horn to warn our people that Rhiannon had been killed, and to flee the city. Just after she got out the warning call, the Blueblood Matron slaughtered her. But it gave our people enough time to run. To survive." Silver lined Bronwen's dark eyes. "It is my honor to blow this horn again today. Not to warn our people, but to rally them."

None of the Thirteen looked Bronwen's way, but Manon knew they heard each word.

Bronwen put a hand on her leather breastplate. "Telyn is here today. In the hearts of every Crochan who got out, who made it this far. All of them who fell in the witch wars are with us, even if we cannot see them."

Manon thought of those two presences she'd felt while fighting the Matrons and knew Bronwen's words to be true.

"It is for them that we fight," Bronwen said, her stare falling to the approaching army. "And for the future we stand to gain."

"A future we all stand to gain," Manon said, and met the eyes of the Thirteen. Though they did not smile, the fierceness in their faces spoke enough.

Manon turned to Glennis. "You truly intend to fight?"

Glennis nodded, firm and unyielding. "Five hundred years ago, my mother chose the future of the royal bloodline over fighting beside her loved ones. And though she never regretted her choice, the weight of what she left behind wore on her. I have carried her burden my entire life." The crone gestured to Bronwen, then to Asterin. "All of us who fight here today do so with someone standing invisible behind us."

Asterin's gold-flecked black eyes softened a bit. "Yes," was all Manon's Second said as her hand drifted to her abdomen.

Not in memory of the hateful word branded there, of what had been done to her.

In memory of the stillborn witchling who had been thrown by Manon's grandmother into the fire before Asterin had a chance to hold her.

In memory of the hunter whom Asterin had loved, as no Ironteeth ever had loved a man, and had never gone back to, for shame and fear. The hunter who had never stopped waiting for her to return, even when he was an old man.

For them, for the family she had lost, Manon knew her Second would fight today. So it might never happen again.

Manon would fight today to make sure it never did, too.

"So we come to it after five hundred years," said Glennis, her voice unwavering yet distant, as if pulled into the depths of memory. The rising sun bathed the white walls of Orynth in gold. "The final stand of the Crochans."

As if the words themselves were a signal, Bronwen lifted the horn of Telyn Vanora to her lips and blew.

Most believed the Florine River flowed down from the Staghorns, right past the western edge of Orynth before cutting across the lowlands.

But most didn't know that the ancient Fae King had built his city wisely, digging sewers and subterranean streams that carried the fresh mountain water directly into the city itself. All the way beneath the castle.

A torch lifted high, Lysandra peered into one of those underground waterways, the dark water eddying as it flowed through the stone tunnel and out the city walls. Her breath curled in front of her as she said to the group of Bane soldiers who'd accompanied her, "Lock the grate once I'm out."

A grunt was her only confirmation.

Lysandra frowned at the heavy iron grate across the subterranean river, the metal bands as thick as her forearm. It had been Lord Murtaugh who'd suggested this particular route of attack, his knowledge of the waterways beneath the city and castle beyond even Aedion's awareness.

Lysandra braced herself for the plunge, knowing the water would be cold. Beyond cold.

But Morath was moving, and if she did not get into position soon, she might very well be too late.

"Gods be with you," one of the Bane soldiers said.

Lysandra gave the man a tight smile. "And with you all."

She didn't let herself reconsider. She just walked right off the stone ledge.

The plunge was swift, bottomless. The cold ripped the air from her lungs, but she was already shifting, light and heat filling her body as her bones warped, as skin vanished. Her magic pulsed, draining quickly at the expenditure making this body required, but then it was done.

Distantly, above the surface, the Bane swore. Whether in fear or awe, she didn't care.

Surfacing enough to gulp down a breath, Lysandra submerged again. Even in this form, the cold tore at her, the water murky and dim, but she swam with the current, letting it guide her on its way out of the ancient tunnel.

Beneath the city walls. Into the wider Florine, where the cold grew nearly unbearable. Thick blocks of ice drifted overhead, veiling her from enemy eyes.

She swam down the river, right along the eastern flank of Morath's host, and waited for her signal.

The Crochans took to the skies, a wave of red that swept over the city and its walls.

Atop the southern section of the wall, Ren at his side, Aedion tipped his head back as he watched them soar into the air above the plain.

"You really think they can fight against that?" Ren nodded toward the oncoming sea of Ironteeth witches and wyverns.

"I think we don't have any other choice but to hope they can," Aedion said, unslinging his bow from across his back. Ren did the same.

At the silent signal, archers down the city walls took up their bows.

Scattered amongst them, Rolfe's Mycenians positioned their fire-lances, bracing the metal contraptions on the wall itself.

Morath marched. There would be no more delays, no more surprises. This battle would unfold.

Aedion glanced toward the curve of the Florine, the ice sheets glaringly bright in the morning sun. He shut out the dread in his heart. They were too desperate, too outnumbered, for him to deny Lysandra the task she'd taken on today.

A look over his shoulder had Aedion confirming that Bane soldiers had the catapults primed atop the battlements, the Fae royals ready to use their depleted magic to levitate the enormous blocks of river-stone into place. And on the city walls, Fae archers remained watchful as they waited for their own signal.

Aedion nocked an arrow into his bow, arm straining as he pulled back the string.

As one, the army gathered on the city walls did the same.

"Let's make this a fight worthy of a song," Aedion said.

CHAPTER 85

Manon and the Thirteen shot into the skies as the Crochan army flowed below, a red tide rushing toward the sea of black ahead.

Forcing the Ironteeth legion to choose: their ancient enemies or their new ones.

It was a test, and one Manon had wanted to make early. To see how many of the Ironteeth would heed the command to plow forward, and how many might break from their orders, the temptation of battling the Thirteen too much to bear. And a test, she supposed, for the Matrons and the Heirs who led their legion—would they fall for it? Split their forces to swarm the Ironteeth, or continue their assault on the Crochans?

Higher and higher, Manon and the Thirteen rose, the two armies nearing each other.

The Crochans didn't hesitate as their swords glinted in the sun, pointing toward the oncoming wyverns.

The Ironteeth had not trained against an enemy able to fight back. An enemy who could be airborne, smaller and faster, and strike where they were weakest: the riders. That was the Crochans' goal—to bring down the riders, not the beasts.

But to do so, they'd need to brave the snapping jaws and spiked tails, the poison coating them. And if they could navigate around the wyverns, then the matter would remain of facing the flying arrows, and the trained warriors atop the beasts. It would not be easy, and it would not be quick.

The Thirteen rose so high that the air became thin. High enough that Manon could see to the very back of the host, where the horrific, unmistakable bulk of Iskra Yellowlegs's wyvern flew.

A challenge and a promise of a confrontation to come. Manon knew, despite the distance, that Iskra had marked her.

No sign of Petrah. Or of the two remaining Matrons. Who had replaced the Yellowlegs crone to become High Witch, Manon didn't know. Or care. Perhaps her grandmother had convinced them not to appoint Iskra or a new one just yet—to clear the way for her own path to queendom.

Just as Manon's head turned light at the altitude, fifty or so wyverns peeled away from the enemy's host. Flying upward—racing for them, beasts freed of their tether. Hungry for the glory and bragging rights that killing the Thirteen would win.

Manon smiled.

The two armies slammed into each other.

Loosing a breath, Manon yanked once on Abraxos's reins.

Her fierce-hearted wyvern flung out his wings as he arched—and plummeted.

The world tilted while they twisted and plunged down, down, down, the Thirteen falling with them. They tore through wisps of cloud, the clashing army blurring, the castle and city looming below.

And when the Ironteeth were close enough that Manon could see they were Yellowlegs and Bluebloods, Abraxos banked sharply to one side and a current launched him right into the heart of them.

The Thirteen snapped into formation behind her, a battering ram that smashed through the Ironteeth.

Manon's bow sang as she fired arrow after arrow.

At the first spray of blue blood, some part of her slipped away.

But she kept firing. And Abraxos kept flying, ripping apart wing and throat with his tail and teeth.

And so it began.

Even in the river, the thunder of marching feet rumbled past Lysandra.

They didn't see the large white snout that periodically broke through the ice floes to huff down a breath. The sky was dark now, thick with the clashing of wyverns and Crochans.

Bodies occasionally plunged into the river, Ironteeth and Crochan alike.

The Crochans who thrashed, who were still alive, Lysandra covertly carried to the far shore. What they made of her, they didn't say. She didn't linger long enough to let them.

The Ironteeth who fell into the river were dragged to the bottom and pinned to the rocks.

She'd had to look away each time she did it.

Lysandra's snout broke the surface as a sharp horn shattered over the din, right from the city walls. Not a warning call, but an unleashing.

Lysandra dove to the bottom. Dove and then pushed *up*, mighty tail thrashing to launch her toward the surface.

She broke from the ice and the water, arcing through the air, and slammed right into Morath's eastern flank.

Soldiers screamed as she unleashed herself in a whirlwind of teeth and claws and a massive, snapping tail.

Where the white sea dragon moved, black blood sprayed.

And just when the soldiers mastered their terror enough to launch arrows and spears at the opalescent scales enforced with Spidersilk, she twisted and flipped back into the deep river, vanishing beneath the ice. Spears plunged into the turquoise waters, missing their mark, but Lysandra was already racing past.

The sea dragon's body—river dragon, she supposed—didn't slow. She pushed it to its limit, the great lungs working like a bellows.

The river curved, and she used it to her advantage as she leaped from the water again.

The soldiers, so focused on the damage she'd done up ahead, didn't look her way until she was upon them.

She had all of a glance to the city walls, where a wave of black now crashed against them, siege ladders rising and arrows flying, bursts of flame amid it all, before she returned to the river's icy depths.

Black blood streamed from her maw, from her tails and claws, as she doubled back, the shadow of the witches warring overhead upon the ice above her.

So she fought, the ice floes her shield. Attacking, then moving; destabilizing the eastern flank with every assault, forcing them to flee from the river's edge to crowd the center ranks.

Slowly, the turquoise waters of the Florine clouded blue and black.

Still, Lysandra kept ripping bites from the side of the behemoth that launched itself upon Orynth.

The heat off the firelances scorched Aedion's cheek, warming his helmet to near-discomfort.

A small price, as the bursts of flame sent the Valg foot soldiers at the walls scrambling back. Where their archers felled the enemy, more came. And where the firelances melted them away, only scorched earth and melted armor remained. But there was not enough—not even close.

Above, beyond the walls, the Ironteeth and Crochans clashed.

So violently, so quickly, that a blue mist hung in the skies from the bloodshed.

He couldn't determine who had the upper hand. The Thirteen fought amongst them, and where they plunged into the fray, Ironteeth and their mounts tumbled. Crushing Valg foot soldiers beneath them.

Iron siege ladders rose again, aiming for the city walls. Answering blasts from the firelances sent those already on them to the ground as charred corpses. But more Valg scrambled up, the fear of flame not enough to deter them.

Sprinting to the nearest ladder, Aedion nocked arrow after arrow, firing at the soldiers creeping up its rungs. Clean shots through the gaps in the dark armor.

The archers around him did the same, and the Bane soldiers behind him settled into fighting stances, waiting for the first to breach the walls.

At the city gates, flame blasted and raged. He'd concentrated many of the Mycenians at either of the two gates into Orynth, their most vulnerable weakness along the walls.

That the fire kept flaring as it did told him enough: Morath was making its push there.

Rolfe's order to *Conserve fire!* set a pit of dread forming in his gut, but Aedion focused on the siege ladder. His bow twanged, and another soldier tumbled away. Then another.

Down the wall, Ren had taken on the other nearby siege ladder, the lord's bow singing.

Aedion dared a glance to the army ahead. They had amassed close enough now.

Falling back, letting an archer take his place, he lifted his sword, signaling the Bane at the catapults, the Fae royals and archers near them. *"Now!"*

Wood snapped and groaned. Boulders as large as wagons soared over the walls. Each had been oiled, and gleamed in the sun while they rose.

And when the boulders reached their peak, just as they began to plummet toward the enemy, the Fae archers unleashed their flaming arrows.

They struck the oil-slick boulders right before the stones slammed into the earth.

Flame erupted, flowing right into the holes that Aedion had ordered drilled into the rock, right into the nest of the explosive powders they'd again taken from the precious reserves of Rolfe's firelances.

The boulders blasted apart in balls of flame and stone.

Along the city walls, soldiers cheered at the carnage that the smoking ruins revealed. Nothing but melted, squashed, or shattered Valg grunts. Every place the six catapults had fired upon now had a ring of charred ground around it.

"*Reposition!*" Aedion roared. The Bane were already heaving against the wheels that would rotate the catapults on their wooden stands. Within seconds, they had aimed at another spot; within seconds, the Fae royals were lifting more oiled boulders from the stockpile Darrow had acquired over weeks and weeks.

He didn't give Morath a chance to recover. "*Fire!*"

Boulders soared, flaming arrows following.

The explosions on the battlefield shook the city walls this time.

Another cheer went up, and Aedion motioned the Bane and Fae royals to halt. Let Morath think that their stock was depleted, that they only had a few lucky shots in their arsenal.

Aedion turned back to the siege ladder as the first of the Valg grunts cleared the walls.

The man was killed before his feet finished touching the ground, courtesy of a waiting Bane soldier.

Aedion unstrapped the shield from across his back and angled his sword as the wave of soldiers crested the walls.

But it was not a Valg foot soldier who appeared next, climbing over the ladder with ease.

The young man's face was cold as death, his black eyes lit with unholy hunger.

A black collar was clasped around his throat.

A Valg prince had come.

CHAPTER 86

"Focus on the ladder," Aedion snarled to the soldiers shrinking from the handsome demon prince who stepped onto the city walls as if he were merely entering a room.

He wore no armor. Nothing but a black tunic cut to his lithe body.

The Valg prince smiled. "Prince Aedion," purred the thing inside it, drawing a sword from a dark sheath at his side. "We've been waiting for you."

Aedion struck.

He did not have magic, did not have anything to combat the dark power in the prince's veins, but he had speed. He had strength.

Aedion feinted with his sword, that ordinary, nameless sword, and the prince swung with his own blade—just as Aedion slammed his shield into the man's side.

Driving him back. Not toward the ladder, but to the Mycenian who wielded the firelance—

The Mycenian was dead.

The prince chuckled, and a whip of dark power lashed for Aedion.

Aedion ducked, shield rising. As if it would do anything against that power.

Darkness struck metal, and Aedion's arm sang with the reverberations. But the pain, the life-draining agony, did not occur.

Aedion instantly parried, a slash upward that the Valg prince dodged with a hop to the side.

The demon's eyes were wide as he took in the shield. Then Aedion.

Then the Valg prince hissed, "Fae bastard."

Aedion didn't know what it meant, didn't care as he took another blast upon his shield, the battlements already slick with blood both black and red. If the Mycenian nearby was dead, then there was another down by Ren's ladder—

The Valg prince unleashed blast after blast of power.

Aedion took each one upon his shield, the prince's power bouncing off as if it were a spray of water upon stone. And for every burst of power sent his way, Aedion swung his sword.

Steel met steel; darkness clashed with ancient metal. Aedion had the vague sense of soldiers Valg and human alike halting as he and the demon prince battled their way across the city wall.

He kept his feet beneath him, as Rhoe had taught him. As Quinn had taught him, and Cal Lochan. As all his mentors and the warriors he'd admired above all others had taught him. For this moment, when he would be called to defend Orynth's very walls.

It was for them he swung his sword, for them he took blow after blow.

The Valg prince hissed with every blast, as if enraged that his power could not break that shield.

Rhoe's shield.

There was no magic in it. Brannon had never borne it. But one of them had forged it, one of the unbroken line of kings and queens who had come after him, who had loved their kingdom more than their own lives. Who had carried this shield into battle, into war, to defend Terrasen.

And as Aedion and the Valg prince fought along the walls, as that ancient shield refused to yield, he wondered if there was a different sort of power in the metal. One that the Valg could never and would never understand. Not true magic, not as Brannon and Aelin had. But something just as strong—stronger.

That the Valg might never break, no matter how they tried.

Aedion's sword sang, and the Valg prince roared as Aedion connected with his arm, slashing deep.

Black blood sprayed. Aedion leaped upon the advantage, shoving with the shield and stabbing with his blade.

But the prince had been waiting.

Had set a trap, his own body as the bait.

And as Aedion slammed into the Valg prince, the demon drew a dagger from his sword belt and struck. Right where Aedion's armor exposed just a sliver near his armpit, vulnerable with the outstretched position of his arm.

The knife plunged in, rending flesh and muscle and bone.

Pain, white-hot and blinding, threatened to make him splay his hand, to drop his sword. Only Aedion's training, only those years of work, kept his feet under him as he leaped back, wrenching free of the knife.

The Valg prince chuckled, and Aedion was dimly aware of the fighting along the walls, the shouting and dying and flares of fire, as the prince smiled down at the bloodied dagger.

Bringing it to his sensual mouth, the prince dragged his tongue along the blade. Licked Aedion's blood clean off. "Exquisite," the demon breathed, shuddering with pleasure.

Aedion backed away another step, his arm burning and burning and burning, blood pooling inside his armor.

The prince stalked after him.

A whip of dark power launched for Aedion, and he again took it on his shield. Let it send him tumbling to the ground, landing atop the ironclad body of one of the Bane.

His breath turned sharp as the knife that had stabbed him.

The prince paused before Aedion. "Feasting on you will be a delight."

Aedion hefted his shield over himself, bracing for the blow.

The prince made to lift the bloodied dagger to his mouth again, eyes rolling back in his head.

Those eyes went wide as an arrow broke the skin of his throat. Right above the collar.

The prince gagged, whirling toward the arrow that had come not from Aedion, but from behind. Right into the path of Ren Allsbrook and the firelance he bore in his arms.

Ren slammed his hand into the release hatch, and flame erupted.

Aedion ducked, coiling his body beneath his shield as the flame threatened to melt his own bones.

The world was heat and light. Then nothing. Only the shouts of battle and dying men.

Aedion managed to lower his shield.

Where the Valg prince had been, a pile of ashes and a black Wyrdstone collar remained.

Aedion panted, a hand going to his bleeding side. "I had him."

Ren only shook his head, and pivoted on a boot, unleashing the firelance upon the nearest Valg soldiers.

The Lord of Allsbrook turned back to him, mouth open to say something. But Aedion's head swam, his body plunging into a coldness he'd never known. Then there was nothing.

⁓

The battle was so much worse than Evangeline had imagined.

The sound alone made her quake in her bones, and only delivering messages to Lord Darrow where he stood on one of the higher castle balconies saved her from curling into a ball.

Her breath was a ragged, dry thing as she raced back onto the balcony, to where Darrow stood by the stone railing, two other Terrasen lords beside him. "From Kyllian," Evangeline managed to say, bobbing a curtsy, as she had each time she'd delivered a message.

Battles were no place for manners, she knew—Aelin certainly would have said that. But she kept doing it, the curtsying, even when her legs trembled. Couldn't stop herself.

Kyllian's messenger had met her at the castle stairs, and now waited for Darrow's reply. It was as close to the fighting as she'd gotten. Not that being up here was any better.

Pressing herself against the stones of the tower wall, Evangeline let Darrow read the letter. The Crochans and wyverns were so much closer up here. This high, she stood on their level, the world a blur below. Evangeline laid her palms flat against the icy stones, as if she could draw some strength from them.

Even with the roar of battle, she heard Darrow declare to the other lords, "Aedion has been wounded."

Evangeline's stomach dropped, nausea—oily and thick—surging. "Is he all right?"

The two other lords ignored her, but Darrow looked her way. "He has lost consciousness, and they have moved him into a building near the wall. Healers are working on him as we speak. They will move him here as soon as he is capable of withstanding it."

Evangeline staggered to the balcony rail, as if she might see that building amid the sea of chaos by the city walls.

She had never had a brother, or a father. She hadn't yet decided which one she would like Aedion to be. And if he was so injured that it warranted a message to Darrow—

She pressed a hand to her stomach, trying to contain the bile that burned her throat.

Murmuring sounded, and then there was a hand on her shoulder. "Lord Gunnar will see to delivering my reply," Darrow said. "You will remain here with me. I might have need of you."

The words were stern, but the hand on her shoulder was kind.

SARAH J. MAAS

Evangeline only nodded, sick and miserable, and clung to the balcony rail, as if her grip might somehow keep Aedion on this side of life.

"Hot refreshments, Sloane," Darrow ordered, his voice brooking no room for argument.

The other lord peeled away. Evangeline didn't know how long passed after that. How long it took until the lord arrived, and Darrow pressed a scalding mug into her fingers. "Drink."

Evangeline obeyed, finding it to be broth of some sort. Beef, maybe. She didn't care.

Her friends were down there. Her family, the one she'd made.

Far out, near the river, a blur of motion was her only indication that Lysandra still lived.

No word arrived about Aedion's fate.

So Evangeline lingered on the tower, Darrow silent beside her, and prayed.

CHAPTER
87

Even moving as fast as they could, the khagan's army was too slow. Too slow, and too large, to reach Terrasen in time.

In the week that they'd been pushing northward, Aelin begging Oakwald, the Little Folk, and Brannon for forgiveness as she razed a path through the forest, they were only just now nearing Endovier, and the border mere miles beyond it. From there, if they were lucky, it'd be another ten days to Orynth. And would likely become a disaster if Morath had kept forces stationed at Perranth after the city's capture.

So they'd chosen to skirt the city on its western flank, going around the Perranth Mountains rather than cutting to the lowlands for the easier trek across the land. With Oakwald as their cover, they might be able to sneak up on Morath at Orynth.

If there was anything left of Orynth by the time they arrived. They were still too far for the ruk riders to do any sort of scouting, and no messengers had crossed their paths. Even the wild men of the Fangs, who had remained with them and now swore to march to Orynth to avenge their kin did not know of a faster path.

Aelin tried not to think of it. Or about Maeve and Erawan, wherever they might be. Whatever they might have planned.

Endovier, the only outpost of civilization they'd seen in a week, would be their first news since leaving the Ferian Gap.

She tried not to think of that, either. Of the fact that they would be passing through Endovier tomorrow, or the day after. That she'd see those gray mountains that had housed the salt mines.

Lying on her stomach atop her cot—no point in making anyone set up a royal bed for her and Rowan when they would be marching within a few hours—Aelin winced against the stinging burn along her back.

The clink of Rowan's tools and the crackle of the braziers were the only sounds in their tent.

"Will it be done tonight?" she asked as he paused to dip his needle in the pot of salt-laced ink.

"If you stop talking," was his dry reply.

Aelin huffed, rising onto her elbows to peer over a shoulder at him. She couldn't see what he inked, but knew the design. A replica of what he'd written on her back this spring, the stories of her loved ones and their deaths, written right where her scars had been. Exactly where they'd been, as if he had their memory etched in his mind.

But another tattoo lay there now. A tattoo that sprawled across her shoulder bones as if it were a pair of spread wings. Or so he'd sketched for her.

The story of them. Rowan and Aelin.

A story that had begun in rage and sorrow and become something entirely different.

She was glad to have him leave it at that. At the happiness.

Aelin rested her chin atop her hands. "We'll be near Endovier soon."

Rowan resumed working, but she knew he'd listened to every word, thought through his response. "What do you want to do about it?"

She winced at the sting of a particularly sensitive spot near her spine.

"Burn it to the ground. Blast the mountains into rubble."

"Good. I'll help you."

A small smile curved her lips. "The fabled warrior-prince wouldn't tell me to avoid carelessly expending my strength?"

"The fabled warrior-prince would tell you to stay the course, but if destroying Endovier will help, then he'll be right there with you."

Aelin fell silent while Rowan continued working for another few minutes.

"I don't remember the tattoo taking this long the last time."

"I've made improvements. And you're getting a whole new marking."

She hummed, but said nothing more for a time.

Rowan kept at it, wiping away blood when necessary.

"I don't think I can," Aelin breathed. "I don't think I can stand to even look at Endovier, let alone destroy it."

"Do you want me to?" A calm, warrior's question. He would, she knew. If she asked him, he'd fly to Endovier and turn it into dust.

"No," she admitted. "The overseers and slaves are all gone anyway. There's no one to destroy, and no one to save. I just want to pass it and never think of it again. Does that make me a coward?"

"I'd say it makes you human." A pause. "Or whatever a similar saying might be for the Fae."

She frowned at her interlaced fingers beneath her chin. "It seems I'm more Fae these days than anything. I even forget sometimes—when the last time was that I was in my human body."

"Is that a good or bad thing?" His hands didn't falter.

"I don't know. I *am* human, deep down, Faerie Queen nonsense aside. I had human parents, and their parents were human, mostly, and even with Mab's line running true . . . I'm a human who can turn into Fae. A human who wears a Fae body." She didn't mention the immortal life span. Not with all they had ahead of them.

"On the other hand," Rowan countered, "I'd say you were a human with Fae instincts. Perhaps more of them than human ones." She felt him smirk. "Territorial, dominant, aggressive . . ."

"Your skills when it comes to complimenting women are unparalleled."

His laugh was a brush of hot air along her spine. "Why can't you be both human and Fae? Why choose at all?"

"Because people always seem to demand that you be one thing or another."

"You've never bothered to give a damn what other people demand."

She smiled slightly. "True."

She gritted her teeth as his needle pierced along her spine. "I'm glad you're here—that I'll see Endovier again for the first time with you here."

To face that part of her past, that suffering and torment, if she couldn't yet look too closely at the last several months.

His tools, the numbing pain, halted. Then his lips brushed the top of her spine, right above the start of the new tattoo. The same tattoo he'd had Gavriel and Fenrys inking on his own back these past few days, whenever they stopped for the night. "I'm glad to be here, too, Fireheart."

For however much longer the gods would allow it.

⁓

Elide slumped onto her cot, groaning softly as she bent to untie the laces of her boots. A day of helping Yrene in the wagon was no easy task, and the prospect of rubbing salve into her ankle and foot seemed nothing short of divine. The work, at least, kept the swarming thoughts at bay: what she'd done to Vernon, what had befallen Perranth, what awaited them at Orynth, and what they could ever do to defeat it.

From the cot opposite hers, Lorcan only watched, an apple half peeled in his hands. "You should rest more often."

Elide waved him off, yanking away her boot, then her sock. "Yrene is pregnant—and throwing up every hour or so. If she doesn't rest, I'm not going to."

"I'm not entirely certain Yrene is fully human." Though the voice was gruff, humor sparked in Lorcan's eyes.

Elide fished the tin of salve from her pocket. Eucalyptus, Yrene had said, naming a plant Elide had never heard of, but whose smell—sharp and

yet soothing—she very much enjoyed. Beneath the pungent herb lay laven-
der, rosemary, and something else mixed in with the opaque, pale liniment.

A rustle of clothing, and then Lorcan was kneeling before her, Elide's
foot in his hands. Nearly swallowed by his hands, actually. "Let me," he
offered.

Elide was stunned enough that she indeed let him take the tin from
her grip, and watched in silence as Lorcan dipped his fingers into the
ointment. Then began rubbing it into her ankle.

His thumb met the spot on her ankle where bone ground against bone.
Elide let out a groan. He carefully, with near-reverence it seemed, began
easing the ache away.

These hands had slaughtered their way across kingdoms. Bore the
faint scars to prove it. And yet he held her foot as if it were a small bird, as
if it were something . . . holy.

They had not shared a bed—not when these cots were too small, and
Elide often passed out after dinner. But they shared this tent. He'd been
careful, perhaps too careful, she sometimes thought, to give her privacy
when changing and bathing.

Indeed, a tub steamed away in the corner of the tent, kept warm courtesy
of Aelin. Many of the camp baths were warm thanks to her, to the eternal
gratitude of royal and foot soldier alike.

Alternating long strokes with small circles, Lorcan slowly coaxed the
pain from her foot. Seemed content to do just that all night, should she
wish it.

But she was not half-asleep. For once. And each brush of his fingers
on her foot had her sitting up, something warming in her core.

His thumb pushed along the arch of her foot, and Elide indeed let out
a small noise. Not at the pain, but—

Heat flared in her cheeks. Grew warmer as Lorcan looked up at her
beneath his lashes, a spark of mischief lighting his dark eyes.

Elide gaped a bit. Then smacked his shoulder. Rock-hard muscle
greeted her. "You did that on purpose."

Still holding her gaze, Lorcan's only answer was to repeat the motion.

Good—it felt so damned *good*—

Elide snatched her foot from his grip. Closed her legs. Tightly.

Lorcan gave her a half smile that made her toes curl.

But then he said, "You are well and truly Lady of Perranth now."

She knew. She'd thought about it endlessly during these hard days of travel. "This is what you really wish to talk about?"

His fingers didn't halt their miraculous, sinful work. "We haven't spoken of it. About Vernon."

"What of it?" she said, trying and failing for nonchalance. But he looked up at her from beneath his thick lashes. Well aware of her evasion. Elide loosed a breath, peering up at the tent's peaked ceiling. "Does it make me any better than Vernon—how I chose to punish him in the end?"

She hadn't regretted it the first day. Or the second. But these long miles, as it had become clear that Vernon was likely dead, she'd wondered.

"Only you can decide that, I think," Lorcan said. Yet his fingers paused on her foot. "For what it's worth, he deserved it." His dark power rumbled through the room.

"Of course you'd say that."

He shrugged, not bothering to deny it. "Perranth will recover, you know," he offered. "From Morath's sacking. And all Vernon did to it before now."

That had been the other thought that weighed heavily with each mile northward. That her city, her father and mother's city, had been decimated. That Finnula, her nursemaid, might be among the dead. That any of its people might be suffering.

"That's if we win this war," Elide said.

Lorcan resumed his soothing strokes. "Perranth will be rebuilt," was all he said. "We'll see that it is."

"Have you ever done it? Rebuilt a city?"

"No," he admitted, his thumbs coaxing the pain from her aching bones. "I have only destroyed them." His eyes lifted to hers, searching and open. "But I should like to try. With you."

She saw the other offer there—to not only build a city, but a life. Together.

Heat rose to her cheeks as she nodded. "Yes," she whispered. "For however long we have."

For if they survived this war, there was still that between them: his immortality.

Something shuttered in Lorcan's eyes at that, and she thought he'd say more, but his head dipped. Then he began to unlace her other boot.

"What are you doing?" Her words were a breathless rush.

His deft fingers—gods above, those *fingers*—made quick work of her laces. "You should soak that foot. And soak in general. As I said, you work too hard."

"You said I should rest more."

"Because you work too hard." He jerked his chin toward the bath as he pulled off the boot and helped her rise. "I'll go find some food."

"I already ate—"

"You should eat more."

Giving her privacy without the awkwardness of her needing to ask for it. That's what he was trying to do.

Barefoot before him, Elide peered into his granite-hewn face. Shrugged out of her cloak, then jacket. Lorcan's throat bobbed.

She knew he could hear her heart as it began racing. Could likely scent every emotion on her. But she said, "I need help. Getting into the bath."

"Do you, now." His voice was near-guttural.

Elide bit her lip, her breasts becoming heavy, tingling. "I might slip."

His eyes drifted down her body, but he made no move. "A dangerous time, bath time."

Elide found it in herself to walk toward the copper tub. He trailed a few feet behind, giving her space. Letting her steer this.

Elide halted beside the tub, steam wafting past. She tugged the hem of her shirt from her pants.

Lorcan watched every move. She wasn't entirely certain he was breathing.

But—her hands stalled. Uncertain. Not of him, but this rite, this path. "Show me what to do," she breathed.

"You're doing just fine," Lorcan ground out.

But she gave him a helpless look, and he prowled closer. His fingers found the loose hem of her shirt. "May I?" he asked quietly.

Elide whispered, "Yes."

Lorcan still studied her eyes, as if reading the sincerity of that word. Deeming it true.

Gently, he pulled the fabric from her. Cool air kissed her skin, pebbling it. The flexible band around her breasts remained, but Lorcan's gaze remained on her own. "Tell me what you want next," he said roughly.

Hand shaking, Elide grazed a finger over the band.

Lorcan's own hands shook as he unbound it. As he revealed her to the air, to him.

His eyes seemed to go wholly black as he took in her breasts, her uneven breathing. "Beautiful," he murmured.

Elide's mouth curled as the word settled within her. Gave her enough courage that she lifted her hands to his jacket and began unbuckling, unbuttoning. Until Lorcan's own chest was bare, and she ran her fingers over the smattering of dark hair across the sculpted planes. "Beautiful," she said.

Lorcan trembled—with restraint, with emotion, she didn't know. That darling purr of his rumbled into her as she pressed her mouth against his pectoral.

His hand drifted to her hair, each stroke unbinding her braid. "We only go as far and long as you want," he said. Yet she dared to glance down his body—to what strained under his pants.

Her mouth went dry. "I—I don't know what I'm doing."

"Anything you do will be enough," he said.

She lifted her head, scanning his face. "Enough for what?"

Another half smile. "Enough to please me." She scoffed at the arrogance, but Lorcan brushed his mouth against her neck. His hands bracketed her waist, his thumbs grazing her ribs. But no higher.

Elide arched into the touch, a small sound escaping her as his lips brushed just beneath her ear. And then his mouth found hers, gentle and thorough.

Her hands twined around his neck, and Lorcan lifted her, carrying her not to the bath, but to the cot behind them, his lips never leaving hers.

Home. This, with him. This was home, as she had never had. For however long they might share it.

And when Lorcan laid her out on the cot, his breathing as uneven as her own, when he paused, letting her decide what to do, where to take this, Elide kissed him again and whispered, "Show me everything."

So Lorcan did.

~

There was a gate, and a coffin.

She had chosen neither.

She stood in a place that was not a place, mist wreathing her, and stared at them. Her choices.

A thumping pounded from within the coffin, muffled female screams and pleading rising.

And the gate, the black arch into eternity—blood ran down its sides, seeping into the dark stone. When the gate had finished with the young king, this blood was all that remained.

"You're no better than me," Cairn said.

She turned to him, but it was not the warrior who had tormented her standing in the mists.

Twelve of them lurked there, formless and yet present, ancient and cold. As one they spoke. "Liar. Traitor. Coward."

The blood on the gate soaked into the stone, as if the gate itself devoured even this last piece of him. The one who had gone in her place. The one she'd let go in her place.

The thumping from within the coffin didn't cease.

"That box will never open," they said.

She blinked, and she was inside that box—the stone so cold, the air stifling. Blinked, and she was pounding on the lid, screaming and screaming. Blinked, and there were chains on her, a mask clamped over her face—

⁓

Aelin awoke to dim braziers and the pine-and-snow scent of her mate wrapped around her. Outside their tent, the wind howled, setting the canvas walls swaying and swelling.

Tired. She was so, so tired.

Aelin stared into the dark for long hours and did not sleep again.

⁓

Even with the cover of Oakwald, despite the wider path that Aelin incinerated on either side of the ancient road running up through the continent like a withered vein, she could feel Endovier looming. Could feel the Ruhnn Mountains jutting toward them, a wall against the horizon.

She rode near the front of the company, not saying much as the morning, then the afternoon passed. Rowan stayed by her side, always remaining on her left—as if he might be a shield between her and Endovier—while she sent out plumes of flame that melted ancient trees ahead. Rowan's wind stifled any smoke from alerting the enemy of their approach.

He'd finished the tattoos the night before. Had taken a small hand mirror to show her what he'd done. The tattoo he'd made for them.

She'd taken one look at the spread wings—a hawk's wings—across her back and kissed him. Kissed him until his own clothes were gone, and she was astride him, neither bothering with words, or capable of finding them.

Her back had healed by morning, though it remained tender in a few spots along her spine, and in the hours that they'd ridden closer to Endovier, she'd found the invisible weight of the ink to be steadying.

She'd gotten out. She'd survived.

From Endovier—and Maeve.

And now it was upon her to ride like hell for the North, to try to save her people before Morath wiped them away forever. Before Erawan and Maeve arrived to do just that.

But it did not stop the heaviness, that tug toward the west. To look to the place that she had taken so long to escape, even after she'd been physically freed.

After lunch, she found Elide on her right, riding in silence under the trees. Riding taller than she'd seen the girl before. A blush on her cheeks.

Aelin had a feeling she knew precisely why that blush bloomed there, that if she looked behind to where Lorcan rode, she'd find him with a satisfied, purely male smile.

But Elide's words were anything but those of a lovesick maiden.

"I didn't think I'd really get to see Terrasen again, once Vernon took me out of Perranth."

Aelin blinked. And even the blush on Elide's face faded, her mouth tightening.

Of all of them, only Elide had seen Morath. Lived there. Survived it.

Aelin said, "There was a time when I thought I'd never see it again, too."

Elide's face grew contemplative. "When you were an assassin, or when you were a slave?"

"Both." And maybe Elide had come to her side just to get her to talk, but Aelin explained, "It was a torture of another kind, when I was at Endovier, to know that home was only miles away. And that I would not be able to see it one last time before I died."

Elide's dark eyes shone with understanding. "I thought I'd die in that tower, and no one would remember that I had existed."

They had both been captives, slaves—of a sort. They had both worn shackles. And bore the scars of them.

Or, Elide did. The lack of them on Aelin still ripped at her, an absence that she'd never thought she'd regret.

"We made it out in the end, though," Aelin said.

Elide reached over to squeeze Aelin's hand. "Yes, we did."

Even if she now wished for it to be over. All of it. Her every breath felt weighed down by it, that wish.

They continued on after that, and just as Aelin spied the fork in the road—the crossroads that would take them to the salt mines themselves—a warning cry went up from the rukhin, soaring along the edge between the forest and mountains.

Aelin instantly had Goldryn drawn. Rowan armed himself beside her, and the entire army pausing as they scanned the woods, the skies.

She heard the warning just as a dark shape shot past, so large it blotted out the sun above the forest canopy.

Wyvern.

Bows groaned, and the ruks were racing by, chasing after that wyvern. If an Ironteeth scout spotted them—

Aelin readied her magic. The wyvern banked toward them, barely visible through the latticework of branches.

But light flared then. Blasted back the rukhin—harmlessly.

Not light. But ice, flickering and flashing before it turned to flame.

Rowan recognized it, too. Roared the order to hold their fire.

It was not Abraxos who landed at the crossroads. And there was no sign of Manon Blackbeak.

Light flashed again. And then Dorian Havilliard stood there, his jacket and cape stained and worn.

Aelin galloped down the road toward him, Rowan and Elide beside her, the others at their backs.

Dorian lifted a hand, his face grave as death, even as his eyes widened at the sight of her.

But Aelin sensed it then.

What Dorian carried.

The Wyrdkeys.

All three of them.

CHAPTER 88

Aedion's arm and ribs were on fire.

Worse than the searing heat of the firelances, worse than any level of Hellas's burning realm.

He'd regained consciousness as the healer began her first stitches. Had clamped down on the leather bit she'd offered and roared around the pain while she sewed him up.

By the time she'd finished, he'd fainted again. He woke minutes later, according to the soldiers assigned to make sure he didn't die, and found the pain somewhat eased, but still sharp enough that using his sword arm would be nearly impossible. At least until his Fae heritage healed him— faster than mortal men.

That he hadn't died of blood loss and could attempt to move his arm as he ordered his armor strapped back on him and stumbled into the city streets, aiming for the wall, was thanks to that Fae heritage. His mother's, yes, but mostly from his father.

Had Gavriel heard, across the sea or wherever their hunt for Aelin had taken him, that Terrasen was about to fall? Would he care?

It didn't matter. Even if part of him wished the Lion were there. Rowan and the others certainly, but the steady presence of Gavriel would have been a balm to these men. Perhaps to him.

Aedion gritted his teeth, swaying as he scaled the blood-slick stairs to the city walls, dodging bodies both human and Valg. An hour—he'd been down for an hour.

Nothing had changed. Valg still swarmed the walls and both the southern and western gates; but Terrasen's forces held them off. In the skies, the number of Crochans and Ironteeth had thinned, but barely. The Thirteen were a distant, vicious cluster, ripping apart whoever flew in their path.

And down at the river . . . red blood stained the snowy banks. Too much red blood.

He stumbled a step, losing sight of the river for a moment while soldiers dispatched the Valg grunts before him. When they passed, Aedion could scarcely breathe while he scanned the bloodied banks. Soldiers lay dead all around, but—there. Closer to the city walls than he'd realized.

White against the snow and ice, she still fought. Blood leaking down her sides. Red blood.

But she didn't retreat into the water. Held her ground.

It was foolish—unnecessary. Ambushing them had been far more effective.

Yet Lysandra fought, tail snapping spines and giant maw ripping off heads, right where the river curved past the city. He knew something was wrong then. Beyond the blood on her.

Knew Lysandra had learned something that they had not. And in holding her ground, tried to signal them on the walls.

His head spinning, arm and ribs throbbing, Aedion scanned the battlefield. A group of soldiers charged at her. A whack of her tail had the spears snapped, their bearers along with them.

But another group of soldiers tried to charge past her, on the riverside.

Aedion saw what they bore, what they tried to carry, and swore. Lysandra smashed apart one longboat with her tail, but couldn't reach the second cluster of soldiers—bearing another.

They reached the icy waters, boat splashing, and Lysandra lunged. Right as she was swarmed by another group of soldiers, so many spears and lances that she had no choice but to face them. Allowing the boat, and the soldiers carrying it, to slip past.

Aedion noted where those soldiers were headed, and began shouting his orders. His head swam with each command.

In Lysandra sneaking to the river through the tunnels, she'd had the element of surprise. But it had also revealed to Morath that another path existed into the city. One right below their feet.

And if they got through the grate, if they could get inside the walls . . .

Fighting against the fuzziness growing in his head, Aedion began signaling. First to the shifter holding the line, trying so valiantly to keep those forces at bay. Then to the Thirteen, perilously high in the skies, to get back to the walls—to stop Morath's creeping before it was too late.

High up, the cries of the wind bleeding into those of the dying and injured, Manon saw the general's signal, the careful pattern of light that he'd shown her the night before.

A command to hurry to the walls—immediately. Just her and the Thirteen.

The Crochans held the tide of the Ironteeth at bay, but to fall back, to *leave*—

Prince Aedion signaled again. *Now. Now. Now.*

Something was wrong. Very wrong.

River, he signaled. *Enemy*.

Manon cast her gaze to the earth far below. And saw what Morath was covertly trying to do.

"*To the walls!*" she called to the Thirteen, still a hammer behind her, and made to steer Abraxos toward the city, tugging on the reins to have him fly high above the fray.

Asterin's warning cry reached her a heartbeat too late.

Shooting from below, a predator ambushing prey, the massive bull aimed right for Abraxos.

Manon knew the rider as the bull slammed into Abraxos, claws and teeth digging deep.

Iskra Yellowlegs was already smiling.

The world tilted and spun, but Abraxos, roaring in pain, kept in the air, kept flapping.

Even as Iskra's bull pulled back his head—only to close his jaws around Abraxos's throat.

CHAPTER 89

Iskra's bull gripped him by the neck, but Abraxos kept them in the air.

At the sight of those powerful jaws around Abraxos's throat, the fear and pain in his eyes—

Manon couldn't breathe. Couldn't think around the terror rushing through her, so blinding and sickening that for a few heartbeats, she was frozen. Wholly frozen.

Abraxos, *Abraxos*—

Hers. He was hers, and she was his, and the Darkness had chosen them to be together.

She had no sense of time, no sense of how long had passed between that bite and when she again moved. It could have been a second, it could have been a minute.

But then she was drawing an arrow from her nearly depleted quiver. The wind threatened to rip it from her fingers, but she nocked it to her bow, the world spinning-spinning-spinning, the wind roaring, and aimed.

Iskra's bull bucked as her arrow landed—just a hairsbreadth from his eye.

But he did not let go.

He didn't have the deep grip to rip out Abraxos's throat, but if he crunched down long enough, if he cut off her mount's air supply—

Manon unleashed another arrow. The wind shifted it enough that she struck the beast's jaw, barely embedding in the thick hide.

Iskra was laughing. Laughing as Abraxos fought and could not get free—

Manon looked for any of the Thirteen, for anyone to save them. Save him.

He who mattered more than any other, whom she would trade places with if the Three-Faced Goddess allowed it, to have her own throat gripped in those terrible jaws—

But the Thirteen had been scattered, Iskra's coven plowing their ranks apart. Asterin and Iskra's Second were claw-to-claw as their wyverns locked talons and plunged toward the battlefield.

Manon gauged the distance to Iskra's bull, to the jaws around the neck. Weighed the strength of the straps on the reins. If she could swing down, if she was lucky, she might be able to slash at the bull's throat, just enough to pry him off—

But Abraxos's wings faltered. His tail, trying so valiantly to strike the bull, began to slow.

No.

No.

Not like this. Anything but this.

Manon slung her bow over her back, half-frozen fingers fumbling with the straps and buckles of the saddle.

She couldn't bear it. Wouldn't bear it, this death, his pain and fear before it.

She might have been sobbing. Might have been screaming as his wingbeats faltered again.

She'd leap across the gods-damned wind, rip that bitch from the saddle, and slit her mount's throat—

Abraxos began to fall.

Not fall. But dive—trying to get lower. To reach the ground, hauling that bull with him.

So Manon might survive.

"*PLEASE.*" Her scream to Iskra carried across the battlefield, across the world. "*PLEASE.*"

She would beg, she would crawl, if it bought him the chance to live.

Her warrior-hearted mount. Who had saved her far more than she had ever saved him.

Who had saved her in the ways that counted most.

"*PLEASE.*" She screamed it—screamed it with every scrap of her shredded soul.

Iskra only laughed. And the bull did not let go, even as Abraxos tried and tried to get them closer to the ground.

Her tears ripped away in the wind, and Manon freed the last of the buckles on her saddle. The gap between the wyverns was impossible, but she had been lucky before.

She didn't care about any of it. The Wastes, the Crochans and Ironteeth, her crown. She didn't care about any of it, if Abraxos was not there with her.

Abraxos's wings strained, fighting with that mighty, loving heart to reach lower air.

Manon sized up the distance to the bull's flank, ripping off her gloves to free her iron nails. As strong as any grappling hook.

Manon rose in the saddle, sliding a leg under her, body tensing to make the jump ahead. And she said to Abraxos, touching his spine, "I love you."

It was the only thing that mattered in the end. The only thing that mattered now.

Abraxos thrashed. As if he'd try to stop her.

Manon willed strength to her legs, to her arms, and sucked in a breath, perhaps her last—

Shooting from the heavens, faster than a star racing across the sky, a roaring form careened into Iskra's bull.

Those jaws came free of Abraxos's neck, and then they were falling, twisting.

Manon had enough sense to grab onto the saddle, to cling with everything she had as the wind threatened to tear her from him.

His blood streamed upward as they fell, but then his wings spread wide, and he was banking, flapping up. He steadied enough that Manon swung into the saddle, strapping herself in as she whirled to see what had occurred behind her. Who had saved them.

It was not Asterin.

It was not any of the Thirteen.

But Petrah Blueblood.

And behind the Heir to the Blueblood Witch-Clan, now slamming into Morath's aerial legion from where they'd crept onto the battlefield from high above the clouds, were the Ironteeth.

Hundreds of them.

Hundreds of Ironteeth witches and their wyverns crashed into their own.

Petrah and Iskra pulled apart, the Blueblood Heir flapping toward Manon while Abraxos fought to stay upright.

Even with the wind, the battle, Manon still heard Petrah as the Blueblood Heir said to her, "A better world."

Manon had no words. None, other than to look toward the city wall, to the force trying to enter through the river grates. "The walls—"

"Go." Then Petrah pointed to where Iskra had paused in midair to gape at what unfolded. At the act of defiance and rebellion so unthinkable that many of the Morath Ironteeth were equally stunned. Petrah bared her teeth, revealing iron glinting in the watery sunlight. "*She's mine.*"

Manon glanced between the city walls and Iskra, turning toward them once more. Two against one, and they would surely smash her to bits—

"*Go,*" Petrah snarled. And when Manon again hesitated, Petrah only said, "For Keelie."

For the wyvern Petrah had loved—as Manon loved Abraxos. Who had fought for Petrah to her last breath, while Iskra's bull slaughtered her.

So Manon nodded. "Darkness embrace you."

Abraxos began soaring for the wall, his wingbeats unsteady, his breathing shallow.

He needed to rest, needed to see a healer—

Manon glanced behind her just as Petrah slammed into Iskra.

The two Heirs went tumbling toward the earth, clashing again, wyverns striking.

Manon couldn't turn away if she wished.

Not as the wyverns peeled apart and then banked, executing perfect, razor-sharp turns that had them meeting once more, rising up into the sky, tails snapping as they locked talons.

Up and up, Iskra and Petrah flew. Wyverns slashing and biting, claws locking, jaws snapping. Up through the levels of fighting in the skies, up through Crochans and Ironteeth, up through the wisps of clouds.

A race, a mockery of the mating dance of the wyverns, to rise to the highest point of the sky and then plummet down to the earth as one.

Ironteeth halted their fighting. Crochans stilled in midair. Even on the battlefield, Morath soldiers looked up.

The two Heirs shot higher and higher and higher. And when they reached a place where even the wyverns could not draw enough air into their lungs, they tucked in their wings, locked claws, and plunged headfirst toward the earth.

Manon saw the trap before Iskra did.

Saw it the moment Petrah broke free, golden hair streaming as she drew her sword and her wyvern began to circle.

Tight, precise circles around Iskra and her bull as they plummeted.

So tight that Iskra's bull did not have the space to open its wings. And when it tried, Petrah's wyvern was there, tail or jaws snapping. When it tried, Petrah's sword was there, slashing ribbons into the beast.

Iskra realized it then.

Realized it as they fell and fell and fell, and Petrah circled them, so fast that Manon wondered if the Blueblood Heir had been practicing these months, training for this very moment.

For the vengeance owed to her and Keelie.

The very world seemed to pause.

Petrah and her wyvern circled and circled, blood from Iskra's wyvern raining upward, the beast more frantic with every foot closer to the earth.

But Petrah had not opened her wyvern's wings, either. Had not pulled on the reins to bank her mount.

"Pull out," Manon breathed. "Bank now."

Petrah did not. Two wyverns dropped toward the earth, dark stars falling from the sky.

"*Stop*," Iskra barked.

Petrah didn't deign to respond.

They couldn't bank at that speed. And soon Petrah wouldn't be able to bank at all. Would break herself on the ground, right alongside Iskra.

"*Stop!*" Fear turned Iskra's order into a sharp cry.

No pity for her kindled in Manon. None at all.

The ground neared, brutal and unyielding.

"*You mad bitch, I said stop!*"

Two hundred feet to the earth. Then a hundred. Manon couldn't get down a breath.

Fifty feet.

And as the ground seemed to rise to meet them, Manon heard Petrah's only words to Iskra like they had been carried on the wind.

"*For Keelie.*"

Petrah's wyvern flung out its wings, banking sharper than any wyvern Manon had ever witnessed. Rising up, wing tip grazing the icy ground before it shot back into the skies.

Leaving Iskra and her bull to splatter on the earth.

The boom rumbled past Manon, thundering through the world.

Iskra and her bull did not rise again.

Abraxos gave a groan of pain, and Manon twisted in the saddle, her heart raging.

Iskra was dead. The Yellowlegs Heir was dead.

It didn't fill her with the joy it should have. Not with that vulnerable grate on the city wall under attack.

So she snapped the reins, and Abraxos soared for the city walls, and then Sorrel and Vesta were beside her, Asterin coming in fast from behind. They flew low, beneath the Ironteeth now fighting Ironteeth, the Ironteeth still fighting Crochans. Aiming for the spots where the river flowed right up to their sides.

Already, a longboat had reached them. Already, arrows were flying from the small grate—guards frantic to keep the enemy at bay.

The Morath soldiers were so preoccupied with their target ahead that they did not look behind until Abraxos was upon them.

His blood streamed past her as he landed, snapping with talons and teeth and tail. Sorrel and Vesta took care of the others, the longboat soon in splinters.

But it was not enough. Not even close.

"The rocks," Manon breathed, steering Abraxos toward the other side of the river.

He understood. Her heart strained to the point of agony at pushing him, but he soared to the other side of the river and hauled one of the smaller boulders back across. The Thirteen saw her plan and followed, swift and unfaltering.

Every one of his wingbeats was slower than the last. He lost height with each foot they crossed the river.

But then he made it, just as another group of Morath soldiers were trying to enter the small, vulnerable passage. Manon slammed the stone into the water before it. The Thirteen dropped their stones as well, the splashes carrying over the city walls.

More and more, each trip across the river slower than the last.

But then there were rocks piled up, breaking the surface. Then rising above it, blocking out all access to the river tunnel. Just high enough to seal it over—but not give a leg up to the Morath soldiers swarming on the other bank.

Abraxos's breathing was labored, his head sagging.

Manon twisted in the saddle to order her Second to halt piling the rocks, but Asterin had already done so. Her Second pointed to the city walls above them. "*Get inside!*"

Manon didn't waste time arguing. Snapping Abraxos's reins, Manon sent him flying over the city walls, his blood raining on the soldiers fighting there.

He made it to the castle battlements before his strength gave out.

Before he hit the stones and slid, the boom of impact ringing across Orynth.

He slammed into the side of the castle itself, wings limp, and Manon was instantly freeing herself from the saddle as she screamed for a healer.

The wound to his neck was so much worse than she'd thought.

And still he'd fought for her. Stayed in the skies.

Manon shoved her hands against the deep bite wound, blood rushing past her fingers like water through a cracked dam. "Help is coming," she told him, and found her voice to be a broken rasp. "They're coming."

The Thirteen landed, Sorrel sprinting into the castle to no doubt drag a healer out if she had to, and then there were eleven pairs of hands on Abraxos's neck.

Staunching the flow of his blood. Pressing as one, to keep that precious blood inside him while the healer was found.

Manon couldn't look at them, couldn't do anything but close her eyes and pray to the Darkness, to the Three-Faced Mother as she held her hands over the bleeding gashes.

Racing footsteps sounded over the battlement stones, and then Sorrel was there beside Manon, her hands rising to cover his wounds, too.

An older woman unpacked a kit, warning them to keep applying pressure.

Manon didn't bother to tell her that they weren't going anywhere. None of them were.

Even while the battle raged in the skies and on the land below.

⁓

Lysandra could barely draw in breath, each flap of her wings heavier than the last as she aimed for the place where she'd seen Manon Blackbeak and her coven go crashing to the castle battlements.

She'd shifted into a wyvern herself, using the chaos of the Ironteeth rebels' arrival as a distraction, but the draining of her magic had taken its toll. And the fighting, the wounds that even she could not staunch . . .

Lysandra spied the two figures hauling a familiar golden-haired warrior up the castle stairs just as she hit the battlements, the witches whirling toward her.

But Lysandra willed herself to shift, forcing her body to do it one last time, to return to that human form. She'd barely finished shoving on the pants and shirt she'd stashed in a pack by the castle wall when Ren Allsbrook and a Bane soldier reached the top of the battlements, a half-conscious Aedion between them.

There was so much blood on him.

Lysandra ran for them, ignoring her deep limp, the splintering pain rippling in her left leg, in her right shoulder. Down the battlements, a healer worked on the injured Abraxos, the Thirteen, coated in his blood, now standing vigil.

"What happened?" Lysandra skidded to a halt before Aedion, who managed to lift his head to give her a grim smile.

"Valg prince," Ren said, his own body coated in blood, face pale with exhaustion.

Oh gods.

"He didn't walk away," Aedion rasped.

Ren snapped, "And you didn't rest long enough, you stupid bastard. You tore your stitches."

Lysandra ran her hands over Aedion's face, his brow. "Let's get you to a healer—"

"I've already seen one," Aedion grunted, setting his feet on the ground and trying to straighten. "They brought me up here to *rest*." As if such a thing was a ridiculous idea.

Ren indeed unlooped Aedion's arm from around his shoulder. "Sit down, before you fall and crack your head on the stones." Lysandra was inclined to agree, but then Ren said, "I'm heading back to the walls."

"Wait."

Ren turned toward her, but Lysandra didn't speak until the Bane soldier helped Aedion to sit against the side of the castle itself.

"Wait," she said again to Ren when he opened his mouth, her heart thundering, nausea coiling in her gut. She whistled, and Manon Blackbeak and the Thirteen looked her way. She waved them over, her arm barking in pain.

"You're hurt," Aedion growled.

Lysandra ignored him as the witches stalked over, so much blood and gore on all of them.

She asked Manon, "Will Abraxos live?"

A shallow nod, the Witch-Queen's golden eyes dull.

Lysandra didn't have it in her for relief. Not with the news she'd flown back so desperately to deliver. She swallowed the bile in her throat, then pointed to the battlefield. To its dark, misty heart. "They have the witch tower up again. It's moving this way. I just saw it myself. The witches have gathered atop it."

Absolute silence.

And as if in answer, the tower erupted.

Not toward them, but skyward. A flash of light, a boom louder than thunder, and then a portion of the sky became empty.

Where Ironteeth, rebels and the faithful alike, had been fighting, where Crochans had been weaving between them, there was nothing.

Just ash.

Lysandra's voice broke as the tower continued moving. A straight, unbreakable line toward Orynth. "They mean to blast apart the city."

Hands and arms coated in Abraxos's blood, Manon stared at the battlefield. Stared at where all those witches, Ironteeth and Crochan fighting for either army, had just . . . vanished.

Everything her grandmother had claimed about the witch towers was true.

And it was not Kaltain and her shadowfire that fueled that blast of destruction, but Ironteeth witches.

Young Ironteeth witches who offered themselves up. Who made the Yielding as they leaped into the mirror-lined pit within the tower.

An ordinary Yielding might take out twenty, thirty witches around her. Maybe more, if she was older and more powerful.

But a Yielding amplified by the power of those witch mirrors . . . One blast, and the castle looming above them would be rubble. Another blast, maybe two, and Orynth would follow it.

Ironteeth swarmed the tower, a vicious wall keeping the Crochans and rebel Ironteeth out.

A few Crochans indeed tried to break through those defenses.

Their red-clad bodies fell to the earth in pieces.

Petrah, now within the confines of her coven, even made a run for the tower. To rip it down.

They were beaten back by a swarm of Ironteeth.

The tower advanced. Closer and closer.

It would be within range soon. Another few minutes, and that tower would be close enough for its blast to reach the castle. To wipe away this army, this remnant of resistance, forever.

There would be no survivors. No second chances.

Manon turned to Asterin and said quietly, "I need another wyvern."

Her Second only stared at her.

Manon repeated, "*I need another wyvern.*"

Abraxos was in no shape to fly. Wouldn't be for hours or days.

Aedion Ashryver rasped, "No one is getting through that wall of Ironteeth."

Manon bared her teeth. "*I am.*" She pointed at the shape-shifter. "You can carry me."

Aedion snarled, "*No.*"

But Lysandra shook her head, sorrow and despair in her green eyes. "I can't—the magic is drained. If I had an hour—"

"We have five minutes," Manon snapped. She whirled to the Thirteen. "We have trained for this. To break apart enemy ranks. We can get through them. Take apart that tower."

But they all looked at one another. Like they'd had some unspoken conversation and agreement.

The Thirteen stalked toward their own mounts. Sorrel clasped Manon's shoulder as she passed, then climbed onto her wyvern's back. Leaving Asterin before Manon.

Her Second, her cousin, her friend, smiled, eyes bright as stars. "Live, Manon."

Manon blinked.

Asterin smiled wider, kissed Manon's brow, and whispered again, "*Live.*"

Manon didn't see the blow coming.

The punch to her gut, so hard and precise that it knocked the wind from her. Sent her to her knees.

She was struggling to get a breath down, to get up, when Asterin reached Narene and mounted the blue mare, gathering the reins. "Bring our people home, Manon."

Manon knew then. What they were going to do.

Her legs failed her, her body failed her, as she tried to get to her feet. As she rasped, "*No.*"

But Asterin and the Thirteen were already in the skies.

Already in formation, that battering ram that had served them so well. Spearing toward the battlefield. Toward the approaching witch tower.

Manon clawed her way to the battlement ledge, and hauled herself to her feet. Leaned against the stones, panting, trying to get air into her lungs so she might find some way to get airborne, find some Crochan and steal her broom—

But there were no witches here. No brooms to be found. Abraxos remained unconscious.

Manon was distantly aware of the shifter and Prince Aedion coming up beside her, Lord Ren with them. Distantly aware of the silence that fell over the castle, the city, the walls.

As all of them watched that witch tower approach, their doom gathering within it.

As the Thirteen raced for it, raced against the wind and death itself.

A wall of Ironteeth rose up before the tower, blocking their path.

A hundred against twelve.

Inside the witch tower, close enough now that Manon could see through the open archway of the uppermost level, a young witch in black robes stepped toward the hollowed interior.

Stepped toward where Manon's grandmother stood, gesturing to the pit below.

The Thirteen neared the enemy in their path and did not falter.

Manon dug her fingers into the stones so hard her iron nails cracked. Began shaking her head, something in her chest fracturing completely.

Fracturing as the Thirteen slammed into the Ironteeth blockade.

The maneuver was perfect. More flawless than any they'd done. A lethal phalanx that speared through the enemy's ranks. Aiming right for the tower.

Seconds. They had seconds until that young witch summoned the power and unleashed the Yielding in a blast of blackness.

The Thirteen punched through the Ironteeth, spreading wide, pushing them to the side.

Clearing a path right to the tower as Asterin swept in from the back, aiming for the uppermost level.

Imogen went down first.

Then Lin.

And Ghislaine, her wyvern swarmed by their enemy.

Then Thea and Kaya, together, as they had always been.

Then the green-eyed demon twins, laughing as they went. Then the Shadows, Edda and Briar, arrows still firing. Still finding their marks.

Then Vesta, roaring her defiance to the skies.

And then Sorrel. Sorrel, who held the way open for Asterin, a solid wall for Manon's Second as she soared in. A wall against whom the waves of Ironteeth broke and broke.

The young witch inside the tower began glowing black, steps from the pit.

Beside Manon, Lysandra and Aedion wrapped their arms around each other. Ready for the end heartbeats away.

And then Asterin was there. Asterin was barreling toward that open stretch of air, for the tower itself, bought with the lives of the Thirteen. With their final stand.

Manon could only watch, watch and watch and watch, shaking her head as if she could undo it, as Asterin removed her leathers, the shirt beneath.

As Asterin rose in the saddle, freed of the buckles, a dagger in hand as her wyvern aimed straight for the tower.

Manon's grandmother turned then. Away from the pit, the acolyte about to leap inside and destroy them all.

Asterin hurled her dagger.

The blade flew true.

It plunged into the acolyte's back, sending the witch sprawling to the stones. A foot away from the drop to the pit.

Asterin drew the twin swords from the sheaths at her hips and slammed her wyvern into the side of the tower. The crack of bone on rock echoed across the world.

But Asterin was already leaping. Already arching through the air, swords raised, wyvern tumbling away beneath, Narene's body broken on impact.

Manon began screaming then.

Screaming, endless and wordless, as that thing in her chest, as her heart, shattered.

As Asterin landed in the witch tower's open archway, swords swinging at the witches who rushed to kill her. They might as well have been blades of grass. Might as well have been mist, for how easily Asterin cut them down, one after another, driving forward, toward the Matron who had branded the letters on stark display across Asterin's abdomen.

UNCLEAN

Twirling, twisting, blades flying, Asterin slaughtered her way toward Manon's grandmother.

The High Witch of the Blackbeak Clan backed away, shaking her head. Her mouth moved, as if she breathed, *"Asterin, no—"*

But Asterin was already there.

And it was not darkness, but light—light, bright and pure as the sun on snow, that erupted from Asterin.

Light, as Asterin made the Yielding.

As the Thirteen, their broken bodies scattered around the tower in a near-circle, made the Yielding as well.

Light. They all burned with it. Radiated it.

Light that flowed from their souls, their fierce hearts as they gave themselves over to that power. Became incandescent with it.

Asterin tackled the Blackbeak Matron to the ground, Manon's grandmother little more than a shadow against the brightness. Then little more than a scrap of hate and memory as Asterin exploded.

As she and the Thirteen Yielded completely, and blew themselves and the witch tower to smithereens.

CHAPTER 90

Manon sank to the stones of the castle battlements and did not move for a long, long while.

She didn't hear those who spoke to her, who touched her shoulder. Didn't feel the cold.

The sun arced and descended.

At some point, she lay down upon the stones, curled against the wall. When she awoke, a wing had covered her, and warm breath whispered across her head as Abraxos dozed.

She had no words in her. Nothing but a ringing silence.

Manon got to her feet, easing past the wing that had shielded her.

The dawn was breaking.

And where that witch tower had stood, where the army had been, only blasted earth remained.

Morath had drawn back. Far back.

The city and walls still stood.

She roused Abraxos with a hand to his side.

He couldn't fly, not yet, so they walked together.

Down the battlement steps. Out through the castle gates and into the city streets beyond.

She didn't care that others followed. More and more of them.

The streets were filled with blood and rubble, all of it gilded by the rising sun.

She didn't feel the warmth of that sun on her face while they walked through the southern gate and onto the plain beyond. She didn't care that someone had opened the gate for them.

At her side, Abraxos nudged aside piles of Valg soldiers, clearing a path for her. For all those who trailed in their wake.

It was so quiet. Inside her, and on the plain.

So quiet, and empty.

Manon crossed the still battlefield. Didn't stop until she reached the center of the blast radius. Until she stood in its heart.

Not a trace of the tower. Or those who had been in it, around it. Even the stones had been melted into nothing.

Not a trace of the Thirteen, or their brave, noble wyverns.

Manon fell to her knees.

Ashes rose, fluttering, soft as snow as they clung to the tears on her face.

Abraxos lay beside her, his tail curling around her while she bowed over her knees and wept.

Behind her, had she looked, she would have seen Glennis. And Bronwen. Petrah Blueblood.

Aedion Ashryver and Lysandra and Ren Allsbrook.

Prince Galan and Captain Rolfe and Ansel of Briarcliff, Ilias and the Fae royals beside them.

Had she looked, she would have seen the small white flowers they bore. Would have wondered how and where they had gotten them in the dead heart of winter.

Had she looked, she would have seen the people gathered behind them, so many they streamed all the way to the city gates. Would have seen the humans standing side by side with the Crochans and Ironteeth.

All come to honor the Thirteen.

But Manon did not look. Even when the leaders who had come with her, walked with her all this way, began to lay their flowers upon the blasted, bloodied earth. Even when their tears flowed, dropping into the ashes alongside their offerings of tribute.

They didn't speak. And neither did the streaming line of people who came after them. A few bore flowers, but many brought small stones to lay on the site. Those who had neither laid down whatever personal effects they could offer. Until the blast site was covered, as if a garden had grown from a field of blood.

Glennis stayed until the end.

And when they were alone on the silent battlefield, Manon's great-grandmother put a hand on her shoulder and said quietly, her voice somehow distant, *"Be the bridge, be the light. When iron melts, when flowers spring from fields of blood—let the land be witness, and return home."*

Manon didn't hear the words. Didn't notice when even Glennis returned to the city looming at her back.

For hours, Manon knelt on the battlefield, Abraxos at her side. As if she might stay with them, her Thirteen, for a little while longer.

And far away, across the snow-covered mountains, on a barren plain before the ruins of a once-great city, a flower began to bloom.

CHAPTER 91

Dorian hadn't believed it—hadn't dared to hope for what he saw.

A foreign army, marching northward. An army he'd grown up studying. There were the khagan's foot soldiers, and the Darghan cavalry. There were the legendary ruks, magnificent and proud, soaring above them in a sea of wings.

He'd aimed as close to the head of the army as he could get, wondering which of the royals had come. Wondering if Chaol was with them. If the presence of this miraculous army meant his friend had succeeded against all odds.

The ruks had spied him then.

Chased him, and he'd begun signaling as he'd neared. Hoping they'd pause.

But then he'd landed at the crossroads. And then he'd seen them. Seen her.

Aelin, galloping for him. Rowan at her side, Elide and the others with her.

Maeve had believed Aelin had headed to Terrasen. And here she was, with the khagan's army.

Aelin's smile faded the moment she grew close. As if she sensed what he bore.

"Where's Manon?" was all she asked.

"Terrasen," he breathed, panting slightly. "And likely with the Crochans, if it went according to plan."

She opened her mouth, eyes wide, but another rider came galloping down the road.

The world went quiet.

The approaching rider halted, another—a beautiful woman Dorian could only describe as golden—right behind.

But Dorian stared at the rider before him. At the posture of the body, the commanding seat he possessed.

And as Chaol Westfall dismounted and ran the last few feet toward Dorian, the King of Adarlan wept.

~

Chaol didn't hide his tears, the shaking that overtook him as he collided with Dorian and embraced his king.

No one said a word, though Chaol knew they were all gathered. Knew Yrene stood behind him, crying with them.

He just held his friend, his brother.

"I knew you'd do it," Dorian said, voice raw. "I knew you'd find a way. For all of it."

The army. The fact that he was now standing.

Chaol only gripped Dorian tighter. "You have one hell of a story to tell yourself."

Dorian pulled back, his face solemn.

A story, Chaol realized, that might not be as happy as his own.

Yet before whatever doom Dorian carried could fall upon them, Chaol gestured to where Yrene had dismounted and now wiped away her tears.

"The woman responsible for this," Chaol said, motioning to his standing, his walking, to the army stretching down the road. "Yrene Towers. A healer at the Torre Cesme. And my wife."

Yrene bowed, and Chaol could have sworn a flicker of sorrow darkened Dorian's eyes. But then his king was taking Yrene's hands, lifting her from her bow. And though that sorrow still edged his smile, Dorian said to her, "Thank you."

Yrene went scarlet. "I've heard so much about you, Your Majesty."

Dorian only winked, a ghost of the man he'd been before. "All bad things, I hope."

Yrene laughed, and the joy on her face—the joy that Chaol knew was for both of them—made him love her all over again.

"I have always wanted a sister," Dorian said, and leaned to kiss Yrene on either cheek. "Welcome to Adarlan, Lady."

Yrene's smile turned softer—deeper, and she laid a hand on her abdomen. "Then you shall be pleased to hear that you'll soon be an uncle."

Dorian whirled to him. Chaol nodded, unable to find the words to convey what flooded his heart.

But Dorian's smile dimmed as he faced where Aelin now leaned against a tree, Rowan and Elide beside her.

"I know," Aelin said, and Chaol knew she didn't mean about the pregnancy.

Dorian closed his eyes, and Chaol laid a hand on his king's shoulder at whatever burden he was about to reveal.

"I retrieved the third from Morath," Dorian said.

Chaol's knees buckled, and Yrene was instantly there, an arm around his waist.

The Wyrdkeys.

Chaol asked Dorian, "You have all three now?"

Dorian nodded once.

A look from Rowan had his cadre peeling off to make sure none from the army got close enough to hear.

"I snuck into Morath to get the third," Dorian said.

"Holy gods," Aelin breathed. Chaol just blinked.

"That was the easy part," Dorian said, paling. The khaganate royals emerged from the ranks, and Dorian smiled at Nesryn. Then nodded to the royals. Introductions would come later.

"Maeve was there," Dorian said to Aelin.

Flame danced at Aelin's fingertips as she rested her hand atop Goldryn. The fire seemed to sink into the blade, the ruby flickering. "I know," she said quietly.

Dorian's brows rose. Aelin just shook her head, motioning him to continue as the cadre returned.

"Maeve discovered my presence, and . . ." Dorian sighed, and the whole story came tumbling out.

When he was done, Chaol was glad Yrene had kept her arm around his waist. Silence fell, thick and taut. Dorian had destroyed Morath.

"I have little doubt," Dorian admitted, "that both Erawan and Maeve survived Morath's collapsing. It likely only served to enrage them."

It didn't stop Chaol from marveling at his friend, the others gawking.

"Well done," Lorcan said, scanning the king from head to toe. "Well done indeed."

Aelin let out an impressed whistle. "I wish I could have seen it," she said to Dorian, shaking her head. Then she turned to Rowan. "Your uncle and Essar came through, then. They kicked Maeve to the curb."

The Fae Prince snorted. "You said your letter was strongly worded. I should have believed you." Aelin sketched a bow. Chaol hadn't the faintest idea what they were talking about, but Rowan went on, "So if Maeve cannot be Queen of the Fae, she will find herself another throne."

"Bitch," Fenrys spat. Chaol was inclined to agree.

"Our worst fears have been confirmed, then," Prince Sartaq said, glancing to his siblings. "A Valg king and queen united." A nod toward Elide. "Your uncle did not lie."

"Maeve has no army now," Dorian reminded them. "Just her power."

Nesryn cringed. "The hybrids she created with the princesses might be disaster enough."

Chaol glanced to Yrene, the woman who held the greatest weapon against the Valg within her own body.

"When did you leave Morath?" Rowan asked.

"Three days ago," Dorian said.

Rowan turned to Aelin, ashen-faced as she remained leaning against the tree. Chaol wondered if she did so only because her own legs might not be able to support her. "Then at least we know that Erawan has not yet come to Terrasen."

"His Ironteeth host went ahead of him," Dorian said.

"We know," Chaol said. "They're already at Orynth."

Dorian shook his head. "That's impossible. They left soon after I did. I'm surprised you didn't see them flying past in the Ruhnns."

Silence.

"The full Ironteeth host isn't yet at Orynth," Aelin said softly. Too softly.

"I counted over a thousand in the host that I flew with," Dorian said. "Many bore soldiers with them—all Valg."

Chaol closed his eyes, and Yrene's arm tightened around him in silent comfort.

"We knew the rukhin would be outnumbered anyway," Nesryn said.

"There won't be anything left of Terrasen for the rukhin to defend," Prince Kashin said, rubbing his jaw. "Even if the Crochans arrived before us."

The Queen of Terrasen pushed off from the tree at last. "We have two choices, then," she said, her voice unwavering despite the hell that swept upon them. "We continue north, as fast as we can. See what there is to fight when we arrive at Terrasen. I might be able to bring down a good number of those wyverns."

"And the other option?" Princess Hasar asked.

Aelin's face was stark. "We have the three Wyrdkeys. We have me.

I can end this now. Or at least take Erawan out of play before he can find us, steal those keys back, and rule over this world and all others."

Rowan started, shaking his head. But Aelin held up a hand. And even the Fae Prince stood down. "It's not my choice alone."

And Chaol realized that it was indeed a queen standing before them, not the assassin he'd dragged out of a salt mine a few miles down the road. Not even the woman he'd seen in Rifthold.

Dorian squared his shoulders. "The choice is also mine."

Slowly, so slowly, Aelin looked at him. Chaol braced himself. Her voice was deadly soft as she said to Dorian, "You retrieved the third key. Your role in this is done."

"Like hell it is," Dorian said, sapphire eyes flashing. "The same blood, the same debt, flows in my veins."

Chaol's hands curled at his sides as he fought to keep his mouth shut. Rowan seemed to be doing the same as the two rulers squared off.

Aelin's face remained unmoved—distant. "You're so eager to die?"

Dorian didn't retreat. "Are you?"

Silence. Utter silence in the clearing.

Then Aelin shrugged, as if the weight of entire worlds didn't hang in the balance. "Regardless of who will put the keys back into the gate, this is a fate that belongs to all of us. So all of us should decide." Her chin lifted. "Do we continue on to war, hope we make it to Orynth in time, and then destroy the keys? Or do we destroy the keys now, and then you continue northward." A pause, horrible and unbearable. "Without me."

Rowan was shaking, whether with restraint or in dread, Chaol couldn't tell.

Aelin said, unwavering and calm, "I would like to put it to a vote."

A vote.

Rowan had never heard of anything so absurd.

Even as part of him glowed with pride that she had chosen now, here, as the moment when that new world she had promised would rise.

A world in which a few did not hold all the power, but many. Beginning with this, this most vital choice. This unbearable fate.

All of them had moved farther down the road, and it was not lost on Rowan that they stood at a crossroads. Or that Dorian and Aelin and Chaol stood in the heart of that crossroads, merely a few miles from the salt mines. Where so much of this had begun, just over a year ago.

There was a dull roar in Rowan's ears as the debate raged.

He knew he should fall on his knees and thank Dorian for retrieving the third key. But he hated the king all the same.

He hated this path they'd been put on, a thousand years ago. Hated that this choice lay before them, when they had already fought so much, given so much.

Prince Kashin was saying, "We march on a hundred thousand enemy troops, possibly more. That number will not change when the Wyrdgate is closed. We will need the Fire-Bringer to cut through them."

Princess Hasar shook her head. "But there is the possibility of that army's collapse should Erawan vanish. Cut off the beast's head and the body could die."

"That's a big risk to take," Chaol said, his jaw tight. "Erawan's removal from all this might help, or it might not. An enemy army this big, full of Valg who might be eager to fill his place, could be impossible to stop at this point."

"Then why not use the keys?" Nesryn asked. "Why not bring the keys north and use them, destroy the army, and—"

"The keys cannot be wielded," Dorian cut in. "Not without destroying the bearer. We're not entirely sure a mortal *could* withstand the power." He nodded toward Aelin, silent and watchful while it took all of Rowan's training not to hurl up his guts. "Just putting them back in the gate requires everything." He added tightly, "From one of us."

Rowan knew he should be arguing against this, should be bellowing.

Dorian went on, "I should do it."

"No." The word broke from Chaol—and Aelin. Her first word since this debate had begun.

But it was Fenrys who asked Chaol, voice deadly soft, "You'd rather my queen die than your king?"

Chaol stiffened. "I'd rather neither of my friends die. I'd rather none of this happen."

Before Fenrys could snarl his answer, Yrene cut in. "So when the Lock is forged and the Wyrdgate is sealed, the gods will be gone?"

"Good riddance," Fenrys muttered.

But Yrene stiffened at the casual dismissal, and put a hand over her heart. "I love Silba. Dearly. When she is gone from this world, will my powers cease to exist?" She gestured to the gathered group.

"Doubtful," Dorian said. "That cost, at least, was never demanded."

"What of the other gods in this world?" Nesryn asked, frowning. "The thirty-six of the khaganate. Are they not gods as well? Will they be sent away, or just these twelve?"

"Perhaps our gods are of a different sort," Princess Hasar mused.

"Can they not help us, then?" Yrene asked, sorrow for the goddess who had blessed her still darkening her golden eyes. "Can they not intervene?"

"There are indeed other forces at work in this world," Dorian said, touching Damaris's hilt. The god of truth—that's who had blessed Gavin's sword. "But I think if those forces had been able to aid us in this manner, they would have done so already."

Aelin tapped her foot on the ground. "Expecting divine handouts is a waste of our time. And not the topic at hand." She fixed her burning stare on Dorian. "We are also not debating who shall pay the cost."

"Why." Rowan's low question was out before he could halt it.

Slowly, his mate turned toward him. "Because we're not." Sharp, icy words. She cut Dorian a look, and the King of Adarlan opened his mouth. "We're not," she snarled.

Dorian opened his mouth again, but Rowan caught his eye. Held his stare and let him read the words there. *Later. We shall debate this later.*

Whether Aelin noted their silent conversation, whether she beheld Dorian's subtle nod, she didn't let on. She only said, "We don't have time to waste on endless debate."

Lorcan nodded. "Every moment we have all three keys is a risk of Erawan finding us, and finally gaining what he seeks. Or Maeve," he added, frowning. "But even with that, I would go north—let Aelin put a dent in Morath's legions."

"Be objective," Aelin growled. She surveyed them all. "Pretend you do not know me. Pretend I am no one, and nothing to you. Pretend I am a weapon. Do you use me now, or later?"

"You are not no one, though," Elide said quietly. "Not to a good many people."

"The keys go back in the gate," Aelin said a bit coldly. "At some point or another. And I go with them. We are deciding whether that is now, or in a few weeks."

Rowan couldn't bear it. To hear another word. "No."

Everyone halted once more.

Aelin bared her teeth. "Not doing anything isn't an option."

"We hide them again," Rowan said. "He lost them for thousands of years. We can do it again." He pointed to Yrene. "She could destroy him all on her own."

"*That* is not an option," Aelin growled. "Yrene is with child—"

"I can do it," Yrene said, stepping from Chaol's side. "If there's a way, I could do it. See if the other healers could help—"

"There will be Valg by the thousands for you to destroy or save, Lady Westfall," Aelin said with that same cold. "Erawan could slaughter you before you even get the chance to touch him."

"Why are you allowed to give up your life for this, and no one else?" Yrene challenged.

"I am not the one carrying a child within me."

Yrene blinked slowly. "Hafiza might be able to—"

"I will not play a game of what-ifs and *mights*," Aelin said, in a tone that Rowan had heard so rarely. That queen's tone. "We vote. Now. Do we put the keys back in the gate immediately, or continue to Terrasen and then do it if we are able to stop that army?"

"Erawan can be stopped," Yrene pushed, unfazed by the queen's words. Unafraid of her wrath. "I know he can. Without the keys, we can stop him."

Rowan wanted to believe her. Wanted more than anything he'd ever desired in his life to believe Yrene Westfall. Chaol, glancing at Dorian, seemed inclined to do the same.

But Aelin pointed at Princess Hasar. "How do you vote?"

Hasar held Aelin's stare. Considered for a moment. "I vote to do it now."

Aelin just pointed to Dorian. "You?"

Dorian tensed, the unfinished debate still raging in his face. But he said, "Do it now."

Rowan closed his eyes. Barely heard the other rulers and their allies as they gave their replies. He walked to the edge of the trees, prepared to run if he began to vomit.

Then Aelin said, "You're last, Rowan."

"I vote no. Not now, not ever."

Her eyes were cold, distant. The way they'd been in Mistward.

"It's decided, then," Chaol said quietly. Sadly.

"At dawn, the Lock will be forged and the keys go back into the gate," Dorian finished.

Rowan just stared and stared at his mate. His reason for breathing.

Elide asked softly, "What is your vote, Aelin?"

Aelin tore her eyes from Rowan, and he felt the absence of that stare like a frozen wind as she said, "It doesn't matter."

CHAPTER
92

Aelin didn't say that asking them to vote hadn't just been about letting them decide, as free peoples of the world, how to seal its fate. She didn't say that it had also been a coward's thing to do. To let someone else decide for her. To choose the road ahead.

They camped that night at Endovier, the salt mines a mere three miles down the road.

Rowan made them set up their royal tent. Their royal bed.

She didn't eat with the others. Could barely touch the food Rowan laid on the desk. She was still sitting in front of it, roast rabbit now cold, poring over those useless books on Wyrdmarks when Rowan said from across the table, "I do not accept this."

"I do." The words were flat, dead.

As she would be, before the sun had fully risen. Aelin shut the ancient tome before her.

Only a few days separated them from Terrasen's border. Perhaps she should have agreed to do this now, but on the condition that it was on Terrasen soil. Terrasen soil, rather than by Endovier.

But every passing day was a risk. A terrible risk.

"You have never accepted anything in your life," Rowan snarled, shooting to his feet and bracing his hands on the table. "And now you are suddenly willing to do so?"

She swallowed against the ache in her throat. Surveyed the books she'd combed through thrice now to no avail. "What am I supposed to do, Rowan?"

"You damn it all to hell!" He slammed his fist on the table, rattling the dishes. "You say to hell with their plans, their prophecies and fates, and you make your own! You do *anything* but accept this!"

"The people of Erilea have spoken."

"To hell with that, too," he growled. "You can start your free world *after* this war. Let them vote for their own damned kings and queens, if they want to."

She let out a growl of her own. "I do not want this burden for one second longer. I do not want to choose and learn I made the wrong choice in delaying it."

"So you would have voted against it, then. You would have gone to Terrasen."

"Does it matter?" She shot to her feet. "The votes weren't in my favor anyway. Hearing that I wanted to go to Orynth, to fight one last time, would have only swayed them."

"You're the one who's about to die. I'd say you get to have a voice in it."

She bared her teeth. "This is my *fate*. Elena tried to get me out of it. And look where it landed her—with a cabal of vengeful gods swearing to end her eternal soul. When the Lock is forged, when I close the gate, I will be destroying another life alongside my own."

"Elena has had a thousand years of existence, either living or as a spirit. Forgive me if I don't give a shit that her time has now come to an end, when you only received twenty years."

"I got to twenty years because of her."

Not even twenty. Her birthday was still months away. In a spring she would not see.

Rowan began pacing, his stalking steps eating up the carpet. "This mess is because of her, too. Why should you bear its weight alone?"

"Because it was always mine to begin with."

"Bullshit. It could have as easily been Dorian. He's willing to do it."

Aelin blinked. "Elena and Nehemia said Dorian wasn't ready."

"Dorian walked into and out of Morath, went toe to toe with Maeve, and brought the whole damn place crashing down. I'd say he's as ready as you are."

"I won't allow him to sacrifice himself in my stead."

"Why?"

"Because he is my *friend*. Because I won't be able to *live* with myself if I let him go."

"He said he would do it, Aelin."

"He doesn't know what he wants. He's barely emerging from the horrors he endured."

"And you aren't?" Rowan challenged, wholly unfazed. "He's a grown man. He can make his own choices—*we* can make choices without you lording over them."

She bared her teeth. "*It's been decided.*"

He crossed his arms. "Then you and I will do it. Together."

Her heart stopped in her chest.

He went on, "You are not forging the Lock alone."

"No." Her hands began shaking. "That is not an option."

"According to whom?"

"According to *me*." She couldn't breathe around the thought—of him being erased from existence. "If it was possible, Elena would have told me. Someone with my bloodline *has* to pay."

He opened his mouth, but beheld the truth in her face, her words. He shook his head. "I promised you we'd find a way to pay this debt—together."

Aelin surveyed the scattered books. Nothing—the books, that scrap of hope they'd offered had amounted to *nothing*. "There isn't an alterna-tive." She dragged her hands through her hair. "*I* don't have an alternative," she amended. No card up her sleeve, no grand reveal. Not for this.

"We don't do it tomorrow, then," he pushed. "We wait. Tell the oth-ers we want to reach Orynth first. Maybe the Royal Library has some texts—"

"What is the point in a vote if we ignore its outcome? *They decided*, Rowan. Tomorrow, it will be over."

The words rang hollow and sickly within her.

"Let me find another way." His voice broke, but his pacing didn't fal-ter. "I *will* find another way, Aelin—"

"There is no other way. Don't you understand? All of this," she hissed, arms splaying. "All of *this* has been to keep you alive. *All* of you."

"With you as the asking price. To atone for some lingering guilt."

She slammed a hand atop the stack of ancient books. "Do you think I *want* to die? Do you think any of this is easy, to look at the sky and wonder if it's the last I'll see? To look at you, and wonder about those years we won't have?"

"I don't know what you want, Aelin," Rowan snarled. "You haven't been entirely forthcoming."

Her heart thundered. "I want it to be over, one way or another." Her fingers curled into fists. "I want this to be *done*."

He shook his head. "I know. And I know what you went through, that those months in Doranelle were hell, Aelin. But you can't stop fighting. Not now."

Her eyes burned. "I held on for this. For *this* purpose. So I can put the keys back in the gate. When Cairn ripped me apart, when Maeve tore away everything I knew, it was only remembering that this task relied upon my survival that kept me from breaking. Knowing that if I failed, all of you would die." Her breathing turned uneven, sharp. "And since then, I've been so damned *stupid* in thinking that perhaps I wouldn't have to pay the debt, that I might see Orynth again. That Dorian might do it instead." She spat on the ground. "What sort of person does that make me? To have been filled with dread when he arrived today?"

Rowan again opened his mouth to answer, but she cut him off, her voice breaking. "I thought I could escape it—just for a moment. And as soon as I did, the gods brought Dorian sweeping right back into my path. Tell me that's not intentional. Tell me that those gods, or whichever *forces* might also rule this world, aren't roaring that I should still be the one to forge the Lock."

Rowan just stared at her for a long moment, his chest heaving. Then he said, "What if those forces didn't lead Dorian into our path so you alone might pay the debt?"

"I don't understand."

"What if they brought you *together*. To not pick one or the other, but to share the burden. With each other."

Even the fire in the braziers seemed to pause.

Rowan's eyes glowed as he blazed ahead. "That day you destroyed the glass castle—when you joined hands, your power . . . I'd never seen anything like it. You were able to meld your powers, to become *one*. If the Lock demands all of *you*, then why not give half? Half of *each* of you—when you *both* bear Mala's blood?"

Aelin slid slowly into her chair. "I—we don't know it will work."

"It's better than walking into your own execution with your head bowed."

She snarled. "How could I ever ask him to do it?"

"Because it is not your burden alone, that's why. Dorian knows this. Has accepted it. Because the alternative is losing you." The rage in his eyes fractured, right along with his voice. "I would go in your stead, if I could."

Her own heart cracked. "I know."

Rowan fell to his knees before her, putting his head in her lap as his arms wrapped around her waist. "I can't bear it, Aelin. I can't."

She threaded her fingers through his hair. "I wanted that thousand years with you," she said softly. "I wanted to have children with you. I wanted to go into the Afterworld together." Her tears landed in his hair.

Rowan lifted his head. "Then fight for it. One more time. Fight for that future."

She gazed at him, at the life she saw in his face. All that he offered.

All that she might have, too.

⁓

"I need to ask you to do something."

Aelin's voice roused Dorian from a fitful sleep. He sat up on his cot. From the silence of the camp, it had to be the dead of night. "What?"

Rowan was standing guard behind her, watching the army camp beneath the trees. Dorian caught his emerald gaze—saw the answer he already needed.

The prince had come through on his silent promise earlier.

Aelin's throat bobbed. "Together," she said, her voice cracking. "What if we forged the Lock together?"

Dorian knew her plan, her desperate hope, before she laid it out. And when she finished, Aelin only said, "I am sorry to even ask you."

"I am sorry I didn't think of it," he replied, and pushed to his feet, tugging on his boots.

Rowan turned toward them now. Waiting for an answer that he knew Dorian would give.

So Dorian said to them both, "Yes."

Aelin closed her eyes, and he couldn't tell if it was from relief or regret. He laid a hand on her shoulder. He didn't want to know what the argument had been like between her and Rowan to get her to agree, to accept this. For Aelin to have even said yes . . .

Her eyes opened, and only bleak resolve lay within. "We do it now," she said hoarsely. "Before the others. Before good-byes."

Dorian nodded. She only asked, "Do you want Chaol to be there?"

He thought about saying no. Thought about sparing his friend from another good-bye, when there was such joy on Chaol's face, such peace.

But Dorian still said, "Yes."

CHAPTER 93

The four of them strode in silence through the trees. Down the ancient road to the salt mines.

It was the only place the scouts weren't watching.

Every step closer made her queasy, a slow sweat breaking down her spine. Rowan kept his hand gripped around hers, his thumb brushing over her skin.

Here, in this horrible, dead place of so much suffering—here was where she would face her fate. As if she had never escaped it, not really.

Under the cover of darkness, the mountains in which the mines were carved were little more than shadows. The great wall that surrounded the death camp was nothing but a stain of blackness.

The gates had been left open, one broken on its hinges. Perhaps the freed slaves had tried to rip it down on their way out.

Aelin's fingers tightened on Rowan's as they passed beneath the archway and entered the open grounds of the mines. There, in the center—there stood the wooden posts where she had been whipped. On her first day, on so many days.

And there, in the mountain to her left—that was where the pits were. The lightless pits they'd shoved her into.

The buildings of the mines' overseers were dark. Husks.

It took all her self-control to keep from looking at her wrists, where the shackle scars had been. To not feel the cold sweat sliding down her back and know no scars lay there, either. Just Rowan's tattoo, inked over smooth skin.

As if this place were a dream—some nightmare conjured by Maeve.

The irony wasn't lost on her. She'd escaped shackles twice now—only to wind up back here. A temporary freedom. Borrowed time.

She'd left Goldryn in their tent. The sword would be of little use where they were going.

"I never thought we'd see this place again," Dorian murmured. "Certainly not like this." None of the king's steps faltered, his face somber as he gripped Damaris's hilt. Ready to meet whatever awaited them.

The pain she knew was coming.

No, she had not ever really escaped at all, had she?

They halted near the center of the dirt yard. Elena had walked her through forging the Lock, putting the keys back into the gate. Though there would be no great display of magic, no threat to any around them, she had wanted to be away. Far from anyone else.

In the moonlight, Chaol's face was pale. "What do you need us to do?"

"Be here," Aelin said simply. "That is enough."

It was the only reason she was still able to endure standing here, in this hateful place.

She met Dorian's inquiring stare and nodded. No use in wasting time.

Dorian embraced Chaol, the two of them speaking too quietly for Aelin to hear.

Aelin only began to sketch a Wyrdmark in the dirt, large enough for her and Dorian to stand in. There would be two, overlapping with each other: Open. Close.

Lock. Unlock.

She'd learned them from the start. Had used them herself.

"No sweet farewells, Princess?" Rowan asked as she traced the mark with her foot.

"They seem dramatic," Aelin said. "Far too dramatic, even for me."

But Rowan halted her, the second symbol half-finished. Tipped back her chin. "Even when you're . . . there," he said, his pine-green eyes so bright under the moon. "I am with you." He laid a hand on her heart. "Here. I am with you here."

She laid her own hand on his chest, and breathed his scent deep into her lungs, her heart. "As I am with you. Always."

Rowan kissed her. "I love you," he whispered onto her mouth. "Come back to me."

Then Rowan retreated, just beyond the unfinished marks.

The absence of his scent, his heat, filled her with cold. But she kept her shoulders back. Kept her breathing steady as she memorized the lines of Rowan's face.

Dorian, eyes shining bright, stepped onto the marks. Aelin said to Rowan, "Seal the last one when we're done."

Her prince, her mate, nodded.

Dorian drew out a folded bit of cloth from his jacket. Opened it to reveal two slivers of black stone. And the Amulet of Orynth.

Her stomach roiled, nausea at their otherworldliness threatening to bring her to her knees. But she took the Amulet of Orynth from him.

"I thought you might be the one who wished to open it," Dorian said quietly.

Here in the place where she'd suffered and endured, here in the place where so many things had begun.

Aelin weighed the ancient amulet in her palms, ran her thumbs along the golden seam of its edges. For a heartbeat, she was again in that cozy room in a riverside estate, her mother beside her, bequeathing the amulet into her care.

Aelin traced her fingers over the Wyrdmarks on the back. The runes that spelled out her hateful fate: *Nameless is my price.*

Written here, all this time, for so many centuries. A warning from Brannon, and a confirmation. Their sacrifice. Her sacrifice.

Brannon had raged at those gods, had marked the amulet and laid all those clues for her to one day find. So she might understand. As if she could somehow defy this fate. A fool's hope.

Aelin turned the amulet back over, brushing her fingers along the immortal stag on its front.

Borrowed time. It had all been borrowed time.

The gold sealing the amulet melted away in her hands, hissing as it dropped onto the icy dirt. With a twist, she pulled apart the two sides of the amulet.

The unearthly reek of the third key hit her, beckoning. Whispered in languages that did not exist in Erilea and never would.

Aelin only dumped the sliver of Wyrdkey into Dorian's awaiting hand. It clinked against the other two, and the sound might have echoed into eternity, into all worlds.

Dorian shuddered, Chaol and Rowan flinching.

Aelin just pocketed the two halves of the amulet. A piece of Terrasen to take with her. Wherever they were about to go.

Aelin met Rowan's stare one last time. Saw the words there. *Come back to me.*

She'd take those words, that face with her, too. Even when the Lock demanded everything, that would remain. Would always remain.

She swallowed past the tightness in her throat. Broke Rowan's piercing stare. And then sliced open her palm. Then Dorian's.

The stars seemed to shift closer, the mountains peering over Aelin's and Dorian's shoulders, as she sliced her knife a third time, down her forearm. Deep and wide, skin splitting.

To open the gate, she must *become* the gate.

Erawan had begun the process of turning Kaltain Rompier into that gate—had put the stone within her arm not for safekeeping, but to prepare her body for the other stones. To turn her into a living Wyrdgate that he might control.

Just one sliver in her body had destroyed Kaltain. To put all three in her own . . .

My name is Aelin Ashryver Galathynius, and I will not be afraid.

I will not be afraid.

I will not be afraid.

"Ready?" Aelin breathed.

Dorian nodded.

With a final look at the stars, one final look at the Lord of the North standing guard over Terrasen mere miles away, Aelin took the shards from Dorian's outstretched palm.

And as she and Dorian joined bloodied hands, as their magic roared through them and wove together, blinding and eternal, Aelin slammed the three Wyrdkeys into the open wound of her arm.

Rowan sealed the Wyrdmarks with a swipe of his foot through the icy earth.

Just as Aelin clapped her palm upon her arm, sealing the three Wyrdkeys into her body while her other hand gripped Dorian's.

It had to work. It had to have been why their paths had crossed, why Aelin and Dorian had found each other twice now, in this exact place. He could accept no other alternative. He couldn't have let her go otherwise.

Rowan didn't breathe. Beside him, he wasn't sure if Chaol did, either.

But while Aelin and Dorian still stood there, heads high despite the fear he scented coursing through them, their faces had gone vacant. Empty.

No flash of light.

No flare of power.

Aelin and Dorian simply stood, hands united, and stared ahead.

Blank. Unseeing. Frozen.

Gone.

Here, but gone. As if their bodies were shells.

"What happened?" Chaol breathed.

Aelin's hand fell from where it had been clapped onto her arm and dangled limply at her side. Revealing that open wound. The black slivers of rock shoved inside it.

Something in Rowan's chest, intricate and essential, began to strain. Began to go taut.

The mating bond.

Rowan lurched forward a step, a hand on his chest.

No. The mating bond writhed, as if in agony, as if in terror. He halted, Aelin's name on his lips.

Rowan fell to his knees as the three Wyrdkeys within Aelin's arm dissolved into her blood.

Like dew in the sun.

CHAPTER 94

As it had been once before, so it was again.

The beginning and end and eternity, a torrent of light, of *life* that flowed between them, two halves of a cleaved bloodline.

Mist swirled, veiling the solid ground beneath. An illusion, perhaps—for their minds to bear where they now stood. A place that was not a place, in a chamber of many doors. More doors than they could ever hope to count. Some made of air, some of glass, some of flame and gold and light.

A new world beyond each; a new world beckoning.

But they remained there, in the crossroads of all things.

In bodies that were not their bodies, they stood amid all those doorways, their power pouring out, pooling before them. Blending and merging, a ball of light, of creation, hovering in midair.

Every ember that flowed from them into the growing sphere before them, into the Lock taking form, would not return. It would not replenish.

A well running dry. Forever.

More and more and more, ripping from them with each breath. Creation and destruction.

The sphere swirled, its edges warping, shrinking. Forming into the shape they'd chosen, a thing of gold and silver. The Lock that would seal all these infinite doors forever.

Still they gave over their power, still the forming of the Lock demanded more.

And it began to hurt.

~

She was Aelin and yet she was not.

She was Aelin and yet she was infinite; she was all worlds, she was—

She was Aelin.

She was *Aelin*.

And by letting the keys into her, they had entered the *true* Wyrdgate. A step, or a thought, or a wish would allow them to access any world they desired. Any possibility.

An archway lingered behind them. An archway that would smell of pine and snow.

Slowly, the Lock formed, light turning to metal—to gold and silver.

Dorian was panting, his jaw stretched tight, as they gave and gave and gave their power toward it. Never to see it again.

It was agony. Agony like nothing she had known.

She was Aelin. She was Aelin and not the things that she'd set in her arm, not this place that existed beyond reason. She was Aelin; she was Aelin; and she had come here to do something, had come here promising to do *something*—

She fought her rising scream as her power rippled away, like peeling skin from her bones. Precisely how Cairn had done it, delighted in it. She had outlasted him, though. Had escaped Maeve's clutches. She had outlasted them both. To do this. To come here.

But she had been wrong.

She couldn't bear it. Couldn't stomach it, this loss and pain and growing madness as a new truth became clear:

They would not leave this place. Would have nothing left anyway. They would dissolve, mist to float into the fog around them.

~

It was agony like Dorian had never known. His very self, unraveled thread by thread.

The shape of the Lock, Elena had told Aelin, did not matter. It could have been a bird or a sword or a flower for all this place, this gate, cared. But their minds, what was left of them as they frayed, chose the shape they knew, the one that made the most sense. The Eye of Elena, born again—the Lock once more.

Aelin began screaming. Screaming and screaming.

His magic ripped away from that sacred, perfect place inside him.

It would kill them to forge it. It'd kill them both. They had come here out of the desperate hope they'd *both* leave.

And if they did not halt, if they did not stop this, neither would.

He tried to move his head. Tried to tell her. *Stop.*

His magic tore out of him, the Lock drinking it down, a force not to be leashed. An insatiable hunger that devoured them.

Stop. He tried to speak. Tried to pull back.

Aelin was sobbing now—sobbing through her teeth.

Soon. Soon now, the Lock would take everything. And that final destruction would be the most brutal and painful of all.

Would the gods make them watch as they claimed Elena's soul? Would he even have the chance, the ability, to try to help her, as he had promised Gavin? He knew the answer.

Stop.

Stop.

"Stop."

Dorian heard the words and for a heartbeat did not recognize the speaker.

Until a man appeared from one of those impossible-yet-possible doorways. A man who looked of flesh and blood, as they were, and yet shimmered at his edges.

His father.

CHAPTER 95

His father stood there. The man he had last seen on a bridge in a glass castle, and yet not.

There was kindness on his face. Humanity.

And sorrow. Such terrible, pained sorrow.

Dorian's magic faltered.

Even Aelin's magic slowed in surprise, the torrent thinning to a trickle, a steady and agonizing drain.

"Stop," the man breathed, staggering toward them, glancing at the ribbon of power, blinding and pure, feeding the Lock's formation.

Aelin said, "This cannot be stopped."

His father shook his head. "I know. What has begun can't be halted."

His father.

"No," Dorian said. "No, you cannot be here."

The man only looked down—to Dorian's side. To where a sword might be. "Did you not summon me?"

Damaris. He had been wearing Damaris within that ring of Wyrd-marks. In their world, their existence, he still did.

The sword, the unnamed god it served, apparently thought he had one truth left to face. One more truth, before his end.

"No," Dorian repeated. It was all he could think to say as he looked upon him, the man who had done such terrible things to all of them.

His father lifted his hands in supplication. "My boy," he only breathed.

Dorian had nothing to say to him. Hated that this man was here, at the end and beginning.

Yet his father looked to Aelin. "Let me do this. Let me finish this."

"What?" The word snapped from Dorian.

"You were not chosen," Aelin said, though the coldness in her voice faltered.

"Nameless is my price," the king said.

Aelin went still.

"Nameless is my price," his father repeated. The warning of an ancient witch, the damning words written on the back of the Amulet of Orynth. "For the bastard-born mark you bear, you are Nameless, yet am I not so as well?" He glanced between them, his eyes wide. "What is my name?"

"This is ridiculous," Dorian said through his teeth. "Your name is—"

But where there should have been a name, only an empty hole existed.

"You . . . ," Aelin breathed. "Your name is . . . How is it that you don't have one, that we don't know it?"

Dorian's rage slipped. And the agony of having his magic, his soul, shredded from him became secondary as his father said, "Erawan took it. Wiped it from history, from memory. An ancient, terrible spell, so power-ful it could only be used once. All so I might be his most faithful servant. Even I do not know my name, not anymore. I lost it."

"Nameless is my price," Aelin murmured.

Dorian looked then. At the man who had been his father. Truly looked at him.

"My boy," his father whispered again. And it was love—love and pride and sorrow that shone in his face.

His father who had been possessed as he had, who had tried to save them in his own way and failed. His father, who had everything taken from him, but had never bowed to Erawan—not entirely.

"I want to hate you," Dorian said, his voice breaking.

"I know," his father said.

"You destroyed everything." He couldn't stop his tears. Aelin's hand only tightened in his.

"I am sorry," his father breathed. "I am sorry for all of it, Dorian."

And even the way his father said his name—he had never heard him speak it like that.

Dismiss him. Throw him into some hell-world. That's what he should do.

And yet Dorian knew for whom he had really brought down Morath. For whom he'd buried that room of collars, the hateful tomb around them.

"I'm sorry," his father said again.

He did not need Damaris to tell him the words were true.

"Let me pay this debt," his father said, stepping closer. "Let me pay this, do this. Does Mala's blood not flow through my veins as well?"

"You don't have magic—not like we do," Aelin said, her eyes sorrowful.

His father met Aelin's stare. "I have enough—just enough in my blood. To help."

Dorian glanced over his shoulder, toward the archway that opened to Erilea. To home. "Then let him," he said, though the words did not come out with the iciness he wished. Only heaviness and exhaustion.

Aelin said softly to his father, "I had planned to before it got to the end."

"Then you will not be alone now," his father replied. Then the man smiled at him—a vision of the king, the father, he might have been. Had always been, despite what had befallen him. "I am grateful—that I got to see you again. One last time."

Dorian had no words, couldn't find them. Not as Aelin turned to him, tears sliding down her face as she said, "One of us has to rule."

Before Dorian could understand, before he could realize the agreement she'd just made, Aelin ripped her hand from his.

And shoved him through that gateway behind them. Back into their own world.

Roaring, Dorian fell.

As the Wyrdgate's misty realm vanished, Dorian saw Aelin take his father's hand.

CHAPTER 96

Rowan had not moved for the hours they'd stood beside Aelin and Dorian and watched them stare at nothing. Chaol had not so much as shifted, either.

The night passed, the stars wheeling over this hateful, cold place.

And then Dorian arched, gulping down air—and collapsed to his knees.

Aelin remained where she was. Remained standing and simply let go of Dorian's hand.

Rowan's very soul halted.

"No," Dorian rasped, scrambling toward her, trying to grip her hand again, to join her.

But the wound on Aelin's hand had sealed.

"No, *no!*" Dorian shouted, and Rowan knew then.

Knew what she had done.

The final deceit, the last lie.

"What happened?" Chaol demanded, reaching to hoist Dorian to his feet. The king sobbed, unbuckling the ancient sword from his side and hurling it away. Damaris thunked hollowly as it hit the earth.

Rowan just stared at Aelin.

At his mate, who had lied to him. To all of them.

"It wasn't enough—the two of us together. It would have destroyed us both," Dorian wept. "Yet Damaris somehow summoned my father, and . . . he took my place. He offered to take my place so she . . ." Dorian lunged, reaching for Aelin's hand, but he'd left the ring of Wyrdmarks.

They now kept him out.

A wall that sealed in Aelin.

The mating bond stretched thinner and thinner.

"She and him—they're going to end it," Dorian said, shaking.

Rowan barely heard the words.

He should have known. Should have known that if their plan failed, Aelin would never willingly sacrifice a friend. Even for this. Even for her own future.

She had known he'd try to keep her from forging the Lock if she'd mentioned that possibility, what she would do if it all went to hell. Had agreed to let Dorian help her only to get herself here. Would likely have dropped Dorian's hand without his father appearing.

Over—she had said so many times that she wished it to be over. He should have listened.

Chaol gripped Dorian, and the young lord said to Rowan, softly and sadly, "I'm sorry."

She had lied.

His Fireheart had lied.

And he would now watch her die.

Hand in hand with her enemy, Aelin allowed the magic to flow again. Allowed it to rage out of her.

The nameless king's power was nothing compared to Dorian's. But it was just enough, as he said. Just enough to help.

She had never intended for Dorian to destroy himself for this. Only for him to give just enough. And then she would have tossed him back into Erilea. So she might finish this alone.

Payment for ten years of selfishness, ten years away from Terrasen, ten years of running.

The agony became a numbing roar. Even the old king was panting through the pain.

Close now. The gold loops and circles of the Lock solidified.

Still more was needed. To bind this place, to bind all worlds.

He would never forgive her.

Her mate.

She had needed him to let her go, needed him to accept it. She would never have been able to do it, to come here, had he been begging her not to, had he been weeping as she had wanted to weep when she had kissed him one last time.

Come back to me, he had whispered.

She knew he'd wait. Until he faded into the Afterworld, Rowan would wait for her to return. To come back to him.

Aelin's magic tore out of her, a piece so vital and deep that she cried out, swaying. Only the king's grip kept her from falling.

The Lock was nearly finished, the two overlapping circles of the Eye almost complete.

Her magic writhed, begging her to stop. But she could not. Would not.

"Soon now," the king promised.

She found the man smiling.

"I was given a message for you," he said softly. His edges blurred, as the last of his power drained away. But he still smiled. Still looked at peace. "Your parents are . . . They are so very proud of you. They asked me to tell you that they love you so very much." He was nearly invisible now, his words little more than a whisper of wind. "And that the debt has been paid enough, Fireheart."

Then he was gone. The last of him flowed into the Lock. Wiped from existence.

She barely felt the tears on her face as she fell to her knees. As she gave and gave her magic, her very self. *My name is Aelin Ashryver Galath—*

A choking scream tore out of her as the last of the Lock sealed.

As the Lock became forged once more, as real as her own flesh.

As Aelin's magic completely vanished.

CHAPTER 97

She could barely move. Barely think.

Gone. Where light and life had flowed within her, there was nothing.

Not an ember. Only a droplet, just one, of water.

She clung to it, shielded it as they appeared, twelve figures through the portal behind her. Filtering into this place of places, this crossroads of eternity.

"It is done, then," said the one with many faces, approaching the Lock that hovered in midair. A flick of a ghostly, ever-changing hand and the Lock floated toward Aelin. Landed on her lap, gold and glittering.

"Summon us our world, girl," said the one with a voice like steel and screams. "And let us go home at last."

The final breaking. To send them back, to seal the gate. She'd use her last kernel of self, the final droplet, to seal the gate shut with the Lock. And then she would be gone.

Once upon a time, in a land long since burned to ash, there lived a young princess who loved her kingdom . . .

"Now," one with a voice like crashing waves ordered. "We have waited enough."

Aelin managed to lift her head. To look at their shimmering figures. Things from another world.

But amongst them, pressed into their ranks as if they held her captive . . .

Elena's eyes were wide. Agonized.

Who loved her kingdom . . .

One of them snapped their ghostly fingers at Aelin. "Enough of this."

Aelin looked up at her, at the goddess who had spoken. She knew that voice. Deanna.

Silently, Aelin surveyed them. Found the one like a shimmering dawn, the heart of a flame.

Mala did not look at her. Or at Elena, her own daughter.

Aelin turned away from the Fire-Bringer. And said to none of them in particular, "I should like to make a bargain with you."

The gods stilled. Deanna hissed, "A bargain? You dare to ask for a bargain?"

"I would hear it," said one whose voice was kind and loving.

The thing in her arm writhed, and Aelin willed it to reveal what they sought.

The portal to their realm. Sunlight over a rolling green country nearly blinded her. They whirled toward it, some sighing at the sight.

But Aelin said, "A trade. Before you fulfill *your* end."

Words were distant, so difficult and pained. But she forced them out.

The gods halted. Aelin only looked at Elena. Smiled softly.

"You have sworn to take Erawan with you. To destroy him," Aelin said, and the one with a voice like death faced her. As if remembering they had indeed promised such an outrageous thing.

"I would like to trade," she said again. And managed to point, with that arm that held all of eternity within it. "Erawan's soul for Elena's."

Mala turned toward her now. And stared.

Aelin said into their silence, "Leave Erawan to Erilea. But in exchange, leave Elena. Let her soul remain in the Afterworld with those she loves."

"Aelin," Elena whispered, and tears like silver flowed down her cheeks.

Aelin smiled at the ancient queen. "The debt has been paid enough."

She had wanted them to debate it—her friends. Had asked for a vote on the gate not just to ease the burden of the choice, but to hear it from them, to hear them say that they could defeat Erawan on their own. That Yrene Towers might stand a chance to destroy him.

So she could make this bargain, this trade, and not seal their doom entirely.

"Don't do it," Elena begged. Begged all those cold, impassive gods. "Don't agree to it."

Aelin said to them, "Leave her be, and go."

"Aelin, *please*," Elena said, weeping now.

Aelin smiled. "You bought me that extra time. So I might live. Let me buy this for you."

Elena covered her face with her hands and wept.

The gods looked among themselves. Then Deanna moved, graceful as a stag through a wood.

Aelin loosed a breath, bowing over her knees, as the goddess approached Elena.

No one but herself. She would allow no one but herself to be sacrificed in this final task.

Deanna laid her hands on either side of Elena's face. "I had hoped for this."

Then she pressed her hands together, Elena's head clasped between them.

A flare of light from Mala, in warning and pain, as Elena's eyes went wide. As Deanna squeezed.

And then Elena ruptured. Into a thousand shimmering pieces that faded as they fell.

Aelin's scream died in her throat, her body unable to rise as Deanna wiped her ghostly hands, and said, "We do not make bargains with mortals. Not any longer. Keep Erawan, if that is what you wish."

Then the goddess strode through the archway into her own world.

Aelin stared at the empty place where Elena had been only heartbeats before.

Nothing remained.

Not even a shimmering ember to send back into the Afterworld, to the mate left behind.

Nothing at all.

CHAPTER
98

It was breaking apart.

The mating bond.

Bowed over his knees, Rowan panted, a hand on his chest as the bond frayed.

He clung to it, wrapped his magic, his soul around it, as if it might keep her, wherever she was, from going to a place he could not follow.

He did not accept it. Would never accept this fate. Never.

Distantly, he heard Dorian and Chaol debating something. He didn't care.

The mating bond was breaking.

And there was nothing he could do but hold on.

⌒

One by one, the gods strode through the archway into their own world. Some sneered down at her as they passed.

They would not take Erawan.

Would not . . . would not do *anything*.

Her chest was hollow, her soul gutted out, and yet this . . .

And yet this . . .

Aelin clawed at the mist-shrouded ground-that-was-not-ground as the last of them vanished. Until only one remained.

A pillar of light and flame. Shining in the mists.

Mala lingered on the threshold of her world.

As if she remembered.

As if she remembered Elena, and Brannon, and who knelt before her. Blood of her blood. The recipient of her power. Her Heir.

"Seal the gate, Fire-Bringer," Mala said softly.

But the Lady of Light still hesitated.

And from far away, Aelin heard another woman's voice.

Make sure that they're punished someday. Every last one of them.

They will be, she'd sworn to Kaltain.

They had lied. Had betrayed Elena and Erilea, as they had believed themselves betrayed.

Their green sun-drenched world rippled away ahead.

Groaning, Aelin climbed to her feet.

She was no lamb to slaughter. No sacrifice on an altar of the greater good.

And she was not done yet.

Aelin met Mala's burning stare.

"Do it," Mala said quietly.

Aelin looked past her, toward that pristine world they had sought to return to for so long. And realized that Mala knew—saw the thoughts in her own head.

"Aren't you going to stop me?"

Mala only held out a hand.

In it lay a kernel of white-hot power. A fallen star.

"Take it. One last gift to my bloodline." She could have sworn Mala smiled. "For what you offered on her behalf. For fighting for her. For all of them."

Aelin staggered the few steps to the goddess, to the power she offered in her hand.

"I remember," Mala said softly, and the words were joy and pain and love. "I remember."

Aelin took the kernel of power from her palm.

It was the sunrise contained in a seed.

"When it is done, seal the gate and think of home. The marks will guide you."

Aelin blinked, the only sign of confusion she could convey as that power filled and filled and filled her, melding into the broken spots, the empty places.

Mala held out her hand again, and an image formed within it. Of the tattoo across Aelin's back.

The new tattoo, of spread wings, the story of her and Rowan written in the Old Language amongst the feathers.

A flick of Mala's fingers and symbols rose from it. Hidden within the words, the feathers.

Wyrdmarks.

Rowan had hidden Wyrdmarks in her tattoo.

Had inked Wyrdmarks all over it.

"A map home," Mala said, the image fading. "To him."

He'd suspected, somehow. That it might come to this. Had asked her to teach him so he might make this gamble.

And when Aelin looked behind her, to the archway into her own world, she indeed could . . . *feel* them. As if the Wyrdmarks he'd secretly inked onto her were a rope. A tether home.

A lifeline into eternity.

One last deceit.

Another voice whispered past then, a fragment of memory, spoken on a rooftop in Rifthold. *What if we go on, only to more pain and despair?*

Then it is not the end.

That power flowed and flowed into Aelin. Her lips curved upward.

It was not the end. And she was not finished.

But they were.

"To a better world," Mala said, and walked through the doorway into her own.

A better world.

A world with no gods. No masters of fate.

A world of freedom.

Aelin approached the archway to the gods' realm. To where Mala now walked across the shimmering grass, little more than a shaft of sunlight herself.

The Lady of Light halted—and lifted an arm in farewell.

Aelin smiled and bowed.

Far out, striding over the hills, the gods paused.

Aelin's smile turned into a grin. Wicked and raging.

It did not falter as she found the world she sought. As she dipped into that eternal, terrible power.

She had been a slave and a pawn once before. She would never be so again.

Not for them. Never for them.

The gods began shouting, running toward her, as Aelin ripped open a hole in their sky.

Right into a world she had seen only once. Had accidentally opened a portal into one night in a stone castle. Distant, baying howls cracked from the bleak gray expanse.

A portal into a hell-realm. A door now thrown open.

Aelin was still smiling when she closed the archway into the gods' world.

And left them to it, the sounds of their outraged, frightened screams ringing out.

There was still one last task to seal the gate forever.

Aelin unfurled her palm, studying the Lock she had forged. She let it float into the heart of this misty, door-filled space.

She was not afraid. Not as she opened her other palm, and power poured forth.

Mala's final gift. And defiance.

The force of a thousand exploding suns ruptured from Aelin's palm.

Lock. Close. Seal.

She willed it, willed it, and willed it. Willed it to close as she offered over her power.

But not that last bit of self.

The debt has already been paid enough.

A map home, a map inked in the words of universes, would lead the way.

More and more and more. But not all.

She would not give it up. Her innermost self.

She would not surrender.

They would not take this lingering kernel of her.

She would not yield it.

Light flowed through the Lock, fracturing like a prism, shooting to all those infinite doorways.

Closing and sealing and shutting. An archway to everywhere now sealing.

They would not destroy her. They would not be *allowed* to take this.

Come back to me.

More and more and more, Mala's last power funneling out of her and into the Lock.

They would not win. They couldn't take it—couldn't have her.

She refused.

She was screaming now. Screaming and roaring her defiance.

A beam of light shot to the archway behind her. Beginning to seal it, too.

She would live. She would *live*, and they could all go to hell.

A better world. With no gods, no fates.

A world of their own making.

Aelin bellowed and bellowed, the sound ringing out across all worlds.

They would not beat her. They would not get to take this, this most essential kernel of self. Of soul.

Once upon a time, in a land long since burned to ash, there lived a young princess who loved her kingdom . . . .

Her kingdom. Her home. She would see it again.

It was not over.

Behind her, the archway slowly sealed.

The odds were slim; the odds were insurmountable. She had not been destined to escape this—to reach this point and still be breathing.

Aelin's hand drifted to her heart and rested there.

It is the strength of this *that matters,* her mother had said, long ago. *Wherever you go, Aelin, no matter how far, this will lead you home.*

No matter where she was.

No matter how far.

Even if it took her beyond all known worlds.

Aelin's fingers curled, palm pressing into the pounding heart beneath. *This will lead you home.*

The archway to Erilea inched closed.

World-walker. Wayfarer.

Others had done it before. She would find a way, too. A way home.

No longer the Queen Who Was Promised. But the Queen Who Walked Between Worlds.

She would not go quietly.

She was not afraid.

So Aelin ripped out her power. Ripped out a chunk of what Mala had given her, a force to level a world, and flung it toward the Lock.

The final bit. The last bit.

And then Aelin leaped through the gate.

CHAPTER 99

She was falling.

Falling and being thrown.

The Wyrdgate sealed behind her, and yet she was not home.

As it closed, all worlds overlapped.

And she now fell through them.

One after another after another. Worlds of water, worlds of ice, worlds of darkness.

She slammed through them, faster than a shooting star, faster than light.

Home.

She had to find *home*—

Worlds of lights, worlds of towers that stretched to the skies, worlds of silence.

So many.

There were so many worlds, all of them miraculous, all of them so precious and perfect that even as she fell through them, her heart broke to see them.

Home. The way *home*—

She fumbled for the tether, the bond in her soul. Inked into her flesh.

Come back to me.

Aelin plunged through world after world after world.

Too fast.

She would hit her own world too fast, and miss it completely.

But she could not slow. Could not stop.

Tumbling, flipping over herself, she passed through them one by one by one by one by one.

It is the strength of this *that matters. Wherever you go, Aelin, no matter how far, this will lead you home.*

Aelin roared, a spark of self flashing through the sky.

The tether grew stronger. Tighter. Reeling her in.

Too fast. She had to slow—

She plummeted into the last of herself, into what remained, grappling for any sort of power to slow her racing.

She passed through a world where a great city had been built along the curve of a river, the buildings impossibly tall and glimmering with lights.

Passed through a world of rain and green and wind.

Roaring, she tried to slow.

She passed through a world of oceans with no land to be seen.

Close. Home was so close she could nearly smell the pine and snow. If she missed it, if she passed by it—

She passed through a world of snowcapped mountains under shining stars. Passed over one of those mountains, where a winged male stood beside a heavily pregnant female, gazing at those very stars. Fae.

They were *Fae*, but this was not her world.

She flung out a hand, as if she might signal them, as if they might somehow help her when she was nothing but an invisible speck of power—

The winged male, beautiful beyond reason, snapped his head toward her as she arced across his starry sky.

He lifted a hand, as if in greeting.

A blast of dark power, like a gentle summer night, slammed into her.

Not to attack—but to slow her down.

A wall, a shield, that she tore and plunged through.

But it slowed her. That winged male's power slowed her, just enough.

Aelin vanished from his world without a whisper.

And there it was.

There it was, the pine and the snow, the snaking spine of the mountains up her continent, the tangle of Oakwald to the right, the Wastes to the left. A land of many peoples, many beings.

She saw them all, familiar and foreign, fighting and at peace, in sprawling cities or hidden deep within the wilds. So many people, revealed to her. Erilea.

She threw herself into it. Grabbed the tether and bellowed as she hauled herself toward it. Down it.

Home.

Home.

Home.

It was not the end. She was not finished.

She willed herself, willed the world to halt. Just as the Wyrdgate slammed shut with a thunderous crack, all other doors with it.

And Aelin plunged back into her own body.

⁓

The Wyrdmarks faded into the rocky ground as the sun rose over Endovier.

Rowan was on his knees before Aelin, readying for her last breaths, for the end that he hoped would somehow take him, too.

He'd make it his end. When she went, he'd go.

But then he'd felt it. As the sun rose, he'd felt it, that surge down the frayed mating bond.

A blast of heat and light that welded the broken strands.

He didn't dare to breathe. To hope.

Even as Aelin collapsed to her knees where the Wyrdmarks had been.

Rowan was instantly there, reaching for her limp body.

A heartbeat echoed in his ears, into his own soul.

And that was her chest, rising and falling. And those were her eyes, opening slowly.

The scent of Dorian's and Chaol's tears replaced the salt of Endovier as Aelin stared up at Rowan and smiled.

Rowan held her to his chest and wept in the light of the rising sun.

A weak hand landed on his back, running over the tattoo he'd inked. As if tracing the symbols he'd hidden there, in a desperate, wild hope. "I came back," she rasped.

She was warm, but . . . cold, somehow. A stranger in her own body.

Aelin sat up, groaning at the ache along her bones.

"What happened?" Dorian asked, held upright by the arm Chaol had around his waist.

Aelin cupped her palms before her. A small lick of flame appeared within them.

Nothing more.

She looked at Rowan, then Chaol, and Dorian, their faces so haggard in the rising light of day.

"It's gone," she said quietly. "The power." She turned her hands, the flame rolling over them. "Only an ember remains."

They didn't speak.

But Aelin smiled. Smiled at the lack of that well within her, that churning sea of fire. And what did remain—a significant gift, yes, but nothing beyond the ordinary.

All that remained of what Mala had given her, in thanks for Elena.

But—

Aelin reached inward, toward that place inside her soul.

She put a hand to her chest. Put a hand there and felt the heart beating within.

The Fae heart. The cost.

She had given all of herself. Had given up her life.

The human life. Her mortality. Burned away, turned to nothing but dust between worlds.

There would be no more shifting. Only this body, this form.

She told them so. And told them what had occurred.

And when she was done, when Rowan remained holding her, Aelin held out her hand once more, just to see.

Perhaps it had been a final gift of Mala's, too. To preserve this piece of her that now formed in her hand—this droplet of water.

Her mother's gift.

What Aelin had saved until the end, had not wanted to part with until the very last dregs of her were given to the Lock, to the Wyrdgate.

Aelin held out her other hand, and the kernel of flame sputtered to life within it.

An ordinary gift. A Fire-Bringer no more.

But Aelin all the same.

CHAPTER
100

A prodding kick from Kyllian had Aedion awake before dawn.

He groaned as he stretched out on the cot in the Great Hall, the space still dim. Countless other soldiers slumbered around him, their heavy breathing filling the room.

He squinted at the small lantern that Kyllian held above him.

"It's time," Kyllian said, his eyes weary and red-rimmed.

They'd all looked better. Been better.

But they were still alive. A week after the Thirteen had sacrificed themselves and pushed back Morath's tide, they were alive. The witches' lives had bought them a full day of rest. One day, and then Morath had marched on Orynth's walls again.

Aedion slung the heavy fur cloak he'd been using for a blanket over his shoulders, wincing at the throbbing ache in his left arm. A careless wound, when he'd taken his attention off his shield for a moment and a Valg foot soldier had managed to slice him.

But at least he wasn't limping. And at least the wound the Valg prince had given him had healed.

Slinging his shield over that same shoulder, he scooped up his sword and belted it at his waist as he picked his way through the labyrinth of sleeping, exhausted bodies. A nod to Kyllian had the man striding for the city walls.

But Aedion turned left upon leaving the Great Hall, aiming for the north tower.

It was a lonely, cold walk to the room he sought. As if the entire castle were a tomb.

He knocked lightly on the wooden door near the top of the tower, and it immediately opened and shut, Lysandra slipping into the hall before Evangeline could stir in her bed.

In the flickering light of Aedion's candle, the shadows etched on Lysandra's face from a week of fighting from sunup to sundown were starker, deeper. "Ready?" he asked softly, turning back down the stairs.

It had become their tradition—for him to see Lysandra upstairs at night, then come to meet her in the morning. The only bright point in their long, horrible days. Sometimes, Evangeline accompanied them, narrating her time running messages and errands for Darrow. Sometimes, it was only the two of them trudging along.

Lysandra was silent, her graceful gait heavier with each step they descended.

"Breakfast?" Aedion asked as they neared the bottom.

A nod. The eggs and cured meats had given way to gruel and hot broth. Two nights ago, Lysandra had flown off in wyvern form after the fighting had ceased for the day, and returned an hour later with a hart clutched in each taloned foot.

That precious meat had been gone too soon.

They hit the bottom of the tower stairwell, and Aedion made to aim for the dining hall when she stopped him with a hand on his arm. In the dimness, he turned toward her.

But Lysandra, that beautiful face so tired, only slid her arms around his waist and pressed her head to his chest. She leaned enough of her weight into him that Aedion set down his candle on a nearby ledge and wrapped his arms tightly around her.

Lysandra sagged, leaning on him further. As if the weight of exhaustion was unbearable.

Aedion rested his chin atop her head and closed his eyes, breathing in her ever-changing scent.

Her heartbeat thundered against his own as he ran a hand down her spine. Long, soothing strokes.

They hadn't shared a bed. There was no place to do so anyway. But this, holding each other—she'd initiated it the night the Thirteen had sacrificed themselves. Had stopped him at this very spot and just held him for long minutes. Until whatever pain and despair eased enough that they could make the trek upstairs.

Lysandra pulled away, but not wholly out of his arms. "Ready?"

"We're running low on arrows," Petrah Blueblood said to Manon in the blue-gray light just before dawn. They strode through the makeshift aerie atop one of the castle's towers. "We might want to consider assigning some of the lesser covens to stay behind today to craft more."

"Do it," Manon said, surveying the still-unfamiliar wyverns who shared the space with Abraxos. Her mount was already awake. Staring out, solitary and cold, toward the battlefield beyond the city walls. Toward the blasted stretch of earth that no snow had been able to wipe away entirely.

She'd spent hours staring at it. Could barely pass over it during the endless fighting each day.

Her chest, her body, had been hollowed out.

Only moving, going through every ordinary motion, kept her from curling up in a corner of this aerie and never emerging.

She had to keep moving. Had to.

Or else she would cease to function at all.

She didn't care if it was obvious to others. Ansel of Briarcliff had sought her out in the Great Hall last night because of it. The red-haired warrior had slid onto the bench beside her, her wine-colored eyes missing none of the food that Manon had barely eaten.

"I'm sorry," Ansel had said.

Manon had only stared at her mostly untouched plate.

The young queen had surveyed the solemn hall around them. "I lost most of my soldiers," she said, her freckled face pale. "Before you arrived. Morath butchered them."

It had been an effort for Manon to draw her face toward Ansel. To meet her heavy stare. She blinked once, the only confirmation she could bother to make.

Ansel reached for Manon's slice of bread, pulling off a chunk and eating it. "We can share it, you know. The Wastes. If you break that curse."

Down the long table, some of the witches tensed, but did not look toward them.

Ansel went on, "I'll honor the old borders of the Witch Kingdom, but keep the rest." The queen rose, taking Manon's bread with her. "Just something to consider, should the opportunity arise." Then she was gone, swaggering off to her own cluster of remaining soldiers.

Manon hadn't stared after her, but the words, the offer, had lingered.

To share the land, reclaim what they'd had but not the entirety of the Wastes . . . *Bring our people home, Manon.*

The words had not stopped echoing in her ears.

"You could stay off the battlefield today, too," Petrah Blueblood now said, a hand on her mount's flank. "Use the day to help the others. And rest."

Manon stared at her.

Even with two Matrons dead, Iskra with them, and no sign of Petrah's mother, the Ironteeth had managed to remain organized. To keep Manon, Petrah, and the Crochans busy.

Every day, fewer and fewer walked off the battlefield.

"No one else rests," Manon said coldly.

"Everyone else manages to sleep, though," Petrah said. When Manon held the witch's gaze, Petrah said unblinkingly, "You think I do not see you, lying awake all night?"

"I do not need to rest."

"Exhaustion can be as deadly as any weapon. Rest today, then rejoin us tomorrow."

Manon bared her teeth. "The last I looked, *you* were not in charge."

Petrah didn't so much as lower her head. "Fight, then, if that is what you wish. But consider that many lives depend on you, and if you fall because you are so tired that you become sloppy, they will *all* suffer for it."

It was sage advice. Sound advice.

Yet Manon gazed out over the battlefield, the sea of darkness just becoming visible. In an hour or so, the bone drums would beat again, and the screaming din of war would renew.

She could not stop. Would not stop.

"I am not resting." Manon turned to seek out Bronwen in the Crochans' quarters. She, at least, would not have such ridiculous notions. Even if Manon knew Glennis would side with Petrah.

Petrah sighed, the sound grating down Manon's spine. "Then I shall see you on the battlefield."

The roar and boom of war had become a distant buzz in Evangeline's ears by midday. Even with the frigid wind, sweat ran down her back beneath her heavy layers of clothes as she made yet another sprint up the battlement stairs, message in hand. Darrow and the other old lords stood as they had these past two weeks: along the castle's walls, monitoring the battle beyond the city.

The message she'd received, straight from a Crochan who had landed so briefly that her feet had hardly touched the ground, had come from Bronwen.

Rare, Evangeline had learned, for either the Ironteeth or the Crochans to report anything to the humans. That the Crochan soldier had found *her*, had known who she was . . . It was pride, more than fear, that had Evangeline running up the stairs, then across the battlements to Lord Darrow.

Lord Darrow, Murtaugh at his side, had already stretched out a hand by the time Evangeline slid to a stop.

"Careful," Murtaugh warned her. "The ice can be treacherous."

Evangeline nodded, though she fully planned to ignore him. Even if she'd taken a spill down the stairs yesterday that thankfully no one had witnessed. Especially Lysandra. If she'd glimpsed the bruise that now bloomed over Evangeline's leg, the matching one on her forearm, she'd have locked her in the tower.

Lord Darrow read the message and frowned toward the city. "Bronwen reports they've spotted Morath hauling a siege tower to the western wall. It will reach us in an hour or two."

Evangeline looked past the chaos on the city walls, where Aedion and Ren and the Bane fought so valiantly, out beneath the melee in the skies, where witches fought witches and Lysandra flew in wyvern form.

Sure enough, a massive shape was lumbering toward them.

Evangeline's stomach dropped to her feet. "Is—is it one of those witch towers?"

"A siege tower is different," Darrow said with his usual gruffness. "Thank the gods."

"Still deadly," Murtaugh said. "Just in a different way." The old man frowned at Darrow. "I'll head down there."

Evangeline blinked at that. None—*none* of the older lords had gone to the front.

"To warn them?" Darrow asked carefully.

Murtaugh patted the hilt of his sword. "Aedion and Ren are stretched thin. Kyllian, too, if you want to keep telling yourself that he's the one leading them." Murtaugh didn't so much as lower his chin to Darrow, who stiffened. "I'll handle the western wall. And that siege tower." A wink at Evangeline. "We can't all be brave messengers, can we?"

Evangeline made herself smile, even though dread pooled in her. "Should—should I warn Aedion that you'll be there?"

"I'll tell him myself," Murtaugh said, and ruffled her hair as he walked by. "Be careful on the ice," he warned her again.

Darrow didn't try to stop him as Murtaugh walked off the battlements. Slow. He looked so slow, and old, and frail. And yet he kept his chin high. Back straight.

If she'd been able to choose a grandfather for herself, it would have been him.

Darrow's face was tight when Murtaugh disappeared at last.

"Old fool," Darrow said, worry in his eyes as he turned to the battle raging ahead.

CHAPTER 101

Human no more.

Aelin's breath rasped in her ears—her permanently arched, immortal ears—with each step back toward the camped army. Rowan remained at her side, a hand around her waist.

He hadn't let go of her once. Not once, since she'd come back.

Since she'd walked through worlds.

She could see them still. Even walking in silence under the trees, the darkness yielding toward the grayish light before dawn, she could see each and every one of those worlds she'd broken through.

Perhaps she'd never stop seeing them. Perhaps she alone in this world and all others knew what lay beyond the invisible walls separating them. How much *life* dwelled and thrived. Loved and hated and struggled to claw out a living.

So many worlds. More than she could contemplate. Would her dreams forever be haunted by them? To have glimpsed them, but been unable to explore—would that longing take root?

Oakwald's branches formed a skeletal lattice overhead. Bars of a cage. As her body, and this world, might be.

She shook off the thought. She had lived—lived, when she should have died. Even if her mortal self . . . that had been killed. Melted away.

The outer edges of the camp neared, and Aelin peered down at her hands. Cold—that was a trace of cold now biting into them.

Altered in every way.

Dorian said as they approached the first of the rukhin, "What are you going to tell them?"

The first words any of them had spoken since they'd begun the trek back here.

"The truth," Aelin said.

She supposed it was all she had to offer them, after what she'd done.

She said to Dorian, "I'm sorry—about your father."

The chill wind brushed the strands of Dorian's hair off his brow. "So am I," he said, resting a hand atop Damaris's hilt.

At his side, Chaol kept silent, though he glanced at the king every now and then. He'd look out for Dorian. As he always had, Aelin supposed.

They passed the first of the ruks, the birds eyeing them, and found Lorcan, Fenrys, Gavriel, and Elide waiting by the edge of the tents.

Chaol and Dorian murmured something about gathering the other royals, and peeled away.

Aelin remained close to Rowan as they approached their court. Fenrys scanned her from head to toe, nostrils flaring as he scented her. He staggered a step closer, horror creeping across his face. Gavriel only paled.

Elide gasped. "You did it, didn't you?"

But it was Lorcan who answered, stiffening, as if sensing the change that had come over her, "You—you're not human."

Rowan snarled in warning. Aelin just looked at them, the people who'd given so much and chosen to follow her here, their doom still remaining. To succeed, and yet to utterly fail.

Erawan remained. His army remained.

And there would be no Fire-Bringer, no Wyrdkeys, no gods to assist them.

"They're gone?" Elide asked softly.

Aelin nodded. She'd explain later. Explain it to all of them.

God-killer. That's what she was. A god-killer. She didn't regret it. Not one bit.

Elide asked Lorcan, "Do you—do you feel any different?" The lack of the gods who'd watched over them.

Lorcan peered up at the trees overhead, as if reading the answer in their entangled branches. As if searching for Hellas there. "No," he admitted.

"What does it mean," Gavriel mused, the first rays of sun beginning to gild his golden hair, "for them to be gone? Is there a hell-realm whose throne now sits vacant?"

"It's too early for that sort of philosophical bullshit," Fenrys said, and offered Aelin a half smile that didn't quite meet his eyes. Reproach lay there—not for her choice, but in not telling them. Yet he still tried to make light of it.

Doomed—that lovely, wolfish grin might be in its final days of existence.

They might all be in their last days of existence now. Because of her.

Rowan read it in her eyes, her face. His hand tightened on her waist. "Let's find the others."

⁓

Standing inside one of the khagan's fine war tents, Dorian held his hands out before a fire of his own making and winced. "That meeting could have gone better."

Chaol, seated across the fire, Yrene in his lap, toyed with the end of his wife's braid. "It really could have."

Yrene frowned. "I don't know how she didn't walk out and leave everyone to rot. I would have."

"Never underestimate the power of guilt when it comes to Aelin Gala-thynius," Dorian said, and sighed. The fire he'd summoned fluttered.

"She sealed the Wyrdgate." Yrene scowled. "The least they could do is be grateful for it."

"Oh, I have no doubt they are," Chaol said, frowning now as well. "But the fact remains that Aelin promised one thing, and did the opposite."

Indeed. Dorian didn't quite know what to think of Aelin's choice. Or that she'd even told them about it—about trading Erawan for Elena. The gods betraying her in turn.

And then Aelin destroying them for it.

"Typical," Dorian said, trying for humor and failing. Some part of him still felt as if he were in that place-of-places.

Especially when some part of him had been given up.

The magic that had felt bottomless only yesterday now had a very real, very solid stopping point. A mighty gift, yes, but he did not think he'd ever again be capable of shattering glass castles or enemy strongholds.

He hadn't yet decided whether it was a relief.

It was more power, at least, than Aelin had been left with. Gifted with, it sounded like. Aelin had burned through every ember of her own magic. What she now possessed was all that remained of what Mala had given her to seal the gate—to punish the gods who had betrayed them both.

The idea of it still made Dorian queasy. And the memory of Aelin choosing to throw him out of that non-place still made him grind his teeth. Not at her choice, but that his father—

He'd think about his father later. Never.

His nameless father, who had come for him in the end.

Chaol hadn't asked about it, hadn't pushed. And Dorian knew that whenever he was ready to talk about it, his friend would be waiting.

Chaol said, "Aelin didn't kill Erawan. But at least Erawan can never bring over his brothers. Or use the keys to destroy us all. We have that. She—you *both* did that."

There would be no more collars. No more rooms beneath a dark fortress to hold them.

Yrene ran her fingers through Chaol's brown hair, and Dorian tried to fight the ache in his chest at the sight. At the love that flowed so freely between them.

He didn't resent Chaol for his happiness. But it didn't stop the sharp slicing in his chest every time he saw them. Every time he saw the Torre healers, and wished Sorscha had found them.

"So the world was only partly saved," Yrene said. "Better than nothing."

Dorian smiled at that. He adored his friend's wife already. Likely would have married her, too, if he'd had the chance.

Even if his thoughts still drifted northward—to a golden-eyed witch who walked with death beside her and did not fear it. Did she think of him? Wonder what had become of him in Morath?

"Aelin and I still have magic," Dorian said. "Not like it was before, but we still have it. We're not entirely helpless."

"Enough to take on Erawan?" Chaol said, his bronze eyes wary. Well aware of the answer. "And Maeve?"

"We'll have to figure out a way," Dorian said. He prayed it was true.

But there were no gods left to pray to at all.

～

Elide kept one eye on Aelin while they washed themselves in the queen's tent. One eye on the deliciously warm water that had been brought in.

And kept warm by the woman in the tub beside her own.

As if in defiance of the horrible meeting they'd had with the khaganate royals upon Aelin's unexpected return.

Triumphant. But only in some regards.

One threat defeated. The other fumbled.

Aelin had hid it well, but the queen had her tells, too. Her utter stillness—the predatory angle of her head. The former had been present this morning. Utter stillness while she'd been questioned, criticized, shouted at.

The queen had not been this quiet since the day she'd escaped Maeve.

And it was not trauma that bowed her head, but guilt. Dread. Shame.

Nearly shoulder-deep in the high, long tubs, Elide had been the one to suggest a bath. To give Prince Rowan a chance to fly high and wide and take some of the edge off his temper. To give Aelin a moment to settle herself.

She'd planned to bathe this morning anyway. Though she'd imagined a different partner in the bath beside hers.

Not that Lorcan knew that. He'd only kissed her temple before striding off into the morning—to join Fenrys and Gavriel in readying the army to move out. Keep plunging northward.

Aelin scrubbed at her long hair, the flowing mass of it draped over her body. In the light of the braziers, the tattoos on the queen's back seemed to flow like a living black river.

"So your magic is still there?" Elide blurted.

Aelin slid turquoise eyes over to her. "Is your water warm?"

Elide snorted, dragging her fingers through the water. "Yes."

"You wish to know how much, exactly."

"Am I allowed to know?"

"I wasn't lying in the meeting," Aelin said, voice still hollow. She'd stood there and taken every shouted question from Princess Hasar, every frown of disapproval from Prince Sartaq. "It's . . ." She lifted her arms, and positioned her hands in the air above each other, a foot of space between them. "Here's where the bottom was before," she said, wriggling her lower fingers. She lifted her bottom hand until it hovered two inches from her top hand. "Here's where it is now."

"You've tested it?"

"I can feel it." Those turquoise eyes, despite all she'd done, were heavy. Solemn. "I've never felt a bottom before. Felt it without having to look for it." Aelin dunked her sudsy scalp in the water, scrubbing free the bubbles and oils. "Not so impressive, is it?"

"I never cared if you had magic or not."

"Why? Everyone else did." A flat question. Yes, when they'd been children, so many had feared what manner of power Aelin possessed. What she'd grow into.

"Who you are isn't your magic," Elide said simply.

"Isn't it?" Aelin rested her head on the back of the tub. "I liked my magic. Loved it."

"And being human?" Elide knew she shouldn't have dared ask, but it slipped out.

Aelin glanced sidelong at her. "Am I still human, deep down, without a human body to possess?"

Elide considered. "I suppose you're the only person who can decide that."

Aelin hummed, dunking under the water again.

When she emerged, Elide asked, "Are you afraid? Of facing Erawan in battle?"

Aelin hugged her knees, her tattoo flexing across her back. She was quiet for a long while.

"I am afraid of not reaching Orynth in time," she said at last. "If Erawan chooses to drag his carcass up there to fight me, I'll deal with it then."

"And Maeve? What if she arrives with Erawan, too?"

But Elide knew the answer. They would die. All of them.

There had to be some way—some way to defeat both of them. She supposed Anneith would be of no help now. And perhaps it was time for her to rely upon herself anyway. Even if the timing could have been far better.

"So many questions, Lady of Perranth."

Elide blushed, and reached for the soap, scrubbing her arms down. "Sorry."

"Do you now see why I didn't have you take the blood oath?"

"The Fae males challenge you all the time."

"Yes, but I like having you not bound to me." A soft sigh. "I didn't plan for any of this."

"For what?"

"To survive the Lock. The gate. To actually have to . . . rule. To live. I'm in uncharted territory, it seems."

Elide considered. Then pulled the golden ring from her finger. Silba's ring—not Mala's.

"Here," she said, extending the ring between their tubs, suds dripping off her fingers.

Aelin blinked at the ring. "Why?"

"Because between the two of us, you're more likely to face Erawan or Maeve."

Aelin didn't reach for it. "I'd rather you keep it."

"And I'd rather you have it," Elide challenged, holding the queen's stare. She asked softly, "Haven't you given enough, Aelin? Won't you let one of us do something for you?"

Aelin glanced down to the ring. "I failed. You realize that, don't you?"

"You put the keys back in the gate. That is not failure. And even if you had failed in that, I would give this ring to you."

"I owe it to your mother to see that you survive this."

Elide's chest tightened. "You owe it to my mother to *live*, Aelin." She leaned closer, practically pushing the ring into Aelin's face. "Take it. If not for me, then for her."

Aelin stared at the ring again. And then took it.

Elide tried not to sigh as the queen slid it onto her finger.

"Thank you," Aelin murmured.

Elide was about to answer when the tent flaps opened, icy air howling in—along with Borte. "You didn't invite me for a bath?" the rukhin asked, frowning dramatically at the queen.

Aelin's lips curved upward. "I thought rukhin were too tough for baths."

"Do you see how nice the men keep their hair? You think that doesn't imply an obsession with cleanliness?" Borte strode across the royal tent and plopped onto the stool beside the queen's tub. Not at all seeming to care that the queen or Elide were naked.

It took all of Elide's will not to cover herself up. At least with Aelin in the adjacent tub, the lip of the bath was high enough to offer them privacy. But with Borte sitting *above* them like this—

"Here are my thoughts," Borte declared, flicking the end of one of her braids.

Aelin smiled slightly.

"Hasar is cranky and cold. Sartaq is used to these conditions and doesn't care. Kashin is trying to make the best of it, because he's so damned nice, but they're all just a *little* nervous that we're marching on a hundred thousand soldiers, potentially more on the way, and that Erawan is *not* out of commission. Neither is Maeve. So they're pissed. They like you, but they're pissed."

"I'd gathered as much," Aelin said drily, "when Hasar called me a stupid cow."

It had taken all of Elide's restraint not to lunge for the princess. And from the growl that had come from the Fae males, even Lorcan, gods above, she knew it had been just as difficult for them.

Aelin had only inclined her head to the princess and smiled. Just as she was smiling now.

Borte waved off Aelin's words. "Hasar calls everyone a stupid cow. You're in good company." Another smile from Aelin at that. "But I'm not here to talk about that. I want to talk about you and me."

"My favorite subject," Aelin said, chuckling slightly.

Borte grinned. "You're alive. You made it. We all thought you'd be dead." She drew a line across her neck for emphasis, and Elide cringed. "Sartaq is probably going to have me leading one of the flanks into battle, but I've done that. Been good at that." That grin widened. "I want to lead *your* flank."

"I don't have a flank."

"Then who shall you ride with into battle?"

"I hadn't gotten that far," Aelin said, lifting a brow. "Since I expected to be dead."

"Well, when you do, expect me to be in the skies above you. I'd hate for the battle to be dull."

Only the fierce-eyed rukhin would have the nerve to call marching on a hundred thousand soldiers *dull*.

But before Aelin could say anything, or Elide could ask Borte whether the ruks were ready against the wyverns, the ruk rider was gone.

When Elide looked to Aelin, the queen's face was somber.

Aelin nodded toward the tent flaps. "It's snowing."

"It's been snowing with little rest for days now."

Aelin's swallow was audible. "It's a northern snow."

The storm slammed into the camp, so fierce that Nesryn and Sartaq had given the ruks orders to hunker down for the day and night.

As if crossing into Terrasen days earlier had officially put them into brutal winter.

"We keep going north," Kashin was saying, lounging by the fire in Hasar's sprawling tent.

"Like there is another option," Hasar snipped, sipping from her mulled wine. "We've come this far. We might as well go all the way to Orynth."

Nesryn, seated on a low sofa with Sartaq, still wondered what, exactly, she was doing in these meetings. Wondered at the fact that she sat with the royal siblings, the Heir to the khaganate at her side.

Empress. The word seemed to hang over her every breath, every movement.

Sartaq said, "Our people have faced odds like this before. We'll face them again."

Indeed, Sartaq had stayed up long into the night these weeks reading the accounts and journals of khaganate warriors and leaders from generations past. They'd brought a trunk of them from the khaganate—for this reason. Most Sartaq had already read, he'd told her. But it never hurt to refresh one's mind.

If it bought them a shot against a hundred thousand soldiers, she wouldn't complain.

"We won't be facing them at all if this storm doesn't let up," Hasar said, frowning toward her sealed tent flaps. "When I return to Antica, I am never leaving again."

"No taste for adventure, sister?" Kashin smiled faintly.

"Not when it's in a frozen hell," Hasar grumbled.

Nesryn huffed a soft laugh, and Sartaq slipped his arm around her shoulders. A casual, careless bit of contact.

"We keep going," Sartaq said. "All the way to the walls of Orynth. We swore as much, and we do not renege on our promises."

Nesryn would have fallen in love with him for that statement alone. She leaned into him, savoring his warmth, in silent thanks.

"Then let us pray," Kashin said, "that this storm does not slow us so much that there's nothing left of Orynth to defend."

CHAPTER
102

They had cleared a small chamber near the Great Hall for his viewing.

The room lit by whatever candles could be spared, the ancient stones were cast in flickering relief around the table where they'd laid him.

Lysandra lingered in the doorway as she gazed toward the sheet-draped body at the back of the room.

Ren knelt before him, head bowed. As he had done for hours now. Ever since word had come at sundown that Murtaugh had fallen.

Hewn down by Valg foot soldiers as he sought to staunch their flow over the city walls courtesy of one of their siege towers.

They had carried Murtaugh back from the city wall, a throng of soldiers around him.

Even from the skies, flying in with the witches after Morath had given the order to halt once more, Lysandra had heard Ren's scream. Had seen from high above as Ren ran down the battlements to the body borne through the city streets.

Aedion had been there within seconds. Had kept Ren upright as the young lord had sobbed, and had half carried him here, despite the fresh wounds on the prince.

And so Aedion had stayed. Standing vigil beside Ren all this time, a hand on his shoulder.

Lysandra had come with Evangeline. Had held the stunned girl while she cried, and lingered while Evangeline strode to Murtaugh's body to press a kiss to his brow. As much as the sheet would allow them to see, after what the Valg had done.

She had escorted her ward from the chamber just as Darrow and the others arrived.

Lysandra hadn't bothered to look at Darrow, at any of them who hadn't dared to do what Murtaugh had done. His death, they'd learned, had rallied the men at the wall. Made them topple that siege tower. A lucky, costly victory.

Lysandra had helped Evangeline bathe, made sure she got a hot meal, and tucked her into bed before returning.

Finding Aedion still beside Ren, his hand still on the kneeling lord's shoulder.

So she'd lingered here, at the doorway. Her own vigil, while the well of her power refilled, while the wounds she'd sustained healed over inch by inch.

Aedion murmured something to Ren, and withdrew his hand. She wondered if they were his first words in hours.

Aedion turned toward her then, blinking. Hollowed out. Gutted. Exhausted and grieving and bearing a weight she couldn't stand to see.

Even Aedion's usual stalking gait was barely more than a trudge.

She followed him out, glancing back only once to where Ren still knelt, head bowed.

Such terrible silence around him.

Lysandra kept pace beside Aedion as he turned toward the dining hall. At this hour, food would be scarce, but she'd find it. For both of them. Would go hunting if she needed to.

She opened her mouth to tell Aedion just that.

But tears slid down his face, cutting through blood and grime.

Lysandra stopped, tugging him into a halt.

He didn't meet her eyes as she wiped his tears away from one cheek. Then the other.

"I should have been at the western wall," he said, voice breaking.

She knew no words would comfort him. So she wiped Aedion's tears again, tears he would only show in this shadowed hall, after all others had found their beds.

And when he still didn't meet her stare, she cupped his face, lifting his head.

For a heartbeat, for eternity, they stared at each other.

She couldn't stand it, the bleakness, the grief, in his face. Couldn't endure it.

Lysandra rose onto her toes and brushed her mouth over his.

A whisper of a kiss, a promise of life when death hovered.

She pulled away, finding Aedion's face as distraught as it had been before.

So she kissed him again. And lingered by his mouth as she whispered, "He was a good man. A brave and noble man. So are you." She kissed him a third time. "And when this war is over, however it may end, I will still be here, with you. Whether in this life or the next, Aedion."

He closed his eyes, as if breathing in her words. His chest indeed heaved, his broad shoulders shaking.

Then he opened his eyes, and they were pure turquoise flame, fueled by that grief and anger and defiance at the death around them.

He gripped her waist in one hand, the other plunging into her hair, and tipped her head back as his mouth met hers.

The kiss seared her down to her ever-changing bones, and she wrapped her arms around his neck as she held him tightly.

Alone in the dark, quiet hall, death squatting on the battlefield nearby, Lysandra gave herself to that searing kiss, to Aedion, unable to stop her moan as his tongue flicked against hers.

The sound was his unleashing, and Aedion twisted them, backing her against the wall. She arched, desperate to feel him against all of her. He growled into her mouth, and the hand at her hip slid to her thigh, hoisting it around his waist as he ground into her, exactly where she needed him.

Aedion tore his mouth from hers and began to explore her neck, her jaw, her ear. She breathed his name, running her hands down his powerful back as it flexed under her touch.

More. More. More.

More of this life, this fire to burn away all shadows.

More of him.

Lysandra slid her hands to his chest, fingers digging into the breast of his jacket, seeking the warm skin beneath. Aedion only nipped at her ear, dragged his teeth along her jaw, and seized her mouth in another plundering kiss that had her moaning again.

Footsteps scuffed down the hall, along with a pointed cough, and Aedion stilled.

Loud—they must have been so loud—

But Aedion didn't budge, though Lysandra unwrapped her leg from around his waist. Just as the sentry walked past, eyes down.

Walked past *quickly*.

Aedion tracked the man the entire time, nothing human in Aedion's eyes. An apex predator who had found his prey at last.

No, not prey. Never with him.

But his partner. His mate.

When the sentry had vanished around the corner, no doubt running to tell everyone what he'd interrupted, when Aedion leaned to kiss her again, Lysandra halted him with a gentle hand to his mouth. "Tomorrow," she said softly.

Aedion let out a snarl—though one without any bite.

"Tomorrow," she said, and kissed him on the cheek, stepping out of his arms. "Live through tomorrow, fight through tomorrow, and we'll . . . continue."

His breathing was ragged, eyes wary. "Was this from pity?" A broken, miserable question.

Lysandra slid her hand against his stubble-coated cheek and pressed her mouth against his. Let herself taste him again. "It is because I am sick of all this death. And I needed you."

Aedion made a low, pained sound, so Lysandra kissed him a final time. Went so far as to run her tongue along the seam of his lips. He opened for her, and then they were tangled in each other again, teeth and tongues and hands roaming, touching, tasting.

But Lysandra managed to extract herself again, her breathing as jagged as his own.

"Tomorrow, Aedion," she breathed.

⁓

"We have enough left in our arsenal for our archers to use for another three days, maybe four if they conserve their stores," Lord Darrow said, arms crossed as he read through the tally.

Manon didn't dislike the old man—part of her even admired his iron-fisted control. But these war councils each evening were beginning to tire her.

Especially when they brought bleaker and bleaker news.

Yesterday, there had been one more standing in this chamber. Lord Murtaugh.

Today, only his grandson sat in a chair, his eyes red-rimmed. A living wraith.

"Food stores?" Aedion asked from the other side of the table. The general-prince had seen better days, too. They all had. Every face in this room had the same bleak, battered expression.

"We have food for a month at least," Darrow said. "But none of that will matter without anyone to defend the walls."

Captain Rolfe stepped up to the table. "The firelances are down to the dregs. We'll be lucky if they last through tomorrow."

"Then we conserve them, too," Manon said. "Use them only for any higher-ranking Valg that make it over the city walls."

Rolfe nodded. Another man she begrudgingly admired—though his swaggering could grate.

It was an effort not to look to the sealed doors to the chamber. Where Asterin and Sorrel should have been waiting. Defending.

Instead, Petrah and Bronwen stood there. Not as her new Second and Third, but just representatives from their own factions.

"Let's say we make the arrows last for four days," Ansel of Briarcliff said, frowning deeply. "And make the firelances last for three, if used conservatively. Once they're out, what remains?"

"The catapults still work," provided one of the silver-haired Fae royals. The female one.

"They're for inflicting damage far out on the field, though," said Prince Galan, who, like Aedion, bore Aelin's eyes. "Not close fighting."

"Then we have our swords," Aedion said hoarsely. "Our courage."

The latter, Manon knew, was running low, too.

"We can keep the Ironteeth at bay," Manon said, "but cannot also aid you at the walls."

They were indeed fighting a relentless tide that did not diminish.

"So is this the end, then?" Ansel asked. "In four, five days, we offer our necks to Morath?"

"We fight to the last of us," Aedion growled. "To the very last one."

Even Lord Darrow did not object to that. So they departed, meeting over.

There wasn't anything else to discuss. Within a few days, they'd all be a grand feast for the crows.

CHAPTER
103

The storm had halted their army entirely.

On the first morning, it raged so fiercely that Rowan hadn't been able to see a few feet before him. Ruks had been grounded, and only the hardiest of scouts had been sent out—on land.

So the army sat there. Not fifty miles over Terrasen's border. A week from Orynth.

Had Aelin possessed her full powers—

Not her full powers. Not anymore, Rowan reminded himself as he sat in their war tent, his mate and wife and queen on the low-lying sofa beside him.

Aelin's full powers were now . . . he didn't quite know. Where they'd been at Mistward, perhaps. When she still had that self-inflicted damper. Not as little as when she'd arrived, but not as much as when she'd encircled all of Doranelle with her flame.

Certainly not enough to face Erawan and walk away. And Maeve.

He didn't care. Didn't give a shit whether she had all the power of the sun, or not an ember.

It had never mattered to him anyway.

Outside, the wind howled, the tent shuddering.

"Is it always this bad?" Fenrys asked, frowning at the shaking tent walls.

"Yes," Elide and Aelin said, then shared a rare smile.

A miracle, that smile on Aelin's mouth.

But Elide's faded as she said, "This storm could last days. It could dump three feet."

Lorcan, lingering near the brazier, grunted. "Even once the snow stops, there will be that to contend with. Soldiers losing toes and fingers to the cold and wet."

Aelin's smile vanished entirely. "I'll melt as much as I can."

She would. She'd bring herself to the edge of burnout to do it. But together, if they linked their powers, the force of Rowan's magic might be enough to melt a path. To keep the army warm.

"We'll still have an army who arrives at Orynth exhausted," Gavriel said, rubbing his jaw.

How many days had Rowan seen him gaze northward, toward the son who fought in Orynth? Wondering, no doubt, if Aedion still lived.

"They're professionals," Fenrys said drily. "They can handle it."

"Going the long way around will only increase the exhaustion," Lorcan said.

"The last we heard," Rowan said, "Morath held Perranth." A pained wince from Elide at that. "We won't risk crossing too close to it. Not when it would mean potentially getting entangled in a conflict that would only delay our arrival in Orynth and thin our numbers."

"I've looked at the maps a dozen times." Gavriel frowned to where they were laid out on the worktable. "There's no alternative way to Orynth—not without drawing too close to Perranth."

"Perhaps we'll be lucky," Fenrys said, "and this storm will have hit the entire North. Maybe freeze some of Morath's forces for us."

Rowan doubted they'd be that lucky. He had a feeling that any luck they possessed had been spent with the woman sitting beside him.

Aelin looked at him, grave and tired. He could not imagine what it felt like. She had yielded all of herself. Had given up her humanity, her magic. He knew it was the former that left that haunted, bruised look in her eyes. That made her a stranger in her own body.

Rowan had taken the time last night to reacquaint her with certain parts of that body. And his own. Had spent a long while doing so, too. Until that haunted look had vanished, until she was writhing beneath him, burning while he moved in her. He hadn't stopped his tears from falling, even when they'd turned to steam before they hit her body, and there had been tears on her own face, bright as silver in the flame, while she'd held him tight.

Yet this morning, when he'd nuzzled her awake with kisses to her jaw, her neck, that haunted look had returned. And lingered.

First her scars. Then her mortal, human body.

Enough. She had given enough. He knew she planned to give more.

A rukhin scout called for the queen from the tent flaps, and Aelin gave a quiet command to enter. But the scout only poked in her head, her eyes wide. Snow covered her hood, her eyebrows, her lashes. "Your Majesty. Majesties," she corrected, glancing at him. Rowan didn't bother to tell her he was simply and would forever be *Your Highness*. "You must come." The scout panted hard enough for her breath to curl in the chilled air leaking through the tent flaps. "All of you."

It took minutes to don their warmer layers and gear, to brace for the snow and wind.

But then they were all inching through the drifts, the scout guiding them past half-buried tents. Even under the trees, there was little shelter.

Yet then they were at the edge of the camp, the blinding snows roaring past. Veiling what the scout pointed to as she said, "Look."

At his side, Aelin stumbled a step. Rowan reached for her to keep her from falling.

But she hadn't been falling. She'd been lurching forward—as if to run ahead.

Rowan saw at last what she beheld. Who emerged between the trees.

Against the snow, he was nearly invisible with his white fur. Would have been invisible were it not for the golden flame flickering between his proud, towering antlers.

The Lord of the North.

And at his feet, all around him . . . The Little Folk.

Snow clinging to her lashes, a small sound came out of Aelin as the creature nearest curled its hand, beckoning. As if to say, *Follow us.*

The others gaped in silence at the magnificent, proud stag who had come to greet them.

To guide home the Queen of Terrasen.

But then the wind began to whisper, and it was not the song that Rowan usually heard.

No, it was a voice that they *all* heard as it streamed past them.

Doom is upon Orynth, Heir of Brannon. You must hurry.

A chill that had nothing to do with the cold skittered down Rowan's skin.

"The storm," Aelin blurted, the words swallowed by the snow.

You must hurry. We will show you the way, swift and unseen.

Aelin only stilled. Said to that voice, as ancient as the trees, as old as the rocks between them, "You have already helped me so many times."

And you have given much yourself, Heir of Brannon. We who remember him know he would have made such a choice, had he been able to do so. Oakwald shall never forget Brannon, or his Heir.

Aelin straightened, scanned the trees, the snow-whipped wind.

Dryad. That was the word he sought. Dryad. A tree spirit.

"What is your cost?" Aelin asked, her voice louder now.

"Do you really want to ask?" Fenrys muttered. Rowan snarled at him.

But Aelin had gone still as she waited for the dryad to answer. The voice of Oakwald, of the Little Folk and creatures who had long cared for it.

A better world, the dryad replied at last. *Even for us.*

~

The army was a flurry of activity as it hauled itself into preparing to march—to race northward.

But Aelin dragged Rowan into their tent. To the pile of books Chaol and Yrene had brought from the southern continent.

She ran a finger over the titles, searching, scanning.

"What are you doing?" her mate asked.

Aelin ignored the question and hummed as she found the book she sought. She leafed through it, careful not to tear the ancient pages. "A stupid cow I might be," she muttered, rotating the book to show Rowan the page she sought, "but not without options."

Rowan's eyes danced. *You're including me in this particular scheme, Princess?*

Aelin smirked. *I wouldn't want you to feel left out.*

He angled his head. "We need to hurry, then."

Listening to the ruckus of the readying army beyond their tent, Aelin nodded. And began.

CHAPTER
104

The sweat and blood on him quickly freezing, Aedion panted as he leaned against the battered city walls and watched the encamped enemy pull back for the night.

A sick sort of joke, a cruel torment, for Morath to halt at each sundown. As if it were some sort of civility, as if the creatures who infested so many of the soldiers below required light.

He knew why Erawan had ordered it so. To wear them down day by day, to break their spirits rather than let them go out in raging glory.

It wasn't just the victory or conquest that Erawan desired, but their complete surrender. Their begging for it to be over, for him to end them, rule them.

Aedion ground his teeth as he limped down the battlements, the light quickly fading, the temperature plummeting.

Five days.

The weapons they'd estimated running out in three or four days had lasted until today. Until now.

Down the wall, one of the Mycenians sent a plume of flame onto the

Valg still trying to scale the siege ladder. Where it burned, demons fell away.

Rolfe stood by the woman wielding the firelance, his face as bloodied and sweaty as Aedion's.

A black-armored hand clamped onto the battlement beside Aedion as he passed by, grappling for purchase.

Barely looking, Aedion slammed out his ancient shield. A yelp and fading cry was his only confirmation that the rogue soldier had gone tumbling to the ground.

Rolfe smiled grimly as Aedion halted, the weight of his armor like a thousand stones. Overhead, Crochans and Ironteeth flew slowly back across the city walls, red capes drooping over brooms, leathery wings beating irregularly. Aedion watched the sky until he saw the riderless wyvern he looked for every day, every night.

Spotting him, too, Lysandra banked and began a slow, pained descent toward the city wall.

So many dead. More and more each day. Those lost lives weighed his every step. Nothing he could do would ever make it right—not really.

"The archers are out," Aedion said to Rolfe by way of greeting as Lysandra drew closer, blood both her own and from others on her wings, her chest. "No more arrows."

Rolfe jerked his chin toward the Mycenian warrior still setting off her firelance in sputtering fits and bursts.

Lysandra landed, shifting in a flash, and was instantly at Aedion's side, tucked under his shield arm. A soft, swift kiss was their only greeting. The only thing he looked forward to every night.

Sometimes, once they'd been bandaged and eaten something, he'd manage to get more than that. Often, they didn't bother to wash up before finding a shadowed alcove. Then it was nothing but her, the sheer perfection of her, the small sounds she made when he licked up her throat, when his hands slowly, so slowly, explored each inch of her. Letting her set the pace, show him and tell him how far she wished to go. But not that final joining, not yet.

Something for them both to live for—that was their unspoken vow.

She reeked of Valg blood, but Aedion still pressed another kiss to Lysandra's temple before he looked back at Rolfe. The Pirate Lord smiled grimly.

Well aware that these would likely be their final days. Hours.

The Mycenian warrior aimed her firelance again, and the lingering Valg tumbled away into the darkness, little more than melted bones and fluttering cloth.

"That's the last of it," Rolfe said quietly.

It took Aedion a heartbeat to realize he didn't mean the final soldier of the evening.

The Mycenian warrior set down her firelance with a heavy, metallic thud.

"The firelances are done," Rolfe said.

Darkness fell over Orynth, so thick even the flames of the castle shriveled.

On the castle battlements, Darrow silent at her side, Evangeline watched the trudging lines of soldiers come in from the walls, from the skies.

Bone drums began to beat.

A heartbeat, as if the enemy army on the plain were one massive, rising beast now readying to devour them.

Most days, they only beat from sunup to sundown, the noise blocked out by the din of battle. That they had started it anew as the sun vanished . . . Her stomach churned.

"Tomorrow," Lord Sloane murmured from where he stood beside Darrow. "Or the day after. It will be done then."

Not victory. Evangeline knew that now.

Darrow said nothing, and Lord Sloane clapped him on the shoulder before heading inside.

"What happens at the end?" Evangeline dared ask Darrow.

The old man gazed across the city, the battlefield full of such terrible darkness.

"Either we surrender," he said, voice hoarse, "and Erawan makes slaves of us all, or we fight until we're all carrion."

Such stark, harsh words. Yet she liked that about him—that he did not soften anything for her. "Who shall decide what we do?"

His gray eyes scanned her face. "It would fall upon us, the Lords of Terrasen."

Evangeline nodded. Enemy campfires flickered to life, their flames seeming to echo the beat of their bone drums.

"What would you decide?" Darrow's question was quiet, tentative.

She considered it. No one had ever asked her such a thing.

"I should have very much liked to live at Caraverre," Evangeline admitted. She knew he did not recognize it, but it didn't matter now, did it? "Murtaugh showed me the land—the rivers and mountains right nearby, the forests and hills." An ache throbbed in her chest. "I saw the gardens by the house, and I would have liked to have seen them in spring." Her throat tightened. "I would have liked for that to have been my home. For this . . . for all of Terrasen to have been my home."

Darrow said nothing, and Evangeline set a hand on the castle stones, gazing to the west now, as if she could see all the way to Allsbrook and the small territory in its shadow. To Caraverre.

"That's what Terrasen has always meant to me, you know," Evangeline went on, speaking more to herself. "As soon as Aelin freed Lysandra, and offered to let us join her court, Terrasen has always meant home. A place where . . . where the sort of people who hurt us don't get to live. Where anyone, regardless of who they are and where they came from and what their rank is can dwell in peace. Where we can have a garden in the spring, and swim in the rivers in the summer. I've never had such a thing before. A home, I mean. And I would have liked for Caraverre, for Terrasen, to have been mine." She chewed on her lip. "So I would choose to fight. Until the very end. For my home, new as it is. I choose to fight."

Darrow was silent for so long that she peered up at him.

She'd never seen his eyes so sad, as if the weight of all his years truly settled upon them.

Then he only said, "Come with me."

She followed him down the battlements and into the warmth of the castle, along the various winding hallways, all the way to the Great Hall, where a too-small evening meal was being laid out. One of their last.

No one bothered to look up from their plates as Evangeline and Darrow passed between the long tables crammed with drained and injured soldiers.

Darrow didn't look at them, either, as he went right up to the line of people waiting for their food. Right up to Aedion and Lysandra, their arms looped around each other while they waited their turn. As it should have been from the start—the two of them together.

Aedion, sensing Darrow's approach, turned. The general looked worn through.

He knew, then. That tomorrow or the day after would be their last. Lysandra gave Evangeline a small smile, and Evangeline knew that she was aware, too. Would try to find a way to get her out before the end.

Even if Evangeline would never allow it.

Darrow unbuckled the sword at his side and extended it to Aedion.

Silence began to ripple through the hall at the sight of the sword—Aedion's sword. The Sword of Orynth.

Darrow held it between them, the ancient bone pommel gleaming. "Terrasen is your home."

Aedion's haggard face remained unmoved. "It has been since the day I arrived here."

"I know," Darrow said, gazing at the sword. "And you have defended it far more than any natural-born son would ever be expected to. Beyond what anyone might ever reasonably be asked to give. You have done so without complaint, without fear, and have served your kingdom nobly." He extended the sword. "You will forgive a proud old man who sought to do so as well."

Aedion slid his arm from Lysandra's shoulder, and took the sword in his hands. "Serving this kingdom has been the great honor of my life."

"I know," Darrow repeated, and glanced down to Evangeline before he looked to Lysandra. "Someone very wise recently told me that Terrasen is not merely a place, but an ideal. A home for all those who wander, for those who need somewhere to welcome them with open arms." He inclined his head to Lysandra. "I formally recognize Caraverre and its lands, and you as its lady."

Lysandra's fingers found Evangeline's and squeezed tight.

"For your unwavering courage in the face of the enemy gathered at our doorstep, for all you have done to defend this city and kingdom, Caraverre shall be recognized, and yours forevermore." A glance between her and Aedion. "Any heirs you bear shall inherit it, and their heirs after them."

"Evangeline is my heir," Lysandra said thickly, resting a warm hand on her shoulder.

Darrow smiled slightly. "I know that, too. But I should like to say one more thing, on this perhaps final night of ours." He inclined his head to Evangeline. "I never fathered any offspring, nor did I adopt any. It would be an honor to name such a wise, brave young lady as my heir."

Absolute silence. Evangeline blinked—and blinked again.

Darrow went on in the stunned quiet, "I should like to face my enemies knowing that the heart of my lands, of this kingdom, will beat on in the chest of Evangeline. That no matter the gathering shadow, Terrasen will always live in someone who understands its very essence without needing to be taught. Who embodies its very best qualities." He gestured to Lysandra. "If that is agreeable to you."

To make her his ward—and a lady . . . Evangeline clasped Darrow's hand. He squeezed back.

"I . . ." Lysandra blinked, and turned to her, eyes bright. "It is not my call, is it?"

So Evangeline smiled up at Darrow. "I would very much like that."

⁓

The bone drums beat all night long.

What new horrors would be unleashed with the dawn, Manon didn't know.

Sitting beside Abraxos in the aerie tower, she stared with him at the endless sea of blackness.

It would be over soon. The desperate hope of Aelin Galathynius had flickered out.

Would any be able to escape once the city walls were breached? And where would they even go? Once Erawan's shadow settled, would there be any stopping him?

Dorian—Dorian could. If he had gotten the keys. If he had survived.

He might be dead. Might be marching on them right now, a black collar around his throat.

Manon leaned her head against Abraxos's warm, leathery side.

She would not be able to see her people home. To bring them to the Wastes.

Tomorrow—in her wicked, old bones she knew it would be tomorrow that the city walls fell at last. They had no weapons left beyond swords and their own defiance. That would only last so long against the endless force waiting for them.

Abraxos shifted his wing so that it shielded her from the wind.

"I would have liked to have seen it," Manon said quietly. "The Wastes. Just once."

Abraxos huffed, nudging her gently with his head. She stroked a hand over his snout.

And even with the darkness squatting on the battlefield, she could picture it—the rolling, vibrant green that flowed to a thrashing gray sea. A shining city along its shore, witches soaring on brooms or wyverns in the skies above it. She could hear the laughter of witchlings in the streets, the long-forgotten music of their people floating on the wind. A wide, open space, lush and evergreen.

"I would have liked to have seen it," Manon whispered again.

CHAPTER 105

Blood rained over the battlefield.

Blood and arrows, so many that as they found marks in Lysandra's flank, her wings, it barely registered.

Morath had been reserving its arsenal. Until today.

With the dawn, they had unleashed such a torrent of arrows that getting into the skies had been a lethal gauntlet. She had not wanted to know how many Crochans had fallen, despite the best efforts of the rebel Ironteeth to shield them with their wyverns' bodies.

But most had made it into the air—and right into the onslaught of the Ironteeth legion.

Below, Morath swarmed with an urgency she had not yet witnessed. A black sea that crashed against the city walls, breaking over it every now and then.

Siege ladders went up faster than they could be taken down, and now, the sun barely cresting, siege towers inched forward.

Lysandra barreled into an Ironteeth witch—a Blackbeak, from the dyed leather band on her brow—and tore her from the saddle before ripping out the throat of her wyvern.

One. Only one out of the mass in the skies.

She dove, picking another target.

Then another. And another. It would not be enough.

And where the Ironteeth legion had been content to engage them in battle these past few weeks, today they pushed. Drove them back foot by foot toward Orynth.

And there was nothing Lysandra, nor any of the Crochans or rebel Ironteeth, could do to stop it.

So witches died.

And below them, on the city walls, soldiers from so many kingdoms died as well.

The final stand, the last few hours, of their desperate alliance.

Manon's breath was a rasp in her throat, her sword arm aching.

Again and again, they rallied and drove against the Ironteeth legion.

Again and again, they were shoved back. Back toward Orynth. Toward the walls.

The Crochan lines were foundering. Even the Ironteeth rebels had begun to fly sloppily.

How had they fought and fought and still come to this? The Thirteen had given up their lives; her chest was hollowed out, the din of battle still a distant roar over the silence in her head. And yet it had come to this.

If they kept it up, they would be overrun by nightfall. If they did not reconfigure their plan of attack, they would have nothing left by dawn. Enough remained of her shredded spirit to find that unacceptable. To rage against that end.

They had to retreat to the city walls. To regroup and use Orynth, the mountains behind it, to their advantage. The longer they lingered in the open air, the deadlier it would become.

Manon freed the horn from her side and blew twice.

Crochan and Ironteeth whirled toward her, eyes wide in shock. Manon blew the horn again.

Fall back, the horn bleated. *Fall back to the city.*

The western gate to the city shuddered.

Where intricate, ancient carvings had once graced the towering iron plates, now only dents and splattered blood remained.

A thunderous boom echoed throughout the city, the mountains, and Aedion, panting as he fought atop the battlements above the gates, dared to look away from his latest opponent. Dared to survey the wake of the battering ram's latest blow.

Soldiers filled the passageway to the gate, more lining the streets beyond it. As many as could be spared from the walls.

Soon now. Soon the western gate would yield. After thousands of years, it would finally sunder.

The Sword of Orynth was slick in his bloodied hand, his ancient shield coated with gore.

Already, people were fleeing to the castle. The brave souls who had lingered in the city all this time, hoping against hope that they might survive. Now they ran, children in their arms, for the castle that would be the final bastion against Morath's hordes. For however long that would be.

Hours, perhaps.

Manon had given the order to pull back, and Crochans and Ironteeth landed upon the wall by the still-steady southern gate, some joining the battle, others holding the line against the enemy aerial legion on their tails.

The western gate shuddered again, rocking inward, the wood and metal and chains they'd reinforced it with buckling.

Aedion sensed the enemy rushing at his exposed left and lifted his shield, so infinitely heavy. But a riderless wyvern intercepted the soldier, ripping the man in two before hurling his remains off the battlements.

With a flash of light, Lysandra was there, snatching up clothes, sword, and shield from a fallen Silent Assassin. "Tell me where to order Manon and the others stationed in the city," she said, panting hard. A gash ran down her arm, blood leaking everywhere, but she didn't seem to notice it.

Aedion tried to sink into that cool, calculating place that had guided him through other battles, other near-defeats. But this was no near-defeat.

This would be a defeat, pure and brutal. A slaughter.

"Aedion." His name was a frantic plea.

A Valg soldier rushed them, and Aedion split the man from navel to nose with a swipe of the Sword of Orynth. Lysandra barely blinked at the black blood that sprayed onto her face.

The western gate buckled, iron screaming as it began to peel apart.

He had to go—had to go down there to lead the fight at the gate.

Where he'd make his last stand. Where he'd meet his end, defending the place he'd loved most. It was the least he could do, with all the warriors who had fallen thanks to him, to his choices. To fall himself for Terrasen.

A death worthy of a song. An end worthy of being told around a fire.

If in Erawan's new world of darkness, flames would be allowed to exist.

The Morath Ironteeth legion barreled into their rebel kin; the exhausted Crochans alit on the stones as they guzzled down water, checked injuries. A breath before their final push.

Along the wall, Valg soldiers surged and surged and surged over the battlements.

So Aedion leaned in, and kissed Lysandra, kissed the woman who should have been his wife, his mate, one last time. "I love you."

Sorrow filled her beautiful face. "And I you." She gestured to the western gate, to the soldiers waiting for its final cleaving. "Until the end?"

Aedion hefted his shield, flipping the Sword of Orynth in his hand, freeing the stiffness that had seized his fingers. "I will find you again," he promised her. "In whatever life comes after this."

Lysandra nodded. "In every lifetime."

Together, they turned toward the stairs that would take them down to the gates. To death's awaiting embrace.

A horn cleaved through the air, through the battle, through the world.

Aedion went still.

Whirled toward the direction of that horn, to the south. Beyond Morath's teeming ranks. Beyond the sea of blackness, to the foothills that bordered the edge of Theralis's sprawling plain.

Again, that horn blared, a roar of defiance.

"That's no horn of Morath," Lysandra breathed.

And then they appeared. Along the edge of the foothills. A line of golden-armored warriors, foot soldiers and cavalry alike. More and more and more, a great line spreading across the crest of the final hill.

Filling the skies, stretching into the horizon, flew mighty, armored birds with riders. Ruks.

And before them all, sword raised to the sky as that horn blew one last time, the ruby in the blade's pommel smoldering like a small sun . . .

Before them all, riding on the Lord of the North, was Aelin.

CHAPTER
106

Through the ancient, forgotten pathways of Oakwald, through the Perranth Mountains, the Lord of the North and Little Folk had led them. Swift and unfaltering, racing against doom, they had made their last push northward.

They had barely stopped to rest. Had left any unnecessary supplies behind.

The ruk scouts had not dared to fly ahead for fear of being discovered by Morath. For fear of ruining the advantage in surprise.

Six days of marching, that great army hurrying behind her.

Inhospitable terrain smoothed out. Little rivers froze over for their passing. The trees blocked out the falling snow.

They had traveled through the night yesterday. And when dawn had broken, the Lord of the North had knelt beside Aelin and offered himself as her mount.

There was no saddle for him; none would ever be permitted or needed. Any rider he allowed on his back, Aelin knew, would never fall.

Some had knelt when she rode by. Even Dorian and Chaol had inclined their heads.

Rowan, atop a fierce-eyed Darghan horse, had only nodded. As if he had always expected her to wind up here, at the head of the army that galloped the final hours to the edge of Orynth.

She had fitted her battle-crown to her head, along with the armor she'd gathered in Anielle, and outfitted herself with whatever spare weapons Fenrys and Lorcan handed to her.

Yrene, Elide, and the healers would remain in the rear—until ruks could carry them into Orynth. Dorian and Chaol would lead the wild men of the Fangs on the right flank, the khaganate royals on the left, Sartaq and Nesryn in the skies with the ruks. And Aelin and Rowan, with Fenrys, Lorcan, and Gavriel, would take the center.

The army had spread out as they'd neared the foothills beyond Orynth, the hills that would take them to the edge of Theralis's plain, and offer their first view of the city beyond it.

Heart hammering, the Lord of the North unfaltering, Aelin had ascended the last of those hills, the highest and steepest of them, and looked upon Orynth for the first time in ten years.

A terrible, pulsing silence went through her.

Where a lovely white city had once glittered between river and plain and mountain . . .

Smoke and chaos and terror reigned. The turquoise Florine flowed black.

The sheer size, the *booming* of the massive army that thundered against its walls, in the skies above it . . .

She hadn't realized. How large Morath's army would be. How small and precious Orynth seemed before it.

"They're almost through the western gate," Fenrys murmured, his Fae sight gobbling down details.

The khagan's army fanned out around them, across the hill. The crest of a wave soon to break. Yet even the Darghan soldiers hesitated, horses shifting, at the army between them and the city.

Rowan's face was grave—grave, yet undaunted, as he took in the enemy.

So many. So many soldiers. And the Ironteeth legion above them.

"The Crochans fight at the city walls," Gavriel observed.

Indeed, she could barely make out the red cloaks.

Manon Blackbeak had not broken her vow.

And neither would she.

Aelin glanced at her hand, hidden beneath the gauntlet. To where a scar should have been.

I promise you that no matter how far I go, no matter the cost, when you call for my aid, I will come.

There would be no time for speeches. No time to rally the soldiers behind her.

They were ready. And so was she.

"Sound the call," Aelin ordered Lorcan, who lifted a horn to his lips and blew.

Down the line, heralds from the khaganate sent up their own horns in answer. Until they were all one great, bellowing note, racing toward Orynth.

They blew the horns again.

Aelin drew Goldryn from its sheath across her back and hefted her shield as she lifted the sword to the sky. As a thread of her magic pierced the ruby in the pommel and set it glowing.

The Darghan soldiers pointed their *suldes* forward, wood creaking, horsehair whipping in the wind.

Down the line, Princess Hasar and Prince Kashin trained their own spears at the enemy army. Dorian and Chaol drew their blades and aimed them ahead.

Rowan unsheathed his sword, a hatchet in his other hand, his face like stone. Unbreakable.

The horns blew a third and final time, the rallying cry singing out across the bloody plain.

The Lord of the North reared up, jutting Goldryn higher into the sky, and Aelin unleashed a flash of fire through the ruby—the signal the army behind her had awaited.

For Terrasen. All of it, for Terrasen.

The Lord of the North landed, the immortal flame within his antlers shining bright as he began the charge. The army around and behind her flowed down the hillside, gaining with each step, barreling toward Morath's back ranks.

Barreling toward Orynth.

Toward home.

Onward into battle they charged, undaunted and raging.

The queen atop the white stag did not balk with each gained foot toward the awaiting legions. She only flipped her sword in her hand— once, twice, shield arm tucking in tight.

The immortal warriors at her side did not hesitate, either, their eyes fixed upon the enemy ahead.

Faster and faster, the khaganate's cavalry galloping beside her, the front line forming, holding, as they neared the first of Morath's back lines.

The enemy turned toward them now. Pointed spears; archers racing into position.

The first impact would hurt. Many would go down before they even reached it.

But the front line had to make it. They could not break.

From the enemy lines, an order arose. *"Archers!"*

Bowstrings groaned, targets were fixed.

"Volley!"

Great iron arrows blotted out the sun, aiming for the racing cavalry.

But ruks, golden and brown and black as night, dove, dove, dove from the skies, flying wing to wing. And as those arrows arced toward the earth, the ruks intercepted them, taking the brunt as they shielded the charging army beneath them.

Ruks went down.

And even the queen leading the charge wept in rage and grief as the birds and their riders crashed to the earth. Above her, taking arrow after arrow, shield raised to the skies, a young rider roared her battle cry.

The front lines could not break.

Ironteeth witches on wyverns banked toward them, toward the ruks soaring for their exposed back.

In the city, along Orynth's walls, a white-haired queen bellowed, *"Push! Push! Push!"*

Exhausted witches took to the skies, on broom and beast, swords lifting. Racing for the front of the aerial legion turning to the ruks. To crush the Ironteeth legion between them.

On the bloody ground, Morath aimed spears, pikes, swords, anything they bore at the thundering cavalry.

It was not enough to stop them.

Not when shields of wind and flame and blackest death locked into place—and sliced into the front lines of Morath.

Felling the soldiers braced for battle. Exposing those behind still waiting to raise weapons.

Leaving Morath wide open for the golden army as it slammed into them with the force of a tidal wave.

CHAPTER
107

Rowan's breath was a steady rasp in his throat as he charged through the lines of Valg soldiers, screaming ringing out around him. Nearby, cutting a swath through Morath's masses, Aelin and the Lord of the North fought. Soldiers swarmed, but neither queen nor stag balked.

Not when Aelin's flame, reduced as it was, kept any in her blind spots from landing a blow.

The Darghan cavalry shoved Morath back, and above them, ruks and wyverns clashed.

Beasts, feathered and scaled, crashed to the earth.

Still Borte fought above the queen, guarding her from the Ironteeth who spotted that white stag, as good as a banner amid the sea of darkness, and aimed for her. At Borte's side, her betrothed guarded their flank, and Falkan Ennar, in ruk form, guarded her other.

His Darghan horse fearless, Rowan swept out his left arm, hatchet singing. A Valg head tumbled away, but Rowan was already slashing with his sword at his next opponent.

The odds were against them, even with the planning they'd done. Yet if they could liberate the city, regroup and restock, before Erawan and Maeve arrived, they might stand a chance.

For Erawan and Maeve would come. At some point, they would come, and Aelin would want to face them. Rowan had no intention of letting her do so alone.

Rowan glanced toward Aelin. She had plowed farther ahead, the front line spreading out, swarms of Morath soldiers between them. Stay close. He had to stay close.

A Crochan swept by, shooting past Rowan to rise up, up, up—right to the unprotected underbelly of an Ironteeth witch's wyvern.

Sword raised, the witch raced along its underside, swift and brutal.

Where she passed, blood and gore rained.

The beast groaned, wings splaying, and Rowan threw out a gust of wind. The wyvern crashed onto Morath's ranks with a boom that sent his own damned horse plowing away.

When the shuddering wings had stilled, when Rowan had steadied his horse and felled the soldiers rushing at him, he again searched for Aelin.

But his mate was no longer near him.

No, charging ahead, a vision of gold and silver, Aelin had gotten so far away that she was nearly beyond sight. There was no sign of Gavriel, either.

Yet Fenrys battled near Rowan's other side, Lorcan on his left—a dark, deadly wind lashing out in time with his sword.

Once, they had been little more than slaves to a queen who had unleashed them across the world. Together, they had taken on armies and decimated cities.

He had not cared then whether he walked off those distant battle-fields. Had not cared whether those kingdoms fell or survived. He had been given his orders, and had executed them.

But here, today . . . Aelin had given them no order, no command other than the very first they'd sworn to obey: to protect Terrasen.

So they would. And together, they would do so, cadre once more.

They would fight for this kingdom—their new court. Their new home.

He could see it in Fenrys's eyes as he cut a soldier in two with a deep slice to the middle. Could see that vision of a future on Lorcan's raging face as the warrior wielded magic and blade to rip through the enemy ranks.

Cadre, yet more than that. Brothers—the warriors fighting at his side were his brothers. Had stayed with him through all of it. And would continue to do so now.

It steeled him as much as the thought of his mate, still fighting ahead. He had to get to her, keep close. They all did. Orynth depended upon it.

No longer slaves. No longer raging and broken.

A home. This would be their home. Their future. Together.

Morath soldiers fell before them. Some outright ran as they beheld who battled closer.

Perhaps why Maeve had gathered them in the first place. Yet she had never been able to fully harness it—their potential, their true might. Had chosen shackles and pain to control them. Unable to comprehend, to even consider, that glory and riches only went so far.

But a true home, and a queen who saw them as males and not weapons . . . Something worth fighting for. No enemy could withstand it.

Lorcan and Fenrys battling at his side, Rowan gritted his teeth and urged his horse after Aelin, into the chaos and death that raged and raged and did not stop.

~

Aelin had come.

Had escaped Maeve, and had come.

Aedion couldn't believe it. Even as he saw the army that fought with her. Even as he saw Chaol and Dorian leading the right flank, charging with the front lines and wild men of the Fangs, the king's magic blasting in plumes of ice into the enemy.

Chaol Westfall had not failed them. And had somehow convinced the khagan to send what appeared to be the majority of his armies.

But that army was inching toward Orynth, still far across Theralis.

Morath did not halt its assault on Orynth's two gates. The southern held strong. But the western gate—it was beginning to buckle.

Lysandra had shifted into a wyvern and soared with the desperate, final push of Manon Blackbeak and the Crochans toward the Ironteeth legion, hoping to crush it between them and the ruks. The shifter now fought there, lost amid the fray.

So Aedion charged down to the western gate, a battle cry on his lips as his men let him right up to the iron doors and the enemy army just visible through the sundering plates. The moment the gate opened, it would be over.

Aedion's drained legs shook, his arms strained, but he held his ground. For whatever few breaths he had left.

Aelin had come. It was enough.

Dorian's magic snapped out of him, felling the charging soldiers. Side by side with Chaol, the wild men of the Fangs around them, they cleared a path through Morath's ranks, their swords plunging and lifting, their breath a burn in their throats.

He had never seen battle. Knew he never wished to again. The chaos, the noise, the blood, the horses screaming—

But he was not afraid. And Chaol, riding near him, breaking soldiers between them, did not hesitate. Only slaughtered onward, teeth gritted.

For Adarlan—for what had been done to it and what it might become.

The words echoed in his every panting breath. *For Adarlan.*

Morath's army stretched ahead, still between them and the battered walls of Orynth.

Dorian didn't let himself think of how many remained. He only thought of the sword and shield in his hands, Damaris already bathed in blood, of the magic he wielded to supplement his strikes. He wouldn't shift—not yet. Not until his weapons and magic began to fail him. He'd never fought in another form, but he'd try. As a wyvern or a ruk, he'd try.

Somewhere above him, Manon Blackbeak flew. He didn't dare look up long enough to hunt for a gleam of silver-white hair, or for the shimmer of Spidersilk-grafted wings.

He did not see any of the Thirteen. Or recognize any of the Crochans as they swept overhead.

So Dorian kept fighting, his brother in soul and in arms beside him.

He'd only let himself count at the end of the day. If they survived. If they made it to the city walls.

Only then would he tally the dead.

There was only Aelin's besieged city, and the enemy before it, and the ancient sword in her hand.

Siege towers neared the walls, three clustering near the southern gate, each teeming with soldiers.

Still too far away to reach. And too distant for her magic.

Magic that was already draining, swift and fleeting, from her veins.

No more endless well of power. She had to conserve it, wield it to her best advantage.

And use the training that had been instilled in her for the past ten years. She had been an assassin long before she'd mastered her power.

It was no hardship to fall back on those skills. To let Goldryn draw blood, to engage multiple soldiers and leave them bleeding out behind her.

The Lord of the North was a storm beneath her, his white coat stained crimson and black.

That immortal flame between his antlers didn't so much as flutter.

Overhead the skies rained blood, witch and wyvern and ruk alike dying and fighting.

Borte still covered her, engaging any Ironteeth who swooped from above.

Minutes were hours, or perhaps the opposite was true. The sun peaked and began its descent, shadows lengthening.

Rowan and the others had been scattered across the field, but an icy blast of wind every now and then told her that her mate still fought, still killed his way through the ranks. Still attempted to reach her side once more.

Slowly, Orynth began to loom closer. Slowly, the walls went from a distant marker to a towering presence.

The siege towers reached the walls, and soldiers poured unchecked over the battlements.

Yet the gates still held.

Aelin lifted her head to give the order to Borte and Yeran to bring the siege towers down.

Just in time to see the six Ironteeth wyverns and riders slam into the ruks.

Sending Borte, Falkan, and Yeran scattering, ruk and wyvern screaming as they hit the earth and rolled.

Clearing the path overhead for a gargantuan wyvern to come diving for Aelin.

She blasted a wall of flame skyward as the wyvern stretched out its claws for her, for the Lord of the North.

The wyvern banked, rising, and dove again.

The Lord of the North reared, holding his ground as the wyvern aimed for them.

But Aelin leaped from his back, and slapped his flank with the flat of her sword, throat so broken from roaring that she couldn't form the words. *Go.*

The Lord of the North only lowered his head as the wyvern barreled toward them.

She did not have enough magic—not to turn the thing into ashes.

So Aelin threw her magic around the stag. And stepped from the orb of flame, shield up and sword angled.

She braced herself for the impact, took in every detail on the wyvern's armor, where it was weakest, where she might strike if she could dodge the snapping jaws.

The carrion on its breath was a hot blast as its maw opened wide.

Its head went tumbling to the ground.

Not tumbling so much as smashing.

Beneath a spiked, massive tail. Belonging to an attacking wyvern with emerald eyes.

Aelin crouched as the riderless wyvern whirled on the gaping Iron-teeth witch, still atop her beheaded mount.

With one slamming sweep of the tail, the green-eyed wyvern impaled the witch on its spikes—and sent her body hurling across the field.

Then the flash and shimmer. And a ghost leopard now hurtled toward her, and Aelin toward it.

She flung her arms around the leopard as it rose up, massive body almost knocking her to the ground. "Well met, my friend," was all Aelin could manage to say as she embraced Lysandra.

A horn blared from the city—a frantic call for help.

Aelin and Lysandra whirled toward Orynth. Toward the three siege towers against the walls by the southern gate.

Emerald eyes met those of turquoise and gold. Lysandra's tail bobbed.

Aelin grinned. "Shall we?"

He had to get to her side again.

A battlefield separating them, Rowan slaughtered his way toward Aelin, Fenrys and Lorcan keeping close.

Pain had become a dull roar in his ears. He'd long since lost track of his wounds. He remembered them only because of the iron shard an arrow to his shoulder had left when he wrenched it free.

A foolish, hasty mistake. The iron shard was enough to keep him from shifting, from flying to her. He hadn't dared to pause long enough to fish it from him, not with the teeming enemy. So he kept fighting, his cadre with him. Their horses charged bold and dauntless beneath them, gaining ground, but he could not see Aelin.

Only the Lord of the North, bounding across the battlefield, aiming for Oakwald.

As if he had been set free.

Fenrys, face splattered with black blood, shouted, "Where is she?"

Rowan scanned the field, heart thundering. But the bond in his chest glowed strong, fire-bright.

Lorcan only pointed ahead. To the city walls by the southern gate.

To the ghost leopard tearing through the droves of Morath soldiers, spurts of flame accompanying her as a golden-armored warrior raced at her side.

To the three siege towers wreaking havoc on the walls.

With the towers' open sides, Rowan could see everything as it unfolded.

Could see Aelin and Lysandra charge up the ramp within, slicing and shredding soldiers between them, level after level after level. Where one missed a soldier, the other felled him. Where one struck, the other guarded.

All the way up, to the small catapult near its top.

Soldiers screamed, some leaping from the tower as Lysandra shredded into them.

While Aelin threw herself at the rungs lining the catapult's wheeled base, and began pushing.

Turning it. Away from Orynth, from the castle. Precisely as Aelin had told him Sam Cortland had done in Skull's Bay, the catapult's mechanisms allowed her to rotate its base. Rowan wondered if the young assassin was smiling now—smiling to see her heaving the catapult into position.

All the way to the siege tower at its left.

On the second tower, a red-haired figure had fought her way onto the upper level. And was turning the catapult toward the third and final tower.

Ansel of Briarcliff.

A flash of Ansel's sword, and the catapult snapped, hurling the boulder it contained. Just as Aelin brought down Goldryn upon the catapult before her.

Twin boulders soared.

And slammed into the siege towers beside them.

Iron groaned; wood shattered.

And the two towers began to topple. Where Ansel of Briarcliff had gone to escape the destruction, even Rowan could not follow.

Not as Aelin remained atop the first siege tower, and leaped upon the now-outstretched arm of the catapult, jutting over the battlefield below. Not as she shouted to Lysandra, who shifted again, a wyvern rising up from a ghost leopard's leap.

Grabbing the catapult's outstretched arm in one taloned foot while plucking up Aelin in another.

With a mighty flap, Lysandra ripped the catapult from its bolts atop the tower. And twisting, she swung it into the final siege tower.

Sending it crashing to the ground. Right onto a horde of Morath soldiers trying to batter their way through the southern gate.

Wide-eyed, the three Fae warriors blinked.

"That's where Aelin is," was all Fenrys said.

Salkhi remained airborne. So did Sartaq, Kadara with him.

That was all Nesryn knew, all she cared about, as they took on wyvern after wyvern after wyvern.

They were so much worse in battle than she'd anticipated. As swift and fearless as the ruks might be, the wyverns had the bulk. The poisoned barbs in their tails. And soulless riders who weren't afraid to destroy their mounts if it meant bringing down a ruk with them.

Close now. The khaganate's army had pushed closer and closer to besieged Orynth, flaming and shattered. If they could continue to hold their advantage, they might very well break them against the walls, as they had destroyed Morath's legion in Anielle.

They had to act swiftly, though. The enemy swarmed both city gates, determined to break in. The southern gate held, the siege towers that had been attacking it moments ago now in ruins.

But the western gate—it would not remain sealed for long.

Salkhi rising up from the melee to catch his breath, Nesryn dared to gauge how many rukhin still flew. Despite the Crochans and rebel Ironteeth, they were outnumbered, but the rukhin were fresh. Ready and eager for battle.

It was not the number of remaining rukhin that snatched the breath from her chest.

But what came up behind them.

Nesryn dove. Dove for Sartaq, Kadara ripping the throat from a wyvern midflight.

The prince was panting, splattered with blue and black blood, as Nesryn fell into flight beside him. "Put out the call," she shouted over the din, the roar of the wind. "Get to the city walls! To the southern gate!"

Sartaq's eyes narrowed beneath his helmet, and Nesryn pointed behind them.

To the secondary dark host creeping at their backs. Right from Perranth, where they had no doubt been hidden.

The rest of Morath's host. Ironteeth witches and wyverns with them.

This battle had been a trap. To lure them here, to expend their forces defeating this army.

While the rest snuck behind and trapped them against Orynth's walls.

The western gate sundered at last.

Aedion was ready when it did. When the battering ram knocked through, iron screaming as it yielded. Then there were Morath soldiers everywhere.

Shield to shield, Aedion had arranged his men into a phalanx to greet them.

It was still not enough. The Bane could do nothing to stop the tide that poured from the battlefield, pushing them back, back, back up the passageway. And even Ren, leading the men atop the walls, could not halt the flow that surged over them.

They had to shut the gate again. Had to find a way to get it shut.

Aedion could barely draw breath, could barely keep his legs under him.

A warning horn rang out. Morath had sent a second army. Darkness shrouded the full extent of their ranks.

Valg princes—lots of them. Morath had been waiting.

Ren shouted down to him over the fray, "They cleared the southern gate! They're getting as many of our forces as they can behind the walls!"

To regroup and rally before meeting the second army. But with the western gate still open, Morath teeming through, they'd never stand a chance.

He had to get the gate shut. Aedion and the Bane stabbed and slashed, a wall for Morath to break against. But it would not be enough.

A wyvern came crashing toward the gate, flipping across the ground as it rolled toward them. Aedion braced for the impact, for that huge body to shatter through the last of the gate.

Yet the felled beast halted, squashing soldiers beneath its bulk, right at the archway.

Blocking the way. A barricade before the western gate.

Intentionally so, Aedion realized as a golden-haired warrior leaped from the wyvern's saddle, the dead Ironteeth witch still dangling there, throat gushing blue blood down the leathery sides.

The warrior ran toward them, a sword in one hand, the other drawing a dagger. Ran toward Aedion, his tawny eyes scanning him from head to toe.

His father.

CHAPTER 108

Morath's soldiers clawed and crawled over the fallen wyvern blocking their path. They filled the archway, the passage.

A golden shield held them at bay. But not for long.

Yet the reprieve Gavriel bought them allowed the Bane to drain the last dregs of their waterskins, to pluck up fallen weapons.

Aedion panted, an arm braced against the gate passageway. Behind Gavriel's shield, the enemy teemed and raged.

"Are you hurt?" his father asked. His first words to him.

Aedion managed to lift his head. "You found Aelin," was all he said.

Gavriel's face softened. "Yes. And she sealed the Wyrdgate."

Aedion closed his eyes. At least there was that. "Erawan?"

"No."

He didn't need the specifics on why the bastard wasn't dead. What had gone wrong.

Aedion pushed off the wall, swaying. His father steadied him with a hand to the elbow. "You need rest."

Aedion yanked his arm out of Gavriel's grip. "Tell that to the soldiers who have already fallen."

"You will fall, too," his father said, sharper than he'd ever heard, "if you don't sit down for a minute."

Aedion stared the male down. Gavriel stared right back.

No bullshit, no room for argument. The face of the Lion.

Aedion just shook his head.

Gavriel's golden shield buckled under the onslaught of the Valg still teeming beyond it.

"We have to get the gate shut again," Aedion said, pointing to the two cleaved but intact doors pushed against the walls. Access to them blocked by the Morath grunts still trying to break past Gavriel's shield. "Or they'll overrun the city before our forces can regroup." Getting behind the walls would make no difference if the western gate was wide open.

His father followed his line of sight. Looked upon the soldiers trying to get past his defenses, their flow forced to a trickle by the wyvern he'd so carefully downed before them.

"Then we shall shut them," Gavriel said, and smiled grimly. "Together."

The word was more of a question, subtle and sorrowful.

Together. As father and son. As the two warriors they were.

Gavriel—his father. He had come.

And looking at those tawny eyes, Aedion knew it was not for Aelin, or for Terrasen, that his father had done it.

"Together," Aedion rasped.

Not just this obstacle. Not just this battle. But whatever would come afterward, should they survive. Together.

Aedion could have sworn something like joy and pride filled Gavriel's eyes. Joy and pride and sorrow, heavy and old.

Aedion strode back to the line of the Bane, motioning the soldier beside him to make room for Gavriel to join their formation. One great push now, and they'd secure the gate. Their army would enter through the southern one, and they'd find some way to rally before the new army reached the city. But the western one, they'd clear it and seal it. Permanently.

Father and son, they would do this. Defeat this.

But when his father did not join his side, Aedion turned.

Gavriel had gone directly to the gate. To the golden line of his shield, now pushing back, back, back. Shoving that wall of enemy soldiers with it, buckling with every heartbeat. Down the passage. Through the archway.

No.

Gavriel smiled at him. "Close the gate, Aedion," was all his father said.

And then Gavriel stepped beyond the gates. That golden shield spreading thin.

No.

The word built, a rising scream in Aedion's throat.

But Bane soldiers were rushing to the gate doors. Heaving them closed.

Aedion opened his mouth to roar at them to stop. To *stop, stop, stop.*

Gavriel lifted his sword and dagger, glowing golden in the dying light of the day. The gate shut behind him. Sealing him out.

Aedion couldn't move.

He had never halted, never ceased moving. Yet he could not bring himself to help with the soldiers now piling wood and chains and metal against the western gate.

Gavriel could have stayed. Could have stayed and pushed his shield back long enough for them to shut the gates. He could have remained here—

Aedion ran then.

Too slow. His steps were too slow, his body too big and heavy, as he shoved through his men. As he aimed for the stairs up to the walls.

Golden light flashed on the battlefield.

Then went dark.

Aedion ran faster, a sob burning his throat, leaping and scrambling over fallen soldiers, both mortal and Valg.

Then he was atop the walls. Running for their edge.

No. The word was a beat alongside his heart.

Aedion slaughtered the Valg in his way, slaughtered any who came over the siege ladder.

The ladder. He could fight his way down it, get to the battlefield, to his father—

Aedion swung his sword so hard at the Valg soldier before him that the man's head bounced off his shoulders.

And then he was at the wall. Peering toward that space by the gate.

The battering ram was in splinters.

Valg lay piled several deep around it. Before the gate. Around the wyvern.

So many that access to the western gate was cut off. So many that the gate was secure, a gaping wound now staunched.

How long had he stood there, unable to move? Stood there, unable to do anything while his father did *this*?

It was the golden hair he spotted first.

Before the mound of Valg he'd piled high. The gate he'd shut for them. The city he'd secured.

A terrible, rushing sort of stillness took over Aedion's body.

He stopped hearing the battle. Stopped seeing the fighting around him, above him.

Stopped seeing everything but the fallen warrior, who gazed toward the darkening sky with sightless eyes.

His tattooed throat ripped out. His sword still gripped in his hand.

Gavriel.

His father.

⁓

Morath's army pulled back from the secured western gate. Pulled back and retreated to the arms of the advancing army. To the rest of Morath's host.

Limping from a deep gash in his leg, his shoulder numb from the arrow tip that remained lodged in it, Rowan drove his blade through the face of a fleeing soldier. Black blood sprayed, but Rowan was already moving, aiming for the western gate.

Where things had gone so, so still.

He'd only aimed for it when he'd spied Aelin battling her way toward the distant southern gate, Ansel with her, after they'd brought the siege towers down around it. It was through the secured gate that the bulk of their army now hurried, the khagan's forces racing to get behind the city walls before they were sealed.

They had an hour at most before Morath was again upon them— before they were forced to shut the southern gate as well, locking out any left behind to be driven right against the walls.

The western gate would remain sealed. The downed wyvern and heaps of bodies around it would ensure that, along with any inner defenses.

Rowan had seen the golden light flaring minutes ago. Had battled his way here, cursing the iron shard in his arm that kept him from shifting. Fenrys and Lorcan had peeled away to pick off any Morath grunts trying to attack those fleeing for the southern gate, and overhead, ruks bearing the healers, Elide and Yrene with them, soared into the panicking city.

He had to find Aelin. Get their plans in motion before it was too late.

He knew who likely marched with that advancing host. He had no intention of letting her face it alone.

But this task—he knew what lay ahead. Knew, and still went.

Rowan found Gavriel before the western gate, dozens of the dead piled high around him.

A veritable wall between the gate and looming enemy host.

The light faded with each minute. Lingering Morath soldiers and Iron-teeth fled toward their oncoming reinforcements.

The khagan's army tried to kill as many as they could as they hurtled for the southern gate.

They had to get inside the city. By any means possible.

Hoisting up siege ladders that had been knocked to the earth only minutes or hours earlier, the khagan's army climbed the walls, some bearing the injured on their backs.

His magic little more than a breeze, Rowan gritted his teeth against his throbbing leg and shoulder and hauled away the Morath grunt half-sprawled over Gavriel.

Centuries of existence, years spent waging war and journeying through the world—gone. Rendered into nothing but this still body, this discarded shell.

Rowan's knees threatened to buckle. More and more of their forces scaled the city walls, an orderly but swift flight into a temporary haven.

Keep going. They had to keep going. Gavriel would wish him to. Had given his life for it.

Yet Rowan lowered his head. "I hope you found peace, my brother. And in the Afterworld, I hope you find her again."

Rowan stooped, grunting at the pain in his thigh, and hauled Gavriel over his good shoulder. And then he climbed.

Up the siege ladder still anchored beside the western gate. Onto the walls. Each step heavier than the last. Each step a memory of his friend, an image of the kingdoms they had seen, the enemies they had fought, the quiet moments that no song would ever mention.

Yet the songs would mention this—that the Lion fell before the western gate of Orynth, defending the city and his son. If they survived today, if they somehow lived, the bards would sing of it.

Even with the chaos of the khaganate soldiers and Darghan cavalry streaming for the city, silence fell where Rowan strode down the battlement stairs, bearing Gavriel.

He barely managed a grateful, relieved nod to a battered and bloody Enda and Sellene, catching their breath with a cluster of their cousins by the remnants of their catapults. His blood and kin, yet the warrior over his shoulder—Gavriel had also been family. Even when he had not realized it.

The impossible, hideous weight at his shoulder grew worse with every step to where Aedion stood at the foot of the stairs, the Sword of Orynth dangling from his hand.

"He could have stayed," was all Aedion said as Rowan gently set Gavriel down on the first of the steps. "He could have stayed."

Rowan looked at his fallen friend. His closest friend. Who had gone with him into so many wars and dangers. Who had deserved this new home as much as any of them.

Rowan closed Gavriel's unseeing eyes. "I will see you in the Afterworld."

Aedion's golden hair hung limp with blood and sweat, the ancient sword in his hands caked with black blood. Soldiers streamed past him, down the battlement stairs, yet Aedion only stared at his father. A blood-ied rock in the stream of war.

Then Aedion walked into the streets. Tears and screaming would come later. Rowan followed him.

"We need to prepare for the second part of this battle," Aedion said hoarsely. "Or we won't last the night." Already, Enda and Sellene were using their magic to haul fallen blocks of debris against the western gate. The stones wobbled, but moved. It was more power than Rowan could claim.

Rowan turned to climb back up the walls, and didn't dare let himself look behind them—to where he knew soldiers were moving Gavriel deeper into the city. Somewhere safe.

Gone. His friend, his brother was gone.

"Your Highness." A panting, blood-splattered ruk rider stood on the battlement wall. He pointed to the horizon. "Darkness veils much of it, but we have an estimate for the oncoming army." Rowan braced himself. "Twenty thousand at a minimum." The rider's throat bobbed. "Their ranks are filled with Valg—and six *kharankui*."

Not *kharankui*. But the six Valg princesses who had infested them.

Rowan willed himself to shift. His body refused.

Gritting his teeth, he peeled back the armor on his shoulder and reached for the wound. But it had sealed. Trapping the iron shard within. Keeping him from shifting—from flying to Aelin. Wherever she was.

He had to get to her. Had to find Fenrys and Lorcan and find her. Before it was too late.

But as the night fell, as he freed a dagger and lifted it to the sealed wound in his shoulder, Rowan knew it might already be.

Even though the gods were now gone, Rowan still found himself praying. Through the agony as he ripped open his shoulder, he prayed. That he might reach Aelin in time.

They had survived this long, against all odds and in defiance of ancient prophecies. Rowan dug his knife in deeper, seeking the iron shard wedged within.

Hurry—he had to hurry.

CHAPTER
109

Chaol's back strained, pain lashing down his spine. Whether from his wife's healing within the castle walls or from the hours of fighting, he had no idea.

Didn't care, as he and Dorian galloped through the southern gate into Orynth, the two of them little more than unmarked riders amid the army racing in. Bracing for the impact of the fresh host marching toward them.

Night would soon fall. Morath would not wait until dawn. Not with the darkness that hovered above them like some sort of awful cloud.

What flew and scuttled in that darkness, what waited for them . . .

Dorian was nearly slumped in his saddle, shield strapped over his back, Damaris sheathed at his side.

"You look how I feel," Chaol managed to say.

Dorian slid sapphire eyes toward him, a spark of humor lighting the haunted depths. "I know a king shouldn't slouch," he said, rubbing at his blood-and-dirt-splattered face. "But I can't bring myself to care."

Chaol smiled grimly. "We have worse to worry about."

Much worse.

They hurried toward the castle, turning up the hill that would take them to its doors, when a horn cut across the battlefield.

A warning.

With the view the hill offered, they could clearly see it. What sent the soldiers racing toward them with renewed urgency.

Morath was picking up speed.

As if realizing that their prey was on its last legs and not wishing to let them recover.

Chaol glanced to Dorian, and they reined their horses back toward the city walls. The khagan's soldiers did so as well, running down the hills they'd been scaling.

Back toward the battlements. And the hell soon to be unleashed upon it once more.

Slumped against a dead wyvern, Aelin drained the last of her waterskin.

Beside her, Ansel of Briarcliff panted through her gritted teeth while healer's magic pulled the edges of her wound together. A nasty, deep slice to Ansel's arm.

Bad enough that Ansel hadn't been able to hold a weapon. So they had halted, just as the tide of the battle had shifted, their enemy now fleeing Orynth's walls.

Aelin's head swam, her magic down to the dregs, her limbs leaden. The roar of battle still buzzed in her ears.

Covered in gore and mud, no one recognized either queen where they'd fallen to their knees, so close to the southern gates. Soldiers ran past, trying to get into the city before the army at their backs arrived.

Just a minute. She needed to only catch her breath for a minute. Then they'd hurry to the southern gate. Into Orynth.

Into her home.

Ansel swore, swaying, and the healer shot out a hand to brace her.

Not good. Not at all.

Aelin knew what and who marched toward them.

Lysandra had returned to the skies long ago, rejoining the rebel Iron-teeth and Crochans. Where Rowan now was, where the cadre was, she didn't know. Had lost them hours or days or lifetimes ago.

Rowan was safe—the mating bond told her enough. No mortal wounds. And through the blood oath, she knew Fenrys and Lorcan still breathed.

Whether she could say that for the rest of her friends, she didn't know. Didn't want to know, not yet.

The healer finished Ansel, and when the woman turned, Aelin held up a hand. "Go help someone who needs it," Aelin rasped.

The healer didn't hesitate before she hurried off, sprinting toward the sound of screaming.

"We need to get into the city," Ansel murmured, leaning her head against the ironclad hide behind her. "Before they shut the gate."

"We do," Aelin said, willing strength to her exhausted legs so she might stand. Assess how far away that final, crushing host was.

A plan. She'd had a plan for this. They all had.

But time hadn't been on her side. Perhaps her luck had faded with the gods she'd destroyed.

Aelin swallowed against the dryness in her mouth and grunted as she got to her feet. The world swayed, but she stayed upright. Managed to grab the reins of a passing Darghan rider and order her to stop.

To take the red-haired queen half-delirious on the ground.

Ansel barely protested when Aelin heaved her into the saddle behind the soldier.

Aelin stood beside the felled wyvern, watching her friend until she'd passed through the southern gate. Into Orynth.

Slowly, Aelin turned to the rising wave of darkness.

She had doomed them.

Behind her, the southern gate groaned shut.

The boom echoed into her bones.

Soldiers left on the field shouted in panic, but orders went out. Form the lines. Ready for battle.

She could do this. Adjust the plan.

She still scanned the skies for a white-tailed hawk.

No sign of him.

Good. Good, she told herself.

Aelin shut her eyes for a heartbeat. Put a hand on her chest. As if it might steady her, prepare her, for what squatted in the approaching darkness.

Soldiers shouted as they rallied, the screams of the injured and dying ringing throughout, wings booming everywhere.

Still Aelin remained there for a moment longer, just beyond the gates to her city. Her home. Still she pressed her hand to her chest, feeling the heart thundering beneath, feeling the dust of every road she had traveled these ten years to return here.

For this moment. For this purpose.

So she whispered it to herself, one last time. The story.

Her story.

Once upon a time, in a land long since burned to ash, there lived a young princess who loved her kingdom . . .

Yrene had halted her healing only for a few minutes. Her power flowed, strong and bright, undimming despite the work she'd been doing for hours.

But she'd stopped, needing to see what had happened. Hearing that their soldiers, with victory in hand, had fled back to the city walls, had only sent her running for the castle battlements faster, Elide with her. As she had been all day, helping her.

Elide winced as they took the stairs up to the battlements, but made no complaint. The lady scanned the crowded space, looking for someone, something. Her gaze settled on an old man, a child with remarkable red-gold hair beside him. Messengers approached him, then darted away.

A leader—someone in charge, Yrene realized after Elide did, already limping to them.

The old man faced them as they approached, and started. At the sight of Elide.

Yrene stopped caring about the introductions as her gaze landed on the battlefield.

On the army—*another* army—marching on them, half veiled in darkness. Six *kharankui* at their front lines.

The khagan's soldiers had gathered by the walls, both outside and within the city. The southern gate now stood closed.

Not enough. Not nearly enough to face what marched, fresh and unwearied. The *creatures* she could just barely make out teeming within its ranks. Valg princesses—there were Valg princesses amongst them.

Chaol. Where was *Chaol*—

Elide and the old man were speaking. "We cannot face that number of soldiers and walk away," the lady said, her voice so unlike any tone Yrene had heard from her. Commanding and cold. Elide pointed to the battlefield. The darkness—holy gods, the darkness—that massed over it.

A chill slithered over Yrene's body.

"Do you know what that is?" Elide asked too quietly. "Because I do."

The old man only swallowed.

Yrene knew it then. What was in that darkness. Who was in it.

Erawan.

The last of the sun vanished, setting the bloodied snows in hues of blue.

A flash of light flared behind them, and the child whirled, a sob breaking from her throat as a stunningly beautiful woman, bloodied and battered, appeared. She wrapped a cloak around her naked body like a gown, not even shivering with the cold.

A shape-shifter. She opened her arms to the girl, embracing her.

Lysandra, Chaol had called her. A lady in Aelin's court. Unknown niece to Falkan Ennar.

Lysandra turned to the old man. "Aedion and Rowan sent up the order, Darrow. Any who can are to evacuate immediately."

The old man—Darrow—just stared toward the battlefield. At a loss for words as that army prowled closer and closer and closer.

As two figures took form at its head.

And walked, unhindered, toward the city walls, darkness swarming around them.

Erawan. The golden-haired young man. She'd know it if she were blind.

A dark-haired, pale-skinned woman strode at his side, robes billowing around her on a phantom wind.

"Maeve," Lysandra breathed.

People began screaming then. In terror and despair.

Maeve and Erawan had come. To personally oversee Orynth's fall.

They stalked toward the city gates, the darkness behind them gathering, the army at their backs swelling. Pincers clicked within that darkness. Creatures who could devour life, joy.

Oh gods.

"Lord Darrow," Elide cut in, sharp and commanding. "Is there a way out of the city? Some sort of back door through the mountains that the children and elderly could take?"

Darrow dragged his eyes from the approaching Valg king and queen.

It was helplessness and despair that filled them. That broke his voice as he said, "No route that will allow them to escape in time."

"Tell me where it is," Lysandra ordered. "So they might try, at least." She grabbed for the girl's arm. "So Evangeline might try to run."

A defeat. What had seemed like a triumphant victory was about to become an absolute defeat. A butchering.

Led by Maeve and Erawan, now a mere hundred yards from the city walls.

Only ancient stone and iron stood between them and Orynth.

Darrow hesitated. In shock. The old man was in shock.

But Evangeline pointed a finger. Out toward the gates, toward Maeve and Erawan. "Look."

And there she was.

In the deepening blues of descending night, amid the snow beginning to fall, Aelin Galathynius had appeared before the sealed southern gate.

Had appeared before Erawan and Maeve.

Her unbound hair billowed in the wind like a golden banner, a last ray of light with the dying of the day.

Silence fell. Even the screaming stopped as all turned toward the gate.

But Aelin did not balk. Did not run from the Valg queen and king who halted as if in delight at the lone figure who dared face them.

Lysandra let out a strangled sob. "She—she has no magic left." The shifter's voice broke. "She has nothing left."

Still Aelin lifted her sword.

Flames ran down the blade.

One flame against the darkness gathered.

One flame to light the night.

Aelin raised her shield, and flames encircled it, too.

Burning bright, burning undaunted. A vision of old, reborn once more.

The cry went down the castle battlements, through the city, along the walls.

The queen had come home at last.

The queen had come to hold the gate.

CHAPTER 110

Her name was Aelin Ashryver Whitethorn Galathynius.

And she would not be afraid.

Maeve and Erawan halted. So did the army poised behind them, a final blow of the hammer, ready to land upon Orynth.

The magic in her veins was little more than a sputtering ember.

But they did not know that.

Her shaking hands threatened to drop her weapons, but she held firm. Held fast.

Not one more step.

Not one more step toward Orynth would she allow them to make.

Maeve smiled. "What a very long way you've traveled, Aelin."

Aelin only angled Goldryn. Met Erawan's golden stare.

His eyes flared as he took in the sword. Remembered it.

Aelin bared her teeth. Let the flame she fed into the sword glow brighter.

Maeve turned to the Valg king. "Shall we, then?"

But Erawan looked at Aelin. And hesitated.

She would not have long. Not long at all until they realized that the power that made him hesitate was no more.

But she had not remained outside the southern gate to defeat them.

Only to buy time.

For those in the city she loved so greatly to get away. To run, and live to fight tomorrow.

She had made it home.

It was enough.

The words echoed with her every breath. Sharpened her vision, steeled her spine. A crown of flame appeared atop her head, swirling and unbreakable.

She could never win against both of them.

But she wouldn't make it easy. Would take one of them down with her, if she could. Or at least slow them enough for the others to enact their plan, to find a way to either halt or defeat them. Even if either option seemed unlikely. Hopeless.

But that was why she remained here.

To give them that slim shred of hope. That will to keep fighting.

At the end of this, if that was all she was able to do against Erawan and Maeve, she could go to the Afterworld with her chin held high. She would not be ashamed to see those she had loved with her heart of wildfire.

So Aelin sketched a bow to Erawan and said with every remaining scrap of bravado she possessed, "We've met a few times, but never as we truly are." She winked at him. Even as her knees quaked, she winked at him. "Pretty as this form is, Erawan, I think I miss Perrington. Just a little bit."

Maeve's nostrils flared.

But Erawan's eyes slitted in amusement. "Was it fate, you think, that we encountered each other in Rifthold without recognizing the other?"

Such casual, easy words from such horrible, corrupt filth. Aelin made herself shrug. "Fate, or luck?" She gestured to the battlefield, her wrecked city. "This is a far grander setting for our final confrontation, don't you think? Far more worthy of us."

Maeve let out a hiss. "Enough of this."

Aelin arched a brow. "I've spent the past year of my life—ten years, if you consider it another way—building to this moment." She clicked her tongue. "Forgive me if I want to savor it. To talk with my great enemy for longer than a moment."

Erawan chuckled, and the sound grated down her bones. "One might think you were trying to delay us, Aelin Galathynius."

She beckoned to the city walls behind her. "From what? The keys are gone, the gods with them." She threw them a smile. "You did know that, didn't you?"

The amusement faded from Erawan's face. "I know." Death—such terrible death beckoned in his voice at that.

Aelin shrugged again. "I did you a favor, you know."

Maeve murmured, "Don't let her talk. We end this now."

Aelin laughed. "One would think *you* were afraid, Maeve. Of any sort of delay." She turned to Erawan once again. "The gods had planned to drag you with them. To rip you apart." Aelin gave him a half smile. "I asked them not to. So you and I might have this grand duel of ours."

"How is it that you survived?" Maeve demanded.

"I learned to share," Aelin purred. "After all this time."

"Lies," Maeve spat.

"I do have a question for you," Aelin said, glancing between the two dark rulers, separated from her by only the swirling snow. "Will *you* be sharing power? Now that you're both trapped here." She gestured to Maeve with her burning shield. "Last I heard, you were hell-bent on sending *him* home. And had gathered a little army of healers in Doranelle so you might destroy him the moment you got the chance."

Erawan blinked slowly.

Aelin smiled. "What *will* you do with all those healers now, Maeve? Have you two discussed that?"

Darkness swirled around Maeve's fingers. "I have endured enough of this prattling."

"I have not," Erawan said, his golden eyes blazing.

"Good," Aelin said. "I *was* her prisoner, you know. For months. You'd be surprised how much I picked up. About her husband—your brother. About the library in his castle, and how Maeve learned so many interesting things about world-walking. Will you share that knowledge, Maeve, or is that not part of your bargain?"

Doubt. That was doubt beginning to darken Erawan's eyes.

Aelin pressed, "She wants you out, you know. Gone. What did she even tell you when your Wyrdkey went missing? Let me guess: the King of Adarlan snuck into Morath, killed the girl you'd enslaved to be your living gate, destroyed your castle, and Maeve arrived just in time to try to stop him—but failed? Did you know that she worked with him for days and days? Trying to get the key from you?"

"That is a *lie*," Maeve snapped.

"Is it? Shall I repeat some of the things you said in your most private meetings with Lord Erawan here? The things the King of Adarlan told *me*?"

Erawan's smile grew. "You always had a flair for the dramatic. Perhaps you are lying, as my sister claims."

"Perhaps I am, perhaps I am not. Though I think the truth of your new ally's backstabbing is far more interesting than any lie I might invent."

"Shall we tell you another truth, then?" Maeve crooned. "Do you wish to know who killed your parents? Who killed Lady Marion?"

Aelin stilled.

Maeve waved a hand to Erawan. "It wasn't him. It wasn't even the King of Adarlan. No, he sent a low-ranking Valg prince to do it. He couldn't even be bothered to go himself. Didn't think anyone important was really necessary to do the deed."

Aelin stared at the queen. At the Valg king.

And then arched a brow. "Is that some attempt to unnerve me? You're thousands of years old, and that is all you can think of to say?" She laughed again, and pointed to Erawan with Goldryn. She could have sworn he flinched away from the flaming blade. "I feel sorry for you, you know.

That you've now shackled yourself to that immortal bore." She sucked on a tooth. "And when Maeve sells you out, I suppose I'll feel a little bit sorry for you then, too."

"See how she talks?" Maeve hissed. "That has always been her gift: to distract and babble while—"

"Yes, yes. But, as I said: you have the field. There's nothing left that can really stop you."

"Except for you," Erawan said.

Aelin pressed her shield against her chest. "I'm flattered you think so." She flicked up her brows. "Though I think the two hundred healers we've got in the city right now might be a little offended that you forgot them. Especially when I've watched them so diligently expel your Valg grunts from the hosts they infected."

Erawan stilled. Just a fraction.

"Or is that another lie?" Aelin mused. "A risky thing for you to do, then—to enter this city. My city, I suppose. To see who's waiting for you. I heard you went to an awful lot of trouble to try to kill one of my friends this summer. Silba's Heir. If I were you, I might have been more thorough in trying to end her. She's here, you know. Came all this way to see you and repay the favor." Aelin let her flame grow brighter as Erawan again hesitated. "Maeve knew. She knows that the healers are here, waiting for you. And will let them at you. Ask her where her owl is—the healer she keeps chained to her. To protect her from you."

"Don't listen to her nonsense," Maeve spat.

"She even made a bargain: to spare their lives in exchange for ridding her of you." Aelin waved Goldryn toward Orynth. "You're walking into a trap the moment you enter the city. You, and all your little Valg friends. And only Maeve will be left standing in the end, Lady of All."

Maeve's shadows rose in a wave. "I have had enough of this, Aelin Galathynius."

Aelin knew Maeve would go on ahead, without Erawan. Work without him, if need be.

The dark king looked toward Maeve and seemed to realize it, too.

Maeve's black hair flowed around her. "Where is the King of Adarlan? We would have words with him." Simmering, vicious rage pulsed from the queen.

Aelin shrugged. "Off fighting somewhere. Likely not bothering to think about you." She inclined her head. "A valiant effort, Maeve, to try to divert the conversation." She turned to Erawan. "The healers are waiting for you in there. You'll see I'm telling the truth. Though I suppose it will be too late by then."

Doubt. That was indeed doubt in Erawan's eyes. Just a crack. An open doorway.

And it would now be upon Yrene—Yrene and the others—to seize it.

She had not wanted to ask, to plan this. Had not wanted to drag anyone else in.

But she trusted them. Yrene, her friends. She trusted them to see this through. When she was gone. She trusted them.

Maeve stepped forward. "I hope you have enjoyed yourself these past few moments." She bared her too-white teeth, all traces of that cool grace vanished. Even Erawan seemed to blink in surprise at it—and again hesitate. As if wondering whether Aelin's words had struck true. "I hope you are entertained by your prattling idiocy."

"Eternally so," Aelin said with a mocking bow. "I suppose I'll be more entertained when I wipe you from the face of the earth." She sighed skyward. "Gods above, what a sight that will be."

Maeve extended a hand before her, darkness swirling in her cupped palm. "There are no gods left to watch, I'm afraid. And there are no gods left to help you now, Aelin Galathynius."

Aelin smiled, and Goldryn burned brighter. "I am a god."

She unleashed herself upon them.

Rowan pried free the shard of iron from his shoulder as Maeve and Erawan arrived.

As Aelin went to meet them before the walls of Orynth.

His magic guttered within his veins, but he clapped a hand to his bleeding arm as he ran for the southern gate. Willed the healing.

Flesh stung as it knitted together—too slowly. Too damn slowly.

But he couldn't fly with a shredded wing, as he'd surely have if he shifted now. Block after block, through the city that would have been his home, he ran for the southern gate.

He had to get to her.

A warning shout from the battlements had him throwing up a shield on instinct. Just as a siege ladder collided with the wall above him.

Morath's footsoldiers spilled over it, into the awaiting blades of both khagan soldier and Bane warrior. Too many.

Ironteeth clashed with Crochans above them—Ironteeth bearing several Morath footsoldiers apiece. They deposited them on the battlements, on the streets.

People screamed. Further into the city, people were screaming. Fleeing.

Only a few blocks to the southern gate—to Aelin.

And yet . . . those screams of terror and pain continued. Families. Children.

Home. This was to be his home. Already was, if Aelin were with him. He would defend it.

Rowan drew his sword and hatchet.

Fire burst beyond the walls, bathing the city in gold. She couldn't have more than an ember. Against Erawan and Maeve, she should already be dead. Yet her flame still raged. The mating bond held strong.

White flashed beside him, and then there was Fenrys, stained with blood and snarling at the soldiers pouring over the walls. One neared them, and a swipe of a mighty paw was all it took for the grunt to be in pieces.

A swipe—and then a burst of black wind. Lorcan.

They halted for all of a heartbeat. Both males looked to him in question. They knew full well where Aelin was. What the plan had been.

Another blast of flame from beyond the walls.

But the screams of the innocent in the city . . . She would never forgive him for it. If he walked away.

So Rowan angled his weapons. Turned toward the screaming. "We swore an oath to our queen and this court," he snarled, sizing up the soldiers pouring over the walls. "We will not break it."

~

Even three of the great powers of the realm battling before the city gates was not enough to halt the war around them.

Morath swarmed, and the exhausted khaganate army turned to meet them once more. To meet the new horrors that emerged, beasts of snapping teeth and baying howls, ilken sailing above them. No sign of the Valg princesses, not yet. But Elide knew they were out there. Morath had emptied its darkest pits for this final destruction.

And on the plain, before the gates, fire and darkness blacker than the fallen night warred.

Elide didn't know where to look: at the battle between the armies, or the one between Maeve and Erawan, and Aelin.

Yrene remained beside her, Lord Darrow, Lysandra, and Evangeline watching with them.

A flare of light, an answering wave of darkness.

Aelin was a fiery whirlwind between Maeve and Erawan, the fighting swift and brutal.

She had no power left. Before the Wyrdgate had ripped it from her, Aelin might have been able to face one of them and emerge triumphant. But left with a whisper of power, and after a day of wielding it on this battlefield . . .

Maeve and Erawan didn't know.

They didn't know that Aelin was only deflecting, not attacking. That this drawn-out dance was not for the spectacle, but because she was buying them all time.

Down in the dark beyond the walls, soldiers died and died. And in the city, as siege ladders breached the battlements, Morath surged into Orynth.

Still Aelin held the gate against Erawan and Maeve. Didn't let them get one step closer to the city. The final sacrifice of Aelin Galathynius for Terrasen.

The moment they realized Aelin had nothing left, it would be over. Any amusement they felt at this shallow exchange of power and skill would vanish.

Where were the others? Where was Rowan, or Lorcan, or Dorian? Or Fenrys and Gavriel? Where were they, or did they not know what occurred before the city gates?

Lysandra's breathing was shallow. Nothing—the shifter could do nothing against them. And to offer Aelin assistance might be the very thing that made Erawan and Maeve realize the queen was deceiving them.

There was no gentle voice at Elide's shoulder. Not anymore. Never again would she hear that whispering, wise voice guide her.

See, Anneith had always murmured to her. *See*.

Elide scanned the field, the city, the queen battling the Valg rulers.

Aelin did nothing without reason. Had gone out there to buy them time. To wear the Valg rulers down, just a bit. But Aelin could not defeat them.

There was only one person who could.

Elide's eyes landed on Yrene, the healer's face ashen as she watched Aelin.

The queen would never ask. Never ask that of them, of Yrene.

But she might leave a path open. Should they, should Yrene, wish to take it.

Noticing her stare, Yrene tore her attention away from the battle. "What?"

Elide looked to Lysandra. Then to the city walls, to the flash of ice and flame along them.

She saw what they had to do.

CHAPTER
111

Nesryn had not anticipated the ilken. How terrible even a few dozen would be.

Nimble and vicious, they swept over the front lines of Morath's teeming ranks. Black as the fallen night and more than eager to meet the ruks in combat.

Sartaq had given the order to unleash whatever burning arrows they could find. The heat of one scorched Nesryn's fingers as she picked a target amongst the dark fray and fired.

The flame speared into the night, right for an ilken poised to tear into a Darghan horse. The arrow struck true, and the ilken's shriek reached even Nesryn's ears. The Darghan rider stabbed deep with his *sulde*, and the ilken's screeching was cut off. A lucky, brave blow.

Nesryn was reaching for another arrow and supplies when the Darghan rider fell.

Not dead—the ilken was not dead, but feigning it. The beautiful horse's scream of pain rent the night as talons ripped open its chest. Another slash and the rider's sternum was shredded.

Nesryn fumbled for the flint to light the oil-soaked cloth around the arrowhead.

Up and down the battlefield, ilken attacked. Riders, both equine and rukhin, fell.

And looming at the back of the battlefield, as if waiting for their grand entrance, waiting to pick off what was left of them, a new sort of darkness squatted.

The Valg princesses. In their new, *kharankui* bodies. Erawan's final surprise.

Nesryn aimed and fired her arrow, scanning for Sartaq. The prince had led a unit of rukhin deeper into the enemy lines, a battered Borte, Falkan, and Yeran flanking him.

A desperate, final push.

One that none of them were likely to walk or fly away from.

~

Yrene's breath was tight in her throat, her heart a wild beat through her entire body, yet the fear she thought she'd yield to had not taken over. Not yet.

Not as Lysandra, in ruk form, landed on the city walls, steadily enough that Yrene and Elide could quickly dismount. Right where Chaol and Dorian fought, a desperate effort to keep the Valg off the walls.

The smallest of their concerns. For nearby, slaughtering their way closer—those were ilken.

Silba save them all.

Chaol saw her first. His eyes flared with pure terror. "*Get back to the castle.*"

Yrene did no such thing. And as Dorian turned, she said to the king, "We have need of you, Your Majesty."

Chaol shoved from the wall, his limp deep. "*Get back to the castle.*"

Yrene ignored him again. So did Dorian as the king gutted the Valg before him, shoved the demon over the wall, and hurried to Yrene. "What is it?"

Elide pointed to the southern gate. To the fire that flared amid the attacking darkness.

Dorian's blood-splattered face drained of color. "She has nothing left."

"We know," Elide said, her mouth tightening. "Which is why we need you."

Chaol must have realized the plan before his king. Because her husband whirled to her, shield and sword hanging at his sides. "You can't."

Elide quickly, succinctly, explained their reckless, mad idea. The Lady of Perranth's idea.

Yrene tried not to shake. Tried not to tremble as she realized that they were, indeed, about to do this.

But Elide merely climbed onto the shifter's leathery back and beckoned the king to follow. And Dorian, to his credit, did not hesitate.

Yet Chaol dropped his sword and shield to the bloody stones, and gripped Yrene's face between his hands. "You can't," he said again, voice breaking. "You *can't*."

Yrene put her hands atop Chaol's and brought them brow to brow. "You are my joy," was all she said to him.

Her husband, her dearest friend, closed his eyes. The reek of Valg blood and metal clung to him, and yet beneath it—beneath it, that was his scent. The smell of home.

Chaol at last opened his eyes, the bronze of them so vivid. Alive. Utterly alive. Full of trust, and understanding, and pride.

"Go save the world, Yrene," he whispered, and kissed her brow.

Yrene let that kiss sink into her skin, a mark of protection, of love that she'd carry with her into hell and beyond it.

Chaol turned to where Dorian sat with Elide atop the shifter, the love on her husband's face hardening to something fierce and determined. "Keep her safe," was all Chaol said. Perhaps the only order, Yrene realized, he would ever give his king. Their king.

It was why she loved him. Why she knew that the child in her womb would never spend a single moment wondering if it was loved.

Dorian bowed his head. "With my life." Then the king offered a hand to help Yrene onto Lysandra's back. "Let's make it count."

Manon's chest burned with each inhale, but Abraxos flew unfalteringly through the melee.

So many. Too many.

And the new horrors that Morath had unleashed, the ilken amongst them . . .

Screams and blood filled the skies. Crochan and Ironteeth and ruks—those were *ruks*—fought for their very existence.

Any hope of victory that Aelin Galathynius had brought with her was slipping away.

Manon and Abraxos smashed through the Ironteeth lines, diving to rip apart ilken and foot soldier. Wind-Cleaver was a leaden weight in her hand. She could no longer discern her sweat from blood.

The Queen of Terrasen had come, an army with her, and it would still not be enough.

Lorcan knew Maeve had come. Could feel her presence in his bones, a dark, terrible song through the world. A Valg song.

He fought far down the city walls, Whitethorn and Fenrys nearby, Aedion unleashing himself upon soldier after soldier with a ferocity that Lorcan knew came from deep, brutal grief.

Gavriel was dead. Had died to give his son and those at the western gate a chance to shut them again.

Lorcan tucked away the pang in his chest at the thought of it. That the Lion was no more. Which of them would be next?

Light flared beyond the wall. Darkness devoured it. Too swiftly, too easily.

Aelin had to be insane. Must have lost all her wits, if she thought she could take on not just Maeve, but Erawan, too.

Yet Rowan halted. Would have been run through by a Valg soldier if Lorcan hadn't hurled a dagger straight through the demon's face.

With a nod to Lorcan and Fenrys, Rowan shifted, a hawk instantly soaring over the walls.

Lorcan looked to Fenrys. Found the male bristling. Aware of the change beyond the walls. It was time.

"We finish this together," Fenrys snarled, and shifted as well, a white wolf leaping clean off the battlements and into the city streets below. Toward the gate.

Lorcan glanced at the castle, where he knew Elide was watching.

He said his silent farewell, sending what remained of his heart on the wind to the woman who had saved him in every way that mattered.

Then Lorcan ran for the gate—to the dark queen who threatened all he'd come to want, to hope for. He'd come to *hope*. Had found there was something better out there. *Someone* better.

And he'd go down swinging to defend all of it.

~

It was a dance, and one that Aelin had spent her entire life practicing.

Not just the movements of her sword, her shield. But the smirk she kept on her face as she met each blast of darkness, as she realized over and over and over who her dance partners were.

Where they advanced a step, Aelin sent out a plume of fire. Didn't let her own doubt show, didn't dare wonder if they could tell that the fire was mostly color and light.

They still dodged it. Avoided it.

Waiting for her to plunge down deep, to make that killing blow they anticipated.

And though her fire deflected the darkness, though Goldryn was a burning song in her hand, she knew their power would break through soon.

The keys were gone. And so was the Fire-Bringer.

They would have no use for her. No need to enslave her, save to torment her.

It could go either way. Death or enslavement.

But there would be no keys, no ability for Erawan to craft more Wyrd-stone, or bring in his Valg to possess others.

Aelin lunged with Goldryn, spearing for Erawan as she raised her shield against Maeve. She sent a wave of flame searing for their sides, herding them closer together.

Erawan blasted it back, but Maeve halted. Halted while Aelin leaped away a step, panting.

The coppery tang of blood coated her mouth. A herald of the looming burnout.

Maeve watched Aelin's flame sizzle through the snow, melting it down to the dried grasses of Theralis. An undulating sea of green in the warmer months. Now a muddy, blood-soaked ruin.

"For a god," Maeve said, their first words since this dance had begun minutes or hours or an eternity ago, "you do not seem so willing to smite us."

"Symbols have power," Aelin panted, smiling as she flipped Goldryn in her hand, the flame hissing through the air. "Strike you down too quickly and it will ruin the impact." Aelin drew up every shred of swaggering arrogance and winked at Erawan. "She wants me to wear you down, you see. Wants me to tire you, so those healers up in the castle can finish you off with little trouble."

"*Enough.*" Maeve slammed out her power, and Aelin lifted her shield, flame deflecting the onslaught.

But barely. The impact rippled into her bones, her blood.

Aelin didn't let herself so much as wince as she hurled a whip of flame toward Maeve, and the dark queen danced back. "Just wait—she'll spring the trap shut on you soon enough."

"She is a liar and a fool," Maeve spat. "She seeks to drive us apart because she knows we can defeat her together." Again, that dark power rallied around Maeve.

The dark king only stared at Aelin with those golden, burning eyes, and smiled. "Indeed. You—"

He paused. Those golden eyes lifted above Aelin. Above the gates and wall behind her. To something high above.

Aelin didn't dare to look. To take her attention away for that long. To hope.

But the gold in Erawan's eyes glowed. Glowed—with rage and perhaps a kernel of fear.

He twisted his head toward Maeve. "There are healers in that castle."

"Of course there are," Maeve snapped.

Yet Erawan stilled. "There are *skilled* healers there. Ripe with power."

"Straight from the Torre Cesme," Aelin said, nodding solemnly. "As I told you."

Erawan only looked at Maeve. And that doubt flickered again.

He glanced to Aelin. To her fire, her sword. She bowed her head.

Erawan hissed at Maeve, "If she spoke true, you are carrion."

And before Aelin could muster an ember to strike, a dark, sinewy form swept from the blackness behind Erawan and snatched him up. An ilken.

Aelin didn't waste her power trying to down them, not with the ilken's defenses against magic. Not with Maeve tracking Erawan as he was carried into the skies. Over the city.

Against two Valg rulers, she should have already been dead. Against the female before her, Aelin knew it was still just a matter of time. But if Yrene, if her friends, could take down Erawan . . .

"Just us, then," Maeve said, lips curving into that spider's smile. The smile of the horrendous creatures that launched themselves at Orynth.

Aelin lifted Goldryn again. "That's precisely how I wanted it," she said. Truth.

"But I know your secret, Heir of Fire," Maeve crooned, and struck again.

CHAPTER 112

Atop the highest tower of the castle of Orynth, on the broad balcony that overlooked the world far below, the healer sent out another flare of power.

The white glow seared the night, casting the tower stones in stark relief.

A beacon, a challenge to the dark king who battled Aelin Galathynius below.

Here I am, the power sang through the night. *Here I am.*

Erawan answered.

His rage, his fear, his hatred filled the wind as he swept in, carried in an ilken's gangly limbs. He smiled at the young healer whose hands glowed with pure light, as if already tasting her blood. Savoring the destruction of what she offered, the gift she'd been given.

His sheer presence set people in the castle below screaming as they fled.

Not death incarnate, but something far worse. Something nearly as ancient, and almost as powerful.

The ilken swept over the tower, dropping him onto the balcony stones. Erawan landed with the grace of a cat, barely winded as he straightened.

As he smiled at her.

⌒

"I never thought you'd do it, you know," Maeve said, her dark power coiling around her as Aelin panted. A cramp had begun low in her back and now lashed its way up her spine, down her legs. "That you'd be foolish enough to put the keys back into the gate. What happened to that glorious vision you once showed me, Aelin? Of you in this very city, your worshipping masses crying your name. Was it simply too dull for you, to be revered?"

Aelin rallied herself with every breath, Goldryn still burning bright.

Let her talk—let her gloat and ramble. Every second she had to recover, to regain a fraction of her strength, was a blessing.

Erawan had taken the bait, had let the doubt she'd planted take root in his mind. She had known it was only a matter of time until he sensed Yrene's power. She only prayed Yrene Towers was ready to meet him.

"I had always hoped that you and I were true equals, in a way," Maeve went on. "That you, more than Erawan, understood the true nature of power. Of what it means to wield it. What a disappointment that deep down, you wished to be so ordinary."

The shield had become unbearably heavy. Aelin didn't dare look behind her to see where Erawan had gone. What he was doing. She'd felt Yrene's flare of power, had dared hope it might even be a signal, a lure, but nothing since then. It had drawn Erawan away, though. It was enough.

The darkness around Maeve writhed. "The Queen Who Was Promised is no more," she said, clicking her tongue. "Now you're nothing but an assassin with a crown. And a commoner's gift of magic."

Twin whips of brutal power speared for Aelin's either side.

Throwing up her shield, swinging Goldryn with her other arm, Aelin deflected, flame flashing.

The shield buckled, but Goldryn burned steady.

But she felt it. The familiar, unending pain. The shadows that could devour.

Pressing closer. Eating away at her power.

Maeve glanced to the blazing sword. "Clever of you, to imbue the sword with your own gifts. No doubt done before you yielded everything to the Wyrdgate."

"A precaution, should I not return," Aelin panted. "A weapon to kill Valg."

"We shall see." Maeve struck again. Again.

Forcing Aelin to concede a step. Then another.

Back toward the invisible line she'd drawn between them and the southern gate.

Maeve stalked forward, her dark hair and robes billowing. "You have denied me two things, Aelin Galathynius. The keys I sought." Another whip of power sliced for Aelin. Her flame barely deflected it this time. "And the great duel I was promised."

As if Maeve opened the lid to a chest on her power, plumes of darkness erupted.

Aelin sliced with Goldryn, the fire within the blade unfaltering. But it was not enough. And as Aelin retreated another step, one of those plumes snapped across her legs.

Aelin couldn't stop the scream that shattered from her throat. She went down, shield scattering in the icy mud.

Training kept her fingers clenched on Goldryn.

But pressure, unbearable and slithering, began to push into her head.

"Wake up."

The world shifted. Snow replaced by firelight. The ground for a slab of iron.

The pressure in her head writhed, and Aelin bowed over her knees, refusing to acknowledge it. Real—this battle, the snow and blood, *this* was real.

"Wake up, Aelin," Maeve whispered.

Aelin blinked. And found herself in the iron box, Maeve leaning over the open lid. Smiling. "We're here," the Fae Queen said.

Not Fae. Valg. Maeve was *Valg*—

"You've been dreaming," Maeve said, running a finger over the mask still clamped to her face. "Such strange, wandering dreams, Aelin."

No. No, it had been *real*. She managed to lift her head enough to peer down at herself. At the shift and too-thin body. The scars still on her.

Still there. Not wiped away. No new skin.

"I can make this easy for you," Maeve went on, brushing Aelin's hair back with gentle, loving strokes. "Tell me where the Wyrdkeys are, swear the blood oath, and these chains, this mask, this box . . . all of it will go away."

They hadn't yet begun. To tear her apart.

All of it a dream. One long nightmare. The keys remained unbound, the Lock unforged.

A dream, while they'd sailed here. Wherever here was.

"What say you, niece? Will you spare yourself? Yield to me?"

You do not yield.

Aelin blinked.

"It's easier, isn't it," Maeve mused, bracing her forearms against the lip of the coffin. "To remain here. So you needn't make such terrible choices. To let the others share the burden. Bear its cost." A hint of a smile. "Deep down, that's what haunts you. That wish to be *free*."

Freedom—she'd known it. Hadn't she?

"It's what you fear most—not me, or Erawan, or the keys. That *your* wish to be free of the weight of your crown, your power, will consume you. Embitter you until you do not recognize your own self." Her smile widened. "I wish to spare you from that. With me, you shall be free in a way you've never imagined, Aelin. I swear it."

An oath.

She had sworn an oath. To Terrasen. To Nehemia. To Rowan.

Aelin closed her eyes, shutting out the queen above her, the mask, the chains, the iron box.

Not real.

This was not real.

Wasn't it?

"I know you're tired," Maeve went on, gently, coaxingly. "You gave and gave and gave, and it was still not enough. It will never be enough for them, will it?"

It wouldn't. Nothing she had ever done, or would do, would be enough. Even if she saved Terrasen, saved Erilea, she'd still need to give more, do more. The weight of it already crushed her.

"Cairn," Maeve said.

Strolling footsteps sounded nearby. Scuffing on stone.

Tremors shook her, uncontrollable and unsummoned. She knew that gait, knew—

Cairn's hateful, sneering face appeared beside Maeve's, the two of them studying her. "How shall we start, Majesty?"

He'd spoken the words to her already. They had done this dance so many times.

Bile coated her throat. She couldn't stop shaking. She knew what he'd do, how he'd begin. Would never stop feeling it, the whisper of the pain.

Cairn ran a hand over the rim of the coffin. "I broke some part of you, didn't I?"

I name you Elentiya, "Spirit That Could Not Be Broken."

Aelin traced her metal-encrusted fingers over her palm. Where a scar should be. Where it still remained. Would always remain, even if she could not see it.

Nehemia—Nehemia, who had given everything for Eyllwe. And yet . . .

And yet, Nehemia had still felt the weight of her choices. Still wished to be free of her burdens.

It had not made her weak. Not in the slightest.

Cairn surveyed her chained body, assessing where he would begin. His breathing sharpened in anticipatory delight.

Her hands curled into fists. Iron groaned.

Spirit that could not be broken.

You do not yield.

She would endure it again, if asked. She would do it. Every brutal hour and bit of agony.

And it would hurt, and she would scream, but she'd face it. Survive against it.

Arobynn had not broken her. Neither had Endovier.

She would not allow this waste of existence to do so now.

Her shaking eased, her body going still. Waiting.

Maeve blinked at her. Just once.

Aelin sucked in a breath—sharp and cool.

She did not want it to be over. Any of it.

Cairn faded into the wind. Then the chains vanished with him.

Aelin sat up in the coffin. Maeve backed away all of a step.

Aelin surveyed the illusion, so artfully wrought. The stone chamber, with its braziers and hook from the ceiling. The stone altar. The open door and roar of the river beyond.

She made herself look. To face down that place of pain and despair. It would always leave a mark, a stain on her, but she would not let it define her.

Hers was not a story of darkness.

This would not be the story. She would fold it into herself, this place, this fear, but it would not be the whole story. It would not be *her* story.

"How," Maeve simply asked.

Aelin knew a world and a battlefield raged beyond them. But she let herself linger in the stone chamber. Climbed from the iron coffin.

Maeve only stared at her.

"You should have known better," Aelin said, the lingering embers within her shining bright. "You, who feared captivity and did all this to avoid it. You should have known better than to trap me. Should have known I'd find a way."

"How," Maeve asked again. "How did you not break?"

"Because I am not afraid," Aelin said. "Your fear of Erawan and his brothers drove you, destroyed you. If there was ever anything worthwhile to destroy."

Maeve hissed, and Aelin chuckled. "And then there was your fear of Brannon. Of me. Look what it brought about." She gestured to the room around them, the world beyond it. "This is all you'll have left of Doranelle. This illusion."

Maeve's power rumbled through the room.

Aelin's lips pulled back from her teeth. "You hurt my mate. Hurt the woman you tricked him into thinking was his mate. Killed her, and broke him."

Maeve smiled slightly. "Yes, and I enjoyed every moment of it."

Aelin answered the queen's smile with one of her own. "Did you forget what I told you on that beach in Eyllwe?"

When Maeve merely blinked at her again, Aelin attacked.

Blasting with a shield of fire, she drove Maeve to the side—and launched a spear of blue flame.

Maeve dodged the assault with a wall of dark power, but Aelin went on the offensive, striking again and again and again. Those words she'd snarled to Maeve in Eyllwe rang between them: *I will kill you.*

And she would. For what Maeve had done, to her, to Rowan and Lyria, to Fenrys and Connall and so many others, she'd wipe her from memory.

Half a thought and Goldryn was again in her hand, the blade singing with flame.

Even if it took her last breaths, she'd go down swinging for this.

Maeve met her each blow, and they burned and raged through the room.

The altar cracked. Melted away.

The hook from the ceiling dissolved into molten ore that hissed upon the stones.

She blasted away the spot where Fenrys had sat, chained by invisible bonds.

Again and again, the last embers of her fire rallying, sweat beading on her brow, Aelin struck at Maeve.

The iron coffin heated, glowing red. Only here, in this illusion, might it do so.

Maeve had thought to trap her once more.

But the queen would not be the one walking away this time.

Aelin pivoted, driving Maeve back. Toward the smoldering coffin.

Step by step, she pushed her toward it. Herded her.

Darkness fanned through the room, blocking the rain of fiery arrows that shot for Maeve, and the queen dared to glance over a shoulder to the red-hot fate that awaited her.

Maeve's face went whiter than death.

Aelin rasped a laugh, and angled Goldryn, gathering her power one last time.

But a flicker of motion caught her eye—to the right.

Elide.

Elide stood there, terror written over her features. She reached a hand for Aelin in warning, "Watch—"

Maeve sent a whip of black for the Lady of Perranth.

No—

Aelin lunged, fire leaping for Elide, to block that fatal blow.

She realized her mistake within a heartbeat. Realized it as her hands passed through Elide's body, and her friend disappeared.

An illusion. She had fallen for an illusion, and had left herself open, vulnerable—

Aelin twisted back toward Maeve, flames rising again, but too late.

Hands of shadow wrapped around her throat. Immovable. Eternal.

Aelin arched, gasping for any bit of air as those hands squeezed and squeezed—

The chamber melted away. The stones beneath her became mud and snow, the roar of the river replaced by the din of battle. They flashed between one heartbeat and the next, between illusion and truth. Warm air for bitter wind, life for sure death.

Aelin wreathed her hands in flame, ripping at the shadow lashed around her throat.

Maeve stood before her, robes billowing as she panted. "Here is what shall happen, Aelin Galathynius."

Plumes of shadow shot for her, snapping and tearing, and no flame, no amount of sheer will could keep them at bay. Not as they tightened, wrenching away any breath to scream.

Her fire guttered.

"You will swear the blood oath to me. And then you and I will fix this mess you've made. You, and the King of Adarlan will *fix* what you have done. You may be Fire-Bringer no longer, but you will still have your uses."

A wind kissed with snow brushed past her. *No.*

Another flash of light behind Aelin, and Maeve paused.

The shadows squeezed, and Aelin arched again, a soundless scream breaking through her.

"You may be asking yourself why I'd ever think you'd agree to it. What I might have against you." A low laugh. "The very things that you seek to protect—that's what I shall destroy, should you defy me. What is most precious to you. And when I have finished doing that, you will kneel."

No, *no—*

Darkness pulsed from Maeve, and Aelin's vision wavered.

A wave of ice-kissed wind blasted it back.

Just enough for her to get a breath down. To lift her head and see the tattooed hand that now stretched down for her. Reaching for her—an offer to rise. Rowan.

Behind him, two others appeared. Lorcan and Fenrys, the latter in wolf form.

The cadre, who had not halted that day to help her at Mistward—but who did so now.

But Rowan kept his hand outstretched to Aelin, that offer to stand unfaltering, and didn't take his eyes off Maeve as he bared his teeth and snarled.

But it was Fenrys who struck first. Who had been waiting for this moment, this opportunity.

Fangs bared, fur bristling, he charged at Maeve. Going right for her pale throat.

Aelin struggled, and Rowan shouted his warning, but too late.

Lost in his vengeance, his fury, the white wolf leapt for Maeve.

A whip of darkness slashed for him.

Fenrys's yelp of pain echoed through her bones before he hit the ground. Blood leaked from the wound—the deep slash down his face.

So fast. Barely more than a blink.

Rowan's and Lorcan's power surged, rallying to strike. Fenrys struggled to his feet. Again, darkness snapped for him. Ripped across his face. As if Maeve knew precisely where to strike.

Fenrys went down again, blood splattering on the snow. A flash of light, and he shifted into his Fae form. What she'd done to his face—

No. *No*—

Aelin managed to rally enough air to rasp, "*Run.*"

Rowan glanced at her then. At the warning.

Just as Maeve struck once more.

As if she had been holding back her power—waiting for them. For this.

A wave of blackness enveloped her mate. Enveloped Lorcan and Fenrys, too.

Their magic flared, illumining the darkness like lightning behind a cloud. Yet it was not enough to free themselves from Maeve's grip. Ice and wind blasted against it, again and again. Brutal, calculated strikes.

Maeve's power swelled.

The ice and wind stopped. The other magic within the darkness stopped. Like it had been swallowed.

And then they began screaming.

Rowan began screaming.

CHAPTER 113

Erawan panted as he approached. "Healer," he breathed, his unholy power emanating from him like a black aura.

She backed away a step, closer to the balcony rail. The dark king followed her, a predator closing in on long-awaited prey.

"Do you know how long I have looked for you?" The wind tossed his golden hair. "Do you even know what you can *do*?"

She hesitated, slamming into the balcony rail behind her, the drop so hideously endless.

"How do you think we took the keys in the first place?" A hateful, horrible smile. "In my world, your kind exists, too. Not healers to us, but executioners. Death-maidens. Capable of healing—but also *un*healing. Unbinding the very fabric of life. Of worlds." Erawan smirked. "So we took your kind. Used them to unbind the Wyrdgate. To rip the three pieces of it from its very essence. Maeve never learned it—and never shall." His jagged breathing deepened as he savored each word, each step closer. "It took all of them to hew the keys from the gate—every one of the healers amongst my kind. But you, with your gifts—it would only take you to do it again. And with the keys now returned to the gate . . ." Another smile. "Maeve thinks I left to kill you, destroy you. Your little fire-queen thought so, too. She could not conceive that I *wanted* to find you. Before Maeve. Before any harm could come to you. And now that I have . . . What fun you and I shall have, Yrene Towers."

Another step closer. But no more.

Erawan went still. Tried and failed to move.

Looked at the stones of the balcony then. At the bloody mark he'd stridden across, too focused on his prey to notice.

A Wyrdmark. To hold. To trap.

The young healer smiled at him, and the white light around her hands winked out as her eyes shifted from gold to sapphire. "I'm not Yrene."

⁓

Erawan whipped his head to the skies as Lysandra, in ruk form, came sweeping around the tower from where she'd been hiding on its other side, Yrene clutched in her talons.

Erawan's power swelled, but Yrene was already glowing, bright as the far-off dawn.

Lysandra opened her talons, delicately dropping Yrene to the balcony stones, light streaming off her as she sprinted headfirst to Erawan.

Dorian shifted back into his own body, healing light pouring off him, too, as he encircled his power around the Wyrdmark that held Erawan. The tower door burst open, Elide flying out of it just as Lysandra shifted, landing on a ghost leopard's silent feet upon the balcony.

Erawan didn't seem to know where to look. Not as Dorian sent out a punch of his healing light that knocked him off balance. Not as Lysandra leaped upon the dark king, pinning him to the stones. Not as Elide, Damaris in her hands, plunged the blade deep through Erawan's gut, and between the stones below.

Erawan screamed. But the sound was nothing compared to what came out of him as Yrene reached him, hands like burning stars, and slammed them upon his chest.

The world slowed and warped.

Yet Yrene was not afraid.

Not afraid at all of the blinding white light that erupted from her, searing into Erawan.

He arched, shrieking, but Damaris held him down, that ancient blade unwavering.

His dark power rose, a wave to devour the world.

Yrene did not let it touch her. Touch any of them.

Hope.

It was hope that Chaol had said she carried with her. Hope that now grew in her womb.

For a better future. For a free world.

It was hope that had guided two women at opposite ends of this continent ten years ago. Hope that had guided Yrene's mother to take up that knife and kill the soldier who would have burned Yrene alive. Hope that had guided Marion Lochan when she chose to buy a young heir time to run with her very life.

Two women, who had never known each other, two women who the world had deemed ordinary. Two women, Josefin and Marion, who had chosen hope in the face of darkness.

Two women, in the end, who had bought them all this moment. This one shot at a future.

For them, Yrene was not afraid. For the child she carried, she was not afraid.

For the world she and Chaol would build for that child, she was not afraid at all.

The gods might have been gone, Silba with them, but Yrene could have sworn she felt those warm, gentle hands guiding her. Pushing upon Erawan's chest as he thrashed, the force of a thousand dark suns trying to rip her apart.

Her power tore through them all.

Tore and shredded and ripped into him, into the writhing worm that lay inside.

The parasite. The infection that fed on life, on strength, on joy.

Distantly, far away, Yrene knew she was incandescent with light, brighter than a noontime sun. Knew that the dark king beneath her was nothing more than a writhing pit of snakes, biting at her, trying to poison her light.

You have no power over me, Yrene said to him. Into the body that housed that parasite of parasites.

I shall rip you apart, he hissed. *Starting with that babe in your—*

A thought and Yrene's power flared brighter.

Erawan screamed.

The power of creation and destruction. That's what lay within her.

Life-Giver. World-Maker.

Bit by bit, she burned him up. Starting at his limbs, working inward.

And when her magic began to slow, Yrene held out a hand.

She didn't feel the sting of her palm cutting open. Barely felt the pressure of the callused hand that linked with hers.

But when Dorian Havilliard's raw magic barreled into her, Yrene gasped.

Gasped and turned into starlight, into warmth and strength and joy.

~

Yrene's power was life itself. Pure, undiluted life.

It nearly brought Dorian to his knees as it met with his own. As he handed over his power to her, willingly and gladly, Erawan prostrate before them. Impaled.

The demon king screamed.

Glad. He should be glad of that pain, that scream. The end that was surely to come.

For Adarlan, for Sorscha, for Gavin and Elena. For all of them, Dorian let his power flow through Yrene.

Erawan thrashed, his power rising only to strike against an impenetrable wall of light.

And yet Dorian found himself saying, "His name."

Yrene, focused upon the task before her, didn't so much as glance his way.

But Erawan, through his screaming, met Dorian's stare.

The hatred in the demon king's eyes was enough to devour the world.

But Dorian said, "My father's name." His voice did not waver. "You took it."

He hadn't realized that he wanted it. Needed it, so badly.

A pathetic, spineless man, Erawan seethed. *As you are—*

"Tell me his name. Give it back."

Erawan laughed through his screaming. *No.*

"Give it back."

Yrene looked to him now, doubt in her eyes. Her magic paused—just for a heartbeat.

Erawan leapt, his power erupting.

Dorian blasted it back, and lunged for the demon king. For Damaris.

Erawan's shriek threatened to crack the castle stones as Dorian shoved the blade deeper. Twisted it. Sent their power funneling down through it.

"Tell me his name," he panted through his teeth. Yrene, clinging to his other hand, murmured her warning. Dorian barely heard it.

Erawan only laughed again, choking as their power seared him.

"Does it matter?" Yrene asked softly.

Yes. He didn't know why, but it did.

His father had been wiped from the Afterworld, from every realm of existence, but he could still have his name given back to him.

If only to repay the debt. If only so Dorian might grant the man some shred of peace.

Erawan's power surged for them again. Dorian and Yrene shoved it back.

Now. It had to be now.

"Tell me his name," Dorian snarled.

Erawan smiled up at him. *No.*

"Dorian," Yrene warned. Sweat slid down her face. She couldn't hold him for much longer. And to risk her—

Dorian sent their power rippling down the blade. Damaris's hilt glowed. *"Tell me—"*

It is your own.

Erawan's eyes widened as the words came out of him.

As Damaris drew it from him. But Dorian did not marvel at the sword's power.

His father's name . . .

Dorian.

I took his name, Erawan spat, writhing as the words flowed from his tongue under Damaris's power. *I wiped it away from existence. Yet he only remembered it once. Only once. The first time he beheld you.*

Tears slid down Dorian's face at that unbearable truth.

Perhaps his father had unknowingly hidden his name within him, a final kernel of defiance against Erawan. And had named his son for that defiance, a secret marker that the man within still fought. Had never stopped fighting.

Dorian. His father's name.

Dorian let go of Damaris's hilt.

Yrene's breathing turned ragged. Now—it had to be now.

Even with the Valg king before him, something in Dorian's chest eased. Healed over.

So Dorian said to Erawan, his tears burning away beneath the warmth of their magic. "I brought down your keep." He smiled savagely. "And now we'll bring you down as well."

Then he nodded to Yrene.

Erawan's eyes flared like hot coals. And Yrene unleashed their power once more.

Erawan could do nothing. Nothing against that raw magic, joining with Yrene's, weaving into that world-making power.

The entire city, the plain, became blindingly bright. So bright that Elide and Lysandra shielded their eyes. Even Dorian shut his.

But Yrene saw it then. What lay at Erawan's core.

The twisted, hateful creature inside. Old and seething, pale as death. Pale, from an eternity in darkness so complete it had never seen sunlight.

Had never seen *her* light, which now scalded his moon-white, ancient flesh.

Erawan writhed, contorting on the ground of whatever this place was inside him.

Pathetic, Yrene simply said.

Golden eyes flared, full of rage and hate.

But Yrene only smiled, summoning her mother's lovely face to her heart. Showing it to him.

Wishing she knew what Elide's mother had looked like so she might show him Marion Lochan, too.

The two women he had killed, directly or indirectly, and never thought twice about it.

Two mothers, whose love for their daughters and hope for a better world was greater than any power Erawan might wield. Greater than any Wyrdkey.

And it was with the image of her mother still shining before him, showing him that mistake he'd never known he made, that Yrene clenched her fingers into a fist.

Erawan screamed.

Yrene's fingers clenched tighter, and distantly, she felt her physical hand doing the same. Felt the sting of her nails cutting into her palms.

She did not listen to Erawan's pleas. His threats.

She only tightened her fist. More and more.

Until he was nothing but a dark flame within it.

Until she squeezed her fist, one final time, and that dark flame snuffed out.

Yrene had the feeling of falling, of tumbling back into herself. And she was indeed falling, rocking back into Lysandra's furry body, her hand slipping from Dorian's.

Dorian lunged for her hand to renew contact, but there was no need.

No need for his power, or Yrene's.

Not as Erawan, golden eyes open and unseeing as they gazed at the night sky above, sagged to the stones of the balcony.

Not as his skin turned gray, then began to wither, to decay.

A life rotting away from within.

"Burn it," Yrene rasped, a hand going to her belly. A pulse of joy, a spark of light, answered back.

Dorian didn't hesitate. Flames leaped out, devouring the decaying body before them.

They were unnecessary.

Before they'd even begun to turn his clothing to ash, Erawan dissolved. A sagging bit of flesh and brittle bones.

Dorian burned him anyway.

They watched in silence as the Valg king turned to ashes.

As a winter wind swept over the tower balcony, and carried them far, far away.

CHAPTER
114

She was dead.

Aelin was dead.

Her lifeless body had been spiked to the gates of Orynth, her hair shorn to her scalp.

Rowan knelt before the gates, the armies of Morath streaming past him. It wasn't real. Couldn't be. Yet the sun warmed his face. The reek of death filled his nose.

He gritted his teeth, willing himself out, away from this place. This waking nightmare.

It didn't falter.

A hand brushed his shoulder, gentle and small.

"You brought this upon yourself, you know," said a lilting female voice.

He knew that voice. Would never forget it.

Lyria.

She stood behind him, peering up at Aelin. Clad in Maeve's dark armor, her brown hair braided back from her delicate, lovely face.

"You brought it upon her, too, I suppose," his mate—his lie of a mate—mused.

Dead. Lyria was dead, and Aelin was the one meant to survive—

"You would pick her over me?" Lyria demanded, her chestnut eyes filling. "Is that the sort of male you have become?"

He couldn't find any words, anything to explain, to apologize.

Aelin was dead.

He couldn't breathe. Didn't want to.

❧

Connall was smirking at him. "Everything that happened to me is because of you."

Kneeling on that veranda in Doranelle, in a palace he'd hoped to never see again, Fenrys fought the bile that rose in his throat. "I'm sorry."

"Sorry, but would you change it? Was I the sacrifice you were willing to make in order to get what you wanted?"

Fenrys shook his head, but it was suddenly that of a wolf—the body he had once loved with such pride and fierceness. A wolf's form—with no ability to speak.

"You took everything I ever wanted," his twin went on. "*Everything.* Did you even mourn me? Did it even matter?"

He needed to tell him—tell his twin everything he'd meant to say, wished he'd been able to convey. But that wolf's tongue did not voice the language of men and Fae. No voice. He had no voice.

"I am dead because of you," Connall breathed. "I suffered because of you. And I will never forget it."

Please. The word burned on his tongue. *Please—*

❧

She couldn't endure it.

Rowan kneeling there, screaming.

Fenrys sobbing toward the darkened skies.

And Lorcan—Lorcan in utter silence, eyes unseeing as some untold horror played out.

Maeve hummed to herself. "Do you see what I can do? What they are powerless against?"

Rowan screamed louder, the tendons in his neck bulging. Fighting Maeve with all he had.

She couldn't endure it. Couldn't stand it.

This was no illusion, no spun dream. This, their pain—this was real.

Maeve's Valg powers, at last revealed. The same hellish power that the Valg princes possessed. The same power she'd endured. Defeated with flame.

But she had no flame to help them. Nothing at all.

"There's indeed nothing left for you to bargain with," Maeve said simply. "But yourself."

Anything but this. Anything but this—

"You are nothing."

Elide stood before him, the lofty towers of a city Lorcan had never seen, the city that should have been his home, beckoning on the horizon. The wind whipped her dark hair, as cold as the light in her eyes.

"A bastard-born nobody," she went on. "Did you think I'd sully myself with you?"

"I think you might be my mate," he rasped.

Elide snickered. "Mate? Why would you ever think you were entitled to such a thing after all you have done?"

It couldn't be real—it wasn't real. And yet that coldness in her face, the distance . . .

He'd earned it. Deserved it.

Maeve surveyed them, the three males who had been her slaves, lost to her dark power as it ripped through their minds, their memories, and laughed. "Pity about Gavriel. At least he fell nobly."

Gavriel—

Maeve turned to her. "You didn't know, did you?" A click of her tongue. "The Lion will roar no longer, his life the asking price for defending his cub."

Gavriel was dead. She felt the truth in Maeve's words. Let them punch a hole through her heart.

"You could not save him, it seems," Maeve went on. "But you can save them."

Fenrys screamed now. Rowan had fallen silent, his green eyes vacant. Whatever he beheld had drawn him past screaming, beyond weeping.

Pain. Unspeakable, unimaginable pain. As she had endured—perhaps worse.

And yet . . .

Aelin didn't give Maeve time to react. Time to even turn her head as she grabbed Goldryn where it lay beside her and hurled it at the queen.

It missed Maeve by an inch, the Valg queen twisting aside before the blade buried itself deep in the snow, steaming where it landed. Still burning.

It was all Aelin needed.

She lashed out, flame spearing into the world.

But not for Maeve.

It slammed into Rowan, into Fenrys and Lorcan. Struck their shoulders, hard and deep.

Burning them. Branding them.

⁓

Aelin was dead. She was dead, and he had failed her.

"You are a lesser male," Lyria said, still studying the gate where Aelin's body swayed. "You deserved this. After what was done to me, you deserved this."

Aelin was dead.

He did not wish to live in this world. Not for a heartbeat longer.

Aelin was dead. And he—

His shoulder twinged. And then it *burned*.

As if someone had pressed a brand to it. A red-hot poker.

A flame.

He looked down, but beheld no wound.

Lyria continued on, "You bring only suffering to those you love."

The words were distant. Secondary to that burning wound.

It singed him again, a phantom wound, a memory—

Not a memory. Not a memory, but a lifeline thrown into the dark. Into an illusion.

An anchor.

As he had once anchored her, hauling her from a Valg prince's grip.

Aelin.

His hands curled at his sides. Aelin, who had known suffering as he did. Who had been shown peaceful lives and still chosen him, exactly as he was, for what they had both endured. Illusions—those had been illusions.

Rowan gritted his teeth. Felt the thing wrapped around his mind. Holding him captive.

He let out a low snarl.

She had done this—done it before. Torn into his mind. Twisted and taken from him this most vital thing. *Aelin*.

He would not let her take it again.

~

Lorcan roared at the brand that shredded through his senses, through Elide's mocking words, through the image of Perranth, the home he wanted so badly and might never see.

Roared, and the world rippled. Became snow and darkness and battle.

And Maeve. Poised before them, her pale face livid.

Her power lunged for him, a striking panther—

Elide now lay in a grand, opulent bed, her withered hand reaching for his. An aged hand, riddled with marks, the delicate blue veins intertwining like the many rivers around Doranelle.

And her face . . . Her dark eyes were filmy, her wrinkles deep. Her thinned hair white as snow.

"This is a truth you cannot outrun," she said, her voice a croak. "A sword above our heads."

Her deathbed. That's what this was. And the hand he brushed against hers—it remained young. He remained young.

Bile coated his throat. "Please." He put a hand to his chest, as if it'd stop the relentless cracking.

Faint, throbbing pain answered back.

Elide's breaths rasped against his ears. He couldn't watch this, couldn't—

He dug his hand harder into his chest. To the pain there.

Life—life was pain. Pain, and joy. Joy *because* of the pain.

He saw it in Elide's face. In every line and age mark. In every white hair. A life lived—together. The pain of parting because of how wonderful it had been.

The darkness beyond thinned. Lorcan dug his hand into the burning wound in his shoulder.

Elide let out a hacking cough that wrecked him, yet he took it into his heart, every bit of it. All that the future might offer.

It did not frighten him.

Again and again, Connall died. Over and over.

Connall lay on the floor of the veranda, his blood leaking toward the misty river far below.

His fate—it should have been his fate.

If he walked over the edge of the veranda, into that roaring river, would anyone mark his passing? If he leaped, his brother in his arms, would the river make a quick end for him?

He didn't deserve a quick end. He deserved a slow, brutal bloodletting.

His punishment, his just reward for what he'd done to his brother. The life he'd allowed to be set in his shadow, had always known remained in his shadow and hadn't tried, not really, to share the light.

A burn, violent and unflinching, tore through him. As if someone had shoved his shoulder into a furnace.

He deserved it. He welcomed it into his heart.

He hoped it would destroy him.

Pain. The thing she had dreaded inflicting upon them most, had fought and fought to keep them from.

The scent of their burned flesh stung her nostrils, and Maeve let out a low laugh. "Was that a shield, Aelin? Or were you trying to put them out of their misery?"

As he knelt beside her, Rowan's hand twitched at whatever horror he beheld, right over the edge of his discarded hatchet.

Pine and snow and the coppery tang of blood blended, rising to meet her as his palm sliced open with the force of that twitch.

"We can keep at this, you know," Maeve went on. "Until Orynth lies in ruin."

Rowan stared sightlessly ahead, his palm leaking blood onto the snow.

His fingers curled. Slightly.

A beckoning gesture, too small for Maeve to note. For anyone to note—except for her. Except for the silent language between them, the way their bodies had spoken to each other from the moment they'd met in that dusty alley in Varese.

A small act of defiance. As he had once defied Maeve before her throne in Doranelle.

Fenrys sobbed again, and Maeve glanced toward him.

Aelin slid her hand along Rowan's hatchet, the pain a whisper through her body.

Her mate trembled, fighting the mind that had invaded his once more.

"What a waste," Maeve said, turning back to them. "For these fine males to leave my service, only to wind up bound to a queen with hardly more than a few drops of power to her name."

Aelin closed her hand around Rowan's.

A door flung open between them. A door back to himself, to her.

His fingers locked around hers.

Aelin let out a low laugh. "I may have no magic," she said, "but my mate does."

Waiting to strike from the other side of that dark doorway, Rowan hauled Aelin to her feet as their powers, their souls, fused.

The force of Rowan's magic hit her, ancient and raging. Ice and wind turned to searing flame.

Her heart sang, roaring, at the power that flowed from Rowan and into her. At her side, her mate held fast. Unbreakable.

Rowan smiled—fierce and feral and wicked. A crown of flame, twin to her own, appeared atop his head.

As one, they looked to Maeve.

Maeve hissed, her dark power massing again. "Rowan Whitethorn does not have the brute power that you once did."

"Perhaps he doesn't," Lorcan said from a step behind them, his eyes clear and free, "but together, we do." He glanced to Aelin, a hand rising to the angry red burn marring his chest.

"And beyond us," Aelin said, sketching a mark through the snow with the blood she'd spilled—her blood, and Rowan's—"I think they have plenty, too."

Light flared at their feet, and Maeve's power surged—but too late.

The portal opened. Exactly as the Wyrdmarks in the books Chaol and Yrene had brought from the southern continent had promised.

Precisely to where Aelin had intended. Where she had glimpsed as she'd tumbled back through the Wyrdgate. Where she and Rowan had ventured days ago, testing this very portal.

The forest glen was silvered in the moonlight, the snows thick. Strange, old trees—older than even those in Oakwald. Trees that could only be found north of Terrasen, in the hinterlands beyond.

But it was not the trees that made Maeve halt. No, it was the teeming mass of people, their armor and weapons glinting beneath their heavy furs. Amongst them, large as horses, wolves growled. Wolves with riders.

Down the battlefield, portal after portal opened. Right where Rowan and the cadre had drawn them in their own blood as they fought. All to be opened upon this spell. This command. And beyond each portal, that teeming mass of people could be seen. The army.

"I heard you planned to come here, you see," Aelin said to Maeve, Rowan's power a symphony in her blood. "Heard you planned to bring the *kharankui*-princesses with you." She smiled. "So I thought to bring some friends of my own."

The first of the figures beyond the portal emerged, riding a great silver wolf. And even with the furs over her heavy armor, the female's arched ears could be seen.

"The Fae who dwelled in Terrasen were not wiped out so thoroughly," Aelin said. Lorcan began grinning. "They found a new home—with the Wolf Tribe." For those were humans also riding those wolves. As all the myths had claimed. "And did you know that while many of them came here with Brannon, there was an entire clan of Fae who arrived from the southern continent? Fleeing you, I think. All of them, actually, don't really like you, I'm sorry to say."

More and more Fae and wolf-riders stepped toward the portal, weapons out. Beyond them, stretching into the distance, their host flowed.

Maeve backed away a step. Just one.

"But you know who they hate even more?" Aelin pointed with Goldryn toward the battlefield. "Those spiders. Nesryn Faliq told me all about how their ancestors battled them in the southern continent. How they fled *you* when you tried to keep their healers chained, and then wound up having to battle your little friends. And when they came to Terrasen, they still remembered. Some of the truth was lost, grew muddled, but they remembered. They taught their offspring. Trained them."

The Fae and their wolves beyond the portals now fixed their sights on the *kharankui* hybrids at last emerging onto the plain.

"I told them I'd deal with you myself," Aelin said, and Rowan chuckled, "but the spiders . . . Oh, the spiders are all theirs. I think they've been waiting a while for it, actually. The Ironteeth witches, too. Apparently, the Yellowlegs weren't very kind to those trapped in their animal forms these ten years."

Aelin let out a flare of light. The only signal she needed to give.

For a people who had asked for only one thing when Aelin had begged them to fight, to join this last battle: to return home. To return to Orynth after a decade of hiding.

Her flame danced over the battlefield. And the lost Fae of Terrasen, the fabled Wolf Tribe who had welcomed and protected them at their sides, charged through the portals. Right into Morath's unsuspecting ranks.

Maeve had gone deathly pale. Paled further as magic sparked and surged and those spider-hybrids went down, their shrieks of surprise silenced under Asterion blades.

Yet Rowan's hand tightened on Aelin's, and she peered up at her mate. But his eyes were on Fenrys. On the dark power Maeve still had wrapped around him.

The male remained sprawled in the snow, his tears silent and unending. His face a bloodied ruin.

Through the roar of Rowan's power, Aelin felt for the threads leading from her heart, her soul.

Look at me. Her silent command echoed down the blood oath—to Fenrys.

Look at me.

"I suppose you think you can now finish me off in some grand fashion," Maeve said to her and Rowan, that dark power swelling. "You, who I have wronged the most."

Look at me.

His shredded face leaking blood, Fenrys looked, his eyes blindly turning toward hers. And clearing—just slightly.

Aelin blinked four times. *I am here, I am with you.*

No reply.

"Do you understand what a Valg queen is?" Maeve asked them, triumph on her face despite the long-lost Fae and wolf-riders charging onto the battlefield beyond them. "I am as vast and eternal as the sea. Erawan and his brothers *sought* me for my power." Her magic flowed around her in an unholy aura. "You believe yourself to be a God-Killer, Aelin Galathynius? What were they but vain creatures locked into this world? What were they but things your human mind cannot comprehend?" She lifted her arms. "*I* am a god."

Aelin blinked again at Fenrys, Rowan's power gathering within her veins, readying for the first and likely final strike they'd be able to land, Lorcan's power rallying beside theirs. Yet over and over, Aelin blinked to Fenrys, to those half-vacant eyes.

I am here, I am with you.

⌇

I am here, I am with you.

A queen had said that to him. In their secret, silent language. During the unspeakable hours of torment, they had said that to each other.

Not alone.

He had not been alone then, and neither had she.

The veranda in Doranelle and bloodied snows outside Orynth blended and flashed.

I am here, I am with you.

Maeve stood there. Before Aelin and Rowan, burning with power. Before Lorcan, his dark gifts a shadow around him. Fae—so many Fae and wolves, some riding them—pouring on to the battlefield through holes in the air.

It had worked, then. Their mad plan, to be enacted when all went to hell, when they had nothing left.

Yet Maeve's power swelled.

Aelin's eyes remained upon him, anchoring him. Pulling him from that bloodied veranda. To a body trembling in pain. A face that burned and throbbed.

I am here, I am with you.

And Fenrys found himself blinking back. Just once.

Yes.

And when Aelin's eyes moved again, he understood.

⁓

Aelin looked to Rowan. Found her mate already smiling at her. Aware of what likely awaited them. "Together," she said quietly. Rowan's thumb brushed against hers. In love and farewell.

And then they erupted.

Flame, white-hot and blinding, roared toward Maeve.

But the dark queen had been waiting. Twin waves of darkness arched and cascaded for them.

Only to be halted by a shield of black wind. Beaten aside.

Aelin and Rowan struck again, fast as an asp. Arrows and spears of flame that had Maeve conceding a step. Then another.

Lorcan battered her from the side, forcing Maeve to retreat another step.

"I'd say," Aelin panted, speaking above the glorious roar of magic through her, the unbreakable song of her and Rowan, "that you haven't wronged us the most at all."

Like alternating punches, Lorcan struck with them. Fire, then midnight death.

Maeve's dark brows narrowed.

Aelin flung out a wall of flame that pushed Maeve back another step. "But him—oh, he has a score to settle with you."

Maeve's eyes went wide, and she made to turn. But not fast enough.

Not fast enough at all as Fenrys vanished from where he knelt, and reappeared—right behind Maeve.

Goldryn burned bright as he plunged it through her back.

Into the dark heart within.

CHAPTER 115

Maeve's dark blood leaked onto the snow as she fell to her knees, fingers scrabbling at the burning sword stuck through her chest.

Fenrys stepped around her, leaving the sword where he'd impaled her as he walked to Aelin's side.

Embers swirling around her and Rowan, Aelin approached the queen.

Baring her teeth, Maeve hissed as she tried and failed to pry free the blade. "*Take it out.*"

Aelin only looked to Lorcan. "Anything to say?"

Lorcan smiled grimly, surveying the Fae and wolf-riders wreaking havoc on the spiders. "Long live the queen." The Faerie Queen of the West.

Maeve snarled, and it was not the sound of a Fae or human. But Valg. Pure, undiluted Valg.

"Well, look who stopped pretending," Aelin said.

"I will go anywhere you choose to banish me to," Maeve seethed. "*Just take it out.*"

"Anywhere?" Aelin asked, and let go of Rowan's hand.

The lack of his magic, his strength, hit her like plunging into an ice-cold lake.

But she had plenty of her own.

Not magic, never again as it had been, but a strength greater, deeper than that.

Fireheart, her mother had called her.

Not for her power. The name had never once been about her power.

Maeve hissed again, clawing at the blade.

Wreathing her fingers in flame, Aelin offered her hand to Maeve. "You came here to escape a husband you did not love. A world you did not love."

Maeve paused, studying Aelin's hand. The new calluses on it. She winced—winced in pain at the blade shredding her heart but not killing her. "Yes," Maeve breathed.

"And you love this world. You love Erilea."

Maeve's dark eyes scanned Aelin, then Rowan and Lorcan, before she answered. "Yes. In the way that I can love anything."

Aelin kept her hand outstretched. The unspoken offer in it. "And if I choose to banish you, you will go wherever it is we decide. And never bother us again, or any other."

"*Yes*," Maeve snapped, grimacing at the immortal blade piercing her heart. The queen bowed her head, panting, and took Aelin's outstretched hand.

Aelin drew close. Just as she slid something onto Maeve's finger.

And whispered in Maeve's ear, "Then go to hell."

Maeve reared back, but too late.

Too late, as the golden ring—Silba's ring, Athril's ring—shone on her pale hand.

Aelin backed to Rowan's side as Maeve began to scream.

Screaming and screaming toward the dark sky, toward the stars.

Maeve had wanted the ring not for protection against Valg. No, she *was* Valg. She'd wanted it so that no other might have it.

Yet when Elide had given it to Aelin, it had not been to destroy a Valg queen. But to keep Aelin safe. And Maeve would never know it—that gift and power: friendship.

What Aelin knew had kept the queen before her from becoming a mirror. What had saved her, and this kingdom.

Maeve thrashed, Goldryn burning, twin to the light on her finger.

Immunity from the Valg. And poison to them.

Maeve shrieked, the sound loud enough to shake the world.

They only stood amongst the falling snow, faces unmoved, and watched her.

Witnessed this death for all those she had destroyed.

Maeve contorted, clawing at herself. Her pale skin began to flake away like old paint.

Revealing bits of the creature beneath the glamour. The skin she'd created for herself.

Aelin only looked to Rowan, to Lorcan and Fenrys, a silent question in her eyes.

Rowan and Lorcan nodded. Fenrys blinked once, his mauled face still bleeding.

So Aelin approached the screaming queen, the creature beneath. Walked behind her and yanked out Goldryn.

Maeve sagged to the snow and mud, but the ring continued to rip her apart from within.

Maeve lifted dark, hateful eyes as Aelin raised Goldryn.

Aelin only smiled down at her. "We'll pretend my last words to you were something worthy of a song."

She swung the burning sword.

Maeve's mouth was still open in a scream as her head tumbled to the snow.

Black blood sprayed, and Aelin moved again, stabbing Goldryn through Maeve's skull. Into the earth beneath.

"Burn her," Lorcan rasped.

Rowan's hand, warm and strong, found Aelin's again.

And when she looked up at him, there were tears on his face.

Not at the dead Valg queen before them. Or even at what Aelin had done.

No, her prince, her husband, her mate, gazed to the south. To the battlefield.

Even as their power melded, and she burned Maeve into ash and memory, Rowan stared toward the battlefield.

Where line after line after line of Valg soldiers fell to their knees midfight with the Fae and wolves and Darghan cavalry.

Where the ruks flapped in amazement as ilken tumbled from the skies, like they had been struck dead.

Far out, several shrill screams rent the air—then fell silent.

An entire army, midbattle, midblow, collapsing.

It rippled outward, that collapsing, the stillness. Until all of Morath's host lay unmoving. Until the Ironteeth fighting above realized what was happening and veered southward, fleeing from the rukhin and witches who now gave chase.

Until the dark shadow surrounding that fallen army drifted away on the wind, too.

Aelin knew for certain then. Where Erawan had gone.

Who had brought him down at last.

So Aelin wrenched her sword free of the pile of ashes that had been Maeve. She lifted it high to the night sky, to the stars, and let her cry of victory fill the world. Let the name she shouted ring out, the soldiers on the field, in the city, taking up the call until all of Orynth was singing with it. Until it reached the shining stars of the Lord of the North gleaming above them, no longer needed to guide her way home.

Yrene.

Yrene.

Yrene.

CHAPTER
116

Chaol awoke to warm, delicate hands stroking over his brow, his jaw.

He knew that touch. Would know it if he were blind.

One moment, he'd been fighting his way down the battlements. The next—oblivion. As if whatever surge of power had gone through Yrene had not only weakened his spine, but his consciousness.

"I don't know whether to start yelling or crying," he said, groaning as he opened his eyes and found Yrene kneeling before him. A heartbeat had him assessing their surroundings: some sort of stairwell, where he'd been sprawled over the lowest steps near a landing. An archway open to the frigid night revealed a starry, clear sky beyond. No wyverns in it.

And cheering. Victorious, wild cheering.

Not one bone drum. Not one snarl or roar.

And Yrene, still stroking his face, was smiling at him. Tears in her eyes.

"Feel free to yell all you like," she said, some of those tears slipping free.

But Chaol just gaped at her as it hit him what, exactly, had happened. Why that surge of power had happened.

What this remarkable woman before him had done.

For they were calling her name. The army, the people of Orynth were calling her name.

He was glad he was sitting down.

Even if it did not surprise him one bit that Yrene had done the impossible.

Chaol slid his arms around her waist and buried his face in her neck. "It's over, then," he said against her skin, unable to stop the shaking that took over, the mix of relief and joy and lingering, phantom terror.

Yrene just ran her hands through his hair, down his back, and he felt her smile. "It's over."

Yet the woman he held, the child growing within her . . .

Erawan might have been over, his threat and army with it. And Maeve with it, too.

But life, Chaol realized—life was just beginning.

⁓

Nesryn didn't believe it. The enemy had just . . . collapsed. Even the *kharankui*-hybrids.

It was as unlikely as the Fae and wolves who had simply *appeared* through holes in the world. A missing army, who had wasted no time launching themselves at Morath. As if they knew precisely where and how to strike. As if they had been summoned from the ancient myths of the North.

Nesryn alit on the blood-soaked city walls, watching the rukhin and allied witches chase the Ironteeth toward the horizon. She would have been with them, were it not for the claw-marks surrounding Salkhi's eye. For the blood.

She had barely the breath to scream for a healer as she dismounted.

Barely the breath to unsaddle the ruk, murmuring to the bird as she did. So much blood, the gouging lines from the ilken sentry deep. No sheen of poison, but—

"Are you hurt?" Sartaq. The prince's eyes were wide, his face bloodied, as he scanned her from head to toe. Behind him, Kadara panted on the battlements, her feathers as bloody as her rider.

Sartaq gripped her shoulders. "Are you hurt?" She'd never seen such panic in his face.

Nesryn only pointed to the now-still enemy, unable to find the words.

But others did. One word, one name, over and over. *Yrene.*

Healers raced up the battlements, aiming for both ruks, and Nesryn allowed herself to slide her arms around Sartaq's waist. To press her face against his armored chest.

"Nesryn." Her name was a question and a command. But Nesryn only held him tightly. So close. They had come so, so close to utter defeat.

Yrene. Yrene. Yrene, the soldiers and people of the city shouted.

Sartaq ran a hand down her matted hair. "You know what victory means, don't you?"

Nesryn lifted her head, brows narrowing. Behind them, Salkhi patiently stood while the healer's magic soothed over his eye. "A good night's rest, I hope," she said.

Sartaq laughed, and pressed a kiss to her temple. "It means," he said against her skin, "that we are going home. That you are coming home—with me."

And even with the battle freshly ended, even with the dead and wounded around them, Nesryn smiled. Home. Yes, she would go home with him to the southern continent. And to all that waited there.

⁓

Aelin, Rowan, Lorcan, and Fenrys lingered on the plain outside the city gates until they were certain the fallen army was not going to rise. Until the khagan's troops went between the enemy soldiers, nudging and prodding. And received no answer.

But they did not behead. Did not sever and finish the job.

Not for those with the black rings, or black collars.

Those whom the healers might yet save.

Tomorrow. That would come tomorrow.

The moon had reached its peak when they wordlessly decided that they had seen enough to determine Erawan's army would never rise again. When the ruks, Crochans, and rebel Ironteeth had vanished, chasing the last of the aerial legion into the night.

Then Aelin turned toward the southern gate to Orynth.

As if in answer, it groaned open to meet her.

Two arms flung wide.

Aelin looked to Rowan, their crowns of flame still burning, undimmed. Took his hand.

Heart thundering through every bone in her body, Aelin took a step toward the gate. Toward Orynth. Toward home.

Lorcan and Fenrys fell into step behind them. The latter's wounds still leaked down his face, but he had refused Aelin and Rowan's offers to heal him. Had said he wanted a reminder. They hadn't dared to ask of what—not yet.

Aelin lifted her chin high, shoulders squaring as they neared the archway.

Soldiers already lined either side.

Not the khagan's soldiers, but men and women in Terrasen armor. And civilians amongst them, too—awe and joy in their faces.

Aelin looked at the threshold of the gate. At the ancient, familiar stones, now caked in blood and gore.

She sent a whisper of flame skittering over them. The last dregs of her power.

When the fire vanished, the stones were again clean. New. As this city would be made anew, brought to greater heights, greater splendors. A beacon of learning and light once more.

Rowan's fingers tightened around hers, but she did not look at him as they crossed the threshold, passing through the gate.

No, Aelin only looked at her people, smiling broadly and freely, as she entered Orynth, and they began to cheer, welcoming her home at long last.

CHAPTER 117

Aedion had fought until the enemy soldier before him had slumped to his knees as if dead.

But the man, a black ring on his finger, was not dead at all.

Only the demon inside him.

And when soldiers of countless nations began to cheer, when word spread that a Torre Cesme healer had defeated Erawan, Aedion simply turned from the battlements.

He found him by scent alone. Even in death, the scent lingered, a path that Aedion followed through the wrecked streets and throngs of celebrating, weeping people.

A lone candle had been lit in the empty barracks room where they'd set his body atop a worktable.

It was there that Aedion knelt before his father.

How long he stayed there, head bowed, he didn't know. But the candle had nearly burned down to its base when the door creaked open, and a familiar scent flitted in.

She said nothing as she approached on silent feet. Nothing as she shifted and knelt beside him.

Lysandra only leaned into him, until Aedion put his arm around her, tucking her in tight.

Together, they knelt there, and he knew her grief was as real as his. Knew her grief was for Gavriel, but also for his own loss.

The years he and his father would not have. The years he'd realized he *wanted* to have, the stories he wished to hear, the male he wished to know. And never would.

Had Gavriel known that? Or had he fallen believing his son wished nothing to do with him?

He couldn't endure it, that potential truth. Its weight would be unbearable.

When the candle sputtered out, Lysandra rose, and took him with her.

A grand burial, Aedion silently promised. With every honor, every scrap of stately regalia that could be found in the aftermath of this battle. He'd bury his father in the royal graveyard, amongst the heroes of Terrasen. Where he himself would be buried one day. Beside him.

It was the least he could do. To make sure his father knew in the Afterworld.

They stepped into the street, and Lysandra paused to wipe away his tears. To kiss his cheeks, then his mouth. Loving, gentle touches.

Aedion slid his arms around her and held her tightly under the stars and moonlight.

How long they stood in the street, he didn't know. But then a throat cleared nearby, and they peeled apart to turn toward its source.

A young man, no older than thirty, stood there.

Staring at Lysandra.

Not a messenger, or a soldier, though he wore the heavy clothes of the rukhin. There was a self-possessed purpose to him, a quiet sort of strength in his tall frame as he swallowed.

"Are you—are you Lady Lysandra?"

Lysandra angled her head. "I am."

The man took a step, and Aedion suppressed the urge to push her behind him. To draw his sword on the man whose gray eyes widened—and shone with tears.

Who smiled at her, broad and joyous.

"My name is Falkan Ennar," he said, putting a hand on his chest.

Lysandra's face remained the portrait of wary confusion.

Falkan's smile didn't waver. "I have been looking for you for a very, very long time."

And then it came out, Falkan's tears flowing as he told her.

Her uncle. He was her uncle.

Her father had been much older than him, but ever since Falkan had learned of her existence, he'd been searching for her. Ten years, he'd hunted for his dead brother's abandoned child, visiting Rifthold whenever he could. Never realizing that she might have his gifts, too—might not wear any of his brother's features.

But Nesryn Faliq had found him. Or they'd found each other. And then they had figured it out, a bit of chance in this wide world.

His fortune as a merchant was hers to inherit, if she would like.

"Whatever you wish," Falkan said. "You shall never want for anything again."

Lysandra was crying, and it was pure joy on her face as she flung her arms around Falkan and embraced him tightly.

Aedion watched, silent and ripped open. Yet happy for her—he would always be happy for her, for any ray of light she found.

Lysandra pulled away from Falkan, though. Still smiling bright, more lovely than the night sky above. She laced her fingers with Aedion's and squeezed tight as she answered her uncle at last, "I already have everything I need."

Hours later, still sitting on the balcony where Erawan had been blasted away into nothing, Dorian didn't quite believe it.

He kept staring at that spot, the dark stain on the stones, Damaris jutting up from it. The only trace left.

His father's name. His own name. The weight of it settled into him, not a wholly unpleasant thing.

Dorian flexed his bloodied fingers. His magic lay in scraps, the tang of blood lingering on his tongue. An approaching burnout. He'd never had one before. He supposed he'd better become accustomed to them.

On shaking legs, Dorian yanked Damaris from the stones. The blade had turned black as onyx. A swipe of his fingers down the fuller revealed it was a stain that would not be cleansed.

He needed to get off this tower. Find Chaol. Find the others. Start helping the injured. And the unconscious soldiers on the plain. The ones who had not been possessed had already fled, pursued by the strange Fae who had appeared, the giant wolves and their riders amongst them.

He should go. Should leave this place.

And yet he stared at the dark stain. All that remained.

Ten years of suffering and torment and fear, and the stain was all that remained.

He turned the sword in his hand, its weight heavier than it had been. The sword of truth.

What had the truth been in the end? What was the truth, even now?

Erawan had done this, slaughtered and enslaved so many, so he might see his brothers again. He wanted to conquer their world, punish it, but he'd wanted to be reunited with them. Millennia apart, and Erawan had not forgotten his brothers. Longed for them.

Would he have done the same for Chaol? For Hollin? Would he have destroyed a world to find them again?

Damaris's black blade didn't reflect the light. It didn't gleam at all.

Dorian still tightened his hand around the golden hilt and said, "I am human."

It warmed in his hand.

He peered at the blade. Gavin's blade. A relic from a time when Adarlan had been a land of peace and plenty.

And it would be that way once more.

"I am human," he repeated, to the stars now visible above the city.

The sword didn't answer again. As if it knew he no longer needed it.

Wings boomed, and then Abraxos was landing on the balcony. A white-haired rider atop him.

Dorian stood, blinking, as Manon Blackbeak dismounted. She scanned him, then the dark stain on the balcony stones.

Her golden eyes lifted to his. Weary, heavy—yet glowing. "Hello, princeling," she breathed.

A smile bloomed on his mouth. "Hello, witchling." He scanned the skies beyond her for the Thirteen, for Asterin Blackbeak, undoubtedly roaring her victory to the stars.

Manon said quietly, "You will not find them. In this sky, or any other."

His heart strained as he understood. As the loss of those twelve fierce, brilliant lives carved another hole within him. One he would not forget, one he would honor. Silently, he crossed the balcony.

Manon did not back away as he slid his arms around her. "I am sorry," he said into her hair.

Tentatively, slowly, her hands drifted across his back. Then settled, embracing him. "I miss them," she whispered, shuddering.

Dorian only held her tighter, and let Manon lean on him for as long as she needed, Abraxos staring toward that blasted bit of earth on the plain, toward the mate who would never return, while the city below celebrated.

Aelin strode with Rowan up the steep streets of Orynth.

Her people lined those streets, candles in their hands. A river of light, of fire, that pointed the way home.

Straight to the castle gates.

To where Lord Darrow stood, Evangeline at his side. The girl beaming with joy.

Darrow's face was stone-cold. Hard as the Staghorns beyond the city as he remained blocking the way.

Rowan let out a low growl, the sound echoed by Fenrys, a step behind them.

Yet Aelin let go of her mate's hand, their crowns of flame winking out as she crossed the last few feet to the castle archway. To Darrow.

Silence fell down the illuminated, golden street.

He'd deny her entry. Here, before the world, he would throw her out. A final, shaming slap.

But Evangeline tugged on Darrow's sleeve—as if in reminder.

It seemed to spur the old man into speech. "My young ward and I were told that when you went to face Erawan and Maeve, your magic was heavily depleted."

"It was. And shall remain so forever."

Darrow shook his head. "Why?"

Not about her magic being whittled to nothing. But why she had gone to face them, with little more than embers in her veins.

"Terrasen is my home," Aelin said. It was the only answer in her heart.

Darrow smiled—just a bit. "So it is." He bowed his head. Then his body. "Welcome," he said, then added as he rose, "Your Majesty."

But Aelin looked to Evangeline, the girl still beaming.

Win me back my kingdom, Evangeline.

Her order to the girl, all those months ago.

And she didn't know how Evangeline had done it. How she had changed this old lord before them. Yet there was Darrow, gesturing to the gates, to the castle behind him.

Evangeline winked at Aelin, as if in confirmation.

Aelin just laughed, taking the girl by the hand, and led that promise of Terrasen's bright future into the castle.

Every ancient, scarred hall brought her back. Snatched her breath away and set her tears running. At the memory, how they'd been. At how they now appeared, sad and worn. And what they would become once more.

Darrow led them toward the dining hall, to find whatever food and refreshment might be available in the dead of night, after such a battle.

Yet Aelin took one look at who waited in the faded grandeur of the Great Hall, and forgot about her hunger and thirst.

The entire hall grew silent as she hurtled for Aedion, and flung herself onto him so hard they rocked back a step.

Home at last; home together.

She had the vague sense of Lysandra joining Rowan and the others behind her, but didn't turn. Not as her own joyous laugh died upon seeing Aedion's haggard, weary face. The sorrow in it.

She laid a hand on his cheek. "I'm sorry."

Aedion closed his eyes, leaning into her touch, mouth wobbling.

She didn't remark on the shield across his back—her father's shield. She had never realized he carried it.

Instead she asked softly, "Where is he?"

Wordlessly, Aedion led her from the dining hall. Down the winding passageways of the castle, their castle, to a small, candlelit room.

Gavriel had been laid on a table, a wool blanket obscuring the body she knew was shredded beneath. Only his handsome face visible, still noble and kind in death.

Aedion lingered by the doorway as Aelin walked up to the warrior. She knew Rowan and the others stood by him, her mate with a hand on Aedion's shoulder. Knew Fenrys and Lorcan bowed their heads.

She stopped before the table where Gavriel had been laid. "I wished to wait to offer you the blood oath until after your son had taken it," she said, her quiet voice echoing off the stones. "But I offer it to you now, Gavriel. With honor, and gratitude, I offer you the blood oath." Her tears plopped onto the blanket covering him, and she wiped one away before drawing her dagger from the sheath at her side. She pulled his arm from beneath the covering.

A flick of the blade had her slicing his palm open. No blood flowed beyond a slight swelling. Yet she waited until a drop slid to the stones. Then opened up her own arm, dipped her fingers into the blood, and let three drops fall into his mouth.

"Let the world know," Aelin said, voice breaking, "that you are a male of honor. That you stood by your son, and this kingdom, and helped to save it." She kissed the cold brow. "You are blood-sworn to me. And you shall be buried here as such." She pulled away, stroking his cheek once. "Thank you."

It was all there was left to say.

When she turned away, it was not Aedion alone who had tears streaking down his face.

She left them there. The cadre, the brotherhood, who now wished to say farewell in their own way.

Fenrys, his bloodied face still untended, sank to a knee beside the table. A heartbeat later, Lorcan did the same.

She'd reached the door when Rowan knelt as well. And began to sing the ancient words—the words of mourning, as old and sacred as Terrasen itself. The same prayers she'd once sung and chanted while he'd tattooed her.

Rowan's clear, deep voice filling the room, Aelin looped her arm through Aedion's, and let him lean on her as they walked back to the Great Hall. "Darrow called me 'Your Majesty,'" she said after a minute.

Aedion slid his red-rimmed eyes to her. But a spark lit them—just a bit. "Should we be worried?"

Aelin's mouth curved. "I thought the same damn thing."

⁓

So many witches. There were so many witches, Ironteeth and Crochan, in the halls of the castle.

Elide scanned their faces as she worked with the healers in the Great Hall. A dark lord and dark queen defeated—yet the wounded remained. And since she had strength left in her, she would help in whatever way she could.

But when a white-haired witch limped into the hall, an injured Crochan slung between her and another witch Elide did not recognize . . . Elide was halfway across the space, across the hall where she had spent so many happy childhood days, by the time she realized she'd moved.

Manon paused at the sight of her. Gave the wounded Crochan over to her sister-in-arms. But made no move to approach.

Elide saw the sorrow on her face before she reached her. The dullness and pain in the golden eyes.

She went still. "Who?"

Manon's throat bobbed. "All."

All of the Thirteen. All those fierce, brilliant witches. Gone.

Elide put a hand to her heart, as if it could stop it from cracking.

But Manon closed the distance between them, and even with that grief in her battered, bloodied face, she put a hand on Elide's shoulder. In comfort.

As if the witch had learned how to do such things.

Elide's vision stung and blurred, and Manon wiped away the tear that escaped.

"Live, Elide," was all the witch said to her before striding out of the hall once more. "Live."

Manon vanished into the teeming hallway, braid swaying. And Elide wondered if the command had been meant for her at all.

Hours later, Elide found Lorcan standing vigil by Gavriel's body.

When she'd heard, she had wept for the male who had shown her such kindness. And from the way Lorcan knelt before Gavriel, she knew he had just finished doing the same.

Sensing her in the doorway, Lorcan rose to his feet, an aching, slow movement of the truly exhausted. There was indeed sorrow on his face. Grief and regret.

She held open her arms, and Lorcan's breath heaved out of him as he pulled her against him.

"I hear," he said onto her hair, "that you're to thank for Erawan's destruction."

Elide withdrew from his embrace, leading him from that room of sadness and candlelight. "Yrene is," she said, walking until she found a quiet spot near a bank of windows overlooking the celebrating city. "I just came up with the idea."

"Without the idea, we'd be filling the bellies of Erawan's beasts."

Elide rolled her eyes, despite all that had happened, all that lay before them. "It was a group effort, then." She bit her lip. "Perranth—have you heard anything from Perranth?"

"A ruk rider arrived a few hours ago. It is the same there as it is here: with Erawan's demise, the soldiers holding the city either collapsed or fled. Its people have reclaimed control, but those who were possessed will need healers. A group of them will be flown over tomorrow to begin."

Relief threatened to buckle her knees. "Thank Anneith for that. Or Silba, I suppose."

"They're both gone. Thank yourself."

Elide waved him off, but Lorcan kissed her.

When he pulled away, Elide breathed, "What was that for?"

"Ask me to stay," was all he said.

Her heart began racing. "Stay," she whispered.

Light, such beautiful light filled his dark eyes. "Ask me to come to Perranth with you."

Her voice broke, but she managed to say, "Come to Perranth with me."

Lorcan nodded, as if in answer, and his smile was the most beautiful thing she had ever seen. "Ask me to marry you."

Elide began crying, even as she laughed. "Will you marry me, Lorcan Salvaterre?"

He swept her up into his arms, raining kisses over her face. As if some final, chained part of him had been freed. "I'll think about it."

Elide laughed, smacking his shoulder. And then laughed again, louder.

Lorcan set her down. "What?"

Elide's mouth bobbed as she tried to stop her laughing. "It's just . . . I'm Lady of Perranth. If you marry me, you will take my family name."

He blinked.

Elide laughed again. "Lord Lorcan Lochan?"

It sounded just as ridiculous coming out.

Lorcan blinked at her, then howled.

She'd never heard such a joyous sound.

He swept her up in his arms again, spinning her. "I'll use it with pride every damned day for the rest of my life," he said into her hair, and when he set her down, his smile had vanished. Replaced by an infinite tenderness as he brushed back her hair, hooking it over an ear. "I will marry you, Elide Lochan. And proudly call myself Lord Lorcan Lochan, even when the whole kingdom laughs to hear it." He kissed her, gently and lovingly. "And when we are wed," he whispered, "I will bind my life to yours. So we will never know a day apart. Never be alone, ever again."

Elide covered her face with her hands and sobbed, at the heart he offered, at the immortality he was willing to part with for her. For *them*.

But Lorcan clasped her wrists, gently prying her hands from her face. His smile was tentative. "If you would like that," he said.

Elide slid her arms around his neck, feeling his thundering heartbeat raging against hers, letting his warmth sink into her bones. "I would like that more than anything," she whispered back.

CHAPTER 118

Yrene slumped onto the three-legged stool amid the chaos of the Great Hall. The story was familiar, though the setting slightly altered: another mighty chamber turned into a temporary sick bay. Dawn was not far off, yet she and the other healers kept working. Those bleeding out wouldn't be able to survive without them.

Human and Fae and witch and Wolf—Yrene had never seen such an assortment of people in one place.

Elide had come in at some point, glowing despite the injured around them.

Yrene supposed they all wore that same smile. Though her own had faltered in the past hour, as exhaustion settled in. She'd been forced to rest after dealing with Erawan, and had waited until her well of power had refilled only just enough to begin working again.

She couldn't sit still. Not when she saw the thing that lay beneath Erawan's skin every time she closed her eyes. Forever gone, yes, but . . . she wondered when she'd forget him. The dark, oily feel of him. Hours ago, she hadn't been able to tell if the retching that ensued was from the memory of him or the babe in her womb.

"You should find that husband of yours and go to bed," Hafiza said, hobbling over and frowning. "When was the last time you slept?"

Yrene lifted her head—heavier than it had been minutes ago. "The last time you did, I'd wager." Two days ago.

Hafiza clicked her tongue. "Slaying a dark lord, healing the wounded . . . It's a wonder you're not unconscious right now, Yrene."

Yrene was about to be, but the disapproval in Hafiza's voice steeled her spine. "I can work."

"I'm ordering you to find that dashing husband of yours and go to sleep. On behalf of the child in your womb."

Och. When the Healer on High put it like *that* . . .

Yrene groaned as she stood. "You're merciless."

Hafiza just patted her shoulder. "Good healers know when to rest. Exhaustion makes for sloppy decisions. And sloppy decisions—"

"Cost lives," Yrene finished. She lifted her eyes toward the vaulted ceiling high, high above. "You never stop teaching, do you?"

Hafiza's mouth cracked into a grin. "This is *life*, Yrene. We never stop learning. Even at my age."

Yrene had long suspected that love of learning was what had kept the Healer on High young at heart all these years. She just smiled back at her mentor.

But Hafiza's eyes softened. Grew contemplative. "We will remain for as long as we are needed—until the khagan's soldiers can be transported home. We'll leave some behind to tend for any remaining wounded, but in a few weeks, we will go."

Yrene's throat tightened. "I know."

"And you," Hafiza went on, taking her hand, "will not return with us."

Her eyes burned, but Yrene whispered, "No, I won't."

Hafiza squeezed Yrene's fingers, her hand warm. Strong as steel. "I shall have to find myself a new heir apparent, then."

"I'm sorry," she whispered.

"Whatever for?" Hafiza chuckled. "You have found love, and happiness, Yrene. There is nothing more that I could ever wish for you."

Yrene wiped away the tear that slipped out. "I just—I don't want you to think I wasted your time—"

Hafiza crowed with laughter. "Wasted my time? Yrene Towers—Yrene Westfall." The ancient woman cupped Yrene's face with her strong, ancient hands. "You have saved us *all*." Yrene closed her eyes as Hafiza pressed a kiss to her brow. A blessing and a farewell.

"You will stay in these lands," Hafiza said, her smile unwavering. "But even with the ocean dividing us, we will remain linked here." She touched her chest, right over her heart. "And no matter the years, you will forever have a place at the Torre. Always."

Yrene put a shaking hand over her own heart and nodded.

Hafiza squeezed her shoulder and made to walk back to her patients.

But Yrene said, "What if—"

Hafiza turned, brows rising. "Yes?"

Yrene swallowed. "What if, once I have settled in Adarlan, and had this babe . . . When the time is right, what if I established my own Torre here?"

Hafiza cocked her head, as if listening to the cadence of the statement while it echoed into her heart. "A Torre Cesme in the North."

Yrene went on, "In Adarlan. In Rifthold. A new Torre to replenish what Erawan destroyed. To teach the children who might not realize they have the gift, and those who will be born with it." Because many of the Fae streaming in from the battlefield were descendants of the healers who had gifted the Torre women with their powers—long ago. Perhaps they would wish to help again.

Hafiza smiled anew. "I like that idea very much, Yrene Westfall."

With that, the Healer on High walked back into the fray of healing and pain.

But Yrene remained standing there, a hand drifting to the slight swelling in her belly.

And she smiled—broad and unfalteringly—at the future that opened before her, bright as the oncoming dawn.

⁓

Sunrise was near, yet Manon could not sleep. Had not bothered to find a place to rest, not while the Crochans and Ironteeth remained injured, and she had not yet finished her count of how many had survived the battle. The war.

There was an empty space inside her where twelve souls had once burned fiercely.

Perhaps that was why she had not found her bed, not even when she knew Dorian had likely procured sleeping arrangements. Why she still lingered in the aerie, Abraxos dozing beside her, and stared out at the silent battlefield.

When the bodies were cleared, when the snows melted, when the spring came, would a blasted bit of earth linger on the plain before the city? Would it forever remain as such, a marker of where they fell?

"We have a final count," Bronwen said behind her, and Manon found the Crochan and Glennis emerging from the tower stairwell, Petrah at their heels.

Manon braced herself for it as she waved a hand in silent request.

Bad. But not as bad as it could have been.

When Manon opened her eyes, the three of them only stared at her. Ironteeth and Crochan, standing together in peace. As allies.

"We'll collect the dead tomorrow," Manon said, her voice low. "And burn them at moonrise." As both Crochans and Ironteeth did. A full moon tomorrow—the Mother's Womb. A good moon to be burned. To be returned to the Three-Faced Goddess, and reborn within that womb.

"And after that?" Petrah asked. "What then?"

Manon looked from Petrah to Glennis and Bronwen. "What should you like to do?"

Glennis said softly, "Go home."

Manon swallowed. "You and the Crochans may leave whenever you—"

"To the Wastes," Glennis said. "Together."

Manon and Petrah swapped a glance. Petrah said, "We cannot."

Bronwen's lips curved upward. "You can."

Manon blinked. And blinked again as Bronwen extended a fist toward Manon and opened it.

Inside lay a pale purple flower, small as Manon's thumbnail. Beautiful and delicate.

"A bastion of Crochans just made it here—a bit late, but they heard the call and came. All the way from the Wastes."

Manon stared and stared at that purple flower.

"They brought this with them. From the plain before the Witch-City."

The barren, bloodied plain. The land that had yielded no flowers, no life beyond grass and moss and—

Manon's sight blurred, and Glennis took her hand, guiding it toward Bronwen's before the witch tipped the flower into Manon's palm. "Only together can it be undone," Glennis whispered. "Be the bridge. Be the light."

A bridge between their two peoples, as Manon had become.

A light—as the Thirteen had exploded with light, not darkness, in their final moments.

"When iron melts," Petrah murmured, her blue eyes swimming with tears.

The Thirteen had melted that tower. Melted the Ironteeth within it. And themselves.

"When flowers spring from fields of blood," Bronwen went on.

Manon's knees buckled as she stared out at that battlefield. Where countless flowers had been laid atop the blood and ruins where the Thirteen had met their end.

Glennis finished, "Let the land be witness."

The battlefield where the rulers and citizens of so many kingdoms, so many nations, had come to pay tribute. To witness the sacrifice of the Thirteen and honor them.

Silence fell, and Manon whispered, her voice shaking as she held that small, impossibly precious flower in her palm, "And return home."

Glennis bowed her head. "And so the curse is broken. And so we shall go home together—as one people."

The curse was broken.

Manon just stared at them, her breathing turning jagged.

Then she roused Abraxos, and was in the saddle within heartbeats. She did not offer them any explanation, any farewell, as they leaped into the thinning night.

As she guided her wyvern to the bit of blasted earth on the battlefield. Right to its heart.

And smiling through her tears, laughing in joy and sorrow, Manon laid that precious flower from the Wastes upon the ground.

In thanks and in love.

So they would know, so Asterin would know, in the realm where she and her hunter and child walked hand in hand, that they had made it.

That they were going home.

Aelin wanted to, but could not sleep. Had ignored the offers to find her a room, a bed, in the chaos of the castle.

Instead, she and Rowan had gone to the Great Hall, to talk to the wounded, to offer what help they could for those who needed it most.

The lost Fae of Terrasen, their giant wolves and adopted human clan with them, wanted to speak to her as much as the citizens of Orynth. How they had found the Wolf Tribe a decade ago, how they'd fallen in with them in the wilds of the mountains and hinterlands beyond, was a tale she'd soon learn. The world would learn.

Their healers filled the Great Hall, joining the Torre women. All descended from those in the southern continent—and apparently trained by them, too. Dozens of fresh healers, each bearing badly needed supplies. They fell seamlessly into work alongside those from the Torre. As if they had been doing so for centuries.

And when the healers both human and Fae had shooed them out, Aelin had wandered.

Each hallway and floor, peering into the rooms so full of ghosts and memory. Rowan had walked at her side, a quiet, unfaltering presence.

Level by level they went, rising ever higher.

They were nearing the top of the north tower when dawn broke.

The morning was brutally cold, even more so atop the tower standing high over the world, but the day would be clear. Bright.

"So there it is," Aelin said, nodding toward the dark stain on the balcony stones. "Where Erawan met his end at the hands of a healer." She frowned. "I hope it will wash off."

Rowan snorted, and when she looked over her shoulder, the wind whipping her hair, she found him leaning against the stairwell door, his arms crossed.

"I mean it," she said. "It'll be odious to have his mess there. And I plan to use this balcony to sun myself. He'll ruin it."

Rowan chuckled, and pushed off the door, going to the balcony rail. "If it doesn't wash off, we'll throw a rug over it."

Aelin laughed, and joined him, leaning into his warmth as the sun gilded the battlefield, the river, the Staghorns. "Well, now you've seen every hall and room and stairwell. What do you make of your new home?"

"A little small, but we'll manage."

Aelin nudged him with an elbow, and jerked her chin to the nearby western tower. Where the north tower was tall, the western tower was wide. Grand. Near its upper levels, hanging over the perilous drop, a walled stone garden glowed in the sunlight. The king's garden.

Queen's, she supposed.

There had been nothing left but a tangle of thorns and snow. Yet she still remembered it, when it had belonged to Orlon. The roses and drooping latticework of wisteria, the fountains that had streamed right over the edge of the garden and into the open air below, the apple tree with blossoms like clumps of snow in the spring.

"I never realized how convenient it would be for Fleetfoot," she said of the secret, private garden. Reserved *only* for the royal family. Sometimes just for the king or queen themselves. "To not have to run down the tower stairs every time she needs to pee."

"I'm sure your ancestors had canine bathroom habits in mind when they built it."

"I would have," Aelin grumbled.

"Oh, I believe it," Rowan said, smirking. "But can you explain to me why we're not in there right now, sleeping?"

"In the garden?"

He flicked her nose. "In the suite beyond the garden. Our bedroom."

She'd led him quickly through the space. Still preserved well enough, despite the disrepair of the rest of the castle. One of the Adarlanian cronies had undoubtedly used it. "I want it cleaned of any trace of Adarlan before I stay in there," she admitted.

"Ah."

She heaved a breath, sucking down the morning air.

Aelin heard them before she saw them, scented them. And when they turned, they found Lorcan and Elide walking onto the tower balcony, Aedion, Lysandra, and Fenrys trailing. Ren Allsbrook, tentative and wary-eyed, emerged behind them.

How they'd known where to find them, why they'd come, Aelin had no idea. Fenrys's wounds had closed at least, though twin, red scars slashed from his brow to his jaw. He didn't seem to notice—or care.

She also didn't fail to note the hand Lorcan kept on Elide's back. The glow on the lady's face.

Aelin could guess well enough what that glow was from. Even Lorcan's dark eyes were bright.

It didn't stop Aelin from catching Lorcan's stare. And giving him a warning look that conveyed everything she didn't bother to say: if he broke the Lady of Perranth's heart, she'd flambé him. And would invite Manon Blackbeak to roast some dinner over his burning corpse.

Lorcan rolled his eyes, and Aelin deemed that acceptance enough as she asked them all, "Did *anyone* bother to sleep?"

Only Fenrys lifted his hand.

Aedion frowned at the dark stain on the stones.

"We're putting a rug over it," Aelin told him.

Lysandra laughed. "Something tacky, I hope."

"I'm thinking pink and purple. Embroidered with flowers. Just what Erawan would have loved."

The Fae males gaped at them, Ren blinking. Elide ducked her head as she chuckled.

Rowan snorted again. "At least this court won't be boring."

Aelin put a hand on her chest, the portrait of outrage. "You were honestly worried it would be?"

"Gods help us," Lorcan grumbled. Elide elbowed him.

Aedion said to Ren, the young lord lingering by the archway, as if still debating making a quick exit, "Now's the chance to escape, you know. Before you get sucked into this endless nonsense."

But Ren's dark eyes met Aelin's. Scanned them.

She'd heard about Murtaugh. Knew now was not the time to mention it, the loss dimming his eyes. So she kept her face open. Honest. Warm. "We could always use one more to partake in the nonsense," Aelin said, an invisible hand outstretched.

Ren scanned her again. "You gave up everything and still came back here. Still fought."

"All of it for Terrasen," she said quietly.

"Yes, I know," Ren said, the scar down his face stark in the rising sun. "I understand that now." He offered her a small smile. "I think I might need a bit of nonsense myself, after this war."

Aedion muttered, "You'll regret saying that."

But Aelin sketched a bow. "Oh, he certainly will." She smirked at the males assembled. "I swear to you, I won't bore you to tears. A queen's oath."

"And what will not boring us entail, then?" Aedion asked.

"Rebuilding," Elide said. "Lots of rebuilding."

"Trade negotiations," Lysandra said.

"Training a new generation in magic," Aelin went on.

Again, the males blinked at them.

Aelin angled her head, blinking right back at them. "Don't you lot have anything worthwhile to contribute?" She clicked her tongue. "Three of you are ancient as hell, you know. I'd have expected better from cranky old bastards."

Their nostrils flared. Aedion grinned, Ren wisely clamping his lips together to keep from doing the same.

But Fenrys said, "Four. Four of us are old as hell."

Aelin arched a brow.

Fenrys smirked, the movement stretching his scars. "Vaughan is still out there. And now free."

Rowan crossed his arms. "He'll never be caught again."

But Fenrys's smirk turned knowing. He pointed to the camped Fae army on the plain, the wolves and humans amongst them. "I have a feeling someone down there might know where we could start." He glanced at Aelin. "If you'd be amenable to another cranky old bastard joining this court."

Aelin shrugged. "If you can convince him, I don't see why not." Rowan smiled at that, and scanned the sky, as if he could see his missing friend soaring there.

Fenrys winked. "I promise he's not as miserable as Lorcan." Elide smacked his arm, and Fenrys darted away, hands up as he laughed. "You'll like him," he promised Aelin. "All the ladies do," he added with another wink to her, Lysandra, and Elide.

Aelin laughed, the sound lighter, freer than any she had made, and faced the stirring kingdom. "We promised everyone a better world," she said after a moment, voice solemn. "So we'll start with that."

"Starting small," Fenrys said. "I like it."

Aelin smirked at him. "I rather liked the whole let's-vote-on-the-Wyrdkeys thing we did. So we'll start with more of that, too."

Silence. Then Lysandra asked, "Voting on what?"

Aelin shrugged, sliding her hands into her pockets. "Things."

Aedion arched a brow. "Like dinner?"

Aelin rolled her eyes. "Yes, on dinner. Dinner by committee."

Elide coughed. "I think Aelin means on vital things. On how to run this kingdom."

"You're queen," Lorcan said. "What's there to vote on?"

"People should have a say in how they are governed. Policies that impact them. They should have a say in how this kingdom is rebuilt." Aelin lifted her chin. "I will be queen, and my children . . ." Her cheeks heated as she smiled toward Rowan. "Our children," she said a bit softly, "will rule. One day. But Terrasen should have a voice. Each territory, regardless of the lords who rule it, should have a voice. One chosen by its people."

The cadre looked toward one another then. Rowan said, "There was a kingdom—to the east. Long ago. They believed in such things." Pride glowed in his eyes, brighter than the dawn. "It was a place of peace and learning. A beacon in a distant and violent part of the world. Once the Library of Orynth is rebuilt, we'll ask the scholars to find what they can about it."

"We could reach out to the kingdom itself," Fenrys said. "See if some of their scholars or leaders might want to come here. To help us." He shrugged. "I could do it. Travel there, if you wish."

She knew he meant it—to travel as their emissary. Perhaps to work through all he'd seen and endured. To make peace with the loss of his brother. With himself. She had a feeling the scars down his face would only fade when he willed it.

But Aelin nodded. And while she'd gladly send Fenrys wherever he wished—"The library?" she blurted.

Rowan only smiled. "And the Royal Theater."

"There was no theater—not like in Rifthold."

Rowan's smile grew. "There will be."

Aelin waved him off. "Need I remind you that despite winning this war, we are no longer flush with gold?"

Rowan slid his arm around her shoulders. "Need I remind you that since you beheaded Maeve, I am a Prince of Doranelle once again, with access to my assets and estates? And that with Maeve outed as an imposter, half of her wealth goes to you . . . and the other to the Whitethorns?"

Aelin blinked at him slowly. The others grinned. Even Lorcan.

Rowan kissed her. "A new library and Royal Theater," he murmured onto her mouth. "Consider them my mating presents to you, Fireheart."

Aelin pulled back, scanning his face. Read the sincerity and conviction.

And, throwing her arms around him, laughing to the lightening sky, she burst into tears.

It was to be a day for many meetings, Aelin decided as she stood in a near-empty, dusty chamber and smiled at her allies. Her friends.

Ansel of Briarcliff, bruised and scratched, smiled back. "Your shifter was a good liar," she said. "I'm ashamed I didn't notice it myself."

Prince Galan, equally battered, huffed a laugh. "In my defense, I've never met you." He inclined his head to Aelin. "So, hello, cousin."

Aelin, leaning against the half-decayed desk that served as the lone piece of furniture in the room, smirked at him. "I saw you from a distance—once."

Galan's Ashryver eyes sparked. "I'm going to assume it was during your former profession and thank you for not killing me."

Aelin chuckled, even as Rolfe rolled his eyes. "Yes, Privateer?"

Rolfe waved a tattooed hand, blood still clinging beneath his nails. "I'll refrain from commenting."

Aelin smirked. "You're the Heir to the Mycenian people," she said. "Petty squabbles are now beneath you."

Ansel snorted. Rolfe shot her a look.

"What *do* you intend to do with them now?" Aelin asked. She supposed the rest of her court should have been here, but when she'd dispatched Evangeline to round up their allies, she'd opted to let them rest. Rowan, at least, had gone to seek out Endymion and Sellene. The latter, it seemed, was about to learn a great deal regarding her own future. The future of Doranelle.

Rolfe shrugged. "We'll have to decide where to go. Whether to return to Skull's Bay, or . . ." His sea-green eyes narrowed.

"Or?" Aelin asked sweetly.

"Or decide if we'd rather rebuild our old home in Ilium."

"Why not decide yourself?" Ansel asked.

Rolfe waved a tattooed hand. "They offered up their lives to fight in this war. They should be able to choose where they wish to live after it."

"Wise," Aelin said, clicking her tongue. Rolfe stiffened, but relaxed upon seeing the warmth in her gaze. But she looked to Ilias, the assassin's armor dented and scratched. "Did you speak at all this entire war?"

"No," Ansel answered for him. The Mute Master's son looked to the young queen. Held her stare.

Aelin blinked at the look that passed between them. No animosity—no fear. She could have sworn Ansel flushed.

Sparing her old friend, Aelin said to them all, "Thank you."

They faced her again.

She swallowed, and put a hand over her heart. "Thank you for coming when I asked. Thank you on behalf of Terrasen. I am in your debt."

"We were in your debt," Ansel countered.

"I wasn't," Rolfe muttered.

Aelin flashed him a grin. "We're going to have fun, you and I." She surveyed her allies, worn and battle-weary, but still standing. All of them still standing. "I think we're going to have a great deal of fun."

At midday, Aelin found Manon in one of the witches' aeries, Abraxos staring out toward the battlefield.

Bandages peppered his sides and wings. And covered the former Wing Leader.

"Queen of the Crochans and the Ironteeth," Aelin said by way of greeting, letting out a low whistle that had Manon turning slowly. Aelin picked at her nails. "Impressive."

Yet the face that turned toward her—

Exhaustion. Grief.

"I heard," Aelin said quietly, lowering her hands but not approaching.

Manon said nothing, her silence conveying everything Aelin needed to know.

No, she was not all right. Yes, it had destroyed her. No, she did not wish to talk about it.

Aelin only said, "Thank you."

Manon nodded vaguely. So Aelin walked toward the witch, then past her. Right to where Abraxos sat, gazing toward Theralis. The blasted patch of earth.

Her heart strained at the sight of it. The wyvern and the earth and the witch behind her. But Aelin sat down beside the wyvern. Brushed a hand over his leathery head. He leaned into her touch.

"There will be a monument," she said to Abraxos, to Manon. "Should you wish it, I will build a monument right there. So no one shall ever forget what was given. Who we have to thank."

Wind sang through the tower, hollow and brisk. But then footsteps crunched in hay, and Manon sat down beside her.

Yet Aelin did not speak again, and asked no more questions. And Manon, realizing it, let her shoulders curve inward, let her head bow. As she might never do with anyone else. As no one else might understand—the weight they both bore.

In silence, the two queens stared toward the decimated field. Toward the future beyond it.

CHAPTER
119

It took ten days for everything to be arranged.

Ten days to clear out the throne room, to scrub the lower halls, to find the food and cooks they needed. Ten days to clean the royal suite, to find proper clothing, and outfit the throne room in queenly splendor.

Evergreen garlands hung from the pews and rafters, and as Rowan stood on the dais of the throne room, monitoring the assembled crowd, he had to admit that Lysandra had done an impressive job. Candles flickered everywhere, and fresh snow had fallen the night before, covering the scars still lingering from battle.

At his side, Aedion shifted on his feet, Lorcan and Fenrys looking straight ahead.

All of them washed and brushed and wearing clothes that made them look . . . princely.

Rowan didn't care. His green jacket, threaded with silver, was the least practical thing he'd ever donned. At his side, at least, he bore his sword, Goldryn hanging from his other hip.

Thankfully, Lorcan looked as uncomfortable as he did, clad in black.

If you wore anything else, Aelin had tutted to Lorcan, *the world would turn on its head. So burial-black it is.*

Lorcan had rolled his eyes. But Rowan had glimpsed Elide's face when he'd spotted her and Lysandra in the hall off the throne room moments before. Had seen the love and desire when she beheld Lorcan in his new clothes. And wondered how soon this hall would be hosting a wedding.

A glance at Aedion, clad in Terrasen green as well, and Rowan smiled slightly. Two weddings, likely before the summer. Though neither Lysandra nor Aedion had mentioned it.

The last of their guests finished filing into the packed space, and Rowan surveyed the rulers and allies seated in the front rows. Ansel of Briarcliff kept fidgeting in her equally new pants and jacket, Rolfe draping an arm over the pew behind her as he smirked at her discomfort. Ilias, clad in the white, layered clothes of his people, sat on Ansel's other side, the portrait of unruffled calm. A row ahead, Galan lounged in his princely regalia, chin high. He winked as his Ashryver eyes met Rowan's.

Rowan only inclined his chin back to the young man. And then inclined it toward his cousins, Enda and Sellene, seated near the aisle, the latter of whom had needed a good few hours of sitting in silence when Rowan had told her that she was now Queen of Doranelle. The Fae Queen of the East.

His silver-haired cousin hadn't dressed for her new title today, though— like Enda, she had opted for whatever clothing was the least battle-worn.

Such changes would come to Doranelle—ones Rowan knew he could not predict. The Whitethorn family would rule, Mora's line restored to power at last, but it would remain up to them, up to Sellene, how that reign would shape itself. How the Fae would choose to shape themselves without a dark queen lording over them.

How many of those Fae would choose to stay here, in Terrasen, would remain to be seen. How many would wish to build a life in this war-torn kingdom, to opt for years of hard rebuilding over returning to ease and wealth? The Fae warriors he'd encountered these two weeks had given him no indication, yet he'd seen a few of them gaze toward the Staghorns, toward Oakwald, with longing. As if they, too, heard the wild call of the wind.

Then there was the other factor: the Fae who had dwelled here before Terrasen's fall. Who had answered Aelin's desperate plea, and had returned to their hidden home amongst the Wolf Tribe in the hinterlands to prepare for the journey here. To return to Terrasen at last. And perhaps bring some of those wolves with them.

He'd work to make this kingdom worthy of their return. Worthy of all who lived here, human or Fae or witch-kind. A kingdom as great as it had once been—greater. As great as what dwelled in the far South, across the Narrow Sea, proof that a land of peace and plenty could exist.

The khaganate royals had told him much about their kingdom these days—their policies, their peoples. They now sat together on the other side of the throne room, Chaol and Dorian with them. Yrene and Nesryn also sat there, both lovely in dresses that Rowan could only assume had been borrowed. There were no shops open—and none with supplies. Indeed, it was a miracle that any of them had clean clothes at all.

Manon, at least, had refused finery. She wore her witch leathers— though her crown of stars lay upon her brow, casting its light upon Petrah Blueblood and Bronwen Crochan, seated on her either side.

Aedion's swallow was audible, and Rowan glanced to the open doors. Then to where Lord Darrow stood beside the empty throne.

Not an official throne—just a larger, finer chair that had been selected from the sad lot of candidates.

Darrow, too, stared toward the open doors, face impassive. Yet his eyes glowed.

The trumpets rang out.

A four-note summons. Repeated three times.

Pews groaned as everyone twisted to the doors.

Behind the dais, hidden beyond a painted wooden screen, a small group of musicians began playing a processional. Not the grand, sprawling orchestra that might accompany an event of this magnitude, but better than nothing.

It didn't matter anyway.

Not as Elide appeared in a lilac gown, a garland of ribbons atop her braided black hair. Every step limped, and Rowan knew it was because she had asked Lorcan not to brace her foot. She'd wanted to make this walk down the long aisle on her own two feet.

Poised and graceful, the Lady of Perranth kept her shoulders thrown back as she clutched the bouquet of holly before her and walked to the dais. Lady of Perranth—and one of Aelin's handmaidens. For today.

For Aelin's coronation.

Elide was halfway down the aisle when Lysandra appeared, clad in green velvet. People murmured. Not just at the remarkable beauty, but what she was.

The shape-shifter who had defended their kingdom. Had helped take down Erawan.

Lysandra's chin remained high as she glided down the aisle, and Aedion's own head lifted at the sight of her. The Lady of Caraverre.

Then came Evangeline, green ribbons in her red-gold hair, beaming, those scars stretched wide in utter joy. The young Lady of Arran. Darrow's ward. Who had somehow melted the lord's heart enough for him to convince the other lords to agree to this.

To Aelin's right to the throne.

They had delivered the documents two days ago. Signed by all of them.

Elide took up a spot on the right side of the throne. Then Lysandra. Then Evangeline.

Rowan's heart began thundering as everyone gazed down the now-empty aisle. As the music rose and rose, the Song of Terrasen ringing out.

And when the music hit its peak, when the world exploded with sound, regal and unbending, she appeared.

Rowan's knees buckled as everyone rose to their feet.

Clad in flowing, gauzy green and silver, her golden hair unbound, Aelin paused on the threshold of the throne room.

He had never seen anyone so beautiful.

Aelin gazed down the long aisle. As if weighing every step she would take to the dais.

To her throne.

The entire world seemed to pause with her, lingering on that threshold.

Shining brighter than the snow outside, Aelin lifted her chin and began her final walk home.

Every step, every path she had taken, had led here.

The faces of her friends, her allies, blurred as she passed by.

To the throne that waited. To the crown Darrow would place upon her head.

Each of her footfalls seemed to echo through the earth. Aelin let some of her embers stream by, bobbing in the wake of her gown's train as it flowed behind her.

Her hands shook, yet she clutched the bouquet of evergreen tighter. Evergreen—for the eternal sovereignty of Terrasen.

Each step toward that throne loomed and yet beckoned.

Rowan stood to the right of the throne, teeth bared in a fierce grin that even his training could not contain.

And there was Aedion at the throne's left. Head high and tears running down his face, the Sword of Orynth hanging at his side.

It was for him that she then smiled. For the children they had been, for what they had lost.

What they now gained.

Aelin passed Dorian and Chaol, and threw a nod their way. Winked at Ansel of Briarcliff, dabbing her eyes on her jacket sleeve.

And then Aelin was at the three steps of the dais, and Darrow strode to their edge.

As he had instructed her last night, as she had practiced over and over in a dusty stairwell for hours, Aelin ascended the three steps and knelt upon the top one.

The only time in her reign that she would ever bow.

The only thing she would ever kneel before.

Her crown. Her throne. Her kingdom.

The hall remained standing, even as Darrow motioned them to sit.

And then came the words, uttered in the Old Language. Sacred and ancient, spoken flawlessly by Darrow, who had crowned Orlon himself all those decades ago.

Do you offer your life, your body, your soul to the service of Terrasen?

She answered in the Old Language, as she had also practiced with Rowan last night until her tongue turned leaden. *I offer all that I am and all that I have to Terrasen.*

Then speak your vows.

Aelin's heart raced, and she knew Rowan could hear it, but she bowed her head and said, *I, Aelin Ashryver Whitethorn Galathynius, swear upon my immortal soul to guard, to nurture, and to honor Terrasen from this day until my very last.*

Then so it shall be, Darrow responded, and reached out a hand.

Not to her, but to Evangeline, who stepped forward with a green velvet pillow.

The crown atop it.

Adarlan had destroyed her antler throne. Had melted her crown.

So they had made a new one. In the ten days since it had been decided she was to be crowned here, before the world, they had found a master goldsmith to forge one from the remaining gold they'd stolen from the barrow in Wendlyn.

Twining bands of it, like woven antlers, rose to uphold the gem in its center.

Not a true gem, but one infinitely more precious. Darrow had given it to her himself.

The cut bit of crystal that contained the sole bloom of kingsflame from Orlon's reign.

Even amid the shining metals of the crown, the red-and-orange blossom glowed like a ruby, dazzling in the light of the morning sun as Darrow lifted the crown from the pillow.

He raised it toward the shaft of light pouring through the bank of windows behind the dais. The ceremony chosen for this time, this ray of sun. This blessing, from Mala herself.

And though the Lady of Light was forever gone, Aelin could have sworn she felt a warm hand on her shoulder as Darrow held up the crown to the sun.

Could have sworn she felt them all standing there with her, those whom she had loved with her heart of wildfire. Whose stories were again inked upon her skin.

And as the crown came down, as she braced her head, her neck, her heart, Aelin let her power shine. For those who had not made it, for those who had fought, for the world watching.

Darrow set the crown upon her head, its weight heavier than she'd thought.

Aelin closed her eyes, letting that weight, that burden and gift, settle into her.

"Rise," Darrow said, "Aelin Ashryver Whitethorn Galathynius, Queen of Terrasen."

She swallowed a sob. And slowly, her breathing steady despite the heartbeat that threatened to leap out of her chest, Aelin rose.

Darrow's gray eyes were bright. "Long may she reign."

And as Aelin turned, the call went up through the hall, echoing off the ancient stones and into the gathered city beyond the castle. *"Hail, Aelin! Queen of Terrasen!"*

The sound of it from Rowan's lips, from Aedion's, threatened to send her to her knees, but Aelin smiled. Kept her chin high and smiled.

Darrow gestured to the awaiting throne, to those last two steps.

She would sit, and the ceremony would be done.

But not yet.

Aelin turned to the left. Toward Aedion. And said quietly, but not weakly, "This has been yours from the day you were born, Prince Aedion."

Aedion went still as Aelin pushed back the gauzy sleeve of her gown, exposing her forearm.

Aedion's shoulders shook with the force of his tears.

Aelin didn't fight hers as she asked, lips wobbling, "Will you swear the blood oath to me?"

Aedion just fell to his knees before her.

Rowan silently handed her a dagger, but Aelin paused as she held it over her arm. "You fought for Terrasen when no one else would. Against all odds, beyond all hope, you fought for this kingdom. For me. For these people. Will you swear to continue to do so, for as long as you draw breath?"

Aedion's head bowed as he breathed, "Yes. In this life, and in all others, I will serve you. And Terrasen."

Aelin smiled at Aedion, at the other side to her fair coin, and sliced open her forearm before extending it to him. "Then drink, Prince. And be welcome."

Gently, Aedion took her arm and set his mouth to her wound.

And when he withdrew, her blood on his lips, Aelin smiled down at him. "You said you wanted to swear it before the entire world," she said so only he could hear. "Well, here you go."

Aedion choked out a laugh and rose, throwing his arms around her and squeezing tightly before he backed to his place on the other side of the throne.

Aelin looked to Darrow, still waiting. "Where were we?"

The old lord smiled slightly and gestured to the throne. "The last piece of this ceremony."

"*Then lunch,*" Fenrys muttered, sighing.

Aelin suppressed her smile, and took the two steps to the throne.

She halted again as she turned to sit.

Halted at the small figures who poked their heads around the throne room doors. A small gasp escaped her, enough that everyone turned to look.

"*The Little Folk,*" people murmured, some backing away as small figures darted through the shadows down the aisle, wings rustling and scales gleaming.

One of them approached the dais, and with spindly greenish hands, laid their offering at her feet.

A second crown. Mab's crown.

Taken from her saddlebags—wherever they had wound up after the battle. With them, it seemed. As if they would not let it be lost once more. Would not let her forget.

Aelin picked up the crown they had laid at her feet, gaping toward the small gathering who clustered in the shadows beyond the pews, their dark, wide eyes blinking.

"The Faerie Queen of the West," Elide said softly, though all heard.

Aelin's fingers trembled, her heart filling to the point of pain, as she surveyed the ancient, glimmering crown. Then looked to the Little Folk. "Yes," she said to them. "I will serve you, too. Until the end of my days."

And Aelin bowed to them then. The near-invisible people who had saved her so many times, and asked for nothing. The Lord of the North, who had survived, as she had, against all odds. Who had never forgotten her. She would serve them, as she would serve any citizen of Terrasen.

Everyone on the dais bowed, too. Then everyone in the throne room.

But the Little Folk were already gone.

So she placed Mab's crown atop the one of gold and crystal and silver, the ancient crown settling perfectly behind it.

And then finally, Aelin sat upon her throne.

It weighed on her, nestled against her bones, that new burden. No longer an assassin. No longer a rogue princess.

And when Aelin lifted her head to survey the cheering crowd, when she smiled, Queen of Terrasen and the Faerie Queen of the West, she burned bright as a star.

~

The ritual was not over. Not yet.

As the bells rang out over the city, declaring her coronation, the gathered city beyond cheered.

Aelin went to greet them.

Down to the castle gates, her court, her friends, following her, the crowd from the throne room behind. And when she stopped at the sealed gates, the ancient, carved metal looming, the city and world awaiting beyond it, Aelin turned toward them.

Toward all those who had come with her, who had gotten them to this day, this joyous ringing of the bells.

She beckoned her court forward.

Then smiled at Dorian and Chaol, at Yrene and Nesryn and Sartaq and their companions. And beckoned them forward, too.

Brows rising, they approached.

But Aelin, crowned and glowing, only said, "Walk with me." She gestured to the gates behind her. "All of you."

This day did not belong to her alone. Not at all.

And when they all balked, Aelin walked forward. Took Yrene Westfall by the hand to guide her to the front. Then Manon Blackbeak. Elide Lochan. Lysandra. Evangeline. Nesryn Faliq. Borte and Hasar and Ansel of Briarcliff.

All the women who had fought by her side, or from afar. Who had bled and sacrificed and never given up hope that this day might come.

"Walk with me," Aelin said to them, the men and males falling into step behind. "My friends."

The bells still ringing, Aelin nodded to the guards at the castle gates.

They opened at last, and the roar from the gathered crowds was loud enough to rattle the stars.

As one, they walked out. Into the cheering city.

Into the streets, where people danced and sang, where they wept and clasped their hands to their hearts at the sight of the parade of waving, smiling rulers and warriors and heroes who had saved their kingdom, their lands. At the sight of the newly crowned queen, joy lighting her eyes.

A new world.

A better world.

CHAPTER
120

Two days later, Nesryn Faliq was still recovering from the ball that had lasted until dawn.

But what a celebration it had been.

Nothing as majestic as anything in the southern continent, but the sheer joy and laughter in the Great Hall, the feasting and dancing . . . She would never forget it, as long as she lived.

Even if it might take her until her dying day to feel rested again.

Her feet still ached from dancing and dancing and dancing, and she'd spotted both Aelin and Lysandra grousing about it at the breakfast table just an hour ago.

The queen had danced, though—a sight Nesryn would never forget, either.

The first dance had been Aelin's to lead, and she had selected her mate to join her. Both queen and consort had changed for the party, Aelin into a gown of black threaded with gold, Rowan into black embroidered with silver. And what a pair they had been, alone on the dance floor.

The queen had seemed shocked—delighted—as the Fae Prince had led her into a waltz and had not faltered a step. So delighted that she'd crowned them both with flames.

That had been the start of it.

The dance had been . . . Nesryn had no words for the swiftness and grace of their dance. Their first as queen and consort. Their movements had been a question and answer to each other, and when the music had sped up, Rowan had spun and dipped and twirled her, the skirts of her black gown revealing Aelin's feet, clad in golden slippers.

Feet that moved so quickly over the floor that embers sparked at her heels. Trailed in the wake of her sweeping dress.

Faster and faster, Aelin and Rowan had danced, spinning, spinning, spinning, the queen glowing like she'd been freshly forged as the music gathered into a clashing close.

And when the waltz slammed into its triumphant, final note, they halted—a perfect, sudden stop. Right before the queen threw her arms around Rowan and kissed him.

Nesryn was still smiling about it, sore feet and all, as she stood in the dusty chamber that had become the headquarters for the khaganate royals, and listened to them talk.

"The Healer on High says it will be another five days until the last of our soldiers are ready," Prince Kashin was saying to his siblings. To Dorian, who had been asked into this meeting today.

"And you will depart then?" Dorian asked, smiling a bit sadly.

"Most of us," Sartaq said, smiling with equal sadness.

For it was friendship that had grown here, even in war. True friendship, to last beyond the oceans that would separate them once more.

Sartaq said to Dorian, "We asked you here today because we have a rather unusual request."

Dorian lifted a brow.

Sartaq winced. "When we visited the Ferian Gap, some of our rukhin found wyvern eggs. Untended and abandoned. Some of them now wish to stay here. To look after them. To train them."

Nesryn blinked, right along with Dorian. No one had mentioned this to her. "I—I thought the rukhin never left their aeries," Nesryn blurted.

"These are young riders," Sartaq said with a smile. "Only two dozen." He turned to Dorian. "But they begged me to ask you if it would be permissible for them to stay when we leave."

Dorian considered. "I don't see why they couldn't." Something sparked in his eyes, an idea formed and then set aside. "I would be honored, actually."

"Just don't let them bring the wyverns home," Hasar groused. "I never want to see another wyvern for as long as I live."

Kashin patted her on the head. Hasar snapped her teeth at him.

Nesryn chuckled, but her smile faded as she found Dorian smiling sadly at her, too.

"I think I'm about to lose another Captain of the Guard," the King of Adarlan said.

Nesryn bowed her head. "I . . ." She hadn't anticipated having this conversation. Not right now, at least.

"But I will be glad," Dorian went on, "to gain another queen whom I can call friend."

Nesryn blushed. It deepened as Sartaq smirked and said, "Not queen. Empress."

Nesryn cringed, and Sartaq laughed, Dorian with him.

Then the king embraced her tightly. "Thank you, Nesryn Faliq. For all you have done."

Nesryn's throat was too tight to speak, so she hugged Dorian back.

And when the king left, when Kashin and Hasar went to find an early lunch, Nesryn turned to Sartaq and cringed again. "Empress? Really?"

Sartaq's dark eyes glittered. "We won the war, Nesryn Faliq." He tugged her close. "And now we shall go home."

She'd never heard such beautiful words.

Chaol stared at the letter in his hands.

It had arrived an hour ago, and he still hadn't opened it. No, he'd just taken it from the messenger—one of the fleet of children commanded by Evangeline—and brought it back to his bedroom.

Seated on his bed, the candlelight flickering through the worn chamber, he still couldn't bring himself to crack the red wax seal.

The doorknob twisted, and Yrene slipped in, tired but bright-eyed. "You should be sleeping."

"So should you," he said with a pointed look to her abdomen.

She waved him off, as easily as she'd waved off the titles of *Savior*, and *Hero of Erilea*. As easily as she waved off the awed stares, the tears, when she strode by.

So Chaol would be proud for both of them. Would tell their child of her bravery, her brilliance.

"What's that letter?" she asked, washing her hands, then her face, in the ewer by the window. Beyond the glass, the city was silent—sleeping, after a long day of rebuilding. The wild men of the Fangs had even remained to help, an act of kindness that Chaol would ensure did not go unrewarded. Already, he had looked into where he might expand their territory—and the peace between them and Anielle.

Chaol swallowed. "It's from my mother."

Yrene paused, her face still dripping. "Your . . . Why haven't you opened it?"

He shrugged. "Not all of us are courageous enough to take on Dark Lords, you know."

Yrene rolled her eyes, dried her face, and plopped down on the bed beside him. "Do you want me to read it first?"

He did. Damn him, but he did. Wordlessly, Chaol handed it to her.

Yrene said nothing as she opened the sealed parchment, her golden eyes darting over the inked words. Chaol tapped a finger on his knee. After a long day of healing, he knew better than to try to pace. Had barely made it back here with the cane before he'd sunk to the bed.

Yrene put a hand to her throat as she turned the page, read the back.

When she lifted her head again, tears slid down her cheeks. She handed him the letter. "You should read it yourself."

"Just tell me." He'd read it later. "Just—tell me what it says."

Yrene wiped at her face. Her mouth trembled, but there was joy in her eyes. Pure joy. "It says that she loves you. It says that she has missed you. It says that if you and I are amenable to it, she would like to come live with us. Your brother Terrin, too."

Chaol reached for the letter, scanning the text. Still not believing it. Not until he read,

I have loved you from the moment I knew you were growing in my womb.

He didn't stop his own tears from falling.

Your father informed me of what he did with my letters to you. I informed him I shall not be returning to Anielle.

Yrene leaned her head against his shoulder while he read and read.

The years have been long, and the space between us distant, his mother had written. *But when you are settled with your new wife, your babe, I would like to visit. To stay for longer than that, Terrin with me. If that would be all right with you.*

Tentative, nervous words. As if his mother, too, did not quite believe that he'd agree.

Chaol read the rest, swallowing hard as he reached the final lines.

I am so very proud of you. I have always been, and always will be. And I hope to see you very soon.

Chaol set down the letter, wiped at his cheeks, and smiled at his wife. "We're going to have to build a bigger house," he said.

Yrene's answering grin was all he'd hoped for.

~

The next day, Dorian found Chaol and Yrene in the sick bay that had been moved to the lower levels, the former in his wheeled chair, helping his wife tend to a wounded Crochan, and beckoned them to follow.

They did, not asking him questions, until he found Manon atop the aerie. Saddling Abraxos for his morning ride. Where she'd been each day, falling into a routine that Dorian knew was as much to keep the grief at bay as it was to maintain order.

Manon stilled as she beheld them, brows narrowing. She'd met Chaol and Yrene days ago, their reunion quiet but not chilly, despite how poorly Chaol's first encounter with the witch had gone. Yrene had only embraced the witch, Manon holding her stiffly, and when they'd pulled apart, Dorian could have sworn some of the paleness, the gauntness, had vanished from Manon's face.

Dorian asked the Witch-Queen, "Where do you go, when everyone leaves?"

Manon's golden eyes didn't leave his face.

He hadn't dared ask her. They hadn't dared speak of it. Just as he had not yet spoken of his father, his name. Not yet.

"To the Wastes," she said at last. "To see what might be done."

Dorian swallowed. He'd heard the witches, both Ironteeth and Crochans, talking about it. Had felt their growing nerves—and excitement. "And after?"

"There will be no after."

He smiled slightly at her, a secret, knowing smile. "Won't there be?"

Manon asked, "What is it that you want?"

You, he almost said. *All of you.*

But Dorian said, "A small faction of the rukhin are remaining in Adarlan to train the wyvern hatchlings. I want them to be my new aerial legion. And I would like you, and the other Ironteeth, to help them."

Chaol coughed, and gave him a look as if to say, *You were going to tell me this when?*

Dorian winked at his friend and turned back to Manon. "Go to the Wastes. Rebuild. But consider it—coming back. If not to be my crowned rider, then to train them." He added a bit softly, "And to say hello every now and then."

Manon stared at him.

He tried not to look like he was holding his breath, like this idea he'd had mere minutes ago in the khaganate royals' chamber wasn't coursing through him, bright and fresh.

Then Manon said, "It is only a few days by wyvern from the Wastes to Rifthold." Her eyes were wary, and yet—yet that was a slight smile. "I think Bronwen and Petrah will be able to lead if I occasionally slip away. To help the rukhin."

He saw the promise in her eyes, in that hint of a smile. Both of them still grieving, still broken in places, but in this new world of theirs . . . perhaps they might heal. Together.

"You could just marry each other," Yrene said, and Dorian whipped his head to her, incredulous. "It'd make it easier for you both, so you don't need to pretend."

Chaol gaped at his wife.

Yrene shrugged. "And be a strong alliance for our two kingdoms."

Dorian knew his face was red when he turned to Manon, apologies and denials on his lips.

But Manon smirked at Yrene, her silver-white hair lifting in the breeze, as if reaching for the united people who would soon soar westward. That smirk softened as she mounted Abraxos and gathered up the reins. "We'll see," was all Manon Blackbeak, High Queen of the Crochans and Ironteeth, said before she and her wyvern leaped into the skies.

Chaol and Yrene began bickering, laughing as they did, but Dorian strode to the edge of the aerie. Watched that white-haired rider and the wyvern with silver wings become distant as they sailed toward the horizon.

Dorian smiled. And found himself, for the first time in a while, looking forward to tomorrow.

CHAPTER
121

Rowan knew this day would be hard for her.

For all of them, who had become so close these weeks and months.

Yet a week after Aelin's coronation, they gathered again. This time not to celebrate, but to say farewell.

The day had dawned, clear and sunny, yet still brutally cold. As it would be for a time.

Aelin had asked them all to stay last night. To wait out the winter months and depart in the spring. Rowan knew she'd been aware her request was unlikely to be granted.

Some had seemed inclined to think it over, but in the end, all but Rolfe had decided to go.

Today—as one. Scattering to the four winds. The Ironteeth and Cro-chans had left before first light, vanishing swiftly and quietly. Heading westward toward their ancient home.

Rowan stood beside Aelin in the castle courtyard, and he could feel the sorrow and love and gratitude that flowed through her as she took them in. The khaganate royals and rukhin had already said their good-byes, Borte the most reluctant to say farewell, and Aelin's embrace with Nesryn Faliq had been long. They had whispered together, and he'd known what Aelin offered: companionship, even from thousands of miles away. Two young queens, with mighty kingdoms to rule.

The healers had gone with them, some on horseback with the Darghan, some in wagons, some with the rukhin. Yrene Westfall had sobbed as she had embraced the healers, the Healer on High, one last time. And then sobbed into her husband's arms for a good while after that.

Then Ansel of Briarcliff, with what remained of her men. She and Aelin had traded taunts, then laughed, and then cried, holding each other. Another bond that would not be so easily broken despite the distance.

The Silent Assassins left next, Ilias smiling at Aelin as he rode off.

Then Prince Galan, whose ships remained under the watch of Ravi and Sol in Suria and who would ride there before departing to Wendlyn. He had embraced Aedion, then clasped Rowan's hand before turning to Aelin.

His wife, his mate, his queen had said to the prince, "You came when I asked. You came without knowing any of us. I know I've already said it, but I will be forever grateful."

Galan had grinned. "It was a debt long owed, cousin. And one gladly paid."

Then he, too, rode off, his people with him. Of all the allies they'd cobbled together, only Rolfe would remain for the winter, as he was now Lord of Ilium. And Falkan Ennar, Lysandra's uncle, who wished to learn what his niece knew of shape-shifting. Perhaps build his own merchant empire here—and assist with those foreign trade agreements they'd need to quickly make.

More and more departed under the winter sun until only Dorian, Chaol, and Yrene remained.

Yrene embraced Elide, the two women swearing to write frequently.

Yrene, wisely, just nodded to Lorcan, then smiled at Lysandra, Aedion, Ren, and Fenrys before she approached Rowan and Aelin.

Yrene remained smiling as she looked between them. "When your first child is near, send for me and I will come. To help with the birth."

Rowan didn't have words for the gratitude that threatened to bow his shoulders. Fae births . . . He didn't let himself think of it. Not as he hugged the healer.

For a moment, Aelin and Yrene just stared at each other.

"We're a long way from Innish," Yrene whispered.

"But lost no longer," Aelin whispered back, voice breaking as they embraced. The two women who had held the fate of their world between them. Who had saved it.

Behind them, Chaol wiped at his face. Rowan, ducking his head, did the same.

His good-bye to Chaol was quick, their embrace firm. Dorian lingered longer, graceful and steady, even as Rowan found himself struggling to speak past the tightness in his throat.

And then Aelin stood before Dorian and Chaol, and Rowan stepped back, falling into line beside Aedion, Fenrys, Lorcan, Elide, Ren, and Lysandra. Their fledgling court—the court that would change this world. Rebuild it.

Giving their queen space for this last, hardest good-bye.

⁓

She felt as if she had been crying without end for minutes now.

Yet this parting, this final farewell . . .

Aelin looked at Chaol and Dorian and sobbed. Opened her arms to them, and wept as they held each other.

"I love you both," she whispered. "And no matter what may happen, no matter how far we may be, that will never change."

"We will see you again," Chaol said, but even his voice was thick with tears.

"Together," Dorian breathed, shaking. "We'll rebuild this world together."

She couldn't stand it, this ache in her chest. But she made herself pull away and smile at their tear-streaked faces, a hand on her heart. "Thank you for all you have done for me."

Dorian bowed his head. "Those are words I'd never thought I'd hear from you."

She barked a rasping laugh, and gave him a shove. "You're a king now. Such insults are beneath you."

He grinned, wiping at his face.

Aelin smiled at Chaol, at his wife waiting beyond him. "I wish you every happiness," she said to him. To them both.

Such light shone in Chaol's bronze eyes—that she had never seen before. "We will see each other again," he repeated.

Then he and Dorian turned toward their horses, toward the bright day beyond the castle gates. Toward their kingdom to the south. Shattered now, but not forever.

Not forever.

~

Aelin was quiet for a long time afterward, and Rowan stayed with her, following as she strode up to the castle battlements to watch Chaol, Dorian, and Yrene ride down the road that cut through the savaged Plain of Theralis. Until even they had vanished over the horizon.

Rowan kept his arm around her, breathing in her scent as she rested her head against his shoulder.

Rowan ignored the faint ache that lingered there from the tattoos she'd helped him ink the night before. Gavriel's name, rendered in the Old Language. Exactly how the Lion had once tattooed the names of his fallen warriors on himself.

Fenrys and Lorcan, a tentative peace between them, also now bore the tattoo—had demanded one as soon as they'd caught wind of what Rowan planned to do.

Aedion, however, had asked Rowan for a different design. To add Gavriel's name to the Terrasen knot already inked over his heart.

Aedion had been quiet while Rowan had worked—quiet enough that Rowan had begun telling him the stories. Story after story about the Lion. The adventures they'd shared, the lands they'd seen, the wars they'd waged. Aedion hadn't spoken while Rowan had talked and worked, the scent of his grief conveying enough.

It was a scent that would likely linger for many months to come.

Aelin let out a long sigh. "Will you let me cry in bed for the rest of today like a pathetic worm," she asked at last, "if I promise to get to work on rebuilding tomorrow?"

Rowan arched a brow, joy flowing through him, free and shining as a stream down a mountain. "Would you like me to bring you cakes and chocolate so your wallowing can be complete?"

"If you can find any."

"You destroyed the Wyrdkeys and slew Maeve. I think I can manage to find you some sweets."

"As you once said to me, it was a group effort. It might also require one to acquire cakes and chocolate."

Rowan laughed, and kissed the top of her head. And for a long moment, he just marveled that he could do it. Could stand with her here, in this kingdom, this city, this castle, where they would make their home.

He could see it now: the halls restored to their splendor, the plain and river sparkling beyond, the Staghorns beckoning. He could hear the music she'd bring to this city, and the laughter of the children in the streets. In these halls. In their royal suite.

"What are you thinking about?" she asked, peering up at his face.

Rowan brushed a kiss to her mouth. "That I get to be here. With you."

"There's lots of work to be done. Some might say as bad as dealing with Erawan."

"Nothing will ever be that bad."

She snorted. "True."

He tucked her in closer. "I am thinking about how very grateful I am. That we made it. That I found you. And how, even with all that work to be done, I will not mind a moment of it because you are with me."

She frowned, her eyes dampening. "I'm going to have a terrible headache from all this crying, and you're not helping."

Rowan laughed, and kissed her again. "Very queenly."

She hummed. "I am, if anything, the consummate portrait of royal grace."

He chuckled against her mouth. "And humility. Let's not forget that."

"Oh yes," she said, winding her arms around his neck. His blood heated, sparking with a power greater than any force a god or Wyrdkey could summon.

But Rowan pulled away, just far enough to rest his brow against hers. "Let's get you to your chambers, Majesty, so you can commence your royal wallowing."

She shook with laughter. "I might have something else in mind now."

Rowan let out a growl, and nipped at her ear, her neck. "Good. I do, too."

"And tomorrow?" she asked breathlessly, and they both paused to look at each other. To smile. "Will you work to rebuild this kingdom, this world, with me tomorrow?"

"Tomorrow, and every day after that." For every day of the thousand blessed years they were granted together. And beyond.

Aelin kissed him again and took his hand, guiding him into the castle. Into their home. "To whatever end?" she breathed.

Rowan followed her, as he had his entire life, long before they had ever met, before their souls had sparked into existence. "To whatever end, Fireheart." He glanced sidelong at her. "Can I give you a suggestion for what we should rebuild first?"

Aelin smiled, and eternity opened before them, shining and glorious and lovely. "Tell me tomorrow."

A Better World

Brutal winter gave way to soft spring.

Throughout the endless, snowy months, they had worked. On rebuilding Orynth, on all those trade agreements, on making ties with kingdoms no one had contacted in a hundred years. The lost Fae of Terrasen had returned, many of the wolf-riders with them, and immediately launched into rebuilding. Right alongside the several dozen Fae from Doranelle who had opted to stay, even when Endymion and Sellene had returned to their lands.

All across the continent, Aelin could have sworn the ringing of hammers sounded, so many peoples and lands emerging once more.

And in the South, no land worked harder to rebuild than Eyllwe. Their losses had been steep, yet they had endured—remained unbroken. The letter Aelin had written to Nehemia's parents had been the most joyous of her life. *I hope to meet you soon*, she'd written. *And repair this world together.*

Yes, they had replied. *Nehemia would wish it so.*

Aelin had kept their letter on her desk for months. Not a scar on her palm, but a promise of tomorrow. A vow to make the future as brilliant as Nehemia had dreamed it could be.

And as spring at last crept over the Staghorns, the world became green and gold and blue, the stained stones of the castle cleaned and gleaming above it all.

Aelin didn't know why she woke with the dawn. What drove her to slip from under the arm that Rowan had draped over her while they slept. Her mate remained asleep, exhausted as she was—exhausted as they all were, every single evening.

Exhausted, both of them, and their court, but happy. Elide and Lorcan— now Lord Lorcan Lochan, to Aelin's eternal amusement—had gone back to Perranth only a week ago to begin the rebuilding there, now that the healers had finished their work on the last of the Valg-possessed. They would return in three weeks, though. Along with all the other lords who had journeyed to their estates once winter had lightened its grasp. Everyone would converge on Orynth, then. For Aedion and Lysandra's wedding.

A Prince of Wendlyn no longer, but a true Lord of Terrasen.

Aelin smiled at the thought as she slipped on her dressing robe, shuffling her feet into her shearling-lined slippers. Even with spring fully upon them, the mornings were chill. Indeed, Fleetfoot lay beside the fire on her little cushioned bed, curled up tightly. And as equally exhausted as Rowan, apparently. The hound didn't bother to crack open an eye.

Aelin threw the blankets back over Rowan's naked body, smiling down at him when he didn't so much as stir. He much preferred the physical rebuilding—working for hours on repairing buildings and the city walls— to the *courtly bullshit*, as he called it. Meaning, anything that required him to put on nice clothing.

Yet he'd promised to dance with her at Lysandra and Aedion's wedding. Such unexpectedly fine dancing skills, her mate had. *Only for special occasions*, he'd warned after her coronation.

Sticking out her tongue at him, Aelin turned from their bed and strode for the windows that led onto the broad balcony overlooking the city and plain beyond. Her morning ritual—to climb out of bed, ease through the curtains, and emerge onto the balcony to breathe in the morning air.

To look at her kingdom, their kingdom, and see that it had made it.

See the green of spring, and smell the pine and snow of the wind off the Staghorns. Sometimes, Rowan joined her, holding her in silence when all that had happened weighed too heavily upon her. When the loss of her human form lingered like a phantom limb. Other times, on the days when she woke clear-eyed and smiling, he'd shift and sail on those mountain winds, soaring over the city, or Oakwald, or the Staghorns. As he loved to do, as he did when his heart was troubled or full of joy.

She knew it was the latter that sent him flying these days.

She would never stop being grateful for that. For the light, the *life* in Rowan's eyes.

The same light she knew shone in her own.

Aelin reached the heavy curtains, feeling for the handle to the balcony door. With a final smile to Rowan, she slipped into the morning sun and chill breeze.

She went still, her hands slackening at her sides, as she beheld what the dawn had revealed.

"Rowan," she whispered.

From the rustle of sheets, she knew he was instantly awake. Stalking toward her, even as he shoved on his pants.

But Aelin didn't turn as he rushed onto the balcony. And halted, too.

In silence, they stared. Bells began pealing; people shouted.

Not with fear. But in wonder.

A hand rising to her mouth, Aelin scanned the broad sweep of the world.

The mountain wind brushed away her tears, carrying with it a song, ancient and lovely. From the very heart of Oakwald. The very heart of the earth.

Rowan twined his fingers in hers and whispered, awe in every word, "For you, Fireheart. All of it is for you."

Aelin wept then. Wept in joy that lit her heart, brighter than any magic could ever be.

For across every mountain, spread beneath the green canopy of Oakwald, carpeting the entire Plain of Theralis, the kingsflame was blooming.

≫ ACKNOWLEDGMENTS ≪

Finishing up a series that I've been working on for (literally) half of my life is no easy task. But finding a way to properly thank all the people who have played a part in making this dream of mine come true is equally daunting.

I suppose I should start with my parents, to whom this book is dedicated and whose love for reading inspired my own. Thank you for reading to me every night when I was growing up, for never telling me I was too old for fairy tales, and for empowering me to follow my dreams.

None of this would have been possible without my fearless and lovely agent, Tamar Rydzinski. Tamar: You signed me when I was a twenty-two-year-old unpublished writer, and believed in this series when no one else did. Working with you these past ten years has been a privilege and a joy—thank you for being my champion, my fairy godmother, and most important, my friend.

Over the course of this series, I've had the honor of working with several fantastic editors. To Margaret Miller: thank you for taking a chance on this book, and for your insightful and genius editorial guidance throughout the years. I am a better writer for having worked with you. To Michelle Nagler and Cat Onder: thank you for your support, your vision, and your kindness. To Laura Bernier: thank you for all your help with *Tower of Dawn*—working with you on it was such a delight. To Bethany Strout:

Thank you so freaking much for all your wonderful and crucial feedback on *Kingdom of Ash*. You helped me shape this book into something I'm truly proud of. And to Kamilla Benko: we haven't been working together that long, but it's already such a pleasure!

To Lynette Noni: thank you, thank you, thank you for your insanely brilliant notes on this book, for reading it multiple times, and for all those last-minute catches. I'm so glad our paths crossed in Australia all those years ago.

To the entire team at Bloomsbury, present and past, who have worked so tirelessly on these books: Cindy Loh, Cristina Gilbert, Kathleen Farrar, Nigel Newton, Rebecca McNally, Emma Hopkin, Lizzy Mason, Erica Barmash, Emily Ritter, Alona Fryman, Alexis Castellanos, Courtney Griffin, Beth Eller, Jenny Collins, Phoebe Dyer, Nick Parker, Lily Yengle, Frank Bumbalo, Donna Mark, John Candell, Yelena Safronova, Melissa Kavonic, Oona Patrick, Liz Byer, Diane Aronson, Kerry Johnson, Christine Ma, Linda Minton, Chandra Wohleber, Jill Amack, Emma Saska, Donna Gauthier, Doug White, Nicholas Church, Claire Henry, Lucy MacKay-Sim, Elise Burns, Andrea Kearney, Maia Fjord, Laura Main Ellen, Sian Robertson, Emily Moran, Ian Lamb, Emma Bradshaw, Fabia Ma, Grace Whooley, Alice Grigg, Joanna Everard, Jacqueline Sells, Tram-Anh Doan, Beatrice Cross, Jade Westwood, Cesca Hopwood, Jet Purdie, Saskia Dunn, Sonia Palmisano, Catriona Feeney, Hermione Davis, Hannah Temby, Grainne Reidy, Kate Sederstrom, Hali Baumstein, Charlotte Davis, Jennifer Gonzalez, Veronica Gonzalez, Elizabeth Tzetzo. Thank you from the bottom of my heart for making this series a reality. I adore you all.

To the team at the Laura Dail Literary Agency: you guys are badasses and I love you. To Giovanna Petta and Grace Beck: thanks *so much* for your help. To Jon Cassir and the team at CAA: thank you for being so fantastic to work with, and for finding such good homes for my books. To Maura Wogan and Victoria Cook: thank you for being such a stellar legal team. To David Arntzen: thank you for all your guidance and kindness these years. To Cassie Homer: thank you for being the best damn assistant out there! To Talexi: thank you for the gorgeous covers!

ACKNOWLEDGMENTS

A heartfelt and massive thank-you to all my marvelous publishers around the world: Bosnia: Sahinpasic, Brazil: Record, Bulgaria: Egmont, China: Honghua Culture, Croatia: Fokus, Czech Republic: Albatros, Denmark: Tellerup, Estonia: Pikoprit, Finland: Gummerus, France: Editions du Seuil, Georgia: Palitra, Germany: DTV Junior, Greece: Psivhogios, Hungary: Konyvmolykepzo, Israel: Kor'im, Italy: Mondadori, Japan: Villagebooks, Korea: Athena, Lithuania: Alma Littera, Netherlands: Meulenhof/Van Goor, Norway: Gyldendal, Poland: Wilga, Portugal: Marcador, Romania: RAO, Russia: Azbooka Atticus, Serbia: Laguna, Slovakia: Slovart, Slovenia: Ucila International, Spain: Santillana & Planeta, Sweden: Modernista, Taiwan: Sharp Point Press, Thailand: Nanmee Books, Turkey: Dogan Kitap, Ukraine: Vivat. I'm keeping my fingers crossed that I'll get to meet all of you in person one day!

I would not have gotten this far if it was not for some of my very first readers: the Fictionpress community. How can I convey my gratitude for all you have done? Your love for these characters and this world gave me the courage to try to get published. Thank you for staying until the very end.

One of the best parts of this journey has been the friends I've made along the way. Thank you and endless love to Louisse Ang, Steph Brown, Jennifer Kelly, Alice Fanchiang, Diyana Wan, Laura Ashforth, Alexa Santiago, Rachel Domingo, Jessica Reigle, Jennifer Armentrout, Christina Hobbs, Lauren Billings, and Kelly Grabowski. To Charlie Bowater: Getting to know you has been such a highlight of my career, and your incredible art has inspired me in so many ways. Thank you for all your hard work (and for being a total genius).

To my family: Thank you for your unwavering love. It has carried me farther than you know. To my in-laws, Linda and Dennis: thank you for taking such good care of Josh and me these past few months (okay, let's be honest: for the past fourteen years!), and for being such wonderful and selfless grandparents.

To *you*, dear reader: Thank you from the bottom of my heart for *everything*. None of this would have been possible without you. I could write another thousand pages about how grateful I am, and will always be. But in the end, all I can think to say is that I hope that your dreams, whatever they may be, come true. I hope you pursue those dreams with your whole heart; I hope you work toward them no matter how long it takes, no matter how unlikely the odds. Believe in yourself, even if it feels that the world does not. Believe in yourself, and it will carry you farther than you could imagine. You can make it. You *will* make it. I'm rooting for you.

To Annie, my canine companion and (other) best friend: You sat by my side (. . . or in my lap, or on the couch, or at my feet) while I wrote these books. If I could, I'd gift you an endless supply of rabbit chews for all your unconditional love—and for all the happiness you've brought me. I love you forever and ever, baby pup.

To Josh, my husband, my *carranam*, my mate: What can I say? I've known you for almost as long as I've been working on these books—and what a journey it's been. Every day, I wake up with joy and gratitude in my heart because I get to walk this road with you. Thank you for taking such good care of me, for being my best friend, for making me laugh, and for carrying me when I felt like I couldn't go on. I wouldn't have made it without you, and I'm so excited and blessed to go on this next leg of the journey with you.

And lastly, to Taran: You were the destination all along, buddy. You were the thing I walked toward my entire life without even knowing it. You are perfect, you are wonderful, you are my pride. You won't remember these early months, but I find it strangely fitting that these books are ending at the same moment you've arrived. It truly is one chapter of my life closing and the next beginning.

So, now that I'm at this crossroads, I want you to know that no matter where your own path carries you, Taran, I hope you find joy, and wonder, and luck along the way. I hope you are guided by courage and compassion and curiosity. I hope you keep your eyes and your heart open, and that you always take the road less traveled. But mostly, I hope you know that no matter the road, no matter how far it carries you, I love you. To whatever end.